SILENCE
UNLOCKED

A women's fictional biography set in 1890 to 1933

By

Janet M Reeves

CONTENTS

The Elkson Family

Ellen (Ellie) Elkson; born 1881

Grandma Jane Elkson; born 1818

David (Dave) Elkson, Ellie's father; born 1857

Jeannie Elkson, Ellie's mother; born 1859

Stephen Elkson, Ellie's brother; born 1884

George Elkson, Ellie's brother; born 1886

Edwin Elkson, Ellie's brother; born 1887

Sarah Elkson, Ellie's sister; born 1890

John (Jack) Elkson; Ellie's brother; born 1893

Hannah Elkson (nee Nelson), George's wife; born 1886

Annie Elkson, Edwin's wife; born 1888

Laura McLean, Jack Elkson's fiancée, born 1893

Thomas (Tom) Elkson, son of George and Hannah; born 1912

Rebecca Elkson, daughter of George and Hannah; born 1914

Richard Elkson, son of George and Hannah; born 1922

Alice Elkson, daughter of George and Hannah; born 1923

Becky Nelson, sister of Hannah Elkson; born 1891

Alice Nowell (nee Elkson) Sister of David Elkson born 1856

Arthur Nowell (husband of Alice.) Ellie's uncle born 1857

Hugh Nowell (son of Alice and Arthur Nowell) Ellie's cousin born 1880

This book is dedicated to Jean and Jim,
who helped me to unlock the silence.

PROLOGUE

(Hartsbeck 1933)

Nine mourners wound their way towards the freshly dug grave. Black-cloaked, the parson waited with open prayer book and a heavy heart. The grieving mother, seventy-four years old and trembling with Parkinson's disease, leant on the arm of Stephen, her eldest son. Two more of her sons followed with their wives. A younger man, dark-suited, his clerical collar alone marking his calling, brought up the rear escorting two middle-aged women in ill-fitting coats and faded black hats. All were relatives or acquaintances of Ellie Elkson, whose body they had come to bury in the cemetery of their home town of Hartsbeck.

Their eyes were drawn to the low, curved headstone at the head of the grave-pit. No more than two feet high and three feet across, it was a dwarf of a stone among the tall edifices of surrounding graves. Plainly cut and the colour of clean sand, the memorial already bore the name of Ellie's father:

David Elkson, died 22nd June 1921 aged 64 years.'

Carved above David's name were the words-

In loving memory of

There was space beneath for others to be added, in their turn. Ellie's name would not be written there until after the death of her mother in 1937, when the stone would read:-

Also Jeannie, his wife, who died 18th April 1937 aged 78 years

Also Ellen, their daughter, who died 15th September 1933.

On this day, the 28th of September, nineteen hundred and thirty three, only David Elkson's remains awaited those of his elder daughter.

"Thank goodness your Dad didn't live to see this," Jeannie murmured to Stephen as she leaned against him.

Stephen noted the slightness of her failing body and tucked his arm firmly around her waist. He remembered how strong she'd once been.

Only those of Ellie's own generation, or older, were at the graveside. The younger folk, Ellie's nieces and nephews, had been persuaded to go about their daily business. There was too much horror about this death. Too many questions floating around. They could only speak of it silently, inside their own heads. It seemed as if they were listening, stunned and waiting for the meaning of it all to be revealed. For Stephen, Ellie's manner of death was a coded message, which once cracked, would reveal the hidden truths behind all their lives.

As the coffin was lowered into the earth, the Rev Owen Griffiths, Vicar of Hartsbeck, reminded them that Ellie was being buried in consecrated ground, beside her father, who'd loved her and grown proud of her.

The polished wooden casket bore no flowers or loving messages but beneath the lid, Ellie's body had been carefully dressed in her uniform and Stephen had placed a photograph of Ellie's younger sister, Sarah, between her folded hands. Hugh, Ellie's clergyman cousin, had tucked a small, carved wooden box, beside her. The Elkson's housekeeper, Gertie Foster, had pressed the box into Hugh's hands before the coffin was closed,

"This ought to go with her. It came from you. Will you put it in with her, please sir?"

These were the only obvious, outward expressions of their relationship with Ellie. Now even these were hidden inside her coffin, soon to be covered with heavy, Hartsbeck clay. The dejected cortege cast their handfuls of earth into the grave. Owen said a final prayer and almost unnoticed, a conspiracy of silence closed around the life of Ellen Elkson.

It was a conspiracy, which lasted for four decades, until new generations began to ask questions and the silence surrounding Ellie's life was unlocked...

PART ONE

HARTSBECK 1890-1899

CHAPTER 1

Expectations in Aspen Lane

"Sparrows light, sparrows bright, bless our home and do not roam!" chanted nine year old Ellie Elkson. Standing in a patch of sunshine in her brown cotton frock and cream pinafore and throwing crumbs into the air she appeared at one with the homely brown birds. It was 12th May in the year eighteen hundred and ninety. Florence Nightingale was seventy years old to the day, forty-six years since her first foray into nursing. In London's East End the first council houses were being built and slum clearances had begun. Infant mortality rates were high and Dr. Frederick Truby King, the international pioneer in mother and baby care, was thirty two years old and the lilac bush and the clematis in the Elkson's small back garden in Lancashire hung heavy with blooms.

Her crumbs all gone, Ellie tipped back her head and shading her eyes against the brightness of the sky, watched the sparrows flitting to and from their nests in the eaves of the stone terraced house which was her home. These tiny birds made her think of her school friends, who had died last autumn in the fever epidemic. Some old tale, told to her by her Norfolk grandfather, of seabirds being the souls of drowned sailors, lingered in her memory and linked the lively sparrows to her vanished playfellows and made her smile.

"I wish I could fly like you," she whispered.

A tiny butterfly with brown tipped wings brushed past Ellie's cheek and the child, raising her arms, spun round and round, a brown swirl in a fusion of green and yellow light.

"Ellie! Where are you, girl? Come here, quickly now!" her mother shouted from the kitchen.

Ellie's mood plummeted. She hurried inside. To linger would make her mother out of sorts for most of the day. Jeannie Elkson was sitting, bent forward, in the old rocking chair by the open kitchen door. She rocked backwards and forwards, roughened hands clasped across her pregnant belly, eyes squeezed shut. The room behind her was too warm for comfort; the kitchen fire had to be lit every morning, even in summertime, for cooking and heating water. Ellie's first waking sound had always been of her Dad stumbling about, raking the clinkers, emptying the ash bucket and laying and relighting the fire.

Panic rose in Ellie, she had never seen her mother like this. "Mam! What's the matter?"

Jeanie snapped open her eyes and straightened up with a sigh.

"Nothing to get het up about, lass. I needed to sit in a bit of draught; it's too hot in here."

She rubbed the small of her back then re-twisted and pinned up the thick rope of her hair which had come loose. Two small boys, George four and Stephen six years old, stood near her. They were dressed for school in long, grey shorts and shirts and held hands as they waited, wide-eyed and silent. Playing on the rug at their feet was two year old Edwin, washed, dressed and fed by Ellie half an hour previously. Edwin had objected, he was to be three in a month's time and thought himself too old to be treated as the baby any more.

"I want you to take the boys along to school. Tell your teacher you're needed at home and come straight back here. Your dad went off early. He's had to go into Preston to do with work. Take young Edwin to school as well and ask if he can go in with the baby class, just for today."

"But Mam, it's Nature Study and I'm to read out my composition about the ramble over Whalley Nab and Bert Lee and I were going to show the class the nature specimens we found."

Disappointment threatened rebellion in Ellie but her mother's next words knocked all selfish thoughts from her head.

"Can't be helped. You'll do as I say. Oh, on the way knock on Annette Hamilton's door and tell her to come over, baby is on its way," Jeannie wiped away a few beads of perspiration from her top lip.

"Ooh, Mam!" Stephen and George gave a skip and looked at each other their faces splitting into wide grins.

Ellie took charge. "Don't worry Mam, I'll tell Annette and I'll run all the way back from school. Now come along boys. Oh George, you scamp, where are your clogs?"

"There, by the door, they were muddy last night. Stop it, Ellie! You're hurting me,"

Ellie pushed George's protesting feet into his clogs. Ignoring Edwin's wails, she took the two youngest by the hand and marched all three of them out of the house and down the road. The sight of Annette Hamilton, standing at her front door having just waved her own offspring off to work, steadied the anxious little group. Even Edwin stopped wailing aimlessly and changed his cries to-

"'Nette, Nette," as he pulled towards her.

Plump and rosy- cheeked, wrapped around in the cleanest of print frocks and white aprons, Annette looked to Ellie as good and wholesome as a freshly baked loaf wrapped in a clean white cloth. She bent down and took Edwin in her arms as she listened to Ellie's message and answered in her precise English. To Annette, English was a second language, German was her native tongue.

"Well now, Ellie, isn't it just the perfect day for a baby to come? You will have your chance to help me at last, my liebling!"

Ellie wanted to dance with excitement. Up until now she had been sent out of the way when a birth was imminent and even this time she was not sure whether they would let her stay in the actual room. Annette sensed Edwin's bewilderment and replaced the small boy on his feet before reaching into her apron pocket and pulling out three toffees wrapped in shiny paper. She looked down into three pairs of round, questioning eyes;

"My word, Edwin! What a big boy you are, going to school; and George and Stephen, quite the scholars! Your new brother or sister is going to be so proud of you."

The boys stood tall and beamed at her. She chuckled and gave them each a toffee.

"Thank you, Mrs Hamilton," said Stephen.

"No sucking them in class now!" she said, pinching their cheeks playfully. Annette unwrapped Edwin's sweet and popped it into his mouth.

"Don't you dare dribble on your clean clothes, my lad."

"I'll keep mine for the new baby," said George, pocketing it carefully.

The woman and the young girl caught each other's eyes, brimming with mirth.

"Off you go now! Be quick back, Ellie, I shall be needing you."

Ellie looked impatiently at her three brothers and hoped she wouldn't be delayed at the school. St. Mark's elementary school was only two streets away and if she gave Edwin a piggy-back they could be there in ten minutes. Stephen helped hoist Edwin onto her back, then he took charge of George and they set off at a gentle trot.

Annette watched them go. She'd been looking forward to a bit of a rest and a chance to put her own house in order. Also, if truth be known, Jeannie Elkson wasn't her favourite person, a bit reserved and stand-offish, too wrapped up in her own family- and bossy. She rebuked herself,

"Now Annette, stop being so selfish, that's not the way. You can be just as stiff as Jeannie, when you're in the mood. Think of the baby coming and little Ellie and remember that Jeannie Elkson has her troubles."

It was well known that Dave Elkson, Jeanie's husband, had recently taken to drinking more than was good for him or his family.

Annette hurried into her cottage to check her midwifery bag. Her husband, who was disabled, had been picked up earlier by his friend Harry who was a farmer up at Greenshaw hamlet, about two miles away. Dick was a gifted artist and planned to spend the day on the farm, sketching and painting the spring- time activities. His illustrations were to be part of a series of articles about farm life which Harry was writing for the local newspaper. Annette had been relieved to see her husband's spirits lift when Harry arrived. Dick and his wheel chair and artist's equipment were soon packed into the farm cart and he'd waved cheerily to Annette as he and Harry bounced away.

Annette had been born in Switzerland. When she was sixteen she'd worked in a sanatorium in the Swiss Alps, learning about the care of patients with respiratory diseases. After three years she'd accompanied one of the patients back to their home in England. Annette had decided to stay and during her first year in England, she'd met and married Dick Hamilton and they'd come to live in Hartsbeck.

As well as her experience in the Sanatorium, Annette had a treasury of home nursing and midwifery skills, learnt from her mother in the remote mountain village where she had been brought up. Quickly recognising the needs of the community, she'd soon put her skills to good use and earned the respect of most of the doctors in Hartsbeck.

Annette and Dick had two children, Bertha and Joel. A third child had been expected when an accident at the coal pit where Dick was a foreman caused Annette to lose the baby and Dick both his legs. Annette always said that God had taken their family in hand and carried them through the trauma. Twelve years had gone by since the accident and the experience seemed to have sweetened, rather than embittered Annette's nature. She was called on constantly, for her medical skills, by families who couldn't afford doctor's bills.

Ellie had been four years old, when Annette had helped to nurse her through an attack of measles. Nurse and child had grown fond of each other. During the five years since then, Ellie had visited Annette's home whenever she could. Fascinated, she would watch Dick, busy at his work-bench in the back room of the cottage.

Despite Dick's disability, there was none of the air of gloom or resentment which Ellie sometimes felt in her own home. To the child, the Hamilton's house had seemed filled with warmth and love and plenty of teasing and laughter. Enjoying a break from the responsibility of being the eldest of her family, Ellie had relaxed into an easy friendship with Bertha and Joel. Best of all, she began to learn from Annette about looking after sick people and how to fight against illness.

Annette had told her of tiny creatures, "too small to see with your eyes," called germs.

"They carry nasty diseases that come from cess pits and lavatories and vermin, such as rats and mice, cockroaches, flies and fleas and from not washing properly with our good friend, Mr. SOAP."

Ellie would laugh as she pictured Mr. Soap, with arms and legs and a cheerful face, bowing and smiling as he washed away every nasty invader of their lives.

Being often with Annette, the girl had picked up pieces of information about childbirth from conversations between this unofficial midwife and the women of the neighbourhood. When Ellie asked her own mother about such things she was told sharply to "wait till you are older, you're not ready to worry your head about such things. You've enough to do at school and at home. No doubt your time will come, my lady. Sufficient unto the day–"

Jeannie had a habit of ending her remarks with this unsatisfactory phrase, but Ellie did not dare to ask her what it meant. Now that she was nine years old, Ellie's interest was even stronger.

"Annette, my greatest wish is to help with a birthing. When can I help you?" Ellie had kept pestering.

On this morning of Jeannie Elkson's labour Annette sighed, as she realised that Ellie's wish was at last to come true.

"God forbid that anything should go wrong," she murmured as she fixed a small straw hat on top of her fair, neat cottage-bun styled hair. She dropped to her knees, as she always did before leaving home and bowed her head to pray. She thanked God for the new day and the chance to serve Him; she asked a blessing on all in childbirth, especially Jeannie Elkson. She asked God to guard her own thoughts and her quick tongue and to guide her hands in all their tasks, "and please help young Ellie to cope with her first birthing."

Her prayer ended, Annette remained still, resting in the peace of the moment. Rising from her knees, she threw a shawl round her shoulders and pencilled a note to say, if anyone needed her she was at number 174, Aspen Lane. Satisfied the self-appointed midwife picked up her ready- packed bag and left the house. She fixed the note to her front door, hid the key behind a loose brick and with the swinging strides of one brought up to mountain walking she was away up the street to the larger, terraced houses where the Elksons lived.

CHAPTER 2

Ellie's first birthing.

Ellie was not held up at the school. Teachers were used to children being needed at home during school hours, particularly elder sisters. Miss Prior, Ellie's class teacher, was sympathetic.

"I'll make sure Stephen and George have their meal at lunchtime, Ellie. Miss Gordon in the baby class will see to Edwin for today. Nowadays, she's used to toddlers coming in from time to time. I'll walk your brothers home myself, after school. Maybe you'll have some good news for us, by then."

Miss Prior looked thoughtfully at Ellie, "I have something I think you might enjoy, my dear. Just a minute."

The teacher rummaged in a cupboard and brought out a thick book. It had a picture on the cover of a baby's face peering through a watery colour-wash of greens and blues.

"There's always a lot of waiting, when a baby's coming. If you have time on your hands, you may like to read this. It's 'The Water Babies,' by Charles Kingsley. Take your time over it, there's no rush to bring it back."

Ellie gasped with pleasure and took the book, clasping it in her arms. Her family called her a real bookworm but she didn't care, books opened new worlds to her.

"Thank you, Miss Prior; I'll take good care of it but I must hurry home now. Thank-you for looking after my brothers."

Ellie escaped before Miss Prior could say anything else and raced all the way home.

Annette had already taken Jeannie upstairs and made sure her patient had emptied her bowels, before helping her on with a nightgown and into bed. A wooden crib had been brought in and as soon as Ellie arrived, Annette handed her a pile of, baby- sized sheets and blankets.

"Take these, Ellie, they've been warmed. Make up the crib with them, ready for baby."

Entranced with this task, Ellie lined the crib. She made it as soft and comfy as possible, imagining the tiny form nestling there, like some small animal in its den.

"Good girl, I could just curl up into it myself. Now, find as many old newspapers as you can and four of your mothers' largest clean towels. Also, we'll need two more large basins. I've put plenty of water to heat on the stove downstairs but I'll deal with that."

Jeannie half -raised herself on the bed. She didn't like her house being taken over and attempted to assert her authority.

"Ellie, I've put towels ready for the birthing in the big kitchen drawers near the stove; they should be nicely aired and warm by now. Bring in the big wash basins from the boys' bedrooms. And, Ellie, you can stay here with me and help Annette this time-Aah!" Jeannie subsided into silence as pain washed over her.

"What will happen?" Ellie asked Annette, feeling suddenly nervous and not at all sure whether she wanted this, Annette smiled fondly at her and said, with just the hint of her German-Swiss accent:

"I was just your age when I began to help my mother with the births. Your mother's pains tell her baby is getting ready to come. Just now they are small pains and not often, soon they will get stronger and more often, until the baby comes."

Annette patted Ellie's hands comfortingly, "You mustn't be frightened. Don't worry if your mother shouts out when the birth pains become very strong, most women do that! There will be some blood and watery stuff. It is a little bit messy having a baby but it is soon over and then—then we have a new life in our hands. Alright my little one?"

Ellie had listened carefully, trying not to feel sick.

"Yes Annette, I think so."

"Now, let's have a toffee to cheer ourselves up!" said Annette and fished two liquorice sweets in shiny paper from her pocket, un-wrapping them she popped one into Ellie's mouth, the other into hers. Ellie sucked and the delicious spicy-sweetness calmed her fears.

Annette made a cup of soothing herbal tea for Jeannie and poured cool lemonade for herself and Ellie.

"It can be a long wait. I'd find yourself something to do, Ellie, or go into the garden, if you want. I'll call you."

Annette took some knitting from her bag and made her-self comfortable in a chair near to the bed.

"You could make yourself useful peeling the potato's for dinner and scrubbing the kitchen down!" said Jeannie.

"Now then Jeannie, Ellie tells me the boys are having their meal at school and the kitchen's just fine and Ellie needs to conserve her strength."

Ellie didn't want to leave the room so she brought 'The Water Babies' and curled herself comfortably on the green, padded top of the bedding box under the window. She opened the book and was soon lost in the world of young Tom and the Irish woman. The sooty chimney-sweep's lad reminded her of the men she saw coming home from work in the coal pits. She remembered their red-rimmed eyes in faces begrimed with coal dust and the white-rimmed mouths, where they'd licked or sweated the black dust away. Worst of all was their hawking coughs and spitting into the gutter, as they tried to clear the foul pit dust from their chests and lungs. But she remembered something else, something uplifting. A lot of the men had whistled as they walked, lively foot- tapping tunes, vying with each other. Tired women in aprons, some with babes in their arms would come hurrying and laughing to their front doors or windows, to see them pass.

The bedding-box, where Ellie rested, made a soft bright spot in a room of heavy, dark- wood furniture. A deep-set wardrobe and a man's tall-boy, took up the whole of one wall. Against another wall stood a chest-of-drawers and a wooden washstand holding two porcelain basins, one with a pink flowery pattern the other quite plain and beside them two water jugs, large and pot-bellied. Under the bed, were two white chamber pots for night-time use.

The herbal tea had a soporific effect and Jeannie was dozing, when a loud hammering on the front door made them all jump. A boy was shouting but they couldn't tell what he said. Ellie ran downstairs and opened the door to a thin, grubby-looking boy, about her own age, "Greg Jones, whatever is it?" she asked. "Mrs Hamilton-Annette, i- is she 'ere? It's me Mam. She's fallen down t' cellar steps and the babbie's coming too soon. She's screaming 'er 'ead off; I can't do nothing. She wants Annette, now!"

Annette called from the top of the stairs,

"It's alright Gregory. Go home and tell your Mam, I'm on my way. Put a pillow under her and sit and hold her hand till I come, try and keep her calm. Can you do that?"

"Yes, Mrs Hamilton," and the boy was gone, running like a chased rabbit.

Ellie was horrified, "but Annette, what'll we do here? You can't leave me with mother like this. You can't!."

"Yes I can; I must. You saw that poor boy. Your mother won't be ready to give birth for a while yet and I'll be back within the hour. Look at me Ellie! You can cope. Your mother's had three children and all straight forward. She's strong and healthy, which is more than I can say for Greg's mother. I'll sort Mrs Jones out and send Greg for Dr. Waters. I'll be back long before your mother's ready."

"Well, I suppose it'll be alright."

"Course it will, keep her comfy and calm just as I told Greg. I'm counting on you Ellie. Now I must wash my hands in that carbolic soap, to kill any nasty germs before going," Annette made herself ready as she spoke..

"Good old Mr. Soap," laughed Ellie, though she really wanted to scream and stamp her foot and force Annette to stay. Instead she swallowed hard and watched Annette leave. Slowly she walked back into the bedroom and sat beside her mother. Jeannie lay on the bed, sometimes at rest, sometimes writhing with spasms of pain making her clutch the bedclothes and bite her lips. For a moment Ellie was frozen with fear, then a hot, steely determination entered her and reaching out, she took her mother's hand.

"Mammy, can I do anything for you," the child whispered her own small fists clenching and unclenching in time to her mother's pains.

"Open the window a bit Ellie, there's a good girl. It's getting that warm in here. And pull the curtain to, the light's hurting my eyes. Aaaaagh!"

Jeannie Elkson gasped as another bout of pain surged through her. Ellie struggled with the heavy sash window and by straining her neck and shoulders she managed to push it up an inch. They heard the sound of the steam tram, chugging and wheezing its way up their street from the town. Looking out Ellie saw her class on their way back to school after a nature walk, her friend Emily and silly Suzanne, from lower down the street, were giggling together; they carried bunches of wild bluebells for the classroom table. Bert Lee who was in the local naturalists' society with Ellie, was at the back with a group of boys, he looked up and waved when he saw her at the window. Ellie felt a surge of envy, but her mother's low moaning reminded her of the importance of what she was doing. Going to school with your friends was commonplace, she could do that any day, but this day, with her mother having a baby, would never come again. At least not with this baby! She waved to Bert, then drew the heavily patterned curtains across the window dimming the harsh glare, softer light filtered in between the patterns, pleasantly dappling the walls and ceiling.

"You're sweating Mummy," Ellie touched the moisture on her mother's forehead and brought a damp cloth from the wash-basin and gently wiped her mother's face and clenched hands,

"Eeh, that's grand Ellie. You're a born nurse. Will you give me a sip of water, I'm that dry? It's hard work bringing a baby into the world."

Ellie had never known her mother be so gentle with her. She took the glass of water, ready on the bedside table and supporting her mother's head, helped her to drink. Another contraction began before she had finished and Ellie found herself gripped and pulled tightly against her mother's writhing body and felt all the powerful energy and force. The glass went flying scattering water over the bedding but did not break as it rolled onto the matting beside the bed.

"That was a fierce one. The baby won't be so long now. Is everything ready? Where's Annette?"

Jeannie's breath came in short sharp gasps, as she tried to talk. Ellie told herself not to worry, her mother had already had four babies.

"She'll be back soon Mummy, she had to go to Greg Jones's mother, but she said she'll be back before our baby comes."

"Well, if she's much longer you'll have to help me. You're quite sensible enough. Now, wash your hands with the carbolic."

Another fierce contraction gripped Jeannie. When it had passed she ordered Ellie to take off the top bedclothes and pull her nightie up over her knees. Ellie hesitated feeling suddenly sick; this was for real, suppose she did something wrong.

"Oh Annette please come back. Dear God, please make Annette come now," she prayed.

"Oh let me do it; this is no time for prudishness!" Jeannie yanked off the top bedclothes and wriggled her nightie up to her knees. Ellie saw there was a rubber sheet tucked underneath her mother's lower body and was glad Annette had prepared everything.

Ellie knew, from Annette, that things could go wrong at births. The wise Swiss woman had explained to her that a lot of families in Hartsbeck were poor and many of the women who gave birth were not strong. Childhood illnesses such as diphtheria, gastric problems, measles and scarlet fever, had sapped their strength. Poor diet and bad sanitation didn't help, nor did working long hours at the mill or the crowded conditions in which they lived.

"Sometimes five children, sleeping in one bed!" Annette had told her. "All these things weaken their defences and then giving birth isn't so easy."

13

The Elkson family was lucky. Ellie and her brother Stephen had been born over the small grocery shop in Preston, Lancashire, which had been run by her parents. Their home had been clean and they'd never been short of food and always there'd been books to look at and interesting people, rich and poor, coming into the shop. Then, when Ellie was six, they'd moved here to the mill town of Hartsbeck, twenty miles east of Preston.

Hartsbeck spread itself in a deep, wide fold of the moors, its' streets and factories surrounded by wooded cloughs, as by medieval moats. You could find your way into the cloughs without even leaving the town; from the dusty streets you were suddenly in a place of deep-flowing, rocky streams, their steeply-wooded banks rioting with wild flowers in spring and summer and in autumn bursting with hips and haws, beech-nuts and horse-chestnuts. Deep in the earth beneath Hartsbeck, dense forests had sunk and decimated over millions of years, silently fossilising into the rich, black gold that kept industrial Britain going; coal. Coal pits, brick works, cotton mills and engineering works spawned all over the growing town. Ellie's father had taken a well-paid office job in one of the new engineering works and their way of life had become very comfortable. Then her brothers George and Edwin had been born.

Now here she was, a skinny nine year old girl with lively brown eyes, in her brown school dress and pinafore, white socks and brown boots, her straight, dark hair scraped back and tied with the plainest of brown ribbons, helping her new brother or sister to enter the world. Ellie looked at her mother's face contorted with pain, Jeannie had stuffed a corner of the pillowcase into her mouth and was biting on it hard. Ellie's insides turned over as she realised Annette might not be back in time. Never mind, mother would know what to do, wouldn't she?

Jeannie pushed the pillowcase from her mouth. Panting hard she instructed Ellie, "Now child. In a minute I'm going to push real hard and I want you to watch between my legs to see if the top of the baby's head shows. Ellie was too scared to feel embarrassed, as a gush of watery blood flowed out from between her mother's legs and something smooth, pale and slightly curved just peeped out from the widening opening,

"I see it Mammy! It's there! I see it!"

Jeannie gave one great push and the baby's head came out. Ellie grabbed one of the clean towels and leaning forward supported the tiny head, then, easily and quickly, came the shoulders and a squirming little body covered in blood-streaked slime. Ellie caught the tiny creature in the towel just as Annette came rushing into the room throwing off her hat and coat and briskly washing her hands with the carbolic soap and water put ready earlier.

"Well now, didn't you come quickly? I think you wanted to come to your big sister!" Annette took over, checking the baby and wiping mucous from its nose and mouth so that it squawked and cried out, drawing its first real breath.

"You're hurting it!" Ellie wanted to cry herself and pull the baby from Annette who was deftly tying and cutting the ropy cord,

"No child, and she's not an 'it,' she's a healthy baby girl, God bless her! A sister for you, Ellie and a second daughter for you, Mrs Elkson."

"But you've cut part of her!" Ellie looked at the bluish rope which had trailed from the baby and into her mother.

"That's the cord that joined your sister to your mother when she was growing inside her but she doesn't need it now, it had to be cut. I'll tell you more about it another time. Now, I need to sort out your mother."

Annette worked as she talked, wrapping the baby in a clean towel and handing her over to Ellie.

"You hold your sister close to you in that towel; she's used to being inside your mother and will be feeling a bit strange."

Ellie carried her sister to the window while Annette saw to the afterbirth and helped Jeannie to use the chamber pot. Then she cleaned and washed the weary woman.

A small, almost care-worn face peered out of the thick white towel, filmy bluish eyes seemed to wander over Ellie's face and a tiny hand pushed out from the towelling folds, miniature fingers waved, testing the air and Ellie touched their tips lightly with her own gigantic fingers. Her sister's hand reached and touched and clutched at Ellie's. Once again Ellie's insides turned over, this time with love for the tiny human being she held closely against her. Years later, this moment and this love would lead Ellie into an unbearably dark place, but for now they were both safe, warm and in the light.

CHAPTER 3

The listening place

The door of St. Mark's Church was wide open, letting in a late September breeze to dilute the smell of old books and distant damp in stone and wood, of furniture polish and a musky mixture of fading and fresh flowers. Young people and elderly, wandered in quietly, emanating an aura of lavender and mothballs from their Sunday clothes.

Ellie loved the smell of the church; it calmed her. Whatever had been happening in the family or with her friends, the worries, petty jealousies and arguments, all stopped at the church door. A calm descended and she knew there would be at least an hour's respite from the see-saw existence of everyday life.

Her brothers, George and Edwin had already disappeared through the vestry door to don their choir robes of royal blue and white. As the service started, the choir processed out of the vestry and down the side aisle, twelve choir boys aged between seven and eleven years were followed by ten adult male choristers, similarly robed, who stared over the heads of the boys as if they would not deign to look down at them. It was their show of dignity. These men came from all walks of life. Gangly and spotty Tony Dearing, just eighteen who was a fettler at Leigh's cotton mill; his close friend Bert Lee who worked at Oak Farm; Vernon Hindle, retired bank clerk, bowed and shaky on his legs at seventy and eight other men of varying ages and occupations. Millworkers and a mill owner; engineers and a foundry man, teachers and a tram driver; all equal in their office as choristers of St. Mark's Parish Church.

Ellie stood to sing and watched over her open hymn book as her two brothers walked sedately among the other boys, down the side aisle to the back of the church. George caught his sister's eye with a large and obvious wink as he passed, trying to sing around a suspicious lump in the side of his cheek. Hot embarrassment surged through Ellie.

"Oh no," she prayed silently, "not a gobstopper."

Surreptitiously she moved her eyes to see if anyone else had noticed but people appeared engrossed in the hymn and the choir, having reached the back, turned to process down the central aisle towards the East end.

"Ah well," Ellie told herself, "the choir master will deal with him, thank goodness Dad isn't here. George should be safe till after the service, as long as he keeps that gobstopper under control."

Stephen, now nine, was not in the choir.

"Tom Dearing says he's what you call a 'groaner'- can't sing a tune but groans along, all on one note." George had delighted in breaking this news at the Sunday dinner table on the day Stephen had been discreetly asked to leave the choir. His toneless meanderings had become too much for those singing next to him and they'd finally complained to the choirmaster. It didn't worry Stephen one bit because he was then given the enviable job of pumping the organ bellows, allowing the music to flow freely from the fingers of the organist, Miss Salter, through the organ pipes, to lead the whole congregation and choir.

"You lot wouldn't get anywhere, without me pumping the organ," he boasted.

This was proved true on the day he fell asleep in the organ loft and missed his cue. There was a considerable delay and much sighing and groaning from the organ and giggles in the congregation before the music rose crazily to its full volume with the voices of choir and people responding in rapturous relief. There were no girls in the choir. Mr. Bamford, the choirmaster was steeped in the traditional belief that the purity of a boy's soprano was essential to sacred music.

"Perhaps we females shouldn't sing the hymns at all," mused Ellie and joined in the verses of 'Praise to the Holiest in the Heights', with added gusto. At twelve years old, Ellie, as the eldest child, was conscious of her place in the family and was often put in charge of her siblings. She would be leaving St. Mark's school at the end of this term. As well as being expected to find a part time job, to help supplement the family income, the rest of her time would be spent helping mother to run the home and care for the younger ones. However, today, she was blissfully alone in the family pew. Mother, who was expecting another baby next month had stayed at home and three year old Sarah, who was grizzly and had a cough, had stayed with her. Their father was sleeping off a late night celebrating the win of the Preston Grasshoppers, the Rugby team in which he played fly- half.

"It's the fly-half that's the play-maker. In my position, I have the power to dictate the pattern of play," he would boast sitting back in his easy chair by the fire, entertaining the boys with the highlights of the latest match.

"He must be alright because his team mates seem to like him well enough," Ellie had replied to her mother's snappy remark –"Oh take no notice. It's just your dad's Big Talk!"

"Anyway," said Jeannie, "if he keeps drinking like this, he'll not be fit to play and probably lose his job at the engineering works into the bargain."

The hymn had finished and Ellie settled back in her pew. She stared at the shafts of light criss-crossing the empty spaces above and around them. The shafts coming through the plain glass of the upper windows was clear and alive with dancing dust particles; others were infused with colour from the stained glass pictures of bible stories and saints in the lower windows and from the great East window over the altar, which showed Christ in a rainbow of glory. She loved to watch the light move softly over the mellow stone walls and pillars; jewel-like reds and greens, blues and violets that hovered like visitors from another world, too beautiful to stay long in one place. When she'd been too young to understand the words of the service going on around her, Ellie had imagined God in those shafts of light, pouring into the church and touching everyone and everything and she would smile up at the windows and whisper in her childish way, "Hello God."

Ellie and others of her age had recently moved up into a higher Sunday School class, taken by Miss Broughton, the Deaconess at St. Marks. A gentle, serious woman of thirty-one years, Deaconess Broughton was a vicar's daughter from Aberdeen. The girls thought her a romantic figure. She wore her fair hair in a Grecian plait, wound like a crown around her head and was fond of poetry and the writings of the mystics, such as Julian of Norwich. She was a good teacher and in her soft Scottish brogue encouraged the girls to look and listen for signs of God's spirit in everything around them.

"You are beginning to open your 'inward eye and ear'," Deaconess Broughton would tell her group of enraptured young girls, "and starting to discern all sorts of meanings in the things around you."

The service ended and Ellie met Stephen and George in the churchyard. They were unusually thoughtful, chattering together as they walked home.

"I like looking at the pictures in the church windows," said George. "It's clever the way they cut the pieces and fit them into shapes of people and flowers and animals and the colours are stunning. During the sermons I work out the stories in them. My favourite is the one with the disciples in the boat, with the storm raging round them."

Ellie spoke shyly of her delight in watching the light from the windows, "I imagine it as God just touching everyone lightly, almost like a breath, brightening and transforming everyone and everything it touches and bringing a kind of blessing and acceptance to our feeble efforts at worship."

Stephen turned to look at her with his intent, short-sighted, grey eyes. He needed to concentrate to see clearly and smiled in the direction of Ellie's face under her floppy, wide- brimmed hat.

"You have some strange thoughts Ellie; I think you must be a mystic like Joan of Arc. Now, when I look at those windows, I like to think of science and industry working together with nature. The effect of the natural light on coloured glass made in our factories from natural minerals. Then the artist, bringing them all together to draw out the beauty of it all," and Stephen gesticulated wildly with his hands, to include everything around them.

"You sound a bit of a mystic yourself! St. Elkson of the hills and mills," teased Ellie. Stephen tipped Ellie's hat from her head and the debate ended with laughter and hair pulling and a race home for Sunday lunch. They dashed into the house panting and dishevelled. Mum scolded them wearily, pushing damp strands of hair off her forehead and placing her hand over the ache in the small of her back. Her main shot as usual was aimed at Ellie,

"It's not fitting behaviour in the streets for a Sunday. If it wasn't for the work I've put in and good food spoiling, I'd send you three up to bed with no dinner. Ellie, you're the eldest; can't you keep any control over your brothers when I'm not with you. Wash your hands and come tidy to the table children, your father will be down in a few minutes."

Ellie picked up Sarah from where she was playing on the floor. She wiped the child's dribbling nose and sitting down at the table, took her onto her lap. As soon as father had taken his place and the food served, she mashed up a portion of the dinner on her own plate to feed to her sister. Sarah's mouth opened eagerly like a small bird,

"She must be feeling better, mother, she can't wait for her dinner."

"Thank the Lord for that, I thought she might be coming down with something, but it must be just a cold."

"There's measles at school. They might have to close, if it gets worse," said Edwin.

"That's all we need," said Jeannie looking hard again at Sarah, who after a couple of mouthfuls was pushing the spoon away and turning her head from the food.

CHAPTER 4

A country holiday 1893

Sarah did have measles, followed, a week later, by Edwin and George. Ellie and Stephen had already had the disease, so Ellie was able to take her turn at nursing. Dr Waters, their family doctor, called in daily to check on them all. Thanks to him and to Annette Hamilton and her medical skills, all three children recovered.

Ellie had learnt much as she'd tended her brothers and baby sister by shielding their eyes from the light, dabbing their livid rashes with camomile and thinking up all sorts of diversions to take their minds from their discomfort. Edwin had been particularly ill and was left with a cough he found difficult to shake off; he would wake with it during the night so that the whole family began to suffer from broken sleep.

Three children from the infant class at St. Mark's died, as a result of measles and the school was closed until the epidemic had died down.

When George started being cheeky to Dr Waters and playing practical jokes on him, Dave decided his children had recovered sufficiently for the whole family to go away to the country for two weeks. He arranged for them to go to their friends, the Procters. The Procters had a farm near Dorby Bridge, a small village about eleven miles away, in the heart of the Ribble Valley. The Elksons had a holiday there most years and it always seemed like Heaven to the children.

"Fresh air and good farm food is what you all need. That'll set you up," Dave decided, looking at his weary wife and pale, listless children.

He sent them all off on the train as far as Clitheroe. Here they were met at the station by Herbert Proctor in his horse-drawn cart, which had been made comfortable for them with bales of straw covered with thick horse rugs. Jeannie and the children piled into the cart and Herbert drove them through the winding country lanes to Dorby Bridge. They crossed the river which ran through the village, then climbed the hillside by a rough track enclosed by dry stone walls. Edwin stood up in the cart to see the rolling view of sloping moorlands and sheep. It was not flat moorland but undulating with rocky hillocks and crevices some large, some small reminders of the flow of ice-age glaciers. The rivulets of small streams ran down from the moor to slide under the dry stone-walls and gather in the wet, green ditch that ran along the edge of the lane.

"Look, the grass is changing to purple," croaked Edwin, his throat and chest still affected by his dose of measles.

"That's the heather blooming," George told him importantly,

"There'll be bilberries, this time of year," smiled mother, "you'll have to pick some for Mrs Procter to make a pie."

Ellie leaned back against the side of the cart breathing in the fresh, clear air and watching the moorland birds soaring up into the sky where they hovered over the places where their nests must be. In spite of the bumpy ride, her tired body relaxed in contentment. Then round a bend in the road 'Wingate Farm' came into view and the children gave a loud cheer.

Dave joined them at the end of the first week, relieved to see his children rosy- cheeked and full of merriment. It was three o'clock in the afternoon when he arrived. Ellie, Sarah and the boys were sitting round the large well- scrubbed table in the farmhouse kitchen drinking mugs of creamy milk and tucking into a plate of home-made ginger biscuits. They jumped up in excitement to greet their father.

Sarah cried out "Dada, dada!" and held out her chubby arms. Flinging off his hat and coat he took the little girl and tossed her nearly to the ceiling, catching her as she came down chortling with delight.

"Not just after she's had a mug of milk," protested Ellie and Dave handed the child back to her sister with pretended remorse.

23

"We're going down to the river when we've finished this. Come with us dad," pestered Edwin, "I caught lots of water snails yesterday but I want to find a water- beetle. It's smashing down there!"

"Give me time to walk in," laughed Dave, "Where's your mother?"

"She's having a lie down. Come here Dave, I want a quiet word with you." Dave followed the sound of the womanly voice into a stone-floored scullery, where Jenny Procter was busy churning butter. She spoke quietly so the children wouldn't hear.

"Jeannie took the children bilberry picking over the moor this morning and it was a bit much for her. You want to watch that wife of yours Dave, make this the last bairn, or you'll be losing her."

Jenny Procter looked sternly at her old friend. Dave reddened angrily, then his holiday mood got the better of him and he whirled Jenny round in his arms.

"You've no room to talk Jenny Procter, seven bairns in as many years. Who keeps your Herbert in order? Perhaps I should have a word with him."

"Oh go on with you, Dave Elkson, you never change. I'm a lot stronger than Jeannie and life's a deal healthier out here than in that smoky mill town. Anyways, two of mine are twins. Go and see your Jeannie and I'll make you a cup of tea before you go down to the beck. You'd better put rubber boots on, there's a pair your size behind the back door. Oh, and another thing," she lowered her voice even further, "be gentle with your Ellie, she's reached that delicate stage this last week, her emotions are up and down like a yo-yo."

Dave raised an eyebrow. Jennie smiled and tapped her nose; she knew he understood exactly what she meant. Having been brought up around animals, which do what comes naturally for all to see, there was no prudery about this farmer's daughter, now become a hard-working farmer's wife. Even though she wrapped it up in oblique language, she saw no reason for hiding the fact from Dave that his eldest daughter had begun her menstrual cycle for the first time and needed to be treated with sensitivity. Sighing a big man's sigh, Dave went in search of his wife.

He found her fast asleep in the bedroom under the eaves, which was always theirs when they stayed here. The white-washed ceiling sloped down to the casement window that looked out over the fields at the back of the farm towards the heathery slopes of the Trough of Bowland. It was a bright Indian summer day, sporting snatches of brilliant blue sky between fair-weather clouds. Groups of hardy moorland sheep methodically cropped the tough grass, lifting their heads to gaze lazily about and soak in the last of the summery warmth before autumn took hold. Jeannie stirred and Dave looked down at her, his heart giving a lurch when he saw the deep frown lines on her forehead and the tight set of her mouth, even in sleep. Under the slight tan, from the wind and sunshine of her week's holiday, he noticed an anaemic paleness and her hands were thin and work-worn, as they rested on the taught swelling of her belly.

"I promise you Jeannie, there'll be no more bairns after this one."

He bent down and kissed her softly so as not to wake her, then crept away to have a mug of strong hot tea and a scone straight from the oven and spread thickly with butter. Fortified, he found the rubber boots and walked down to the village where his children were already engrossed in their chosen pursuits on the river bank. He stopped before they were aware of him and watched them. They were like young creatures of the wild, set free in their true environment. Stephen had waded out in a sheltered part of the river and was now kneeling on the large flat rocks and scooping up pebbles from the river bed. He was examining them for fossils, or evidence of mineral deposits. The small canvas knapsack, slung around his neck, was bulging with his finds. George and Edwin were trawling the water, under the bank, with a string-handled jam jar each. Ellie sat on a short plank of wood attached by two lengths of rope to a strong old oak tree, she swung on this seat with Sarah on her lap. Both girls were wrapped up in warm coats, with scarves wound round their heads, in case of sudden chill.

"It may seem warm, but it is autumn," had been their mother's warning. Ellie didn't mind, she'd been feeling chilly and the extra warmth helped ease the nagging discomfort of her first period. She was filled with a gentle tiredness, which made her feel soft and womanly and she gave her father a dreamy smile as he joined them. They stayed on the river bank until five o'clock, when Jimmy, the Procter's eldest son, arrived leading Brom, the carthorse.

"Mum says its 'ome time; tea'll be on' table in 'alf an hour," said Jimmy in his slow friendly voice. "Come on little 'uns, Brom's come to give you a ride 'ome, 'e's just been for new shoes so 'es proud as punch!"

Dave watched as George and Edwin came running and Sarah stretched out her arms shrieking, "me too, me too!!" Jimmy lifted the small boys into place and carefully placed Sarah between them, wedging her in firmly. Brom knew his own way back so Jimmy just walked beside the horse with his long arm stretched up to Sarah to keep her safe. The children laughed as they swayed their way up the track to the farm, their legs sticking out straight on either side of the huge animal's wide, warm back. Ellie remembered when she had first ridden Brom, the dry warmth of his waxy coat against the bare skin of her legs and the hot smell of horse sweat wafting over her as he moved. It seemed such a short time since she was a child. She had ridden Brom alone with Jimmy's Dad beside her and still felt the sense of elation as she had entered the farm-yard to be greeted by shouts of admiration from the farm hands. Now she was walking beside the little ones as they rode aloft and she had become a woman, no longer a child or even a young girl, but a real woman. She gave herself a secret, happy smile.

On the third of October, 1893, three weeks after their return home, Jeannie, helped by Ellie and Annette, was delivered of her final child, a boy. It proved to be the hardest of Jeannie's deliveries but Annette worked her through it, watched closely by Ellie. They chose the name John for the boy but he was always known as Jack.

Now, Ellie was needed at home more than ever. She was soon fully involved with cooking, cleaning, laundry-work and entertaining the 'tinies' as Sarah and Jack were labelled by their brothers.

CHAPTER 5

Planting the sycamore. 1897.

For five years all ran as smoothly in the Elkson household as is possible with a family of eight. Stephen had his twelfth birthday on 6th June 1895. At the end of that school year he left the elementary school and began an apprenticeship in engineering at the Lucas Engineering Works in Hartsbeck; the same firm that employed his father as a financial clerk.

Dave Elkson's spirits had lifted after the birth of his fourth son. Since then he'd approached his work with fresh zeal and despite the occasional drink, he came home early each night, sober and ready to enjoy his own hearthside. A knee injury had pulled him out of the rugby team for the season. This left him free to tend his garden, much to the delight of Edwin and Sarah who loved to dig and plant and watch things grow.

On the 18th September, 1897, Edwin's tenth birthday, Dave arrived home with a tiny sycamore sapling in a brown paper bag. After an extra special family high tea, of bacon, eggs, mushrooms, tomatoes and potato cakes, Dave took the sapling and disappeared into the back garden with Edwin, each carried a large spade.

"I want you all to come out, in about twenty minutes," Dave called over his shoulder, "and bring a cup of water each, when you come."

The other children, who had started to follow Edwin, skipped back inside.

"George and Stephen you can do the washing up, that should use up the time nicely" said Jeannie "I'll give Jack a wash now and Ellie, you can see to Sarah, so we won't have to bother getting them ready for bed later.

When it was time, Dad called them outside. Mother led the way carrying a large jug of water with Jack toddling beside her in his night things. Ellie followed with a giggling Sarah who was hugging a coat over her nightie. George and Stephen loped behind. Each brother and sister carried an old cup. They found Dad and Edwin, sleeves rolled up, leaning on their spades and looking with satisfaction at the deep hole they had dug.

"Now then," said Dad, "This is Edwin's tenth birthday and as he has shown such an interest in gardening, we are going to plant a sycamore tree, in his honour."

Edwin looked suitably pleased but Ellie could see real pride and excitement in the way he gripped his spade. Sarah was jumping up and down. Ellie put her arm round her sister and smiled with contentment. She looked round the family group, all sharing peaceably in this glad moment and tried to fix it in her memory.

"We are growing older so quickly, how long will we be together like this?" she wondered as she listened to her father.

"If tended right, this sapling should grow, over the years, into a great spreading tree and should be here for your grandchildren to see, aye and to climb an' all. Sycamore's make good climbing trees."

Everyone laughed when they saw the fragile looking plant, which Dave drew from the long paper bag.

"Trees need their roots in plenty of water, so I want all you young ones to pour your cups of water into the hole. Good thinking, Mother, you've brought a jug full!"

Jeannie filled the cups and they all trooped round the hole, pouring in their libations as they went, till there was a generous puddle in the bottom; Jack leant right over and had to be hauled back by the seat of his pants. Then Edwin was called upon to kneel down and take the sapling. He took it in his small, square hands and carefully held the thinly trailing roots over the hole and lowered the young tree into its watery bed. They had left a cone-shaped mound of earth in the centre of the hole, so that when Edwin laid the root ball on top of the cone, its longer, thready roots, splayed out and dangled freely on either side. Dad spaded the soil into the hole till the sapling stood firm and strong then Edwin took his spade and put the last of the earth round the top pressing it firmly with his boots.

"Now then lads and lasses, this tree needs looking after, nurturing. You'll need to feed the soil Edwin and make sure it doesn't dry out, or get too wet. It's firm enough now but as it grows taller you'll need to put a strong stake beside it to support it, till it's well established and strong enough to support its height and weight on its own. The rest we leave to God and nature. And no pulling it up to see what's happening, the roots will need to grow long and deep before the upper part of the tree can grow properly. Right young Edwin, what do you say to that?"

"It's splendid Dad, thank you. I'll look after it. It's something right special, it'll always remind me of this and of you and everything,"

Edwin, blushing and grinning and looking shy all at once, spread his hands to indicate the whole garden and the family and all that it meant. The setting sun bathed them in a golden rosy light and Ellie tried to lock it all in her memory. They lingered in the stillness, each feeling entirely happy to be there, alive and together.

"Maybe, in a few million years or so, someone will dig it up as a fossil," said Stephen, at which everyone laughed and they all trooped indoors to have a slice of birthday cake. After the infants were in bed, the older ones had a noisy card game, which Edwin was cleverly allowed to win and bedtime was reached in peace. Dave and Jeannie watched fondly as the children went off to bed. As soon as they were alone, Dave took his wife in his arms and kissed her.

"We're not doing too badly by them lass, are we?" he said.

"They'll do for now," smiled Jeannie kissing him back. "What will be their future? Well, we'll have to wait and see. Times are changing. By the way, Dave, Ellie's nearing the end of her confirmation classes. The Vicar's announced that the Bishop is coming next month, to confirm those who've been prepared and give them their first Communion. Your mother is very keen for all her grandchildren to be confirmed. What do you think?"

"I think we should ask Ellie if this is what she wants. I've no objection if she chooses to be confirmed but I don't hold in pushing it onto young folks if they've no leaning towards it; my mother needs to realise she can't control people. I puzzle over some of the Church's teachings myself but I've a great respect for the Reverend Chadwick, he's done a lot of good with the youngsters round here. I'm not so sure of that Deaconess. She seems to have her head in the clouds, needs to be a bit more down to earth! I had to laugh, when our Ellie said she was going up on the Tops 'to meditate' like Deaconess Broughton told them. Meditating, at Ellie's age, I ask you? What's the woman thinking about? Filling young girls' heads with such airy-fairy nonsense?"

"The girls certainly seem to take to her, Dave. At Ellie's age, I'm not sure they know whether they've a leaning towards the Church or not. We agreed that we'd let Ellie go to the confirmation classes and then make up her mind, in the light of them."

"Well, we've done that. Has it got her anywhere? She doesn't seem much different to me apart from her 'meditations.'"

"Oh Dave, there's a lot more to life than what we see every day. Some days I'm that sure of God I think I could touch Him and others He's in a bit of a mist, a long way away. What do you really think, love?"

"I think, Mrs Elkson, that I love you very much and it's time we were upstairs in bed," bending over his wife he kissed her tenderly and laughing quietly, they wound their way upstairs.

CHAPTER 6

Sarah attends a funeral. 1898.

S arah lay on her bed resting after a Sunday dinner of beef and Yorkshire pudding with roasted potatoes, carrots, runner beans and cabbage. All the vegetables were from their own garden and there had been far more of these on their plates than beef. The family had more money, now that Ellie had a part-time job at the grocer's shop on the corner of Aspen Lane, so they could have afforded more meat but mother insisted it was better for them to eat vegetables. Mother had made up for it by serving plenty of good rich gravy, full of softly-boiled onions. This had been followed by a slightly heavy jam pudding, made by Ellie the previous day. Sarah thought her elder sister hadn't learnt the knack of turning out sponges as light as mother's but, with hot custard, nobody had complained. Sarah had managed to exchange her own half- full pudding plate, with Edwin's quickly emptied one, when no-one else was looking. Leaving food was a major sin but she really had been too full; Edwin was never full, thank goodness.

A half hour's rest on their beds for the Elkson children before the they walked up to afternoon Sunday School, was a family rule and Sarah lay contentedly, having what she called, "a good think." Ellie being older, was allowed to sit downstairs.

Sarah was mulling over a Wednesday morning two weeks ago. She'd been in the church, for the funeral of eleven year old Joe Shaw. His sister, Lily, was in Sarah's class and the two girls had been partners on a nature walk the previous week. They'd passed near to a deep cut lodge, or man- made pool, about forty feet square. The

31

water had looked dark and cold, set among the sunny, grass covered slopes dotted with white- tufted cotton grass, glossy green bilberry plants and the tiny yellow flowers of the 'treacle mustard.'

"Mi brother drowned in that lodge last Saturday," Lily had confided to Sarah, as matter-of-factly as if she was saying he'd gone down to the shops. Sarah had felt cold inside.

"How awful for you," she'd stammered.

They'd walked on in silence. Eventually Sarah hadn't been able help herself and asked, "How did it happen?"

Lily had shrugged her shoulders, "He'd gone fishing with some bigger lads; He jumped in to cool off and couldn't get out. Funeral's next week."

"Your mum must be upset?" Sarah had tried to imagine Lily's mother coping with the tragedy.

"Dunno really. She won't say nought about it, 'cept 'e shouldn't 'ave gone; 'e knew 'e weren't allowed. There's that many of us at 'ome, she can't keep 'er eye on all of us," Lily had sniffed and rubbed her nose with a corner of her tattered pinafore, "I miss 'im. 'E were alreet wi' me, were our Joe. 'E were only one year older 'n me."

The thin, sharp-faced child had shaken back her long, straight hair which was so fair as to be almost silver. It was meant to be tied back with a strip of rag but her hair was fine and sparse and hadn't enough body to hold it. With her pale skin and faded clothes, the only real colour about Sarah's companion was her language and feisty spirit.

"Come on Sarah, we'd better look for some more plants! We've only found two sorts; Miss Prior will be right buggered off with us."

Giggling at the forbidden words they'd begun to search the side of the path for interesting specimens.

The following week Joe's school class had gone to his funeral service. Sarah's class was not going but Lily had asked specially if Sarah could come with her, as her friend. Miss Prior had spoken with Sarah's parents and it had been agreed that she should go.

"Wait and walk in with me," whispered Lily, as she stood with her family at the church gate. At a nod from the head teacher, Sarah had stayed with the Shaw family. There'd been nine Shaw children; Joe had been the eldest and now it was Lily. Mrs. Shaw had been a surprise to Sarah. She'd expected a poor, weak, down-trodden little woman, worn out with work and children. She'd certainly looked thin and shabbily dressed but Jessie Shaw had stood proudly upright, with a baby on her arm and her chin in the air. She kept smiling encouragingly at her children and pressed against her husband who drooped beside her, his head down and his arms falling loosely, with a flat cap dangling from his fingers.

"Grief," Lily had whispered to Sarah, "Can't take it; Dad's had too much of it," and she'd tapped the side of her nose knowingly.

Sarah had felt frightened and longed for Ellie. The coffin had arrived and was carried into the churchyard by two of Lily's uncles, on her mother's side. It was so near to Sarah she could have touched the shiny wooden box. Thinking of what was inside it, Sarah had wanted to turn and run but she'd just stood there, her knees trembling. She remembered firm fingers closing over her hand and looking up she'd found Mrs Shaw leaning across to her,

"Don't fret child, we're just saying goodbye to our Joe, Jesus has taken him on a big adventure, don't fret about it." The strong little woman had straightened up and shepherded her family into line as the Vicar, the Revd. Ralph Chadwick walked down the path to greet them. After exchanging a kind word with them the Vicar had turned and the small procession had followed him into the church.

"Do not let your hearts be troubled neither let them be afraid, trust in me—"

Sarah had felt better as soon as she heard Mr. Chadwick speaking the opening words of the funeral service in his warm familiar voice

It was during this service that Sarah had really looked, for the first time, at the stained glass picture that so impressed George. It was of the disciples in a boat, with a storm raging and the figure of Jesus, moving through the waters towards them. The Vicar, thinking of the children, had drawn their attention to it and used the story to help them cope with the traumatic death of young Joe.

"Jesus has promised he will always be there for us in the difficult and sad times of our lives just as he came to the disciples in that awful storm."

Sarah had almost felt the spray from the waves and heard their roar and the sound of the wind as she stared at the window picture. Ralph Chadwick had paused, looking out over his congregation. Sarah remembered she'd wondered what he'd had been thinking at that moment. In fact, the Reverend Chadwick had felt humbled before the people he was preaching to; he knew so many of their daily struggles and as always, wondered at their bravery. "Just how much can a person take before breaking?" he had thought as he looked down at Joe's father and had uttered a silent prayer before continuing.

"There will be lots of storms in our lives but Jesus will be there to help us through. He is here now with the Shaw family in their sadness and with you, Joe's school fellows. He has promised to be with us when we come to our death and to take us home to himself. And so, when young Joe drowned in the Lodge, because it was too cold and deep for him to survive, we trust that Jesus came and like the good shepherd, in that other story of the lost sheep, took Joe up in his arms and carried him to his home in Heaven. Who knows what wonderful times Joe will be having there."

Joe's mother had lifted her head and smiled right up at the Vicar, but her lips had trembled.

Mr. Chadwick had sensibly ended his little homily at that point. Prayers had been said commending Joe to his heavenly Father at which point his earthly father had let out a great groan.

"Shush Harry, you'll upset the young folk," whispered his wife, tapping him firmly on the knee. Mr. Shaw had subsided into meek silence but Sarah had seen tears running quietly down his cheeks.

The service had ended with a hymn which fitted the theme of the Vicar's sermon 'Will your Anchor hold in the storms of life'. It was well-loved by children and adults alike and had a rousing tune, which had lifted everybody's spirits.

When they'd come out of church, Sarah had seen Ellie waiting for her at the gate. After saying goodbye to Lily and her family, Sarah had gone straight home with Ellie. Once there, Sarah had put her head on her sister's shoulder and cried as if her heart would break. Ellie had held her tight, until the sobs ended in hiccups.

"I'll have to find you 'The Water Babies' to read," Ellie had said and told Sarah of the chimney sweep's boy, who'd fallen into the river and been changed into a water-baby. Sarah remembered it had been Ellie's closeness and her soothing voice that had comforted her, rather than the unconvincing idea of Joe Shaw becoming a water-baby. Soon after Ellie had finished her tale, three year old Jack had toddled in, demanding their attention and had soon driven away any dismal thoughts, with his smiles and antics.

All this had happened over two weeks ago; the disturbing event had become a memory, but a significant one. "Jesus has taken Joe on a big adventure", Sarah repeated Mrs. Shaw's words to herself and snuggling down contentedly on her bed, she slept.

CHAPTER 7

The NATS, a bull and other creatures. 1898.

Happily for Sarah there had been two events, in the weeks following Joe's funeral, to lift her spirits. The first was the children's community ramble and picnic with the Hartsbeck Naturalist and Antiquarian Society or the 'NATS.' For the Elkson children, the NATS had become an extended part of their family. They'd been born and bred with a passion for the natural world, Ellie and Stephen had trotted alongside their parents on NATS outings since they were five and four years old. .

Children were always welcome to join the NATS weekly rambles in the countryside. A few keen youngsters even attended the Saturday night lectures when Natural History was explored in substance and theory, by visiting experts or knowledgeable locals, on flora, fauna and rock formation.

However, despite the fascinating specimens and amazing lantern slides, these lectures were not always appealing to children. From the kindness of their hearts and a desire to enthuse a love of nature into the young folk, the NATS organised an annual outing, specifically for children aged seven to twelve years of age. Numbers had to be limited and most of the children came by special invitation. The children of members were always included but every year a particular part of the town was chosen and twenty children invited, from that area, none of whom would normally have the chance of such an outing. This year it was the turn of St. Mark's parish and Miss Prior from St. Mark's school and Mr Chadwick, the Vicar, had been asked to produce names and addresses of needy children.

The day included a country ramble with competitions of bug-hunting and plant and rock collecting. This year it was to be held on the last Saturday in June and fingers were crossed for a fine day. Sadly, the day dawned with a slight threat of rain.

"It could go either way," said old Len Cartwright, shading his eyes with a cupped hand as he studied the sky, turning his gaze in different directions.

"I think the rain clouds are moving west, in which case we'll keep dry and might even catch a bit of sun around lunch time," Len had worked on the railways for twenty years and considered himself an expert on the ways of the weather.

"I'm not so sure," Bill Dobson, retired schoolmaster, licked his forefinger and held it high in the air to feel the direction of the wind, "I think that wind is from the West, in which case the rain clouds will be right over us before long,"

"Oh, what's a drop o' rain amongst friends, them's not 'eavy rain clouds; it'll be a light shower at most and quickly over," Jack Long, who worked for the Parks department, looked knowingly at the sky, before turning to the group which had gathered to decide the fate of the outing.

"Is it on, or is it off?" panted Amy Foster rushing up at the last minute from an early morning cleaning job. "Me and our Gertie have the food all ready to be packed up."

Usually everyone took their own picnic on the rambles but for the children's outing a large communal picnic was always prepared. It was paid for from monies raised throughout the year.

"I think we should let Vincent, as Chairman, make the final decision, otherwise we'll get nowhere. Right everyone?" Len Cartwright looked round at them all,

"Aye, you're right, should be his responsibility,"

"That's what he's there for."

Vincent Moss, forty-six year old carpenter and joiner, and the Nats' Chairman for this year, considered the matter before replying;

"I think we should go with our alternative plan. As we've got some youngsters under seven with us and several who've been ill over the last few months, I think, considering the uncertain weather, we shall keep a little nearer to home. Instead of taking the steam tram to Rooky Bank, we'll set off walking round the edge of the Playing Fields at the top of Aspen Lane. There'll be plenty of plants and insects in the long grasses. Then down into Willow Clough for water plants and bugs and a rock hunt. From there we can carry on up the hill for quarter of a mile to Oak Farm for our picnic lunch and a look at the children's finds."

"Well" said Gertie, "that sounds alright. Mind you, they'll be disappointed about the tram. Just remember, not all the youngsters have waterproofs and some of them aren't very strong. If they catch cold it could be the band to play!"

"The Vicar's wife and I have been round folks we know and managed to gather a collection of children's waterproofs and boots. I think we'll have enough," said the ever resourceful Miss Prior, who knew most of the families in the neighbourhood,

"It's so important for these town children to get out into the fresh air and enjoy a taste of country-side. It's worth risking a wetting, we're not going so far from home, after all," and Miss Prior shook her head earnestly. She turned quite pink and her neat bun of hair quivered with eagerness. She knew just how many children, from the overcrowded homes of industrial workers, had little chance to breathe country-fresh air and enjoy the wonders of the natural world.

Vincent turned to Frank Airey, a large rugged-faced man in his early fifties and the owner of Oak Farm.

"Frank. You kindly offered us shelter in your new barn if it rained."

"Oh Aye, that's right, Vincent. We've just finished building t' barn and it's not in use yet, so it's clean and dry. It's empty too, so there's plenty o' room. We'll carry some straw bales across for you to sit on and my wife says she'll provide hot drinks. You can have a bit of a sit in there, even if it's fine. I've asked young Bert Lee to drive the cart down and carry the picnic up to the farm for you, so you won't have the food to carry. If 'rain comes on 'afore lunch, ye can all go straight to the farm and play games and tell stories or have a good sing song in the barn. That way it'll be a reet good do, whatever the weather."

Frank rubbed his hands and beamed round at everyone, glad to provide such a beneficent solution. A general murmur of assent went through the group. Vincent sighed with relief, "that's settled then. We shall meet outside the school at a quarter to ten, ready to set off at ten o'clock sharp."

By quarter to ten a motley gang of children, aged from seven to twelve, were gathered outside St. Mark's primary school. Some, like Sarah and her brothers, came from the slightly better houses similar to Aspen Lane; others came from the poorer areas of overcrowded streets with back to back houses where disease and infant mortality were rife. Ellie had visited some of these houses with Annette. It had shocked the young girl to see the state of the shared privies standing in rows of stone shelters separated from the dwellings by a narrow ginnel. The stink of them had made her feel sick.

This morning, all the children present had been well-scrubbed so that their usually pallid faces looked pink and raw. Any children arriving without boots were soon fitted out with them. Some of the smallest were weary already, after the walk from their homes. Miss Prior guessed rightly, that most of the poorer children had eaten no breakfast and had been awake much of the night with excitement. She'd come prepared. From a cloth bag slung across her shoulders she produced a large paper package,

"A jam butty for everyone before we start," she declared, opening the parcel and revealing a pile of thick bread sandwiches oozing raspberry jam.

At the same time, a beaming Annette Hamilton hurried up from her house carrying a tray of mugs filled with milk.

"Ooh, Miss!" chorused those who had come hungry. Every child, rich or poor was given a share of bread and jam and a mug of milk. Those who had already eaten breakfast shared theirs with the hungry ones. There was much laughter and chattering as the food worked its vivacious miracle. No distinction by class or wealth was ever taken into account in this group of good-hearted people of equal worth in their common interest in nature in all its' forms. All but one or two of the children relaxed and mixed happily together.

Vincent Moss and the NATS had brought an assortment of equipment. Butterfly nets, ponding nets; jars, large and small, with perforated lids and string handles. There was a pile of bags, made of sacking, to hold rocks and plants. The children were divided into pairs and given a selection of collecting materials. The ponding nets were to be carried by the adults until the Clough was reached. The Vicar and his wife carried the spare waterproofs and first aid materials. Vincent gave instructions about the route and the competitions. Then the adults divided themselves among the children and the grand trek began.

Stephen had his mind set on the rock collecting. He didn't really care about it being a competition, he just wanted the excuse to search for particular rocks he knew ought to be around that area; he'd brought his own strong canvas bag, a small trowel and a strong penknife. He was saving up for a geologist's hammer but today didn't warrant such equipment. It was botany which fascinated Edwin, with its' mad variety of plants and their choices of habitat.

Ellie liked to help Stephen, he knew so much and she tried hard to remember everything he showed and told her about. However, today she had the special care of three of the poorer children and carried a selection of bags, jars and small boxes ready for their eager finds. Like her friend, Bert Lee, she had now reached the age of being one of the helpers.

Sarah and George, as junior members of the NATS, flitted from group to group, ready to help anyone who needed it while collecting whatever struck their fancy and pushing it into the relevant jar, bag or box.

Sarah was with a girl called Lily Shaw when they came across a small butterfly, delicately shaded in muted browns and soft orange, with a black spot in the outer corner of each front wing and two small white dots down the centre of the black spots. They had noticed it feasting on the nectar of a purple clover flower but neither of them wanted to imprison it. They quickly recorded its size, colour and special markings in Sarah's note-book and Lily made a quick sketch of it and they popped a purple clover flower into their bag to remind them.

Len Cartwright came over to them," that butterfly's called the Gatekeeper. They're special up here. They likes to live in the hedgerows and edges of fields and woodlands, just the kinds of places you might find a gate. It fairly loves them wild blackberry blossoms, or brambles as some folks call 'em, but it's enjoying that head of clover right enough. Aah, there she goes, never long in one place."

The small gatekeeper fluttered into the air, hovered around Sarah for a moment, then fluttered in front of them, as they walked along a path towards the hedgerows, which skirted the track they were to take.

"It's leading us," laughed Lily

"Aye, they do say that about the Gatekeeper. She'll look after you; lead you in the right way! In springtime you'll find their chrysalis, hanging from the stalks of the long grasses, all along the edge of the field, marking the path. Friendly sort they are!" and old Mr. Cartwright went away chuckling to himself.

They were in the Clough, looking for quiet pools among the rocks in the busily running brook, where they might find water boatmen, diving-beetles and water-snails, when the rain came. Gently at first so they hardly noticed it, then harder until the Vicar's wife called the children and made them don their waterproofs.

"To the farm," cried Vincent "fast as you can now but mind you don't fall on the stones; we don't want any sprained ankles. Once we get into the lane it'll be easier walking."

Two nine year old lads held back, as the others surged forward across the rough ground. One of these was Ephraim Shaw brother of the late Joe. The other was Geoff Chadwick, one of the vicar's sons.

"Hey, Geoff," Ephraim hissed plucking at the frayed sleeve of his friend's jersey, "I reckon we can find a quicker way and be at the farm before them! That'll show these know- it -all country lovers that we can do as good as them."

"I'm with yer, Eep. Where'll we go?"

"Just wait be'ind this bush till they've gone over the brow; then we'll cross the stream on t' water pipes and through the 'edge into that field. If we run across t' field, we'll be in t' farmyard long afore that lot 'ave walked up the lane."

"We'll be soakin' wet," said Geoff, thinking of his mother.

"Aw do'an be such a chicken!" Eep pushed Geoff in the stomach, then set off, sliding down the bank to where two large cylindrical iron pipes crossed a deeper and swifter flowing part of the stream. Adroitly balancing on the surface of the widest pipe Eep, confident with much practice, stepped quickly across the rounded metal surface to the other bank. Geoff was more cautious and sat on the pipe straddling it with his legs.

"Yer soft ape-orth, you'll be all day," grumbled Ephraim.

Geoff ignored him and pulled himself along the rusty pipe on his bottom, staining the seat of his trousers. Ephraim was up the other bank and nearly at the hedge by the time Geoff was across. The hedge held them up, being thick and prickly but Eep stood on Geoff's shoulders and threw himself over the top. He reached down and pulled Geoff over the lethal thorns, straight into a patch of thickly churned mud. Their waterproofs had protected them from being too badly scratched, except on face and hands but their clothing was ripped in several places. Geoff was beginning to wish he hadn't come, especially as he felt his feet sink deep into the sticky mud, he tried to run after Ephraim but his boots were firmly stuck and sinking deeper.

"Eep!!" he screamed, "I think it's quicksand. Help I'm sinking, I can't get out!"

Ephraim, on his way up the centre of the field, shouted over his shoulder, "don't be daft, it's not that deep- pull yer feet out an' walk on t' grass tufts, it's only muddy at th' edge o' field. Yer should 'a gone wi t' others, yer great soft Mick!"

Geoff pulled and his foot came out, leaving his boot and sock in the mud. He put his bare foot down and struggled in vain to get out of the mess. Tears and snot were running down his face as he slipped and slithered and stuck and tried to retrieve his boot. A sudden cry from Ephraim made him look up to see an animal, standing taller than a cow in the centre of the field they had entered. The enormous creature's dark brown hide rolled in great folds over its gross body and thick set neck. The beast's head was turned towards Ephraim, the tips of its horns had been blunted but the threatening shape was still there and the metal ring through its flaring nostrils proclaimed it to be farmer Airey's famous bull.

"Run Ephraim, it's the BULL!" shouted Geoff.

Now it was Ephraim's turn to be scared. The boy and the bull stared at one another, each frozen in their tracks. The bull moved first, lowering his head and turning round in a circle. The boy set off again across the field towards the distant top gate but he couldn't run, his legs and body felt too heavy and it was painful to breathe.

"HELP, SOMEBODY HELP!!" screamed Geoff sitting down in the mud and backing under the safety of the hedge. "HELP, DAD, HELP!!"

The rest of the group with Miss Prior and Ellie, were walking up the lane on the other side of the hedge, which skirted the field and heard the frantic screams. The Reverend Chadwick and Vincent Moss ran to the top gate leading into the field and saw the bull lower his head again, ready to charge at Ephraim. The vicar vaulted over the gate and moved quickly towards the bull, shaking his walking stick in front of him, shouting as he went. Vincent Moss followed, quietly opening the gate and slipping through, to make his way down the edge of the field to Geoff. As soon as he was in the path of the bull, with Ephraim behind him, the Vicar stood still but continued shouting and shaking his stick in the air and waving his other arm wildly.

"Ephraim, get through the gate as fast as you can." he shouted without turning his face from the bull. The lad tried to hurry to the gate but his wobbly legs slowed him down. Ellie rushed forward and dragged the terrified boy out of the field. Miss Prior pounced on a wiry, ferret of a boy-"Morgan Pearce, run up to the farm and get help, Mr Airey or a farm hand, fast as you can now,"

Morgan ran. "Tell them it's the bull!" Miss Prior yelled after him.

The bull was confused, shaking his head he stopped in his tracks and turned away snorting and tossing his head, he walked round in a circle once more. The Vicar slowly backed towards the gate; he dare not draw attention to Vincent struggling with Geoff at the bottom of the field. Ellie summed up the situation and suggested they move further up the lane above the gate and make a noise and jump up and down to distract the bull from Geoff and Vincent and the Vicar. Soon every child was excitedly jumping up and down in the rain waving their arms madly in the air, the bull, looked, rolled his eyes, snorted and turning his back to them relieved himself prolifically.

"Eeh, look at that! Where's it all come from?" the boys were all admiration, "Ugh, that's disgusting," some of the older girls screwed up their noses; the younger girls stared, as open-mouthed as the boys.

Five minutes later two men arrived from the farm with Morgan. With practised hands they soon made the bull secure. Geoff, now free of the mud was reunited with his sock and boot and shamefacedly shambled up the field with Vincent.

"That'll teach you not to obey orders," barked Major Simpson, ex- army. "If you had been two of my men —

"Now, Major," Miss Prior intervened, "I'm quite sure Geoff and Ephraim, indeed all of us, have learnt a very valuable lesson today. Haven't we? I think an apology is in order to Mr Moss and the Vicar, and to Farmer Airey for disturbing his bull. Ephraim, Geoffrey?"

"Yes, Miss; sorry Miss. Sorry to cause trouble Mr. Moss, thanks Mr. Chadwick for coming to rescue me. You were reet brave. I'm sorry Farmer Airey." Ephraim snuffled and wiped his nose on his sleeve.

"Thank you Mr Moss. I'm sorry dad, mum, Mr. Airey," Geoffrey mumbled, hanging his head.

"Apology accepted," Mr. Moss clapped both boys on their shoulders. "No more to be said young men. Now you will understand that there's always an important reason for doing what you're told, especially on a country walk. You never know what dangers may be lurking!!"

The adults smiled, remembering other walks and other hazards. Farmer Airey shook his head, thinking what could have happened. He looked at the bedraggled children,

"Now then," he bellowed, "on to my barn, before you have to swim there," and the group hurried up the track to the farmyard and the welcoming dry barn, hot drinks and food. Ellie smiled to see her child-hood friend, Bert Lee, helping with the food which he'd brought up in the farm cart.

"They've got you working then Bert," she teased, "even though it looks like women's work," she ducked as Bert threatened her with a basket of sticky buns.

"I'd like to see you bring that farm cart up the hill," Bert handed the basket to Miss Prior.

"Hmm, and there I thought it was old Toby, my favourite cart-horse who did all the hauling!" Ellie ran laughing in amongst the other children as Bert pretended to chase her.

"Ellie, you are now a young woman and too old to be behaving like a young school child. Set an example to the others and don't encourage Bert's attentions." The Vicar's wife spoke sharply and Ellie blushed hotly at the insinuation. She'd been friends with Bert for so long, it hadn't occurred to her that they'd reached the age where childish antics could be misconstrued.

She answered politely, "Yes of course, Mrs. Chadwick, I was forgetting myself in all the excitement."

Mrs Chadwick shook her head sadly, "that's just the time bad things happen, when you are off your guard. Learn the lesson and don't forget. I've seen many a young girl slip into trouble unawares," and she patted Ellie's arm before going to help with the little ones. Ellie knew from Annette about women slipping into trouble. She could have felt insulted but, aware of the Vicar's wife's deep involvement with women's moral welfare, amusement welled inside Ellie as she thought of herself being one of Mrs Chadwick's 'saved' women.

"What does that make Bert Lee?" she wondered, grinning wickedly but only partly understanding.

Once the muddiest children had been cleaned up and the hunger and thirst of all satisfied, the youngsters displayed the plants, bugs and rocks they had collected during the ramble. Bugs were examined first so that those which had survived the ordeal could be released back to the wild. The winner was Stan Simpson, a small waif of a boy with huge grey eyes and an enormous cheeky grin. He'd captured a beautiful diving- beetle from a rocky pool in the Clough. His prize was a pocket-sized magnifying glass and his proud smile nearly split his face in two. Morgan thumped Stan on the back, "Well done young un, what a prize specimen!"

"Couldn't 'ave catched it without you, Morgan, the blighter would have gone under, if there 'adn't bin the two of us."

"Maybe, but 'twas you that spotted the feller!" and the two boys sat together, gloating over the large hard backed beetle moving slowly up and down in the jam jar full of pond water.

The winner of the plant collecting was Susan Ramsden, a sweet, sad-faced, nine year old, one of a family of eight, whose mother was an invalid. Susan rarely had time to enjoy life outside the home and was often missing from school because her mother needed her. Today she was revelling in the freedom and had discovered over twenty two different species of plants, including flowers; grasses; moss; lichens; water- weed and even a few early berries and seed pods. She'd worked alone, enjoying the delightful sensation of not being constantly moithered by the needs of others. Her prize was a beautifully illustrated compendium of wild flowers of the British Isles, just small enough to fit into a pocket but chunky enough to be packed with information on most known species.

The rock competition was won by Lambert Wilkinson, helped by Stephen Elkson. Lambert was a shy, awkward ten year old, whose father was in prison for burglary. The lad fitted in well with Stephen, who tended to be rather silent and terse when engrossed in anything to do with his beloved rocks. Lambert had stuck to Stephen like a limpet during the ramble and had become fascinated at the way his mentor dug and hammered, sniffed at and collected different soils, as well as stones and rocks. Soon, Lambert had been collecting for himself and had a variety of sixteen different coloured stones, pebbles and soils, in a variety of textures. His prize was a lump of grey rock, curiously coiled and patterned, reminding him of a large snail shell.

"This, my boy, is a fossil. About one hundred and seventy million years ago it was a living creature, a shell fish living in the sea, probably the shallower waters near the shore because these markings show they couldn't swim very well. This fossil is called an ammonite and it formed because the hard shell of the creature was preserved under layers of mud and sediment. The natural chemicals surrounding it changed it into rock- form. The process took millions of years. This ammonite was found not so many miles from here! Keep it safe Lambert, it will remind you how short a time we have on this earth, at least, in the form we are now. We need to use the time well, before our bodies become earth and dust. If you want to know more, ask young Stephen here. Now it's time for some fun and games."

Lambert looked with awe at the fossil, it fitted perfectly into his hand and he traced the smooth and rough edges of its exquisitely formed patterns. He felt the stony hardness of its weight and could hardly believe it was not carved by a man's hand but formed by nature over, how many years?

"Is it really mine?" he whispered to Stephen

"Course it's yours. Say, Lambert, if you're really interested, you can come with me when I go fossil - hunting next time. It's grand fun and there are lots of different fossils about."

Lambert felt excited, unbelieving and hopeful all at once. He stared at the older boy.

"I'd like that, Stephen, I really would,"

The two lads solemnly shook hands to bind the arrangement, then, with a mutual sigh, resigned themselves to joining in the noisy games, which were the traditional finale to the day. Later, as it was still raining, Farmer Airey brought out two large farm carts and horses to pull them. Tired and happy the children piled in and were transported back to the school in style.

CHAPTER 8

Grandma Jane's 80th Birthday July 1898

The second event that year, which lifted Sarah's spirits and Ellie's, was a grand family gathering in July, to celebrate Grandma Elkson's eightieth birthday. Grandma Jane, as they all called her, lived in Preston, fifteen miles from Hartsbeck, with her daughter and son-in-law, Alice and Arthur Nowell and their four children. There was eighteen year old Hugh; Lettie at fifteen; Ursula twelve and Gilbert who was ten. Another baby was expected in three months' time. Their large town house was in a quiet street overlooking a tree filled park and was deceptively close to Preston town centre. During the afternoon, Grandma Jane had managed to speak to each of her grandchildren in turn, even four year old Jack had enjoyed a special story- time, all to himself, sitting on a padded leather buffet at her feet.

Imperious and beak nosed, Grandma Jane sat upright in a straight backed arm-chair which was richly upholstered in green and gold brocade. She cut a striking, matriarchal figure, in her full skirted dress of black bombazine, the white crocheted top of a modesty vest, peeping above the frock's square-cut neckline and an exquisite piece of black, pointed lace, resting on the plaited, white coronet of her hair. A silky shawl in a delicate shade of lilac was draped around her thin shoulders, softening the sombre black and suggesting her gentler side.

When it came to Ellie's turn for a private interview, the seventeen year old girl sat nervously beside her grandmother, conscious of some peculiar intention behind Grandma Jane's probing questions.

"Now, Ellie my dear. You will be nineteen in the New Year. If I remember correctly, you were confirmed in church, by the Bishop of Manchester, about a year ago. A bit late but according to your father it was of your own free choice. No doubt you pray and attend Church regularly and receive the Sacrament of Holy Communion?"

Ellie tried not to quail under the penetrating gaze turned upon her.

"Yes Grandma. I go to Holy Communion every month and attend morning and evening prayer every week."

"Good. I hope you go gladly and not because it is expected of you?"

"Sometimes I go gladly; other times I'm not so sure."

Grandma laughed, "I know just what you mean, my dear. If you go gladly 'sometimes', it shows the spark is there and hopefully it will grow to a stronger flame. However, to live your life as a true follower of Christ means a lot more than attending church on Sunday."

Ellie squirmed uncomfortably; whatever was the old lady going to say next? Was this to be a sermon?

"You finished your schooling about four years ago. Am I right?"

"Yes Grandma. I left school when I was fourteen. I'd passed all the exams up to standard seven when I left and Miss Prior allowed me to go to her privately, for extra tuition, for a full year afterwards. I work most days, as an assistant in the grocer's corner shop, but I read a lot and I've been going to some night classes at the Institute."

"Tell me about those. What subjects have you been studying? I wasn't sure whether they allowed young women to attend the classes."

"Oh yes, they'll take anyone who's really interested. I've been going to mathematics, chemistry and biology classes. We sit apart from the boys and in some subjects, such as human physiology, we're taught separately."

"My word! Sciences. I am impressed. Your mother tells me you also help the local midwife in her work and visit the poorer families, when there is sickness. Is this wise, Ellie? Especially with your work in the grocery."

"I'm very careful, Grandma, Mrs Hamilton, the woman I help, won't let me go where she knows there is infectious disease and she insists I wash properly after any visits. She takes me to families who are undernourished through poverty and bad food. A lot of children have rickets and other conditions, just because they don't eat properly or get fresh -air. Sometimes I help her with childbirth; I really love that part. The St. John's ambulance brigade taught us about delivering a baby, as well. I've been a member of the brigade since I was eleven. Annette, that is Mrs Hamilton, also teaches me at her home, about hygiene and the values of different foods and herbs and how to help prevent, as well as treat, diseases. She learnt a lot from her mother in Switzerland."

"Mm," mused Grandma, looking keenly over half rimmed spectacles at the girl and marking her obvious enthusiasm; "Ellie, have you heard of a lady called Florence Nightingale?"

"Oh, yes. I've read about her work in the Crimea. It's very exciting. A friend of mine, who's gone to London to nurse in St. Gabriel's Hospital, sent me some pamphlets written by Miss Nightingale. I like what she says. Life could be so much better for people, if we acted on her advice."

Grandma Jane leaned back in her chair drumming on her knees with bony fingers. She closed her eyes for a moment and Ellie watched, hoping the day hadn't been too much for the old lady. Snake-like, Jane Elkson snapped open her eyes and leaned forward looking straight into Ellie's face, she took hold of one of Ellie's strong firm hands in her own thin trembling ones,

"I've heard of St. Gabriel's, it has a good reputation. Ellie, my dear. I am very old and even if I live another five years or so, my needs are few. I have quite a tidy sum of money invested which was left to me when my husband (your grandfather Elkson) died and from legacies of my own parents. I've enough to help all my grandchildren make something of their lives. I've been pondering and praying over you all as I sit quietly in my chair day after day.

Now, Ellie. Due to Miss Nightingale and others, several good schools of nursing have been established in London Hospitals.

Would you like to join one of these schools and train to become a professional Nurse in the style of Miss Nightingale?"

Ellie felt as if the blood was draining from her; it rushed back suddenly so that her face became hot and red.

"Grandma, I've dreamt of this- but I'd no idea how I could manage it. How can I leave Mother and Dad and the other children? It takes money to go to London and I think you have to pay towards the first year as a probationer nurse. I was saving some of my wages from the shop but the family need most of it and it would take me ages to put enough by."

Grandma Jane leant forward and waved a hand dismissively,

"Don't let any of that stand in your way, Ellie. I'll talk with your Mother and Father. I've told you I have money waiting to be used; I can easily cover the finances. I've ideas for your brothers and sister and your cousins as well. I know Stephen is doing well in his engineering apprenticeship and he has a real bent for geology and most of the sciences. George is interested in the Law. Edwin I'm not sure about yet, or young Jack, but their time will come. Sarah is a happy child, who loves school. Your Aunt tells me she has a musical talent, but she isn't very strong."

"She's always talking about being a teacher when she grows up and she's growing stronger all the time;" Ellie was determined that Sarah shouldn't be side-lined.

"Well, we shall see. I want you to think and pray about what I've said. I am now going make enquiries for you, about nurses' training and as soon as I have definite information you will hear from me. If you are considered acceptable and you are willing to go, I'll arrange for your enrolment in a London teaching hospital and make it all possible for you, my dear."

"You sound like the Fairy Godmother!!" gasped Ellie almost too surprised to say thank you.

"Go on with you lass, I'm just an old woman with too much money but plenty of time to sit and dream what my talented grandchildren might do in the world, with a bit of help. Some folk would call it meddling or manipulating but you've all got the chance to say 'Yes' or 'No' to what I suggest. If you've better ideas of your own, I'm prepared to listen. God is very good, Ellie, never forget that but remember that 'those to whom much is given, much will be required.' Now go and let me have a bit of peace and quiet. It's been a very happy day but now I'm tired." Jane Elkson smiled as she folded her hands and resting her head against the chair back closed her eyes. Ellie crept out of the room and was just closing the door when Grandma called sharply,

"Leave it open, Ellie! I like to hear the noise of family chatter."

Uncle Arthur heard her and laughed, "She doesn't want to miss anything!" he whispered loudly,

"I heard that!" called Grandma.

Ellie and the rest of the family spent a happy, noisy hour, playing cards and guessing games. Then, it was time to say goodbye. On the journey home Ellie was silent, going over and over Grandma's words in her head. Excitement made her want to shout aloud into the night sky and she was glad when Dad started them all singing 'Show me the way to go home' and 'My old man said follow the van.' There was a rare jollity about Dad that night. It infected the whole family as they travelled home in the dark, squashed against each other in the hired farm cart behind the intrepid cart horse. They could have been setting out on any kind of adventure.

CHAPTER 9

A proposition for Ellie.

Three weeks later, Ellie received a letter from Grandma Jane stating that Cousin Hugh was going to drive her over to Hartsbeck, in the horse and trap, on Sunday the twenty first of August.

"I have important news for you Ellie and a proposition. I'm not going to tell you what it is until I've spoken to your mother and father face to face. I don't want to be accused of trying to shape the course of your life behind their backs and I want to temper their reaction, which is sure to be mixed. Cousin Hugh and I hope to arrive no later than eleven o'clock, weather and accidents permitting. We shall expect to take lunch and tea with you all but I'll make a courteous request, concerning that, to your mother in a separate letter."

Jeannie received her letter the same day, the twelfth of August. It gave her just nine days to prepare for the matriarchal visit and she whipped her household into frantic sessions of cleaning and baking.

Sunday the twenty-first was dry and warm and Grandma Jane was helped down from the horse and trap, at precisely eleven o'clock, with no more than a slight stiffness of her joints from the two hour journey.

Dave was delighted to welcome his mother. It was some years since she had travelled to Hartsbeck and she was pleasantly surprised with their house on Aspen Lane.

"It's in a healthier position than your last house, Dave, down in that crowded little street in the town," she remarked looking up the lane to the farmland and the moors beyond.

They ate lunch early. It was a happy meal, with all the family gathered round the dining room table. Jeannie had baked a piece of gammon, stuck with cloves and glazed with honey. She served it with vegetables from their own garden. Afterwards there was sherry trifle made with fresh raspberries, from the last of the crop grown that year by Edwin.

Jeannie had insisted on doing all the cooking herself. "I daren't risk any upsets," she'd stated and Ellie had been delegated to prepare the table and the children and make sure all was kept clean and tidy. Grandma Jane did justice to the meal, despite her age, and declared everything delicious.

"You haven't lost your touch Jeannie. I always envied the way you could make a simple meal taste like a feast."

Jeannie smiled and said she was glad Grandma had enjoyed the food.

While Ellie and Sarah cleared away and washed the dishes, Grandma Jane retired to the front room with Jeannie and Dave for a private discussion. After half an hour raised voices were heard. Dave was shouting and Grandma Jane was banging her stick and ordering him to, "Grow up and listen, David!"

Sarah stared wide-eyed at Ellie, "what's going on?" she whispered.

Ellie had turned white and was gripping the rim of the kitchen sink, "I'm not sure, but it may be about me, Sarah. Grandma wants me to go to London to be a nurse."

"Oh Ellie! Can't you be a nurse here?"

"I want to train in a proper teaching hospital in London and Grandma's offered to help me. That way, I can come back and be better qualified help to change some of the awful conditions here."

"That would be wonderful, Ellie; but why is dad angry."

"I don't know. Maybe he feels bad that it's Grandma who will be paying for me to go and not himself. Also, I expect dad thinks I should stay at home and help with the family. It's my place, as the eldest daughter."

Suddenly the front room door was flung open and Dave stormed out. He snatched his hat from the hall peg and marched, muttering, through the front door and up the street.

"He'll have gone to the 'Dog and Partridge'," said Stephen, who'd been listening from the staircase.

Jeannie Elkson came into the kitchen and saw Ellie's white face. "I think you can guess what that was all about, my girl. I'm not sure what to think. Your grandma wants to speak with you, in the front room."

"The front room, eh!" said Grandma Jane when Ellie was sitting opposite her. "It shows how much your mother thinks you've all risen from the days when it was the parlour." She chuckled quietly but Ellie detected a tremble in the frail hands that clutched and unclutched the walking stick handle.

"Now Ellie, you'll be worried about your father's reaction. Don't be. He'll come round; he's been like that since a child – hot off the mark, but one to see sense when he's had time to cool off and think things over."

"It's a big thing for him to face, if it's about my going to London," said Ellie defensively.

"No doubt, but if you're strong enough to accept it then he will- and so will your mother."

"You said you had important news for me," Ellie realised that they had started the conversation at the wrong end.

"Yes, forgive me Ellie. After our talk on my birthday, I wrote to an old friend of mine. She is a retired Matron of a London hospital and a well-known pioneer of nursing in her day. She's given me the information we need to know. First you will need to have an interview with the Matron of St. Gabriel's, as the hospital of your choice. If accepted you will be a probationary nurse for six weeks, during which time they test your suitability before enrolling you as a student nurse. You should be qualified by the time you are twenty-one. I am willing to finance you during your probationary and student nurse period. I've made provision for this in my will in the event of my death."

Ellie listened in silence. The map of her life was being drawn out before her at an alarming rate.

"Now, Ellie, in the light of your enthusiasm I have already written to the Matron of St. Gabriel's hospital and she has offered you an interview on Monday, 24th October at two o'clock in the afternoon. I hope you are happy with that; preparing for the interview will help you to decide whether it is what you really want to do."

"It's all happening very quickly," replied Ellie.

"Matron does stipulate that you wouldn't be able to start your training until after your nineteenth birthday on the thirtieth of November. That will give you a short breathing place to get used to the idea. Will you go for the interview?"

Ellie hesitated, "May I have a week to think about it and to persuade dad and mother?"

"Yes, of course, but don't try too hard to persuade your parents. They'll come round to it more quickly, if left alone. Make it clear that you want to go, if they ask you but don't argue. Believe an old woman, Ellie; things have a way of working out, if left alone."

Ellie came to her grandma and kissed her, "Thank you for all you're doing for me. I'll make you proud, if they'll have me."

"I'm already proud of you for wanting to try, my dear. Ask your mother if we can have a reviving glass of sherry and then I'll rest a while before tea and that long journey home."

For all her reassurances to Ellie, Jane Elkson was concerned about Dave, her second eldest son. She was anxious when he hadn't come home by the time she left to return to Preston with cousin Hugh. Stephen had dashed down to the 'Dog and Partridge' and seen his father slumped in a chair in the snug, sound asleep. He hurried back to tell Grandma Jane that Dave was safe at the public house but in no condition to come home yet. Jane Elkson travelled home subdued by her son's behaviour and afraid that he was 'going downhill.'

It was true that for some time, Dave Elkson had been suffering from bouts of moodiness and ill- temper. There were periods when he would sit up late into the night with nothing but a bottle of spirits for company but he was always up and away to his work on time, in the morning. These bouts only lasted two or three days and it might be a full two weeks before such a mood hit him again. Ellie soon learnt to keep her siblings out of their father's way at these times. Their presence and noise inflamed his mood and he would shout and hit out at them so that they were hurt and frightened. It was becoming increasingly wearing for her to be always watching and waiting, wondering what his mood would be when he came home. As the eldest she felt responsible for the other children and became edgy and sharp in her own manner to them, constantly afraid they would do something to upset their father.

Stephen was too engrossed in applying himself to his engineering apprenticeship to notice. As part of his contract he was released for two days a week to study maths and sciences at the local technical college and of his own accord attended evening classes at the Mechanics institute. He revelled in the courses provided at the Institute; inorganic chemistry; practical chemistry; geology; magnetism and electricity; the study of light and heat; acoustics and animal physiology. Chemistry and Geology were his real favourites and so good a student was he, that the teachers often employed him to assist them in preparing lessons, or coaching the beginners. He was fascinated by the natural world especially the formation of landscape with its shapes and variety of rocks and soils and the creatures nurtured by these varying habitats. He obtained a camera and became expert at photographing flora and fauna and all things natural in the countryside.

Soon he would finish his apprenticeship and with Grandma Jane's help, hoped to attend college full time and further his qualifications in science. His short-sightedness had been diagnosed and was corrected by a pair of round, rimless spectacles which gave him an attractive air of scholarliness. Young women, of a studious nature, flattered him by vying for his attentions. Stephen was not averse to such flirtations, they were the ideal antidote to keep him human, but the quickly stolen kisses and cuddles were more experimental than leading to any close relationships. Many a young girl imagined she nursed a wounded heart from his chaste, if tender affections.

George, although only twelve, already had a job. He was a water carrier in the iron foundry of the engineering works, where Stephen was apprenticed and where their father was a wages clerk. George had been given the job together with his close friend, Bob Stubbs; between them they carried the heavy water containers to the smelting shops, to cool the white hot metals, as well as the red and sweating labourers who worked them. The two young lads found the work taxing for their young untrained bodies. George longed for the time when he could work with his mind, rather than his body. He watched and listened and learned much from the hardworking men around him and was surprised at how often Annette Hamilton's name and sometimes his sister Ellie's, was spoken among them with real respect.

"Eeh, that Annette, she's such a one. I reckon our Edie wouldn't be 'ere but for 'er helping bring our little Benjamin in t' world," Bob Jones, one of the smelters, said one morning as the men sat drinking from their tea- cans at break time.

"Aye and that young Ellie Elkson wot 'elps 'er, nought seems to phase 'er. She set to and did all our washing last week, when the Missus was sick. She's not afraid of a bit o' dirt that one!"

"Aye, and she don't worry about catching ought. She carried our Sid 'ome when she found him sick with fever in the street when t'other folks wouldn't touch 'im."

That worried George, he didn't like to think of his sister risking her own health or bringing sickness home to the rest of their family. Bob noticed his anxious face,

"She's your sister, isn't she lad? Don't fret. Annette Hamilton teaches your Ellie ways of warding off infection. M' Mam knows a thing or two and she says Annette has more nouse than most doctors."

It didn't stop George worrying. Dave Elkson was hearing similar stories and he too was uneasy. He wanted his girls to grow up with caring natures, but to care to the extent of risking their own skins, and those of their family, was something altogether different.

Bob was right, Annette kept a careful eye on Ellie. In the course of their ministrations Annette and Ellie had to go into some very unsavoury situations. Annette kept a set of easily washed cotton smocks, which could be put on over ordinary clothes and fastened with a belt. She also insisted they wore cotton head-scarves, fastened tightly over their hair. The two women would put these on before setting out on any house visit. Annette always carried clean towels and carbolic soap with her and made sure Ellie scrubbed her hands before and after touching any patient, or anything connected with them. Annette would never knowingly take Ellie into danger. Whenever they had been to a house where they might have been exposed to diphtheria, or other infectious disease, they would go straight back to the Hamilton's home and Annette would pour them both a glass of greenish yellow liquid and insisted that they both gargled with it.

"It's a herbal recipe of my mother's. It will kill any nasty bugs and help to ward off infection and prevent you passing on germs to anyone else. After you've gargled, spit it out, and then drink the rest of the liquid."

Ellie had been apprehensive at first but the taste, though slightly bitter, had a hint of aniseed and was not unpalatable. In any case, her trust in Annette was absolute.

Lying in her bed at night, watching the moving patterns across the ceiling made by the flickering gas lamps in the street outside, she would mull over all she had seen among the poverty stricken back streets of Hartsbeck. She thought of the bread and margarine, which was all some children had for their main meal, with the occasional bits of potato and a scrap of bacon. The cramped streets of back to back houses with their tiny bedrooms where five children slept in one bed, head to toe, or on flat truckle beds which slid under the larger family bed. Old sacks had many uses, as protection from rain, as bedding and even towels in the poorest households and were seldom washed. Coats doubled up as blankets, piled on top of the beds on winter nights for warmth. Bed bugs and other vermin thrived. There was no running water and the lavatories were earth closets or tipplers, standing in rows outside the backs of the houses. Ellie had seen some children, from these districts, come to school engrained with the dirt of several days, covered with sores and smelling of filth and stale urine. Yet, there were others from the same area, who, though their clothes were shabby and mended, were clean and smelt sweet. Ellie was puzzled.

She thought of Aunt Lucy Nelson, who lived with her ten children and husband in a two up two down terraced house in a poorer area of the town. The Elksons had been their next door neighbours for three years before moving to their present, larger house in Aspen Lane.

"Cleanliness is next to Godliness, there can be no excuse for not cleaning yourself and the clothes and home you live in," Aunt Lucy would chunter and lived up to her chuntering.

She wasn't a relative, but had been Aunt Lucy as long as Ellie could remember, a plump, jolly person, whose house she had run in and out of as if it had been her own and who never minded an extra child under her feet. Five of Aunt Lucy's daughters were older than Ellie and had treated the rather serious little girl as one of their younger sisters, jollying her out of her solemn moods.

Annette had told Ellie of families who had no idea how to manage the small amount of money they had each week, so that they couldn't afford soap, when they had to buy food. Even when they had soap, the mothers, badly nourished themselves, were often ill and too weary to set to and clean their own homes and children. Their strength had all gone into endless child- bearing and child–rearing, as well as working at the mill or cleaning and washing in the houses of the wealthy to earn what they could.

"They care for their families as best they can with what little wit and strength they have left and in conditions not fit for animals to live in," Annette fumed.

"Why is Aunt Lucy not like that?"

"Well, your Aunt Lucy's a bit like me. She was brought up on a farm out in the country and grew up strong and healthy with good farm food and plenty of fresh air. She had a good start and that helps to make healthy babies later on. She learnt all about feeding the animals and how to cook wholesome meals for herself and her brothers, using all the animal parts that the wealthy folk won't look at. On top of that her folks sometimes bring in food from the farm and the children take turns to go and stay there for a holiday, now and again. And now the older girls are weavers at the mill, Lucy Nelson doesn't have to go out to work herself."

"That means she's more energy and enough money to buy soap," Ellie surmised,

"Oh your Aunt Lucy's got enough nouse to make her own soap. When she left the farm she went into service as a maid at one of the big mill-owners houses. She learnt all sorts of good cleaning ways. It's a lot cheaper to buy the ingredients and make your own, than buying the brands in the shops. She knows a trick or two with herbs as well. I once caught her walking all through the house with some-thing smouldering on a shovel.

'Sage', she told me, 'burn a bit on shovel - there's nothing better for sweetening the air in a fusty room.'"

"I'll remember that," said Ellie.

Annette had looked at Ellie in a strange way,

"Yes, little Ellie, you will soon be a young woman, ready to make your own home. Don't grow up too quickly; enjoy what's left of your childhood. Maybe I've shown you more than I should of the world's miseries."

"Annette, I've loved helping you. You've shown me things I would never have known about. I'm not a child any more. I'm going to do something about all this misery, see if I don't."

A week after Grandma Jane's visit Ellie was sure she would have to refuse the interview at St. Gabriel's. Her father hadn't come round and was insistent that her mother needed her at home. Apart from making this clear he refused to discuss the matter at all and became increasingly morose as the days passed. Grandma Jane sent a message to say that, as long as Ellie made her decision by the end of September, the interview would remain available. She added that there was no reason why Dave shouldn't allow Jeannie to have some paid help in the house. Most families of their standing had a woman to help with the chores and it didn't cost over much.

CHAPTER 10

Dad's fury

It was early September, 1898. A death had occurred which affected the whole community. Old Mr Lucas, the original owner and founder of the engineering works, which gave employment to so many people in Hartsbeck, had died peacefully in his own bed at eighty-seven years old. All of Hartsbeck was called upon to mourn. Old Lucas had been something of a philanthropist and poured money into many local community projects and charities. Out of respect, all the schools in the town were closed for the day of the funeral. The children, neat and respectful, lined the streets, as the grand cortege passed.

"Now boys remove your caps and bow your heads as the coffin goes by and girls bow your heads and dip a small curtsy, just as you've practised and keep your heads bowed, till the family have passed in their carriages. We're saying goodbye to a grand old man today, someone who 'as done us all a lot of good," said Mr Barnes, a town councillor, clearing his throat and looking sternly at the children from St. Mark's school, lined up, along the main road at the bottom of Aspen Lane.

In his will, Mr. Lucas had asked that a funeral tea should be provided for the people of the town. This was to be served in various schools and church halls. The Elkson's attended the one at St. Mark's school although Stephen was elsewhere with the other Lucas apprentices.

Young Edwin Elkson preferred the old term used by the Hartsbeck folk 'burial with ham' on account of the inevitable ingredients of ham sandwiches, pungent with pickled onions and mustard. The Lucas's had also provided egg and cress, home grown radishes, tomatoes and lettuce, bowls of raspberries and cream, melt-in-the mouth Victoria sandwich cakes and slices of dark fruit cake. When everyone had eaten their fill, the adults and older children set to and helped in clearing away and setting the school rooms to rights.

Jeannie Elkson hauled herself out of the chair from which she had presided over one of the tea tables. She caught sight of George, slipping a slice of fruit cake into his pocket and aiming for the exit. In one swift movement his mother seized his collar from behind,

"Not till you've done your share of the clearing up, young man. Now carry all these dirty pots to the women in the kitchen and stack them ready for washing. When you've done that you can take a plate of food round to old Mr Ramsbottom, he'd have been at the funeral if he had his health."

"Aw mother!" George looked up into his mother's stern face and obeyed, knowing his pocket would be full of sticky crumbs by the time he'd finished. Maybe he could sneak a bit extra onto Mr Ramsbottom's plate and eat it on the way"

"I'll fix him a plateful myself and wrap it for you," said Jeannie scotching George's plan, she hadn't brought up her family without learning a thing or two.

"Where's your Dad gone?" Jeanie asked Ellie, "He was here ten minutes ago helping to stack the chairs and tables."

Ellie looked round, "I think he went out, straight after he'd finished; maybe he's gone home. You take Jack and Sarah and go home yourself Mum, you look worn out. Sarah will help you. I'll help the ladies wash up first."

She turned to Sarah who was pulling young Jack around the slippery floor of the school hall on his bottom. Jack was whooping with delight,

"Sarah, take Jack home with Mother and make sure Mother has a rest. Edwin's off with his friends and George is going to Mr. Ramsbottom's."

An hour later Ellie walked thankfully through their front door on Aspen Lane. Immediately she realised something was very wrong. Jack was screaming from the back of the house and she could hear Dad's voice raised in fury and the sound of loud thumps from the kitchen. She hurried through and found Jack crouching in a corner of the room screaming in terror. Mum was sitting at the table, her head buried in her arms, sobbing quietly. Sarah leant over her, patting her shoulders. Dad was standing opposite them, his face scarlet, shouting and banging the table with his fists. Suddenly he picked up a kitchen chair and threw it across the room; mercifully it missed Jack but one of its legs snapped from the force of the throw.

"That young bastard! He can take his stinking engineering works with him t' Hell! I've worked my brains out for that firm and what thanks do I get. No sooner is the old feller in his grave than it's 'We don't think you are quite up to it anymore, Mr Elkson. Perhaps, in the light of your loyal service, we could find you something less demanding!'"

Dave turned unsteadily and saw Ellie staring at him. His eyes slid about like marbles in jelly, as they tried to focus and she realised he was drunk. The sight of his elder daughter seemed to inflame him more;

"And you, Miss High and Mighty, I know what you're up to – you and your Grandmother, plotting and scheming. Off to London to be a skivvying Nurse. Yes! That's what they are, just skivvies, cleaning up other peoples filth! Mark my words, lass, you'll be back in a week. You'll never stand it, all your romantic notions of curing folk; it's all a dream, a silly, girlish dream. You need a husband, some man that'll bring you down to earth and make a real woman of you. They'll make mincemeat of you down south. You mark my words, mincemeat!"

Staggering against the table, Dave clutched his head, muttering an oath. Turning his back on them all he reeled off upstairs. They heard him blunder his way into the bedroom. The creak of the bed, followed by silence, told them he was safe and would soon be snoring loudly.

Ellie rubbed her own forehead, her head ached and she longed for fresh air but she took the boiling kettle from the hob and made a large pot of tea. She poured a cup and took it to her mother who now was absentmindedly patting her tumbled hair. Sarah had taken up Jack and was rocking him in her arms, singing softly. His screams had become sobs, then hiccups and soon he began to fall asleep with the exhaustion of it all. Ellie poured two more cups, one for Sarah and one for herself, then she flopped down at the table opposite her mother. A despairing bitter feeling seeped through Ellie, could that really have been her own dad in a drunken rage. The words burst from her:

"What is happening to Dad? When did he start to be so bitter and nasty about people? He was always proud of working at Lucas's,"

"It's the drink," murmured Jeannie wearily.

"But why? Why did he have to start drinking like that?" Ellie cupped her chin in her hands and glared across at her mother.

"It's all part of him being in those rugby and cricket teams. They always end up in the 'Dog and Partridge', or the 'Shoulder of Mutton', or some other public house," said Jeannie, a hard edge to her voice

"But all the players do that. They haven't all ended up drunkards," said Ellie.

Sarah stared at them both, her face registering shock,

"Hey, Dad isn't really a drunkard, I know he isn't. He's just upset about his job and old Mr Lucas dying." her voice was a whisper.

"Well maybe not a complete drunkard, Sarah love, but he's well on the way, I grant you, Ellie. There are other things upsetting him. He's been getting bored with his job and he wants a better style of living for us than we have here on Aspen Lane."

"But this is a lot better than when we lived on Pendle Street!" Ellie was perplexed.

"His job with the wages put him on good terms with the bosses, as well as the workers. He got acquainted with people above his station. Your Dad didn't like it that I had no paid help in the house. He saw other wives who had women in to help with the washing and scrubbing and other heavy work such as carrying buckets of coal in for the fire."

"But Dad did most of the carrying of coal and emptying the ashes, and the boys do a lot of the heavy stuff, now that they're old enough. Anyway, we can afford some paid help. It may not be as much as rich folk can afford but it would be enough to ease the load. You're just making excuses for him, Mother. He's becoming a bad lot."

Ellie still smarted from the stinging insults flung at her by her father and spoke harshly. Jeannie continued as if she hadn't heard Ellie.

"Did you see some of the men who came to the funeral? Real toffs some of them, silk shirts and black toppers; all the way from Preston. Every one of them knew your dad. He found it hard, when we came here to Hartsbeck, even though wages clerk is a respectable position. In our little shop in Longmoor, Preston, your dad was his own boss. Then, this afternoon, that young Lucas, before his grandfather was cold in his grave, went into the Dog and Partridge to drink to Old Lucas with the men. There, in front of them all– and our Stephen there as well– told your dad, straight out, that he wasn't up to his job! Dad might have had a bit to drink but after all these years- and in front of all those people." Jeannie shook her head. "It's no wonder your Dad was angry! Stephen brought him home and then went out again, he was that ashamed."

Ten year-old Sarah was finding it hard to think badly of her father.

"It must have been grand when you and dad ran your own shop in Longmoor, before I was born," she sighed, thinking of the old tales she loved to hear. "I know he drinks more than he should but he can be a lot of fun. Do you remember, Ellie, when he took us to the pig farm and had to rescue Jack from the sty and carried him home on his shoulders even though he stank of pig muck?"

"Yes and he frightened away those horrid turkeys, by bending down and gobbling back at them right in their faces," Ellie laughed, searched her memory for the dad they had both adored.

Sarah took up the memory laughing and crying as she recounted it, "And flapping his arms at them and moving his head backwards and forwards just like them. Oh yes! I wet my knickers, I laughed so much, once we got over the fright. They came at us that fiercely."

"So fiercely! Watch your grammar, Sarah," corrected Jeannie automatically. In her own way, she too, wanted her family to move higher in the social scale but would never openly admit it.

Ellie began to recount earlier times, before any of her siblings were born.

"He used to tell me stories when I was very small, sitting on his knee by the fire. He told me about Old Mother Demdyke and the witches of Pendle Hill. It made me shiver but he just laughed and held me tight and told me it was all a very long time ago."

Jeannie gave Ellie a keen look, "Your dad will come round to you, Ellie; he was always fond of you, being his first- born."

Sarah frowned and spoke more sharply than usual, "Ellie, have you made up your mind yet, whether you're going to stay in Hartsbeck? I know you still want to be a nurse."

Ellie felt cornered and annoyed, "That's for me to worry about. You think about what you're going to do, I'll sort myself out, you'll know soon enough."

"But Ellie, what we do depends on what you do! Anyway, you know I want to be a teacher. If you go away, I'll just have to stay and be a pupil teacher in Hartsbeck, or nearby, where I can be close to mother and Jack. I won't be able to go to college and become a real teacher. The boys will be alright, they'll soon make their own way."

"Well, we'll see. There, I've finished my tea. I'm going out now, Sarah."

Ellie took the empty tea things to the sink, then, seeing her younger sister looked tired and near to tears, leaned across and pecked her gently on the cheek,

"I'm sorry I snapped at you. I've got to work things out and make decisions but I'm not ready to talk about it yet. I need to go and think things through. I'll have a walk up on the tops for an hour or so and clear my head. You and Mother have a proper rest..."

Sarah flung her arms round Ellie and hugged her tightly, "I'll see you when you come back. I won't badger you; I know you'll talk to me when you're ready.

CHAPTER 11

Decision on the Tops

Assured that the household had calmed down after Dave's fit of rage, Ellie was content to leave. She pinned on her black straw hat and taking a thick woollen shawl from the peg behind the back door made her escape.

She walked up the steep, cobbled back that ran behind the houses then, at the last house, she crossed the lane into an open field. The lightest of breezes played around her face and hair and ruffled her long skirts. She stared up into the open sky where sheets of thin white cloud softened the deep blue, cirrus stratus; she remembered Stephen telling her the name but couldn't think what type of weather such formations predicted. It didn't matter; it was pleasant stepping along the dry-baked mud of the path that ran beside the hedgerow. Last June there had been Mayflowers, with just a hint of pink, nodding shyly to her from among green horses- tails and the tall- stemmed flowers of the Red-Campion waving over them. The white stars of stitchwort had rioted with purple vetch in the shade of the hedge which had been entwined with delicate pink and white blossoms of the brier-rose, laden with golden pollen. Now the mayflowers were all spent and replaced with seeding sorrel and dock. The red campion sported its deep-cupped, purple-veined seed pods, stiffly frilled by their old, dry sepals. The wild rose and the hawthorn were heavy with rich red and orange hips and haws. As always, Ellie felt a deep thrill at the mysterious beauty of the seasons and all this wild growth. She ran her fingers along the long stalks of dock, the rusty seeds scattering along the ground beside her. Her tired body began to relax and her thoughts to settle.

The path took her over a small railway bridge and down a steeper incline into the small ravine of the Clough, with its clear stream running through grassy banks and bracken, where the children had played on the NAT's outing last spring. Now the clumps of bracken were turning brown.

Today, Ellie didn't want to linger in the close atmosphere of the Clough; she hankered to be up on the tops. There the air would be fresh and clear to help her with the decision she must make and make quickly.

Ellie sighed as she wound her way up the track towards Oak Farm sniffing the faint smell of pig sty and cattle drifting down towards her. A lump came to her throat at a rush of memories of her father taking them up here as children. Sarah was right. He had loved larking about with them and sharing in their lives, until about five years ago. He'd changed so slowly, she'd hardly noticed it happening. Small things, such as snapping at them if they'd joked with him or asked him to play.

He used to enjoy explaining things to them but recently, if they asked a question, his answer would most likely be: "It's time you learnt to find things out for yourselves." Or if the younger ones wanted him to tell them a story, he would brush them off with; "Now you can read, you should be finding your own books and stories."

He'd deliberately been pushing his family away and hiding his old familiar kindliness under a cloak of irritability. Ellie realised that he'd spent more and more time away, playing in his beloved rugby team, or down at the local pub. At home he would disappear, into the front room or the garden, with a bottle of whisky. Ellie had seen her mother's manner towards all of them harden as she'd steeled herself against the emotional hurt to herself and her children.

To escape the situation, Ellie had developed her own interests. She'd joined the local library and the Mechanics Institute and had started to read widely. Her compassion and interest in social problems had been further aroused on reading Mrs Gaskell's 'Mary

Barton' and George Elliot's 'Silas Marner' and 'Adam Bede'. Her interest in science and medicine had drawn her, like a magnet, to know more. Nursing seemed to her to encapsulate all of these.

"Isn't it what I've always wanted, cared about, read about;" she told herself as she walked on up the hill. She knew that nursing was becoming a recognised profession and her heart swelled with excitement. She wouldn't be paid much but she would be able to send some money home to help her mother. In any case, they wouldn't have her at home, to feed and do for, surely that would save something? Anyway, Stephen and George were planning careers for themselves, so why shouldn't she?

She had no worries about the preliminary nursing course. She'd done well in the classes at the Mechanics Institute and her work at the corner- shop had included plenty of scrubbing and cleaning, as well as dealing with some awkward customers. It would all stand her in good stead. She still helped Annette from time to time with her midwifery and home-nursing in the neighbourhood. Illness didn't frighten her, it challenged her. Something inside her longed for this challenge and she wondered if this was what people meant when they spoke about God was calling them to do something.

Even the pigs seemed to be part of the conspiracy to push her decision. She'd taken the path through the farmyard and suddenly the smell of the pigs in her nostrils was stronger than usual. She heard loud grunts and huffs and puffs from the pig sty intermingled with small squeals and the slow shifting of heavy bodies. Peering over the half gate in the wall of the barn which housed the pigs, Ellie saw Bert Lee on his knees beside Sally, the large white sow, four tiny piglets were squirming in the straw and Bert was lifting the sow's tail to see if there were any more. The sow didn't like it and kept turning her head to view Bert through one irate eye. Bert was sweating and Ellie could see that all was not well,

"What's wrong Bert?"

The lad jumped at her voice, "Can't you see she's farrowing. I'm busy, get along with yer, Ellie."

"Shall I fetch Mr. Airey?" Ellie was not put off by Bert's manner, she could see his predicament.

"He's not here. He and Mrs Airey are still with the Lucas family. They were invited back after the funeral, Mrs Airey being a niece of old Lucas. We weren't expectin' Sally to farrow so soon; though I should have seen the signs this morning."

"I can help," said Ellie "I know about birthing, at least human birthing. It can't be much different, can it?"

Before Bert could stop her Ellie took off her shawl and rolling up her sleeves climbed into the pig pen beside him. He thought it would be easier to use her than argue.

"Right then; this is Sally's first litter and she's not sure what to do. She's full of little uns all wantin' to be out and somat's blocking the way. It's not usual for a sow to have any bother with birthing. Piglets are that small they pop out easy as peas; these first four came out alreet. Now she's struggling and if we're not quick to help her, we'll lose sow and piglets and most likely mi job as well."

Ellie looked at the four new borns squirming in the straw and mewling away, their small mouths working,

"Put these to the mother to suckle. They'll be safe and it will distract and comfort Sally, while we get the rest out," Ellie spoke with such authority that Bert did as she said, she was right anyway, he had just panicked too much to think of it.

Feeling the suckling of the tiny piglets, the huge sow gave a great contented sigh and relaxed. Ellie gently massaged Sally's abdomen speaking encouragingly, as she would to a woman in labour. After a few moments another, much larger piglet, pushed its way out,

"By golly, that one must 'ave been 'oldin things up," laughed Bert as three more smaller piglets squirmed through.

By the end of the farrowing there were thirteen piglets, all eagerly suckling.

"I'll 'ave to keep my eye on that big 'un," said Bert "or some of these other little squealers won't get a look in," and he gently picked the offending piglet off its mother and handed it to Ellie who weighed the creature in her hands.

"Quite a weight there, Bert. I'm glad we humans don't have so many at once."

Bert smiled at Ellie and kept his hands on hers as he took back the piglet.

"Ellie, you know I've always been fond of you and you're good around animals. Any road you're not afraid of getting mucked up!"

Ellie laughed self-consciously as she looked at her hands and skirt covered in muck and streaks of blood.

"Would you consider walking out with me, Ellie? I'd be honoured if you would. Farmer Airey hasn't got any children, nor likely to have now. He's said if I carry on as I am, he'll deed the farm to me."

Ellie looked at Bert, dear Bert, with his discerning blue eyes and capable hands. He was the first young man to say anything like this to her. They'd been playmates since they were six years old and then been in the same class at school, they'd danced together at church socials and both belonged to the NATS. Now they'd farrowed a litter of piglets together. Ellie felt a warmth for Bert that was unsettling. She hesitated, gripped by a longing quite new to her. She stared down at the piglets and their mother and in her mind she saw the difficult human births she'd attended in the poorer quarters of Hartsbeck. She knew how she must answer Bert. Gently taking Bert's strong fingers in her own, she spoke firmly.

"Bert, if there was anyone I would choose to walk out with, it would be you. But I can't. I've made up my mind to go to London and train as a nurse. I've been thinking about this for so long and being with Sally today, as she was giving birth, finally made my mind up for me. I have to go; I can do this Bert. There are too many young women out there struggling to bring children into the world and then rear them; too many deaths, too much sickness. I know I can help. If I walked out with you and then married you, I would just become another of these struggling women, I want to be able to help change things for them, for the better."

"Oh, Ellie lass, I've lost the best if I lose you. I thought with all the young 'uns at home you might have decided to stop here in

Hartsbeck and help your mother. Can't you stay and be like Doris Hamilton? She does a lot of good?"

"No Bert. Life's changing fast. I'll need good training and good qualifications to do what I want. That means London."

Ellie felt a familiar steely determination creep through her and straightening up she climbed from the pig pen and smoothed her clothes. Bert was silent, he brought her a pail of fresh water and a towel and she cleaned off the worse of the muck. As they prepared to say goodbye Bert saw a smudge of dirt on her cheek and gently wiped it away with trembling fingers.

"I understand lass, I'm sad, but I'm proud of you. Just let me give you this for luck," and holding her shoulders gently, the young farm lad planted a soft kiss on Ellie's cheek. He let go of her.

"Bert," said Ellie touching her cheek "I'll remember this when I'm slaving away on the wards and feeling homesick in London. Take care of yourself, you'll find a good wife soon enough and whoever she is she'll be lucky to have you."

Despite her determination Ellie was unsettled by Bert's proposal. As she walked on, Ellie mulled over again the rights or wrongs of her ambition. Bertha, Annette's daughter, had been home for a few days. Sitting in Annette's kitchen helping Ellie sew baby clothes for Hartsbeck's poorer maternity case, Bertha had told Ellie fascinating tales about the nurses' training she was taking in London. As she listened, Ellie became more and more assured, that she could do this. Bertha had put on weight and Ellie couldn't help noticing the new strength in her rough red hands, as she manipulated the material for the tiny garments.

"Mind you, it's hard work Ellie. There's lots of scrubbing and cleaning. 'Doing battle with them nasty germs,' as Mam says."

"When was a Hartsbeck lass ever afraid of hard work? But you do get to do proper nursing as well, don't you Bertha?"

"Oh aye, once we finished the seven weeks preliminary course we were let to work with the patients, but the senior nurses and the Ward Sisters watch our every move and are as strict as they come. One false step and you're warned; another and you're on the train back home, Ellie. At first, it's scrubbing and cleaning the patients as well as floors and walls and cupboards. We have coal fires to heat the wards and a room with great fish-kettles of boiling water for sterilising the equipment. There are ward maids to help with the fires and laundry and the roughest cleaning but we're expected to turn our hand to their jobs, if necessary. The classes we have every week would be just up your street, all about how the body works and different diseases and conditions."

Ellie's passionate desire for such knowledge had increased over the years and as she'd listened to Bertha, she'd longed more than ever to go to London and join this great teaching hospital.

"It's a good feeling, Ellie, as if you're part of something grand and new. We really do help cure people of things they'd have died from, a few years back."

"Have you cured anyone, Bertha?"

Bertha had laughed loud and heartily; "Don't ever claim to have cured a patient yourself! You should hear Matron when she's on her high horse."

Bertha had taken the piece of material she was sewing and folded it on top of her head tying it on with a piece of thin ribbon with two bows beneath her chin, mimicking a Matron's strings. Standing up she thrust out her bosom and head held high and with quivering jaw, spoke in the tones of the august matron of St. Gabriel's Hospital:

"Now gels, we're part of a team. If you want an epidemic in the ward or your patients in the mortuary, all you have to do is neglect one tiny item of your job. The doctor's job is 'hit and miss' without your part. Your ward must be a place where patients have no excuse but to recover". Bertha had removed her headdress and resumed her normal voice, "You must try it, Ellie, its' what you've always hankered after. I think you've a real calling."

"How do you get on with the other nurses?" Ellie had asked.

"Well, I was a bit shy at first, till I found out we probationers all felt the same. When I arrived at Victoria Station I met up with another new girl, called Joan,. She picked me out straight away, looking as lost as herself. When we discovered that we were both going to St. Gabriel's, we treated ourselves to tea and buns, to settle our nerves. She's a friendly soul from Durham and a bit of a comic. We've a room with six others in the nurses' home. There isn't time or energy to fall out and Home Sister keeps us all on friendly terms. We don't have any spare money but we get good food and the beds are great. You've to watch out for those nurses a bit higher up than you on the wards; some like to catch you out but most are kindly when they've time to be."

"I've been reading a bit, at the institute, about Florence Nightingale," Ellie had ventured "how she said that women who wanted to be nurses must thoroughly master their subject just as a working man masters his."

"Oh we are trained alright; noses to the grindstone! We have to follow the nurses a year ahead of us and learn from them, while still doing the menial tasks of our own level. But we're doing a proper job Ellie and we're not beholden to anybody else to keep us. It's our own work that's giving us bed and board and we're doing something worthwhile. Why, it don't matter if we never get married. If we do it right, we can stay in nursing till our old age, if we want to."

That had been three weeks ago and since then Ellie had turned Bertha's words over in her mind a thousand times. She walked on over the Tops not noticing her tiredness, or the steepness of the path, or the passing of time. The light breeze turned into something stronger and colder and it began to drizzle with rain. Ellie carried on, wrapping her shawl more tightly round her head. Eventually she came out above the tree line onto the bare moor and turning round looked out over the town of Hartsbeck. The sun was beginning to set behind the mills and factories, a blood red ball, spreading great streaks of fire across the paling sky. The buildings were black sculptures against this living background of colour.

The tall mill buildings and the sloping terraces of grey houses took on a life and beauty not obvious in the daylight. There were a few people about, looking like small creatures scurrying to find their holes. Ellie stood entranced and amazed, impervious to the rain. She knew the struggles and squalor in those streets and she had seen the love and heartache and hopeful lives crumbling under the hopeless burden of ignorance, poverty and disease. She had seen the good life too, clean homes, good food and healthy children. She recognised that some were glad to share their wealth generously. Others, with a cloaked arrogance, did just a little but not enough, to help right the sufferings of the poor.

She looked at the number of church buildings that stood out clearly, around the town. The tall spire of the Baptist church rising high on the slope of a hill and built at the expense of a mill-owner; the Methodists chapels, square and strong no- nonsense buildings; the Roman Catholic churches guarded by sculpted statues; the great edifice of the New Jerusalem Church of the Swedenborgians, with their strange mystical mix of philosophy and the spiritual; the smaller, friendly, Congregational chapels. Dotted here and there, in their parish settings, were the towers and spires of numerous Anglican churches, including their own St. Mark's. Everywhere the Church was in among the people, or rather the people were the church who worshipped in these buildings. Together they looked to God, ministered to one another and tried to make sense of the strangeness of life. Hartsbeck was full of people who had flocked here from all over Great Britain and beyond, to find work in the fast growing industries of the small town. These folk had discovered, through their common humanity and many through their shared Christian faith, that they were not strangers to one another.

Once again Ellie decided that she must learn how to help the mothers and children of communities like this. Thinking of her own Dad, she realised that fathers too needed help in this sticky quagmire of society. She turned and looked down the other side of the hill to the South West where the local Fever Hospital stood, gently lit from within by gas lights, isolated in the middle of fields. How many of her classmates had gone there, to recover or to die, with the dreaded diphtheria or scarlet fever, measles, typhoid or any of the other myriads of infectious illnesses. She knew that more children were recovering in that hospital because trained nurses had come there, from the big cities, bringing new medicines and nursing methods.

To be of any real use, she must go to London, to train at St. Gabriel's, no matter how much her father was against it. He had issues of his own and she mustn't let these stand in the way of her own calling. Her mind was quite settled, she would accept the place offered to her and go to London.

Ellie saw that the sun was fast disappearing and the gas lights were being lit in the streets of the town below. Her way back would be dark, as well as wet. She must have been out for a good hour and a half. Shivering, she set off towards home and as she reached the tree- line a wavering light came towards her up the hill. It was Stephen, carrying the storm lantern.

"Ellie, is that you?" he called

"Yes, it's me. Thanks for coming, I lost track of time."

"Ah well, I'm a good brother sometimes. You sound weary lass, link arms and we'll soon be home. Dad's woken up and is worrying about you."

The two walked home arm- in- arm, the lantern swinging crazily. Their father, sobered up, was standing in the open doorway looking for them.

"Eeh lass," he said to Ellie "I'm that sorry for what I said, I was beside me-self but I'd no right. I don't want to lose you but I've been thinking and I've talked to your mother. Maybe we should let you go to London and see what you can do. I'm not happy about it, I still think you might find you've bitten off more than you can chew but I know you'll do your best. You'll make us right proud, lass." Ellie wasn't blind to her father's struggle concerning her and her heart echoed his pain. Dave opened his arms and Ellie went to him, as she had as a child. He held her close.

"The great soft lumps," said Jeannie when Stephen told her, but she smiled and a weight lifted from her.

As it happened Ellie didn't need to go to London for her interview. The Matron of St. Gabriel's contacted Ellie personally, to say that she was travelling to Preston for a medical conference and if

Miss Elkson would care to meet her there on Friday, the twenty-eighth of October, she would be happy to conduct the interview then and save Miss Elkson the extra journey to London.

Ellie went to Preston on the twenty-eighth in great trepidation but Matron was impressed by her obvious enthusiasm and by her studies. A week later, Ellie received a letter inviting her to start as a probationer nurse at St. Gabriel's on Monday, 12th of December this year. The letter suggested that if she travelled up to London on the Friday beforehand she would have the weekend to settle into the Nurses Home, before her first duties on the Monday morning.

Grandma Jane came again in November, to discuss the final arrangements. All was soon settled as the family sat in the parlour round a roaring fire specially lit to "dispel the horrid autumn chills" from Grandma's, "aging bones". They discussed seriously the proposed careers of the two daughters of the house and the details of Ellie's imminent departure for London on the ninth of December. Dave had accepted that his drinking had been making him irresponsible and ill. He agreed to go away for a cure and to take a less responsible post at the engineering works, at least for the time being. Grandma persuaded them that Jeannie should have some paid help in the house.

"Well," said Grandma Jane, "I was expecting a grand battle on my hands. I don't know whether to be relieved or disappointed."

"Grand Battle?" exclaimed Dave "Eeh Mother, that's not our way but I could always arrange one." and he gave Ellie a sly wink.

"Go on with you lad! Just like your father." laughed Grandma as she kissed them all goodbye, "Ellie hold your head up, you are as good as the next one if not better! Don't forget to write," in a whisper she added, "don't worry about your Dad; I'll make sure the family doesn't go short."

The grand old lady climbed into the trap as if it were a royal carriage and tucked up with rugs and a hot brick to her feet, waved regally to them all as she was driven away.

The weeks passed all too quickly and the night before she was to leave home, Ellie couldn't sleep. Eventually, she crept downstairs to the kitchen. Her hands and feet were icy cold and she crouched down on her haunches in front of the low burning embers of the fire. Being so close to the heat would soon draw out the fiery itchiness of her chilblains but she couldn't help, it she had to feel the warmth. Soon she moved into the wide-armed rocking chair and fell into a wakeful doze, as warmth seeped through her. She could pick out shapes in the room from the glow of the fire and the moonlight coming through the window over the sink. She stared up at the wooden clothes rack, pulled up near the ceiling and secured by a series of pulleys and a strong waxed rope. Draped over the cream- painted wooden slats of the rack was the family laundry. The washed and wrung out clothes would steam gently in the rising heat from the fire, until ready for ironing. Once ironed they would be hung there again to air. Mother was proud of her laundry skills, nowadays a woman came in to help with the heavy washing but the rest was Jeannie's domain. The filled rack was the show piece for her cleanliness and industry, for her prowess in mending and ironing. Even when Ellie helped, her mother hovered over her like a hawk, expecting perfection in every crease, patch, or darn. Dad's shirts hung perfectly pressed and folded, underwear was placed more discreetly on the slats near the wall, shielded from sight by the womenfolk's skirts and blouses. Ellie remembered baby clothes, snow -white nappies, bonnets and knitted coatees, children's vests and night shirts; all hanging there in their turn, over the years.

On alternate weeks the rack would dip crazily under the weight of sheets, pillowcases, towels and table cloths. On fine days, the wet laundry would have had a good blow and a dose of sunshine on the clothes line in the back yard but once ironed, they paraded their spotless glory on the rack. The sight of a full rack had always meant to Ellie that all was well with mother; all was well in their home. Sighing, she allowed herself to wonder if all would be well, once she had left for London. Would everything carry on the same, as if she had never been, or would there be a sense of something missing?

"I don't know what'll happen but they'll have to manage without me. I must go to London," and she fell asleep, there in the kitchen. Two hours later she woke, shivering in the dark, to a dead fire and climbed the stairs to her own bed.

PART TWO

LONDON 1899-1905

CHAPTER 12

Ellie arrives in London. 1899.

Ellie's eyelids drooped and she drifted into a deep doze, full of shifting dreams. A heavy jolt startled her awake and she grimaced as the smell of bad eggs hit her. Stretching, she eased the aching stiffness in her limbs. She was on the train to London at last. The last few weeks had been painful ones for her and all the family. Now, having left them behind, Ellie was revelling in the freedom of following her own vocation.

"Nearly there. Next station, Euston," an elderly passenger declared, folding his newspaper decisively and nudging the young lad slumbering beside him. "Wake up lad, if you want to see anything of our coming into London."

"Umm, oh, righto grandpa," the boy blinked himself awake and like Ellie stared out at the buildings alongside the railway tracks. From open fields the train had quickly entered a gorge of steep embankments, topped by small houses followed by the blank faces of warehouses and then, quite suddenly, she was staring at a landscape of domes and towers as they crossed the River Thames into the great city of London. A surge of emotion welled inside Ellie. The city seemed like a person she half knew and had longed to meet and here she was. She hadn't much luggage. A trunk packed with the articles she was required to take, together with a few small mementos of home, had been sent on a week in advance. It should be waiting for her at the Nurses Home of St. Gabriel's hospital. In case her trunk hadn't arrived, Ellie had with her, a change of underwear, wash things and a night-gown which her mother had stitched by hand. All these were in a leather hold-all embossed with her initials which was a farewell gift from her brothers and now sat on the luggage rack above her head. Sarah had tucked three small parcels in coloured paper inside the folds of the nightgown and ordered Ellie not to open them until she was in her room at the nurses' home. On her knee Ellie held a volume of Sherlock Holmes' detective stories, given to her by Aunt Lucy Nelson. She'd read it intermittently during the journey but her concentration had constantly drifted, either forward to where she was going, or backwards to all she'd left behind. Conan Doyle's descriptions of London scenes both disturbed and excited her. Of course she knew that he was attempting to create a sinister atmosphere but prickles of fear unsettled her, as she thought of entering that predaceous city.

The train hissed and wheezed its way to a juddering stop in the station. Doors slammed, voices shouted. Now that she'd arrived, foreboding and excitement chased each other inside Ellie's stomach. With shaky fingers, she fastened her warm coat and skewered the mandatory black hat to her severely tight bun of hair. Gloves on and clutching her hold-all, Ellie stepped carefully down onto the platform in a haze of sulphurous steam and smoke. The shouting voices were clearer now with sharp commands and questions:

"Carry your bags, Sir, Ma'm?"

"Watch your backs!!"

"Cab, Ladies?"

"Mind the doors!"

Thumps and thuds of heavy objects all around, rushing bodies brushed against her and were gone. Ellie clung to her bag, half expecting it to be snatched away. All in a moment the haze cleared and Ellie heard someone call her name. The station platform came sharply into focus and striding towards her, a broad grin spreading over her face was Bertha Hamilton.

"Welcome to the great metropolis, I just got away in time to meet you. Hey now, you'll be alright in a minute. Just find your feet,"

Ellie had grabbed hold of Bertha's arm her eyes filling with unexpected tears, her legs trembling.

"I knew you'd be feeling like finding the next train home but you'll soon be alright. Come along, we'll find a café and fortify ourselves with tea, buns and a good chat," Bertha linked Ellie's arm and drew her towards the exit. Ellie just smiled and nodded and squeezed Bertha's arm, trying to take in all that was going on around them.

Outside in the street an old man in a threadbare suit stumbled towards them holding out a grubby cloth cap "Something to help keep out the cold Miss?" his eyes were rheumy and his lips had a bluish tinge. Bertha sighed, stopped and fished a halfpenny out of her pocket and dropped it into the man's hat.

"I know I shouldn't and things aren't always what they seem but I can't help it; for old people and children," said Bertha.

"Gawd bless you Miss," wheezed the old man and touched his forehead.

Wheels epitomised London for Ellie on that first afternoon, both the sight and noise of them. Wheels of barrows, top heavy with fruit and vegetables pushed along by cheeky boys; wheels of horse- buses and carts and of swaying, motorised omnibuses overloaded with passengers. A few automobiles, stiffly upright, moved with quick negotiations on their masked tyres with stops and starts, belches of black smoke and the hunting cries of their horns.

Bertha guided her between the wheels and the oil and horse-muck, to the safety of a Lyon's Corner House. They chose a table for two near the window. Strong hot tea and toasted currant teacake, running with butter ,quickly restored Ellie's spirits. Bertha chattered away asking questions about home and Ellie murmured replies automatically, her mind captured by the London life passing the café window. This time the wheels gave place to hats, Ellie had never seen so many. Men in cloth caps, top hats or round bowlers, in all kinds of condition, made of shiny silk or glossy beaver, in blacks and browns, greens or silver grey. Some wore cloth hats with ear-flaps and there was a dark skinned man in a white turban.

The hats of the women floated by like carnival costumes; cartwheel hats in ruched silks and satin; neat bonnets, plain or with a framing of lace or soft fur around the face; richly coloured hats and plain blacks and greys in felt or velour and dozens of hard- rimmed black straws. Amongst them Ellie saw a few women moving in the shadows with grey knitted shawls drawn over their heads. They looked thin and poorly dressed and hugged loose cloth bags close to them. Ellie watched a barrow boy call to one of them and slip some goods from his stall into her bag, the woman nodded and walked on and a girl from the Lyons Corner House stepped outside and placed some packets into the bags of several of these shawled women.

Bertha laughed at Ellie's expression, "At the end of the day the stall holders and shops give away some of their perishable produce to the poor and needy. These women will have families to feed and no wage coming in, for one reason or another. It's not much but it helps keep them alive and out of our clutches!"

"Our clutches? Oh you mean at the hospital. I remember my friend Lily, from school, going to Mr Taylor, the greengrocer, for over-ripe fruit and veg. Her mother would stew them and she always said it made good eating."

Ellie decided that London folk weren't so different from Hartsbeck folk; everything was just on a much larger scale and far less personal.

"Come along, it's nearly lighting up time, we need to get you settled in the Nurses Home. Home Sister will be biting her nails wondering where we are. She fusses over us like a mother hen." Gathering their belongings the two young women left the warm café. Ellie could hardly contain her excitement and relief that she was really on her way to becoming a nurse and an independent woman.

CHAPTER 13

Letters from Ellie.

The Nurses home,
St. Gabriel's Hospital,

London.
21st Dec.1899

Dear Mother and Dad,

I hope all is well with you both, I shall always worry about how you are managing but I expect you will soon find I am not as necessary to the running of the household as you thought.

Well, here I am, safely settled into my room at the Nurses Home. It's much more comfortable than I expected. There are four of us, all probationer nurses, in one large bedroom – a quarter each. Each quarter has a curtained off corner with a rail, where we hang our clothes and we each have a white- wood chest of drawers with a marble top holding a stand mirror and a large porcelain wash bowl. Every morning and evening, we take large metal jugs and collect hot water for washing, from a tap in the bathroom. Once we've washed, we empty the soapy water into buckets in the unused fireplace alcove in our room. We sleep on iron bedsteads, with thin, hard mattresses and are allowed one pillow each, with sheets and pillowcases and one grey, woollen blanket – very coarse and scratchy! Anything extra we have to supply ourselves. My particular friend in the dormitory is called Mattie. She comes from Stoke-on Trent and we seem to understand each other.

You will be pleased to know that Home Sister is like a strict mother to us. Her manner is severe but she has a warm heart. She makes sure we all eat a hearty breakfast before going on duty at 6.30am and bread, butter, jam and hot tea are available whenever we come off duty between meals. Most of our other meals are taken in the hospital dining room. We take it in turns to leave the wards. There is a comfortable sitting room in the Nurses Home called the Common Room, where we can all relax in easy chairs and talk or read, sew or knit, play games or listen to the gramophone. There is another room with desks, where we go for quiet study and lessons from Home Sister or other Medical Staff.

If we go out in the evening we have to be in by 9pm, unless we have a special pass to go to a meeting or the theatre —but I don't expect that will be often as it is too expensive. Home Sister keeps a strict eye on our health and informed us that she has doses and ointments at the ready for sore throats; coughs and sniffles; blistered feet- (yes we are told to expect blisters as nursing is hard on the feet); chapped hands; tummy upsets and irregular bowels! She also accompanied those of us who are Anglicans,(and not on duty) to a service at the local Church on the first Sunday morning. It wasn't compulsory and we could go to another church if we wished. Sister is very devout and leads us all in prayer, morning and evening, as she is expected to do. She says our nursing tasks are all the better for being offered to God and performed with His help. It reminds me of Annette Hamilton, who always said a prayer before going on any of her home visits.

Yes Dad, you were right, there is quite a lot of skivvying for a probationer nurse but that isn't the whole story. We are learning to treat actual patients and apart from the practical side we have a whole syllabus to follow of lessons in anatomy and chemistry, as well as in hygiene and the types of diseases prevalent in different sections of our society. Skills in nursing and the practice of medicine are progressing in leaps and bounds as knowledge increases- it's an exciting time to be alive.

I've hardly been here two weeks and feel a different person already but I do miss you all and wonder how you are. Mother, do take regular rest and Dad keep your eye on those brothers of mine, especially young Jack. Are you missing playing Rugby, Dad? I'm so glad your 'cure' was a success; I see such a lot of heartache, among our patients, as a result of drink, but I know you're not the type to let it beat you-you're made of stronger stuff!

Christmas will soon be here, I'll miss you but it will be extra busy on the wards so I won't have chance to mope.

*Tell Sarah I'm writing her a letter, all to herself. I must write to Grandma
Jane as well. My loving thoughts and my good wishes are always with you.
Have a jolly Christmas.*

Your head-strong daughter, Ellie.

Ellie wondered at herself for daring to write to her father about
his drink problem and realised how much more she could say in a
letter than face to face. She began to write a regular weekly letter
to Grandma Jane, telling the old lady more about the probationary
course and stressing her enthusiasm and gratitude for all that she
was learning.

Grandma Jane read the letters with satisfaction, "The girl's gaining confidence already. She may be a probationer but the authority of her profession comes through. Yes, I'm sure she's in the right
place," and the old lady settled down to continue planning for her
other grandchildren.

In her letter to Sarah, Ellie did her best to entertain her ten year
old sister:

Dearest Sarah,

*How are you, my own little sister? I miss you so much, although I am
quite happily settled here in London. Doesn't that sound grand? I enclose
a picture post- card of one of the Guards outside Buckingham Palace. His
strange hat is called a busby and is made from bear-skin and very warm! I
saw a soldier just like this on my first afternoon off, last Sunday. A group
of us from the Nurses Home walked through a beautiful park, called St.
James's Park, right in the middle of London. It has tree- lined walks and
bridle paths and a small lake with ducks and swans. When we came out of
the park there was Buckingham Palace – right in front of us. I don't think
Queen Victoria was at home, otherwise we might have called at the palace
for tea. Instead, we hurried back to the Nurses' Home for sardines on toast
and fruit cake. We bought the cake ourselves, as a treat. It worked out quite
reasonably, when we shared the cost but there was only a small piece each.
One of my room-mates is Mattie Brierley, from Stoke-on-Trent. We seem to
get on well together.*

The nights are cold in our little beds in the Nurses' Home. Our warm nurses' cloaks make a good extra blanket but we have to wait until lights out to put these on our beds as it would certainly be frowned upon by Home Sister. They tend to fall on the floor and crumple. Please be a dear and ask Stephen to parcel up and send me a blanket from my bed, or even one of the old rugs we used when we went camping. I daren't ask Mother as she would worry and Dad would say, "I told you it would be too tough for her!" We are allowed to provide extra bedding for ourselves but I haven't saved enough money or had any time yet, to go shopping in London.

You will be on holiday from school now. Is there any measles or scarlet fever around? We see so many sick children in the hospital. Make sure you drink your milk and eat an apple every day and go out in the fresh air as much as you can. All this will help you keep well. I hope you will keep on going to the NATS meetings; do tell me what they get up to, they are all such characters. I miss walking on the moors, I long for their wild openness.

Many of the people who live here think Lancashire is all dark, ugly mills and factories with hovels for the workers to live in and the people ignorant and coarse. It would be laughable if it didn't make me so angry! There's plenty of poverty and coarseness in parts of London. I'm often teased for my northern accent but you should hear some of the southern ones; they've no room to talk!

Do write and tell me what's happening to you all. Are George and Edwin still members of the St. John's Ambulance *brigade? You'd find it interesting too and you'd make some good friends. Give Jack a big hug from me and show the boys the post card.*

My work at the hospital is very interesting but it's sad to see so many people suffering. I'm glad I'm doing something to help them and earning my own living at the same time. Work hard at school, Sarah, then you'll be able to do something worthwhile, when you grow up, which won't be so very long. If you still want to be a teacher, make sure you are entered for the College exams. Grandma Jane will help you.

Only five more days to Christmas Day! I expect you have been busy making mince pies and eating them. I can almost smell them baking. They are putting up a huge Christmas tree in the Hospital this week and we shall have a smaller one on our Ward and in the Nurses Home but it won't be like home. Have a happy time together. Think of us singing carols in the wards on Christmas Eve, we've been practising but my voice isn't like yours- I croak in the background.

I must go now, it's time for evening prayers led by the Home Sister and then to bed. We get up at 5.30am tomorrow, for breakfast and more prayers, before we go on duty.

Goodnight my own dear Sarah,

Your loving sister Ellie.

Christmas came and the nurses of St. Gabriel's worked hard to make the season special for their patients. Small gifts and messages reached Ellie from the folk in Hartsbeck. The most poignant gift was from Dick Hamilton, Annette's husband. It was a beautifully orchestrated charcoal drawing, of the Virgin and child. The Virgin Mary, dressed in the typical clothes of a Lancashire mill worker, was sitting on the stone doorstep of a house in one of the poorest, back streets of Hartsbeck. Cast over the virgin's head and shoulders was a worn woollen shawl, its folds falling across her lap to form a nest for the Christ Child. The baby Jesus gazed up at his mother, as she gazed down at him. Mary's skirt was patched and torn and her boots, which rested on the cobblestones of the street, had holes in the toes. Instead of shepherds and angels, cheeky ragged urchins peered round street lamps their thin, hungry faces so real that Ellie almost recognised them as children she knew. Cats, a mangy dog or two and a pouter pigeon strutting in the gutter with his neck craned to see the baby, took the place of ox and ass and sheep of the stable.

A cloth-capped workman with a bag over his shoulder and a woman with a basket of washing had stopped to stare. The two gas lamps gave little light but Dick had used his skill to bring a bright glow from the baby in the Madonna's lap, this was reflected in various ways in the faces of all the onlookers. Almost hidden in the doorway behind the mother and child were two shadowy women's figures, quietly packing things into a bag, just like the one Annette would carry to childbirth. This picture became one of Ellie's most treasured possessions. It was an icon to her, a constant reminder of her home town and her own calling. The depiction of the Christ Child in the centre of it all evoked a strange longing in her.

Annette Hamilton was never far from Ellie's thoughts as she followed the strict hygiene regime drummed into them at St. Gabriel's, much of which she had already learnt from the Hartsbeck midwife. After six weeks as a probationer Ellie wrote to her old mentor, pouring out some of her struggles:

Dear Annette,

I was so very touched by your Christmas gifts, and am sorry I am only now writing to thank you. Your Dick's picture of the Hartsbeck nativity hangs near to my bed and I only need to look at it to feel near you and home. Please thank Dick, he couldn't have thought of anything better. I hope you have been able to find someone else to help you with the maternity and sick visiting. I often think about you and half wish I was with you on your rounds. It was very strange here in the first week, not quite knowing what to expect and experiencing some horrible situations in the hospital. I had a nasty shock when I saw my first case of congenital syphilis in a baby but was amazed at the improvement after a week's dosing with mercury. It's given in the form of a grey powder mixed with the baby's feed.

You will be pleased to know that Home Sister insists we have times of prayer together, twice each day, before we go on duty and before bed. It helps in a way, when Sister places all our work, our experiences good and bad and our patients, into God's hands. It makes you realise there is a much greater reality beyond our own small lives but I wish I knew why there has to be so much suffering. I know a lot of it is brought on by the way people live but some people can't help the situations they are in, they suffer because of the way society is changing. Mankind is certainly moving forward; for some, this means a better life style but for others, it brings even more suffering. Ah well, 'Onward and Upward', as you used to say, at least we are learning to help casualties of this social progress.

Of course, being in a large teaching hospital, we get many of the worse cases. When we have a patient with a broken bone or other minor injury in an otherwise healthy body, it can be quite a relief to look after them! At first, as probationers, we were given most of the cleaning jobs but now we've progressed to washing the actual patients and changing dressings. This can lead to some lively conversations and leg-pulling by the cheekier ones especially the men! I'm certainly not treated as a young lady. Dad would be shocked and mother would die on the spot!

Your Bertha has been very kind; she met me from the train and helped me settle into the Nurses Home. In the first week she was on hand to calm me down when I broke two thermometers, cut my hand open and witnessed my first death, all in the space of an hour. How she knew to appear at that moment, I'll never know. She hauled me out of the sluice room where I'd run to hide, treated my cut, gave me a brisk talking to and pushed me back on the ward. I think it was her familiar face and accent that put me to rights, more quickly than anything.

"Come on, Ellie!" she said "We're Hartsbeck lasses; nothing gets us down, tough as old boots, that's us— get back in there and show 'em. See you later for a cuppa!"

Good old Bertha. I'm sorry she's moving on but she deserves the post as a Staff Nurse in Preston Royal Infirmary. At least you'll be able to see her more often. It was strange being at my first death. Of course I've always known that people die and even some of my own school friends died but, I've never actually seen or touched a dead person or seen their life breath just stop. I'm glad it wasn't a child but an older woman, it seemed more acceptable. Sister asked me to help the trained nurse, to wash and lay out the body. I was in a cold daze as I worked, just doing what I was told. I felt I was intruding, uninvited, on a person's privacy. We worked in silence except when the other nurse had to instruct me. The older nurse was very reverential and gentle in the way she dealt with the woman's body, I think she saw it as a sacred duty. When we'd finished, the woman's face looked so quiet and peaceful and her body at rest; I tiptoed away from the bedside and it was a while before I spoke normally, I found myself whispering as if I was in the library. I expect I shall get used to it, but I dread dealing with a child's death, Annette. I must work extra hard at keeping them alive. Very sick children can be so brave, they put us adults to shame sometimes.

Thank you for reading my ramblings. Give my love to those we used to visit together and please, still mention me in your prayers.

With very great affection to you, my dear friend and teacher,
Ellie Elkson.

Annette's written English was poor but she tried to assuage Ellie's unease at dealing with the dying and the dead. "It is our privilege to do what needs doing, when they can no longer do it themselves," she wrote with Dick's help, "I sheltered you from the deaths in Hartsbeck, I felt you were too young. I hope that you learn as I did, that death can be beautiful and can speak of God's presence. Concentrate on the living, don't let death fill your mind and take time to have fun."

Ellie loved Annette for her words.

It was Sarah who was to become Ellie's chief correspondent, keeping her in touch with news from home. Stephen also wrote occasionally. Mother, always busy, would sometimes send a short note enclosed with Sarah's letter and Dad would ask her to write a message from him at the end. Ellie was content with this, her life was filled from morning to night and she had little time to brood about home.

CHAPTER 14

1902. A Qualified Nurse and new digs.

Ellie woke early on the morning of the 29th August 1902, in her narrow bed in the Nurses' Home. Quiet snuffles told her that her room- mates were still sleeping. She lay on her back, staring at the ceiling. Shadowy reflections of tree-branches moving in the early light crept through the thinly-curtained window.

The previous December she'd had her twenty-first birthday and yesterday she'd received the certificate declaring her to be a fully qualified Nurse. The four years of training and exams were over. Now it was time to choose the next step in her career.

Before their final exams, the probationers had been handed questionnaires, asking if there was a particular path of nursing they would like to pursue. Ellie had no hesitation in declaring that she wanted to specialise in nursing sick children and babies, which would naturally extend to maternity cases and mother-care.

Today, the 29th of August, was the all-important interview with Matron, about her future. Would she be able to convince this formidable woman, of her yearning to improve the lives of children and mothers, especially those struggling in poverty? Perhaps more importantly, would Matron think her suitable to enter this field of nursing?

"Very commendable," said Matron later that morning having listened to Ellie's reasons for choosing paediatrics. Tapping her notepad, the experienced woman fixed a steady eye on her young colleague, "but I am inclined to think you rather idealistic, Nurse Elkson. Your own small contribution may not bring about the great revolution you envisage, my dear."

"But surely, my contribution, alongside that of many others, including the doctors - who are discovering new methods all the time, will count for something?"

Matron's cap-ribbons trembled beneath her protruding chin and she dropped her gaze,

"You are quite right my dear, of course it will. I'm becoming disheartened and rather cynical. Maybe I've have been in this job too long." The older woman rubbed her forehead hard looking suddenly very tired, "but I've no right to quell your enthusiasm."

She pulled a large folder towards her and opened it, running her finger down a list,

"Sister Juniper in Paediatrics has a vacancy. If you are happy to stay with us at St. Gabriel's and to work on Juniper Ward, I am willing to recommend you. How do you feel about that, Nurse?"

"Thank you Matron, I would feel privileged to work with Sister Juniper,"

"Good. I want you to go down to her Ward right away and introduce yourself. I shall write a note for you to give her. Your practical skills and your exam results show you are already a competent nurse. Keep it up my dear and you should go far. Just one word of advice Nurse Elkson; humour, never forget it!"

Matron wrote quickly in a firm hand folded the note and sealed it in an envelope addressed to Sister Juniper and Ellie took her leave with a singing heart.

Ellie realised it was also time to think of leaving the Nurses' Home to find accommodation of her own. The other girls, who'd qualified at the same time, joined her in searching for suitable rooms. They scanned the adverts in the daily newspapers and shop windows. Ellie and her friend Mattie decided to find rooms together and they spent their free time dashing from bed-sits to boarding-houses and becoming more and more bewildered. Coming away from the latest bed-sit on offer the two young nurses had become utterly down-hearted. The bed-sit had been a dingy room, on the second floor of a shabby tenement. The room smelt of old dust and damp, paint peeled from the walls and the corners were spotted with black mould. The bed sagged with use, it had a lever which winched it upright into a cavity in the wall, when not in use and a filthy chenille curtain of faded-green could then be drawn across, hiding the bed. The carpet was shiny with trod-den-in grease and they detected mouse-droppings along its edges. There was one upholstered chair that must have housed a whole colony of bugs. The room's heavy sash-windows were begrimed with dust and soot.

"Oh what the heck does it matter? I'm going to take it," declared Mattie belligerently, "there's nothing to stop me giving it a good scrub and a lick of paint. I can make fresh curtains and put down mouse traps. It's cheap and I'm fed up with traipsing round searching."

"But that awful shared bathroom and toilet. No, Mattie you can't," Ellie was horrified.

"Nothing that a dose of carbolic won't cure, surely we've learnt how to clean toilets if nothing else. They might even pay me to keep it clean!"

"You'd be lucky!" laughed Ellie, "but seriously Mattie, I think there are prostitutes living in the house, the room might have been used by one for her work. Just think, in that bed -ugh—Mattie, you can't go there."

"Well, I'll sleep on it - at least not literally! Anyway we've still got to find somewhere for you. I'd hoped there'd be somewhere we could share but there doesn't appear to be such a place."

Ellie was secretly relieved, she wanted freedom and independence, somewhere quiet to return to after the emotional trauma of hospital life, somewhere to lose her-self in a book, somewhere her friends would come only when invited. She wanted to be able to go out and not have to say where or why, but it wouldn't do to say this to Mattie.

It was next morning in the hospital that Ellie had one of those wind-fall experiences which seem almost miraculous. For the last six weeks she'd been nursing Paul, a boy of twelve, who had been suffer-ing from rheumatic fever. The doctors had been concerned about how they could lessen possible damage to the boy's heart valves.

"With careful nursing, we can prevent any damage to the heart at all!" Ward Sister had stated, with a toss of her head. When the doctors had left the ward she'd turned to Ellie,

"Nurse Elkson, please will you special this boy, Paul, along with Nurse Gibbs and Night Sister. You will monitor him every half hour and keep a constant watch on his temperature and pulse rate; these need to remain roughly parallel. Report to me or a doctor immediately, if the pulse rate remains high after the temperature drops towards normal. I will plan out a suitable diet and I want you to see he has it. Complete bed rest, which means bed-baths and bed –pans, which the lad won't like. Make sure he has gentle limb-manipulation every two hours. Keep his mind occupied. Report anything unusual immediately, to myself or to the doctor."

Ellie worked hard with Paul, calming him and keeping his temperature down with drinks and cool sponging and making him rest to lower his heart rate. She ignored his protests against the bed- pan whisking it in and out so proficiently he soon accepted it. She talked with him about subjects that interested her brothers and brought him books to read. She gently exercised his arms and legs as he lay in bed, increasing the time gradually over the days and weeks. When he was well enough, she encouraged another, more mobile patient, to play quiet board games with him. When she was off duty Nurse Gibbs took over and together the two young women nursed him back to health.

After eight weeks the doctor announced that Paul could be moved to a convalescent home before returning to live with his widowed mother. Mrs Larson, Paul's mother, was overcome with gratitude to the two nurses and in talking with Ellie mentioned that she was going to advertise for a lady-lodger to take a room in her house.

"That way I can earn some extra money and be at home more for Paul. It's been hard for us since my husband was taken, a year ago. We've a small terraced-house that my father-in -law left to us but I've had to take on shop-work and a bit of cleaning, to keep us both."

"How much would you be asking for the room, Mrs Larson?" asked Ellie

"I thought eight shillings a week including breakfast and a bit extra for an evening meal. It's in a decent area, not the best but quiet and respectable."

"That sounds reasonable. I'm looking for new lodgings, myself. Would you allow me to look at the room, Mrs Larson, Now that I'm qualified it's time I moved out of the Nurse's Home and made room for someone else."

Mrs Larson's sad face beamed, "You're welcome to come round and see it, Nurse Elkson. It may not be what you're wanting but if it is, I'd be more than happy to have you as a lodger and Paul would be tickled pink!"

"As long as he doesn't pay me back for the bed-pans," laughed Ellie

"It'll be good to have that wicked boy back home but don't worry, I'll watch him. You won't have any trouble from young Paul."

The accommodation turned out to be more than satisfactory and much to Mattie's delight Mrs Larson had a spare room for her as well, so the two young nurses were able to move in before winter. As there were two of them, Mrs Larsen lowered the rent to six shillings and sixpence a week including an evening meal, when they wanted it. This suited the nurses' pockets much better and left them with more pocket money for themselves.

Mattie was nursing on the cancer Ward,

"There are so many advances taking place, its' quite exciting and the nursing is crucial and specialised. The doctors are very devoted to the work too," Mattie's large, lively face broke into a mischievous grin.

Ellie smiled at her friend. It wasn't going to be too bad, living in the same digs as Mattie. "I'm just glad you won't be sleeping in that awful bed," she said.

CHAPTER 15

Juniper Ward. September 1902-August 1905

Sister Juniper had a warm welcome for young Nurse Elkson onto her children's ward. It was one of the first children-only wards in the hospital and had only been open a year. Before this, children and adults had been nursed together so the new ward was something of an experiment. Ellie soon came to love and admire the middle-aged Sister, with her mixture of efficiency and firm kindliness. Under her watchful-eye, Ellie's nursing skills broadened and deepened.

Sister Juniper spoke plainly to her staff.

"You'll experience tragedy and joy on this ward, plus a lot of down-right common-sense nursing. Not every case is a drama, though some families make them so. You need to learn the knack of bringing people down-to-earth, without belittling their fears. Parents need to be able to trust you, as do the doctors. You'll discover that doctors often turn to you for advice; you are their eyes and ears on the shop-floor, so to speak. Notice every small detail about your patient and try to understand their personalities; unformed as many of them are, as yet, bless them."

Ellie sometimes thought that the parents of her young patients were looking at her with disdain. She imagined the mothers and grandmothers of large families and the harassed fathers, were looking pointedly, at her clean, starched uniform and the nakedness of her wedding finger.

"I just know they are thinking, 'What the dickens does she know about having children and feeding and bringing up a family on next to nothing'," she groaned to Agnes, another newly qualified nurse, on the ward.

Agnes had answered thoughtfully. "It's hard to trust your children to someone else, especially when they are sick. We're strangers to them, not part of their family. On top of that, they're worried in case they are asked to pay money they can't afford. It's no wonder they're suspicious. I suppose we have to earn their trust."

In the end parents had no choice but to trust them; waiting helplessly in the hospital corridors, while Ellie and others like her, worked tirelessly to nurse their children back to health, or ease their way towards death, they fell silent. Some families warmed towards the nurses, others remained cold and withdrawn, resentful of the power that was taken away from them and put into the hands of strangers. Their worries about paying for medical treatment were groundless. The hospital had been built in the 1830's, through a doctor whose dream was to provide free medical care for the poor. Rich philanthropists had come to his aid and several of the aristocracy had also become patrons of the hospital. Annual charity events boosted the funds. Patients were not chrequired to pay towards their care.

Ellie knew that many of the illnesses, of the children brought onto Juniper Ward, were caused by malnutrition and lack of hygiene resulting from poverty and ignorance. This ignorance didn't stop with the working population, Ellie discovered it was present in the medical profession; in local health authorities and even Government circles. She had already realised, from Hartsbeck days that greed, amongst the prospering captains of industry, was often behind the badly overcrowded, inadequate housing conditions of the working classes.

She was shocked to see a number of babies and older children, suffering horribly from the effects of sexually transmitted diseases, such as congenital syphilis, which had been passed on to the child, either in the womb or at the time of birth. These infants had become the innocent victims of disease and the treatments were often long term and dangerous. In treating these cases Ellie learnt that nursing was a serious science dealing with the careful regulation of dangerous substances and constant watching for and recording any chemical changes in blood and urine, caused by the medicines or by the disease. Partnership, between nurse and doctor was a clinical affair of trust. Ellie loved the way the whole medical team worked in harmony, to discover and implement new ways of healing. Recovery, when it came, was often dramatic and then the doctors were seen as mini- gods; the nurses had simply done what was expected of them.

Sister Juniper watched her young nurses at work and made time to have a weekly, individual chat with each of them.

Walking down the ward, one morning, Sister noticed Gladys, a young girl of seven years old who was in the later stages of a tubercular bone disease. Gladys was desperately trying to say something to Ellie. Ellie didn't answer the child but remained concentrated on giving her a dose of medicine. The child slumped disconsolately back on her pillow and said something else to Ellie who turned abruptly and hurried away to the sluice, her face set. Sister went straight to Gladys and found tears were sliding quietly down her cheeks.

"It's not like you to cry, Gladys. What did you say to Nurse Ellie?"

"I'm sorry Sister. I didn't mean to upset her but I wanted to ask her if I could go home for my sister's birthday, but she wouldn't listen, just got on with giving me that nasty brown stuff."

"It's very important for you to have that brown medicine, Gladys; it does make you feel better. Nurse Elkson was probably making sure you had the right dose. What else did you say to her?"

"I just told her she was good at making me take my medicine but I liked Nurse Agnes more, because she makes me feel better and smells of primroses."

"Well then, Gladys, you've got the best of both worlds. Now, as you may not be able to go home, we'll see if your sister can come to you, for an extra special visit. We must buy her a birthday present." Sister Juniper smiled down at the wizened little girl and gently stroked her cheek.

"You make me feel better too," croaked the child and closed her eyes to sleep.

Sister Juniper sighed and decided she must bring up the incident during her next weekly talk with Ellie, which should be tomorrow.

Ellie looked tense and worn as she entered Sister's office the following afternoon.

"Nurse Elkson, when I talk with you each week, I think of your work on the ward, how conscientious you are in your duties and how meticulous in noting and recording, your patients bodily functions and reactions to treatment, scrupulous in following instructions in the measuring and giving of medicine and a real stickler for hygiene and cleanliness. All excellent. Yet, I rarely see you smile, nowadays. Yesterday, I saw you became upset by something Gladys Palmer said. You walked away from her abruptly, a child so sick she hasn't long to live. She was crying. Do you remember what Gladys said to you?"

"Yes, I remember, I can't stop remembering," the small face and poignant words had haunted Ellie ever since yesterday.

Sister settled back in her chair and gave the young woman her full attention. Ellie continued.

"Sometimes I can't bear to look into their small faces. They are so bewildered and can't understand why they feel so bad. I have to stiffen myself, make myself see them as cases, rather than people and try not to relate to them. Only by doing this can I make an efficient job of nursing them. I can't help it Sister. Sometimes I think I'm turning into a machine. All I can do is try to relieve their physical suffering and all the time I'm angry, because I know, so much of this could be prevented."

Sister Juniper nodded and waited for Ellie to say more realising the young woman needed to express her frustration. Ellie needed no encouragement:

"To most of these children, home means poverty, dirt and hunger but they still want to go back there. It's all a vicious circle of disease; poor development and inability to work; depression and the sheer weariness of keeping alive. Juniper Ward is filled with diseased children who could have been healthy and strong, if they had access to decent food and living conditions. I want to find some way of tackling all these problems".

So passionately did she feel about this that Ellie couldn't say any more, she just sat and seethed inwardly. Sister Juniper agreed with much that the young woman said,

"But you can only be a small cog in a large wheel, my dear. What you are talking about involves a whole army of politicians, teachers, community workers, economists, as well as ourselves."

"I know, I just feel on a treadmill, going nowhere," Ellie slumped in her chair.

"Ellie, look at me. When you come in here for these talks I don't just see you as Nurse Elkson, I see you as Ellie, the young woman, who left her family and all that she knew, in the North of England and came here, to train as a nurse. I remember you when you began; an eager, excited girl, with a ready smile and wry sense of humour. I can guess what's happened. You're in the middle of a cosmopolitan city, full of strangers. You see poverty and deformity on the streets every day; you walk past rows of overcrowded tenements and you work in a major teaching hospital where the worst cases come to us day after day and you see no end to it. What you need to look for is the living human spirit and love, among all this misery. When Gladys longs to be at home, she is thinking of the familiar warmth of her mother and sisters, who love her; not of the stinking, over-crowded hovel, we might see. I remember my own early days here, my dear. You have to find a way to keep yourself human and see the larger picture of life, beyond the hospital."

"It's not all as bad as that, Sister. Agnes and I and the other nurses have many a good laugh together," Ellie was anxious to reassure Sister Juniper,

"Yes, and it helps to break the tension, helps you relax. Think how a good laugh or a kind word, even just a smile would help your patients to relax and feel better in themselves."

"Like Agnes smelling of primroses, instead of carbolic," Ellie gave a wry smile.

"Well it makes them realise Agnes is not just a nurse but a young woman who likes to smell nice and that reminds them of other, happy things, outside the hospital. Remember they are missing home and family, however poor that may be."

Ellie lowered her eyes, thinking of her own family so far away in Hartsbeck.

"Ellie, you are sensitive and caring. Try and see beyond the sickness to the person. Help them remember good things and give them hope for something more than the next dose of medicine. Don't be afraid of being upset by their suffering, in that way you share it with them. You'll do yourself more harm by stiffening yourself against their predicament, learn to face it. I believe you belong to the Church of England?" This last question seemed so out of context that Ellie was taken by surprise.

"Yes, I always went to our local church with my family at home and when I first came to St. Gabriel's we went with Home Sister on Sundays."

"I suspect you've dropped off recently. Were you confirmed before you left home?"

"Yes, Sister, when I was fourteen."

"I ask, because over the years, I've found that to take Holy Communion, as regularly as I can, has helped to keep me human and in tune with God and life. To share our lives and whatever is throw at us, with Our Lord, Jesus Christ and have his help constantly, makes an amazing difference. Remember, he too was 'a man of sorrows and acquainted with grief', yet he carries joy and peace with Him."

Sister Juniper, her face quite pink, after this personal revelation, took off her spectacles and rubbed the lenses, briskly, on her handkerchief. Ellie wasn't sure how to reply but the older woman didn't give her time to say anything,

"There now, enough of that. Next year I would like you to consider taking one of the new courses in Midwifery. It is important that you build on the skills you brought with you from Harts beck before you forget them all. Bringing new life into the world will hopefully bring your smile back. Childbirth and midwifery is one of the areas where we are really progressing and saving lives. Thank you for your time, Nurse Elkson. Off you go, before you miss your entire lunch break."

"Thank you, Sister Juniper," Ellie smiled broadly, bobbed a curtsey and hurried away to the dining hall.

Over the next year Ellie gradually found ways to relax in her attitude to her young patients. Another hospital Christmas helped. The air of festivity crept in as nurses and helpers festooned the wards with Christmas decorations, which the children helped to make. Dull eyes grew brighter and there were cheers on the day the janitor carried in a tall Christmas tree. She naturally thought of her family at home in Hartsbeck and could imagine how her small, homesick, patients must feel. Sometimes, Ellie pretended it was one of her brothers or her sister in the hospital bed and she their big sister, trying to cheer them up as she had done when they were small. She told herself that she would have been just as careful in giving medicines if it was Jack or Sarah lying there but her manner would have been warmer, more familiar. Often it worked well and she won a smile and even a giggle, from the child she was tending. One such child was five year old Billy Morgan who had a serious liver complaint. She had started to tell him funny stories as she fed him and was rewarded when his worn, scared little face smiled up at her.

"I wish it was you, as fed me every time. I like your stories," he whispered and was watching eagerly for her, whenever she came on duty.

After a weekend off duty, Ellie hurried to find Billy; his bed was empty. Staff Nurse explained;

"I'm sorry Nurse Elkson but Billy died during the night. They've taken his body to the mortuary."

For a while, Ellie's cold stiffness returned.

"But Ellie, can't you see?" Agnes said in exasperation, "You made Billy Morgan's last few weeks so much happier by making him smile and feel you really cared about him. Don't switch off from them again, please, Ellie. It's important to the little mites."

Ellie agreed, she hated herself when she turned cold and starchy but it was her way of coping.

Billy's death had brought on a wave of homesickness and fear. She was so far from her own family, what if one of them became ill, or died. She had missed all this time away from them.

In February there was a spectacular dry dust-fall, over most of England and Wales. This badly affected many of the local London children, whose lungs and chests were already weakened by the unhealthy city atmosphere. Juniper Ward had an influx of respiratory cases. The nurses had to master new skills and new equipment, as well as continuing to care for their normal intake of patients.

Ellie never forgot going from bed to bed, where children were struggling to breathe properly, doctors barking out orders which the nurses scurried to obey. The holding of spittoons while the tiny chests heaved up the choking, stringy phlegm.

"You would think it was a diphtheria epidemic," Sister Juniper was heard to remark.

"God Forbid!" replied Sir Peter Edwards.

Swept up in this communal drama, Ellie stopped pretending the children on the ward were her own siblings and related to them as themselves. When the crisis was over and they all had time to relax a little, Ellie recognised a change in herself. The warmer manner, she had earlier forced herself to use with the children, had become natural. She had discovered ways of gently teasing her charges as she treated them. Mrs Larson had given her a present of a box of rose scented soap and one evening she daringly used it to wash herself, before going on duty,

"Cor Nurse, you smell like a flower shop tonight. It's lovely. I'd like to give my mum some of that," said little Suzy Greenwood, a cheery nine year old with chronic valvular disease of the heart. Ellie smiled and dropped a light kiss, on Suzy's forehead. Sister Juniper noticed.

"Now you are really nursing the children, Nurse Elkson," she whispered as she passed.

CHAPTER 16

Doctors and Nurses

Ellie gained a calm efficiency, which won her the trust of the doctors who attended the ward.

Some of the older ones, among the higher ranking doctors and consultants, held themselves aloof. They would only relate to the Sisters or to Matron, their instructions being passed down the strict chain of command. However, the nurses came into their own with the 'green' trainee doctors who accompanied the consultants round the wards and were sometimes allowed to perform simple procedures on the patients. The regular hands-on experience of the nurses, rescued many of these would-be medical men from calamity.

One afternoon Ellie had come back from her break to hear the terrified screaming of a two year old boy called Harry, who had a condition which gave him chronic constipation. The poor child's abdomen was painfully swollen and the nurses could only ease his discomfort with regular, gentle enemas. The screams were caused by a young trainee doctor standing over the child with a conical shaped instrument which he was unsuccessfully attempting to insert inside the child's tiny back passage. The other nurses on duty were busy coping with sick children elsewhere on the ward. Suddenly, the ward doors crashed open and Sister Juniper, head-dress bouncing, stormed down upon the young doctor. Panic oozed from him and young Harry continued to buck and scream. Sister's voice reached the doctor before she did,

"How dare you interfere with one of my patients, without one of my nurses being present! What do you think you are doing Dr. Baxter?"

Dr. Baxter paled before this formidable apparition but he spoke back to her.

"Excuse me Sister; I was under the impression that doctors had priority over nurses. Sir Peter Edwards, Consultant, suggested trying this new procedure on children with mega colon like Harry. It means inserting this conical bongie into the bowel once a day and leaving it there for half an hour, apparently it is proving quite successful in such cases."

Ellie trembled at his coolness, knowing Sister Juniper's protective instinct towards her patients,

"That may well be but, even Sir. Peter Edwards himself would not think of touching any of my patients without first consulting me and asking for the presence of a nurse. As you can tell, your approach has been far from successful. Nurse Elkson, please take over from Dr. Baxter and instruct him in the insertion of the instrument into young Harry's rectum."

Ellie reddened, she'd never used an instrument like this.

"Think of it as an enema tube," whispered Sister, "I'll be at the next bed if you need me."

Harry had quietened down at the sound of Sister Juniper's voice. Ellie gave the small boy a hug and told him she was going to make him feel better, she tickled him under the chin until he smiled. Then, lifting the toddler's legs as if she was changing a nappy and holding them up with one hand she gently greased the entrance to the child's anus with petroleum jelly. She took the instrument of torture from the subdued intern and with her small, competent fingers, showed him how to ease it gently in and move it further up inside the child's bowel. Harry wriggled in discomfort but she soothed him with soft words and made him as comfortable as possible with the bongie inside him. The child's eyes were wide with apprehension but he kept them on Ellie and did not cry. She gave him a drink of water and stroked his temple, until the child's eyes drooped and closed with sheer exhaustion. Relieved, Ellie turned to Dr. Baxter. He bowed to her sheepishly,

"I'm very grateful to you nurse, my fingers weren't made for such delicate tasks, I'd be better as a farmer."

"Just practice, Doctor, that's all it needs. You will soon learn to use the tips of your fingers; even farmers have to be able to perform delicate tasks."

Ellie remembered watching Bert Lee and Frank Airey castrating piglets, pinching out each delicate organ with their strong, sensitive finger tips.

Working days on Juniper Ward were mentally demanding. Sick children are not always able to tell you what is wrong, in the way an adult can and Ellie learnt to diagnose a child's immediate condition from their facial expression, or by the way they sat or lay in their beds.

One morning she was listening to the eminent paediatric specialist, Sir Peter Edwards, as he spoke to a group of student doctors who trailed behind him on his rounds. She respected this experienced Senior Doctor who held his dignity but never in the cold, aloof manner, of some Consultants. Sir Peter's bushy eyebrows would rise up and down in a comical fashion, delightful to his small patients and his discerning eyes met their own with a twinkle, as if they shared a secret joke. On this particular day, it was Ellie's turn to stand beside Sir Peter with a bowl of hot water, carbolic soap and hot towels, for him to wash and warm his hands before he touched a child.

"Always begin by noting the child's facial expression. You will learn by experience that each type of disease shows a particular face. In this Ward, you will become familiar with the faces of abdominal disease; acute respiratory disease; disease of muscles and joints; cerebral disease and so on and so on. As that eminent children's specialist, Dr. Hutchinson, is fond of saying, '*the face of a child is a mirror, in a way in which that of a grown up person is not. It is a clean sheet, upon which disease can write.*' What do I mean by that, Gentlemen?"

Often there would be an uncomfortable silence but on this occasion a tall young man, with fair hair which constantly flopped over his eyes, spoke out, in a warm Canadian drawl;

"Surely if the child is under six years old, its face won't bear the lines of hardship and development of character formed from an adult's life-time of experience?"

"Quite so, young man. What does our Nurse have to say to that," Sir Peter turned his eyes towards Ellie, who was staring at the young doctor.

Ellie blushed but answered straight up, just as if she was having a discussion with her brothers;

"You will find signs, in an adult's face, of a life time of good or bad diet; previous illness; emotional conflict; whether they lived in luxury or poverty. Their whole life style will be found there, what job of work they do; whether they have had to breathe bad or fresh air. Also the nature of a person, how they've have learnt to cope with life. Compassion; humour; contentment; bitterness and resentment; all these show up in the lines of the face. Sometimes, even a young child, can reflect some of the parent's anxiety of life and their diseases are often caused by the parents' life style but it's easier to pick up a child's immediate needs from their facial expression, adults learn to mask their feelings and—oh, I'm sorry, Sir Peter, I was carried away."

It was Sister Juniper's meaningful cough that stopped Ellie in mid-sentence. She bit her tongue realising she had said far too much and taken advantage of the situation. She lowered her eyes, hot with embarrassment, not daring to think what the young Canadian must think of her. Sir. Peter's lips twitched and he fixed his gaze on Ellie for a moment,

"Thank you Nurse, most illuminating. Gentlemen, remember your nurses are an invaluable asset to you in your work. I might even go so far as to say, that it is you who are a valuable tool in their work. In other words, you work in an essential partnership. I emphasise, a working partnership!"

The canny consultant swept a meaningful glance around his troop of eligible young men and the blushing, uniformed nurses. Sister Juniper turned and led the group on, her head lifted high in its starched head-dress, Ellie followed with the soapy water and slowly cooling towels.

CHAPTER 17

Theosophy and Eliza Fazakerley 1904

The long working days were incessantly physically and mentally demanding, on Juniper Ward. Spring turned to summer and autumn came again. Each season brought its' own particular sickness and Ellie's expertise broadened with every new case. It had been emotionally trying, several children died during September and October. Learning to deal with bereaved families and the other children in the ward who naturally became subdued and frightened, demanded all Ellie's resourcefulness. She began to question her Christian Faith and wondered again at the suffering of innocent children.

By the middle of October Ellie felt drained and it was no surprise to Sister Juniper when her young nurse fell prey to a nasty head cold.

"You'll not work on my ward with those disgusting germs, threatening my patients and staff. Go home right now, put yourself to bed with whatever cold remedy you like best. I prefer lemon, honey and whisky. Keep warm and sleep, eat lightly and drink plenty of fluids. Come back in a week."

Ellie did as she was told and slept for a full twenty-four hours. Her landlady, Mrs Larsen, was very good, providing her with food and drinks when she could but she was out at work much of the time. Mattie, when not on duty, kept strictly out of the way of Ellie's germs.

"Although, I could do with a week off, you lucky thing! Suck on these and think of me!" she grinned unsympathetically from Ellie's bedroom doorway as she tossed her a bag of sweets before disappearing to the Cancer Hospital.

Ellie had insisted that Paul kept well away from her,

"You've done so well, we don't want a heavy cold to set you back!" she said firmly when Mrs Larsen had sent Paul to her room with something.

"I haven't many books but you are welcome to read any of these. Paul goes down to Boots library every few days, so he can bring you some from there, if you make a list of what you like."

Mrs Larsen placed a beaker of hot lemon and honey (without the whisky) and a small pile of books on the bedside table, then she hurried away to her cleaning job.

Ellie was intrigued by the books. Her head felt clearer and after dipping into some of the lighter material and George Elliot's 'Silas Marner', which she had read before, she searched through the pile for something new and challenging. She found several pamphlets, published by the Theosophy Society, which she'd not heard of before. Flicking through them, Ellie was drawn to the titles of some articles.

'The World Mother as Symbol and Fact,' 'The Astral Plane,' 'The Bliss of the Heaven World,' 'Extracts from the Hindu and Buddhist Scriptures,' 'Death the gateway to bliss.'

Ellie scanned the articles and found herself both puzzled and interested. She finally turned to an article, 'What is Theosophy?' by H.P. Blavatsky and read that the roots of theosophy meant 'lover of truth'. As far as she could tell there was no mention of God in the Theosophist beliefs, despite 'Theo' being in its' name. It was obviously some strange, mystical, religious movement. Madame Blavatsky mentioned several different planes of life, which Ellie found intriguing but hard to grasp.

She settled down to read the story of a 'young woman of purity of mind who possessed untrained psychic gifts'. Apparently this woman, during sleep, had drifted into a scene of great bliss, which she had conjured up in her mind. So entranced and uplifted was she in this scene, that the woman entered a new plane of life. The woman had apparently, risen in her mind- body onto the mental plane. According to the writer, this woman was in a similar state to a person in death. In this state of bliss the woman slept for hours, then woke filled with great peace and joy but with no recollection of what had happened. This rang alarm bells in Ellie's head, she wondered how the experience came to be written down, if the woman didn't remember it?

Ellie shivered, the afternoon was drawing in and she felt a chill in the room as daylight faded. Curling up beneath the covers, she drifted into sleep. Perhaps it was the return of a slight fever, or memories of what she had read but Ellie dreamt vividly. In her dream she was walking into a wood lit by shafts of golden sunlight beaming down, between the trees. Beneath the trees were banks of wood anemones, white pink-tipped cups nestling among dark green leaves. Clusters of primroses and violets glowed gem-like, among tree roots and mossy stones. Smooth rocks, like bleached bone, jutted through the hard-trodden earth of the pathway. Out, beyond the wood, were open swathes of chalk- green grass with a few deep pink, field orchids. She was conscious of butterflies and especially a small brown one, with dark- tipped wings, the Gatekeeper, which flew ahead of Ellie and her companion. Lazily, she wondered who it could be, walking beside her. She was completely at ease with whoever it was. Ellie turned and it was Sarah, her sister, smiling broadly at her.

Much later, Ellie was woken by Mrs Larsen, rattling the curtain rings as she drew the drapes across the window. She had already lit the gas and the gentle humming and warm yellow light was comforting.

"I see you've been reading my Theosophy pamphlets," Mrs Larsen looked at her uneasily.

"Oh, yes, I was intrigued by them. I'm not sure I understood it all but I had a lovely dream afterwards and feel much better."

"Ah! Did you now? That is interesting. Maybe you've got a gift. I started going to the Theosophists when my husband died. I can't say that I really understand it but somehow, they help me feel a bit nearer to him. I go with my neighbour, Mrs Gregory. We would be pleased to take you along to one of the meetings. An educated woman, like you, would understand it more than we do and you'd be able to talk with the more advanced members, they could explain it better than I can."

"I'll think about it Mrs Larsen. It may do me good to get involved with something other than nursing."

Ellie was strangely drawn to the idea of theosophy and yet repelled, at the same time. She knew her sister would be upset and Cousin Hugh certainly would warn her away from such teachings and tell her to get involved with a church, if she wanted an outside interest.

It was the fascination Theosophy seemed to have with death and the spirit world that appealed to her. The number of deaths and the suffering of children on Juniper Ward troubled her. It would help her, if she could be persuaded that there was some mystical answer behind the suffering among such innocents. Mrs Larsen came back carrying a jug of hot water and left Ellie to wash and use the chamber pot.

In three days Ellie's cold was much better but she had been given a week off and dare not return to work before then. The weather had turned sunny and it was tempting to venture outside so she dressed warmly and walked down the road to the shops opposite the underground station. She discovered the branch of Boots' library visited by Paul. The library was at the back of the well-stocked Chemist shop. On her way through, Ellie treated herself to a bag of coltsfoot cough drops and bought a bottle of Pulmer Bailey, (a bitter, watery medicine, that her mother had always dosed them with when they had colds. She also bought two prettily packaged tablets of soap, rose-scented for Mattie and lavender for Mrs Larsen, as a thank you for their care of her.

Passing behind a dark wood screen into the library section was like entering some quiet lawyer's office or a gentleman's private study. Three walls were lined with bookcases approximately seven feet high and immediately opposite the entrance was a low curved wooden counter polished so that it glowed in the mellow gas light. A small window high in the wall behind the counter let in a small amount of daylight and a bright faced woman of about thirty years old sat behind the counter welcoming Ellie with a happy smile.

"You are my first customer today, Ma'am, how can I help you? Are you a member of the library?"

"No, this is the first time I've been. May I look through the books first, before I decide to join?"

"Certainly. You'll find we cover a wide spectrum. Over here, we have novels and other works of fiction, which are popular amongst most women but nothing too racy. Then we have men's fiction but of course you don't have to stick to either category, it's just for convenience. Then we have a classical collection and a poetry section. There is a small children's collection and the shelves on the left are all nonfiction, factual material. If we don't have what you are looking for we might be able to obtain it for you. Our stock circulates through branches all over the country." The young woman leant over the counter, waving her hands in all directions, as she spoke. Her eagerness was confusing and Ellie was glad when another customer arrived. Stout, well dressed and gently wheezing, the new arrival stopped just within the library entrance leaning heavily on her folded umbrella. The eager assistant lifted a flap in the counter and darted out,

"Mrs Fazakerley, what a pleasure. How are you?" and a high backed stool was whisked out of a corner and placed so that the older lady could sit.

"Thank you my dear. I am a little better today and was determined to change my library books. I've read these at least three times and felt I'd go mad without something new to titillate my brain."

Ellie suppressed a smile and turned to the nonfiction shelves. The books here were in subject order and she recognised two or three of the geology and scientific volumes that Stephen used to read. She was searching for something more about Theosophy and high on the top shelf spied a thin volume 'Theosophy, its influence for today.' Spying a portable contraption of three steps attached to a long polished pole, Ellie manoeuvred it across and climbed the steps to reach the book and stayed there, leafing through the closely printed pages. There was a chapter on the influence of theosophy on English literature and she was surprised to read that several of the well-known poets such as William Blake and W.B. Yeats and the authors Charles Kingsley, Oscar Wilde and Bernard Shaw were listed and some of these were on the register of members of the society, past and present. Climbing down from the ladder, she found the poetry section and a volume Blake's poems. Turning to the counter Ellie felt the room spin ever so slightly. This was her first time out after being in bed for two whole days and another half day just sitting in her room. It must have shown in her face, the assistant left Mrs Fazakerley and hurried over to Ellie, relieving her of her books

"Are you alright my dear, you have gone very pale," Mrs Fazakerley had risen from her chair. "Sit here; I have hogged the seat long enough. No, I insist. We can't have you swooning like a lady in one of our Miss. Curtis's novels,"

Ellie's knees trembled and she sat quickly on the high stool bending her head towards her knees. In a moment she was well again and felt foolish as she looked at the two anxious faces staring down at her,

"I'm perfectly alright now," she assured them, "this is my first time out after being in bed with a cold and I had quite forgotten when I became engrossed in the books. I should have known I had overdone things."

"Well now, what a coincidence, this is my first time out after a bout of bronchitis. My name is Eliza Fazakerley and I'm reasonably respectable. Nobody to be frightened of anyway! Do let us celebrate our recovery together, over tea and cakes. There is a tea shop just next door which I can recommend. Miss. Curtis here has sorted me out with fresh books so I shall go and book us a table. Please, do join me in five minutes. That is, if you've nothing better to do."

"Thank you, that would be lovely," "stammered Ellie. "My name is Ellen Elkson- Miss Ellen Elkson and I think I'm respectable, some of the time!"

The middle aged lady threw back her head and laughed the velvet flowers on her hat wobbling in accompaniment; then she swept away with her umbrella and bag of books, leaving a warm smell of camphor and cloves.

Miss Curtis was delighted,

"It is so nice when people make friends among my books," she babbled, "You will find Mrs Fazakerley quite delightful, if rather opinionated. Now I see you have chosen some books, oh how interesting, Theosophy and Blake. You may choose a third book if you wish but first let me register you as a member. It costs one shilling to join and that will last you for three months. I need your name and address and place of work, that is, if you have one."

"Do you have any of the stories of Oscar Wilde?" queried Ellie, after giving Miss Curtis her details. She remembered her childhood reading of 'The Selfish Giant' and 'The Happy Prince' and was wondering how they fitted in with the author's interest in Theosophy. Miss Curtis went straight to the right shelf and brought her 'The Picture of Dorian Gray.'

"Don't go having nightmares, it's a creepy tale. You may keep the books for three weeks and then renew them if you need to, Miss Elkson."

"Thank you," said Ellie, accepting her books in a green canvas bag, with the Boots' logo.

"You look so much better," gushed Miss Curtis, "the tea shop is first on the right as you leave our shop. Thank you for patronising our branch. I look forward to your next visit."

They exchanged formal smiles and Ellie hurried to find her new acquaintance.

CHAPTER 18

In the teashop with Eliza

When she arrived in the tea shop she found that Mrs Fazakerley had ordered two glasses of a sparkling white wine and a plate of sweet biscuits. She sounded like some wonderful goddess of plenty with her smiling greeting:

"My dear, I insist you share a medicinal glass of wine with me before we have our hot tea. I do hope you're not teetotal! It will do us both good."

"No I'm not teetotal, thank you. As I'm on sick leave I shall enjoy it but I didn't realise they provided wine in tea shops,"

"Not many do, just a few have a licences and I think I know most of them," Mrs Fazakerley gave a fruity chuckle.

The two women sipped their wine and nibbled biscuits for half an hour chatting together like old friends. Ellie was amazed at herself, she was usually timid and withdrawn with new people.

She learnt that Mrs Fazakerley had been widowed during the last Boer War and had no children or dependants but had been left well provided for.

"I was well loved by my husband, Harry, and I loved him. Of course, I miss him but he was a soldier and I had learnt to pursue an active and interesting life, when he was away. I certainly wasn't just going to wait around at home, improving the house and staring at walls. Sadly we had no children. When Harry died, in November, 1902, I was devastated for a time and then was able to continue following the pursuits I had cultivated when he was away. Well most of them. I'm slowing down now, with age and my silly chest."

Mrs Fazakerley patted her chest affectionately then turned the conversation to Ellie,

"Tell me of your family; from your accent you're from the North of England, I would say Lancashire?"

"Yes from Hartsbeck, about fifteen miles from Preston."

"I know of it. They make wonderful cotton prints there and brick, good red brick."

"That's right!" said Ellie delighted and surprised

"Does your family work in textiles or brick?"

"Neither. My father is a clerk in one of the large engineering works and my mother stays at home to keep house for my four brothers and my sister. I'm the eldest and the first to leave home."

"How very brave to venture so far. What brought you to London?"

"I came to train as a nurse in St. Gabriel's teaching hospital. I saw so much sickness and child mortality brought about through ignorance and lack of care in Hartsbeck, that I wanted to join the nursing profession and help do something about it. London seemed the best place to train."

"I expect you cut your teeth on tales of Florence Nightingale? She's certainly spread her message around."

Did Ellie hear a note of cynicism in the older woman's voice? She looked at her over the rim of her wine glass. Mrs Fazakerley laughed,

"You've found me out. Yes I have a slight grudge against Miss Nightingale. That doesn't stop me admiring the woman and the inspiration she's been, to such as yourself. No, it's just that my husband told me about other women who were out there, caring for the troops, some even before Miss Nightingale. These women realised what was needed and provided what they could out of their own meagre resources. They were idolised by the soldiers but hadn't the money or power to rouse the Government backing, like Florence."

"But surely they would have been glad when she arrived and was able to draw on her assets to make things happen?"

"Oh they were, but their own ideas and pioneering work were never acknowledged. Miss. Nightingale had all the publicity and the glory and it helped that she did. People responded to her call as a heroine. But I like to think of those other women. One in particular my husband used to tell me about was Mary Seacole. She was an hotelier, half Irish and half Jamaican and when no-one would fund her to go out as a nurse she went to the Crimea off her own bat- took some of her best kitchen staff and built a hotel near the front."

"A hotel? That sounds an odd thing to do! It wasn't exactly a holiday resort."

"Yes, she called it, 'The British Hotel.' The wounded and any-one needing a break from the fighting were brought to her and she provided for them out of her own pocket. She made sure they had good wholesome food. Harry said her rice pudding was a favourite - without milk mind you. She gave them ham and chicken, fresh vegetables and a clean, dry place with comfortable beds, to stay in till they recovered."

"Did she know how to treat their wounds and doctor the sick?"

"Oh yes, she knew all sorts of successful traditional West Indian remedies for cholera and typhoid and for helping wounds to heal. The doctors worked with her. She even went out on the battlefield searching for and tending the wounded. Yet, when she came home after the Crimean War she was bankrupt, having used up her fortune in caring for the troops and was going to be put in a debtors' prison. Nobody honoured her but the soldiers found out and they wouldn't let her down. They held some amazing public events to raise funds for her and made sure she was set up for the rest of her life. The Queen had to acknowledge her in the end; the Prince of Wales had seen her work at first hand and thought the world of her. He made a sculpture of her."

Ellie felt uncomfortable but her respect for Miss Nightingale went far beyond what had been achieved in the Crimea; without her influence Nursing would not have progressed to the professional status and reputation it had now achieved.

"What do your brothers and sisters do?" Mrs Fazakerley deftly changed tack.

Ellie told her about Stephen who was now nineteen and studying sciences,

"He's obsessed with geology and spends all his spare time travelling around discovering rocks and fossils,"

"Sounds deadly interesting," said Miss Fazakerley in her gravely cynical tone.

Ellie was nettled.

"Oh, when he talks about it, he brings it all alive. He also collects moths and butterflies," she didn't describe how he killed and pinned them into boxes, not wanting a remark about "another deadly interest."

Ellie moved on quickly to George, who at seventeen, was junior clerk with the solicitors' firm of Drake and Son, with a view to moving on to serve his articles with Mr Drake and become a fully qualified lawyer. Then Edwin, who at fifteen was also a junior office clerk but in a firm of accountants.

"Although his first love is botany and photographing wild birds."

"A healthy foil to labouring over figures in a stuffy office," murmured Mrs Fazakerley

"Then there's my Sarah, who's twelve. She loves music, plays the piano and sings beautifully. She studies and helps mother at home but she'd like to train as a teacher in a few years' time. Then there's Jack the youngest and a real scamp. He's nine and still at school. I expect we've all spoilt him but he's a grand lad."

"My, you're all aiming high in the world. Everything is changing so fast, we certainly need all these professional people in order to help us find our way around and survive in today's society. Does your family attend a church my dear?"

The question came so abruptly, that alarm bells rang in Ellie's head. It reminded her of Sister Juniper.

"Well yes, we attend the local parish church at home and as children we went to the church primary school. Sarah and Jack are still there, at the same school."

"You mean Church of England, I presume?"

"Yes, why do you ask?"

"When you nearly fainted in Boots' library I picked up your books and noticed one on Theosophy and the other was poems of

William Blake. Now I happen to know that, in Hartsbeck, there is a large branch of the Swedenborgian' Church,"

"Yes, I know it. They call it, the New Church, it's a huge building and has attracted lots of people. Some girls I studied with at the institute were members. It's a lively church."

"It's the largest Swedenborgian church building in England. They follow the teachings of Emmanuel Swedenborg, which are very much akin to theosophy. I thought, after seeing your reading material and now finding out you are from Hartsbeck, that maybe you were from that church."

"Well, no. What a strange coincidence. I didn't really know what the New Church was all about. There are a lot of Non-conformist and Anglican churches in Hartsbeck and Roman Catholic. I presumed the New Church was just another, like them. I think it's' full name is 'The New Jerusalem Church'. Are you a member?"

"No, not altogether. I have close friends who are trying to persuade me. They haven't completely convinced me but I am very interested. What's your interest in theosophy?"

Then began a long talk in which Ellie described how she had read her land-lady's pamphlets. How she had been wrestling with the questions of the suffering and deaths of children and of mothers dying from the results of childbirth. She went on to tell of her blissful dream, of walking in the woods with her sister, which seemed to fit in with a passage she had been reading in the Theosophy journal.

"Could death really be such a blissful state? I'd like to think so," finished Ellie, turning inquiring eyes on the older woman.

"Maybe, but the suffering and grief left behind when a child dies is certainly not a blissful state," Mrs Fazakerley's eyes filled with tears and her mouth set in a grim line.

"I told you Harry and I couldn't have children but there was one, a little boy. He lived only a few minutes after he was born but his eyes opened and his little body trembled in my arms before he went. I hope he went into a state of bliss but I didn't and neither did my husband. There was a moment of utter peace, straight after he died and the nurse asked his name, I said Luke. She laid her hand on our son's tiny head and spoke a simple prayer commending Luke to God's keeping. I felt utterly empty, for a very long time and so did Harry. There's still an empty space- if I allow myself to think—."

Tentatively Ellie stretched out her hand and laid it briefly over her companion's shaking one. Mrs Fazakerley smiled and straightened herself,

"Well, we will just depress ourselves if we talk of such things. Let's have a bowl of this café's excellent soup as its past lunchtime and I'm rather peckish."

The soup came, a rich, steaming, beef broth full of onions and other vegetables and a hunk of bread to go with it. Soon the two convalescents felt fully restored.

"My landlady has invited me to go with her to one of her Theosophy meetings. I feel quite tempted to go; there is something about it that fascinates me," confided Ellie.

"You feel it might give you some ready-made answers to the problems of life? My dear only life itself can reveal its meaning. You've got to live it and even then, you realise there's far more you don't know than what you think you know."

"Well, yes but it must help to hear someone else's ideas,"

"As long as you don't let your mind become addled by cranks. You've plenty of good common sense but it can be poisoned by manipulative brain- boxes and spiritual eccentrics!"

Ellie laughed at the robust warning.

"Oh Mrs Fazakerley, it can't be so dangerous, surely?"

"You'd be surprised. I tell you what, my dear. Would you allow me to come with you, if you decide to go to one of these meetings? My Swedenborgian friends would be tickled pink but I would like to know what it is that has such a hold on them. Also, with my cynical outlook, I might be able to protect you; if it does turn out to be 'so dangerous.'"

"Alright, let's do it together. I'll find out when Mrs Larson is willing to take me and I'll ask if you may come too. How do I get in touch with you?"

The two women exchanged addresses and decided they could also meet at Boots' library or leave messages there with Miss. Curtis.

"If we are to be friends, you must call me Eliza," said Mrs Fazakerley extending her strong square hand to Ellie as they rose to go home.

"Thank you Eliza. Then you must call me Ellie."

A firm handshake sealed the beginning of a lasting friendship. Ellie was glad of the warm companionship of the outwardly sensible, Eliza, who must have been at least twenty years her senior but with the spirit of someone much younger.

"I suppose I need a mother figure," Ellie smiled and realised that she hadn't really smiled, from sheer enjoyment, for a very long time.

CHAPTER 19

The Theosophy Meeting, Great Russell Street. 1904

By the end of the week Ellie was back at work and had little time or energy for anything else. However, she was becoming used to the daily demands of Juniper Ward and learning to relax and switch off when she came off duty. Mrs Larson usually had some kind of stew simmering on the hob, for Ellie and Mattie to help themselves, whatever time they came home.

"I didn't realise there could be so many different kinds of stew," said Mattie, dishing out two generous plates of fish stew including potatoes, carrots and onions. Mrs Larson was a clever cook and manager. Rabbit stew one day would be followed the next by a rabbit and mushroom pie. The small amount of meat in a beef stew would be supplemented with the addition of tasty suet dumplings and cheap, neck of lamb made a Lancashire hotpot which delighted even Ellie. Their schedules didn't often coincide but when they did the two young nurses sat over their evening meal and talked "till the cows came home" as Jeannie Elkson would have said.

At last Mrs Larson suggested an evening when she could take Ellie and Eliza to a meeting of the Theosophical Society. It was to be held the following Monday, 7th November at 7.30pm in the notorious Bloomsbury district of London at a house on Great Russell Street. Ellie was free and Eliza sent a note to say she would cancel all her engagements for that evening and accompany them.

"My word, she must be keen," exclaimed Mrs Larson.

Ellie smiled imagining the twinkle in her friend's eyes and the rise of one eyebrow to signify a wild exaggeration.

Ellie was tingling with fear and anticipation as the three women took the underground to Gt. Russell Street and climbed up into the district of Bloomsbury. The tall houses loomed over the pavements and the gas street-lights cast giant, shifting shadows around them as they walked. Occasionally they passed an open door. Glancing through one, Ellie saw a man lolling on a chaise-longue, smoking from a long pipe attached to a large bulbous glass container of bubbling, colourless liquid. The man's eyes seemed to meet hers through the open doorway, they lingered languorously staring at, Ellie knew not what; she was quite certain he wasn't focusing on her.

"He's smoking opium," whispered Eliza, "you're probably part of his dream world, not really there. You might appear in a poem later, 'strange lady of the night who floated by and cast on me her liquid eye,'" Eliza droned out the words dreamily.

Ellie spluttered, "behave yourself Eliza, or we won't be allowed into the meeting."

"My lips are sealed," mocked Eliza.

The headquarters of the Theosophical Society was in a narrow but imposing, stone built house, about four storeys high. They climbed an outside staircase, grateful for the iron-wrought handrails, to an apartment on the first floor.

Silently they followed Mrs Larson, through a half open door and along a dimly lit corridor. They could hear people chattering and entered a large gas-lit room. Chairs were set out in semi-circular rows in front of a raised podium on which stood a carved reading desk which was draped with a cloth embroidered with strange emblems. The same emblems were painted large, on banners hanging over the windows.

"Don't be overawed, Ellie, it's all for effect. Just pretty pictures, "whispered Eliza. In the sputtering gaslight the symbols on the banners trembled and seemed alive.

"Pretty? I call them spooky!" said Ellie and tipped her head round to examine them better. She made out a large serpent coiled in a perfect circle, the tip of its pointed tail entering its open mouth. Above this was a smaller circle containing a crooked-legged cross and above it a strange character in Arabic style lettering. Inside the circle, the two conjoined triangles of the Star of David enclosed another small cross which was topped by a round loop, Ellie wondered if this was some primitive style of crucifix. Mrs Larson leant forwards and whispered across that the symbols on the banner were the Society's seal and would be explained during the evening.

"I know that one in the middle- the cross with the loop. It's an ancient Egyptian symbol for eternal life; they called it the key of the Nile," murmured Eliza.

"I thought it might be a primitive crucifix," whispered Ellie.

"I think some Eastern Christians may have adopted it as such." replied Eliza. Ellie cast her companion a sideways glance wondering how she knew so much,

"Shhhh, they're about to begin," Mrs Larson settled back in her chair, a fixed expression sliding over her face.

Ellie realised the lighting in the room had been dimmed. The familiar smell of gas held a spicy, more exotic scent. A faint sound of music sounded from far away, gradually coming nearer. It was a high, sweet melody, reminding Ellie of the shepherd's pipe her brother Stephen had brought home from Turkey. Stringed instruments joined the pipe producing a strange, wailing beauty, which soothed Ellie and she relaxed in her chair, her eyelids drooping.

"Incense and Indian mystical music. Don't become bewitched," Eliza lightly nipped the back of Ellie's hand, making her jump.

Movement from the back of the podium drew their attention. Two men and a woman entered from behind a dark, velvet curtain and moved to sit on three ornately carved, chairs facing the audience. The men wore black waist-coats and tail suits with white cravats and the woman was swathed from neck to toe in fitted black satin, relieved only by a loose scarf of a pale, diaphanous material.

The mystical music faded away and the silence in the room became intense. The three on the stage sat as if listening and waiting for something. Ellie found she was doing the same, till a surreptitious dig from Eliza's elbow caused a giggle to rise in her throat, she disguised it as a cough which brought the eyes of the woman in black searching in her direction, the eyes were staring and stony grey. Ellie sat motionless, willing not to be seen and was relieved when one of the men stood and began to speak. He was a small, lean man, probably in his early forties, with a quiff of mousey-brown hair, brushed away from his forehead and pale eyes. He fluttered his hands as he welcomed everybody and introduced himself and the others on the podium in a high- clipped, educated voice. The man's name was Brendon James. He explained, for those who had come for the first time, that the music followed by silence was intended to help them leave behind the worry and busyness of their everyday lives and enter into a different spiritual place, a quieter and more receptive space, more receptive to less obvious things–

"Which are always there but we are not always aware of them in the clamour of our daily lives."

The quiet little man encouraged them to sit comfortably with their feet flat on the floor and their hands resting loosely in their laps.

"Now, close your eyes and breath slowly and deeply, in and out, i-i-i-in –n-n and ou- ou- out," he lengthened the vowels to slow the rhythm of their breathing. When he was satisfied that everyone was doing as he asked, he stopped talking and the mysterious music took over again, for a few minutes, then another silence. Before it became oppressive, Mr James brought them all to attention:

"Now; open your eyes, Ladies and Gentlemen, before we go to sleep or become restless again. Our guest for this evening, Madam Greta Bechstein, will now address our gathering",

He bowed to the lady in black who rose regally, her hair a dark coronet around her head. She glided towards the tall reading desk, where a sheaf of papers was laid ready. Brendon James resumed his seat and once again Madam Bechstein roved the audience with her steely grey eyes, Ellie felt a chill as they rested briefly on her. The woman began to speak and her voice was deep and warm with the hint of a German accent reminding Ellie of Annette at home. Ellie became captivated. The woman explained the meaning of the symbols on the society's emblem and somehow they made sense to Ellie. Madame Greta spoke of evolution but not just in the animal kingdom as Ellie's brother had spoken of it, but as a great movement taking place in the whole cosmos, involving the planets, the solar systems and galaxies which she spoke of as conscious entities and carefully watched over by the Masters of Ancient Wisdom, "a spiritual hierarchy invisible to us, the highest in their ranks being highly advanced spiritual beings." Frequently the term 'Monads' was mentioned. Monads, she explained, were:

"spiritual units of consciousness which can manifest among us in many forms including angels and human beings, which help us to come closer to our Divine Nature,"

"I know many of us have been feeling lost as we listen to the different churches arguing with the scientists about the creation of the world. As Theosophists, evolution does not worry us; indeed we see it as an essential part of our beliefs. Evolution in the material world mirrors our evolution in the spiritual world, we need to seek the guidance of the Monads to evolve in the way of light and not be lured into the ways of darkness."

Madam Greta's honey thick voice flowed on encouraging her listeners to "cultivate selflessness and the traditional virtues of honesty, justice, fortitude, prudence. All are vital to help us to develop our Divine Natures."

Ellie realised that re-incarnation was part of the Theosophist understanding and that theosophists believe there are many planes on which a person can live both physically and spiritually. The more advanced a person becomes spiritually, the more time they spend in the astral planes, in between reincarnations. Death didn't seem to be part of it at all – just a continual passing from one plane to another. Occasionally one could contact those who had gone to another plane, if they wanted to contact us. One moment Ellie thought she had grasped what Madam Greta was saying the next she felt utterly confused and longed to thrash it all out with Eliza over tea and toast.

At last Madam Greta Bechstein sat down and the third person on the platform stood up, he was a short stocky man of late middle age, a few long wisps of greying, dark hair brushed over his round, balding head. He had a cheerful face and was obviously popular with the group as he was greeted with a round of applause.

"It is now left to me to close tonight's gathering with a reading. I have chosen a passage from the new play by our eminent Mr George Bernard Shaw, 'Man and Superman', which, if you are able to pick through the speeches and machinations of his characters, presents the idea of a 'Life Force', a power which seeks to raise mankind, (with our co-operation of course)," a titter ran through the listeners, "to a higher and better existence which, I believe, fits in well with Madam Bechstein's words to us this evening".

The gentleman opened his book and placing spectacles on his nose, read from the speech of Don Juan, from 'Man and Superman'. The little man was skilful in drawing out the character and humour of the speech and made even the dry bits interesting. By the time he had finished Ellie wanted nothing more than to watch the whole play.

"Well, I call that a welcome diversion. I'd had just about all I could take from Madam Greta," said Eliza, pulling on her gloves and smiling.

"I'm sorry you feel like that," said Mrs Larsen, obviously offended. "Madam Blechstein is very high ranking in the society."

"I think that was my problem. Excellent as her lecture was, parts of it were rather over my head. Smaller doses would be better for me to begin with. Now, I don't usually like readings taken out of context but that little man's rendering from 'Man and Superman' was superb. Let's make an occasion to watch the whole play together. My treat Mrs Larsen, as a thank- you for tonight," Eliza linked Mrs Larsen's arm companionably

"Well, I don't know. That sounds very nice, Mrs Fazakerley, I must say. What do you think Ellie?"

"It sounds a wonderful idea, Eliza, but will you meet me in the Brown Leaves Café near the hospital, one day soon? At 12.15pm if possible. I have an hour for lunch all this week. I really need to talk with you."

"Of course, I'm free tomorrow, why not then?"

"That would be lovely."

"Now, I'm going to call us a cab. Its late and starting to rain so I insist on dropping you off on my way home," Eliza held out her umbrella and stopped a passing motor- taxi instructing the driver to go first to Mrs Larsen's home and then to her own. Neither Ellie nor Mrs Larsen had ridden in a motor-taxi before but they accepted it as if it was an everyday occurrence. Eliza Fazakerley must not know their lack of finesse.

Lying in bed an hour later the voice of Madam Greta Bechstein flowed round and round in Ellie's mind. The theosophist's words began to mingle in Ellie's head with the old scientific arguments of her brothers and odd words from the church services of her child-hood. Eventually she must have fallen asleep and woke to the sound of early morning traffic in the street outside. It was time for work again.

CHAPTER 20

Eliza's decision.

Ellie and Eliza met many times over the next year. Together they tried to make sense of Theosophy. They attended meetings and seminar groups at Great Russell Street. Ellie was intrigued by it but Eliza became suspicious of the personalities behind the movement. Madam Blavatsky, the movement's founder, who had died in 1891, had led a rather unsavoury life-style. Eliza had spoken out about this and embarrassed Ellie, during one of the open discussion groups;

"I have always thought that the behaviour of the founders of a movement reflects the authenticity of its teaching. Theosophy would seem to stress purity of thought and action but from what I have read, Madam Blavatsky and other leaders were far from pure and behaved in a sexually immoral way towards younger members of the group as a matter of course."

The group leader was brusque in his answer

"Annie Besant, the present leader, declared that, despite her many falls from grace, Madam Blavatsky's teachings were sound. She said that their founder had been the first to admit that she gave way too readily to the temptations of the flesh but this in no way undermines the teachings and principles underlying Theosophy."

After this Eliza had become increasingly unhappy and cynical about the whole movement.

"All my earlier fears are proving right, Ellie. At one point I hoped my spiritual faith would be deepened by theosophy but I find it humbug and subversive. Do you know, Ellie, it's sent me scurrying back to the dear old Church of England!"

"Eliza! I never thought you would turn to the Anglican Church. The Swedenborgians maybe. I could understand you going to them, but not the Church of England."

Eliza laughed and patted Ellie's hand,

"You've moved a long way from home, Ellie my dear. Be careful not to get lost!"

"But why Eliza, and why not the 'New Church'?"

"Just too much cool philosophy and metaphysics. I needed some honest, warm humanity and even with all the back- biting and bitchiness and superstition, the Church of England is full of humanity."

"If you say so," said Ellie truculently.

"Anyway, I've found a church, in easy walking distance of home. The people that go are quite happy to be flesh and blood individuals, who need of plenty of help in their everyday lives. What's more, they don't turn their noses up at finding that help in God."

"I want something a bit deeper than that."

"Well, you may do but I'm past digging deep. What I need has to be fairly accessible and not too far beneath the surface of things."

"What about all those arguments, in the church, against evolution? All the distrust you had in the truth of some of the biblical stories?" Ellie was not convinced by her friend but Eliza answered with surprising alacrity.

"Ah, now it's you who are staying right on the surface and not looking even just a tiny bit deeper."

Ellie was riled. "Whatever do you mean Eliza? You said yourself you couldn't believe the earth and everything in it was made in seven days and that Noah's Ark couldn't possibly have happened like it says,"

"I was a bit naïve in my thinking, when I said that. I'd only met Christians who took the Bible literally, at face value. I've met a Christian clergyman who explained to me that not everything in the Bible is meant to be taken literally, like a scientific text book. The scriptures are just trying to express all sorts of things about us and God and the world; sometimes picture language is the only way to explain things. You'd be fascinated by what he has to say, Ellie."

"It could be bordering on theosophy - finding hidden spiritual meanings in everything. You've been got at by somebody, Eliza. My brothers Stephen and George have just walked out of their church because the Vicar was preaching against evolution and saying such ideas came from the devil."

"I don't blame them if that's what their Vicar says. Stephen's a scientist and a geologist isn't he? Well he knows a thing or two about evolution and the millions of years it's taken the earth to form. What is sad is that your brothers think they can't stick to their understanding of scientific knowledge and still be Christians. Lots of clergymen believe in the theory of evolution and still hold a firm faith in God and Jesus Christ."

"Oh, honestly Eliza, how can Stephen and George do that? They wouldn't be able to keep their mouths shut. There'd be no end of trouble."

"Well, I think that's just what they should do. I've been reading a book called 'Essays and Reviews' which tells about all sorts of church leaders who didn't keep their mouths shut. They stood together against their colleagues and published strong articles for the same reasons that your brothers walked out."

"That's a bit different from being part of a small community church and standing up against the local Vicar. It could split the congregation apart!"

"Yes, I can see that. It's bound to split the community into those against and those for Church. In another generation or two things might be seen differently, let's hope so. Anyway God isn't restricted to the Church; He wouldn't be God if He was! Now come along my dear, I'm treating you to a glass of champagne and a cream bun. You've been looking peaky again and it'll be just the tonic."

Ellie felt disappointed. She wanted someone to discuss this strange but intriguing Theosophical religion with her, someone outside the Movement but as interested in it as herself. She thought she had such a person in Eliza but now her friend had firmly turned her back on theosophy. Ellie was frightened of being engulfed by the Movement. Eliza had kept her safely on the edge, peering in but

136

prevented from teetering over altogether by the older woman's common sense and humour.

"My dear, I shall still be just as interested, to hear about the goings on from Great Russell Street, as before and I'd be glad to have your opinion about the things I'm discovering from my little Church of St. Stephen's. I rely on you to tell me if I'm going too far!"

"That sounds fair Eliza. I do look forward to our discussions. Here's to our twin ventures on the Spiritual side of life!"

Laughing Ellie and Eliza raised their glasses and sipped the Champagne appreciatively.

CHAPTER 21

A new assignment

By August 1905 Ellie had been on Juniper Ward for over two years. She had become more of a true Nurse. The children she cared for were no longer just patients to her; they were individuals with personalities, which needed to be nurtured as carefully as their sick bodies.

"We will soon need to find you a place as Staff Nurse," Sister Juniper had warned her two months earlier during one of her weekly talks.

There had been no further mention of the midwifery course she had earlier set her heart on. Ellie wondered if she should try to find a post nearer home like Bertha Harrison, but she didn't feel ready to go back to Lancashire just yet, it would be retreating into a backwater life. She talked it over with Eliza in their favourite tea shop,

"I want to be in a place where new things happen. Here, in London I feel the hospitals are at the cutting edge. Men and women come from all over the world, to train in London hospitals."

"That may be so but knowledge travels fast nowadays. I think you'll find hospitals in Lancashire are developing very quickly. I read a lot about such things and have friends in the North. Manchester has an excellent reputation and so has Preston. Even if you were to go to one of the smaller cottage hospitals, as a London trained nurse you would still be spreading your expertise among those who need it? Much as I would miss you and our London adventures, I would hate to think you are beginning to set yourself above your roots, Ellie!"

"Oh, Eliza that's not how I see it at all, what an awful thought but I do feel a different person here, more alive. If I go home I shall become dull little Miss. Elkson getting all her excitement from books, when she's not at work. I would miss you dreadfully but if I'm really needed back home- that's where I must go. I always intended to go back eventually, it just seems too soon. I need to learn so much more."

It was Matron, who solved the problem. She called Ellie to her office.

"Nurse Elkson, I remember, a year ago, urging you consider taking the midwifery course when you left Juniper. I myself have fought long and hard for specialised midwifery training but the courses are experiencing a few hiccups at the moment and I would advise you to delay it. Also, although I said the opposite a year ago, I now think your early experiences in Hartsbeck may be frowned on in professional circles. There has been so much prejudice about the so-called untrained midwives. I think a little more experience will stand you in good stead."

Ellie bristled as she thought of Annette Hamilton and her unparalleled 'untrained' midwifery skills and the trust, her friend had earned, of the doctors in Hartsbeck. Many women would not have survived childbirth but for her.

Matron continued, "You have proved yourself to be a conscientious and caring nurse. Sister Juniper reports that During your time on her ward, she has seen you mature both in your handling of yourself and in your attitude to the children in our care. However, it hasn't been easy for you. You have a sensitivity which, at times, has shown a highly strung nature. You have worked hard at mastering it but I think it would be better if you were to leave London for a while and go to some less turbulent hospital. Hopefully, you would then be able to concentrate on nursing and leadership skills without the trauma of the metropolis."

She's sending me back to Hartsbeck, thought Ellie. Well that answers my dilemma, I suppose but I don't feel happy about it.

Matron's tone had changed to positive, her words clipped and challenging.

"There is a Staff Nurse vacancy coming in two months' time at Doxlee Hospital, a rather special Hospital, within three miles of Oxford. I believe it will be more than suitable for you, if you are happy to apply for it?"

Ellie felt a shock go through her. Staff Nurse! Was she ready for that? Of course she knew it had to come, that was the next step, but Oxford. The very name was tempting; certainly it was not too far from London. Of course they may not want her.

"Well? Have I made you speechless?" Matron waited.

"Th-that sounds very interesting, Matron, would it be on a children's ward? I presume most hospitals now have separate Children's Wards?"

"Well, not quite all, as yet, but in this case, yes. The vacancy is on a Children's Orthopaedic Ward. It's somewhat unusual. Scientists from Oxford and Cambridge are researching the cause and treatment of rickets and scurvy and such like diseases. In fact, any disease which affects the bones and mobility of children. A special trust has enabled several specialist wards to be opened at Doxlee. You will be expected to cooperate with these scientists, for instance, supplying them with patients' blood samples, writing special reports for them and with the doctor's supervision, trying out particular treatments. The research scientists will have access to the wards but are not allowed to be intrusive in their dealings with the patients. Some of the children will be long term but most of them are expected to leave the ward eventually, alive if not always kicking! You have a lot to offer them, Nurse Elkson and you will certainly learn plenty."

Ellie thought hard, she would certainly find orthopaedics interesting, she thought of the children with rickets and malformed limbs that she had known at St. Mark's school in Hartsbeck. Nevertheless, the faces of those Hartsbeck mothers struggling in childbirth flashed across her memory, they must still be her first concern and her answer was hesitant.

"I think I would like that very much, Matron. Thank you, but do I have to make a decision straight away?"

"You are unsure. What's troubling you Nurse Elkson?"

"It's just that I feel very strongly about Midwifery. Since the Midwives Act in 1902 I have been anxious to take up the special Midwifery Training now being given. You yourself and Sister Juniper suggested it to me, quite strongly, a year ago. Eventually I hope to specialise in mother and baby care. How long would I be expected to serve as a Staff Nurse before I can do this?"

"I know you've had this dream for a long time. Let me see," she consulted her papers,

"You are expected to be a Staff Nurse for at least two years. By that time, who knows? You may have become so enamoured by orthopaedics that you want to stay in that field. However, if you're original desire stays intact, that will be the time to apply for mid-wifery training and enter your chosen specialisation. By then the midwifery courses should have recovered from their teething prob-lems and be much improved! Your time in orthopaedics will be well spent, you will learn a lot about the causes of bone and joint prob-lems, which will be of use to you in mother and child care, both ante and post- natal."

Ellie made up her mind, "Thank you Matron; in that case, I am happy to apply for the post, at Doxlee."

By the middle of September, Ellie had been interviewed, offered and had accepted the post at Doxlee. She was to start on the twelfth of December, her brother George's birthday. Her accommodation was to be in the Nurses Home but this time she would have her own room, with facilities for cooking simple meals.

Eliza Fazakerley arranged a farewell supper party at her own home by inviting the few friends Ellie had made since her arrival in London. Mattie came of course and Mrs Larsen and Paul, Lily Curtis the librarian and to Ellie's great surprise, Sister Juniper.

"I thought you would be pleased to see Sister Juniper out of uni-form," gushed Eliza, in her element as hostess.

A month ago Ellie had introduced Eliza to Sister Juniper at a charity tea in aid of the hospital and couldn't understand the sudden mirth between them. It turned out that Sister Juniper was Eliza's old school friend, Agnes Little.

"Hadn't seen each other for donkeys' years," declared Eliza "this strange custom of calling the Sister by the name of her ward- no wonder I didn't recognise who you were until Ellie introduced me."

"After talking with you for a few minutes I began to see the old, or should I say the young Eliza, that I knew. It was as if we'd never had a day apart!"

"We shall keep each other company, when you are away among the dreaming spires of Oxford," enthused Eliza.

Sister Juniper secretly raised her eyebrows and winked at Ellie.

Eliza continued with her introductions: "This is the Reverend Andrew Simpson the Curate at St. Stephen's Church- the one I attend, Ellie. We couldn't have Paul as the only man. The presence of two men will keep our conversation balanced!"

"Now, now- you couldn't have a balanced conversation to save your life, always off at a tangent," teased Sister Juniper shaking her fan at Eliza.

Andrew Simpson bowed to Ellie and his pleasant, open face broke into a happy smile.

"I am glad to meet you, Miss. Elkson, even if I was only invited to double the male attendance. I feel I know something of you already. I roomed with your cousin Hugh at Oxford. He was for ever bringing up "my cousin, who left home to train as a nurse in London" when we discussed women's rights."

The young curate's hair was a startlingly bright ginger and stood up like a stiff brush above narrow sideburns and arched eyebrows but Ellie was more aware of the kind, serious look in his blue eyes as he leant over her.

"My word," she replied "I didn't know my name was known in such illustrious circles."

Eliza beamed at this unexpected success of her choice of guest.

The Reverend Andrew was obviously a great favourite with Eliza. He was the cleric, of the more liberal persuasion, who had won her over with his wholehearted acceptance of the theory of evolution and his sensible understanding of certain parts of the Bible which had always puzzled her. However, what pleased her more was that these open-minded views in no way disturbed his deep faith in God and in Jesus Christ. Conversation slowly gravitated to the subject as the group stood together sipping glasses of fruit punch.

"You are a breath of fresh air, young man," Eliza told him. "I could never understand why it made the slightest difference to God being creator of the universe and everything in it if He did it through evolution rather than according to the book of Genesis! To me it's so obvious that those early biblical stories are myths, beautiful and memorable but written by people without the scientific knowledge that we have. They were as convinced of God's handiwork in creation as we are, just described it more picturesquely."

"It's good to hear you say that, Mrs Fazakerley. You'd be surprised how many good Christian folk think that we're disloyal and cocking a snoot at the Bible and our Christian beliefs by accepting new ideas of science and scholarship. It's a shock to some Christians, as if the very foundations of all they've believed in were being shaken. We need to be sensitive and tread gently on people's understanding."

Ellie was sure his hair glowed more brightly as his speech grew more animated. She dared to join in the conversation.

"Two of my brothers have left the Church of England because our Vicar at home stood out against them when they spoke about the wonders of evolution and how exciting they found it. My brother Stephen is keen on geology and gave a paper to our local Naturalist Society on how we can trace the development and age of the earth through the study of rocks. The Vicar was present and he was not pleased!"

"I wish I could have heard that lecture, Miss. Elkson. Did the Vicar speak out against your brother publicly?"

"Only in the Naturalists' meeting, but it was enough. One of the members writes for the local newspaper and reported the incident. It caused a lot of correspondence from readers, for and against. Stephen and George felt honour bound to resign from the choir and leave the Church. It's sad because the Vicar always considered himself a family friend. My sister, Sarah, won't leave the church, or my mother. I'm not sure about father."

"And, you, Miss. Elkson, have you left the church? Is your Faith intact?"

"I'm not sure, Mr Simpson. I've been puzzled by so many things. I struggle to understand the suffering of the families and young children I nurse. I'm horrified at the vast number of infant deaths and the horrid diseases they often have to face, if they do survive. I don't know what purpose is in it. Do we really have a God who cares?"

"You care, Miss. Elkson and many nurses like you. Don't you think God has a part in that? Will He care any less than you? Think of the words of St. Theresa, "Christ hath no body now on earth but ours." He uses our hands to do his work. Can you not believe that?"

"I don't know. Often it seems that we've created the circumstances for disease and misery ourselves, we're so excited by all the new inventions and greedy to have all that our industries offer us. Still, if God is real, it's him who's made us like this. I must admit, Mr Simpson, I have been searching for answers elsewhere," embarrassment filled Ellie after her confused speech.

"Aah! Among the Theosophists I believe. Eliza told me about the meetings you both attended. Are you still involved with them?"

"Their ideas still fascinate me but I am uneasy. Maybe I don't fully understand; I'm reading as much as I can about them. I think I'm grasping hold of what they believe and then the whole meaning vanishes!"

"That's why I love the good old Church of England, down to earth and full of humanity and right in there, amongst poor and rich alike. We're not perfect but then we couldn't be Christians if we were. Jesus died for sinners, not goody goody's. Don't get lost in the mists of these strange beliefs Ellie; they can lead to madness."

"Oh surely not, Andrew. Oscar Wilde and Bernard Shaw are among their number, they have truly great minds."

"Hmm, well they've had their mental struggles! But haven't we all. Come along, Ellie, let's go and eat some of this delicious spread Eliza's provided for us and forget spiritual mysteries for tonight!"

The two young people had slipped naturally into using each other's first names. They laughed and went companionably to the table, which was spread with a sumptuous buffet supper. Their debating changed to which sauce would taste better with which dish.

At the end of the evening, Eliza proposed a toast to Ellie,

"Take with you our love and friendship, Ellie and find your true joy in caring for those who need it,"

Champagne filled glasses were raised and emptied as they all echoed, "To Ellie!"

"God bless her," said Andrew. "Amen to that," said Sister Juniper.

PART THREE

Orthopaedics Then Midwifery 1905-11

CHAPTER 22

Staff Nurse on Snowdon Ward.

Doxlee Hospital was set in the countryside on the outskirts of Oxford and had been converted from a rambling country mansion of the Georgian era. Ellie was to be the Staff Nurse on Snowdon Ward, a bright, airy ward, situated on the ground floor leading straight off the main hallway. At one end it opened out, through French Windows, onto spreading lawns with wide paths to accommodate wheel chairs and people needing space to learn to walk again. There were twelve beds, four along each side and two facing down the ward on either side of the entrance from the main hallway and another two on either side of the French windows. This arrangement gave plenty of space between beds and meant they were in easy view of the Nurses' desk in the centre of the room. Someone had thought it amusing to name the orthopaedic wards after mountains to "encourage the patients to aim high". Sister Snowdon had two other wards under her care so she was also Sister Helvellyn and Sister Ben Nevis. This caused much hilarity as she was a neat, diminutive person, quick and sure in her movements and utterly un-mountain-like.

Having three wards under her care, it was necessary for Sister to allow her Staff Nurses a great deal of responsibility on their own particular Wards. Ellie was excited by the challenge of her new status. The first few weeks she shadowed the Staff Nurse whom she was to replace and soon became familiar with the routine. She deliberately made time to get to know her young patients and their conditions.

The ward was full of strange noises from the heating system of large water pipes snaking around the walls like a great serpent, sometimes as high as the ceiling. The hot water for heating and washing came from a huge boiler heated by a great coal furnace in the hospital basement and the noises came from its labouring through the pipes to reach them.

Two wards of the hospital were isolated from the others and took children with infectious diseases such as polio and forms of tuberculosis, which affected joints and limbs.

There were no infectious diseases on Snowden Ward. All the children here, suffered from conditions caused chiefly by malnutrition, such as rickets or scurvy and all their hidden complications.

Ellie soon discovered that she and her team of nurses had to be constantly alert when nursing these children. Rickets and scurvy didn't just affect the limbs but in its' severest form it also affected the internal organs, such as the liver and kidneys and digestive system. These had to be dealt with first, before other treatments could have their proper effect. With special diet and fresh air and sunshine many of those affected eventually recovered fully and it thrilled her to see bendy and deformed limbs grow straight and strong over the period of her two years at Doxlee.

It would be twenty-three years before the research scientists identified the miraculous vitamin D, which was the essential element in all these cures but the carriers of this vitamin were soon recognised as essential in performing a cure. These carriers were fish, meat and eggs, good milk, commonplace items in the meals of richer families but often scarce in the diet of the poor. The other two essentials were fresh air and sunshine.

All the children who came to Snowden Ward, had lived in the poorest areas of the smoky, town and city centres overshadowed by tall, tenement buildings. They had survived on a diet of bread, potatoes, onions and margarine with the occasional scrap of fish, or meat, or dripping. The quality of sunshine they were exposed to was a poor, weak apology, filtered to them through grime, soot and smoke. As the second or third generation of families who had lived in such environments they had inherited their parents' physical weaknesses on top of their own.

Ellie had been Staff Nurse for six months when a visitor arrived on the ward. She looked up from the notes she was writing to see a thin, pale young woman hovering anxiously in the doorway. She wore an almost clean, much- mended, grey skirt and shawl, a shabby black bonnet dwarfed her sharply etched face. Rising and walking quickly towards her, Ellie tried to put reassurance into her normally brusque voice,

"Can I help you, my dear? Are you looking for someone?"

"Oh, Yes Miss, excuse me Miss. I'm Dorcas Forester; I've come to see my little girl, Mabel."

"Mabel's mother! We've been trying to get in touch with you Mrs Forester, but no-one knew where you had gone!" Ellie couldn't help the sharp edge to her voice.

Dorcas stared down at her feet her face reddening,

"I'm sorry Miss; you see I'm on my own. I tried but I couldn't look after Mabel properly. I couldn't get a job. When she was brought 'ere, I knew she'd be well looked after but it's 'er birthday today. She'll be five years old. I couldn't 'elp meself, I 'ad to come."

"Hmm, about time too. How did you get here? You look very tired Mrs Forester"

"It's Miss Forester. I'm not married. Mabel's dad didn't want to know when I fell pregnant with 'er. 'E just scarpered, 'e's never seen 'er. I got a lift on the Carrier's cart, this morning. I've brought 'er a bit of something. The lady at the front door said as you might let me see 'er but if I can't, would you give 'er this? Please, Miss."

The tiny, frail woman offered Ellie a small parcel wrapped carefully in a piece of brightly flowered material.

Ellie thought of Mabel Forester, a child who had been on the Ward for only three weeks when Ellie had become Staff Nurse, six months ago. Mabel had had the large, square head and grossly distended abdomen, typical of rickets. A large bulge in her lower spine and small limbs bent into grotesque positions meant she had been unable to walk but she would kick her arms and legs frantically. It was this kicking which had impressed Mabel's determined personality on nurses and doctor's alike.

Ellie smiled at Mabel's mother; "Of course you can see her; she's just outside in the garden. Those who are well enough, spend the hour before lunch out in the fresh air; especially on these lovely summer days. Mabel was the first out this morning, she wanted to run on the grass. You can't stop her nowadays!"

"But she can't walk! I thought she'd be in a bed! Are you sure?"

"Come and see. You'll hardly recognise her!"

The two women walked to the french windows and Ellie pointed out a small but lively child dressed in a cotton smock running, only slightly unsteadily, across the lawn with her chubby arms held out before her. They could hear her laughing and shrieking as she chased one of the probationer nurses. Ellie opened the windows and called her inside:

"Mabel, look whose come to visit you!" Aside to Miss Forester she whispered, "Don't be upset if she seems unsure of you or doesn't recognise you, ten months are a very long time in a four year old's life and she's been through a lot."

The child that came to them looked so sturdy and straight, with tight blond curls covering her gently rounded head, her limbs in good proportion to the rest of her body and no signs of the previously gross abdomen and trunk.

"It's a miracle!" gasped the child's mother, "I can't believe it!"

"I know, I felt the same when I saw her changing." Though not all the children recovered so quickly, many did and Sister Snowdon had laughed delightedly when Ellie had expressed her amazement in the gradual speeding up of improvement in rickety children,

"Cod liver oil and sunshine are the essential ingredients for these children, together with plenty of eggs and milk, red meat and green vegetables."

"I always knew it was important to eat a balanced diet but I never imagined it could work such miracles,"

Sister Snowdon gave a short lecture each week on the various diseases and treatments of their patients and about the importance of vitamins and minerals in the diet. There were other symptoms, which needed careful doctoring when the sick children first arrived,

"Children with rickets arrive with nasty digestive problems. These need to be sorted out firs,t in order that they can assimilate the nutrients which will allow their bodies to work against the disease. Babies who are under nine months old and have acute forms of rickets or scurvy will often scream when they are touched or held as their bones and joints can be very sore. You must learn to differentiate this pain, from the pain a child has from colic. Sadly, a rickety infant will often have both. First we try to calm the child's pain in the usual ways, using warm fomentations or poultices; warm water enemas and doses of carminative waters, such as peppermint and dill, between feeds. If these don't work the doctor may resort to asking you to administer opium, in the form of one fortieth or one thirtieth of a grain of codeine, given with glycerine and carminative water. This dosage, according to Dr. Hutchinson, is a very suitable opiate for a young child. I want you all to make yourself familiar with the contents of Dr. Hutchison's book, 'Lectures on Diseases of Young Children,' it was published last year, 1904, so it is quite up to date. Nurses, do not administer any opiate unless the doctor prescribes it. However, if you feel your patient would benefit from such a drug, you may recommend its necessity to the doctor. Remember too, that your young patients will cry from the emotional traumas of fear and separation from loved ones."

Ellie and all her nurses had to be alert to the progression of disease, or rate of recovery, in each patient and be ready to recommend changes in treatment. Working together with the doctors was important. It was easy to think that, once the children were over the critical gastric problems, it was nursing only that they required but there were still medical hurdles which needed a doctor's expertise. Ellie had to discover the best way to use her nursing team and when and how to delegate tasks. She had to be critically aware of the doctors' expectations and to be patient and accommodating towards the research scientists. Perhaps because of the nature of the diseases they were treating the doctors were patient and affable and the scientists anxious not to be in the way. The atmosphere was less stressful than Juniper Ward with its constant turnover of acute cases. Sister

Snowdon met with her Staff Nurses for twenty minutes each day. She encouraged them to observe each of the nurses under them;

"Get to know them as people, notice their moods, their particular strengths and weaknesses. Try to be aware of any emotional problems they may be having, outside or inside the hospital. Report to me any signs of mental instability or uncontrolled anger towards the children."

Remembering how well Sister Juniper had come to know her, Ellie took the advice seriously. To her surprise she found the nurses became happy with her leadership, they respected her efficiency and coolness in emergencies and were quick to obey her commands.

Treating the patients as people with feelings, as well as physical needs was imperative on this ward. It was home to the children for eighteen months, or more. Ellie knew that she herself was not naturally jolly but when she recognised jollity in any of her nurses, she encouraged it. She wanted Snowdon Ward to be a place where children would smile and laugh. It was catching, as she gained in confidence Ellie relaxed and found herself laughing far more, especially when she wandered into the garden among the children who were basking or walking in the sunshine.

CHAPTER 23

Leisure time

Encouraged by letters from Eliza Fazakerley, who knew Oxford well from earlier years, Ellie used part of her time off to go into this celebrated city. She peered through gateways at renowned colleges and caught sight of students and scholars, in gowns and mortar-boards, hurrying along with piles of books under their arms. The sight stirred Ellie's love of reading and she became adept at unearthing second hand bookshops, hidden away down alleys and side streets. She began to broaden her taste and under the advice of the knowledgeable shopkeepers, devoured poetry, essays, novels and plays by authors she'd previously considering too high brow. She continued to dip into Theosophy but also became drawn towards those English Mystics that Deaconess Broughton had been so fond of, in those far off days in Hartsbeck. Julian of Norwich with her 'Revelations of divine love' and St. Teresa of Avila whose works encouraged Ellie to explore her "inner castle" of spirituality.

She delighted in the poems of Emily Dickinson and Francis Thompson, whereas St. John of the Cross with his "dark night of the soul" both appealed to and depressed her. When these subjects became too heavy and her brain addled, she searched out old favourites from her childhood such as Anna Sewell's 'Black Beauty', Wyss's 'Swiss Family Robinson,' Walter Scott's 'Ivanhoe' and the books of Robert Louis Stevenson. She was entranced by the tales of 'King Arthur' and Longfellow's 'Hiawatha' and enjoyed the plays of J.M. Barrie. There was nothing she liked more than wandering through the water meadows on warm summer afternoons to sit beside the river with her books. In winter she would curl up and read by the common room fire in the Nurses Home, or take her book to a secluded table in one of the local teashops.

During the school summer holidays of 1905, Ellie's sister Sarah, now sixteen, came to stay for two weeks. She slept in a guest room of the Nurses' Home and together the sisters explored the countryside. Sarah gathered quantities of wild flowers and grasses, which she carefully pressed, each evening, between layers of newspaper in a flower- press Edwin had given her,

"He may be training as a dry old accountant but he spends all his spare time searching the countryside for plants and bird watching. Oh and gardening, you should see his part of the garden Ellie, it's a real picture. He asked me to gather plants typical of this area but I never expected there to be such a variety! Look at these, Ellie, so delicate and perfectly shaped I wonder what they are?"

They were amused by the antics of insects busily visiting all the wild flowers,

"There's your butterfly," whispered Sarah as the small brownish Gatekeeper butterfly darted ahead of them along the woodland path, "it always reminds me of you, Ellie, small and determined and adventurous."

Sarah wound her arm through Ellie's and a rush of affection drew them together.

They attended musical concerts in Oxford together .In the afternoons, when Ellie was on duty, Sarah would go to four o'clock choral evensong, in one or other of the College Chapels. She had a devout and uncomplicated Christian faith and loved to hear the singing of sacred music by the Oxford choirs,

"It's a taste of Heaven," she whispered to her sister, on the one occasion Ellie was with her. They sat wrapped in the music as it soared above the arches of the ancient buildings or crept softly round them in pure and gentle tones

Even Ellie admitted that, "it does something strange to my insides." Sarah giggled. Over her sixteen years she had developed a deep love of music and her tuneful soprano voice was fast maturing into something rather special. Each fortnight she travelled to her cousins in Preston where she had singing lessons and also sang with a group of talented singers. This Preston singing group was gradually forming into a reputable choir and their audiences came from all over Lancashire. The piano bought for Sarah by her father on her fifteenth birthday was rarely quiet when she was home.

"Mother loves to sit and listen in the evening and I'm working towards a diploma so that, in a year or so, I should be able give private piano and singing lessons at home."

Ellie felt a flicker of homesickness at the life going on without her in the house on Aspen Lane.

"Music gives such a new dimension to people's lives. You can live in the ugliest slum of Hartsbeck yet have a beautiful singing voice. When people realise this, it just changes their whole view of themselves. Even those who don't have such talents are proud of those among their friends or neighbours who have and they all seem to enjoy listening. The Hartsbeck Choral Society has ever so many concerts planned for this winter. Did you know we have our own town orchestra Ellie? Who would have thought there were so many people who could play violins and cellos, flutes and brass instruments to such a high standard, in our small town? Annette's husband Dick, plays the cello, he's really talented and your old friend from the pig farm plays the bassoon."

Ellie laughed, "I don't believe it! Bert Lee? "she said, "Really?"

"Oh yes, and they give excellent concerts of classical music and there's an amateur operatic society as well. We may not be London or Oxford but in our own way, we are a very cultured community."

Sarah turned up her nose in comic fashion. Ellie thought to herself that music was like medicine to people's inner selves, lifting their spirits and healing them emotionally, bringing beauty and joy into struggling lives. She took Sarah's hand and squeezed it, feeling a bond of similarity between the different work they were doing. Sarah's earnest young face flushed with delight as she prattled on excitedly.

"George is still articled to Mr Drake, the solicitor on Barry Street, he'll soon be qualified. Hannah Nelson and George are seeing a lot more of each other. Hannah is a brilliant teacher, even though she's been almost stone deaf since she was twenty. She's worked so hard with George, helping him through his exams and tutoring him in Latin. I think they will marry, they seem very close. Hannah's helping me as well, with mathematics and English. I need a good grade in both these subjects, before I start training as a teacher in the September term."

"How does she manage to teach a class of children if she's so deaf?" Ellie was intrigued.

"Oh, it's easy to forget she's deaf. Hannah learnt to lip-read from her sisters who work in the cotton mill. All the mill-workers are expert lip-readers, they have to be because they can't hear each other speak over the loud clattering of the machinery."

Ellie's nursing instincts were aroused "How did Hannah come to be so deaf? Was it through an illness or an accident?"

"You do ask a lot of personal questions, Ellie, but I suppose the medical side is bound to interest you. As it happens Hannah told me her deafness began after a bout of measles when she was twelve but it wasn't so bad until she had a severe chest and ear infection when she was twenty. She says she can still remember the intense pain that grew until it was like red hot needles in her ears and when it eventually subsided she hadn't been able to hear a thing, apart from the odd whistles and gurgles from inside her head."

"Couldn't anything be done to restore her hearing?" Ellie couldn't help a rising indignation that neglect caused by late diagnosis had probably intensified Hannah's problem. She'd nursed children with just such conditions caused by measles and with careful treatment most had left hospital with their hearing only slightly impaired.

"Apparently the doctor told her parents that he was afraid she would be stone deaf for the rest of her life. She was determined to carry on teaching and with her lip reading skills, clever brain and sensitive nature, she did just that. She's still teaching at night school and secondary school level and produces admirable results among her pupils. She tells every new class that 'it helps that I was born with eyes in the back of my head and a pinch of the second sight! Remember I'm the seventh child of a seventh child,'" and Sarah mimicked Hannah's authoritative tones so well that Ellie had to laugh. A small shadow of regret crept into Ellie's heart as she thought how much time Hannah and Sarah would be able to spend together in Hartsbeck while she was away from them all in London. Her family was growing without her. "Don't let them grow away from me entirely," she whispered silently.

At the end of the fortnight Ellie and Sarah said goodbye as close friends, as well as sisters. They walked together to Oxford Station for Sarah to catch the early morning train.

"I can't wait to start teaching properly, Ellie, I just hope I can make the grade."

"Of course you will! Write and tell me all about it. Now you tell Stephen to take his eyes off the girls and send me copies of some of these wonderful nature photographs he takes, and ask Jack to write me a letter. Give Mother and Dad a hug from me and tell Edwin about the garden at the hospital." Ellie was near to tears as she waved Sarah off loaded with small gifts for all the family.

CHAPTER 24

Dr. Alex Dobson and Dr. Truby King.

Ellie had been in Oxford almost two years when a tall young doctor came striding onto the ward one morning and leant over her desk, where she was busy writing a report.

"Good morning Staff Nurse. May I trouble you for a minute of your valuable time?"

The tone was teasing and had a vaguely familiar Canadian drawl. Ellie looked up and tried to remember where she had seen those lazy, brown eyes before; she waited in silence for his next words. He decided on a more formal approach.

"Staff Nurse, excuse me for interrupting you. I wondered if any of your nurses would be interested in attending a lecture by the famous Dr. Truby King."

Ellie was startled, she had heard of this Dr. King,

"I thought Dr. King lived in New Zealand," she replied, feeling rather foolish.

"You're right, he does but he's paying a flying visit to Oxford. Apparently, his father used to be a student here and then Member of Parliament for the city, before emigrating to New Zealand. The eminent doctor has childhood memories and a soft spot for the place. As soon as we heard he was coming, we jumped at the chance of asking him to speak. Do you think any of your staff will be interested?"

Ellie suddenly remembered, this was the young Canadian trainee who had been on Juniper Ward the day Sir Peter Edwards questioned her about facial expressions revealing illness.

"It's very kind of you to ask us Dr- er- Dobson isn't it?" Ellie was pleased that she knew his name. "It would help if you told me the date and time and the exact title of his lecture, I know his interests are wide."

Dr. Dobson stared at her, "Of course, stupid of me not to say. The lecture will be on the last Friday in September, at 7.30 pm. That will give you three weeks to plan for it. Among other things, he has researched deeply into the field of child nutrition and mother and baby care. It's this area we hope he will address. –I say, don't I know you from somewhere?"

"We've been in each other's company but never introduced," smiled Ellie. "It was during one of Sir Peter Edward's Ward rounds on Juniper, at St. Gabriel's in London. The great man asked us both a question, I'm afraid I got carried away."

"I remember. You took us all by storm, then stopped mid-sentence and blushed like a peony!"

"That was me alright," said Ellie, blushing again and laughing. "I'm Staff Nurse Elkson now and I, for one, would be very interested to hear Dr. Truby King, I've read exciting things about him. I'll ask the rest of the nurses and see how we can arrange things. I'll need to look at the rota. Oh- but I'd better speak to Sister first."

"I've already done that. She sent me in here to ask you."

"That's a relief. It's easy to forget the chain of command when you're a Staff Nurse on these Wards!"

"I'm pleased to meet you again, Staff Nurse Elkson. I'm now fully qualified, Dr. Alex Dobson and have been Houseman here for a year. I've only just started to work in your part of the hospital. I expect we shall be seeing rather a lot of each other over the next few months."

Ellie felt unexpectedly pleased. To cover her personal interest in the young doctor she quickly turned to medical matters:

"You'll find a lot to interest you on Snowdon Ward, the treatments are amazingly successful. Especially when you see the state of some of the children when they first come to us."

They both turned at a burst of laughter from the other end of the Ward and cries of, "I beat you Nurse! I did! I did!"

A small boy had come in from the garden swinging along on a pair of crutches followed closely by a breathless, pink faced, nurse. The boy sat down on one of the beds and the panting nurse sank onto the chair beside him, fanning herself and laughing,

"You won fair and square, Lenny, I'm fair beat!!"

Lennie fished a bag of sweets from his bedside locker and nurse and boy sat and recovered together, sucking contentedly.

"Bit like a holiday home!" commented Alex.

"You should have seen the poor lad when he came to us eight months ago, miserable as sin and hardly able to sit up, never mind stand. Now look at him!"

"Seems you work miracles on Snowdon," and Dr. Dobson flashed her an impish grin as he left the Ward.

That first lecture from Dr. Truby King was a turning point for Ellie. She accompanied four other nurses from Snowdon to the Victoria Lecture Hall, in the teaching block of the hospital. They looked with interest at the row of eminent, middle aged physicians sitting down one side of the hall. Ellie was pleased to see two women among them.

"Dr. Jane Bradley and Dr. Jessica Trump," whispered Staff Nurse Judith Thompson, from Helvellyn Ward, seated next to Ellie. "Both in obstetrics. Good to see women amongst the almighty males!" and she dug Ellie gently in the side.

Ellie felt a rush of pride for these women. She knew of the battles they had faced to be accepted in their field and noticed how uprightly they sat, heads held high, their facial expressions set. Two male doctors walked over and shook their hands warmly before sitting down, deliberately declaring in public, their support for these female colleagues.

A contingent of nurses in uniform had arrived from London, among them Ellie spotted Sister Juniper. There were several other women, not in uniform but dressed soberly in business-like costumes with tailored jackets over long dark skirts, their hair pinned up severely under plain felt hats. Judith Thompson kept up a whispered commentary,

"There's Miss Margaret Brea and Mrs Bedford Fenwick the one who fought for registration of nurses and midwives and that's her husband Dr. Bedford Fenwick. I'm sure that's Maria Firth. And there's Dr. Glover from the Lying-in Hospital"

Judith's eyes were popping out of her head with rising excitement and Ellie's brain reeled as she heard the celebrated names. Their names had become famous through their writings in the "Nurses' Notes' journal and other medical magazines devoured by rising young nurses and some doctors. They were also known from Parliamentary debates on Nursing and Midwifery legislation, which had been argued over for years. Ellie and her colleagues had performed their nursing tasks, well aware that a war for the recognition and progress of their chosen career was being fought. Here they sat, in the same room with these visionary giants who were the chief warriors in that war.

At half past seven exactly three people stepped through the doors leading directly onto the lecture platform, a small, bald headed man with a beaming face leading a slim, confident-looking woman and followed by tall gentleman with a slight stoop. The tall man seemed lost in his own thoughts as he raised his large head with strangely expressionless eyes, to look across the hall. The platform party seated themselves in front of the audience. When all was quiet the bald headed man stood up, beaming happily at everyone.

"Nurses and medical men and women, Ladies and Gentlemen, welcome. I am Dr. Lucas Graham and it is with enormous pleasure that I bring to you this evening, Dr. Gerda Jacobi who will introduce our guest speaker, Dr. Frederick Truby King, who has agreed to honour us with his presence, during a very brief visit from New Zealand. Dr. King and I are no strangers, we worked together at Glasgow Royal Infirmary, when we were young and handsome in 1887."

A faint titter ran through the audience, and Dr. Graham beamed across at Dr. King who nodded in acknowledgement. "I will say no more but invite Dr. Gerda Jacobi to introduce Dr. King and his topic for tonight. Dr. Jacobi!"

Ellie leant forward eagerly; she had read an article by Dr. Jacobi and recognised her as one of those who had spoken out for the training and registering of Midwives.

Dr. Jacobi rose nervously and addressed the audience her voice growing stronger as she warmed to her topic

"Ladies and Gentlemen, many of you will know that I am concerned about the extreme poverty and unacceptable living conditions endured by certain groups of people in our society. Recently, we have been made even more aware of this in the survey of 'London life and labour', by Mr Jack Booth, that well known Christian gentleman. Poverty brings with it disease and deprivation of many kinds. Together with ignorance, it contributes to the problems of women in childbirth and the immense variety of infantile diseases. The high rates of infant and maternal mortality blight our own nation, together with many other nations of our world. Dr. Truby King has applied his brilliant mind to these issues and it is with great anticipation that I introduce him to you this evening. Dr. King began his medical career as resident surgeon at the Glasgow Royal Infirmary in 1887. While in Glasgow he met and married his wife, Bella, who we know also writes regular articles on mother and baby care for the general public. Dr. King went on to hold the post of medical superintendent of the Wellington General Hospital in New Zealand and since 1889 he has been the Medical Superintendent at Seacliffe Mental Hospital. We have heard of his innovative and successful ideas in the field of psychiatric medicine, including his research into the effects of nutrition on diseases of the mind. However, Dr. King has recently thrown his energies into the field of mother-craft and child-care and this is the subject he has agreed to focus on this evening. Please welcome Dr. Frederick Truby King!"

Dr. Jacobi turned to Dr. King who rose and took her hand, bowing over it.

"He's going to kiss it," whispered the celebrity-struck Nurse Thompson,

"No he isn't, don't be daft and keep quiet!" Ellie hissed, annoyed at her colleague.

They watched the great man arrange his lecture notes on the reading desk. He poured a glass of water from the carafe on the table beside him and took a drink before clearing his throat and fixing his audience with a slow, melancholy gaze. He had captured them already; every eye was fixed upon him.

The lecture from Dr. King floated in and out of Ellie's head for months afterwards. She smiled ruefully when she realised she had almost succumbed to Nurse Thompson's hero-worshipping mentality. At first his appearance had distracted her, the large head with its thatch of thick dark hair above a wirily slim body. When he spoke she noted the strength of his jutting chin and full lips and the dark, thin moustache, which gave a disconcertingly debonair impression. As he warmed to his subject his dark, brooding eyes flashed with fervour and his whole demeanour was intense with the desire that they should all understand and believe him. Several of his comments became etched on Ellie's mind.

"I am always at my best in the face of opposition or fighting for a forlorn hope," was one most of the nurses present related to as afterwards it became a hospital catch phrase which they flung cheerily at each other when faced with a difficulty. He spoke of the importance of nutrition in the prevention and cure of many diseases. In relation to new born babies he roared out his personally coined phrase, "Remember, doctors, nurses, ladies and gentlemen! When a baby feeds, "Breast fed, is best fed!" he repeated it several times explaining the qualities and advantages of breast milk. "As medical professionals you must encourage expectant mothers to come to you and don't forget to teach them that 'breast fed is best fed'. This means that expectant mothers and mothers of new borns must be well nourished in order for them to be healthy in themselves and to produce good breast milk for healthy babies. Breast-feeding mothers need time to build themselves up and replenish their milk between feeds and so my rule for them is 'Feed only by the clock'! Ignore the untimely clamouring of the greedy infant. Giving in to the child not only leads to an exhausted and therefore incompetent mother but also leads to that child developing a weak character and a weak digestion!"

He then spoke at length of a formula, which he had worked on for some time. This formula was as exact a replica of breast milk as he could devise.

"If your mothers are unable to feed their infants from the breast or if the mother is no longer there to feed her baby, then this formula is an excellent substitute."

He described many of the preparations, which were often fed to babies, as being,

"Utterly unsuitable for their developing digestive systems to cope with and in most cases, void of the nutrients needed for healthy growth. Where these nutrients are present, they are in a form which the infant metabolism is ill equipped to assimilate and are often prepared and given in the most unhygienic of ways. No wonder we have multiple infant deaths from that insidious killer, infant diarrhoea. I have observed this in New Zealand but it is no less a problem here in England. Last year, in the North West of England, the number of recorded infant deaths was one hundred and seventy nine to every thousand babies born. A good proportion of those deaths were from diet related illnesses, such as diarrhoea. If they do manage to survive their first year or so, many of the children from poorer classes go on to untold suffering from the manifold diseases of malnutrition, including scurvy and rickets." "That's where we come in!" whispered one of the nurses from Snowdon, looking sideways at Ellie with pride, Ellie smiled at her.

As she listened to the doctor's description of the technicalities of producing his formula, Ellie was amazed at the foresight and determination of the man. Not content to treat his patients' symptoms, he had delved into the root causes of these malignant diseases and was determined to wipe out conditions, which contributed to their increase.

Suddenly she was sitting on the edge of her seat taking in his next words,

"Poverty may always be with us but ignorance must be eradicated. I call upon all you nurses here tonight, to consider your role in this fight against ignorance and deprivation which are a blight on our society. We need an army of nurses who will go into our communities and homes and teach mothers the proper way to care for their children and the proper way to care for their own health and that of their husbands. We need nurses who will help to build healthy babies, rather than patch sick ones. Could you be such a Nurse? Remember the future of a nation depends upon the health of its children. In New Zealand, we are building such a team of community nurses and have already founded the Royal New Zealand Society for the Health of Women and Children. I would like to see such societies in every country in the world. The fate of mothers and children, here in England, is in your hands. Thank you for your attention. Now act upon it."

Dr. Truby King sat down to a standing ovation. Ellie found tears were streaming down her cheeks as she stood and clapped with the rest of medical personnel and visitors in the audience. She didn't notice the two or three doctors who stayed in their seats, hands folded firmly in their laps but she did see Dr. Alex Dobson standing and clapping enthusiastically, his gaze turned towards her, a wide grin spreading over his face.

CHAPTER 25

Christmas Ball at Doxlee

Although Ellie's obligatory two years as a Staff Nurse ended on the twelfth of December, 1907, she stayed on in her post until early in 1908. Christmas 1907 was one of the most memorable of Ellie's life. First there was carol singing round the wards on Christmas Eve. All those off duty joined in and having donned brightly coloured scarves and hats walked from ward to ward carrying a lit storm lantern. The janitor carried an accordion which he played quietly as they walked and accompanying them with gusto when they sang. In each ward the nurses on duty joined with them to sing the old, well known Christmas hymns. There had been practices of course, Ellie discovered she had a fairly decent voice and was an adequate part of the back-up for the more gifted singers, who sang glorious descants to some of the carols.

The chaplain came with them and read the story of the Saviour's birth and said prayers in each ward. He did it in such a warm and gentle manner that the children hung on his words expectantly and Ellie felt she was hearing the story for the first time. He made her heart yearn to understand the full meaning of the coming of the Christ child.

The second special event was the Christmas Ball. This was a grand affair, held annually for the hospital staff, in the week between Christmas and New Year. The venue was to be one of the large assembly halls in the medical school block.

Ellie was among those allowed to be off duty for the event. The older ones among the staff covered the duties for that evening; they declared they'd had their share of such balls in the past. Each nurse was expected to have a male partner for the ball and Ellie's heart raced when Alex Dobson begged her to allow him to be her escort. She agreed, of course.

Nurses roamed the Oxford shops for ball-gown materials and the Nurses Home became a veritable dressmakers' sewing room. Ellie shied away from the pastel colours favoured by most of her colleagues and chose a silky material in a rich, russet colour. It shimmered in the light and reminded her of autumn leaves. She decided the easiest way would be to make a long, softly-flared skirt and a sleeveless tunic of the russet silk which would hang over it. She would sew a border of matching lace around the bottom of the tunic and wear a cream blouse underneath it. She described these ideas to her mother in a letter and two days later a package arrived by post. Ellie was with a group of nurses who had just come off duty. They had rushed across to the nurse's home for tea and the next onslaught on their ball attire. The package was there waiting,

"Open it Ellie, it must be something for your dress, it's soft and squashy!"

She opened the package to find a dainty blouse of creamy coloured lace. She shook it out and the girls gasped at the gently gathered sleeves and softly shaped neckline."

"Try it on," they urged.

"Later," said Ellie, "let's get changed and have tea first."

There was a note with the blouse and Ellie wanted a quiet moment to read it in the privacy of her room. Her eyes filled with tears at her mother's words, neatly penned in her familiar script.

"My darling Ellie,

I would so like to see you dressed for your first ball but if this blouse will do, I will be able to imagine you wearing it. I have had it laid by since my honeymoon. You and I never had much time together as mother and daughter. My time and energy seemed so taken up with the boys and then the newborns and your dad. I have missed you Ellie, but I'm so proud of you. Wear the blouse with my love. Mother."

This small act of her mother's brought her suddenly very close and Ellie had a pang of remorse that she had distanced herself from her over the past few years.

She went into the common room wearing the blouse and the others declared it "just perfect".

In the end Ellie abandoned the idea of a tunic and made a sleeveless vest of the silky russet material to be worn underneath the lace blouse. The russet showed through the lace complementing the material of the skirt and a wide sash, of the same silky material, finished it off perfectly.

Home Sister also insisted that the nurses should know the steps to the most popular dances. Most of them knew the old favourites from childhood such as the Polka, the Military Two step and the Gay Gordons but Sister wanted to be sure her charges would not let her down in the waltz. Twice a week, the large landing of the Nurses Home became a dance school. Home Sister brought her gramophone and put on records of appropriate music while the nurses whirled and stumbled round to her instructions until they mastered the arm holds and the one-two-three, one- two- three, intricacies of the waltz.

On the evening before the ball they had a mannequin parade along the top landing of the hostel in front of Home Sister. Beside her stood a large box full of pieces of jewellery, artificial flowers and leaves, ribbons and decorative hair pieces which she proceeded to match to each young woman as they paraded past. When it was Ellie's turn, Sister cocked her head to one side and peered at her like a bird before diving her hands into the box. She produced a large cream coloured rose of artificial silk and a decorative hair clip made in the shape of a butterfly from glowing orange-brown garnets set in tortoise shell. She pinned the rose onto the right hand side of Ellie's sash and the hairclip into Ellie's dark hair. Both complemented all the colours of her outfit.

"My, you really are my woodland elf tonight," said Dr. Alex Dobson when he arrived the following evening, handsomely attired in black evening tails, to escort her to the ball. Ellie laughed, "I thought my dress might make me an autumn leaf, but Home Sister's hair decoration turned me into a butterfly. It's very like the small brown butterfly that my sister and I always loved, they call it the Gatekeeper!"

"You may need its protection tonight," whispered Alex brushing her hair with his lips as they passed through the door and Ellie's heart missed a beat. Alex had told her he came from a Franco-Albertan family, which meant his parents were French-speaking Canadians and that he had some French blood running through his veins. Tonight, French blood whispered 'romance', to Ellie's fired imagination.

Coloured fairy lights marked the route from the accommodation blocks to the ball room. Each in their bright dancing slippers and on the arm of an escort, the nurses made their way, like the princesses of the old fairy story, to wear out their slippers in dancing the night away.

An unobtrusive watch was kept by those in charge and the nurses were all delivered back to their sleeping quarters by one o'clock in the morning. Their romantic desires and those of their escorts had been carefully kept within the holds and music of the dance floor; or so it would seem. What thoughts and dreams ruffled those maidens' attempts to sleep that night, were secrets to them alone. Certainly, whenever Ellie closed her eyes, she was circling the dance floor in the arms of Dr. Alex Dobson, his laughing eyes looking tenderly down at her as the waltz beat out its insistent one-two-three, one-two-three.

CHAPTER 26

London and Midwifery, 1907

After two weeks of hearty Christmas and New Year celebrations in Oxford, both on and off duty, Ellie returned to London. She had applied for and received papers admitting her to train in Midwifery at one of the reputable Lying-in Hospitals and was to begin the last week in January. As soon as she arrived at the hospital she was shown straight into Matron's office where the course was explained to her,

"Staff Nurse Elkson, we're very happy to have you with us. Now, I want you to understand that we have fought long and hard to obtain recognition as a professional midwifery service. We are, however, still in our infancy and there are those who regard us as flies in the ointment. We are being carefully watched and have to prove ourselves super- competent, super- knowledgeable and super- intelligent in the way we apply our skills. We also need to keep sweet relationships with various other departments of the medical and nursing professions.

During your training here, you must follow exactly the instructions given. I know you have had earlier experience of helping what we sometimes call a 'wise woman', with deliveries in your home town. The practices of many of these good women have always been clean and skilful, others have not. Either way, none of them will have known the advantages of modern medicine. You must try to put on one side what you learnt as a girl in Hartsbeck and concentrate on what we teach you. Do you understand this Nurse Elkson?"

"Yes Matron, I do understand but I must tell you that the woman I helped in Hartsbeck was an excellent midwife and nurse and improved the lot of many families in our town. It was she who encouraged me to come to London, to train as a nurse. She was one of the good 'wise women' and ahead of her time."

"That's good to hear. No doubt you will find the best of what you experienced with her in some of our methods but you must be open minded and prepared to learn new ways.

The course will last six months. If you pass you will then spend a probationary year practising midwifery under supervision and according to our methods. Throughout your probationary year your work and character will be scrutinised by the Central Midwives Board. At the end of the year they will make an assessment. The Central Midwives Board will consist of no less than five doctors and ten other people, one appointed by the Royal British Nurses Association. If your work is satisfactory and you are proved to have a good character you will be accepted as a Certified Midwife. Do you have any questions Staff Nurse?"

"Yes Matron. As a Certified Midwife what will my role be?"

"According to the Midwives Act, which to our great relief, was passed in 1902, you will, legally, be allowed to attend women in child-birth without the presence of a qualified practitioner, that is, a doctor."

Matron's stern face became suddenly effused with smiles; she spread out her hands and continued as if speaking in public;

"We feel doors have at last been opened for us which were long closed. We hope to turn the tide of child-birth and make it a much safer and dare I say, enjoyable experience, than it has been of earlier years."

Matron's stern manner returned, "Staff Nurse, at the moment we are all constantly aware that any of us could do something to close those doors again. Don't let that fear spoil your delight in midwifery, never lose the joy of bringing a new life into the world."

"I won't, Matron," Ellie determined to keep her word.

"Now, because of the often unpredictable nature of your work, you will be required to live on the hospital premises. Any time you wish to spend outside the hospital must be requested for from the Home Sister, even in off duty hours. Remember you have to show a good character on and off duty."

She rang a small hand bell on her desk and in came a bustling, dainty young nurse in a perfectly fitted grey uniform dress under a spotlessly white apron. The young woman's head bobbed importantly beneath her white starched cap with its' ribbons tied firmly beneath her chin.

"Ah, Staff Nurse Norton. This is Staff Nurse Elkson, please escort her to the Nurses Home in E block and introduce her to Home Sister. Make sure her new uniform fits her as well as yours does, your appearance does you credit, nurse. Good luck Nurse Elkson, I look forward to your time with us."

The broad faced, broad shouldered woman stood up, her Matron's strings fluttering. She took Ellie's hand in a firm grip. Ellie felt the woman's strength willing her to be steadfast.

"God bless you my dear," she said unexpectedly and Ellie warmed to her.

"Thank you Matron, I will do my best here."

Staff Nurse Norton led Ellie away to the accommodation block, "She certainly has the knack of winning us round. I've been on the course for two months and I think most of us would die for her and the cause!"

Ellie chuckled, "Her enthusiasm is certainly infectious."

Ellie soon became fully immersed in her new work. When a letter arrived from Sarah in Hartsbeck asking questions about women's protests in London, she realised that she had had no time to think about what was happening in the world at large. Ellie wrote back,

London,
March 1908

"Dear Sarah,

Thank you for your letter. I am pleased that you are showing such an interest in politics!

Political unrest and fights for women's suffrage seem to pass us by here in the Lying-in Hospital; although you could say we are on the front line of improving 'woman's lot'! We are busy from morning to night, or night till

morning depending on our duties. When not nursing we are studying and attending lectures, sleeping or eating.

So much has to be fitted into these six months and then we are out on probation! As nurses and midwives, we all feel we are doing our bit for the rights of women and for the Nation. After all, we're in a woman's profession and working to improve the lot of every mother and child.

You too, Sarah, are in the swim regarding raising the status of women. As a teacher you'll soon be part of a worthy profession and have the means to influence children of both genders! I believe the protests here are spasmodic and dramatic. I admire the women brave enough to risk life and limb but we must all use our own situations to further the cause. I'm so glad you passed your exams with good grades and have started your teacher training.

I'm sad today because we lost a baby and then a mother during the night. It's a pity we couldn't have given the living, motherless baby to the mother whose baby was still born- like Bert Lee did with the orphan lambs on Oak Farm. Do you remember? Still, human beings are far more complicated than farm animals, it wouldn't do nowadays.

No matter how well we train to deliver babies safely, it's the condition the mothers arrive in that's the real enemy. If they are weak from illness or malnutrition then it's a hard battle. It's frustrating that so many babies are born with diseases caught by their mothers, from husbands or other men, who are sexually promiscuous. We need to educate the men, as well as the women, about breeding children! I expect I'm becoming a bore on this subject but at the moment it fills my whole life. I swing from joy to furious anger, to real sorrow, time and again during the course of a day.

I'm glad to hear about the woman from London speaking to you Hartsbeck folk about temperance and the dangers of alcohol. Believe me she's right, many of our mother and baby tragedies here have been caused by the 'demon drink'!

By the way, if you want to keep healthy and beautiful, drink at least two pints of water a day; boiled is best (but cool it first.). It's all the rage amongst our nurses at the moment!

I'll try and drop a note to the boys but in the meantime please thank Stephen and Edwin for the splendid wild life photographs they sent. I was intrigued by the one of homo-sapiens laying electric tramlines down the centre of their local habitat. It caught the flames from the welding magnificently. Edwin must have taken that one; it took the patience of a bird- watcher to wait for the right moment!

I expect those electric trams will be running properly by the time I'm next in Hartsbeck. You write of so many changes, I wonder if I shall recognise my old home town. I won't miss the noise and dirt of those old, bone-shaking steam trams. Do you remember how ill you were when I took you up the valley on one as a child! We had to get off two stops early and walk! I must close now, work calls again!

My love to you all, Ellie."

As she folded Sarah's letter away Ellie half wished she was back in the midst of Hartsbeck life. Her home town was coming alive in a way she had never expected.

"I really ought to go back and nurse in the local hospital, or as a community midwife, when I've qualified", mused Ellie to her old friend Eliza Fazakerley.

They were enjoying a cup of tea in their favourite café on a much needed half day off duty. Ellie found it strange to be back with Eliza, meeting in the same old haunts. The nursing experiences in Oxford had changed Ellie, giving her an open confidence, which Eliza had been pleased to note on their first meetings after Ellie's return. Now Eliza sensed her friend was on edge with the never ending demands of the midwifery course. She was alarmed by Ellie's pale, strained face and the tired look in her dark eyes. The older woman knew better than to remark, she remembered Ellie had a sharp tongue when her strength to perform her work was challenged. Instead Eliza said, "I'm a little peaky today so I'm going to order us a glass of champagne each. No, you must join me, I hate drinking alone and I need a tonic."

Ellie laughed and relaxed. She knew very well what her friend was doing, she had seen that searching look and loved Eliza for her kindness and tact.

"In that case, I can't refuse. It's a good job I'm not on duty till tomorrow morning. I'll be able to sleep it off!"

"You and your temperance ways, a small glass of champagne and you think you're on your way to being a drunkard. We'll have a bite to eat as well, to absorb the alcohol, Miss. Prude!"

"I must admit, because I hardly ever drink alcohol, a small amount affects me quite quickly! I've seen such horrid cases of children and babies being badly harmed by mothers and fathers under the influence. I've a friend on the course who's trying to make us all drink pints of water every day. She swears it's the way to true health and beauty, she's very persuasive."

"Well, it's not a new notion. Look at all the famous Spa towns, they've made their fortunes selling glasses of water or baths full of it, since the sixteen hundreds. Now you can enjoy a glass of spa water in luxurious surroundings and wash it down later with brandy or champagne!" Eliza lifted her champagne glass and winked at Ellie.

"Ah, but I'm not talking about la - di - dah spa waters with special mineral properties. This friend of mine means your common, everyday tap water, preferably boiled and drunk hot or cooled. She swears it cleanses the system of the toxins that are lining up to attack us from inside. In fact, on her days off she often goes on a water fast; eating nothing and drinking copious amounts of water."

"Let's hope she has access to a good plumbing system!" Eliza was determined to keep their conversation light; she had an inkling that Ellie was becoming a little obsessed with her own health.

Ellie smiled but felt aggravated that Eliza wasn't taking her seriously. She'd started to suffer from headaches and indigestion, which kept her from sleeping properly and on the advice of her colleague, was planning to try water therapy. She had hoped to gain Eliza's support. Anyway, today it was good to enjoy Eliza's company and forget the hospital for a few hours. Lifting her champagne glass she drank a toast:

"To good plumbing, long may it serve us," which started them giggling like silly schoolgirls.

The hilarity didn't last long, the waitress, who brought their meal, had a birth mark in the form of a port wine stain on one side of her forehead and cheek. Ellie, catching sight of it, remembered the baby she had helped deliver the week before whose face had been a livid purple mass, the lips thick and dark and the eyes bloodshot and sunk in folds of strangely textured skin with blood vessels thickly marbling the surface. The more experienced trainee midwife beside her managed to disguise a gasp of horror, as she cut the cord. She asked Ellie for cool cloths in an attempt to calm the angry facial tissues.

"No," the midwifery tutor, observing the delivery, stopped them. "Give me the baby for a moment." She smiled at the anxious mother as she wrapped a towel round the infant

"Your little girl just needs a bit of extra cleaning up before we give her to you," and she took the baby from the room.

"There's something wrong isn't there? It might be my first baby but you can't fool me," the mother was in her late thirties. Her face had been white with the exertion of a difficult birth, her blond hair dark with sweat but she was immediately on the alert, regarding her baby.

"Sister will be back in a minute, you can hear your baby squalling, not much wrong with those lungs!" Ellie and her colleague had done their best to sound cheerful as they washed and tidied up the anxious mother.

"Penny for your thoughts, Ellie," Eliza's voice penetrated Ellie's reverie and she quickly explained the whole incident to Eliza, her tongue loosening as they sipped their champagne.

"How terrible! What happened to the child? I know these things calm down sometimes, after a day or so but this sounds more serious,"

"You're right it wasn't just your normal birthmark, the baby's face wasn't going to recover. There were complications with the development of blood vessels and the skin on the baby's head. The baby was healthy in other ways, although the doctor suspected she would be mentally subnormal which would show as she grew older."

"How did the mother react, did she reject her?"

"That was the amazing thing; you'd have thought she would. I've seen mothers reject much less disfigured babies. This mother demanded to see her baby. The doctor had kept the child in a quiet room for a while, hoping her face would calm down a little as she recovered from the birth, but it didn't. In the end Sister explained to the mother about her baby's disfigured face."

"O dear, how did she react?" Eliza's eyes were wide with concern.

"The mother just said, "bring her to me," when she saw the baby's face her eyes filled with tears and she put out her arms to take the child." Ellie's voice quavered, "Then she said,

'Come to your mother little one. There now, you'll be alright, I love you. God bless you my sweetheart, you're safe with me," and tears pouring down her cheeks she kissed that poor little face and took the babe to her breast as normal as you please."

Eliza blew her nose and wiped her eyes.

"I can tell you Eliza, we stood there almost worshipping them. Not a dry eye among us. I've never seen mother love like it."

"What about the father?"

"He was angry at first and wanted to know why his child should be born like this. He wanted somebody to blame. It was terrible to see a man cry as much as he did. Then he saw how his wife handled the little one and he calmed down. We left the three of them together for a while. When we went back he was holding the baby on his knee, and tickling her, he said to us-

"If my wife can handle this, then so can I. Our little girl will need all the love we can give her. She's going to have a hard enough time as it is but she's ours and we love her. God bless her."

"Well that does my heart good, you don't often hear things like that but I'm sorry for them all the same, it won't be easy." Eliza slowly shook her head.

Ellie didn't speak of other deformed babies she had seen delivered, or of the occasional still birth. Instead, she cheered Eliza up by talking of happier births and amusing incidents concerning first time fathers.

"Come to the theatre with me, now that you are back in London," declared Eliza, as they prepared to say goodbye after a good two hours in the café, "I'll find something jolly and we'll go to a matinee on your next afternoon off, my treat, its miserable going on my own.-That is if you've nothing better to do?"

Ellie thought ruefully of her meagre nurses wages and knew that without Eliza's invitations her off duty hours would be rather colourless.

"That would be wonderful, I'll let you know when- Eliza it's been so good to talk with you but I hope my stories haven't depressed you."

"Good gracious, not at all! I come across some very sad cases in my work at the Church. It's just good to hear it from someone who is helping to change things around."

"I'm only a small part of a team," smiled Ellie.

"We all are. Just remember, Ellie, the world is full of good and bad but they often get so mixed together, we can't see the difference till we feel the hurt. I would be in a real muddle if I couldn't turn to God and that's a fact. This ordinary little church I've found, keeps me on an even keel. Some people think it must be boring, joining in the same prayers, week by week but for me it's a joy and a lifeline, a real reassurance of God's love. I don't know why I was so slow to see it before. Oh dear, do I sound like a Bible thumper."

Ellie surveyed her large, rosy cheeked friend. Eliza exuded brightness and joy of life, from her gaudy silk hat dripping with velvet pansies and yellow silk roses, to her ample body wrapped in a voluminous purple cape.

"Oh yes, a real Bible thumper;" Ellie laughed, "Only you don't need a Bible, you just need to be you!" Ellie kissed Eliza's cheek affectionately and they went their separate ways.

CHAPTER 27

Ellie joins Dr Truby King's Team

Ellie's six months midwifery training and the nine months probationary period passed quickly.

Eliza had made sure that Ellie enjoyed the lighter side of life by
arranging off duty visits to the theatre, concerts and art galleries and
providing sumptuous teas and suppers which sometimes included
her church friends and Sister Juniper. It was true that Eliza noticed
that Ellie ate sparingly of the rich food provided at these gatherings
and occasionally refused an invitation because she was "on a water
fast," but on the whole Ellie seemed in good spirits.

Dr. Alex Dobson was still in Oxford but occasionally come up
to London. As he always made a bee-line for Ellie, he soon became
included in Eliza's invitations. Ellie wondered what he did when he was
back in Oxford. They didn't correspond when they were apart but whenever he came to London he sought her out. She asked him about this.

"Alex, I'm always surprised when you suddenly contact me to say
you're in London and can we meet but when you are back in Oxford,
you never write or seem to want to keep in touch."

"Ellie! It works both ways, when have you ever written to me? I
tend to get lost in my work when I'm in Oxford but I have a good
excuse to spend time with you when I'm in London. After all I'm a
lonely alien from a far- away land; I need my friends, few as they are."

'When you've time for them', thought Ellie, but she gave him a
quiet smile.

"Point taken. We have both become too absorbed in our work
and need something, or someone, to shake us out of it."

In the spring of 1909 Ellie passed her midwifery probationary period and took a position as a Community Nurse in London's East End. Part of her time was spent at one of the newly established Mother and Baby Clinics and partly visiting families in their own homes. As they were often on call, even when off duty, Ellie and her colleagues lived in the Community Nurses' House. As a senior nurse Ellie had her own bedroom and the atmosphere was much freer than in the nurses' home at the hospital. She loved her work and came to know the people of the community well. Her brother Stephen, who at twenty-four was still a keen scientist, occasionally came up to London by train to visit the Science museums and attend some of the Royal Societies open lectures. He visited her on these occasions and encouraged her to buy a bicycle. Stephen impressed upon her that it was the very best way to travel and was all the rage nowadays, especially in Hartsbeck. Of course Ellie had known this in Oxford but didn't deflate him by mentioning it. Also several of her colleagues at the clinic already had bicycles.

Going with her brother to choose a suitable model was a hilarious experience. Stephen perched his spectacles on the end of his nose, pushed back his quiff of light brown hair, clasped his hands behind him and addressed the shopkeeper as, "My good man."

Ellie, not to be outdone, forced a grim, aloof expression on her own face, as they were shown the latest models. The shopkeeper's face fell when they eventually plumped for a second-hand Rudge-Whitworth standard model. Even this would have been far above their price range, but Stephen managed to beat his 'good man' down to four guineas.

"I'll go halves with you. I didn't send you anything for your twenty-first birthday, or any other birthday since you've been here and I've been earning a decent wage for a few years now –so you can't refuse!" Stephen insisted.

Two guineas was still a lot of money to Ellie. However, when the salesman realised her profession he threw in the lights, puncture kit and promise of a free repair service, should the bicycle ever break down.

"We need our Community Nurses; you're doing a cracker of a job, lady. My daughter, Lily, owes her life to you lot!"

Stephen was impressed and Ellie glowed.

The bicycle was a great success. Ellie had no problem riding from the Community Nurses' House to the Clinic in Pimlico and to her home visits. She came to be a familiar figure cycling through the back streets and the homeless men sitting at street corners would hail her as she passed them in the early morning. When she rode home on dark evenings she found to her surprise the same men lurking in dark corners. Initially this alarmed her, until one foggy evening she had stopped to find her bearings and a man stepped out of the shadows frightening her so that she nearly fell. The man chuckled kindly;

"Now then nurse, don't you be a'feared when you see us. We're all'us watching out for you; you'll come to no 'arm whilst we're on the streets. If you gets into trouble just call out, we'll be there! Now, I take it you're going home?" He quickly set her on the right way again.

Touched by their kindness, Ellie felt relieved at the presence of these street sleepers. The streets were notoriously dangerous but her presumption, that all men who were homeless were dangerous thugs, had been quickly quashed.

Ellie worked in this community post for eighteen months. The hardship and tragedies she saw made her once again seek out the other- worldliness of Theosophy. She read the story of Siddhartha and Buddhism. This opened up to her a different view of humanity and understanding of suffering and also spoke of a world in harmony which she thought would interest Stephen. She struggled with the eightfold path of Buddhism and thought sadly, that only a chosen few would manage to follow it meticulously to full enlightenment. On her visits to families in the community, Ellie discovered that several of the older, bereaved women, sought solace in Spiritualism. Thinking about this led her even more deeply into Theosophy.

Eliza gently tried to draw her friend back to the Christian faith but Ellie wanted an escape from the reality around her. Christianity was too real, too involved with humanity as it is and too wrapped up in the personal God. Christ on the cross seemed to emphasise suffering. Somehow Ellie couldn't quite get beyond it to its redeeming message and the resurrection. She couldn't, or wouldn't, see the living Christ that Eliza revelled in. Theosophy appealed to her with its strangely different worlds of spirits and angels, realms of ethereal beauty and rainbow- type auras, which could bring colour to the sad, grey world and Ellie grasped at it, in an attempt to push away the dark ills of life which seemed to crowd in on her.

"Ellie, you're looking through your own dark glasses," Eliza would tell her. "The world isn't as grey as you say. Even in the worst of the slums you've surely heard the laughter and singing, or it's not the East End I used to know! It's your own spirit that's growing jaded and heavy."

Her elderly friend was usually able to lift her spirits for a while but then they would slip back and Ellie would feel driven to search out her acquaintances in the 'Theosophy' circles.

Eliza discussed Ellie's moods with her friend Sister Juniper. They wondered if, on top of everything else, Ellie was having problems of a romantic nature brought about by her friendship with Dr Alex Dobson.

CHAPTER 28

A wedding is announced.

When news arrived from Hartsbeck revealing that Sarah's prediction concerning Hannah and George had been correct, Ellie was a confusion of joy and despair. From Sarah's letter romance was certainly in the air in the Elkson household and a letter from her mother tried to include Ellie in the excitement at the prospect of a wedding in the family. George was to marry Hannah Nelson. The time spent together studying Latin and the Law with Hannah as George's devoted tutor had obviously led to something far beyond the absorption of academic knowledge, as Sarah's letter described.

> *174, Aspen Lane,*
> *Hartsbeck, Lancs.*
> *27th March, 1910*

.......*"It's been so romantic, Ellie. You know that Hannah is the seventh of ten children. It seems she was really clever at school but was given to bouts of bronchitis in the winter which gave her even more time to study at home.. Anyway, her teacher wanted Hannah to stay on at school and take exams for college and train to become a teacher instead of following her sisters into the mill. Her father declared he couldn't possibly afford to pay the college fees, it wouldn't be fair on the family but four of Hannah's sisters insisted that she must be given her chance as the clever one and the cotton- mill would be bad for her chest. They paid her fees out of their own wages. When Hannah qualified as a teacher she soon earned enough to pay back the money to her sisters. Of course, she'll have to give up teaching in school, when she marries George.*

I think it's such a stupid rule that says all women teachers must be spinsters! I expect she'll take some private pupils at home. She's brilliant at maths and knows a lot about English literature. She really helped me pass my exams.

I know you all lived next door to Hannah's family when you were small but did you know that George first met Hannah again, as an adult at the Hartsbeck NATS, about four years ago! Hannah's a keen botanist. Anyway, it was during a NATS' Lecture last year, entitled, 'Flowers in Shakespeare,' that George proposed. Tom Brierly was sitting next to George at the time and told me all about it. Apparently, George underlined a passage in his 'Collected works of Shakespeare', put a marker in the place, closed it up and passed it along the rows to Hannah. She read it and blushed like a rose. She took her pencil and underlined some other lines and passed the Shakespeare back to George. Tom said George's face cracked into a wide grin when he read what she'd marked. Nobody knows what words they were but George went to see Hannah's father the following day. As it was Sunday he stayed there for lunch, then brought Hannah back to our house for tea and announced that they were engaged to be married. You should have seen our Dad, he ordered Mum to bring out the Sherry bottle and we all drank a toast to the 'Happy Couple!' Even mum refused her usual half glass and declared that this was an occasion for a full one! Dear old dad, he didn't have more than the one glass. He's been very strict with himself, ever since the time he was so drunk after old Mr Lucas died.

We missed you being with us, Ellie; I do hope you can have time off to come to the wedding. They are planning it for May or June next year, 1911. Hannah and George will both be twenty five by then and though George will still be a solicitor's clerk, he will be fully articled and on his way to becoming a full-fledged solicitor.

Please write Ellie, we never seem to hear from you nowadays.

Your own, loving little sister; Sarah.

PART FOUR

HARTSBECK 1911-1913.

CHAPTER 29

Wedding preparations. May 1911.

Sarah sat on her mother's bed holding a telegram from Ellie. It was seven o'clock in the morning on Wednesday 10th May, 1911, three days before George's wedding. Ellie had been expected home that afternoon. The telegram had just arrived and its brevity increased its hurtfulness.

[Sorry can't make wedding. Epidemic here. All leave cancelled. Ellie.]

"Oh, what a shame!" Jeannie Elkson sat up in bed flushed with consternation, "I do hope Ellie's alright, she doesn't say if she's caught whatever it is. Oh dear, whatever will George say. He might think it's just an excuse not to come. Telegrams are so brief, they don't tell you much."

"You pay by the letter, or is it the word, I'm not sure. I know you've got to be as short as possible. I'm sure we'd be told if Ellie was ill. Don't worry, Mother, Ellie will write as soon as she can. It is sad but it's all part of her job. I expect she's devastated, she was really looking forward to coming home."

"I suppose so, bless you Sarah, you always see the best side. Now you go along and let me get up and dressed. We've mountains to move before Saturday!!"

George was upset, far more than he admitted. A studious, thoughtful lad, he remembered Ellie caring for him as a child, when his mother had been preoccupied with Sarah and Jack. There were only four years between Ellie and himself but his older sister had been quite capable by the time she was eight. He remembered her firm hands scrubbing his face and pushing him into clothes and boots and marching him off to school with Edwin. He remembered the discussions on the way home from church and the stories she would read or make up, to send them off to sleep at night. He remembered too, how she would bathe and dress his raw hands, when at twelve he'd taken a job as a water carrier at the iron foundry. His friend, Bob Stubbs had worked alongside him. Now look at them both, he was almost a solicitor and Bob a partner in an ironmongery business. Bob was to be his Best Man at the wedding on Saturday.

George knew Ellie must remember Hannah as a child, when the Elksons and the Nelsons had been neighbours and little Ellie had run in and out of Auntie Lucy's home as if it was her own, but he had wanted Ellie to meet the adult Hannah and for her to be proud of them both on their wedding day.

On the evening after the telegram arrived George went round to the Nelson's home; Hannah was in the kitchen with her sister Becky, who was to be her bridesmaid with Sarah. They had been putting the finishing touches to Becky's bridesmaid dress when George knocked at the door.

"I'll leave you two together," said Becky trying to bundle dress and sewing things into an old pillowcase to carry from the room.

"Please stay Becky. I've just come with some news from our Ellie. You'll be interested, even though it's not good news,"

"Oh dear. What's happened George?" Hannah was concerned by his sad expression.

Becky sat down again and with a nod from Hannah, took a section of lacy collar from the bag and started to stitch again. The collar wouldn't give much away about the dresses, which George shouldn't see before the wedding. A bonnie girl of nineteen years, Becky was apprenticed as a sewer at the Hartsbeck clothing and household linen factory, so her skills were a bonus for the wedding entourage.

George took out Ellie's telegram and read it to them, his voice sharp and controlled. The girls waited in silence.

"Why is it more important for her to be caring for sick strangers in London, instead of being up here among her own family," George couldn't keep the irritation out of his voice.

Becky rose to Ellie's defence "She can't help it George. If there's anything I've learnt from being in the St. John's Ambulance brigade it's that sickness and accident don't come to order and often they choose the worst times possible."

She was a keen member of the St. John's ambulance brigade and a great admirer of Ellie. One day she hoped to leave the factory and become a full time nurse herself.

"Becky's right, George. It's sad she can't be with us but it's her duty to stay where she is. She'll be as upset as we are. Keep your fingers crossed that you and I will both be at the Church on Saturday!!"

Hannah always put things in proportion; she might be warm and sympathetic but she wasn't soft and she faced situations realistically.

"You're so matter of fact," grumbled George.

"Comes from being one of ten," Hannah said, gently stroking George's cheek,

"Now, sit yourself down and talk to our Becky. I'm going to make a pot of tea and then we'd better check the details for tomorrow's wedding rehearsal."

Hannah went into the scullery and George sat down opposite Becky. He asked how she liked her job at the factory.

"It's a good place to work, everybody's friendly. Mind you, I've only been sewing sheets and pillowcases for the past year. I don't think they dare let me loose on anything more delicate!" She laughed good -naturedly as she bent over her fine stitching on the delicate collar.

Her older sister Carrie came through at that moment, buttoning her coat ready to go out. Carrie was plump and jolly and an experienced cotton weaver. She was proud of her family's place in the cotton industry and didn't like to hear her young sister belittling herself.

"Nonsense! You've nimble enough fingers. It's just that the largest orders from the factory are for bedding and they need quick, competent sewers like you, to keep up with demand! Sorry George, I didn't mean to ignore you! How are you, lad! Ready for the big day? Hannah's just told me Ellie can't come. That's a shame. I was looking forward to seeing her again; she was in and out of here as a little 'un, when they lived next door. I'd be fifteen in those days. You won't remember it, you were only a month or so when your family left that house. Sorry I can't stay. I'm in a rush to meet some friends; we're off to the pictures. Tata then!" With a quick wave she was out of the back door and away.

The Nelson's and the Elkson's had lost touch over the years and George mused over this unexpected reunion of the two families as he watched Becky at her work. She was said to be the prettiest by far of Hannah's family, except for their beautiful sister Lily who Hannah said she could just remember. With her bright blue eyes, fair pink and white skin and golden curls, Lily had apparently been stolen away by the gypsies, when she was four years old. Hannah had only been six at the time and George was sure she embellished the memory. Annette Hamilton, who knew Hannah's mother well, had her own thoughts about Lily's disappearance. A bad fever epidemic had swept through Hartsbeck at the time and Annette had an idea that the little girl had died of the fever and the kidnap had been a story to keep the other children from fretting. It did seem strange; families were used to the death of little ones at that time and didn't usually hide it from the other children. Maybe, as this particular fever was so virulent, Mrs Nelson wanted to prevent panic spreading amongst her family and neighbours. It remained a mystery. Hannah would turn it into a joke against herself.

"No gypsy would have wanted to steal me away. I was a plain and sallow-skinned child, not really much different from now."

Whenever she said this, George would simply look at her strong, sensitive face and deep, deep eyes and shake his head.

"Your beauty is more than skin deep, Hannah. You're a woman in a million!"

George sat silently, thinking of this and watching Becky's needle dipping in and out with each small stitch bringing his marriage

191

nearer. Hannah came back with the tea tray and soon the three of them were sipping the hot, strong brew and putting their heads together over the final details of the wedding.

CHAPTER 30

Hannah Nelson

George had eventually left Hannah and her sisters to their wedding preparations and walked slowly home, lost in thought. It seemed strange to him that he had agreed so readily to being married in Hannah's parish church. He'd found it exhilarating when he and Stephen had declared they didn't believe in the church anymore and walked out of the church choir practice one Friday evening. He realised it must have been at least ten years ago. They'd both declared they wouldn't ever be coming back. It had caused a ripple in the waters of St. Mark's community, especially as several more of St. Mark's congregation followed suit.

Dear old Mr Chadwick, the open hearted Vicar of their childhood days, had retired the year before and unfortunately for George and Stephen the next Vicar, the Reverend Matthew Shaw, came from a strict, narrow wing of the church. He was young and inexperienced, fresh from his second curacy and filled with a crusading evangelical spirit. The young priest was devout and caring in his way but narrow-minded and unbending in his understanding of the Bible and Christian doctrine. At that time he saw Charles Darwin and his ilk as instruments of the devil and young, deluded boys like George, in need of saving from such influences.

After the 'walk-out' by the two boys, this zealous young Vicar was round at 174, Aspen Lane in no time, eager to talk things through with the boys. The humdinger of an argument ensued about science and religion with neither side listening to the other. George and Stephen shooting out their partly formed ideas freshly gathered from their exciting encounters with evolutionary science and a few jumbled Marxist notions. These had been fed to them by the men they had met in the factories and one particularly popular teacher of the time. George had smiled ruefully, when he told Hannah about the church incident, as they sat together in the front parlour at Aspen Lane, one Sunday afternoon.

"You were angry young lads, believing you knew the way to put the world to rights. None of you were prepared to hear what the other was saying. Honestly George, these same arguments have been going on for decades. I know for a fact, that at the time you were arguing with the Reverend Shaw, the Archbishop of Canterbury, Frederick Temple and other Church leaders, were happily taking on board the theory of evolution and didn't think it affected Christian beliefs one bit, except so far as to make creation even more amazing and exciting and God an even more ingenious Creator!"

"Well, we were hot-headed but there was more to it than that. Dad had been part of a debating society in his early days before rugby and cricket took over. He used to tell us about the meetings they had out at the Harpers Arms in Preston and similar groups that met near here, at the White Horse. They discussed politics and read Karl Marx and French Revolution fanatics such as Edmund Burke and William Godwin. There was an atheist, who came to speak, called Bradlaugh, Dad said he had a real golden tongue and won a lot of men over with his talk about the impossibility of God. It was all quite radical material and strongly elevated the cause of the working man against the bosses. Anyway, Dad still had some of these books and Stephen and I used to read them - quite fiery stuff some of it. The older men down at the foundry where Bob and I were water carriers were full of it and some still met at the local pubs for debates. Stephen and I went along sometimes, quite a few of the men from the NATS would be there. It was inspiring stuff but didn't get much farther than talk!"

"Thank goodness for that! Would you want French revolution tactics here?"

"No, I don't think they'd go so far! If anything the Hartsbeck people are more liberal in their politics!"

"Oh, I'm not so sure, there's a good few on the side of Capitalism; think of the Captains of Industry and mill owners in this area. Money can be persuasive, whether you've got it or whether you haven't."

"Our Ellie was a little firebrand when it came to speaking out about the living conditions of some of the poorer families in Hartsbeck,"

"She was right to speak out but it's not always clear as to which political party is best able to improve matters."

George looked at Hannah admiringly; she had a far-sightedness that transcended party politics. He agreed with her views. He was beginning to lean towards right wing politics as he saw more and more what good could be done by wealth in the hands of far-sighted philanthropists, or channelled wisely for the good of all levels of society, by the Government, both local and national.

George's youthful vision had been for a gradual levelling out of wealth over the whole of society so that none had too much and none had too little but as he saw more of life, he realised this was probably an unobtainable Utopian Dream.

Since he'd begun his solicitor's training, George had seen into the personal lives of all sorts of men and women, from working class; middle class; to the small town aristocracy and rich business people. He was amazed at the way people coped with poverty and tragedy, with success and failure, with material loss, sickness and old age, bereavement and loneliness. He met young married couples experiencing the ups and downs of family life and wondered how he would manage, as a husband and father.

In Hannah he'd found someone who had the patience to look at life quietly and learn from it. If she couldn't find the solution to a situation straight away, she simply waited for the answer to reveal itself in its own good time. "Life's mysteries eventually come clearer to us, we can't rush these things," she would say. Dear Hannah, how he loved her.

"You're so well read, Hannah," he remembered saying to her last spring, as they'd taken a day to walk together in the countryside, just at the time their friendship was turning into courtship. "I'm beginning to believe that all that poetry and literature you read, is proving a deeper fount of wisdom, than all the factual stuff my brothers and I read," and he'd taken her hand in his as they'd walked along the shady country lanes.

"Mm, flattery will get you nowhere; I'll believe that when I see you with a copy of Keats or Shelley,"

George chuckled to himself, remembering how Hannah had parried his smooth talking.

"I'd rather have you read them to me," George pictured himself looking into the depths of her eyes, which had seemed full of visions at that moment.

Those deep greenish-blue eyes were Hannah's best feature, wide set and fringed with dark lashes. In certain lights and moods they looked like deep, darkly shining pools and it intrigued George to see them change again, to their own soft colour. Her long brown hair she kept loosely coiled and pinned up but always a few stray wisps escaped, to drop enticingly round her strong square face with its snub nose and wide, full mouth.

Many times on that walk, George had gazed at her, hardly daring to believe this remarkable woman had agreed to marry him.

At last, amused by his secret glances, Hannah had given George a gentle push, saying-"You'll eat me up with your greedy eyes, George Elkson!"

Then he'd grasped hold of her and kissed her fiercely on the lips. She'd kissed him back. He remembered that kiss. That day George and Hannah had felt so close, they couldn't bear to part at the end of the walk.

"Come home with me. Mother will have supper on by now and our Becky and the others will be home from the St. John's Ambulance," Hannah had urged.

George loved going to Hannah's happy, clean, untidy home. He enjoyed being with her plump, jolly mother and her teasing, warm hearted father and the sisters and brother still at home. Mr Nelson worked as a twister at the cotton mill and was an intelligent, self-educated man, who enjoyed a good banter with his prospective son-in-law. This was the background that had helped to form Hannah and George was at home in it.

George had taken his time walking home, retracing his memories and thoughts of Hannah but a sudden shiver in the cool of the spring evening made him quicken his step, as he shivered he hoped the weather would be milder for their wedding in three days' time.

Meanwhile, back in the Nelson's kitchen Hannah and Becky had finished sewing and talking about the wedding and settled down by the fire with a large jug of hot cocoa, keeping warm on the hob, for any others in the family who might join them.

"I'm glad you wanted to get married in church, Hannah. It was good that George agreed. You must have been worried about his reaction when you told him," said Becky.

"Oh, I wasn't too worried, he just needed a nudge to be more open in his understanding of 'church'."

Hannah had her own thoughts of God, which went far beyond the teachings and weekly services in the local church. Unlike Ellie and George, she wasn't unhappy with the church but she envisaged it as much larger than the visible institution, bound by rules and doctrines. She'd pondered over the different facets of Christian beliefs and sensed that they were bringing her near to almost understanding, the vibrant, living mystery, underlying all of life, both the mundane and the exotic. She believed this mystery was what the church clung on to; wondered about; rejoiced in and kept sacred. Cousin Hugh would tell her to call this living mystery, God, and earth her Christianity in the person of Jesus Christ, "Otherwise you're like a kite flying high and uncontrolled, let Him hold your kite string."

Hannah laughed, "Hugh, I'm sure if Jesus is the person we believe him to be, he's content to let me fly free, in order to find him."

It was Hugh's turn to laugh, "You've got me there Hannah; but don't fly too far away and keep us in touch with what you find."

Becky gave the cocoa jug a stir, "You always go into a dream in church," she teased her sister, "It's as if you're listening to something quite different from what the rest of us hear. I have to give you a dig to tell you we're on to the next bit, or to stand up, or kneel down. What does go on in your head, when we're in church, Hannah?"

"For one thing, I enjoy a bit of peace from my cheeky sisters; also, I can't hear properly what's being said or sung, all the sound seems to come from a great way off and changes into a mysterious min-gling of noises, something like that bit from Shakespeare's play, 'The Tempest'- "be not a-feared the isle is full of noises, sounds and sweet airs that give delight and hurt not, sometimes a thousand twanging instruments are round my ears and sometimes voices"- and the rest. It all becomes a background for my thoughts, I can read the service well enough and it starts me thinking. I suppose I just get lost in my thoughts."

Just then Carry arrived back from the pictures and Polly, (another older unmarried sister), came in with their mother from visiting a neighbour. Dad Nelson was already in bed and asleep, ready for his early morning start.

"I'll say goodnight, girls. I'm getting too old to burn the candle at both ends," he'd called out earlier, on his way upstairs.

"So, it's just us, tonight," sighed mother, as she filled four cups with cocoa from the jug.

"Soon, it'll be just Becky, Polly, Carry and me and your dad," she handed round the cocoa and sank back into an easy chair.

"Come on, mum, that's still five of us at home. It's not like you to come over maudlin. We'd better ask our Hannah, to tell us one of her stories. That'll cheer you up," said Carry.

Lily Nelson smiled. In the days when there had been ten young ones at home, Hannah's story telling had been a life-saver. Her favourites had been from the ancient myths; Nordic legends from the lands of fiords, deep forests and the midnight sun, mixed with stories of the gods and heroes of ancient Greece and Rome, or of King Arthur and his knights and sometimes, the fairy tales of the brothers Grimm.

"We don't want anything horrid, like those three old crones with only one eye that they passed between them, or the witch who poked the fire with her nose and ate people," Becky shuddered at the thought.

"I don't feel like telling a story tonight but I'll give you a poem, something with a bit of romance and adventure. What about Keats's, Eve of St. Agnes?"

Her sisters nodded in agreement. They were all thinking that this could be the last time they would ever sit together, like this. They turned out the lamps and settled back in the firelight, then Hannah recited the evocative poem, about the forbidden love and mystical marriage of the young couple, Madeline and Porphyro, and how they fled away together, one stormy night, far from those who wanted to part them. Hannah's memory was perfect and she lived the words as she spoke them, carrying her small audience with her. They sighed deeply as she recited the final verse,

"And they are gone: ay, ages long ago
These lovers fled away into the storm,"

The final lines spoke of the death of Madeline's old nurse, Angela, and an old beadsman who'd helped the couple,

"Angela the old
Died palsy-twitched, with meagre face deform;
The Beadsman, after thousand Aves told,
For aye unsought for slept among his ashes cold."

"I suppose that'll be your dad and me, when you've all gone off with your romantic heroes," said Lily, smiling mischievously and thoroughly enjoying her daughter's discomfiture.

"Don't be daft mum. I'll still be here with you and you've got to be ready for all the grandchildren!" declared Polly and with warm hugs and laughter, the little group washed up the cocoa things and went to bed.

Hannah lay thinking for some time that in years to come her wedding to George would be just a memory, even for them. Later still it would become a long- ago story, possibly passed on to great, great grandchildren, or more probably, forgotten, like a precious jewel hidden away in deep folds of black velvet and lost. Still, the effects of their love and marriage would hopefully go on, for generations; if they had children. She fell into a sleep filled with warm hopes.

George was glad he'd agreed to a church wedding. The Vicar from Hannah's parish church, Canon Bertram Scott, was middle-aged, astute, with five children and a hearty extrovert of a wife who thought nothing of going into a sick person's home (be they rich or poor) and scrub, wash, cook or nurse- whatever was needed- or, as some people would hint, "even if it wasn't."

The Canon had spoken to the young couple about marriage. He had the advantage of years of the rather wearing but mainly happy experience, of his own marriage and as well as ministering in the ups and downs of the married life of his parishioners from a variety of backgrounds.

George and Hannah had gone to the Vicarage to put up the marriage banns and Canon Scott had talked with them for at least an hour. He probed them with so many personal questions that by the end, Hannah and George felt they'd learnt more about each other, than in all the years of their friendship.

"The clever old so and so," George thought to himself.

Sighing gently, the Canon looked piercingly at the young couple and ended his conversation with words of advice,

"It's good to have God alongside you in this matter of marriage and bringing up children. He understands the quirks and mysteries of our human natures much better than we do! Now I want you both to do your best to pray together each night before getting into bed, or whenever it's most suitable. You'd be surprised how many marriages would be stronger and happier, if each couple did this. Oh, and get to know each other. I know you love each other, but take time to become friends. Misunderstandings can be soothed away by sexual relations, in the early years of marriage and so they should. Be sure to enjoy those precious moments! But as you grow older you need something more, a deeper kind of love and real friendship. Work on it my dears, work on it, learn to forgive and be good to each other."

He ended with a prayer of blessing for their life together.

As they were leaving the Vicarage, Mrs Scott bustled out of the kitchen and spoke directly to Hannah; "Never forget, my dear, when all else fails, the way to a man's heart is through his stomach!"

Hannah took a sideways glance at the rather corpulent Vicar and suppressed a rising giggle.

CHAPTER 31

George and Hannah are married

By the wedding day itself, all the mountains envisaged by Jeannie Elkson had been moved and Lily Nelson, having already married off one son and three daughters, was feeling the usual internal fluttering of the mother of the bride. Hannah was unflapable, she helped Becky into the simple cream coloured bridesmaid's dress and tied a sash of lilac silk round her waist so that it dropped in two long ribbons from a large bow at the back.

A rap on the front door announced the arrival of Sarah, a coat hiding her own bridesmaid finery, which matched Becky's. Hannah arranged a small coronet of jewel like anemones in purple, mauve, red and white on her sister's fair hair, which hung loosely to her shoulders.

"She's still young enough not to put it up, it looks so pretty," said her mother. Hannah placed a similar coronet on Sarah's hair which was partially up, in deference to her profession as a teacher but two long, thickly curling tendrils, had been allowed to hang loose to the nape of her neck, in deference to her youthful, unmarried state.

Becky and Sarah helped Hannah into her wedding outfit, a two piece in white lace over Satin. The skirt flowed into a short train.

"Perhaps I should have worn a hat," murmured Hannah nervously, as her mother arranged a waist length, tulle veil, over her daughters carefully dressed hair and secured it with a crown of orange blossom.

"Oh no, Hannah, the veil is just right- not too fancy and it softens your face," her mother reassured her, feeling tears pricking behind her eyes.

Becky was dancing in delight and Sarah placed into Hannah's hands her bouquet of white carnations, trailing green leaves and lilies of the valley, with a sprig of white heather for luck. Lucy Nelson looked quietly charming in her best navy blue two-piece of slubbed satin, freshened by a new silk blouse of forget-me-not blue. She looked in the mirror, to adjust her large brimmed navy hat, freshly trimmed with a tiny bunch of silk forget-me-nots, and saw a comfortably plump face looking back at her with crinkly laughter wrinkles and a slight frown line between her brows, "Just to show my life hasn't been all a bunch of roses," she thought with satisfaction as she drew on her navy blue gloves and picked up her handbag.

"Come along bridesmaids it's time we were off to the church," she declared and touched Hannah's cheek lightly with her finger,

"God bless you, my Hannah," she said.

"Thank you Mum; for everything," replied Hannah and watched as her mother left the room, followed by the two bridesmaids who quickly gathered up their white gloves and posies of anemones.

Hannah and her father followed, a quarter of an hour later. Hannah thought her father had never looked so distinguished, standing before her in his smart, tailed suit and waistcoat, his silvery hair smoothed down with water- (he refused to use oil, or pomade)- and his face shaved and shining with cleanliness. He bowed and offered his arm;

"Come along then lass, let's get this done!" he paused as he caught sight of their reflection in the mirror over the mantelpiece and his eyes filled up, "You look a fair picture, Hannah – it fair shines out of you! I mind the day you were born—"

"None of that Dad, you'll have us in tears, before we've even set off. You look wonderful yourself, Dad, I'm so proud of you."

They came out of the house to the smiles and waves of what seemed to be all their neighbours. Hannah felt like royalty as she climbed into the wedding car, waving to these people she'd known most of her life.

George and his best man were sitting at the front of the church, Bob craning his head round every few minutes to look towards the back, at last he leant nearer and whispered,

"Hannah's just arriving; we'd better stand up".

George rubbed the palms of his hands surreptitiously across the knees of his trousers; it would be terrible to offer Hannah a sweaty, damp, hand in marriage. He stood up gingerly, legs as wobbly as a new-born foal. The organ changed its tune to 'O Love divine and golden', the hymn Hannah had chosen and the church was filled with throat clearing, thuds and rustles as wedding guests and well-wishers rose to their feet,

"Here we go," said Bob and together the groom and the best man walked forward to the bottom of the chancel steps.

"O Love divine and golden,

Mysterious depth and height,

To Thee the world beholden,

Looks up for life and light—"

The well- known words and tune of the hymn made George's heart swell. He couldn't deny that the Church still held for him, some of the undefinable mystery of life. He was glad for Hannah and himself, that their relationship would be sealed in the presence of this great mystery that Hannah, and maybe even he, called God. Hannah joined him as the final verse rang out,

"God bless these hands united,

God bless these hearts made one!

Unsevered and unblighted,

May they through life go on,

Here in earth's home preparing

For the bright home above,

And there forever sharing

It's joy, where God is Love"

In his short sermon the Vicar declared that there would inevitably be difficult times during Hannah and George's marriage but these should be welcomed. If a marriage was to be strong the couple must learn how to face problems together but to face them recognising their love and commitment to each other.

"Let difficulties draw you closer together, not drive you apart!" he boomed "and remember God is present as a rock in your lives,

He will keep you firm and faithful throughout all life's storms. If you let Him!!"

Dave and Jeannie Elkson found themselves searching for each other's hands and squeezing them tightly.

After the service and in between photographs, George and Hannah mingled separately among the crowd that had gathered to greet them. George, as usual, had one hand tucked behind his back and his head bowed in concentration towards whoever spoke to him. His face wore a bemused smile as he accepted accolades, concerning his new wife, from men and women he didn't know and who came from all walks of life. They'd come, not as guests but as bystanders, to see their beloved teacher married. Hannah was overwhelmed by their kindness and moved among them, smiling and talking. A well dressed, pleasant faced young man came over to George.

"Congratulations Mr Elkson. My name's John Townley, I'm a clerk in the corporation offices. I want to wish Mrs Elkson and yourself, every happiness. I'm one of your wife's old pupils. We all thought the world of Miss Nelson. We'd have done anything for her, even before she went deaf, but when it happened- well it spurred us on even further. She's a grand teacher and we were all determined not to let her down. That's not to say we didn't sometimes take advantage, when her back was turned but I reckon she always knew. She has a sixth sense, Mr Elkson; you won't put anything over on that one!"

"I wouldn't want to, Mr Townley; she's one in a million. I'm very fortunate to have such a woman as my wife. Thank you for your kind words."

As one and another came to him with similar remarks, George began to feel he could never live up to his wife's reputation.

George himself was just on the verge of his law career, his reputation had yet to be built and he was still serving his articles with Drake and Son. By the end of this year his articles would be completed and after one final exam, he would be fully qualified, but what then? As society became more upwardly mobile, there was more need for the services of a solicitor by people in all walks of life. George could be assured of a place with Drake's, but would he remain just a jobbing solicitor, doing the firm's bread and butter work, or would he be able to rise higher. For weeks he had been wondering if he should choose a more specialised area of the legal profession, but today was not the time to dwell on such things.

"This is my wedding day!" he said aloud and filled with uncharacteristic boyishness George flung his top hat into the air, with a whoop of joy.

At that moment, a cloud which had hovered ominously for the last half hour, decided to shed its load. Hannah, laughing as the drops showered over her like a blessing, gathered up her short train and skipped over to her husband, her other hand protecting her veil with its sprig of orange blossom.

"Hannah, your bouquet, you left it in the church!"

Sarah, the dutiful bridesmaid, hurried up to them. She was clutching Hannah's bouquet of white flowers together with her own posy of colourful anemones. As if by magic, Bob, the best man, appeared with a large black umbrella and together they hurried to the open topped car, loaned to them for the day, by the Drake family. It was driven by Lewis Drake, Mr. Drake's only son who was five years younger than George. The handsome young Lewis was red faced from struggling to bring up the car's hood, before the rain soaked the seats; his own clothes and hair becoming drenched in the process. The two bridesmaids and the rest of the guests, climbed into a variety of horse or motor driven vehicles.

Stephen Elkson looked dapper in a fashionably cut grey suit with a silver-grey waistcoat and cravat. He was now a mining engineer and in the next few months would qualify as an Associate Member of the Manchester Geological and Mining society. His studious, slightly withdrawn air was emphasised by round spectacles, which disguised blue eyes that twinkled, in a charming way, at any member of the female sex who took his eye and his boyish figure and slightly unruly hair, drew them to him irresistibly. Stephen made the most of it, he already had one broken heart to his name and there would be many more before he was forty. The broken hearts were unintentional on his part, he enjoyed an innocent dalliance with a woman but his work and his passion for geology and natural history always took precedence and he expected his lady friends to accept this and treat him as casually as he seemed to treat them. As a mining engineer he had to travel around the country, and occasionally overseas. His understanding of the wild life and geology of the areas he covered was uncanny; he seemed to have an understanding of the earth's substance at his fingertips in the same way that his brother Edwin had green fingers when growing plants. Stephen was one of those fortunate people whose work and hobbies were entwined, each enhancing the other. His holidays and time off were generally spent walking the countryside with a camera, specimen bag, geologists hammer and insect net; or mounting and cataloguing his specimens and developing his photographs. Occasionally, he persuaded a lady friend to accompany him but they rarely did so more than once. He often wished Ellie was at home, she'd always been eager to see his finds and go with him when she could; even Edwin had other things to occupy his time nowadays.

Today, at the wedding, Stephen had three young women fluttering around him, like moths to a flame. Ena Barnes, who worked alongside George at Drake's solicitors; Gladys Heyworth whose father owned the local stationers and had printed out today's wedding invitations and Susannah Pickup, a teacher friend of Sarah's.

"Safety in numbers," said Stephen to Edwin, catching his younger brother's disapproving frown.

As the rain started Stephen linked arms with Ena and Susannah and turned to Gladys with a mischievous twinkle,

"Come along Glad Eyes, you sit next to me in the carriage. He gallantly handed the other two girls into one of the horse- driven carriages, then turned and almost lifted the blushing Gladys into the seat facing them before springing up to sit beside her.

"What a charmer," grinned Edwin and looked fondly down at the sweet, smiling lass at his side, "Stephen certainly knows how to choose and handle his women!"

"Thank goodness you don't, Edwin Elkson; you'd never have looked at me otherwise!"

"You wouldn't have looked at me, Annie, if I'd been like that. I'm just glad of the day I found you," and shyly he put his arm round her, proud to show off this lass as his own. Annie Reed was bright and small as a sparrow, kind to a fault, quiet but full of fun and best of all, happy to be with him. Her outfit was in dove grey with white trimmings, cut out and sewn by herself and her sister, at their kitchen table. Neat and fresh and beautifully fitted to her small figure, it didn't matter that it wasn't the latest fashion, or that the material wasn't the most expensive, Annie just looked good in it and Edwin couldn't take his eyes off her.

Aunt Alice Nowell from Preston was standing next to her sister-in-law Jeannie Elkson and watching Edwin and Annie as they searched for a place together in one of the vehicles.

"They'll be next, mark my words," whispered Alice to Jeannie.

Jeannie sighed, life was moving along quickly for her offspring but she felt as if she wasn't moving at all. She was just standing still in the wings, seeing their lives unfolding as in some kind of drama, ready to prompt if any of them forgot their lines but otherwise helplessly watching it all happen. She wondered about Ellie. Was her eldest daughter sad not to be with them, or was she so wrapped up in her nursing that it would just be a passing regret? She'd begun to miss Ellie recently, longing for her practicality and the time to sit down and talk together, as they used to do.

"I do wish Ellie could have been here," she spoke her thoughts aloud and Alice Nowell looked at her quizzically as they were both ushered into a waiting motor vehicle. There was a period of raising hoods, cranking of starter handles and soothing of nervous horses, before the cavalcade set off on the mile long trek to the wedding reception in the newly opened Ambulance Drill Hall.

As soon as they were settled in the back seats of the car, Alice asked, "How old is Ellie? I know she was old enough to help at your Sarah's birth and she's a good bit older than our three but I can't think what year she was born. You were still in Preston weren't you?"

"Yes, we still had the shop, it was 1881. She'll be thirty this year,"

"Do you think she's ever likely to marry?"

"Not while she's nursing; it's not allowed,"

"She's very wrapped up in it, isn't she?"

"Yes, it's a real calling for her but I do wish she'd would come and nurse nearer home. Maybe, if she met someone she wanted to marry, she'd give up nursing and settle down to a home and family of her own but I think she's too dedicated to her work."

"I admire her for it. Granny Jane would be proud of her. It took guts to leave home like she did and go to London; they don't always take kindly to folk from the North; they think we still wear wode and dress in animal skins."

"Oh Alice, go on with you; they're not as ignorant as all that!"

"No, but some of them think we are! Despite places like that," and Alice pointed through the car window to the edifice of the Hartsbeck Public Library, opened eleven years ago through the gift of the great philanthropist, Andrew Carnegie. Year by year more and more people flocked to make use of it.

"Let's hope Ellie and anyone else that goes up to London from here, shows them how wrong they are," Alice spoke indignantly and threw herself back against the seat.

Jeannie remembered how Dave had once said they would tear Ellie to shreds in London, well they hadn't but Jeannie often wondered if, at times, it had come near to happening.

She mused about Sarah too. Now that her younger daughter had qualified as a teacher and had a good position in the local church primary school, she wondered if Sarah would also become so dedicated to her work, that she would forgo marriage. If they wanted to marry, female teachers had to give up their career straight away. It was considered that the distraction and practicalities of caring for a husband and children would be detrimental to their pupils. Jeannie sighed again; her daughters had turned out to be visionaries, determined to do their bit to improve the lot of mankind! The boys might feel the same but for them it didn't mean sacrificing the chance of a wife and children. Something was wrong. Where would the next generation come from, if women decided to take jobs and not marry? Jeannie sighed again, forgetting that teacher Hannah Nelson had just chosen to marry her son.

"I expect human nature will step in somewhere," she muttered, much to Alice's irritation.

"It always does, what do you think is happening today! You're doing far too much sighing and muttering for your son's wedding day, Jeannie Elkson. Here we are at the Drill Hall, now for heaven's sake put a smile on and cheer up. Here's your Dave and he's still sober! Jump out, they're waiting for you in the reception line," and she gave Jeannie an affectionate push.

Friends and family had worked hard decorating the barn -like hall with flowers and coloured streamers. Long trestle tables had been set with white cloths and sparkling glass and silverware and more tables were laden with a sumptuous buffet and a wedding cake fit for the King and Queen. The cake was a gift, proudly made by the cookery class of the school where Hannah had taught.

As most of the Elksons and the Nelsons were members of the St. John's Ambulance brigade, the Drill Hall was a fitting venue and its recent festive opening by Sir Robert Baden Powell himself gave it a novel and auspicious atmosphere.

The wedding reception went well, the food was excellent and abundant; the alcoholic drink provided was just enough to make people cheery and relaxed. Speeches were pithy but not too embarrassing. When George and Hannah eventually left for their home, a large iron horse-shoe and a pair of old clog irons, attached to the back bumper of their car, struck bright sparks as they were dragged along the road, causing much amusement and cheering in the streets of Hartsbeck. At home the couple changed from their wedding finery and Edwin drove them to the railway station, where they took a train to Scotland.

A week together in the highland rain and sunshine was an ideal for forging their new closeness. They were glad of the tranquillity of mountains, waterfalls, lochs and wildlife. One particular incident unsettled Hannah. Exhausted after a long days walking she had fallen asleep on the large double- bed and had a disturbing dream about George's sister, Ellie. She woke with a sense of foreboding, sure that her sister-in-law was in some kind of danger. The superstition that, as the seventh child of a seventh child, she had inherited 'the second sight,' had been told to her since she was a child and Hannah felt sure that Ellie was under some kind of threat. George laughed it off at first but when she persisted, he became angry with his new wife and spoke scathingly of her so-called second sight:

"Ideas like that come from sheer ignorance. The only thing Ellie's in danger from is her own self-importance. Believing herself too indispensable, to come to her own brother's wedding!"

Hurt and humiliated, Hannah stormed out of the guest-house. She walked along the riverside until, cold and subdued, she shook off her foreboding and her anger and made her way slowly back, wondering what reception she would receive from George. Mrs White, the elderly lady who ran the guesthouse, met Hannah as she came through the gate and together they turned to admire the sunset.

"I think o' my husband, on evenings like this," the old woman's musical brogue soothed Hannah, "I've been widowed nigh on twenty years but I still listen for the gate opening and my Doug's whistle, at the time he'd be coming home from work. We brought a lot of love to each other and that's what I ken. You'll no' be without difficult times in a marriage but it's the love that counts. Now, lassie just you go into that husband of yours and give him a lot of loving. Go on now!"

Chuckling, Mrs White turned and limped slowly away to her own part of the house. Hannah went in to find George and told him what the old lady had said,

George, already undressed and in bed had opened his arms wide saying, "Well, Mrs Elkson, what are you waiting for?"

Giggling like a school girl Hannah had thrown off her clothes, snuggled into George's arms and loved him.

A week later the young couple returned to their new, rented home in Hartsbeck, at number 99, Aspen Lane. It was a terraced house, higher up the lane than Jeannie and Dick's home. It was the end house of the last terrace, which meant it bordered on farmland.

Just beyond their new home, the town street became the country lane up which Ellie had walked, onto the tops, twelve years ago.

Hannah's dream of foreboding about Ellie still weighed on her mind. She wrote to her sister-in-law saying she had been concerned about her and enclosed the letter with a piece of wedding cake. Ellie wept when she opened the white box containing the slice of ornately-iced, fruit cake, wrapped in waxed paper. The family's obvious disapproval towards her, for not going to the wedding, had left her feeling horribly desolate. George's cryptic note sent in the first flush of his disappointment and her mother's letter, lecturing her on family responsibilities "which you seem to have relinquished completely," had cut her to the quick. Thoughts of home had always supported her but now she felt her family had no understanding of her situation.

It was two years later, on a rare visit to Hartsbeck, that Ellie told Hannah about the danger she'd been in at the time of their honeymoon.

"It happened on a morning I'd been delivering a baby in a fever-ridden area of the city. The new mother, Tilly Jones, asked me if I'd mind visiting another home, two doors away." Ellie quoted the young woman's exact words, so deeply was the incident engraved on her memory;

"It's a Mrs. Prosser, she's six little uns, all under seven. I know they're not on your list, Sister and it isn't as if she's just given birth, but they're in a terrible bad way with the fever and they can't afford to have the doctor. She cried when I said I'd ask you to look in, she were that relieved."

"I didn't hesitate. We'd been told to look out for cases such as this. I told Tilly I'd go as soon as I'd settled her and the baby. Suddenly she grabbed my arm, and almost hissed at me- "it's not like here, Sister, the Prosser's house is filthy and you'll have to leave if her hubbie shows up; there's things going on round here that's not right and he's part of it."

"I was surprised at the woman's vehemence. I put it down to her having just given birth, after a long night's labour. Then the neighbour who'd come to help, chipped in;"

"She's right. You watch your back in that house, Sister,"

"Intrigued, I went straight round to the Prosser's. No-one answered my knock but the door was unlocked and I walked straight in shouting 'Mrs Prosser, it's the nurse calling,.' Then the smell hit me and I was nearly sick. I'm not squeamish, Hannah but the stink and the horror of what I saw—" Ellie had gone quiet for a moment, remembering and sipping her tea, before continuing:

"Piles of dirty rags lay scattered on the floor and I realised that humped on top of them, were the bodies of children. One of the small bodies moved and these huge eyes stared up at me out of an ancient-looking face. I presumed it was a girl, by the length of her hair. She made a slurred, croaking sound and tried to get up but slumped back onto the pile of rags and closed her eyes. I knelt down and felt the child's head. It was clammy but not hot. I went round examining the other five children. They were all out for the count. Some had been sick and all had wet and soiled themselves. Three of them showed a fever- rash. I thought there was something odd, about the way they were sleeping. The first little girl moaned and opened her eyes again and I saw that the pupils were large and dark and then I realised, the children had been drugged."

"Oh Ellie, how dreadful. Where was their mother?" Hannah was mesmerised.

"I shouted her name again and began to search the house for Mrs Prosser. I found her slumped in an old armchair in the kitchen, obviously under the influence of some strong opiate. She had on a filthy night gown and her skin was grey and unwashed. I took hold of her by the shoulders and shook her hard. It was like shaking an old mattress. A kind of far-away groan and a slight movement of the head showed she was at least alive. I was that angry, I filled a pan with cold water from the sink and flung it over the woman! She jerked awake for a moment but soon sank back, to wherever the drugs had taken her. Suddenly I sensed a shadow in the room and turned round to find a real burly figure of a man in the doorway. He spoke in a horrid low voice,–'And just what do you think you're doing, whoever you are! Who gave you leave to come in here!"

213

I was frozen with fear, I think I stammered out that I was Nursing Sister Elkson from the Community Clinic and had been called to the house to attend to some sick children'.—

"Busy bodying that's what you're doing. Well, you won't get out of here to go and tell what you've seen. I'll teach yer a lesson first, then I'll make you disappear so as no-one will ever find you,' he started to move towards me." Ellie shivered at the memory.

"I noticed a back door, leading from the kitchen and prayed it wasn't locked. I faced the man, he looked deranged, I daren't take my eyes from his face but I kept edging towards the back door. I said, 'Don't be silly. The clinic knows where I am. If you harm me you won't get away with it!' He didn't believe me. His next words made my blood run cold. 'Oh; who says so, my little beauty. You were never here. You never arrived." I'm sure Mr Prosser, for that's who it was, was slightly drugged himself. He leered horridly at me, grabbed my jacket and ripped it off. 'You might be scraggy but you've still g-got -got tits.'"

Ellie had blushed frantically as she repeated this to Hannah. "Then he said, 'We'll 'ave a bit of fun, before I dispatch you, so to speak' He grunted with laughter and tried to tear at the cotton of my uniform blouse. The strength of the material delayed him and I kicked him hard, up between his legs. I overbalanced and fell against the fire place and saw the iron poker. I struck him on the temple with it. That sent him reeling, he'd pitched right into his wife's chair and I made a dash for the back door. It was bolted, I struggled with bolts but Mr Prosser had recovered and reached me before I could open it. He pulled me to him and planted a hard, foul- smelling kiss on my lips, probing inside my mouth with his tongue. I bit down hard on his horrid tongue; he yelped and I tried to push him away but he was too strong."

Ellie sobbed and a shocked Hannah wondered about going for the brandy, but Ellie continued. "Suddenly A woman's voice shouted from the front door, 'Alright Mrs Prosser? I've come to see if Sister Elkson's been round?' It was Tilly Jones's neighbour. I screamed out and shouted for the police. This distracted Mr Prosser enough for me to push passed him and dash towards the front door. Hannah, I've never run so fast in all my life. I stumbled over one child, then another and caught my head on the door frame; my hair was flying loose and all the time I could hear Mr Prosser, coming after me. Tilly Jones's neighbour had opened the front door. She grabbed hold of me and pulled me outside. It was lucky Mr Prosser hadn't locked the front door when he came in, or maybe he'd been upstairs, when I first entered the house. Anyway, when he realised he'd lost me he must have beaten a retreat through the back door. The police found it wide open. They've never found him."

"What happened to Mrs. Prosser and the children?"

"It turned out that Mr Prosser was involved with a dealer in narcotics and opium and had been drugging his family too, when it pleased him. This time it was Mrs Prosser who'd given the children opium, when they all had the fever and she was at the end of her tether. All the children survived, except one, the youngest; a little boy, just one year old. The opium was too strong for him. Once they were out of hospital the Waifs and Strays Society took care of the children and placed them, and their mother, in suitable establishments. They'd be cared for and be helped to find employment, when they become of age."

Ellie had surprised herself. It was the first time she'd poured out the full story to anyone, except her superiors. They'd given her a strict telling off for going into such a situation unaccompanied and without them knowing. Afterwards, she'd just had to get over it and carry on.

Hannah had listened unobtrusively but now she did go for the brandy.

"Let's refill the tea-pot and have a drop of this with it. I need it as much as you, after hearing all that, Ellie. What a shocking experience," she squeezed Ellie's shoulder as she passed, knowing Ellie didn't like fuss. Ellie was suddenly embarrassed at her outpouring.

"Hannah; I want you to promise me that you won't tell a word of this to my brothers, or mother, or Sarah. It would frighten them and really, there's no need."

Hannah felt honoured that Ellie had confided in her and gave her promise; "I understand. George would be moving heaven and earth to make you come back home and the others would be upset. I know you too well, to think you'd give up your nursing to save your own skin. I'll not tell them, Ellie, but thank you for telling me."

This revelation from Ellie was to be given in September, 1912 and made Hannah wonder even more about her so-called gift of second-sight, but she kept any such notions to herself.

By September of 1911 George had completed his articles and had discussed with Hannah his ambition to become a partner in Drake and Son, Solicitors. She still helped George at home with his studies and research but in relation to his professional work, he had to be strict about client confidentiality and couldn't discuss any but the most routine problems.

Hannah needed to keep her brain stretched but was not the kind of person to become frustrated and had the ability to discover the exciting and fascinating in the most mundane areas of life. She enjoyed her home life but didn't entirely desert her teaching and took the occasional pupil at home, giving extra Latin and Maths lessons. Always hospitable to her neighbours Hannah was often interrupted by local children who were stuck with their homework knocking at her door.

"Mi Father says, 'tek it round to Mrs Elkson, she'll put you right', so I've come. Please, can you help me?" would be the plea.

More often than not she could and did. She would throw down what she was doing, sit at the table with her young visitor's homework spread out before her and those ever escaping fronds of hair pinned back with a paper clip, or whatever she could find to hand. One evening, Tony Atkinson from across the road came in tears with a demonic maths question.

"I'm in real trouble if I don't get it right, my teacher showed me four times and I still can't understand it!"

It proved to be a knotty problem, even for Hannah and eventually she sent the frantic boy home saying,

"Leave it with me."

She sat up till the early hours of the morning until she'd solved the problem, then painstakingly copied out the whole method, as well as the answer. Before breakfast she hurried across to young Tony's and went through it with him, before he set of for school.

"I can understand it, when you tell me," a relieved Tony thanked her.

"That teacher will get nowhere, if he puts his pupils in such a panic," fumed Hannah to George over breakfast,

"I'm glad your brain isn't being wasted, Hannah, I sometimes think I've dragged you away from your true profession."

"I came willingly, George. Anyway, nothing is ever wasted. I'll always find a way to use my brain!!"

They laughed but George felt uneasy, would his Hannah eventually become frustrated with her lot?

By the end of March 1912 Hannah knew she was expecting their first baby. "The doctor says the birth date should be in September," Hannah glowed with anticipation as she broke the news to George. "Hannah, this is wonderful news. Now I really will go for the partnership with Mr Drake, we have real responsibilities ahead. I'll take great care of you my love, you must tell me anything you need." George took Hannah gently into his arms as if she were fragile china.

Hannah laughed at him, "It's not an illness George. I won't break if you touch me! In fact, now I'm over the first few months, I've never felt so well before."

"You do look beautiful, but I'm still going to take special care of you."

"Well, I won't object to that," Hannah laughed and she pressed George's hand against her, over the place where she knew their child was growing.

CHAPTER 32

Jack branches out

No, it wasn't Hannah but young Jack Elkson, who was becoming frustrated. At seventeen years old he wasn't yet sure what he wanted to do with his life, nothing that was on offer in Hartsbeck appealed to him. His main interests were inspired by his time in the St. John's Ambulance Brigade and by sport. He was fascinated in the working of the human body and took seriously the lessons, down at the Ambulance Drill Hall, in the bandaging and dressing of wounds, how to splint broken bones and give first aid in a variety of situations, including the fearful case of a punctured lung. He borrowed books on anatomy and medicine from the public library and poured over them in the evenings and wet afternoons.

All the family were in the St. John's Ambulance Brigade but Jack had gone farther than any of them. He'd already taken the highest certificate in First Aid and Basic Nursing and kept up with any changes in the latest methods of treatment. When there was a town parade or the band was playing in the local park, drawing crowds of people, Jack was the first to volunteer to be on duty and he'd soon become used to treating the ills and accidents of the human body. His cheery grin and competent manner had made him a popular member of the Ambulance corps, with young and old alike. He was no saint and could be mischievous but no patient had ever suffered because of this.

Much to his dad's delight, Jack was in the local cricket team and also played Rugby for the Grasshoppers in Preston in his father's old position of fly half. Dave would sit down with him and talk through the different moves. They would discuss tactics late into the night, always ending with Dave's reminiscences of his finest moments in the game. Jack was the sturdiest among his brothers and confident in his bearing. Sarah was sure it was his long, finely chiselled nose, which gave a strength and maturity to his young face with its full generous lips and straight steady gaze.

Jack's growing strength and intelligence was urging him to do something radically different, something energetic and adventurous. When he unearthed an old newspaper dated 1903 and saw the headline, 'New World, New Life'. His imagination was immediately fired.

The article stated that there were vast tracts of land for sale, in Canada, for the sum of ten dollars for every 160 acres. A settler would gain the freehold of the land after three years, if he'd fenced the land, built a house on it, dug a well, put up a stable and cultivated a certain proportion of it. Of course, in order for him to survive, the settler would have had to complete these demands before the hard frost of the first year.

Jack knew that people had flocked to Canada to buy up plots of land, some alone, some with their families. There must be all kinds of settlements out there by now, ready to offer work for young men and maybe there were still plots of land for sale. In any case there would be all kinds of openings in Canada, maybe in the cities, certainly in the medical schools. A new country would have all kinds of medical needs and he knew there was a university in Montreal.

The more Jack thought about it the more he felt he would have a better chance of doing well in Canada than here in England. Also, there was a girl in Jack's life, Laura, another keen member of the brigade. They had been friends since they were both fifteen and felt completely at home with each other. Her father, a local doctor was one of the instructors at the Drill Hall and without any formal understanding, the two young people constantly sought each other's company and always partnered one another for dances and group outings.

One evening in July, five months before Jack's nineteenth birthday, he was walking home with Laura after being on ambulance duty in the park. During the hot, summer afternoon, they'd worked together over a fainting mother; a man with an attack of angina; a child with sunstroke and a boy with a sprained ankle. Both felt the satisfaction of work well done. Jack took Laura's hand and swung it companionably as they walked,

"Laura, I've a funny feeling we're meant to spend our whole lives together. I haven't had much experience in this but I think of you as part of me," he said, trying to be matter of fact but sounding shy and uncertain.

Laura, a great fan of Jane Austen's novels, had stopped and given him a slow coquettish smile that began with her lips and ended with her eyes laughing into his. She raised her hand affectedly to her cheek and replied teasingly,

"Why, Mr Elkson, I do believe you might be right. I think my feelings for you might possibly reflect your own. My dear, Jack could this possibly be luurve," placing her hand across her bosom, Laura acted a state of acute palpitations. Jack blushed and laughingly, lunged at her. A mock fight had ended with a chaste kiss and then another deeper, tenderer one, which made them realise a new depth in their relationship. They had walked on in silence, holding each other's hands. They began to talk together of Canada and made imaginary plans which became more serious as the year progressed.

The chief obstacle to Jack's dream was finance. He had a little money, invested for him by Granny Jane before she died. It wouldn't be enough but it was a start. Laura didn't have any money of her own as yet.

Their parents were anxious about the growing closeness of the young couple's relationship and constantly advised them to- "Take your time", "don't rush into things", "you've all your lives ahead of you."

Jack knew he had to find a job, any job, and save all the money he could earn, although his conscience told him that he ought to give some to his mother to help with his board. He groaned, it could take him years to save enough.

One night, in early August, Jack was talking with some of the leaders at the Ambulance Drill Hall, about going to Canada. A district officer, Leonard Morris, was visiting them that evening and heard the conversation. As a foreman at the local brick-works Leonard had become a good judge of character and he knew of Jack's reputation in the brigade. He rubbed his chin thoughtfully.

"I read sum-mat last month in the Red Cross News Letter; it was about wanting to send travelling clinics out to Canada,"

Jack was all ears. Leonard went on speaking in his slow thoughtful way.

"Apparently some of these settlements, like you were mentioning Jack, on the prairies and in the mountainous areas farther East, are very isolated. It's difficult to travel the long distances to the nearest town on foot, or horseback, or in horse-drawn vehicles and few of the poorer settlers have motor vehicles. They have real problems if they need a doctor, or other medical aid such as a dentist. Some churches and other charitable organisations have been putting money together to send out fully equipped, horse-drawn caravans with medical expertise on board, to travel around the settlements. They're asking for volunteers from the St. John's Ambulance Brigade and the Red Cross to be part of each team."

He turned and shouted across the room, "Anybody seen a copy of the last Red Cross Newsletter around?"

Somebody found one pinned to the notice board and brought it across. Sure enough there was the article. It ended with a plea for experienced, St. John's Ambulance trained men or women over nineteen years of age, to volunteer to go with the medical teams, for twelve months at a time. Passage and keep would be given by the church charity which was providing the clinics. Just before the end of the twelve months, another team would be sent out to take their place. An added note said that "experience in dentistry would be a valuable asset."

Jack looked across at Laura; she was teaching some of the new cadets at the other end of the hall. His mouth went dry. It wasn't quite the way he'd imagined it and it would be voluntary work, not paid but he would have the passage to Canada and he would be involved with work he loved. Surely if he wanted to, he could stay on after the twelve and find paid employment. He could send for Laura when he was settled, or maybe Laura could be a volunteer and come out with him. It sounded ideal.

"Do you think they'd have me? Would they think me experienced enough? I'll be nineteen on the third of October?"

Leonard looked at him kindly, "I don't know lad, we could always ask. It would be a grand opportunity for you. I tell you what, I'll come home with you now and we'll talk it over with your mother and father."

"Alright," agreed Jack, in a state of semi-shock, "let me tell Laura about it first," He dashed across the hall to where she was engrossed in correcting a cadet's attempt to apply a splint.

"Laura, Len's found something really exciting about Canada, we might be able to go with the brigade. Come over and hear what Len has to say."

Leaving her charges to practise bandaging, a bewildered Laura allowed Jack to pull her across to Len who quickly explained the situation. At first she expressed doubt, then shock and finally a cautious excitement.

"I can hardly believe it! It seems too good to be true. I'll have to think about it before I decide for myself but I think you should go for it Jack, it's just what you need."

Sarah wrote to Ellie in a fine state:

174, Aspen Lane,
Hartsbeck.
August 17th 1912

Dear Ellie,

Such excitement in our little household. Jack has a yearning to go to Canada and it appears that Leonard Morris, a district official from the St. John's Ambulance, has found a way for him to go!

About three weeks ago, Leonard Morris, came home with Jack from the brigade meeting. They both sat down with Mum and Dad for a serious talking session. I was in and out with tea, my ears wagging like nobody's business. They seemed to settle the whole matter there and then. It was decided that Jack should apply to go to Canada, as a St. John's Ambulance volunteer, with some travelling clinics that are being financed by charity. Letters were written and signed by Leonard and Mum and Dad and Jack and posted, two weeks ago. The reply came yesterday, asking Jack to go to Preston for an interview on Monday next. Can you imagine mother and father deciding to let either of us do such a thing so quickly? What it is to be a boy! Although I suppose you were Jack's age, when you went to London but what a fuss that caused!

As soon as he'd read all the information about the clinics and the Canadian settlers' need for dental treatment, Jack went to see Mr Lewis, our dentist. He took Jack very seriously and gave him some books on dentistry to study. He's also allowing Jack to sit in on some of his treatments, with the patient's permission of course! I wouldn't like Jack messing about with my teeth but Jack thinks it will give him a better chance of being accepted, if he can show some understanding of dentistry. Mr Lewis agrees.

Laura McLean is volunteering as well. It's not certain whether they'll be in the same team but it will help them both to have a taste of the land where they dream of settling.

Ellie, do you ever feel that life is going far too fast! I pray every night that God will use each one of us for his glory and for the good of others in the world but then I'm shocked when He seems to be taking me at my word! That sounds very arrogant. I'm sure God has His own plans, without my foolish prayers influencing Him. On that note I'd better finish, before I make a complete fool of myself, which I do very often.

My fondest love to you dearest Ellie; please, please, write soon. Your own Sarah.

Ellie laid down the letter and sighed deeply. She was thankful to hear the news from home and to know she was still inside the family loop but for a moment she felt like an exile. She'd left home, of her own choice, fourteen years ago and her life had changed dramatically. The environment she lived in and her type of work was all so alien from anything her parents and siblings had experienced and she couldn't just visit them on a whim. It seemed to her that all 'those old familiar' places and people were being swept from her on a strong tide.

CHAPTER 33

Thirty and an Exile

Much to Ellie's delight, it was Jack, himself, who wrote to her a few weeks later.

Hartsbeck,
24th August, 1912

Dear Ellie,

"At last," you will be saying, "a letter from Jack. Something out of the ordinary must have happened." And indeed it has, Ellie. I am so excited I can hardly contain myself. I've been accepted, as part of a team of St. John's Ambulance volunteers, to go to Canada with a band of mobile clinics. We embark on October 2nd, from Liverpool and should arrive at Montreal in Canada on 12th October. Then we have to take the Canadian Pacific railway across to Alberta and be ready to roll with the mobile clinics by 29th October. If all goes well and I'm not eaten by wolves or grizzly bears, I should be back in England sometime in November 1913.

Three others from Hartsbeck are going as part of our team; Mrs Freda Sowerby and her husband, Humphrey. They've been married five years and can't have children, so they are really happy to be doing this together. Freda is a qualified nursing sister but because she's married, she can't work officially, as such. As this is a voluntary scheme, she's allowed to join us in her professional capacity. Herbert Sowerby is a motor mechanic, as well as St John's Ambulance trained, so he'll be very useful driving and maintaining the clinic van; although in some areas we've been told we will have to use horses.

I'm pleased about the Sowerby's, for selfish reasons, as the other person on our team is my friend, Laura McLean. I'm over the moon that she's coming; we've been close friends for five years and hate being apart. I think her parents only said 'yes', because the Sowerby's will be there as chaperones. There is a chance Laura and I may decide to marry and settle in Canada at some stage, so this adventure will give us a taste of the life out there. We'll be travelling and sleeping under canvas, most of the time, which should be great fun; although eight or nine months in those conditions, is nothing like a week in a tent, on one of Stephen's expeditions. He recently organised a camping trip to Cartmel Fell, with those of the Hartsbeck NATS who were fools enough to go- that included me of course. Actually, we had a great time. Stephen is a walking encyclopaedia of natural history; birds, plants, geology and creepy-crawlies. Is there any topic, in natural science that he doesn't know something about? Edwin is particularly good on birds. Laura and I were very impressed. Stephen's a lot more fun than an encyclopaedia thank goodness, he'll go to any lengths to hook a specimen. Some of the older ones find him too adventurous, he always leads us off the known paths and we had one or two near mishaps -on the edges of precipices and in deep 'sucking' bogs- to name a few!

George and Hannah's baby is expected in September, hopefully before I leave. I can't believe I'm going to be an uncle and you an auntie. Uncle Jack and Auntie Ellie! Will you be able to come for a holiday about then? I could say goodbye properly to you and you'd be here for the baby. Wouldn't it be great if you were to deliver him or her! We've had some lessons at the Drill Hall on how to deliver a baby, in an emergency, but only using a dummy. I think I could manage it but hope I never have to —I think you do an amazing job, Ellie; you were so brave to go off to London on your own to nurse but by George, we missed you at first and still do. Anyway, you must be very busy. Write soon and tell me if you think I'm a fool. Please ask your friend Dr. Dobson to send me some tips about Canada.

Your ever loving brother,

Jack.

P.S. You might like to know I've been helping Mr Lewis, the dentist, and find it fascinating. He said I can come and train with him, if I want to, when I come back from Canada. It's a good profession- everyone needs a dentist!

Jack's letter took Ellie by surprise and it made her feel old. She was, after all, the eldest of the family. When she left home Jack had only been six years old; Sarah had been nine and Edwin twelve; George must have been fifteen and Stephen sixteen or seventeen. She herself had been Jack's age, eighteen, or had she just gone nineteen? It was hard to remember. Now she was thirty years old.

Ellie's depressed spirits were partly due to her having succumbed, at last, to one of the fevers the nurses had been busy fighting among their patients. As she was normally healthy, well- nourished and hygiene conscious, her bout was a fairly mild one but she'd spent two weeks in the nurses' sick bay. The first week was one of feverish nights and days, with attacks of diarrhoea and vomiting which left her weak and listless. The second week had been filled with hours of sleeping and drinking beef tea and other invalid food delights.

Three other nurses had been in the sick bay with Ellie; one was her friend Louise Walker, who had been so keen to persuade the other nurses about the healing properties of water. This turned into an obsession for Louise, during her illness. She called over and over again for boiled water to drink. Of course cooled, boiled water was all they'd been given during the first week, until they could manage food without violent reactions. After drinking copious amounts, Louise had become paranoid about the quality of the water;

"Has this water been boiled?" she would demand, "are you sure? Where did it come from? Who boiled it? How long has it been boiled for? It should be boiled at least two minutes, longer if possible, but no less."

The little maid who prepared our food and drink, under strict supervision, was reduced to tears by Louise's demands and refused to do it anymore. She had to be replaced.

Louise began to refuse to take the water. Delirious with fever, she had struggled out of bed to the kitchen demanding to boil it herself. She had been far too weak and collapsed, at her first attempt, before reaching the kitchen. The next time she managed to sneak in and boil some water but was trembling so much she spilt it over her legs and had to be treated for scalds. The doctor decided she needed sedating. Once her fever abated, the obsession died down and Louise had laughed at herself, when she heard how she'd behaved.

"I still say drinking plenty of clean water is good for us but I must have gone a bit too far, this time," she'd stared ruefully at her bandaged legs.

Strangely, once they'd recovered, it was Ellie who became almost obsessive about water and its curative powers. She came across accounts of the dramatic water treatments of the 1860's, which some physicians still held in high regard even in the light of more advanced medical discoveries. One article strongly encouraged taking regular water fasts. The individual took a few days' rest, if possible, and ate and drank nothing except copious amounts of water, to cleanse all the internal organs, including the blood. This was supposedly beneficial for: - "rheumatic conditions of the joints including gout; skin conditions; congestive conditions of the respiratory tract; every digestive problem under the sun; problems of a feminine nature and also, could possibly aid the treatment of some forms of cancer and in all cases, will promote a feeling of youthful vigour, having cleansed away the toxins of modern living."

Most of these bodily ills make their presence felt, to some degree, in young women by the age of thirty and although Ellie had escaped anything so serious as cancer, she was conscious of other physical niggles.

The plausible, scientific way in which the article described the natural benefits of water, fed Ellie's imagination. It appealed to her curiosity in all things medical. She had begun to practice its recommendations. Her interest was aroused even more when she'd discovered that the article was written by a member of the Theosophical Society. The author stated that the age-old beliefs in the mystical nature of water and the use of such a pure, natural element, in the treatment of human ills, were in agreement with the theosophist philosophy of life.

Ellie's appetite for theosophy had again been wetted. She'd read all the material she could find by theosophists and whenever she had the time, she'd attended the meetings in Great Russell Street.

She was still searching for a deeper understanding of the suffering and sordidness she came across every day and which were clouding her view of life. The occult flavour of the theosophy meetings and the teachings, drew Ellie to them with a peculiar fascination but they did little to ease the darkness that was creeping over her spirit.

Her nursing colleagues had noticed the debilitating effects upon her, of the water fasts. She would start a two day fast when off duty but it inevitably overlapped into her working hours.

"Ellie, you've got to eat something, you're white as a sheet and thin as a lath. Look how your hands are trembling," her colleague, Agnes Greenwood, told her, as she tucked into her own breakfast of toast, eggs and tea while opposite her, Ellie sipped on a glass of water. The two nurses had begun their training together in 1899 and were happy to be working together again but Agnes was shocked at the change in Ellie from the eager, healthy young woman she'd worked with ten years ago.

"It's a waste of time, if I don't keep it up," snapped Ellie, conscious that her legs seemed like jelly, her head ached and she felt slightly sick.

"Well I think you are losing any of the good effects through sheer energy loss," Agnes snapped back.

When Agnes had gone from the room Ellie had spread a slice of bread with butter and jam and devoured it with a glass of milk. Her body had relaxed with relief and the slight feeling of sickness wore off but she'd felt defeated, she should have been strong enough to resist food until the evening.

As usual, Eliza Fazakerley was the one to raise a corner of the cloud from her friend, starting with an apt quote, as they sat over tea and muffins in their favourite café.

"A young man never considers himself mortal, until he is thirty", or something like that; Charles Lamb, 'Essays of Elia',"

"Good job I'm a woman then," Ellie's response held a bitter note, not lost on her friend.

"Come, come Ellie! Look at me, nearly twice your age and still full of 'joie de vivre'!"

"Hmm, maybe, but there was a time when I thought you were going downhill. It was when we first met, if you remember."

"Yes, I remember. Good friends and a second wind, have made all the difference since then! Not to speak of a few unmentionables, like the Church and resurgence of Faith – there's really nothing quite like it for providing a new lease of life!"

Eliza laughed her lazy, guttural laugh and reaching across gave Ellie a gentle dig. Ellie, however, was in no mood for levity and stared morosely at the tea table.

"I'll become an elderly spinster. My most exciting leisure activity is choosing a different kind of cake in a tea shop,"

Eliza ignored the remark and changed tack.

"What's happened to your young doctor friend? You haven't mentioned him recently."

"Oh, he's still in Oxford. We don't have much opportunity to meet."

Eliza looked thoughtful, "something's happened between you hasn't it? You don't have to tell me but I'm happy to listen if you want me to."

Ellie didn't think there was much point in talking to Eliza about her relationship with Alex.

"There really isn't anything to tell, Eliza." She looked pointedly at the clock, "Oh no! is that the time? I must be going I've a meeting at five. Thank you for tea, Eliza and putting up with my miseries. Take care, my dear friend," she bent down and pecked Eliza on the cheek before leaving.

Eliza stayed where she was in the tea shop, frowning as she watched her young friend hurry away.

"All is not well with Staff Nurse Elkson, Eliza, not well at all. You must think of something." Gathering her things together Eliza set off to walk home, on the way she saw that the door of St. Stephen's church was open and went inside. The quietness and the soft light shone through the stained glass of the arched windows. The altar seemed to gather the light to itself, the shining brass cross and candlesticks silently bearing witness to all that they stood for; Christ in the midst of our sufferings; Christ the light of the world; Christ the friend of sinners; Christ who takes away the sins of the world.

"Have mercy on us all," murmured Eliza as she sank down gratefully on one of the warmly polished wooden pews and bowed her head. Kneeling was difficult for her now but she bowed her head in reverence to the one she had come to love and trust,

"Lord, it's only me again, Eliza," she became aware of a familiar peace enfolding her and the strong sense of someone listening expectantly, she continued.

"It's my friend, Ellie, I'm sure you know what's troubling her, I want to help her but I'm a bit flummoxed and frightened of doing the wrong thing. I've always been one for blundering in with the best of intentions. I blame myself for going with her to that Theosophy Meeting, even though I tried to make her see the cracks in it. I know I've got to let her find her own way but I'm so afraid she'll get badly hurt. All sorts of things are happening in her family too, which is unsettling for her. I can only leave everything in your hands. Please watch over her brothers and sister in Hartsbeck and keep walking with her, Lord, even if she takes dangerous paths, don't leave her on her own, stay with her and if you will Lord, use me to help her before I'm too old."

Eliza sat on in the pew for twenty minutes resting completely in her Lord, as she'd learnt to do over the last few years. When her anxious spirit had calmed down and she felt refreshed, Eliza breathed a word of thanks. Then she made for home, carrying the rich peace of her time in the church with her.

CHAPTER 34

A New Challenge for Ellie

Ellie had left the teashop annoyed with herself for reacting badly to Eliza's mention of Alex Dobson. She hurried on to the five o'clock meeting, which had been called by the Matron of the community nurses.

Ellie and her nursing colleagues listened expectantly as Matron addressed them. She explained to them that the well-known Dr. Frederick Truby King, was planning to return to England in about eight months' time so that he could represent New Zealand at the international 'Child Welfare Conference',

"While he is here, Dr. Truby King is offering to run a course in London based on his child welfare programmes which is becoming known as the 'Mother care Movement.' In New Zealand he has a team of specialist nurses trained according to his methods and he is well known for founding the Royal New Zealand Society for the Health of Women and Children. Since his methods have been adopted in New Zealand, they have experienced a significant fall in the infant mortality rate and natal deaths. His appointment to represent New Zealand at the Child Welfare Conference, speaks volumes for his reputation. We all hope his presentations at the conference will give a very positive impression for the future of the 'Mothercraft' movement."

Matron paused dramatically and glared round at them over her spectacles; they all knew her cautious fascination with Dr. King's ideas. She continued,

"Financially, we can only afford to allow four nurses from this clinic to attend the course; it will run alongside your work here with the Community Clinic. You would attend Dr King's classes for two hours on alternate Tuesdays and Thursdays from 4pm till 6.30pm. There will be nurses and doctors from other medical establishments attending. Remember, you are not obliged to agree with all that Dr. King promotes but it will be extremely valuable for you to train, under such an eminent specialist, in the field of mother craft and child welfare and he has much to teach us. Please sign your name on the notice board if you wish to join the course. You must leave it to our discretion, if there are more than four. Thank you Nurses that will be all. Staff Nurse Elkson may I have a word, please."

Ellie went to the Matron in trepidation,

"I particularly want you to attend this course, Staff Nurse. I feel you will benefit from it. I think that at some time in the future, Dr. King may want to establish a team of specialist nurses here in England to spread his ideas among the mothers. From what I have heard of you, I think you may find this particularly relevant to your calling... You are of course not bound by what I suggest but please think about it positively. You can be assured of a place, if you would like it."

"Thank you Matron. I certainly would like a place on the course. I heard Dr. King lecture when I was in Oxford and have long been an admirer of his work."

"Good, that's settled. All the details are on the notice board; present your-self at the right place at the right time! That will be all, Staff Nurse."

"Thank you, Matron." Ellie walked as far as the door when Matron called her back,

"My dear, there is another reason I think this course would be good for you. I think you need a slight change of direction. I know how you feel about safer child birth for the poor but there is a new and rather vulnerable group of women who need help with child birth and child care. You could even say they need help even more than the poorer members of society who have family and old friends on their doorsteps."

Matron was choosing her words carefully. She needed to per-suade Ellie to visualise the needs of a less impoverished group of women. She had watched Ellie with concern for some time and had seen the gradual decline in her health and spirits. Matron understood the nurses who served under her. She sensed that Ellie lacked a certain toughness of character necessary to deal with the rougher side of society on a daily basis. She realised that Ellie was being emotionally dragged down by the sordidness and recognised the stoic manner adopted to mask the guilt she obviously felt at her own weakness. Staff Nurse Elkson was beginning to buckle under the strain and needed to be rescued from this environment. Matron thought she'd hit on the ideal solution. Trying not to sound as if she was giving a lecture, she spoke to Ellie firmly and with conviction;

"Society has been going through rapid changes in your lifetime. It has become a mobile society. There are many women now who marry, what could be considered, above or below their station. Either by choice or circumstance, they have stepped out of the environment where they were born and brought up. They lose much of the support that environment gave them whether from lower or upper class. You know from your brothers and sister, that young men and women are entering professions, such as the law and accountancy and teaching. Whole groups of people are rising to higher standards of living, newly moneyed people need new housing and people are moving away from their roots and extended families. Young women are starting families away from support of family and friends, they are lonely and isolated and many are frightened and depressed.

Their husbands now have enough money to pay for a short term private midwife- cum- children's nurse to live-in for the births of their children and the first two or three months afterwards. Agencies are being set up with lists of nurses with suitable qualifications and recommendations for this purpose. To my mind, you, Staff Nurse Elkson, would be ideally suited for this. I believe a qualification earned under the tuition of Dr. Truby King would strongly increase your eligibility. I have been asked to look out for nurses suitable for such positions and I am sure this would be your forte."

Matron stopped and waited for Ellie's response. Ellie stood gaping at Matron, she needed time to consider what had been said but it sounded as if she was being offered important work in a new sphere. She felt the challenge and decided to take it,

"I think I could do that, Matron, I can see the problems you speak of and - er –yes, I think this is an area I would find interesting. Thank you. Matron."

Dismissed once again, Ellie hurried away.

Her miseries were evaporating and being replaced by excitement. She felt the inevitability of fate taking hold of her and was amazed at the appearance of this new opportunity so soon after she'd felt her life was going nowhere. Her sister's letter came to mind and she smiled as she whispered, "Dearest Sarah, the tide of life does change very quickly, you are quite right." Her sister's prayers didn't enter her mind.

The next surprise was a letter from Dr. Alex Dobson to say he was returning to London and that he also had been invited to attend Dr. King's course.

"Our paths seem destined to meet yet again, beneath the Truby King star," he wrote and Ellie had felt a warm, youthful surge and thought that perhaps thirty was not so old after all.

CHAPTER 35

Farewell to Jack

Ellie was delighted that she was able to be home for the celebration following the birth of her first nephew. "I am giving you three weeks leave, Nurse Elkson," Matron had been firm, "You have been very run down and although you are recovering well, three weeks at home should build you up to full strength. Plenty of moorland air, my girl. I could do with a few lungs full myself!"

Ellie had laughed, Matron was one of the few people who had a romantic view of Northern England; she had spent holidays in her childhood on her grandparents' farm in the Yorkshire Dales. Too young then to be aware of the privations and hardships, her memory was of idyllic summer days among open moorlands and gorges with waterfalls and narrow rivers foaming over rocky boulders, clean stone cottages and fresh farm food. Most people pictured the area as full of smoky mill towns, spawned haphazardly beneath drab, grey skies. Hartsbeck had both. The town had its quarries; coal mines; mills and smoke but its setting between high, moorland hills and picturesque cloughs and streams, gave it a sense of growing out of a wild and beautiful landscape. Stephen used to say that if you listened carefully, you would here it say, "You are welcome to take what you need of my clay for your bricks, coal for your fires and industries, my water for your cotton mills, my grass for your sheep and cattle, my soil for your crops, my trees and my land for your homes and your leisure. But when you are gone, the scars you have made will soon repair and I shall be as wild and beautiful as ever I was." Ellie smiled at the memory and thanked Matron for allowing her such a long holiday.

"We shall expect to reap the benefits when you come back hale and hearty," was Matron's sharp response.

Ellie had hoped to be home for the birth of George and Hannah's baby, but young Thomas decided to make his appearance on the 6th of September, 1913, two weeks earlier than expected.

It was early evening and the lights of the station had just been lit as Ellie arrived at Hartsbeck on the 19th September. She was over-whelmed by the sight of changed but familiar faces waiting for her. After the first shock of seeing her father's thick, brown hair now thin and white and the lines and wrinkles on her mother's once smooth and bonny face, Ellie quickly recognised the same parents she'd always known and felt a rush of affection at her mother's firm kiss and her father's warm hug.

Edwin was there with a shy young lady on his arm, who he intro-duced as "Miss Annie Reed." Annie's smile of greeting expressed a warm and kindly nature and Ellie was satisfied that if this young woman was his intended, Edwin had chosen well.

Sarah rushed across and kissed Ellie before pushing a handsome young lad forward, "You won't recognise Jack. He's grown a bit since you last saw him, Ellie,"

"Jack! I'd recognise that cheeky grin anywhere. Oh, but it's been so long, you are quite grown up," unable to help herself Ellie put out her arms and embraced her young brother, he hugged her back with a strength that showed no trace of embarrassment.

"Good to see you too, sis," his voice already had the deep tones of a man; Ellie laughed and squeezed his hand.

"Come along now, Edwin and Jack. Take your sister's bags. Act like the gentlemen you're meant to be!"

Ellie smiled and exchanged a glance with Sarah; mother had lost none of her stern manner, especially towards her sons.

They all clambered into a waiting motor taxi, which took them home to Aspen Lane for high tea. After tea, Ellie and Sarah walked up the lane to George and Hannah's house to see baby Thomas.

The whole family enjoyed Ellie's holiday with them. Jack was especially glad that Ellie was home for the farewell party, arranged for Laura, himself and the Sowerby's, at the Ambulance Drill Hall. The Hartsbeck Ambulance corps turned out in force and representatives came from the whole Preston District and even from the main headquarters in London. The families and particular friends of those leaving for Canada, were also invited. There were demonstrations of First Aid and a hilarious comedy sketch of an imaginary incident in Canada, involving a dangerous mountain climb, a river in flood and a talking grizzly bear with an injured tail. All this was followed by a grand feast of pies and sandwiches, trifles, jellies and cakes and gallons of hot tea. Then came the emotional speeches, wishing the adventurers well and reminding them that the honour of the St. John's Ambulance Brigade was at stake.

"I know it is in good hands with the group that has been chosen from Hartsbeck. We promise to take care of each one of them and in spite of grizzly bears, dangerous terrain and swollen rivers, we shall endeavour to bring them home safely at the end of their tour of duty." declared the Brigade Officer from London in an attempt to reassure all those present.

"He'd better make sure they come home safely, or I'll be after him," whispered Dave in Jeannie's ear.

"Shush, behave yourself," Jeannie reddened and glanced round to see if anyone had heard but no-one was looking at them.

Two days later the families trooped down to the railway station to wave the pioneers off on the first stage of their journey. They were to travel to Liverpool and take a steamer to Montreal, from there, they would travel West, into the more remote parts of Canada. Ellie swallowed hard as she watched the bright young faces of Laura and Jack pressed to the window of their carriage. The train creaked into life and Laura's parents and the Elkson family waved hats and handkerchiefs until the train disappeared in a cloud of steam. The folk on the platform were suddenly very quiet.

Dr. McLean was the first to recover. "Now then everyone, I suggest we all repair to the Station Hotel for some medicinal, light refreshment, to lift our spirits."

This was exactly what they did. The ladies took tea or sherry and the gentlemen had whatever they preferred!

Once Jack had gone, Ellie's holiday became quieter and more relaxed. She was able to appreciate just being at home.

During the day when Sarah was teaching and the men folk were at work, Ellie would spend time at number 99, Aspen Lane with Hannah and Thomas.

While Hannah rested, Ellie would wheel Thomas out in his pram both of them enjoying the September sunshine. She would take him up the lane towards the tops for an hour. Often, when she returned, her mother would have walked up from number 174, to join them for a cup of tea. She would bring a freshly baked cake, or scones and home-made jam from the raspberries Edwin grew in the back garden. They chatted about all sorts. In the normal run of things, Hannah and Ellie would probably not have been attracted to each other but because they were now thrown together, they found all sorts of things to interest them about each other. Hannah was intrigued by Ellie's interest in Theosophy,

"It has a lot in common with some of the teachings in Hinduism," mused Hannah, "have you ever read any of the Upanishads, Ellie?"

"No, but I think I've heard that mentioned in one of the Theosophy talks. What are they?"

"Part of the ancient Hindu scriptures. I happen to have a copy of some of them, in translation of course! I'll let you borrow it."

"Thank you, Hannah; I'd be very interested in that."

Although Ellie was known as a bookworm, she was slightly wary of her intellectual sister- in- law's offer. Privately, she thought it could be well over her head and wondered if Hannah was showing off her knowledge. Hannah seemed to realise how it must seem and laughed,

"It sounds as if I'm showing off, but I only know that piece of information because the minister from the New Church came to visit us last week and George was asking him what his church believed. Apparently the New Church borders on Theosophy and he mentioned the Upanishads. He thought I might be interested to read them, whilst I was at home with Thomas. He's leant me a copy. I didn't like to refuse; in any case it's good to broaden one's mind. I'm sure he wouldn't mind me lending it to you, as long as you return it before going back to London."

This gave Ellie a chance to air her knowledge,

"Ah yes. The Swedenborgians. They certainly have angels and auras and astral planes in common with us Theosophists." Ellie brought herself up short, this was the first time she had actually aligned herself with the group. She quickly changed tack, "How did you know that I thought you were showing off a bit?"

"Well didn't you? I'd have thought it if I were you. Nevertheless, I'm supposed to have the second sight! Did you know I'm the seventh child of a seventh child?" Hannah's mouth twitched mischievously

"No. Is that significant?" Ellie was intrigued, and a conversation on old superstitions followed leading on to talk of mediums and spiritualism. This was a part of Theosophy Ellie was tempted to explore next and she tried to draw out her sister-in-law on the subject. Perhaps Hannah was a 'chosen one', in touch with the spiritual beings on other planes. Hannah's conscience pricked her, such ideas were not part of her Christian beliefs. She felt she must find a way to redress the balance.

"Hannah, you do know I really wanted to be at your wedding, don't you? I was hurt when George and mother accused me of throwing the family overboard! They didn't show any understanding of the situation I was in," Ellie looked earnestly at Hannah.

"Well, I understood and so did my sisters. They stuck up for you in front of George. He was just disappointed Ellie and a bit childish. I had a strange dream about you when we were on honey-moon, I felt you were under some kind of threat."

It was at this point that Ellie told the story of the Prosser family. After they'd drunk the brandy-fortified tea Hannah deliberately turned from dark to brighter subjects.

"We did miss you at the wedding, Ellie. There was a lovely atmosphere in the church. George and I both said afterwards, that we felt part of something so much greater than ourselves. Your Sarah sang a solo, I know she has a lovely voice. I'm deaf but her notes even managed to penetrate through to me. I'd read the words she sang beforehand, of course, but it was her faith which shone through, Ellie. You talk about bright angels but Sarah's face shone as she sang. She really believes in God and Jesus Christ and the whole gospel message. She's not a Bible thumper but I would honestly say she loves, not just believes in, but loves God."

"What did she sing?" asked Ellie, hurt that Sarah hadn't told her.

"Oh, nothing out of the ordinary, just a simple setting of the twenty third psalm, the one we all learnt by heart at school,"

"'The Lord's my shepherd, I'll not want. He makes me down to lie—' we always got into trouble at that part. I remember Mr George, our teacher, rapping his cane on the desk- 'there's no pause there, it carries straight on –

'He makes me down to lie in pastures green'.-"

"Yes, our teacher was just the same, the pause had to come before going onto–

'He leadeth me the quiet waters by.' It was all rather confusing."

The two women vied with each other in reciting all the verses of the psalm they'd learnt by heart over twenty years since. When they reached the next to the last verse 'in death's dark vale I fear no ill with thee at hand to guide,'

Ellie sighed "It was having to cope with so many deaths in the hospital that made me turn to Theosophy,"

"We have to find our own ways of coping with death but I'd be careful, Ellie. Some of these strange, esoteric ways of thinking can lead us down very dark and dangerous paths. I think I'd rather go with a tried and well- known guide, like Jesus Christ."

"Maybe," said Ellie "if you can find Him."

"I think you've to let Him find you. Don't let's forget the last verse, 'Surely goodness and mercy shall follow me all the days of my life and I shall dwell in the House of the Lord forever'."

They gabbled out the words quickly, both trying to finish first and ended in girlish giggles. Hannah patted Ellie's hand, "never forget those last words Ellie."

Ellie knew she would always remember this time with Hannah but she pictured those families who didn't seem to be followed by goodness and mercy but by heartache and injustice.

Tom was lying in his pram in the back yard, where they could watch and hear him through the open window. It was at this point that a loud squall announced he was awake and needing attention. Both women made to rise, Ellie automatically looking at her watch.

"Go on Ellie, you see to him, please. I'll have him all the time when you've gone. Play with him, while I sort out his clean clothes. You know where things are if he needs changing. He should last another fifteen minutes, before I need to feed him"

Ellie picked her way through the stone paved kitchen and down the step into the back yard, which was part garden, part storage space. She dipped her head to avoid the clean nappies drying on the washing line, catching whatever sunshine and breeze they could. Tom's face was crumpling again, ready for another loud wail when Ellie surprised him by bending over and tickling him under the chin. He stopped mid wail and regarded her solemnly, Ellie scooped him up in her practised arms and holding him firmly, wandered over to a lilac tree in the corner of the garden. The leaves made shadowy patterns, which entranced Tom and took his attention from the fact that Ellie was not his food ticket. Feeling the warm heaviness of his nappy, Ellie circled the yard, talking softly to the infant until they were back inside and she could remove the offending object, wash him and fold and pin a clean nappy round his tiny form. She couldn't help feeling how different it was to be caring for this child of her own blood. Tom was not a patient, she was not his nurse but his Aunt and for that sole reason she was here, picking him up, playing with him and singing nursery rhymes, as well as changing him. A healthy, responsive baby, and as her own brother's son she loved him. Yes, this time she could allow herself to feel real emotion for a child and something tightly coiled inside her, loosened a little. She embraced this feeling and carried it with her when she returned to London and hugged it to her during the lonely nights.

∾

CHAPTER 36

Edwin and Stephen

In May 1913 Edwin married his sweetheart, Annie Reed and they whisked each other away for a fortnight's honeymoon in Estwick, the hidden village discovered by them after being lost in the mist on Ingleborough six years ago. This time Ellie was home for the wedding having taken three days leave. She'd arrived home Thursday night but had to travel back to London on the Sunday.

Returning home late in the evening after this latest wedding, Jeannie and Dave Elkson had settled down in their fireside chairs for a nightcap:

"Well, lass we haven't done too badly by them have we? George and Edwin happily married and both living only a stone's throw away, a bonnie grandson and another grandchild on the way. Our Ellie well set up in her nursing, Stephen a mining engineer, Sarah a qualified teacher, Jack adventuring in Canada and then coming home to be a dentist."

"George a solicitor and Edwin an accountant. Who would have thought it, Dave, when we moved here from Preston twenty-five years ago! Mind you we've had a lot to thank your mother for. I hope it lasts, I sometimes think it's too good to be true."

"It's worrying that keeps you going lass! Accept it. Aye, mother's been good to us but we've worked hard as well and we've been through some tough times together. I've not always been the best and I'm sorry for that, Jeannie."

"Oh, go on with you, Dave Elkson, you had your reasons for how you were and I've not been the easiest to live with. I reckon we've made a good enough couple."

Stephen, his head muzzy after the wedding festivities had changed into his comfortable, every day tweed jacket and trousers and set off in the cool of the May evening, for a late walk on the tops. His love of nature still filled his leisure time and this year he was President of the Hartsbeck NATS, but tonight he just wanted to think and ignored the usually captivating moths and insects that the hour had brought out. He needed to make a decision concerning his everyday working life. Thanks to Grandma Jane, once he'd finished his apprenticeship he'd been able to go to college and further his studies in science gaining good qualifications. Recently two very different job offers had come his way; one in industry and one in education. Whichever he chose would dictate the rest of his life.

As he strode on up the hill past Oak Farm, Stephen noticed the figures of a youngish man and a woman walking well ahead of him, he hoped it wasn't anyone he knew, he didn't want to socialise with so much on his mind. As they came near to a farm gate Stephen saw the man motion to the woman to stop and together they leant over the gate watching the cattle lying in the field and chewing the cud. The two were talking earnestly and suddenly the man seized the woman by the shoulders and pulled her round to face him, Stephen tensed fearing trouble. The man put his arms round the woman and pulled her towards him and for a moment she leaned against him, her head on his chest. Stephen looked away and moved behind a tree, not wanting to embarrass the couple. He looked back over the way he'd come. After a few minutes heavy booted footsteps came stomping towards him down the hill, they quickly passed him and Stephen watched a red faced and breathless Bert Lee kick open the gate to Oak Farm sending an empty bucket clattering across the farmyard as he went. Stephen continued walking up the hill. Now there was only the lone figure of the woman ahead of him, she was walking slowly her head lifted high as she stared at the scenes opening up around her, a shawl hanging loosely from her shoulders and her long skirts swinging with her strides. It was his sister, Ellie. Stephen caught up with her as she reached the summit of the moor.

"Hey there, sis. Looks like we were both drawn to the tops. Two of a kind, eh?" he didn't mention Bert Lee until he saw Ellie's flushed face and the tears running down her cheeks. "Oh, lassie. Whatever's the matter. Was it that Bert Lee? I couldn't help seeing him with you, though I didn't know it was you 'til now. What's he done to upset you?"

"He hasn't done anything wrong, Stephen. He just thinks he's in love with me and has been since we were children. He asked me to marry him once before, the night I came up here to decide whether to go off to London and be a nurse. I said then that I couldn't but he's just asked me again, he told me he's waited for me all these years," Ellie caught her breath and looked into Stephen's face.

"Well, he's an odd sort of bloke, wrapped up in his farming and doesn't socialise much. Still, he's good with animals; anyone will tell you, they'll send for him first if any animal needs attention. He'll help anyone in trouble too, doesn't matter who it is, if they need him he's there. He'll make a good husband if you want him Ellie, but you'd have to give up your nursing."

"I know that Stephen but I'm sorely tempted. I get such longings for a husband and family of my own when I'm in London. It's worse because I'm working with families all the time and helping to bring their children into the world. Just now, when Bert held me, I felt safe and cherished and wished I could be like that always. Then I thought how far I'd come in my nursing career, I can't give it up now; it means too much to me. I had to refuse him, Stephen. The country can't afford to lose too many trained nurses to marriage. Anyway, the populations growing too fast as it is and I should know," she tried to make light of it but Stephen wasn't fooled. He looked at his sister and recognised her womanliness.

"Hasn't there been anyone in London?" he asked and Ellie shook her head. She didn't tell him about Alex Dobson and suddenly wondered how she would answer Alex, if he asked her to marry him.

"Well it's your life, Ellie but I've always thought it wrong just to see women in the light of becoming wives and mothers. We men have all the choices. We can choose to marry, have a family and still follow our career. You've given a good few years to nursing and no-one would think it amiss if you decided that now was your time to give it up and get married. We'd be glad to have you nearby; but I don't think you'll do that Ellie. I think your call to nursing is too strong and I've known you longer than most."

Ellie took her brother's hand and squeezed it, "I've missed you. It's so good to have you to think things through with just like we used to do. I told Bert I couldn't marry him but was regretting what I'd let go, when you came along. Thanks for being a sounding board."

"I may want you to be the same for me. I came up here tonight to make a decision about my own life. I'd be glad to think aloud about it, to you, if you'll listen. You'll be more objective."

"Of course I'll listen. As long as you're not asking me to help you choose between one or other of your lady friends!" said Ellie.

"No, it's nothing like that." Stephen proceeded to tell her that a year ago he'd qualified as an Associate Member of the Manchester Geological and Mining Society. This had put him in touch with several eminent people in his field and given him opportunities to show his abilities. This year he'd been elected to the Fellowship of the Institution of Mining Engineers. A prestigious and lucrative career could well await him in industry and science but Stephen was unsure how he would fair in the cut and thrust of the wider industrial world.

"Now comes the crux of my dilemma, Ellie. I've been offered two jobs, one as a research scientist with a well-established firm of mining engineers, based in Manchester. This particular industry is going from strength to strength and I know I can make a valuable contribution. It's a well-paid position and could lead me on to higher things."

Ellie couldn't detect any real spark of enthusiasm behind Stephen's words.

"And the other one?" she asked.

Stephen sighed, "The other is less prestigious, in the worldly sense. It's a post on the staff of Blackburn Technical College. I'd start with supervision of the science laboratories with some teaching. Then I would move on to teaching all the sciences full-time, to twelve year olds and upwards and also to adult night classes. The technical college is small and provincial, the pay would be less than in industry and it won't be on the cutting edge of research. But it's where we've come from, Ellie. I feel I need to pass on my love of science to youngsters who'll enjoy it now and make good use of it later. Apart from that, I'd have time to carry on my field-work in geology and such like."

Ellie looked at her brother in admiration. A pragmatist, like herself, he didn't trust in fate. He'd always believed he must forge his own way in life and use his intellect and energy to make things happen. After leaving school and before he went to college, Stephen's further education, like her own, had been mainly self-motivated. Like fledglings in their hunger for knowledge they'd both raided the libraries and local Mechanics Institute for books and joined evening classes. They had found champions in the educated men and women who recognised the eager potential among early school-leavers who'd entered apprenticeships or menial jobs. Some of these teachers had learnt their craft in the melee of developing industries; others were university graduates or from training colleges. They encouraged the young folk to aim higher by furthering their education outside working hours.

"The doorways of science and technology are opening for you, our world is on the verge of change. You need to be ready for it," was the message sent out and grasped by such as Stephen and Ellie.

Alongside the explorations of science, classes in Latin and literature, art and philosophy had been introduced. Education had become the desirable experience following hours in the mill, factory or office.

"Well, I am surprised. I thought you'd have jumped at the industrial position and the chance to get away. You're right to see educating future scientists as important, but you're a true scientist with an exceptional brain, which would be invaluable in industry. Whatever you do, Stephen, don't give way to the fear of leaving the familiar. It's not been easy, but I'm glad I decided to leave home to take up nursing."

Ellie was suddenly filled with absolute certainty that, despite the heartaches, she was right to be going back to London and her career.

Stephen was swayed by her words. "Maybe that's it, I'm too cowardly to leave my cosy provincial world when I could be in Manchester, ensconced in a modern, research laboratory, fitted out with the costliest up-to -date equipment and priceless precision instruments. I'd be working alongside eminent scientists and might even find myself on the verge of some vitally important, scientific discovery. I'm tempted, Ellie but I'm frightened that the industrial world would close round me like a prison. I'd become trapped in its narrow agenda. I need my freedom, Ellie."

"Well, being a teacher is no picnic. Ask Sarah. You'll be teaching the same things, year in year out, except for a few scientific advances. You'd have to be really interested in your pupils. Are you sure you're that kind of person Stephen?"

Stephen told Ellie of the philosophy group he'd recently started in Hartsbeck. The group met in a back street of Hartsbeck in a large comfortable room, which had once been a doctor's surgery. They'd begun by discussing the works of Karl Pearson, a favourite of Stephen. Arguments had become heated over the statement that "man is the maker of natural law." Stephen, as leader had discovered he had a natural talent for holding the reigns and steering the debates through the troubled waters of controversy. From Pearson, the group had progressed to Herbert Spencer's, 'First Principles', with its' exploration of sociology including the idea of a gradual weeding out of inferior specimens of humanity (over many generations) to produce a much improved human race.

"Even our quiet Edwin found his voice after reading 'First Principles' and argued about the differences between the terms 'natural selection' and 'survival of the fittest'"

"I thought those terms came from Charles Darwin?" declared Ellie eager to show off her knowledge.

"Charles Darwin first used 'natural selection' and Spencer coined 'survival of the fittest.' Both men used these terms, in their later works."

Stephen went on to tell Ellie about the time someone in the class brought up that a person who was born deaf, "might be considered, by nature, an inferior specimen".

"Well, I'm not 'appy with that," Vernon Heap had stated angrily, "What would that say about our Len? Born stone deaf and can't speak properly, because he can't hear. But 'es t' best cobbler in all t' district -and t' most liked. 'E's as sweet a nature as you could hope for -and intelligent. All the children like 'im and 'is wife thinks t' sun shines out of 'im; only one of their three children was born deaf, like 'is dad, but 'e's getting along fine."

The discussion had rattled on round the group; "Yes, but you'd have preferred it if your boy hadn't been born deaf, Vernon. Len has made a good job of his life but if nature sees best to weed out such imperfections, gradually like, you wouldn't object, would you?"

Stephen had quickly chipped in with, "I think it's how you overcome these things that says whether you're an inferior specimen or not. It can build a strong character, having to face up to being stone deaf and learning how to cope and be an asset to the community. Len has certainly done all that."

Then another of the group, an elderly man who had taught Len at school and urged him into using his skills as a cobbler had spoken up,

"I agree with that. I know, Vernon, that you and your wife were upset when you realised your boy was deaf but I think that Len has developed a higher attribute, through adapting to his deafness. Maybe nature uses such accidents of birth, to stimulate our own evolution as human beings both materially and spiritually. I've watched Len grow up and seen him mature and it's taught me a lot about human nature and the human spirit. I've also seen the reactions of others to him and how they change for the better as they get to know him and realise his highly developed sense of understanding."

"I've seen this in some of my young patients," said Ellie, thoughtfully.

Stephen reflected silently on the philosophy class of the Hartsbeck Naturalists. It had continued reading and debating week after week and Stephen had learnt when to allow the arguments their head and when to reign them in and guide them to smoother paths of reason. He'd honed this skill to such a fine art that none of the group had seemed to notice his gentle easing of their discussions into a different path when he sensed dangerous waters ahead. He'd been teaching them to look into the ideas of the deepest thinkers of their day and to reason for themselves. On occasions, when religious beliefs and politics had been challenged it had taken Stephen's alert mind and skilful prompting to calm the heated arguments and prevent fisti-cuffs.

"Yes", he said out loud, "I am a teacher, not an industrial research scientist."

Decision made, Stephen tapped out and pocketed his pipe. Jumping from the gate, he threw his cap in the air and caught it with a shout of freedom. He would accept the college post. Ellie laughed and linked his arm in hers. As they walked home, their keen eyes searched for the moths and insects of the evening air. They looked up at the darkening skies and wondered about the moon and the bright planet Venus. Ellie could feel Stephen's child-like surge of excitement at the thought of a whole unfathomable universe to reach into and discover.

"I sometimes think that, if I listened hard enough, I'd hear it speaking to me," he chuckled, "but I suppose that wouldn't be considered scientific."

CHAPTER 37

A picnic at Richmond. 1913

Fourteen years after first coming to London, Ellie was walking with Alex Dobson along the bank of the River Thames from Putney Bridge towards Richmond and reminiscing about the afternoon of her arrival.

"I really wasn't sure that I'd be able to stand it, so far away from home. I missed being able to look up and see the high moors above the town and it was peculiar not being in a place where everybody knew everyone. When I first came out of the station Londoners passed each other like strangers - they were strangers to me and to each other- at least it seemed like that. I know that there are some pockets of close-knit communities but in the main, London does seem full of strangers. Now I find it a relief sometimes, to be able to walk through the crowds and feel anonymous. Do you think I'm odd, Alex, to feel that way?"

"Not at all Ellie, I've often felt that way myself. I kept thinking I'd never get used to not seeing a mountain towering over the city. Every township near Jasper, where I come from, seems to be cradled between mountains. From the centre of Jasper it's only a few minutes' walk to the edge of civilisation and there you are, in the forest, walking down to a remote lakeside at the foot of Old Whistler; that's a mountain, by the way."

"It's sounds awe-inspiring, Alex," Ellie spoke softly and gave Alex a timid glance.

Alex spread out his arms towards the lush, green water-meadows dotted with wild flowers. Bushes and tall leafy trees stood etched against the bluey whiteness of the sky, breaking the flatness of the landscape together with the perfect symmetry of a distant stone bridge across the River Thames.

"This also feeds the soul!" he spoke dramatically, walking along with his head thrown back and his arms swinging. Ellie laughed, she almost expected him to burst into song. It was strange to think it was eleven years since they first met. Ellie had hesitated to accept this invitation to go on a picnic with him alone but she felt so at ease with him, almost as if she was with her brother Stephen. Almost, Ellie reminded herself that she was a mature young woman and Alex was in his mid- thirties and definitely not her brother. Again she felt a slight flutter of disquiet, as she became aware of his youthful look-ing, athletic body.

The young doctor stopped and pointed to an inviting patch of grass underneath a shady tree, close to the river's edge;

"I'm starving. Let's sit down here and have lunch, I could eat a whale, never mind a horse!"

Alex laid out his jacket on the grass and they sat on it together to open the satchels of food they had brought. It was one of those clear warm days in late spring, the sky a pale Nordic blue with a few wispy clouds way up high. Ellie's usually sallow cheeks were pink from enjoyment and the brisk walk in the fresh air. They pooled the food they had brought; crisp buttered bread rolls and cheese, tomatoes, spring onions, two small pork pies, russet apples- Alex's favourite of all the English varieties and two large oranges. Then Alex opened a white cardboard box revealing a perfectly iced chocolate cake with tiny crystallized violets and rose petals. He produced a dark brown bottle, with a white phar-macy label declaring it to be 'Freshly made up Baby Milk Formula for New-borns.'

"As recommended by Dr. Frederick Truby King," he informed her seriously.

"Alex, you wouldn't? You can't have—you idiot!" Alex raised one eyebrow and fixed wide open, serious eyes on Ellie,

"I'm assured it's very good for you. Easy to digest and very nourishing and the taste- we'll just try a drop- it could be just what we need after so much rich food." Alex produced two tin cups from his bag and unscrewing the bottle top, poured liquid into the cups. Ellie couldn't see what he was pouring and he told her to close her eyes while he held the cup to her mouth, she tasted delicately,

"It's stout!!"

"Well, fancy that Nurse! No wonder those new-borns, under your care, are flourishing"

"Get on with you Alexander Dobson. I hope you're not trying to get me tipsy!"

"I wouldn't dare. No its Doctor's orders, you need to relax and unwind. You've been working too hard."

Laughing, Ellie took the cup and sipped the refreshing bitterness. It wasn't the first time she'd tried stout, they gave it to new mothers in the hospital to build up their strength and enrich their breast milk and the young nurses had all tried it, when they went off duty. It was an acquired taste and Ellie didn't mind a very little now and again, but here with Alex she was immediately on her guard. She took her time, pretending to sip the stout slowly and pouring most of it away in the grass, when his head was turned.

It had been while attending Dr. Truby King's teaching sessions that the friendship between Ellie and Alex had grown closer. Thirty six year old Alex had decided he needed experience in English methods of midwifery and family and community health practices. Ellie remembered he'd arrived ten minutes late for the first of Dr. Truby King's classes. She'd caught sight of him peering warily through the lecture theatre door, stooping to disguise his height and smiling foolishly through lazy grey eyes,

"I do apologise for my lateness, Dr. King. My name is Dr. Alex Dobson and I'm mighty glad to be here at last."

"We are glad to have you with us Dr. Dobson. I am relieved that at least one other of the male species, is interested in the trials and tribulations of motherhood and rearing of the young."

A titter had run through the assembled nurses and Alex had quickly folded himself into the empty seat beside Ellie. He'd peered over at her lecture notes.

"You haven't missed much, I'll lend you these afterwards," she'd whispered.

Ellie smiled remembering and watched Alex kneeling on the river bank cutting two slices from the rich chocolate cake and carefully placing a delicate, crystallised violet on her slice.

"It reminds me of you, Ellie. Dark, delicate, slightly brittle, but deliciously beautiful," Alex's eyes smiled deep into Ellie's surprised ones. She'd known him for more than five years and he'd never behaved quite like this to her before. She felt a warning tingle.

"Don't worry little Ellie, I haven't brought you here to ravish you. It's just good to have a pleasant few hours in your company. In any case, there are too many people around who would run to your defence." Alex spoke in a humorously dramatic voice, guessing her thoughts.

Ellie chided herself for her fears. Alex was right; there were plenty of other people around, walking and picnicking. She looked at the mothers and fathers with young children, couples both young and elderly, and groups of friends laughing and teasing each other, some playing ball games or exercising dogs. There was no danger and in any case she knew Alex, it wasn't his way. Ellie relaxed and accepting a refill of stout drank it, this time with enjoyment, as she ate the chocolate cake.

"This is a scrumptious Alex. It must be a 'Fortnum and Mason's' special?"

"I hoped you'd think that, but I bought it at a tiny shop near my digs. I've come to know the shopkeeper and she made it specially; she used to work at Fortnum and Masons and knows a few secrets! I told her about you and she said this would be 'just the ticket'. I'm glad you like it, Ellie,"

Alex's hand brushed gently across Ellie's and very timidly she took his fingers in hers, they sat quietly like this, content in each other, watching the sunlight jumping off the water like drops of crystal.

"I could have gone with my ex- landlady to a Theosophy meeting this afternoon but this is so much better."

Alex frowned, "I'm not happy with this ex-landlady of yours, Ellie. Theosophy seems to me to be devious and dangerous, leading to dark and unpleasant ways. I'm very glad you came with me instead."

Ellie did not reply. The fascination of the strange and the mystical, in Theosophy, still captured her imagination. Still, she didn't want to speak of it now, nothing must spoil this perfect afternoon. The quiet contentment returned and the gliding stillness of the Thames was unbroken until the grand arrival of two white swans followed by their adolescent family of four. The long lanky necks and bodies of the younger birds still wore their untidy, probationer habits of brownish- grey.

"They have such dignity, even the cygnets, the 'ugly ducklings', hold themselves like their parents," mused Ellie.

Alex lent down and placed a soft kiss on her cheek; she trembled, then smiled with pleasure. They gathered up the picnic things and wandered further along the river bank towards Richmond, following the swans. The sky began to show the warning colours of sunset. Alex stopped and turned to face Ellie.

"Ellie, you are becoming very special to me. You have a sense of purpose and vision I haven't seen in other girls. I wish so much we could —"

Ellie's heart yearned towards him. She raised her hand to stop him; "Alex, please -not yet."

"Oh Ellie, why not?"

Ellie waited a moment before she spoke, "We're both at the beginning of our careers and we don't know where they will take us. We might hold each other back. You know the rules about nurses not marrying, or even being engaged. I've worked so hard and given up such a lot, to come this far. I must do more. I don't want the distraction of an emotional attachment. Let's carry on as good friends and see what happens."

Ellie wanted to add that Alex was special to her as well. Caution, as usual, held her back.

"Not ready for an emotional attachment?" Alex mimicked Ellie's voice but adding a cruel twist to the tone.

"You sound like one of those romantic novels you women dote on," his face hardened with anger and disappointment; then he saw Ellie's pert little face with its serious intentness and his anger left him.

"I'm not sure I want to be just good friends, little Ellie, but I will try. We'll work alongside each other and we'll enjoy London together and see where all our small adventures take us," the young man sighed deeply.

"That will be good," Ellie searched Alex's eyes and saw his frustration, she took his arm and they walked on in silence. Ellie continued to argue with herself. She knew that she may soon be asked to join the group of Dr King's special nurses, trained to use the 'Truby King' methods. This meant she could be sent anywhere in the country, for months at a time. She felt uneasy about life in general, there were so many people out of work and their children suffering the effects of poverty. She wanted to be available to use her skills for them. Also, there were rumours of unrest in Europe. The newspapers talked of possible war involving the British yet again. Ellie remembered Miss Nightingale's challenges in the Crimea and thought to herself that, if war did come again, nurses would be needed on the battle front.

They'd reached the entrance to Kew Gardens, where they were able to catch a motorbus back to Earls Court. Both felt tired and slightly befuddled. Alex escorted Ellie to the nurses' hostel, dropped a quick kiss on her cheek and said goodnight. Ellie went to her room, undressed, lay on her bed and cried herself to sleep.

She was woken hours later by the clatter of feet as nurses rushed to breakfast. Feeling surprisingly refreshed, Ellie washed and dressed, eager to begin work. Thinking of the previous day, she hoped her response to Alex's proposal hadn't destroyed their friendship. It hadn't. At the next class with Dr. Truby King, Alex was his usual friendly self and they arranged to meet and celebrate after the final session.

CHAPTER 38

Ellie and Dr. Truby King

After the final session and having passed, with distinction, the practical, written and oral exams set by Dr. King, Ellie received a summons to appear before the great doctor. Entering his room, fresh and neat in her newly ironed uniform and the cap of a Senior Staff Nurse, Ellie felt a new confidence in herself which was not lost on Matron who was also present. Matron opened the conversation by introducing Ellie formally,

"Dr King, this is Senior Staff Nurse Elkson, who, you will remember, has just passed your course on Mother and Child Welfare."

"Yes, yes, indeed I remember you. Good morning, Staff Nurse. I trust you didn't find my lectures too mundane, or too controversial," the doctor bowed formally to Ellie.

"Good morning Dr. King. I found your course interesting and extremely helpful, thank you, sir."

"Hmm. You worked alongside that Canadian doctor, Alex Dobson. Would there be any serious attachment between you?"

Matron's eyebrows shot upwards and Ellie was thankful to be able to answer truthfully.

"No, we've become friends through our common interests in medicine and child care but we have no serious intentions."

"Hmm; seems a pity. Still, that may be good news for me. Are you quite sure there is no deeper feeling between you?" The doctor seemed unwilling to let the matter drop and Ellie was puzzled, maybe they'd been seen by the river. She decided she must be honest.

"Dr Dobson and I came to know each other at Doxlee hospital, in Oxford, where I was a staff nurse on the children's orthopaedic ward. It was there, through Dr Dobson, that I first heard you speak, when you came to give a lecture at Doxlee. Dr Dobson and I were drawn to each other because we were both new to the south of England. I came here from Lancashire on my own and he came alone from Canada. Recently Dr Dobson and I discussed our future together and marriage was mentioned. We both decided our work was more important to us. I've worked hard to become a senior staff nurse and been privileged to enter the particular sphere of nursing which is important to me. I am adamant that I want to go forward in my nursing career and not waste what I have achieved so far. Marriage for me is out of the question."

Ellie thought how meagre her achievements must appear to Dr. King and hoped she didn't sound self-important and boastful. She found herself praying silently, "dear God let him believe me; make him take me seriously."

"Good. I could see that you and Dr. Dobson were very much at ease with each other. I'm glad you've been so honest. The fact is, Staff Nurse Elkson that I want to set up a team of nurses, here in England, similar to my team of Plunket Nurses in New Zealand. The name 'Plunket' comes from their chief sponsor, Lady Plunket. I have no idea what name they will be given here! These nurses will be responsible for the well-being of pre and post-natal mothers and babies, in their own family homes. My nurses are expected to include the whole family, father and siblings as well as the mother, in the nurture of a new infant. They will be required to introduce the family to the methods of child-rearing which you learnt about on my course.

As you know, I have already proved these methods to be beneficial in New Zealand. Not only have they brought about a massive decrease in the infant mortality rate there, but they've improved the physical and mental well-being of mothers. This is essential, if women are to bring up their children with strong characters as well as bodies.

In New Zealand, my Plunket Nurses run community centres and mobile clinics as well as leading campaigns for the immunisation of children against some of the worst disabling and killer diseases. I envisage my nurses as an army on active service, working against all that threatens the health of nations."

Dr. King strode about the room as he spoke his hands gripped behind his back his large head nodding rhythmically to emphasise his words. Matron and Ellie seemed almost forgotten.

Suddenly he stopped and turned, staring down at Ellie, his strong chin jutting towards her. She tingled at the determined line of his tightly closed lips and the sharp bristles of his thin moustache and looked upwards straight into his large, compellingly eyes. She saw such a depth of anguish in them, such a huge reservoir of controlled compassion, anger, longing and a questioning intelligence. What beautiful or terrible sights had he seen through those heavy, dog-like eyes? What visions did he have, waiting to be fulfilled? A fragment of the doctor's passion entered Ellie and she told herself that she would give her all, in order to be part of this great man's work.

"So, Staff Nurse Elkson, will you be part of my British team of Nurses. Do you have sufficient confidence in me and what you have learnt of my methods, to spread my message among the families of this land?"

Ellie had no hesitation. She wondered, briefly, if the doctor had hypnotised her. She forgot any misgivings she had about some of his methods and clearing a croak from her voice, spoke up clearly;

"Thank you, Sir. I would deem it a privilege to become one of your nurses,"

Matron frowned and pressed her lips together. Ellie could tell she was uneasy.

"Perhaps we should give Staff Nurse Elkson a little time to think about your proposition," she said "Shall we say that she will let you know in writing, a week from today. There may be other positions she would wish to consider."

"Ah, ever cautious of your chargelings, Matron. You are quite right, of course. I am so anxious for my cause that I tend to forget the wider picture. I wouldn't wish to poach upon your nursing staff. By all means, a week from today, in writing. I shall wait in anticipation, Staff Nurse Elkson. I suspect that may soon be Sister Elkson." he raised an eyebrow as he bowed towards her.

Ellie felt both irritation and gratitude at Matron's intervention. She said goodbye to Dr King and walked away from the interview. It had contained the trace of a theosophist, spiritualist meeting and once the spell was broken, she found the waters of her inner spirit troubled. She chuckled to herself thinking that theosophy had begun to colour her thinking.

The following week was filled with much private soul- searching; endless tea and talk with Eliza; discussions with Alex and cautionary talks from Matron.

After six days Ellie wrote to Dr. King confirming her acceptance to his proposition. Within two months Ellie was on a list of privately- employed nurses, pledged to use and spread the 'Mother and Child Care' methods of Dr. Truby King. The whole enterprise was funded from the private means of wealthy supporters, some from the aristocracy. Groups of Dr King's nurses were placed strategically throughout the country.

Ellie had wondered if she would be sent to Lancashire but found she was to stay in London. She was ensconced with three other nurses, in living accommodation in a delightful Georgian terraced house in Felix Square. The four women, Lettie Parrish, Polly Kent, Bernadette Lowther and Ellie, all arrived on the same afternoon. They had the luxury of a bedroom each and after depositing their belongings, they gathered round the kitchen table with a large pot of tea and a tin of biscuits which had been left for them with a welcome note together with a container of fresh milk in an intriguing cooling device.

"I feel like a kept woman!" said Lettie Parrish, a small, freckle-faced twenty six year old who looked no more than seventeen. With her straight, sandy- coloured hair cut in an attractive bob and her steady light- green eyes, she appeared elf-like and Ellie soon discovered Lettie's manner had an immediate, calming effect on people.

Polly and Bernadette were in their late thirties and were old friends from their probationer days. Both were competent and experienced nurses and midwives.

Polly was also an excellent cook, "I'll cook for us when we're all at home to begin with but you'll have to learn to take your turns. I'm willing to show you if you don't know how!"

"Well that's a grand offer, thanks Polly! I say that those who don't cook wash up and clean," Lettie was relieved, cooking was not her forte.

"I'll fit in, wherever I'm most needed. I'm the eldest of nine children, so I can put my hand to most things domestic," said the strong, large-boned Bernadette.

"I'll take my turn at anything as well; I'm eldest of six," declared Ellie, hoping she could fit in with these open, friendly women. She felt awkward and reserved but they didn't seem to notice and the four of them soon settled into a comfortable routine. Lettie's soft accent reminded Ellie of someone;

"Where do you come from Lettie? Your accent is familiar to me but I can't place it."

"Norfolk, where we speak with the sea creatures," teased Lettie.

"Of course; my brother's wife comes from Norfolk and my grandfather. My grandfather was full of legends of the sea-folk."

"I keep my mermaid's tail well hidden, but watch out when the moon is full," Lettie spoke in a deeply sinister tone. Polly pretended to shiver in her shoes and threw a cushion at Lettie. Bernadette gave a loud laugh, "You remind me of my Irish grannie, with her tales of banshees and hobgoblins."

Ellie was content, home life was going to be relaxed, with these three companions.

Their nursing agency provided them with names and addresses of families who'd booked their services. The four young women divided the clients between them. For the initial visit they went in pairs to the homes of the expectant mothers to assess them in the first stages of pregnancy. From there, one of the pair took charge of the particular family and instructed them in the Truby King methods. The people who approached the agency were mainly from educated, middle class families, who had researched and chosen to employ Dr King's methods. They already understood that fathers and other members of the family had to be involved. This did mean several evening visits, when the fathers were home from work. Two weeks before the mother's expected delivery date, the appointed nurse would take up residence in the home of the family and stay there until the baby was at least a month old. Afterwards, there would be regular visits until the infant was fully weaned. The family paid for the privilege.

Ellie and her two colleagues soon became engaged with families within a radius of twenty miles of Chelsea. As Matron had hoped, Ellie found that working in this middle class environment helped her regain her equilibrium. Her days were more predictable, the homes she visited were orderly, if a little boring. It was exactly what she needed to heal the frayed edges of her mind and personality. There was just enough excitement in the inevitable ups and downs of individual cases to keep her satisfied and engaged in her job.

Even Eliza took advantage of Ellie's knowledge of the increasingly popular Dr Truby King and invited her to speak about his methods to St. Stephen's 'Mothers Union'. Eliza had told Ellie excitedly that their branch leader had told them of a letter from her sister in New Zealand.

"Apparently, Lady Plunket addressed a Mothers' Union meeting in New Zealand, praising them for upholding the sanctity and responsibility of marriage. It appears your Dr King stresses the responsibility of both parents in the training of their offspring, in moral as well as physical health. The Mothers' Union is also working with this precept, so they're eager to hear more. Please say you'll come and give them a talk about it, Ellie?"

"Well, yes. Anything for the cause. Thank you for asking me Eliza. I don't know how good I'll be at public speaking but I do know my subject."

"That's the main thing, Ellie. Oh and the Mothers' Union do stress that the spiritual nurture of children is equally as important as the physical. They include prayer and a Christian way of life in the home as essential, for their own beliefs. They take God, very seriously, into the equation. Please, don't let any of your strange, religious ideas, creep into your talk!"

"I was an Anglican long enough to know the Mothers' Union, Eliza, but I'm no Lady Plunket," gasped Ellie mentally reeling at Eliza's instructions.

"No, you're more authentic; working on the ground so to speak. You are working amongst all sorts of families, in their homes. You'll find our group, at St. Stephen's, a grand bunch; women of all classes, meeting and praying together and very much concerned about children and families."

Ellie was persuaded. She delivered a well- balanced presentation of Dr King's ideas to the members of St. Stephen's branch. As she enumerated and elaborated upon Dr King's twelve essentials for the raising of healthy infants:- "Air and sunshine; water; food; clothing; bathing; muscular exercise and sensory stimulation; warmth; regularity; cleanliness; mothering; management; rest and sleep; Ellie was able to use examples from her experience with children who had not received all these things. She described some of the rickets' cases from Doxlee and it came home to her more forcibly, how revolutionary some of Dr King's essentials actually were. She spoke of the importance Dr King placed on breast feeding and his breast-milk substitutes for non-lactating mothers. She didn't flinch from describing the strict regime of non-cuddling and feeding only by the clock and not on demand and leaving baby to sleep or cry in between feeds or cleansing. "Dr. King believes this helps to strengthen the child's character," she declared.

Afterwards, Ellie was surprised at the lively debate engendered by her talk. The astute questions alerted her to the fact that the rigidity of certain of her mentor's rules aroused suspicion and even enmity.

"I am a mother of six children and each one of them is different in temperament and even regarding robustness of health. If I'd followed Dr Truby King's rules to the letter, three or four of my children may have benefitted but at least two of them would have become nervous wrecks."

Another older woman joined in, "If I simply took care of my children's functional processes and those strictly by the clock and not according to their individual needs, I feel I would be denying them their individuality. Such treatment may even break a child's spirit."

"Staff Nurse Elkson, you may not have experienced motherhood yourself but you had a mother. Do you not recognise the bond of love which needs to be nurtured by cuddling our babies and allowing them to be very much in our presence and with the rest of the family, in their earliest days."

"Indeed I do," remonstrated Ellie," Dr King's methods recognise this but he simply says that the time you give to your baby must be regulated. You must realise that Dr King is looking at all sorts of conditions of family life, not only those of good, educated, Christian homes, such as your own. His methods are helping to lift poorer families out of the trap of mal-nutrition and disease; he is working hard to bring down infant mortality rates and the early death of worn-out mothers. His 'by the clock' regime gives mother time to rest and to produce a better quality of milk. No child- rearing method is perfect, or tailor- made to every child but we need to find ways to rear a healthy nation, for the future."

"The hand that rocks the cradle rules the world, as our founder, Mary Sumner, said". The enrolling member, as the group's leader was called, stood to gather the thoughts of the members together as she thanked Ellie and drew the meeting to a close.

"Thank you Staff Nurse Elkson, for giving up your time to speak to us about this all important topic. You have opened our eyes and given us much food for thought. It's exciting to live in a time when child-rearing has such an important place in the world's eyes. In our prayers we must commit our children and the families of the whole world to God and ask Him to guide us and be alongside us in our ever -day lives. Ladies, let us pray."

The meeting had ended with prayers followed by tea and cake before Ellie could escape, with her own eyes opened to a deeper understanding of motherhood.

Late in November, 1913 a letter had arrived from Jack,

174, Aspen Lane,
Hartsbeck

"Dear Ellie,
I have returned from the most amazing time in Canada. Our project was
successful and very much needed. Laura and I were awed by the beauty and
immensity of Canada and shared times of tragedy and joy with the people we
met. Laura and I have become engaged to be married, *but we shall wait a*
while until I am established in my dental training. She is the most wonderful
young woman, full of compassion and inner strength, which came to the fore
in our Canadian experiences. When you come home, we'll tell you of some of
them.
Our love to you,
Jack (and Laura).

For a moment Ellie regretted her refusal to become engaged to
Alex Dobson, her own Canadian experience, but the satisfaction she
found in her work soon quietened such thoughts.

It was providential that Ellie was able to enjoy this time of regular, satisfying employment, with amicable colleagues. Within ten
months the families of England and the World were to face challenges they had not dreamt of, as the storm of the Great War swept,
without mercy, into their lives.

PART FIVE

1914-1919. THE ELKSONS AND THE GREAT WAR

CHAPTER 39

Jack and Edwin march away.

On the seventh of August, nineteen hundred and fourteen, Dave and Jeannie Elkson were standing among a crowd of people near the entrance to Hartsbeck Railway Station.

"We'll never see them over all these people," moaned Jeannie.

"More to the point, they won't be able to see us!" muttered Dave. "Come on, we'll go higher up that bank." Seizing Jeannie's hand he dragged her across the road and up the embankment overlooking the station entrance.

"But Dave, we won't be able to touch them, or say goodbye properly from here," Jeannie sobbed.

"Come on, lass, we've done that already. We'd never get near enough to them today wherever we were but they'll see us clearly if they look up and I'll holler loud enough to make them hear, don't you fret."

"Don't holler, Dave. Everyone's so quiet today. It'd show Edwin and Jack up,"

"Aye, you're right. Yesterday, when the territorials left to join the East Lancs. Battalion, you couldn't hear yourself think, for the cheering and stamping of the crowds."

"It's different when a hundred men of the St. John's Ambulance set off to the war. It brings home to everyone that there'll be dead and wounded to be seen to; these men aren't going to fight for glory but to pick up the pieces of our fighting lads. Eeh look, Dave, I can see right down the street to the Drill Hall from here. I can see our Sarah, George and Stephen and there's Becky Nelson and Laura, all in their St. John's uniforms, standing along the curb. They stand so straight, I can't bear it, I'm that proud of them all."

As they watched from their high viewpoint, the couple saw a column of men in black and white St. John's Ambulance uniform, march smartly out of the Drill Hall and along the street towards them. The crowd which had collected to see them off was large but silent. Men and boys took off their hats to them as they passed and women either bowed their heads, or gave them steady looks, as if trying to instil strength and courage and healing powers into these young men. The lads were looking surreptitiously into the crowd as they passed, searching for the faces of family and friends. Jack flashed his wide mischievous grin over at Laura and his brothers and sister; he followed it with a solemn salute. Their personal good-byes had been said earlier at home. No tears had been shed, just strong hugs full of meaning and promises to write. Laura was wearing Jack's engagement ring and their lingering embrace spoke of future hopes.

Edwin had eyes only for his young wife, Annie. They exchanged a tender look as he passed her, and then Edwin fixed his eyes on the man in front and marched on with a steady tramp. Last night the young newly-weds had made love slowly and gently, afterwards Edwin had held his small wife close to him in their bed. All night long he'd held her and when she'd woken she was still wrapped in his arms. She'd crept downstairs and made tea for them both. They'd drunk it and had lain together, savouring the last few moments of peace and warmth. As Edwin washed and dressed, Annie hadn't said much. She'd just made sure he had all he needed and had comforted him in all the wifely ways she could, making him a good breakfast and ironing his last minute items. Finally, she'd helped him into his tunic, brushing it down and handing him his cap. Standing back to look at him, she'd spoken in her soft Norfolk accent:

"You'll be alright lad; you'll come back to us. I know it. You'll have a lot to do out there and I know you'll do your best. Remember I love you Eddie Elkson, God go with you, my dearest," as reached up her face and they kissed quickly on the lips. The blood of Norfolk seafarers was in Annie's veins and she'd said her farewells as many a sailor's and fisherman's wife, among her ancestors, had done before and she felt their strength within her.

All Edwin could say was, "I love you Annie, take care of yourself. God keep you safe." Then he'd left the house to go across the road to pick up Jack, at number 174. They'd left together through the back door walking through the small garden. Edwin had stopped by the sycamore tree, planted on his tenth birthday. He'd rubbed his hand up and down the strong trunk.

"Remember when we planted this Jack? No, of course not. You were only just toddling. It was a grand evening, mum and dad and us six children enjoying it together."

Jack stopped thoughtfully and took out his pen knife, "Let's carve our initials on it, Eddie. Who knows if we'll ever come back?"

Jack had carved a deep J.E. as high up as he could reach and Edwin had carved E.E. next to it and the year, 1914, underneath. Then, slapping each other on the back and grinning like naughty school boys, they'd shouldered their kit and set off for the Drill Hall, swinging over the cobbles of the back street. Eddie had fixed in his mind on the weeds growing between the stone sets, the red-seeded sorrel; the pineapple weed with its domed greenish-yellow flower-heads; the tufted grasses and the tiny, flat flowers of the green and brown mosses; all pushing their way up between each cobblestone. He'd thought, how strong their life force must be for them to grow in such conditions.

The march through the town seemed endless. Suddenly, as if at a signal, Jack raised his head as the column of men approached the railway station and his eye caught sight of an elderly couple, frantically waving white handkerchiefs.

"Mum and Dad. There, up there, Eddie -on the embankment," he whispered sideways to his brother. Jack bit his lip hard as it threatened to tremble. He raised his hand in a firm salute while flashing his parents a strong solemn look, followed by a cheeky grin.

"I love you both," he mouthed.

Edwin looked up and gave his gentle smile and kept looking at his parents till he was forced to turn away and march into the station. Dave, watching them go, couldn't help speaking out loud but he didn't shout;

"We love you too, my bonnie lads. Keep safe, God bless you and give you courage."

"God go with you, Edwin and with you Jack," whispered Jeannie standing ramrod straight as she smiled and waved. Her free hand fiercely gripped a nearby railing as her knees began to tremble.

As soon as the boys were out of sight, Jeannie and Dave stumbled down from the bank and waited near the station entrance. They could hear the sonorous voice of the Padre saying a prayer, then came a united 'Amen', followed by the sound of men boarding the train and doors slamming. A whistle blew and they heard the train draw away with a long hiss of steam. The couple stood there, not wanting to move until the last metallic chug of the train had died away. It was here that Stephen and George found them and the family walked slowly home to Aspen Lane, cold and subdued, despite the warmth of the August morning.

The train had been specially commissioned to take companies of ambulance men from four local Lancashire mill towns to Netley Military Hospital, Southampton, for further training before being deployed elsewhere. Laura tried to cheer up Jeannie, by reminding her that Jack and Edwin would be coming home for a short leave before they were sent anywhere abroad. The young woman's cheery prattle kept at bay her own desperate sadness, at her fiancé's departure.

"In any case, they may keep them at the Military Hospital in Southampton for the duration of the war," she continued.

Dave thought the latter highly unlikely, given his youngest son's age, his experience in Canada and his healthy constitution but he kept this to himself. Maybe Edwin would stay at Netley. Jeannie pretended to be comforted by Laura's words and squeezed the girl's hand,

"You're a grand lass, Laura. God willing, he'll be back for you!" and she went to help Sarah who was heating a pan of lamb broth on the hob.

"To put a bit of heart in us," she said but her face was turned to the stove and Jeannie caught the sight of tears on her daughter's cheeks. Hannah hadn't joined, them she was expected to give birth to her second child any day and had stayed at home resting with young Tom and their latest young Irish maid –in- training, Cecilia-Ann.

Jack was to remain at Netley Hospital until the summer of the following year. Edwin a little longer. When they'd arrived at Netley, on the evening of the 7th August, it had been just after sunset. The flag lowering ceremony, with its sounding of the Last Post, was ending. Hearing it, the weary arrivals knew, without a doubt, that they were now part of the military. They stared at the hospital buildings;

"Flippin' heck, Jack! It looks like a palace, not a hospital! Just look at the size of it and the architecture. Look at the stone carving."

The new arrivals were stunned into silence by awe and weariness. Edwin thought he must be dreaming. The building stretched on and on in perfect symmetry, its regimented rows of windows softened by the stone arches containing them. Classical porticos, domes and towers suggested they had arrived at some great emperor's residence. Inside was daunting in a different way. The hospital was known for its long dark wards and corridors, bad design and poor ventilation. For the first time the young recruits breathed in its' lingering, distinctively unpleasant smell. They were taken to a huge dining area and given a meal before being shown to their rather Spartan, dormitory-style sleeping quarters.

The following day the lads from Lancashire were told that their first task, was to help in the erecting and equipping of a special temporary unit, in the grounds of the hospital. This was essential to provide extra training facilities and extra space for war casualties. When that was finished they would start their special military medical training, which would equip them for their duties on the battlefield and for nursing casualties that had been shipped home. After this briefing the lads stood in line for the inevitable personal medical inspections, including the measuring and weighing of each man.

"Don't like this," muttered Ernie Bradshaw who had come out of his father's undertaking business to join the army medical corps, "makes me think of my own job back home, measuring and weighing!"

Jack gave a macabre chuckle, "this way to the shroud department, sirs, we offer a very nice line in khaki. One colour suits all."

"Shut it, Jack. I'm shitting me pants as it is and we haven't done ought yet," hissed Jed Cartwright, their old school friend.

"Silence in the ranks!" a haughty officer's voice rang out and the lads shuffled on in the line.

There followed weeks of preparing and stocking the prefab hospital extension. Then came weeks of medical training, followed by weeks of army training in the wilder areas of Hampshire and Wiltshire. They were given practice after practice of treating and evacuating casualties under fire, through mud and water, over rocky, flat or hilly terrain, with or without cover. Edwin gave thanks for the experience of his escapades with the Hartsbeck Naturalists and from Stephen's unorthodox camping and exploring expeditions. Jack had his tough Canadian adventures to help back him up and though younger, showed a greater aptitude for leadership than Edwin.

CHAPTER 40

Ellie and Netley Military Hospital

Despite being engrossed in her new job, Ellie's thoughts were never far from Jack and Edwin. The war in Europe had already encroached upon her own work. Many of her young mothers were now facing their child-bearing without their husbands. She wondered about Hannah, who'd given birth to a little girl, Rebecca, on the twelfth of August and whether George would soon have to go to war. Or maybe he'd already gone. By December of 1914 Ellie felt she was losing touch with them all, she wasn't even sure whether Jack and Edwin had been posted abroad or were still at Netley. Christmas messages arrived to re-assure her that George was still at home and the two boys were still at Netley. In late January, 1915, a letter from Jack arrived which she opened with apprehension.

Netley Military Hospital
28ᵗʰ January 1915

Dearest Ellie,

You will know that Eddie and I are based, for the time being, at Netley Military Hospital in Hampshire. Since our arrival, last August, to a quiet, almost empty hospital—it's become like a body- repair factory. Ship loads of wounded men arrive daily from France.

Three trains a day carry the wounded to us from Southampton Docks. The alarm is given as soon as the trains are due and everyone rushes to help with the disembarking of stretchers and the walking wounded. We were all fed up, at having to help put up an extra pre-fab extension to the hospital when we first came here – but by Jove, Ellie, we'd be lost without it now!

The injuries are horrible, limbs lost, chest and head wounds and injuries to every other conceivable part of a man's anatomy. On top of that there are the results of gas attacks, blindness and damage to everything respiratory. You can imagine the affect all this has on the men mentally, across the board, be they Officers or men from the ranks. Some are entirely broken in spirit. Others seem to be able to lift themselves above it and joke and sing, jollying us all along, which is a good thing as some of us will soon be going out there. We hear terrible tales of conditions at the front and know that we are desperately needed.

The more of us that are sent to the front, the more replacements we need here. Ellie, you are a fully- trained nurse. Please, please, just come and visit us here. I'm sure when you see what's happening you will feel you must give your services to help in this awful situation. It can't last for ever and when it's all over, you would be able to go back to your mother and baby work. Please come and help us and persuade your nursing friends, we are desperate.

Your ever loving, brother, Jack. xx

Ellie was dumb-struck. Torn between the needs of her lonely mothers, whose husbands were now being torn from them into the war and Jack's heart-rending pleas.

However, in February she went to visit Jack and Edwin and having assessed the situation went straight to the Nursing Agency which employed her and discussed the possibility of her leaving to join the nurses of the RAMC for the duration of the war. The agency tried their best to persuade her to stay, she was curtly reminded that wartime always produced more pregnancies and that "the safe delivery of these babies and the welfare of their mothers are essential."

Thinking of the situation at Netley, Ellie was insistent and the agency allowed her to go. They also generously promised to keep her name on their books, if she wanted to come back, after or during the war. Lettie Parrish was allowed to do the same. Polly and Bernadette stayed on as part of Dr. King's team.

"Somebody's got to keep the home-fires burning, and help bring new generations into the world," they declared cheerily, "but you are both doing the right thing. We'll keep your places warm and make sure our boys have healthy wives and off-spring to come back to."

Polly knew she no longer had the stamina for the rigours of military nursing, in the scale this war required. Bernadette could see the increasing need for midwives at home. They would do their bit with those who needed them here and free others to serve the armed forces.

Ellie and Lettie were both appointed to Netley Hospital where, because of their qualifications, they were each made Senior Staff Nurses. As they were trained as civilian and not military nurses, they were not appointed Sisters. It was hard and gruelling work and the two women found a difference from civilian nursing. For one thing they were often in predicaments where they had to administer emergency treatment which, in a civilian hospital, would not have been considered without a doctor present. Ellie and Lettie rose well to these occasions. Their work as midwives had often put them in emergency situations where they'd had to cope without a doctor.

They were warned that at any time they may be sent to the front and were given classes in medical care on the battle field. There was a camaraderie in the shared horror, filling them with a steely determination to nurse these men through it all, for better or for worse. Patients and medics became part of the same team.

Apart from the horror, there was the lively mischievousness of many of the lads as they recovered. There were periods of blessed quietness, as soldiers began to relax and draw breath from the mayhem of battle, even though some of them knew they would be returning to the front.

There were visits to the wounded from family and loved ones. This was where Ellie saw the military chaplains come into their own. They were always on duty, recognisable by their clerical collars, ready to be approached, ready with a listening ear and a comforting shoulder to cry on.

They held regular services and prayer times in the chapel and made themselves useful around the hospital but never pushed themselves into situations, unless it was appropriate.

One afternoon, Ellie, busy with a patient, noticed a poorly dressed young woman of about nineteen or twenty come onto the ward, searching for her young man. The girl was obviously pregnant and unwell. A nurse guided her towards a soldier called Harry who lay with only his eyes and mouth visible through the bandaging round his head and face. He'd also had part of one leg amputated below the knee. The shock coupled with the smell of gangrene from a neighbouring bed, was too much for the girl. She rose unsteadily to her feet and stumbled from the ward white as a sheet and holding her hand across her mouth. Harry called after her in a croaky voice,

"Betty, Betty!!"

None of the nurses were free to go to her but passing the ward entrance was a dignified, elderly clergyman. Ellie knew him to be high- ranking in the Church of England, he was rather pompous looking and obviously used to ministering to the needs of the upper classes. He seemed the most unapproachable of the Padres. Betty, unable to contain herself lurched against this venerable gentleman and vomited over his shiny black shoes. The whole ward held its breath, watching. The clergyman never hesitated, his arms went round the young woman and he shielded her from the rest of us until she had finished heaving and retching. Then, as gently as if he was her father, he'd led her away down the corridor. Later, when she came back to visit the ward, much recovered, Betty told Harry what had happened. Ellie was just giving Harry his medication so heard all about it.

"I felt so ashamed of mi 'self, Harry, him being one of the Church men and a big nob at that, but he was ever so kind to me. Never mentioned what I'd done to 'is shoes and clothes. He kept his arm round me all the way down the corridor, just comforting like- nothing funny! He just said 'There, there, my poor girl. Let's find somewhere for you to wash, then we'll sit quietly until you feel better.'

He even knew my name. He'd heard you calling it out, and he said, 'If he can call out like that, he's on the way to recovery, my dear.' That's something isn't it Harry, 'cause he'll have seen a lot of men like you. Then he took me to a Ladies' room and said he'd find us both a cup of tea, whilst I freshened myself up. When I came out he was sitting on a bench in the corridor with two cups of tea and two biscuits on a tray. His shoes and his clothes had been all sponged clean. Anyway we took the tray of tea outside in the sunshine. We had such a long talk together and I feel so much better now, Harry."

"I was that worried about you when you ran out like that, I was frightened you were revolted by me and then I got worried for our baby. I wasn't sure what the shock might do to you both," croaked Harry, holding tightly to Bettie's hand.

"I'm tough as old boots, lad. Nurse here, will tell you that it's not so easy to upset babbies, once they're safely settled in here."

Betty patted her growing stomach and looked knowingly up at Ellie who said, "Quite right."

"Harry? I was wondering. Now that I've met the old gent, and we're on speaking terms. Do you think he might marry us, here in the hospital?"

"Betty! Are you sure, lass? Look at me, only one and a half legs and a mangled hand; not to mention what my face is like under these bandages. No, Betty, I'd not ask you to take me on!"

"Take you on! Harry Birtwistle, you are the father of my child. I know we shouldn't have done it but that were the war weren't it and if we get married here and now, then our child has a proper legal father and I have the man I love to be my husband. Oh Harry, do say you'll ask him."

"I do love you Betty. It would be a good thing to do. Our parents would be happier too, if it was done soon as poss. Alright, let's see if this old gent of yours agrees, but what's his proper name? We can't call him, old gent!"

"He's the Venerable Richard Brookhouse, a recently retired Archdeacon, no less! And don't worry about your face, those bandages are coming off tomorrow, you only had superficial cuts and bruises under them," grinned Ellie who'd unashamedly listened in to the whole conversation while tending a nearby patient. She felt ashamed because, at first, she'd thought the 'old gent' to be a snob and the worst kind of advert for Christianity. Well, he'd certainly turned the tables on her. Eliza would be pleased.

The Venerable Richard agreed to the wedding. The young couple were married a week later in the hospital chapel but not by the elderly archdeacon. He arranged for one of the younger chaplains to conduct the service. The 'old gent' himself, in the absence of Betty's father, led the young bride to the altar, where Harry stood beaming, leaning on his crutch, waiting for her.

CHAPTER 41

So many Goodbyes

One breezy, sunny afternoon in March, having just watched another batch of young men leave for the front, Ellie walked across the hospital grounds towards the sea. It was the beginning of her off- duty time and she was glad to be away from the noise and smell of the hospital. She breathed in the salty sea-weed smell, as she came to the sea wall. She'd walked with her back to Southampton and its harbour full of shipping and now looked out over the Solent, beyond the barbed wire and beach defences, to where nature alone seemed to be in charge. Here the sea was ruffled only by the wind and the tides; seabirds cried and swooped, riding the wind and the waves. Monstrous cloud animals and cloud islands, touched by the sunlight into purest white and soft greys, moved slowly across the pale blue sky. Ellie entered a place far-removed from the war. She was leaning against the wall and feeling pleasantly drugged by the natural wonder of the scene, when a hand touched her shoulder. She jumped, and cried out.

"Sorry Ellie, I didn't mean to startle you."

She turned to find Alex Dobson standing beside her. She shook her head, expecting him to disappear but his firm if slightly portly body, wrapped in a trench coat against the breeze, stayed right there and his gentle, smiling grey eyes and untidy fair hair made her want to reach out and touch him.

"Alex! Have they sent you here to work, as well?"

"No, my dear. I've come to see you. They told me you'd probably be walking near the sea. I can see why, it's a world away from in there!" Alex nodded his head back towards the hospital.

"It certainly smells sweeter," smiled Ellie.

"How are you, Ellie? You disappeared so quickly from London, but I got all your messages. How are your brothers?"

For a few minutes they sat on the sea-wall, catching up on the last few months. At last Alex explained his visit.

"I've come to say goodbye, Ellie. The Canadians are entering the war and I must go back to Canada in order to join a regiment. Several of my old friends have written, urging me to come back and sign up with them. I'll need to train first and lose this paunch," Alex patted his rounded stomach. "I hope they'll accept me into the medical corps. I don't think I'd be much good with a gun and a bayonet," he looked ruefully at his doctor's hands.

"You weren't made for killing and wounding, Alex. I don't think many of the men brought here were made that way either. It's all a terrible mess. Just as we thought we were getting somewhere with all the child-birth problems and the poverty."

"Ellie, this war may teach us more than we realise. It's a terrible thing but I always believe that, in the end, we discover new and better things through desperate situations. We've got to believe this, or we'd go mad. We mustn't ever lose hope in what we are about!" Alex's voice cracked and he turned deliberately towards the sea.

"Why should we have to go through such times in order to discover better things? It doesn't make sense, it's cruel and pointless," raged Ellie.

"I'm not saying that we have to go through these wars and killings and wrecking of families and nations, in order to better ourselves. What I'm saying is that it's not the end of the story. I believe better things will come, in the end, as a result. This war is happening, we couldn't prevent it and we can't stop it but we can draw what good we can from it! You watch, mankind will change and most of it will be for the better. But Ellie, dearest; I wish it didn't have to be, I'm afraid I may never see you again."

"Alex, there are too many goodbyes. Each time I say goodbye, to a group of men I've nursed, as they go back to the front and when I remember that my brothers will be sent out to France any day, I

281

know that I may never see any of them again in this life. I daren't think about it and I daren't let myself feel. I'm numb here, inside. Do you know what day it is Alex? It is March 21st, the first day of spring. What a ridiculous joke. Spring should mean new life and all we see is death and destruction."

Alex reached out and took her in his arms. Ellie's words about her feelings were turned to lies, as tears came suddenly and she sobbed unashamedly against Alex's firm chest. When her sobs quietened, Alex tipped Ellie's face to his and they kissed, deeply and warmly. Ellie felt their closeness so intensely that she hardly knew which was her body and which was Alex's, in the depth of their embrace. The warmth stayed with her for a long time after he'd gone.

Alex went back to Canada to join the men of the 4th Canadian Division in their part of the British Expeditionary Force. His last words to Ellie were, "I'll come back for you, my little Ellie. As soon as I can I'll come back and we'll be together."

Ellie had promised him that she'd be waiting for him and in her heart she knew that she would not refuse marriage to him, when he returned.

As he'd hoped, Alex was accepted as a member of the division's medical team. Ten months later Ellie received an official military post card, to say he was well and somewhere in Belgium.

At the beginning of July, 1915, Jack, along with ten others, was told that he'd been selected to join the 52nd Field Ambulance of the Royal Army Medical Corps. By now, Jack had been promoted to Corporal.

"The 52nd Ambulance is part of the 17th Army Division. You will be given passes for forty eight hours leave, to say goodbye to your loved ones before you take ship for France. The exact date of departure will not be given until you return from leave. Your leave begins tomorrow at seven hundred hours, collect your rail passes now from your C.O.

The leave came and went and on 13th July 1915, Jack and his unit left to join the British Expeditionary Force, somewhere in France.

On the morning he embarked, Ellie held her young brother tightly in her arms, she remembered vividly the way she'd held him the day he was born and wished with all her heart for that moment back again. All she could say was,

"Be strong, Jack, save as many lives as you can and come back safe to us."

She couldn't say "God bless you," as Sarah would have done, because Ellie was unsure of God, but with all her might she tried to infuse her brother with courage and love. She thought how strange that within a few months she'd held two men in her arms so passionately when she'd thought she'd long ago ceased to be a demonstrative woman.

Edwin was to stay at Netley for the time being and as he shook his brother's hand, tears welled up behind his eyes. The predicament of the wounded had shocked Eddie more than Jack, who'd already come into contact with horrendous mining and industrial injuries in Canada.

"Keep your spirits up Eddie, whatever happens we've an important job to do and I for one am glad to do it. Be brave lad, you'll be following me out there, before long!"

They embraced and Edwin wished above all that he could go in place of his younger brother.

"If only I had the strong leadership qualities, I'd be going first into danger," he thought. Then he remembered Annie, waiting at home and for her sake, tried to be glad. Jack marched away in the column of young men to the Southampton dockyard, where their ship was waiting. Ellie and Edwin turned back to the hospital. For the rest of the day nursing duties took all Ellie's concentration and energy; she kept her thoughts firmly fixed on the tasks in hand and eventually a sort of calm overtook her. The war was a never- ending phenomenon. Theosophy still intruded into Ellie's thinking from time to time but water-fasts and mystical meditations were definitely out, in these circumstances. This, together with regular, compulsory, Christian services on the hospital wards resurrected in her the bulwarks of the old faith experienced in childhood. It gave a semblance of balance to Ellie's life, enabling her to keep on facing the constant influx of badly wounded, often dying soldiers, arriving from the Western front.

As Eliza put in a letter to Ellie,

"I have often found that, when I've been at my lowest ebb and crying out for help, someone else in need is pushed into my way. In having to help them, I find that my own need is temporarily forgotten and when I do remember it, I wonder whatever I was so upset about. Not that I'm advocating that bad things should happen to other people, in order to help me out of my problems, but it says something about how we tick as human beings. Our well-being really is in serving others. That way we are all serving one another, the served and the servers! Sounds double- Dutch and very preachy but you'll get my meaning I'm sure."

Ellie did and smiled at her friend across the miles from Netley to London.

The next to go was Edwin. Quieter and more of an introvert than Jack, Edwin remained a private in the ambulance corps, steady as a rock and competent at the jobs he was given to do. He was a great comfort to the men as they were brought to the dressing stations, broken and confused. His quiet ways helped to settle their fears as much as his dressings helped to soothe their wounds but inwardly his heart wrenched, each time another bloodied, mud-encrusted young soldier was carried in from the trenches.

Noel Wynne, one of the padres, became Edwin's greatest friend out there, in France. Like so many of those front-line clergymen, Noel would make his way into no-man's land after dark, to help find the wounded and stay with them in the cold and wet, until the stretcher- bearers and medics arrived. Often it would be the padre who would hold and prevent an unconscious young soldier from suffocating in the thick mud and this was how Edwin first met Noel. On his first night as a stretcher- bearer on the front-line, Edwin was picking his way through the darkness out beyond the wire, when he heard a man's voice talking quietly. It was Noel Wynne, standing knee deep in mud and supporting the head of a badly wounded but conscious soldier, "Just keeping away the demons of the dark, till you lot came," he had joked cheerily to Edwin. Once the soldier was carried away, the padre had ploughed on, finding and supporting others, all night long. In the daytime Noel talked with the men; prayed with those who wanted it; took services; buried the dead; wrote letters to bereaved families and stood up for the lads against bullying and cruelty.

"How do you keep going, Padre?" he was often asked.

"By the Grace of God lads, by the Grace of God, same as you," he always replied.

Noel and Edwin enjoyed a mutual interest in ornithology and botany which lifted their thoughts away, for a time, from the suffering around them.

Each day Edwin hoped he might meet up with Jack but it seemed they were positioned in different parts of the Line.

CHAPTER 42

Letters from Hartsbeck, 1915–1918

The letters, which came from Hartsbeck during her time at Netley, impressed upon Ellie the effect the war was having on her home town. The unusual length of a letter from Sarah stressed the emotional impact on those left at home.

174, Aspen Lane,
Hartsbeck,
29th May 1915

Dear Ellie,

"You would be so proud of us, Ellie. You know we've always been part of the St. John's Ambulance corps here in Hartsbeck? Well now we are really involved in training to nurse the wounded, or at least care for those who are convalescent. Do you remember 'Beech Tree Hall'? It's that huge house, belonging to the Edmondson family. They own one of the cotton mills on the way out of Hartsbeck, as you go towards Blackburn. The Hall is on a rise overlooking the mill and it's being turned into a convalescent hospital. As members of the local ambulance brigade we've been encouraged to volunteer to help nurse the soldiers who will be sent there, mainly from the military hospital in Liverpool. Of course we'll be supervised by fully trained nurses, but there is such a huge demand for professional nurses at the front and in the main military hospitals, as well as in the civilian hospitals, that most of the nursing team here is voluntary. We have to fit in our nursing duties with our day jobs and

are attending special classes to prepare us for the type of nursing we'll be expected to do. The Sister Tutor in charge of our training is very strict and told us, we must be as disciplined as if we were paid professionals. Some of the qualified nurses look down their noses at us but Sister seems rather impressed with us.

We've had to knuckle down and prepare Beech Tree Hall for its new role. The Edmondsons decided to leave most of their beautiful furniture and paintings, for the use and enjoyment of the injured men. We've had to strip some of the larger rooms and turn them into hospital wards with iron bedsteads and masses of bedding. You wouldn't believe the amount of sheets and blankets, pillows and pillowcases that have been brought in and we've been unpacking and sorting all these supplies. Local factories and businesses have donated many of the goods.

There is a large games room with a magnificent billiard table and a room for darts and other manly indoor games. Also, there are quiet sitting rooms and the huge garden. So, as the men recover, there will be plenty to occupy them. Do you remember Becky, Hannah's younger sister? She is thinking of training, full- time, as a V.A.D nurse and afterwards transferring to a proper Military Hospital.

You'll have heard of the Pals regiments being formed in towns all over the country, well Hartsbeck has formed its own Pals' regiment, although quite a lot of men from here had already joined up earlier in other regiments. Soldier's pay is a God-send to many families here; they've been on the breadline, mainly with the wages disputes and strikes at the local factories and people being laid off, because of the slump in the cotton trade. The sudden depression in trade came as such a shock.

George, as a solicitor, has been intimately aware of the financial affairs of Hartsbeck. At the end of May last year he remarked, that our little town was more prosperous than it had been for thirty years. Then in June, mills began to close for weeks at a time because of lack of orders. The annual workers' holiday fortnight, was extended -without pay. At least 500 men and women have been put out of work. On top of this, last summer brought even more hardship, when the big engineering works came out on strike for better pay!

Even nature had its pennyworth! A huge thunderstorm in July flooded the machine shop at Lucas's. All production was stopped! Dad came home exhausted that day; he'd been helping to clear up after the flood waters. Even mother joined a group of women detailed to make piles of sandwiches and gallons of tea for the work parties.

It's a bit embarrassing, although a great relief to us, that George is not to go to war. His job is what is called a 'reserved occupation'. Dear old Mr Drake had to choose between allowing his own son to join the army, or George. Both of them are solicitors with the firm but old Mr Drake was only allowed to keep one of them. His son, Lewis, is only twenty years old and was very keen to join up. Mr Drake decided it was better to let Lewis go, as he is single with no commitments. He felt morally obliged to keep George, because of Hannah and the two children. It was a brave decision but George argued against it. He was adamant that Lewis should stay, as he was Mr Drake's only son. In the end, Lewis Drake stole a march on them both, by signing up with a Scottish regiment. He was away before they could stop him. I think Hannah must be relieved, though she doesn't like to mention it. Mother keeps very quiet but I see her following George with her eyes, as if thankful to have one of her sons at home. George has joined the Home Guard; one of his duties is as on the night -watch, guarding the railway viaduct. He heard heavy breathing one night but on investigation discovered it to be a cow. I'm not sure what dad feels.

The depression has affected so many families. Ever since last summer the children in my class have come to school hungry and tired and dirtier than normal. The streets are full of queues at the soup kitchens, set up by the Salvation Army and other churches and organisations.

In your profession, you must know that Hartsbeck already has infant mortality rates higher than the average. I'm sure the numbers have gone even higher, the way things have been going.

No wonder the men flock to join the army. They're given immediate pay, to bring home, as soon as they sign on and the promise of more, on a regular basis. I don't know if they think of the consequences of war, of having to kill or be killed or wounded. The excitement of doing something noble and worthwhile for their country and providing for their loved ones at the same time is infectious. It means the young men can lift up their heads and walk proudly and my word, Ellie, they do just that, marching through the town in their new uniforms, bands playing and flags flying. Then they are gone and the town is left quiet and waiting in uncertainty. Drew's chemical works has been turned into a munitions factory and is advertising jobs for women. It's dangerous work.

At school, most of my children, especially the boys, were full of excitement at first. Then, after a month or so they became subdued and moody, even tearful. Some of them tell me they hear their mothers crying in the night. We teachers have to rack our brains to keep their interest and divert their thoughts and they do make an effort to respond well but are quickly unsettled when news arrives that someone they know has been killed, or wounded, or is missing in action.

I did wonder if I should give up teaching to follow Becky's example and become a full time V.A.D nurse. I decided not to because the number of male teachers enlisting in the forces has badly depleted the teaching staff at St. Mark's. The children and their mothers do need us to help them through the troubles, as well as keeping up the children's education. I feel I'm 'doing my bit for king and country' just by staying put and it would please Mr Asquith, if he knew! It is an enormous responsibility for him to be prime minister in war-time. Stephen, who is very much a Liberal, thinks Mr. Lloyd-George may soon take over from Asquith. I'm not much of a politician but George (who's Conservative) and Stephen, go at it hammer and tongs at times and I pick up things from them relevant to my interests in education and social concerns.

Oh, my dearest Ellie, I wish you were here to talk to like we used to, lying in our beds before going to sleep at night. It's that lonely time, when you can't escape from your own thoughts. You were always so sensible. I'm just thankful that I can pray and pour it all out to God. I'd swear that it's Him that keeps me sane. My dear sister, you are seeing far more of the horrific effects of this war at Netley. I know you struggle with your faith. I shall keep praying for both of us and all the others. I hardly dare imagine what Jack and Edwin are going through but they are never far from my thoughts.

Keep smiling, Ellie,
All my love, Sarah.

On Wednesday, 6th October a letter from Jack arrived at 174, Aspen Lane, it was addressed to Mr and Mrs D. Elkson but Jack's opening greeting was to all the family;

France
Monday,
27ᵗʰ September, 1915

Dear Mum, Dad, George and Hannah, Annie, and of course young Tom and Rebecca,

Hopefully I shall be able to write separately to Stephen and Ellie but in case I don't, please pass on the contents of this letter. I love and miss you all. It's a bit grim out here for the lads but we try to make things more bearable for them, treating the ailments that come from living in muddy trenches with no proper sleep etc. and of course tending the wounded which is on-going. We've learnt when to expect an influx of injuries at certain times each day, especially early evening and morning, the men give these hours unrepeatable names—politely, we see them as the 'rush hours' when no-one here is off-duty. Believe me, I've never seen doctors and nurses work so unceasingly and with such skill in such difficult circumstances. I feel honoured to work alongside them. Men, who we almost gave up for dead, have come through and been sent home alive to their families, though some have lost limbs or have terrible burn and gas injuries. The unseen mental scars are much more difficult to treat.

I've only a few minutes left to tell you that I've recently moved from the field hospital to take charge of a dressing station in the trenches. I've been promoted, which gives me more responsibility. I think of you all before I sleep and when I wake and lots of times in between. I know Edwin is over here somewhere but I haven't heard from, or seen him. Please keep sending letters and parcels, they do arrive eventually and mean such a lot. Thank you for all you are doing. The men suffer from the cold and damp, so any suitable warm clothing is welcome! We keep cheerful. We all enjoyed the drawings from the children in your class, Sarah. We laughed till the tears ran, at some of them. It did us good and triggered off a spate of stories of our own school-days and reminded some of the men of the antics of their own children. Don't tell the school children we laughed– just say they cheered us up no end!

My best love to you all, I hold you in my prayers, as I know you do me - just tell George and Stephen that there are no atheists on the front line! Every man here mutters a prayer as he goes over the top. Oh - I've got to go - 'rush hour' about to begin - God bless you all.

Your own loving son and brother, Jack.

Jack sent another, more personal letter to his fiancée, Laura, but it is not for us to know the contents.

CHAPTER 43

Further news from the Front.

Ellie received no more letters from Jack. On Friday, 7th October, 1915, a message came to 174, Aspen Lane from Archdeacon Southall. It simply said,

> *With deep regret, I must inform you that Sergt. Elkson passed away at 7.20am on Wednesday morning, 6th October.*

Dave was sent for and came home from work at once.

Jeannie's reaction was one of disbelief. "It can't be right, we had a letter from him that very day at twelve o'clock, and we read it as we ate our dinner. I remember, don't you remember Sarah? Dave? You'd both just come in from work for your dinner hour, Wednesday, 6th October, 1915, see it's' here."

She pulled the letter from the mantelpiece, sending a china ornament crashing to the floor, Jeannie ignored the breakage and waved Jack's letter.

Quietly Dave took the letter and pointed to the date written at the top, Monday, 27th September.

"No, Jeannie, love. The letter took over a week to come. Jack wrote this on 27th Sept. It was just coincidence it arrived on the day this message says he died."

Jeannie tried another tactic. She stabbed at the message from the Archdeacon-

"See, the letter says Sergt. Elkson. Jack's not a Sergeant he's a Corporal, and there's no Christian name!"

The ghost of a hope hovered around the family group,

"You're right, Mum, he was only a Corporal. Do you think they could have got it wrong, Dad?" asked Sarah.

Dave sat down and wearily passed his hands over his face.

"I don't know. I doubt it. Anyway, he mentions being promoted. He might well have been made a Sergeant."

Jeannie was walking up and down the room, clutching both letters. She spoke in short, breathless bursts.

"We need to make sure. We have to write. Who do we write to? We must write straight away. Our Ellie would know what to do. We have to get in touch with Ellie. Someone go and tell George and Hannah. It must be a mistake; it must be a mistake. It could be a mistake, couldn't it Dave?"

"Put t' kettle on, Sarah. We need to sit down and think this through over a strong cuppa. Jeannie, sit down here. I'm going across to Annie's and see if she'll ask Fred from the corner shop to take a message to George's office."

At Netley, Ellie had worked a double shift on Friday, 7th October and it was 10.30pm when she came off duty. The battles at the front had been particularly fierce that week and the dead and wounded arriving in the port that day had seemed innumerable.

She was too tense to go straight to bed and instead, made her way to the chapel. There was always a short service of Compline at 11pm. Several of the medical staff were there, seeking strength and peace from that simple service. The chapel was dimly lit and candles burned softly on the altar. The hospital smell was replaced by the lingering sweet spiciness of incense from an earlier Roman Catholic Mass. All denominations shared the chapel. During the service, the Anglican Chaplain read out four names of men from the 52nd Field Ambulance, who had given their lives in the last few days. Men who had left here just three months ago. Ellie lifted her head in disbelief when she heard the name, "Sergeant Jack Elkson," among the four names. She sat without moving, hearing every word of the service, her brain concentrating on shutting out the awful news.

"Keep me as the apple of your eye," the Padre intoned

"Hide me under the shadow of your wings," responded the congregation,

"Save us, O Lord while waking,

And guard us while sleeping,

That awake, we may watch with Christ

And asleep, may rest in peace"

"Now, Lord let your servant go in peace,"

"In peace I will lay myself down to sleep,"

"For you alone, Lord, make us dwell in safety"

"Abide with us, Lord Jesus 'for the night is at hand and the day is now past."

Ellie was slipping into a formless night; dark waves of sound echoed round her.

"As the night watch looks for the morning,

So do we look for you, O Christ."

Gradually, the haunting chant of plain- song died away and people moved quietly from the chapel to work or rest. Ellie did not move. She wanted to stay within the peace of the ancient words and lean against God and never stir again. She wondered vaguely, if this was what it was like for Jack, safe and at peace. The theosophists saw the place of death and afterwards as beautiful and idyllic but they didn't speak of God. Just now Ellie wanted God, a loving vibrant presence who welcomed the dead to their new place and breathed a new kind of life into them. She must have stayed like this for some time, until a loud cough followed by an anxious voice roused her.

"My dear, I think you are very tired. You should go to your quarters now and sleep," the elderly Padre was startled by the look of anguish and bewilderment in Ellie's eyes, as she looked at him.

"Is there something especially troubling you?" he began, taking one of her hands in his.

Before she could say anything, Lettie Parrish burst into the Chapel.

"Oh, I do apologise," Lettie paused, seeing the Padre with her friend.

"Can I help you? You seem in a great hurry my dear."

"An urgent message has come for Nurse Elkson from home, but I'll wait outside till you've finished," Lettie tiptoed back into the corridor.

"Nurse Elkson?" the chaplain stared at Ellie, "Of course, you are Jack Elkson's sister. Oh my dear, was that the first you heard of Jack's death? In the service?"

"Yes," whispered Ellie.

"How terrible for you, to hear the news like that," he clasped her icy cold hands in his and began rubbing warmth into them. "Do you know the nurse who just came in?"

"She's my friend."

"Then I think we should go to her. You need to hear your message from home and you are in shock my dear. Your friend will know what to do for that, better than I."

The old man helped Ellie gently to her feet and guided her to where Lettie was waiting.

"I shall do what I can," he promised "I'll go back into the Chapel and pray for you all and for Jack. He laid a calming hand on Ellie's head, God be with you, my dear. Come back and see me when you can."

He watched as Lettie led Ellie away, then he hobbled back into the chapel to pray. He was a retired priest in his mid- seventies and had come to help out the younger chaplains with the huge burden they had to carry during this war. Too old to be of use at the front, he could perform duties here in the home-land and release those young and fit enough to go. Also he could give some respite to those working day and night here in the hospital.

When Ellie had recovered from the shock, she read the message from home. It was a telegram, brief and distressing.

'Jack presumed dead. Not sure. Mother not convinced. Can you find out more? Sarah.'

As was usual with the death of such a close relative Ellie was given leave to go home to her family. She was to catch an early train to Hartsbeck on Monday morning but, as casualties were arriving thick and fast, she was required to return to Netley by Friday 15th October.

Before leaving, she needed to find out who would know more about her brother's death. Ellie had no doubt that it was Jack, who'd been killed. However, it was obvious that her mother needed proof of a more personal nature and details as to how he'd died. Ellie insisted on being on duty as usual on the Saturday and Sunday before her compassionate leave and discovered that the news of what had happened had already reached the men on her ward. They were full of advice.

"You need to contact one of his mates, someone who was out there with him," Corporal Lu Riley said to her, as she dressed his leg. "The best way to do that is get hold of a list of his battalion and find the address of the wife of one of the Sergeants. Usually, 'Welfare' has an address like that, for relatives to use. Ask her to write to her husband, pronto,"

"Of course, thank you Lu. I'll go to Welfare, in my break."

Ellie went to the welfare office on the hospital site and told them her problem. They gave her an address for the wife of a Sergeant W.D. Beardsall. Sergt. Beardsall was serving with the RAMC in the 52nd Ambulance alongside Jack Elkson. Mrs Beardsall was acting as a welfare contact between concerned relatives and the 52nd. Ellie wrote straight away explaining her mother's dilemma and asked Mrs Beardsall if she would mind writing to her husband, asking him to verify Jack's death. Ellie took the letter back to the Welfare office as they had a quick delivery method for such correspondence. They assured her that Mrs Beardsall could have a message to her husband within a couple of days.

Ellie could do no more. She packed a few things and caught the early train to Hartsbeck on Monday morning. There followed days of tense-waiting and quiet grief. All, except Jeannie, were sure of Jack's death but until the letter from Sergeant Beardsall arrived they dare not mourn openly for fear of her reaction. Sarah, Ellie and Stephen walked up to George and Hannah's home for an hour each evening. Here they talked quietly about the situation and thought about Jack.

They wondered if he would be brought home or would he be buried out there and they spoke of his fiancée, Laura.

On Thursday, Ellie had to leave them all to travel back to Netley. She promised to contact them as soon as she heard from Seargent Beardsall.

CHAPTER 44

Evidence

Two hours after Ellie had left, to return to Netley, a letter from France arrived addressed to Mrs D. Elkson. Jeannie was alone in the house but she put on her coat and went up the road to Hannah's. Tom and Rebecca had gone to Grandma Nelson's, for an hour or so, while Hannah did some house-work.

"It's a letter from France, Hannah. I couldn't face opening it on my own,"

"Come along in, take off your coat and sit down."

The two women sat at the table and opened the letter. Jeannie traced the words with her finger.

> *52nd Field Ambulance*
> *B. E. F.*
> *11/10/15*

Dear Mrs Elkson,

> *I want to express my sympathy with you on the death of your son. I knew him since he joined the Army and I have no hesitation in saying that he was the best Non-Commissioned Officer we had – he will be very hard to replace. He met his end when doing his duty. He went out with a party of bearers under heavy shell fire to rescue a man who had been seriously wounded and who unfortunately died a little later. It may be some consolation for you to know that he died whilst doing his duty and carrying on the best traditions of the Corps to which he belonged.*

> *Yours sincerely,*
> *D. DOUGAL*
> *Capt. R.A.M.C*

The older woman turned a greenish white, and slumped in her chair. Hannah went for the brandy bottle and forced her mother-in-law to take a sip, they stared at the letter again,

"It doesn't say his name and it doesn't mention Dave, his father. It could still be somebody else. Why don't they put his Christian name?" Jeannie was looking for any loophole.

Hannah was non-plussed. It did seem odd. She wondered if the letters were already typed out and just signed and sent to a mother, when her son was killed but no, there was more written here:

"Look mother; this Captain says he knew your son. He writes about how he was killed, he doesn't mention his name but I don't think he thought about that. He knew who he was writing about and knows you are his mother."

"But why doesn't he write Mr and Mrs, he's Dave's son as much as mine?"

"I don't know," Hannah sighed, "maybe its army policy."

Hannah was surprised by her mother-in-law's reaction. She'd always appeared to be such a strong-minded, down-to-earth person but here she was, still refusing to accept that Jack could be dead.

"Until I get a letter with his full name, and convincing evidence, I won't believe it!" Jeannie was firm and sounded rational. She stood up, put on her coat and walked out without another word.

It was a week later that Ellie received a letter from France. She'd gone each day to the Welfare Office to see if a letter had arrived. When it did come, she walked with it out to the sea wall, where she'd said goodbye to Alex. How cold and grey the sea looked now, so different from that day in August when she'd sobbed in his arms. Warmly-wrapped in her thick nurse's cloak and accompanied by the wild sounds of sea and wind and the cries of gulls, she read the letter. As she had expected, it was from Sergeant Beardsall and her heart swelled as she read his words:

France
16/10/15

Dear Miss Elkson,

I received a letter from my wife yesterday, telling me you had written to her for verification of your poor brother's death, and my wife has asked me to write to you, and give you the full details as I know them, which I now do with the greatest regret. I think I can claim to be the last man of the 52nd to see him alive, when he left us at our last position to go to hospital further down the line, and at that time I certainly thought Jack (as we all called him) would pull through alright, and no one was more surprised and sorrowfully shocked than I, when news came through of Jack's death.

If it is any consolation to you and your Mother, in your very sad bereavement, to know what I am going to tell, then I tell you unhesitatingly. While you and your Mother have lost a good brother and dutiful son respectively, we of the 52nd have lost a good, true and jolly chum, respected and loved, as a MAN, by us all and the 52nd has lost one of her best and most efficient N.C.O's, one who could always be relied upon to do his duty no matter what it was and where it may be, he would be right there and do it like a man, to the satisfaction of the officers and N.C.O's and to the credit of the 52nd. His enemy, if he had one (he certainly had not out here) could never accuse him of shirking or cowardice, and he was popular to a degree, with us all, from the C.O. to the bugler boys. His death was brought about by a shrapnel wound in the chest, received while doing his duty in the inky blackness of the night time, when most of our work is done out here.

He answered the call unflinchingly, to attend to a badly wounded case near our own dug-outs, and in saving another life he gave his own, and what more glorious death than that can any man die? He fulfilled the noblest tradition of our very noble and honoured Corps, and we are proud of him and will always hold him in our memories, in the highest esteem. He died, as he had lived, a good and true man. I sincerely trust, that the noble manner in which he met his death will console you and your Mother in your grief and will help you both to bear up, under the affliction the Almighty in His wisdom, has placed upon you, until such time He calls us all together again, in that promised blessed re-union, where we believe there are no more sorrows and partings, and we shall all attain that peace which passeth our understanding. Believe me,

Yours very sincerely,

W.D. BEARDSALL

Sgt R.A.M.C

Ellie wasn't sure even now that this would be enough to convince her mother that it was their Jack, but two more letters arrived from France, which put an end to all doubt. They were from Edwin. One came to Ellie, the other to the family at Hartsbeck. The letters were dated 7th Oct. but both had been delayed. They told a sad tale of how Edwin had arrived on 5th October in the same area of France as Jack. Neither knew the other was there but coming into the dressing station early on Wednesday, 6th October, to start his first spell of duty, Edwin discovered his brother, lying among the other wounded brought in during the night. It was about 7am and a medic had just finished dressing a massive shrapnel wound in Jack's back.

"Jack!" Edwin had stared unbelievingly at his younger brother, some of the trench mud and blood still stuck to his face and hair but in the early morning light it had been unmistakably Jack.

"You know him then?" the medic had asked

"He's m-my b-b-brother," Edwin had stuttered.

"Then you'd better stay with him lad. I'm sorry. We thought he'd pull through but the wound is too deep and he's lost a lot of blood. His lung has collapsed, most likely it's perforated- and there's more internal damage. Be thankful that he's got you, as family, with him at the end. The Padre will be along soon." The young medic had given Edwin a sympathetic pat on the shoulder, before going on to tend more of the wounded.

Edwin had crouched beside his brother and taken his hand, it had been cold but not dead-cold, and Jack's breathing had sounded harsh and laboured.

"Jack?" Edwin had croaked out his brother's name, "Jack, can you hear me?" Jack's eyes had fluttered open and rested on Edwin.

"Eddie," the sound had been hardly a whisper. Edwin had taken out his water bottle and moistened his brother's cracked lips before wiping the mud and blood away from Jack's face. He'd stayed beside the stretcher, holding Jack's hand and talking of home, he'd spoken to Jack of their brothers and sisters and their mother and father and of Laura.

"Laura-I love her- always. –Tell her, Eddie and–and tell mother, I'm sorry." Jack had gasped, his breathing laboured. Edwin, seeing that the end had come had put his arms round his brother and held him gently. At twenty past seven Jack had given three little hiccups and then his breathing had stopped. Edwin had automatically noted the time and then he'd knelt, experiencing the silence and stillness of his brother. With folded hands and closed eyes, Edwin prayed as he'd always done, to the God he trusted;

"Father, take my brother, Jack into your safe keeping. Find him something good to do in your heavenly kingdom."

"May he rest in peace and rise in glory," a familiar voice had finished off Edwin's prayer. It had been his friend, Noel Wynne. They stood together for a moment, caps in hand, heads bent. Then the medics took over and the two friends walked away.

"I'm just glad I was here for him," Edwin had spoken simply.

"Yes, that was a real blessing," Noel had steered his friend to a quiet corner where he could recover.

They'd known that Jack's body, like so many of his fellow soldiers, would not be taken home but buried there in France and that Jack's personal belongings and identity tags would be sent home in a brown paper parcel. Edwin had been thankful that Noel was to take Jack's funeral service.

Edwin could have taken compassionate leave and gone home to his family but determined to do his duty he stayed on in France until the spring of 1917, helping the wounded and the sick, trying to do honour to his brother. Letters came regularly from George, with snippets of family news and amusing tales of Tom and Rebecca, which raised his spirits. In a strange way, he was glad that Jack was buried over there; it made him feel near to him. Then, quite suddenly, Edwin could take no more and was sent home suffering from shell-shock. The stammer he'd developed, while on the front lines, stayed with him for the rest of his life but he remained a hard-working, gentle and caring soul; contented in his faith in God, his fascination of nature and his love for all his family.

Stephen was the next to be sucked into the war-machine. In the same Autumn that Jack was killed, the principal of Blackburn College received a letter requesting that:

"One, Stephen Elkson of 174, Aspen Lane, Hartsbeck, be seconded to the Royal Arsenal, at Woolwich, where he is required to do chemical research."

Stephen also received a similar letter. It came as a relief to him that he was at last to have a specific role in the war, other than his 'reserved occupation' as a teacher. His short sightedness and certain other bodily malfunctions, which he had previously been unaware of, had pronounced him unfit to fight. He'd felt shame, as he'd faced his young students, knowing their fathers and older brothers were fighting at the front and that they couldn't wait to join them.

Jack's death had made Stephen feel his situation to be intolerable and he couldn't pack his bags quickly enough. Jeannie, Dave and Sarah knowing his feelings, waved him off cheerfully. His expertise in mining engineering and science qualified him to become research assistant to Sir. Robert Pickard, one of the chief scientists at the Royal Arsenal in Woolwich. The work he did was top secret and Stephen remained at Woolwich for the remainder of the war. He found deep satisfaction in working with people of the highest calibre, in the scientific world. In his spare time he would roam the local area, seeking out the geological nature of the land and the plants it nurtured. He kept careful records of the specimens he collected, meticulously backed up with explanatory notes. These were of immense future interest to his fellow geologists and also to his students, when he finally returned to teaching.

CHAPTER 45

Becky Nelson at 'Beech Tree Hall'

Back in Hartsbeck the Edmondson's family home, Beech Tree Hall, was fulfilling its new role as an Auxiliary Military Hospital. Members of the local St. John's Ambulance brigade were volunteer members of staff. Among them was Hannah's sister, Becky, who had been working there, every spare minute she had, since November, 1914. To begin with she'd been a general dogsbody, doing whatever job was needed, scrubbing floors; cleaning equipment; doing laundry and kitchen work; making beds; befriending patients and taking messages. She'd become used to the strong smell of carbolic covering other nastier smells of gangrene and vomit and human waste and enjoyed the teasing remarks of the recuperating soldiers, as she went about her work.

"What are you this time, chamber maid, kitchen maid or my maid?" one or other would shout as she scurried past laughingly, avoiding their attempts to catch her.

The high, spacious rooms of the Hall had been transformed into wards for soldiers in various stages of recovery. Some were still bedbound, others able to walk around and use the rest areas and games rooms. On top of these there were treatment rooms; wash rooms; store rooms and sluices; a small operating theatre; kitchens and a communal dining area.

To begin with, most of the patients were convalescent, having been sent from the main military hospital in Liverpool. The majority were recovering well but a few had deeper wounds, psychological as well as physical, which refused to heal properly. As the war progressed and the main hospitals became swamped with casualties, Beech Tree Hall began to receive injured men who were not yet at the convalescent stage. The staff became over-stretched. Matron desperately needed more qualified nurses and approached Becky. Asking her to consider signing on as a full time V.A.D nurse.

"You will receive training on the job and part of each day you will have to attend classes in anatomy and medical procedures, given by local doctors and classes in general nursing, given by myself. We are desperate for more trained nurses, Becky, but I don't want you to think I would ask just anybody. I've seen you at work and among the patients. You are competent, cheerful and hard-working and relate well to the other staff. You have the qualities to make a very good nurse, my dear. Do say you will join the V.A.D."

The tall, vigorous woman looked at Rebecca through very bright, tired eyes and Rebecca agreed.

"I've been hoping you would ask me, Matron, it's what I've longed for but didn't think I would qualify."

"Well, you will need to complete the required number of hours of satisfactory nursing practice as well as the classes I mentioned. Then you will receive a certificate, enabling you to apply for the War Service Bar. Unfortunately for us, you will then be eligible to be sent to any military hospital at home or out in the field. Beech Tree Hall may lose you in the end"

"How long would it take me to earn the certificate?"

"If you do well, it should take you just over twelve months. Even if the war ends during that time, your services will still be needed."

"Will I have to take an exam?" Rebecca was apprehensive

"There will be short written and oral tests, given weekly, about what you have learnt in class. Nothing to be concerned about. Your practical work on the wards will be observed constantly but don't worry; you'll soon forget you're being watched!" "Matron laughed at the horrified expression on the young woman's face. "Once you are qualified and employed through the War Office, you will earn £20 per annum for your first term of employment and this will be raised for each further term that you serve."

Becky looked suitably impressed, the money would be welcome at home.

"Come along! There's work to be done. I'll introduce you to Sister Firth who will sort out your uniform and be in overall charge of you, she's a good sort. Some nurses look down on V.A.D's - but not Sister Firth, she thinks you're all heroines."

By October, 1915, Becky had been accepted and enrolled as a full-time auxiliary nurse in training. She was just twenty four years old and as she was already St. John's Ambulance trained, she was soon involved in proper nursing duties.

One cold night soon after Christmas, Becky was sitting at the desk in the magnificent drawing room of Beech Tree Hall. She was checking the lists of cases at present in the hospital. Looking down at the list of injuries they were dealing with she wondered at the horror of it all. Her thoughts went to her own brothers and Eddie Elkson out there in France. She thought about Jack Elkson and so many other Hartsbeck lads she'd grown up with, now dead. Sighing, she continued to check the records:-

Synopsis of Wounds or Illnesses

A. Bullet Wounds:-	B. Shrapnel Wounds:-
Head *3*	Head... .... *4*
Trunk	Trunk
Nerve.................*2*	Nerve....................... *1*
Soft Parts..............*3*	Bone.......................*2*
Soft Parts................*1*	
Arms and Hands	
Bone.....................*5*	Arms and Hands:-
Soft Parts................*4*	Bone.......................*2*
Soft Parts... ....*3*	
Legs and Feet:-	Legs and Feet:-
Bone *1*	Bone.......................*1*
Soft Parts *3*	Soft Parts...................*7*
Gassed *4*	Miscellaneous..............*46*

Frost Bite 34
Rheumatism……....…..23

RESULT OF CASES TRANSFERRED

To sick furlough …...... .117

To other Hospitals for special treatment.. 2
To Depot 8

Remaining in Hospital .. 21

A hoarse voice from a nearby bed interrupted Becky's thoughts.

"Nurse! Can I have a word with you, please?"

It was Vernon, one of the soldiers suffering from the effects of a gas attack. He was lucky that his eyesight hadn't been affected but his burnt lungs were slow in healing and much of his time was spent in bed- rest. Becky went to him immediately.

"What is it Vernon? Would you like a drink?"

"I wouldn't mind, if there's one going. I could murder a cuppa but- it's not that; I wanted to say som-att to you; nought to do with my health!"

Becky looked round the room, the rest of the men all appeared to be asleep and Vernon's bed was in a quiet alcove on one side of the beautiful Adam fireplace.

"I'll make us both a cup of tea and we can chat comfortably."

Everything needed to make hot drinks was on the ward and five minutes later Rebecca was comfortably ensconced beside Vernon, both with steaming mugs of tea,

"I've been watching you Nurse Nelson. I've been 'ere since you started nursing last November and you've turned out a proper good 'un, you might say a 'natural'. Nought fazes you and you allus cheer us up; even old grumpy guts, 'Arry, 'as a smile when you're around."

"Now you've got me worried, Vernon, I know sweet talk when I hear it. What is it you want from me! I'm not smuggling in any grog for you!" Becky laughed.

"There you are, see. You don't stand no nonsense and your heads screwed on right. You're young, you're strong, and you're a grand nurse. Now then, lass, why don't you apply to go to one of the proper military hospitals, instead of staying here with those of us who are over the worse and just 'ere to finish mending. You could do proper war service, with the men at the front; or even serve with the Royal Navy in one of them hospital ships. I've seen it, love, they're crying out for strong, young things like you."

"I know what you're saying, Vernon, but qualified, experienced nurses are needed here, at Beech Tree Hall, as well. Some of the patients need very careful nursing, if they are to recover enough to lead a decent life,"

"I know that! I was in the Ambulance Corps and I'm not daft but the older qualified nurses and those with children and their own homes to run can manage the nursing here. That way they don't have to leave their homes. You're young, single and free to go. If it weren't for these damned lungs I'd be back at the Front, double quick. I hate the idea of encouraging you to go into danger but believe me, Nurse Nelson, if you'd seen what it's like out there," Vernon slumped back on his pillow panting slightly; "all I can say is they need you, Nurse." To Becky's dismay, she saw tears trickling down his yellowed cheeks.

"Vernon, I'd no idea you were plotting to get rid of me," she teased him gently, "but don't worry, next month I'll have qualified for the War Service Bar, which means I can apply for full military nursing service and then I'll be on my way. I want to apply for Admiralty Service. You're quite right, the navy are crying out for nurses."

Vernon attempted to say more but a fit of coughing stopped him. Rebecca supported him till it was over, then she settled him back on the pillows.

"Now you've tired yourself out. I'm going to give you one of your pills so you'll sleep but thank you for speaking out. You've given me the final push! I'm going to speak to Matron about it tomorrow."

Impulsively she leant across and kissed away the tear on the brave man's cheek.

On 10th November, 1917, Rebecca was called into Matron's office and presented with a certificate embossed with the insignia of the two territorial force associations, the Red Cross and the Order of St. John of Jerusalem. It was headed 'The Central joint V.A.D. Committee' and named the Chairman, the Hon. Arthur Stanley, M.V.O., M.P. and the Vice-Chairmen The Rt. Hon. The Earl of Plymouth, P.C. and the Rt. Hon. Viscount Chilston, P.C.

Her own name had been written beneath them by the Chief of Medical Staff at 'Beech Tree Hall,' Commandant Richard Clegg. Becky felt a thrill of pride as she read the words on the document:

CERTIFICATE OF APPLICATION FOR WAR SERVICE BAR
This is to certify that Miss. Rebecca Nelson
Member of V.A.D. No. 240 County E. Lancs.
Has served, for thirteen months, 2688 hours (1st year) in
Beech Tree Hall Auxiliary Hospital, as Nurse
And is recommended for the War Service Bar.

It was countersigned by the county director, whose name Becky couldn't decipher. Matron was delighted and shook Becky's hand,

"I'm proud of you, Nurse Nelson; you've served us unstintingly here at Beech Tree Hall. You are an outstandingly good nurse, not only in practical medicine, but in the way you relate to the men. You have shown not just sympathy but empathy with them. You've reached the person behind the wounds and the disabilities. It's a rare gift Nurse Nelson and one the patients here have appreciated. Now, as soon as your War Service Bar comes through you will be eligible to be sent to wherever you are needed but until you receive papers to say otherwise, you are required to continue nursing here. We shall try to give you as much experience with the acute cases as possible and you are also to attend training sessions in field medicine, at the army camp near Preston. This will be a three week course starting in January. Do you understand all this Becky?"

"Yes Matron, thank you." As soon as Matron dismissed her, Becky rushed to tell Vernon the news. He grabbed her hand, "I'm routing for you Nurse Becky."

His use of her Christian name brought tears to Becky's eyes. "Thank you Vernon, I'll not let you down," she whispered. Becky's mother and sisters although fearful for her were proud of Becky and considered it no more than her duty. All her sisters who were still at home were members of the St. John's Ambulance brigade but Carrie in particular was the most active. In October of 1917 there was an explosion at Drew's munitions factory. Carry was immediately called on to go and help with the injured. She told her family what had happened. As she'd hurried along the streets in her uniform she was met by a crowd of women in overalls and turbans rushing panic stricken from the factory,

"You're going 't wrong way. Turn round, there's been an explosion at Drew's and likely to be more- and worse," they shouted to her. One woman she knew had grabbed Carrie's arm and tried to drag her with them.

"Can't you see I'm St. John's Ambulance," Carrie shouted back at them. "I've been called to go there in case of injuries." She'd had to push her way against the tide of fleeing people.

"There were some injured but there'd have been a lot more if a policeman hadn't forced his way in and shut the magazine doors. He was killed but he saved a lot of lives," was all she would say afterwards. It was to be many years before Carrie told of the injuries she'd seen that day but she never forgot the bodies with limbs blown off and men and women choking on the yellow gas from the chemicals.

CHAPTER 46

Nurse Rebecca Nelson VAD

It was the late spring of 1918 before Becky received another official letter. Dated the twenty-first of May it had arrived on the twenty second and was, again, headed with the insignia of the Red Cross and the Order of St. John of Jerusalem. Becky's heart beat faster as she read:-

"You are requested to join the Royal Marine Infirmary at Deal for nursing duties on May 25th..You are appointed for one month on probation, and are then expected to sign on for six months if requested to do so. During your residence in the hospital you must conform to the Hospital regulations.

Please write to "Navy, Medical, London," and to me, if you are unavoidably prevented from going. But I trust you will let nothing interfere with your taking up this appointment.

Your luggage must be strictly limited (maximum size of trunk 30in. by 24in. by 12in.)

Regulation indoor uniform only is required for the months' probation. Regulation outdoor uniform is not required unless you sign your contract (if considered satisfactory) at the end of your months' probation. Then it must be obtained immediately and no mufti may be worn. An equipment list can be sent to you on signing your contract, by request. I enclose:-

Railway Warrant for your journey.

Mobilisation Form to be presented to Head Sister on arrival. (Or Sister-in-Charge)

Print of Regulations.

These orders must be acknowledged by post- card, by return of post. In all communications, whether by letter or telegram, please use the word **'allocations'** *at the beginning of your message. On leaving Hospital, for whatever reason, you must report without fail to Devonshire House either in person or by letter.*

No Brassards are worn in the Naval Hospitals at home. These are only worn by members of mobilised detachments working in Auxiliary Hospitals. If you are in possession of a Brassard please return it to your Commandant before reporting at the Hospital to which you are allocated. This does not refer to St. John members' Armlets.

I shall always be glad to know how you are, and if we can help you at any time, we shall be pleased to do so. Please remember that all questions relating to your work or welfare must, in the first instance, be referred through the Sister of your ward to the Head Sister (or Sister-in Charge).

Yours truly,

Margaret Amplewhite pp. G.H.

In the bottom left hand corner were the letters J.W.74 (Naval).

Becky noticed a hurriedly written post-script in pencil at the very top of the letter:-

'As you are needed as soon as possible, there is no time for you to be inoculated. Please report this to the Matron on arrival at the hospital. pp. G.H.'

Becky was at home, sitting round the breakfast table with her mother and two of her sisters when she opened the letter. Three of her brothers were fighting in France, another was with the Royal Navy, and her father was working in the munitions factory.

Mrs Nelson blanched when Rebecca read out the contents. As a mother of ten, she was a pragmatic woman. She knew she couldn't change what was happening in the world, nor how it was affecting her family but that didn't stop the tearing feeling in her guts, when she thought of her boys out there among the death- dealing violence and confusion. Now her Becky was being ordered away from her. The worst of it, was watching this war- machine take control of your own children. They were pawns in a monstrous game of chess but instead of being moved in logical fashion on a chessboard, the players were being moved about in the deranged melee which had become the world's battlefield and she, Lucy Nelson their own mother, was helpless to stop it. She pulled herself together as Josie, her youngest at nineteen, started to cry.

"Why do you have to go, Becky? It's not fair. You don't have to go, women can stay at home. Why did you have to volunteer?" Rebecca, now twenty-eight, had helped to bring Josie up; she was as much a mother- figure, as a sister, to Josie.

"Now then, our Josie, you should be proud of your sister. I know it's hard but Becky's serving her country, just like your brothers are. There's no knowing what would happen to us all and the future generations, if we don't fight this battle to keep Britain the free country it is. Anyway Becky's going to help the lads to get home safely."

"I don't know why you can't stay at 'Beech Tree Hall'," Josie herself had just started working at the Hall as a St. John's volunteer.

"I have to go, Josie love, it's my duty and I want to do this. You must look after the men at the Hall, cheer them up and make sure they get well. Vernon needs a special friend, I won't be there for him, you must befriend him, they need someone young, like you, Josie, keep them smiling."

As soon as she could, Becky escaped to her sister Hannah's on Aspen Lane. She wanted to cuddle and play with Tom and young Rebecca one last time before she left and to break the news to her elder sister. Five year old Rebecca was looking over the gate and saw her aunt hurrying up the hill,

"Auntie Becky, Auntie Becky!" the childish treble made Becky's heart miss a beat and she swept her small niece up into her arms, swinging her round and round both of them laughing and panting, till Rebecca shouted, "stop wobbling me, Auntie!"

Becky set the child down and together they went into the house. Hannah was in the kitchen baking and Tom was sitting on the floor. He was absorbed in taking an old clock to pieces, setting each part down in an orderly pattern. He smiled at his aunt but went straight back to his task.

"He loves taking things apart to see how they work, then fitting them back together, keeps him happy for hours! Old Mr Hammond, from next door, gave him that old clock."

Hannah wiped her hands and put the kettle on. Becky sat at the scrubbed wooden table and took her young namesake on her knee allowing the child to reach up and play with the gold and turquoise pendant, hanging round her neck. She nodded silently at her sister, in answer to the question;

"I take it you've heard from them?"

Hannah took three scones from a batch she had just made and cut and spread them with butter.

"Tom, Rebecca, sit up to the table," she poured milk for the two children and gave them half a scone each and they settled quietly at one end of the table.

The two sisters sat and talked and Hannah read Becky's call-up letter.

Tom and Rebecca drank their milk and ate their scone, covering their faces with buttery crumbs. Tom went back to his clock and eventually Hannah got up and rolled out the pastry, which she had previously left to rest.

The scene brought back a vivid memory from Becky's childhood. Hannah had come home from school with a bag of coins and poured them out on the kitchen table in front of their mother, who was leaning against the table, just as Hannah was doing now. Becky remembered that the coins were all half-pennies and there must have been sixteen or more. Hannah would have been about nine years old and the younger children were open mouthed, at the sight of so much wealth. It was a time when the family was short of everything, father was out of work and they scrimped and saved even on food. Mother had asked sharply how she'd come by the money. When Hannah told her she'd been given it by the school inspector for reciting a poem, mother was suspicious. Hannah explained that the class had all learnt the poem, 'The Ride of Paul Revere' by Longfellow. They were meant to recite it in unison but one by one the others had dropped out until only Hannah was left. The inspector had begun to throw her a half-penny for every line she'd continued to recite. Hannah had carried on, to the very end of the poem, having remembered it all word for word. Then Mother had laughed and asked Hannah what she'd like to spend the money on. Hannah had begged to go to the shop for a quarter of beef dripping for them all to have on their bread for tea. The children had cheered and banged their fists on the table. Such a tea they'd enjoyed that day! Today in 1918, despite the depression, food was far more plentiful for the Nelsons and for Hannah and her family. Becky sighed as she watched Hannah turning her pastry into pies.

Rebecca came and leant against her auntie, sensing something solemn about the occasion. She reached out again, to touch the pretty turquoise pendant. Suddenly Becky wanted desperately to stay in Hartsbeck; she wanted to be able to see Tom and Rebecca every few days, as she had done since they were born. They were changing and growing all the time and even if she was only away for a few months, Becky knew she would miss such a lot. Deep down she knew she would be away far longer.

"Oh, Hannah, it's so quick, now the letter's come. Only three days! I haven't time to get used to it. Good job I've nearly everything ready. The letter sounds so fierce. I don't want to leave you all, now the time's come."

"You'll soon get over that once you're on your way. They certainly give you your orders don't they? There's no denying that they're in charge, even the kind words at the end have a bit of a sting. Telling you to contact them if you need anything but reminding you to go through the correct chain of command first! Make sure they inoculate you as soon as possible, I don't like it that you haven't been done before you go."

Hannah spread pastry over a pie dish and added chopped apple and sugar.

"I'm sure they'll do me as soon as I get there," Becky picked a piece of raw pastry and nibbled it as she had done as a child; she passed a tiny piece to her niece, who spat it out with disgust.

"That's horrid! Why are you going away, Auntie Becky? Tom and I want you to stay. You can sleep in my bed,"

"She's got to go to the War. Aunty Becky's going to save the wounded soldiers, she can't stay Rebecca, don't be silly,"

"I'm not silly," snapped Rebecca stamping her foot and starting to cry, "I want to come with you, Auntie Becky, I can save 'oonded sodjers,"

Tom laughed at her childish pronunciation but their aunt knew she would carry that memory of *'oonded sodjers,* with her into her work wherever she went.

Becky picked up her niece and set her on a chair; she took the pendant from her own neck and fastened it round four year old Rebecca's plump one. The pendant had a delicate fretwork of gold, in a rounded shape, set with tiny turquoise stones and was hung on a fine gold chain.

"Rebecca, this is for you, to keep till you are an old, old lady, so you'll always remember your Auntie Becky. You must let your mummy put it away safely for you, till you are old enough to wear it but I'm sure, whenever you want to, she'll let you look at it. Tom, there's something special for you in this little knap-sack." Becky took a small canvas knap-sack from her shopping bag and handed it to Tom. Inside was her own, worn copy of the 'Song of Hiawatha'. She'd written a short inscription on the fly leaf,

For my nephew, Tom, from Aunt Becky. May you enjoy this as much as I did.

There were also pencils and crayons and a notebook in the bag, Becky fished out a similar one for Rebecca but without a poetry book

Tom stood up looking very solemn, "But, you will be coming back to us won't you, Auntie Becky? You're not going away for ever?"

"When I've finished saving 'oonded sodjers and sailors and maybe air- men too, I'll come back as fast as I can. It's going to be hard work and I'd like to know you were thinking of me sometimes. Now, we are going to march and sing like proper soldiers. Put your knapsacks on troopers!"

Laughing Tom and Rebecca put their knapsacks over their shoulders and marched round the kitchen behind Aunt Becky who had shouldered a broom for a gun. They all sang lustily, "Pack up your troubles in your old kit-bag and smile, smile, smile—," until they had to stop, laughing and breathless.

"Now I really must go," smiled Becky, wiping her face with her hanky.

"You must have my fossil; the one I found with Uncle Stephen," said Tom suddenly and ran off to his bedroom to find his treasure.

"I'll draw you a picture, Auntie," promised Rebecca.

A few minutes later they were saying goodbye. Hannah held her younger sister's hands and gazed into her eyes.

"I'll think of you every day, Becky and every night at six o'clock when I'm putting the children to bed, we'll talk about you and think about what you may be doing,"

"And Rebecca and I will say the prayer you taught us. Every night, without fail," promised Tom and little Rebecca nodded her head in agreement. Auntie Becky put her arms round both children and hugged them tightly, her eyes filling with tears.

Hannah continued "We love you Becky, whatever happens remember that and I'm sure that good will come out of all this, in the end."

"God bless you all! Give George my love, just in case I don't see him before I leave."

Hannah kissed her sister and waved until she was out of sight. She shivered slightly as she went back inside; there was something so final about someone going out of sight. What would happen to her sister; how much would she be changed, when she came back?

Sarah too was sad to say goodbye to Becky. They'd worked together at 'Beech Tree Hall', though Sarah was only a part-time volunteer. They'd both been members of the St. John's Ambulance brigade since they were ten years old and had become good friends. Together they'd followed and discussed Ellie's nursing career and Sarah's older sister had become something of a heroine to Becky. When Sarah became a teacher, Becky had thought she would consider herself too superior to keep the friendship going with a sewer from the textile mill. Not a bit of it, Sarah recognised Becky's true worth and the friendship had become stronger than ever. Hannah had chosen them both to be her bridesmaids. Over recent years they had attended church together and joined the Girl's Friendly Society. Together they'd bemoaned the fact that George and Hannah had decided not to have their babies baptized.

"They must be left free to make up their own minds, when they're old enough," declared George with a firmness that booted no argument.

"Well Becky, I'm going to consider myself a secret God-parent to those children, whatever George thinks. They'll see that someone in the family believes in God and the Church and prays specially for them!"

"I agree, we'll both be self- appointed God- mothers and no-one but God and our-selves will know. What fun, Sarah! We can pray for them and tell them Bible stories, even buy them a Bible each. You can play hymns on your piano and sing to them and no-one will think anything of it!"

"Well, if they've to be equipped to make up their own minds later, they need to know something about the Christian faith!" declared Sarah and they'd laughed at their conspiracy. Hannah had been pleased when she noticed the small ways in which her sister and sister- in -law introduced the Christian Faith into the lives of her children. She herself kept her faith quietly within herself, it was not a churchy faith but she had an awareness of God and sought to under-stand Jesus Christ in a way unfettered by the church's structures. In any case, because of her deafness, she found it difficult to follow the services. She spent time thinking and praying privately but was also wary of her husband's strong views against the Church and didn't want to alienate him.

CHAPTER 47

Becky's heroism.

On May 24th Becky left Hartsbeck and travelled by train to Deal in Kent. The journey took her most of the day and her father had booked for her to stay the night in a small, respectable hotel on the sea front. The following morning she reported to the Matron of the Royal Marine Hospital and began her month on probation. Becky fell into the full nursing routine like a duck into water. She was where she was meant to be and though saddened by the condition of the men she nursed, she was not overwhelmed by the horror of it. Her grounding at 'Beech Tree Hall' stood her in good stead, as did her optimistic nature and ability to relate well to people of all backgrounds. She did fall foul of the chain of command on one occasion. Using her good 'Lancashire common sense,' she had gone straight to the top of the chain with a problem because the 'top' personnel happened to be present at the time. Repercussions and petty jealousies resulted, which caused a bad atmosphere for a while but people moved on and it was soon forgotten. Becky had laughed it off but was unnerved by having so easily rocked the boat. She wrote to Ellie Elkson at Netley about it, knowing she would understand. Ellie reassured her that nursing under the military regime could be a mine-field. Despite her own years of civilian nursing experience, she still had to tread carefully and was often viewed with suspicion. "Don't worry Becky, it's just the military way and we are not used to it. In the end, they are more than thankful to have us."

The incident didn't count against her because, after her one month's probation, Becky was invited to sign on for the next six months under the Auspices of the Admiralty Service.

In September 1918, another challenge hit the overstrained medical teams. Influenza was striking down both patients and staff, causing a huge increase in the work-load. In October, news came that a Royal Navy troop ship was standing off the Goodwin Sands. She had wounded on board but also influenza, which meant a quarantine ban. No-one was allowed to leave the ship until this ban was lifted. Most of the medical staff on board had gone down with influenza, as well as many others of the ship's company. The ship was to be allowed to anchor in the sheltered waters, between the shore and the Goodwin Sands, known as the Downs. An appeal went out for nurses to volunteer to go on board and nurse both the wounded and those with influenza. No nurse was to be forced to perform this duty but, to go voluntarily would be an act of great humanity. Whoever went would remain on board the troop ship, until it was out of quarantine.

Becky didn't hesitate. She was haunted by the thought of those men suffering in shipboard conditions with only the most basic medical aid.

Four other nurses, three orderlies, one doctor and a naval chaplain also volunteered. They were taken in a large dingy to the quarantined ship anchored some way out in the Downs. The sailor who manned the dingy had to stay with them, he wasn't allowed back to shore.

They found the conditions on board to be hellish. There was a constant sound of moaning. The source of this was found in the sailor's sleeping quarters, where at least sixty members of the crew were lying in bunks, hammocks or on the floor in the grips of influenza. In another part of the ship were 180 wounded soldiers. These men were lying on stretchers, mainly uncared for, except by one medic and a few healthy men from among the 230 able-bodied troopers who were being shipped home when the 'flu virus had struck among them. The Captain and another officer were valiantly trying to keep going while themselves suffering the early stages of influenza.

Fresh sheets and bedding, medical supplies, food and fresh water had been brought with them in the dingy and the volunteers quickly went into action. They could have done with three times their number.

The middle-aged doctor was experienced in organising tent hospitals on the battle field and quickly formed work-teams using every able-bodied person on board. Soon the ship became a hospital and the strong smell of disinfectant began to mingle with the stale smell of sick men. Makeshift beds were hurriedly laid in rows on the decks with tarpaulin canopies raised above them; thankfully the weather was dry on that first day. The sick were assessed and divided into groups according to the acuteness or stage of their condition. Water and water vessels were supplied to each person and medication decided upon and administered. Food was prepared for those who could eat. The heads, where the sailors performed ablutions and relieved themselves, had to be cleaned and disinfected. Those too sick to wash themselves had to be bathed where they lay.

The wounded who had escaped influenza, were separated to a different area and wounds dressed and morphine and penicillin administered. The chaplain did whatever job was needed as well as his own. Used to feeding a large family at home, he made himself particularly useful in the galley. The work never stopped, the most rest any of the volunteers could hope for was a staggered half hour each, occasionally. There was hardly time to eat, sleep, or attend to their own sanitary needs.

"Not even time to spit!" gasped another nurse from Lancashire, as she scrambled up and down the ladders between decks. They kept going on adrenalin.

Becky found herself going from bed to bunk, to hammock; setting up drips, sponging fevered bodies, trying to reduce raging temperatures and persuading the men to take fluids and medicines, giving injections and coping with immobile patients' bodily functions. Gradually, after the first week, some of the 'flu victims began to respond to treatment and there was a slight lull, in which the nurses could concentrate on the few who were not responding.

Becky's immune system eventually became so worn down that she contracted influenza herself.

It was on the 23rd October that a telegram came to the Nelson family in Hartsbeck with the news that their daughter Becky had died, while *"fulfilling her duty towards her fellow country-men in a most heroic manner."*

The telegram to the Nelson family was followed by official letters which explained the circumstances of Becky's death. There were also unofficial letters from sailors and colleagues, expressing admiration and gratitude and a warm love for Becky. They told how she'd spent her skills and eventually her life for them.

Piecing together the information from all the letters, Sarah and Hannah worked out just how Becky came to die.

The whole of one wet night when rain drummed on the tarpaulins, and the ship rolled to the shrieking of the wind, Becky had stayed beside one of the petty officers who seemed to be slipping into death. She'd fought tooth and nail to keep him alive, using every skill and bit of knowledge she had, bathing and massaging his limbs, administering medicines and drinks, moving him into positions, which helped his breathing. The young sailor had slowly begun to respond to her ministrations and Becky stayed with him, refusing to be relieved by a colleague.

This young officer was one of the men who'd written to the Nelson family. He seemed a decent young man with a wife and baby and said he owed his life to Nurse Nelson. In his letter he wrote of waking once, towards dawn, to hear her saying something about,

"Here's one of your 'oonded sodjer's, Rebecca, I promise you, I won't let him die."

He went on to say:

'Time and again I woke from a restless sleep to hear her saying, "You're getting better, laddie, just rest, you're getting better." as she held a cool cloth to my aching head.

I recovered and as I was just about the last case of influenza on board, when the vessel was declared out of quarantine. Nurse Becky, as we all called

her, was worn out from no sleep and not much food and collapsed on arrival at the Royal Marine Hospital in Deal. She had little resistance left to fight the influenza when it attacked her; she'd used up her resources in fighting to save us. I heard that she was ill for just one week in the hospital sick-bay, her colleagues did their best but they couldn't save her. I believe her sister-in-law, who's nursing at Netley, came over, just in time to be with her when she died. It's my firm opinion that those volunteer nurses and the doctor saved the lives of most of us sailors on that ship. Only four of the ship's company died of 'flu, though many more had been close to death. Nurse Becky Nelson is up there among the real heroes of this war. She'll always be my hero and my wife's and when she's old enough, I'll tell my little girl all about Nurse Becky.

Such letters drew tears from the loved ones at home who'd been numbed by the shock of Becky's death. The authorities decided that Becky should be brought back to Hartsbeck and buried with full military honours. The Great War was almost over and Becky's funeral was one of the last of the full military funerals to take place in Hartsbeck. The day before the funeral, the Nelson family had met the train at Hartsbeck station bearing Becky's remains from Deal. An escort of sailors and soldiers she had nursed had travelled with her.

"We had to see her home safely, Mrs Nelson," one of the sailors said to Becky's mother, who was standing on the station platform, proud but dejected, surrounded by Becky's remaining brother and sisters, Lucy Nelson had already lost two sons in the war. A detachment of uniformed VAD nurses of the 240th Division, which was Becky's division, stood on the platform to receive her coffin and take it to the Ambulance Drill Hall, where it was to rest overnight, before being taken to the Nelson's home the following morning.

It was an early November day of sunshine and showers. In the small cemetery, on the outskirts of Hartsbeck, bright autumn leaves glowed in the trees or rustled in dry death, underfoot. This burial place was older and nearer to Becky's home than the main town cemetery. A gun carriage was waiting in the street outside the small terraced house. Becky's coffin was lifted carefully onto it and reverently draped with the Union Jack. Neighbours had closed their curtains from respect and stood reverently along the pavement. The Nelson family, including Hannah and George, were led from the house by the Vicar of the church Becky had been a part of since a child. A group of sailors and soldiers shared in the pulling of the gun carriage and the procession left the street where Becky had grown up, for the mile and a half walk to the cemetery. The report in the Hartsbeck Chronicle later in the week stated that:

"There was a strong muster of nurses and other members of St. John's Ambulance Association and large numbers of the general public assembled to witness the interment. The mourners walked from their residence to the cemetery, the route of which was lined with sympathetic spectators. Behind these walked a procession of nurses carrying wreaths and other floral tributes, which made the proceedings very impressive. Soldiers and sailors marched in rank. The procession was silent."

As Becky's body was lowered into her grave, the soldiers prepared to honour her with a full gun salute. Lucy Nelson raised her arm high in the air in protest and walked forward. Hannah's eyes pricked at the dignity of her homely mother, unshapely from years of child- bearing, wrapped around in her ordinary black winter coat and pulled-down felt hat but with her head held high, even in grief.

"No, lads," she said and her voice held a ring of authority. "There's been enough of guns and shooting in this war. Let my daughter go to her grave with thoughts of peace and prayers for healing."

The soldiers lowered their guns and bowed their heads in acknowledgement, the silence was tangible broken only by the call of a moorland bird flying overhead. Then a bugler stepped forward. The notes of the last post rang out over the burial ground. Finally the Vicar recited the old, familiar prayers of committal and the family threw their handfuls of earth into the grave. Afterwards the mourners and their guests moved away to the Ambulance Drill Hall, to share food and memories and hopes for the future.

Ellie had come home for Becky's funeral and processed beside Sarah and other regular and VAD nurses, all of them proudly in uniform, each with a red rose pinned to the white bibs of their aprons. Ellie thought of another memorial service which she had attended earlier that year on 10th April, in St. Paul's Cathedral. It was in honour of all the nurses who had so far died in this terrible war. Great dignitaries had been present, including Queen Alexandra, Princess Victoria and other members of the Royal Family. The Archdeacon of London, the Venerable V.E. Holmes had given a eulogy in praise of the dead nurses. He spoke of all the female nurses who had risen fearlessly to the war-time challenge;

"As women you were offered your chance and you have taken it: women who will be remembered with the soldiers in a never to be forgotten page of history."

He had called on them all, "matrons, sisters and nurses," to remember that they had been entrusted with a great work and because of that work they were gathered there, to worship, in memory of their dead colleagues. He had spoken urgently, reminding them that the future of nursing was dependent on them all and that the sacrifices made by those of their number who had gone to war, would never be forgotten. His final words held a blood chilling warning;

"For nurses and everyone else, the war is not yet over. Four years of murderous conflict has left the population physically and psychologically exhausted, thousands have been left traumatised." He went on to say that "No-one had known how to stop the killing."

Ellie spoke of this to Sarah, as they walked home after the funeral tea. "The service in St. Paul's was very grand and challenging. It was stirring, to be part of all that great company of nurses in uniform and to hear the solemn words, but it's Becky's funeral service and others like them up and down the land, which get to the heart of what the nation's going through."

"It's all so personal," replied Sarah, "we've all been changed, Ellie, we're not the same people we were before all this started. Maybe we've discovered more about ourselves. Women seem stronger, more confident, but we've all been injured one way or another. Family members, who normally would never travel away from their own home area, were whisked away abroad to fight. I hope, in teaching children, I can help the new generation to find their way through the aftermath."

"We've got to pick up the threads and carry on," Ellie remembered the number of times Eliza had quoted this phrase to her.

"May God help us Ellie, otherwise we may never find the way!" The two sisters clung to each other, struck by the horror of all they had seen and been through and lost.

Tom and Rebecca had watched their Aunt Becky's funeral procession pass through the town but were taken to a friend's home during the rest of the ceremony. They'd been awed by the number of people watching and the soldiers and sailors and the nurses carrying wreaths. Rebecca was very quiet afterwards and resolved to herself that, when she grew up, she would do something wonderful, just like her Auntie Becky. She never forgot that resolve, although her vocation was to be in teaching the young women of Hartsbeck how to make happy and healthy homes.

Rebecca was to marry in nineteen thirty nine, at the beginning of the Second World War. After her marriage service, she would take her wedding bouquet to the Ambulance Drill Hall in Hartsbeck and lay it beneath the portrait of VAD Nurse Becky Nelson which hung there and say:

"Auntie Becky, this is for you. You never had a wedding bouquet, only funeral wreaths but they came with so much love. I had no flowers for you on that day but here is my wedding bouquet. Another war is beginning. I will keep thinking of you and make you proud of us, as we are of you."

CHAPTER 48

1919 Ellie in the Spiritualist net

In the spring of 1919 Ellie left Netley and moved back to London and the house in Felix Square. Once again she took up the mantle of Dr Truby King, spreading the message that good parenting was the way to build up a new generation strong in body and in character. Polly had remained in the house, Lettie didn't return but the team of Truby King Nurses had grown to twelve and there were now two accommodation houses.

Dr King had returned to England in 1916 and was at present involved in establishing a Mother-Care training centre, at 29, Trebovir Road, Earls Court. Here instruction in Dr King's methods was given to trained nurses and also to new and expectant mothers, from all walks of life, rich and poor. Dr King had attracted a group of influential and wealthy supporters, including Lady Galway, who worked unstintingly on behalf of the centre. Professional nurses took a three month course before certificates as qualified 'Truby King Nurses'. These Truby King Nurses constantly reminded each other of Dr King's mantra that "a nation moves forward on the feet of its children."

Ellie felt good to be back and part of a movement dealing with new life. She closed off that part of her mind, which was still in shock from the death of Jack and Rebecca, the part which didn't know whether to grieve for Alex's death or to hope for his return. Sometimes she wondered if Alex had moved on to other things and other loves but she couldn't believe that he would end their relationship without telling her. Her heart still raced whenever she knew the post was due.

One day she returned from visiting a young mother, who was struggling to cope with a colicky first baby, to find a letter waiting for her. It was addressed in an unfamiliar, flowing script and been forwarded from Ellie's previous London address with Mrs. Larson. The post-mark was local. The contents of the letter were strange and unsettling. It was from a Mrs Mary Dempster of Charing Cross;

"Dear Miss Elkson,

I hope you won't think it impertinent of me for writing to you. I have your name and address from the attendance registers of some meetings held by the Theosophical Society, which you attended. I heard from various colleagues that you have continued to show an interest in the beliefs of the society, particularly in those dealing with death and beyond.

Since so many families have been devastated by the loss of loved ones during the recent War and from the influenza epidemic, I have felt led, by my own Spirit Guide, to find ways of helping family members come to terms with the death of their loved ones. I am confident that the Spirits want me to help the bereaved of this world, to make contact with those who have been dragged so suddenly into the next life.

Theosophy, as you know, teaches us that it is possible to contact the spirits of those who have passed, through death, into the next sphere of being. I understand that you have lost loved ones in this terrible war and so will understand the devastation of grief. I am sure that you would benefit from contacting your loved ones from beyond the divide. If you would allow me to help you with this, I could then go on to guide you to help others to do the same.

My dear Miss. Elkson, I felt led to write to you and eagerly await your response. If my project to help such families is to work, I shall need many helpers both from this side of the great divide and beyond it.

Also, there are certain spirits who, having passed some hundred years ago or more have gained great wisdom. Such wisdom would help us greatly in our life here. However, these spirits cannot communicate it to us without our help. Our poor world needs the hope of their wisdom, at this time. Our earthly

*sphere is still reeling from the vicious attacks from evil sources, which caused
such a warlike spirit to overtake us!"*

There was more in this vein. The writer's wording became more
esoteric, expressing a view of the world far beyond the simple practicalities of comforting the bereaved. Ellie had the distinct impression
that Mrs Dempster was merely plucking phrases from the annals of
theosophy, without having any clear understanding of her subject and
she wondered if her correspondent's underlying agenda was as noble
as she professed.

Curious, Ellie decided she would agree to meet with the woman.
A flutter of excitement dissipated some of the deathly numbness left
by the war. Ellie sensed that she was entering into something with a
hint of danger and took a guilty pleasure in imagining Eliza's disapproval. For once, she would go her own way. Nevertheless, she wished
she could discuss the letter with her brother Stephen. His scientific
brain would soon pick out the flaws in Mrs Dempster's thought
patterns.

"Oh, what does it matter if Mrs Dempster can't express theosophical arguments clearly? It isn't the easiest of subjects and I'll
soon suss it out if the woman has her own selfish agenda." In her
turmoil Ellie had spoken out loud convincing herself that she
could easily back out of the situation, at any point. There it was;
Ellie was neatly hooked.

"Clever and devious, that's what the woman is. I can't believe that
you don't see right through her Ellie. Alright, go and see her. Find
out what it's all about. But promise me you'll keep me informed of
every little detail. I don't want one of my best friends being caught in
a spirit trap." fumed Eliza when Ellie told her on a visit to her friend.

"I could say that you'd been caught in a spiritual trap, when you
joined the Church!" responded Ellie sharply

"Spiritual is not the same as 'spirit' in this context! The church
is open and above board and doesn't meddle with occult practises,
which is exactly what you would be doing with this Dempster person!"

"Well, I'm going to do it. It's just possible that these practices can help where the church hasn't. There are lots of things we are unaware of, Eliza."

"They've all been tried, my dear, and found lacking– if not dangerous. You could find all this disastrous to your mental health, never mind endangering your eternal soul!"

"Well, if I find myself in danger, you can come and rescue me!" Ellie rose to leave, angry and at odds with Eliza.

Out of real fear for her young friend Eliza couldn't leave things there and leant over to grasp Ellie's sleeve. She spoke out more strongly than usual for her Christian faith;

"Well Ellie, at least the Christian Church has been tried and tested. I've found a real sense of healing there and I certainly wouldn't trust any spirit but the Holy Spirit!" Eliza continued to lay a restraining hand on her friend's arm. Ellie shook it off and left the older woman's house upset but determined to throw in her lot with Mrs Dempster.

Eliza too was upset. She called after Ellie, telling her that she would always be there if she needed her and this must not in any way spoil their friendship.

As soon as Ellie had gone, Eliza put on her hat and coat and walked to St Stephen's church. There she sat and prayed quietly for an end to all the mess the war had left behind and especially for Ellie and the Mrs Dempster's of this world. She could have prayed at home but here, in this ancient church building, she was surrounded by things which witnessed to and affirmed her faith. The prayers and worship of people down the centuries still lingered in the atmosphere and her own prayers mingled with them, touching the very being of God. She, like Ellie, had explored other avenues but found that this way had opened up a new life to her, when she'd been in danger of slipping into despair. A quiet, gravelly voice broke into her thoughts,

"Needing a breath of Heaven?"

It was the vicar calling in on his way home from pastoral duties. He slid into the pew beside Eliza. She smiled at the thin, middle-aged man with his wispy hair and tired, kind eyes. Eliza thought he must be in his early forties but he looked fifty. He'd come back from the war with a limp, from a shrapnel wound. The pain it gave him didn't prevent him walking round his parish, visiting and encouraging, helping people make sense of the toughness of life. She knew he was used as a whipping boy, a shoulder to cry on, a confidante and confessor, advisor, social worker and friend and like herself, needed a constant 'breath of heaven', as he called it to refresh him.

She expressed her feelings to him; "I find reassurance when I come in here. I'm reminded that I'm one among thousands who find that Jesus Christ and His message ring true and that steadies me. It's like being in a ship, steered through storms and fair weather, by a competent and trusty Captain."

"Bless you, Eliza; you're a great comfort to a body like me. Just what I needed to hear, I wish more would listen and understand," his eyes welled up with tears as he patted Eliza's hand and the two sat in comfortable silence, each with their own thoughts and prayers. Then Eliza moved to go home.

"Come and visit me sometime soon, Vicar. I'd like to talk with you. I'm at home every Tuesday afternoon after three o'clock."

"In that case," said the Vicar "I'll call next Tuesday, at half past three."

"The kettle will be on," smiled Eliza and they clasped each other's hands firmly. "Please give my regards to your wife and tell your son I'll look out some more adventure stories for him!"

"He'll be your friend for life," laughed the Vicar, father of two intrepid youngsters, a girl of twelve and a boy of ten. His ten year old son, Jeremy, was frail and asthmatic but with a vivid imagination and a rapacious appetite for adventure and travel stories.

CHAPTER 49

Mrs Dempster; Medium.

Ellie attended a meeting at Mrs Dempster's home, or at least the house where she conducted her communications with the spirits. Ellie wasn't t sure whether it was the house where the medium lived, or if it was a place set up for her by the elders of the Theosophy Society and filled with mystical paraphernalia to create atmosphere. The rooms where they met seemed to have lots of alcoves, some curtained in deep wine- coloured velvet, others with a light, flowing material, reminiscent of water or mist. At that first meeting Mrs Dempster was clothed in a blue dress, which fell around her in loose folds from a round collar. This three inch high, stiff collar, was exquisitely embroidered in a darker blue silk, with the motifs Ellie remembered, from her very first theosophy meeting in Gt. Ormond Street. There was the coiled serpent and the cross with the loop from ancient Egypt; then the swastika (a sacred symbol of Hinduism); and woven among them all was the ancient Egyptian lettering. A plaque on the wall bore the motto of the society, "There is no religion higher than truth."

Mrs Dempster wore no head covering but in her abundantly piled auburn hair, rested a glittering pin in the shape of an alpine rose,

"Out of deference to my spirit guide," she simpered, touching it reverently, "over two hundred years ago, he was a shepherd in the Swiss Alps. This alpine flower image helps to keep us connected."

Ellie's mind flew to memories of Annette, her Swiss friend from Hartsbeck. Annette must be over seventy years old by now and with a pang Ellie realised how many years it was since she had been in touch with her. Was she still alive?

Mrs Dempster rose to welcome Ellie. She flowed across the room to meet her and held out her arms to take both Ellie's hands in hers in a theatrical gesture. The others in the room watched silently. Ellie was sure she detected a smirk, on some faces.

"My dear Miss Elkson, or should I call you Sister. I just knew you would come to our aid. The spirit guides are never wrong and I felt so strongly that I should write to you. Your chosen career of nursing declares you have a nature full of compassion for your fellow human beings. Your sensitivity will allow you to be open to the advances of those trying to reach us from the spirit world. Sit down, my dear. No, not there, this chair, here, next to Mr Jackson, another dear friend who has helped me for some years."

Throughout this welcome Ellie had opened her mouth to speak several times but Mrs Dempster had continued without stopping, as if delivering a well-rehearsed speech in a play. Ellie managed a stuttering, "Thank you," as she sat down next to Mr Jackson and was startled by an amused and very definite wink and lift of an eyebrow from this gentleman.

"She likes her little performances," he whispered, when Mrs Dempster turned her back momentarily, "helps set the scene!"

Then followed a talk and explanation of the spirit world, which Ellie only half recognised from her reading of theosophy. She became more convinced than ever, that Mrs Dempster did not fully understand the subject. However, the talented woman skilfully manipulated her audience and convinced most of them that she was a gifted medium with the ability to communicate with the Spirit world. In no time at all Ellie was almost persuaded to believe in her. With an unnerving aptness Mrs Dempster turned her gaze on Ellie and spoke confidingly;

"You see, my dears, the Spirits don't look for someone with a deep, intellectual understanding of the teachings of our faith. Indeed, such knowledge might get in the way of their attempts to reach us and prevent them from communicating their own messages of higher wisdom to this world. No, they use people of a simpler, open mind, who are willing to offer a blank sheet for them to write on, so to speak,"

Well, thought Ellie, that gets her off the hook as regards intellect but she is clever and what she says could be right. I want to see if she really is in touch with the dead and the Spirits, or if it's all a sham. Even if it's a sham, it may still be a help to the bereaved. Or was Eliza right? Could it disturb people's personalities and unhinge them mentally? Ellie's thoughts were jerked back as Mrs Dempster's manner of address changed.

"However, we do have someone here who is well- known and respected in Theosophical circles and who will take us simpler souls through the theosophical meaning of the 'Septenary Constitution of Man.' I give you, Dr. Melinsky."

Several of those present clapped as a small, bird -like man, with shoulder-length silver hair and wearing a loose, grey tunic and trousers, appeared from one of the curtained alcoves and came to stand in the centre of the room. In a light, wavery voice he spoke for twenty minutes about, what he named to be, "the various constituents of a human being".

Ellie recognised the occasional word but knew it was far beyond her to grasp what he meant in this one afternoon's talk. She would have to read it up in the quietness of her own room.

He spoke of the physical; the astral; of the sthula –sarira and the prana and kam. He described something called 'manas' as being the mind or soul of the human. He spoke of the Buddhi or spiritual soul and the Atman, which he said was the 'inner-spirit' or 'self' of a person, or pure consciousness.

From the book which Hannah had lent her, Ellie recognised that several of these terms were from the Hindu scriptures and were in Sanskrit. *Sthula-sarira* meant the coarse physical body; *Prana* meant the breath of life or the vital spark that brought a body to life; *kam* meant desire.

Dr Melinsky spoke of the inner person as an unbroken, fluid continuity. He spoke of the higher- self and the lower -self and how; '*kam*' can be used for good or evil.

"I fact *kam* comes from the interaction of all the other parts of man.".

"And woman too, I hope," muttered someone close to Ellie. Suppressed giggles travelled round the group.

When he'd finished speaking Mrs Dempster summed it all up, by saying;

"So you see, dear friends, we believe that we are not just the persons we see and relate to here, in this sphere of existence. We are far more complex and our life is not confined to this sphere. When our physical- body and our second-body (which we call linga-sarira) dies and decays, that is far from being the end of us. Oh no; once our real self is no longer burdened by this gross, fleshly body, we are free to go to the next stage of our existence. I intend to demonstrate that it is possible to contact the 'real' personality, of the loved one we knew in this sphere. This will only be possible for a limited time, before they travel further and leave all this behind forever.

There are some who, (when they have travelled much farther into the 'Great Beyond' and gained much wisdom and have evolved into purer spiritual beings), have elected to return to us as Spirit Guides. These guides are so ancient that we could not have known them during their physical lives here. They come to help us in many ways. We hope that we shall meet some of these Guides, in the weeks to come.

Now, I would like you all to gather here again next week, when I will endeavour to make contact with the Spirit World. Please, do not try to get in touch with the Spirits until I have instructed you in this. There is an element of danger; evil does not just belong to this sphere."

She let her penetrating gaze travel round the room and then smiled.

"You have been chosen for this task. It will take courage my dears. You are needed to help in the healing of our nation. I shall leave you now but you will be served with refreshments before you go. Thank you and goodbye, until next week."

With a stately bow Mrs Dempster swept from the room and we were left staring at each other in wary silence. Ellie looked round, half expecting someone to stand up and oppose all that had been said. There was a feeling that something wasn't quite right, that they had been plotting some clandestine act. She could see from the look in their eyes and the way they sat on the edge of their chairs that the others were experiencing the same flutters of excitement and warnings of danger which were welling from the pit of her stomach.

Suspicion was also in the air.

"Pure theatre!" muttered a thin, sallow- faced woman about Ellie's age, as they helped themselves to dainty sandwiches and cups of tea brought in by a maid.

"You think it's all play acting then; no reality behind it?" Ellie queried.

"Oh, contacting loved ones who've died is alright but not all this theosophist mumbo-jumbo. *'Septenary constitution,'* it makes me feel like a department store, one bit of me in the basement with the hardware and household goods, another up on the fourth floor with all the flimsies….lace-trimmed underwear and floating chiffon negligees and yet another part of me among the books and stationary."

"Or torn between the wine and gourmet food with the jewelled evening gowns and plain bread and water with the sturdy weatherproof shoes and coats!" quipped Ellie.

"Exactly! I suppose we all need something from each department but I'd prefer to go 'whole' into each one, rather than cut myself into bits!" The woman's bright, tinkling laugh was infectious and heads looked towards her enquiringly. Ignoring them she turned to Ellie and introduced herself.

"My name is Amelia Antrim, Miss. I've begun to dabble as a straight-forward spiritualist medium. I just try to help people who've lost loved ones. I have private means, so I don't try to make money from it and when the Spirits don't want to play, I help them along with a bit of guidance!" She winked at Ellie and waited for her response.

Ellie was beginning to like Miss Antrim with her mocking, cultured voice and sharp featured face. When she laughed, Ellie thought of a mischievous mouse.

The two women soon became friends. Amelia, as a person of private means, didn't have to work for a living but nevertheless had a job as assistant and receptionist for Dr Richardson, a practitioner of alternative medicine. She lived just two stops on the underground from Ellie and it was easy for them to meet. They travelled together to Mrs Dempster's meetings, although Amelia advised Ellie that they should always have one foot in the door ready to flee and cut contacts with the group, if things became "too fearfully occult."

Eliza met the new friend. She felt that Amelia was an intelligent adventuress and well aware of the dangers of these esoteric schemes. Eliza persuaded herself that although Amelia was "not completely genuine", she would at least keep Ellie from being drawn too deeply into the theosophist treacle by the irresistible lure of Mrs Dempster.

Ellie became interested in Amelia's work with alternative medicine, especially 'water-therapy'. Amelia, on her part, was intrigued by the work of Dr Truby King. The two exchanged books and had many a lively debate, on their common interests.

CHAPTER 50

Truth or Pantomime?

In the following weeks, Mrs Dempster's dramatic presentations of contacting the spirit world intrigued her disciples. They experienced disembodied voices; balls of light which floated round the darkened room. Most intriguing of all was a smoky substance which flowed from Mrs Dempster like a cloud which snaked around her. She called this 'ectoplasm' and stated it to be the physical manifestation of a spirit. There were the usual knocks and table moving and the occasional small object flying through the air. The group gathered round the table were sceptical but happy to believe that, behind the trickery and trappings, Mrs Dempster was definitely in touch with the spirit world. They saw the strange phenomena as clever aids, to help the bereaved feel that their lost loved ones were present.

"Pantomime, that's what it is, a weekly pantomime. Nevertheless, as in all pantomimes there is an element of truth at the bottom of it," was the whispered opinion of Mr Jackson.

Strangely, Mrs Dempster only purported to be in touch with the loved ones of three people in the group and Ellie wasn't one of them.

There was usually an erudite theosophist speaker at the meetings and Ellie couldn't resist delving into the books they mentioned. She became hooked by 'Isis Unveiled: A Master-Key to the Mysteries of Ancient and Modern Science and Religion' written in 1887, by Madame Blavatsky. When Ellie discovered the book's reflections on Darwin's theories of evolution and their impact on religion, she became so excited that she immediately sent a copy to her brother Stephen, now back at the Technical College in Preston. Ellie struggled to understand Madame Blavatsky's theories of the evolution of what she called, 'the root races of humankind,' but found she could grasp the idea that mankind as a whole, was evolving spiritually. Stephen's reply to her was interesting and disappointing:

Hartsbeck
21st November, 1919

Dear Ellie,

Thank you for 'Isis Unveiled', I found it disjointed. I think Mdme. Blavatsky is trying to create a spirituality of her own by using bits from other religions, particularly Eastern ones and those of Ancient Egypt. Try reading something on Theravada Buddhism and on the Hindu scriptures and you'll see what I mean. She takes bits from Judaism and Christianity as well. There is nothing wrong in searching through other faiths to find areas of truth and deeper meaning but don't automatically conclude, that the dear Madame, has hit on the ultimate truth and got it right! Be alert, Ellie, and astute. Madame Blavatsky has a murky, sexually immoral side to her character, which arouses my suspicions. I was interested in her interpretation of Darwinism but thought it disconcerting. There is a twist in her thinking which could result in embracing the very inequality of races which she claims theosophy denies. She implies that we are evolving towards a super-race and that the different races in existence are at different stages, implying some are inferior to others. Have you come across eugenics in your work? I believe Dr. Truby King has expressed thoughts on this subject; he appears to be divided on certain aspects and can well see the dangers. I'd be interested to know what you think of these matters.

Remember, Ellie, you are a darned good children's nurse and midwife. Don't get waylaid into some strange religious cult and ruin your life! I left the Church of England because of a particular scientific stance. During my war service at Woolwich I met many good and knowledgeable people and realised there are those, with integrity of intellect, who see no conflict in being both a modern day scientist and a Christian believer.

I've found out that lots of church members, including many of its leaders, are not against the theory of evolution and happily take on board recent geological discoveries concerning our planet. I would far rather you stayed with one of the tried and tested Churches, than join the theosophists. Surely Christianity speaks with more sense about death than theosophy and offers more comfort?

I'm glad to be back to teaching and out of the war. I was sickened by the way science is used in warfare. I'm determined to instil a moral sense into my students and help them discover the beauty of science. We've a lot to answer for, be careful Ellie. Our way of life on this planet is evolving, both for good and bad. We must do what we can to move it along for good.

I'm becoming boring and pompous aren't I? At least I can escape to my beloved rocks and plants, they don't seem to mind my odd ways.

As for news of home, Mother is constantly tired; most of the family write it off as grief and are sure it will pass. I think the trauma of the war and then losing our Jack may have triggered off some underlying, physical condition. Anyway, Dr. Campbell is keeping his eye on her. Otherwise, we are all well. We are doing what we can to help with the unemployment and aftermath of the war in Hartsbeck. 'As long as the trams keep running!' is a favourite catch-phrase when people meet in the street. The NATS gather every week and uplift our spirits. The natural world is a great healer.

Ah well, Ellie, keep smiling and be thankful that you have important work to do. 'As long as babies keep being born!' should be your catch-phrase.

With love from your ever-aging brother,

Stephen.

At first Ellie felt irritated by her brother's biased response. No doubt, the war had added a wide spectrum of experience to his already analytical mind but she felt patronised, that he should order her to be careful and not dabble in Theosophy. She too, had plumbed new depths of experience since her Hartsbeck years, and had her own valuable insights as a result. She dismissed Stephen's insinuations of Madame Blavatsky's sexual immorality but she did follow his advice and sought out books in the library on Theravada Buddhism and also found an English translation of the Hindu Vedas. She struggled to understand them but gradually some of their meaning came home to her. She became enthralled by the stories of Siddhartha, the young prince who later became the Buddha. His meeting with suffering and hardship in the world and his struggle to understand their purpose resonated in her own life. As she read she felt he was a companion on her own journey.

Ellie also discovered that Madame Blavatsky didn't deny drawing ideas from various religions but aimed to show that they all came from an ancient source of universal Wisdom religion.

The question of eugenics did trouble her. She knew that Dr Truby King had been involved in a political debate about discouraging the 'poor and weaker', lower classes, to 'breed' (the evocative term used by eugenicists) and encouraging those of higher intelligence and strong, healthy bodies, who had proved themselves through success and wealth, to be the main producers of children. The eugenicists hoped that this practice would eventually people the earth with a more superior race of being. To her relief Dr King had steered away from this. Ellie had read of a project to ask wedding couples, of the lower classes, to sign a document agreeing not to have children. Such a declaration would be legally binding and to disobey would be punishable by law. It was this, which had turned Dr King against such a use of eugenics and he had spoken out against the project in strong terms. His vision was to help all classes of the human race to become stronger and healthier, both mentally and physically and for all to be educated:

"That is the way to bring about a better society, not by weeding out a whole group of so called 'weaker breeding-stock,'" he had fumed from his international platforms.

In fact Ellie knew that Dr King was at present in London, establishing a special Mothercraft training centre at number 29, Trebovir Road in the Earls Court district.

Despite Stephen's warning, Ellie continued to accompany Amelia to Mrs Dempster's meetings. Together the two women learnt what they were willing to accept and what to reject from these experiences. Some of the medium's practices they realised were sheer bunkum, or even dangerous meddling in mysteries best left alone but amongst these negative responses the two women found certain ideas which appealed to them.

In January, 1920, Ellie had two weeks leave which she planned to spend in Hartsbeck. Letters from home made her realise that her mother and others in the town, were still grieving for loved ones torn from them so abruptly, by the war. Many families hadn't been able to hold proper funerals, the bodies of their men-folk and some women-folk, lay in graves, known or unknown, overseas. For some, this had left an empty hope, that maybe their loved one was not dead after all. Ellie and Amelia decided that a séance could bring help and comfort to Ellie's family and to their neighbours.

"Come home with me Amelia and help me. You're far more experienced in these matters than I am,"

Amelia rested her chin on her hand and considered.

"Well, I am due some holiday. Yes, if I can persuade Dr Richardson that he can do without me for a fortnight. It will help determine whether what we are doing is worthwhile. Thank you, Ellie, if you're sure it will be alright with your family, I'd love to come home with you."

Ellie wrote to her mother about the proposed visit. She explained about Amelia's gifts as a medium and their desire to help the bereaved.

"Amelia will be happy to conduct a séance for you and any friends you wish to invite, if you think it would help," she concluded.

Jeannie felt her heart quicken at the thought of making contact with Jack and wrote back agreeing to the séance. She told Sarah but kept it secret from the menfolk, sensing a negative reaction.

The two friends arrived in January, to a cold and frosty Hartsbeck and received an uneasy welcome from Ellie's family. Jeannie and Sarah wanted to make their guest feel at home but were anxious at having *a sophisticated London lady* staying with them. Sarah in particular, was unhappy with regard to Amelia's status as a spiritualist medium but tried not to let it interfere with showing good, northern hospitality to Ellie's friend. Stephen greeted Ellie and Amelia brusquely. He had an inkling what this was all about and was not happy. He soon excused himself to go across the road to Edwin's house where he was staying so that Amelia could have a bedroom to herself and Ellie could share with Sarah.

Amelia's manner to her hosts and hostesses was relaxed and friendly and she quickly won over Jeannie Elkson. The two of them were soon chatting over the best way to treat chilblains on feet and hands in this frosty weather. Ellie smiled as she listened to them but was aware of Sarah's unusual quietness. Later, as they undressed for bed Sarah explained,

"I can't agree to this whole thing of trying to contact the spirits of the dead, Ellie. It's wrong. I know it's wrong and the Bible warns us not to do it. I believe Jack and Becky and all those who have died, are now safe with God and at peace from this world. To try and contact them is cruel. If you really could do it, you would be disturbing them in their new life and going against God. Why can't we just help one another to trust God and get on with our everyday, earthly lives? We have to accept that they won't be coming back; trying to reach them is like picking the scab off a wound so that it won't heal properly."

Ellie listened and part of her agreed with her sister but she wasn't going to admit to it.

"The problem that Amelia and I and others like us are trying to address, is that so many have had loved ones torn away from them unexpectedly and in a horribly violent way. Many of them waved goodbye to healthy sons, husbands and fathers. Then, through letters from strangers, they were told their men-folk had been killed in foreign lands,. Some of them haven't even seen the bodies of their loved ones, or been able to give them a proper funeral. Like our Jack,"

Ellie felt her throat tighten as she mentioned her brother and saw that Sarah's eyes had welled up with tears. Sarah reached across and took Ellie's hand in hers,

"It's been hard for you, Ellie, away from home; at least up here we've had each other to talk to."

"I suppose you could say we were fortunate that Edwin was over there with Jack. At least he had one member of his family with him when he died and to attend his funeral. Can't you see how much it would reassure some people, to make contact with their loved one, even if only to say goodbye."

"But, I don't think it would reassure them, it would be so unsatisfactory. A disembodied voice or the movement of an object, it would just make them unsettled and long for more. As for saying goodbye, remember all the goodbyes during the war, on railway stations, on doorsteps; far too many; any more goodbyes would just be too much. Ellie, it's all been too much, we need to let the war go and our dead rest peacefully. I carry so many beautiful memories of Jack and Becky; I wouldn't want the memory of a dubious spiritualist contact to sully them."

"I can see we must agree to differ, Sarah. Don't let's quarrel; don't let it spoil our time together. I've so looked forward to this holiday with you all."

"Oh, Ellie, so have I, you don't know how much. As long as you realise I won't join in the séances. Hannah now, is a different matter. I think you may find she won't be averse to attending. Remember her telling us she was the seventh child of a seventh child, which gives her a kind of 'second sight.'"

The sisters laughed. Soon Ellie turned out the light and slid between the cool, clean sheets of her own bed. Sarah first knelt to say her nightly prayers and then she too climbed into bed.

Over the next two days Jeannie Elkson visited the women of the neighbourhood who'd shown an interest in attending a séance. She had spoken to women who were grieving for dead children, husbands, sisters and brothers or friends.

"They can't seem to settle themselves to anything. The person they've lost keeps coming in between them and ordinary living, just like Jack does with me. He seems to hang around me all the time and I can't shake off the feeling that he's trying to tell me something. These other women say exactly the same about their loved ones. If Ellie and Amelia can help us to be in touch with them, just once, surely it will be a good thing. I don't think it can be as wrong as you say, Sarah."

"Well, mother, you're a grown woman and free to do as you think fit but I refuse to have anything to do with it. I miss Jack terribly and sometimes I feel as if he's very near me. But I know it's wrong to try to contact the spirits of the dead. We believe they're safe in God's hands mother! Leave it at that. It's natural we'll grieve for Jack, and you especially as his mother, but in time the terrible hurt will begin to heal. I've seen it happen to others; give it time mother. We'll struggle through this together."

However, nothing could persuade Jeannie from her desire to make contact with Jack.

Sarah had been right about Hannah, she was easily persuaded to be involved. Brought up in a family where superstition and country folk-lore were given much credibility, Hannah didn't show any aversion to contacting the Spirit world. When Hannah told Amelia that she was the seventh child of a seventh child, Amelia was ecstatic.

"Oh, my dear that will be just perfect. There is nothing the Spirits like better, than the opening that a good superstitious belief produces in the circle. Your decendency will soon get the table rocking."

Hannah had looked quizzically at Amelia and thought to herself, "I think this woman is part humbug. Well, two can play at that game. If she wants the table rocking, I can make sure of that, Spirits or no Spirits."

A séance was planned to take place at Jeannie's house in Aspen Lane on the first Thursday evening of Ellie's stay. The menfolk would be at their weekly gathering of the Debating Society, in an upper room of a local hostelry called 'The Lamb's Fleece'. Their debates went on until ten o'clock and then there was the call of "one for the road," which smoothed over any animosity aroused between them. The men usually came home, in amicable mood, between half past ten and eleven, so the women would be free to hold their séance, quietly among themselves.

"We're just meeting for supper and a gossip. Ladies only," husbands were told.

Hannah took Rebecca with her to Grandma Jeannie's and put her to bed upstairs, before the séance began. Tom was staying overnight with a friend, they were building a model of the ship, 'The Fighting Temeraire', together and it was in its final, crucial stages.

The arrangements seemed perfect and Ellie and Amelia, having made their careful plans, smiled conspiratorially at each other as they went upstairs to change for the event. They had no compunction in having organised a little subterfuge, in case the spirits didn't want to co-operate. After all they'd been warned that the spirits could be fickle and mischievous and as mediums they were very inexperienced. The two friends little realised that they were playing with fire.

CHAPTER 51

The séance

Rebecca peered through the open doorway into her grandmother's parlour, which was at the front of the house. There was a coal fire burning in the grate. It looked full of deep caves glowing red and gold and enticed the child from the chilly hallway towards its warmth.

At six and a half years old she should have been fast asleep in her grandmother's bed upstairs. She knew that her mother was here for a special meeting. When it was over, daddy would come and carry her, half asleep and wrapped in a blanket to their new car and drive mummy and herself home.

Grandma's bedroom had been dark and gloomy and so the child, dressed only in her flannel nightie, had crept downstairs. Now she tiptoed into the parlour and sighing happily curled up on the warm hearth-rug, being careful to keep her nightdress tightly round her and her long straight hair safely down her back, in case of sparks. Heavy velvet curtains were drawn across the bay window, keeping out the winter's night. Two gas wall-lamps gave a dim light and together with the flickering fire, cast moving shadows across the ceiling.

She was staring into the fire, searching for fairy tale pictures, when she heard a door open and the sound of footsteps in the passage. Rebecca decided to hide, she hated it when Grandma was cross and even more if Aunt Ellie was angry. Dark cabinets and chairs loomed shapelessly against the walls but in the middle of the room was a large oval table. It was draped with a cloth of dark, russet-coloured, chenille with a deeply fringed border which, in places, dipped right to the floor. Rebecca knew this table well from Sunday teas and remembered its strange arrangement of wooden legs, which moved to make the table larger. Quick as a flash, she rolled under the table and found a place to crouch between these legs, just as Aunt Ellie came into the room. Rebecca heard her moving pieces of furniture and saw chair legs appearing where the tablecloth didn't quite reach the floor, then a heavy object was placed on the table-top. A large open bag was put on the floor near one of the chair legs but just hidden beneath the cloth. Rebecca wanted to look inside but didn't dare move. Aunt Ellie went to the door and Rebecca wriggled into a sitting position with her arms hugged tightly around her knees.

"Everything is ready; you may all come in now. Please enter quietly and take your seats at the table,"

Aunt Ellie was not speaking in her normal voice. Rebecca wanted to giggle, her Aunt sounded as if she was playing a pretend game, speaking slowly and deeply all on one note. There was some whispering and clearing of throats from the passage, then other ladies came into the room. With much creaking and rustling they sat down, one by one, in the chairs round the table, shuffling their feet under the russet cloth. Desperately wishing she wasn't there, the child tried to find her mother's feet but it was too dark, under the cloth, to make them out clearly.

"Light the table lamp, Ellie, and turn out the wall lights," Rebecca recognised that voice. It belonged to the lady who'd come from London with Aunt Ellie. The cloth began sliding about as someone leaned across the table and Rebecca heard a match strike. Straight away, the room just outside the table cave became much lighter and she saw clearly her mother's shiny, pointed shoes with the tiny patterns on the leather and the buttoned bar and her best lyle stockings. Rebecca's father had taken her mother out to buy the shoes last week, to celebrate his taking on a new client. He said she needed to look smarter, now that he was becoming a respected solicitor in the town. The child put out one finger and just touched the toe of that familiar shoe, she felt better right away, nothing really bad could happen to her if mother was here. Looking round at the other legs and ankles, Rebecca decided that her mother must be one of the youngest there; most of the other feet wore old ladies shoes.

She recognised Mrs Swallow's shoes, flat with scuffed round toes and bulges and her wrinkled, grey woollen stockings. Mrs Swallow kept the corner shop where Rebecca went with Uncle Edwin every Saturday to buy sweets. Mrs Swallow's eyes were often red and swollen, mummy said it was because her two sons hadn't come back from the Great War and it made her cry a lot. Uncle Jack hadn't come back from the Great War. Uncle Edwin said he'd been very brave, saving wounded soldiers but had been shot carrying a wounded man away from the fighting. Aunt Ellie never seemed to have red and swollen eyes but sometimes, Grandma and Auntie Sarah did. Rebecca remembered the special times when she and her mother thought of Auntie Becky, but they did it quietly, without crying.

Rebecca noticed Aunt Ellie's black velvet slippers embroidered with red poppies peeping at her; she remembered they'd been a Christmas present made by Auntie Annie.

The door- bell rang and another lady was quickly ushered into the room.

"I'm so sorry; my husband was late coming home for his dinner."

Rebecca saw a pair of soft grey boots which covered the lady's ankles so her stockings didn't show, the boots had beautiful silky laces and the child knew that this was one of the posh ladies. She thought it must be Mrs McLean, the doctor's wife. The other feet belonged to two women who Rebecca didn't know; they both wore clogs, so they must have come straight from working in the mill.

"Well ladies, we've all had a chance to get to know each other over a cup of tea, except for Mrs McLean. I will quickly put her in the picture. My friend, Miss Antrim, is an experienced medium and has come from London to help us try and meet, in some manner, with our loved ones who have recently gone over to the other side. Mrs Swallow is here to be in touch with her sons Joseph and Matthew who both passed over at the battle of the Somme. Mrs Clarke would like to contact her husband Tony, who died of influenza last year and Mrs Ashworth wants to speak with her son Terry, who was killed at Courcelles in June 1916. My mother and I would both like to contact my youngest brother Jack, who was killed near Ypres and my sister-in-law, Mrs Hannah Elkson, would like to be in touch with her sister, Becky Nelson, who died in the Royal Marine Hospital at Deal, earlier this year. Hannah is a great asset to us at this gathering because she is the seventh child of a seventh child. It is well known that such people have special insights into the Spirit world. Now, Mrs McLean would you like to tell us why you are here?"

"Yes of course. Good evening to you all. Although our daughter, Lucy, was engaged to marry Ellie's brother, Jack, who we loved like a son, I haven't really lost anyone to the Great War in the way that many of you have. I'm here for our little girl, Angela. She died from diphtheria last year; she was only six years old. My husband was so busy attending to other sick folk, that I fear we neglected her and I do so want her to know how much we've always loved her."

Mrs McLean's voice trembled and Rebecca noticed her crossing and uncrossing her feet but she didn't cry. Rebecca had been friends with Angela. She wanted to put her finger on Mrs McLean's shoe, just to say how sorry she was that her little girl had died but the leather looked so soft and thin, she was sure the doctor's wife would feel her touch and that would never do. Rebecca thought of Grandma being angry and of how Uncle Edwin said she used to make him and his brothers scrub the stone flagged kitchen floor from end to end when they'd been naughty. If she were found under the table, Grandma might make her do just that, or something worse.

Now Mrs Antrim was speaking. Rebecca didn't know what a medium was but the woman's voice was warm and soothing.

"I do hope you are all comfortable ladies, Mrs Elkson has provided us with a lovely warm room and pleasant lamplight. It is important that you all feel relaxed and at ease, then our spirit friends will not feel in any way threatened by coming among us. You are free to talk amongst yourselves, until the time we form the circle by holding hands. Talk of pleasant things; don't spoil the calm atmosphere by angry thoughts or expression of any fears. There is nothing to fear. These spirits we wish to contact are our own dear ones, they will not harm us, they will respond only to our loving thoughts of them."

"What happens if we feel sad, or even start crying, will that put them off?" asked Mrs Swallow, her voice thick with anxiety.

"It may do, my dear, just try and think of the happiest times you had with your sons and fill your mind with love for them. Miss Elkson, please lay out the items the ladies have brought."

Aunt Ellie's hand groped under the table cloth feeling for the large soft bag she had placed there, Rebecca sat tight, hoping her aunt wouldn't bend down to look into the bag and see her. A cricket cap and a striped scarf were pulled out and lifted onto the table.

"These belonged to Joseph and Matthew Swallow" said Aunt Ellie in the strange deep voice, "and this to Mr Tony Clarke," a flat cap was taken from the bag, followed by a pair of cycle clips belonging to Terry Ashworth, a pink cardigan, which Rebecca remembered was Angela's favourite and a mouth organ, which had been Uncle Jack's. Rebecca could just remember him playing 'Pop goes the weasel' on it. Uncle Jack had taken it with him to the war, she remembered him whispering to her, that he was going to make the sick soldiers sing again. How did it come to be here? A final rummage in the bag and Aunt Ellie lifted out a piece of lacy material. "Hannah, this is a lace collar which belonged to your Rebecca. Rebecca's chest tightened and she gasped, that was her name but she wasn't dead! Suddenly she wanted to cry, and then she heard her mother's voice.

"Yes, that's my sister Becky's, she wore it for church. One of the patients at Beech Tree Hall gave it to her and she loved it." Rebecca sagged against the table leg with relief; of course it was her Auntie Becky they meant, she'd forgotten her Auntie's full christian name was really the same as hers. Still, Rebecca wished she hadn't come, she didn't like to think of her precious Auntie being dead.

Mrs Antrim now spoke slowly and gently.

"I want each of you, to give your attention to the objects belonging to your particular dear one and use them to help you to think

---

of them. They will also give the spirits of your loved ones something familiar to home in upon."

The ladies had been very quiet, even though they'd been invited to talk together.

"In a moment, I am going to ask Miss Elkson to lift the lid of the musical box. When you hear the tune begin, take the hand of the person on each side of you. Nothing evil can break into this circle of love. If you wish you may close your eyes. Fill your minds with loving thoughts of the ones you wish to contact but be absolutely quiet and still, whatever happens."

Rebecca held her breath, she wasn't holding anyone's hand, would something bad happen to her? She wasn't in the circle. Very, very lightly she touched her mother's shoe, with one finger and Mrs Clarke's shoe with a finger of her other hand. She still felt unhappy and shivery. Suddenly the musical box began to play,

'Home Sweet Home.' The haunting melody filled the silence in the expectant room.

Somebody moaned very slightly, somebody else gave a suppressed sob, and then all went very quiet as the music came to an end.

Out of the silence, Mrs Antrim spoke, in a sing-song whisper, "Come friend Spirits come, we are here to welcome you. Will any of you tell us of the ones we seek?"

The lights in the room seemed to flicker and then steady.

"Aah it is you, Lucian, my dear guide, welcome. Are you able to bring, any of these dear ones, to speak with us tonight? Or do you bring a message from any of them?"

Rebecca saw her mother's legs jerk ever so slightly.

"Oh, our Tom's cap! I saw it move!"

"Shush, Mrs Clarke," someone whispered.

"Tom, are you here. Do you have a message for your wife?" asked the medium.

"Oh, it's moved again," whispered Mrs Clark

"We shall ask you some questions. Tom, move your cap twice if you want to say 'Yes' and once for 'No'. Are you happy on the other side, Tom?"

Rebecca saw her mother's legs jerk again, making the cloth tremble.

"The cap has moved twice. Then you are happy. Do you have a message for your wife Tom? Yes you do. Mrs Clarke, would you like to say something to your husband?"

"NO -I mean yes. I don't know. Tom, did I do right to sell your mother's necklace, we were that short. Tell me I did right, I've been that worried."

"My spirit guide is going to speak for Tom. Quiet everyone."

Mrs Antrim's voice changed but Rebecca, who could only hear, could still tell it was her speaking. The voice she used was high pitched and wavering and the speech very, very slow with a slightly foreign twang,

"Mavis, my dear, if selling my mother's necklace helped you and the family, then it was right. Don't be afraid, there will always be someone to help you. I love you always but I must go now, goodnight sweetheart."

Rebecca could hear a sniffling sound and wondered if Mrs Clark would have to break the circle to get her handkerchief, or, would her eyes and nose just have to run.

"I love you, Tom," whispered Mrs Clark, wishing he'd called her sweetheart when he was alive.

"He's gone in peace," said Mrs Antrim in her own soothing voice. She addressed the Spirits once more.

"Is there anybody else who wants to speak with us? Aah! I think I feel tiny fingers just brushing my cheek, could it be a child."

"The pink cardigan, I'm sure it moved," Mrs Swan's voice. There was no sound from Mrs McLean.

"Lucian, have you guided the spirit of a child to us tonight? You have. Thank you my dear. Will she speak with us? You say she is in the care of a young woman, who has come with her. Do we know the young woman?"

"Look, I saw the lace collar flutter," Mrs Clark's voice again,

"I'm not sure about this," faltered Mrs McLean, Rebecca watched the feet of the doctor's wife twitching nervously and she saw her mother shift slightly so that her knee touched Mrs McLean's comfortingly.

"Lucian! Please help us here? You say you would like Angela's mother to sing to her, her favourite song?"

"Oh no, I can't bear it," Mrs McLean whispered.

"It will help the child to feel at ease,"

"Angela?" the mother spoke the name so tenderly.

"Please, sing to her."

Quietly, in the same way her own mother sometimes sang her to sleep, Rebecca heard Mrs McLean start to sing,

"Do you want a pilot? Signal then to Jesus. Do you want a pilot? Bid Him come aboard. He will safely guide"— the voice faltered and stopped but Hannah Elkson took up the song "across the ocean wide, until you reach the heavenly harbour."

Suddenly a mouth organ could be heard from somewhere picking up and continuing to play the tune.

"Jack!" Aunt Ellie cried out, then all went quiet until the mouth organ stopped playing and Hannah Elkson spoke clearly, "Rebecca, I know you're here, speak to me love."

Rebecca, crouched under the table, just wanting to feel the safety of her mother's arms and answered without thinking,

"Mummy, I'm here; I want to go home now. Please take me home."

"It's Angela! Oh my poppet I want to take you home so much, daddy and I love you very much and we wouldn't have let you go for the world, if we could have helped it."

Shocked but with an intuition beyond her years, Rebecca replied to the yearning in Mrs McLean's voice,

"I know you and daddy love me and I know it wasn't your fault I died. I'm happy now I've heard you say you love me. I will always love you, mummy and daddy."

There was utter silence. Rebecca felt sick at what she'd done and closing her eyes tightly, curled close to the table leg, her head hidden in her arms. Mrs Antrim's normal voice broke in;

"Lucian tells me, that is all for tonight. The Spirits, who came this evening, will not come to us again. They are in bliss; but in time, we shall go to them. Thank you Lucian for your kindness to us." Miss Antrim closed her eyes and let go the hands of the ladies next to her. The others let go of their neighbours' hands and the circle was broken.

"Now ladies, I want you to think on this passage from the New Testament, 'In my Father's house are many mansions and I go to prepare a place for you.' Remember this and commit your loved ones and yourselves into the hands of God. Amen."

"Amen," said all the ladies.

The lights were put on in the room and the gathering broke up. Nobody spoke much, there were just a few pleasantries as people put on their outdoor things and left the house. Rebecca heard her mother speak in a low voice to Angela's mother,

"Don't fret my dear, all is well. I'll come and see you tomorrow,"

The lights were put out and Rebecca lay still in the dark. She must have fallen asleep because she woke to find herself being carried by her father, wrapped in his coat, out to the car.

"Hello Rebecca, what have you been up to?" George said, as he felt his daughter wake in his arms.

"I don't know but it was horrid. I was frightened. I don't think I like Aunt Ellie anymore and mother was there too, but she was kind to Mrs McLean."

"I'm glad to hear it. I don't think your mother was aware that she was part of something very wrong. I think she hoped she could stop anything really bad happening but I do want to know how you came to be there."

"I came down to get warm by the fire and hid under the table when the ladies came in?"

"I see. Well, now you know what can happen when you don't stay in bed as you were told. There will be no more of these shinanikins, so forget all about it and never ever get involved in anything like that again. Do you understand, Madame?"

"Yes, Daddy, I'm sorry," and as far as Rebecca was concerned that was it, but Hannah was treated to a larger dose of her husband's wrath. She'd never seen him so cold with repressed anger. George spoke to her privately in his study, just as if she was the accused in one of his court cases. He stood before her as she sat in his chair and lectured her about the "lying, deceptive, dangerous affair you allowed yourself to be persuaded into. I thought you had more perception, Hannah, and common sense. Surely, it couldn't have been sheer weakness of character that made you take part in a séance. I doubt if I could have misjudged your character so badly. Do you realise how you upset Rebecca, with your foolishness! Luckily she has a strong streak of normality, which I hope will prevent her from being too unsettled by this. You must promise me faithfully, never again to take part in any of my mother's and Ellie's shameful occult practices. I may no longer attend church but even I can see that the Christian Faith is right in condemning such practices. Promise me, Hannah."

Hannah stared up into George's steely blue eyes and for a moment was afraid,

"I promise you George. It was foolish of me. I'll make sure Rebecca's alright," Hannah dropped her gaze, her hands shaking with emotion. George suddenly dropped his lawyer's stance and knelt down beside his wife taking her trembling hands in his.

"We've been through almost more than the human mind can take with this war. Is it any wonder we're confused and look for comfort in strange places," he laid his head on his wife's lap and Hannah gently stroked his hair, feeling the hot tension in his scalp. They remained like this for a while, and then George got up and planted a warm kiss on his wife's cheek.

"Go on, love, make us a cup of tea. We've come through this and no doubt there'll be more to come, good and bad,"

"No doubt, but we keep learning as we go," smiled Hannah with relief, as she went to put the kettle on.

CHAPTER 52

Respite in Hartsbeck

When the truth of Amelia and Ellie's experiments in contacting the dead came to light, there was much anger and disgust among the Elkson family. Amelia left Hartsbeck after staying only one week, feeling she had brought shame on her friend's family.

The worst of the anger came from George and Dave Elkson. Sarah was a little kinder in her attitude, but was definitely against what they had been doing. A frostiness had crept into all their relationships, which was equally reflected in the bitter weather outside. The two friends decided it was best for Amelia to withdraw from the situation and return to London. Ellie would stay on and try to restore friendly relations with her family. She accompanied Amelia to the station for the London train.

"I'm so sorry, Ellie. This is the best way, I'm sure. We must think about this spiritualism very carefully, when you return to London."

They embraced, then Amelia boarded the train and Ellie walked despondently home through the grey streets.

The town looked tired. Men, in shabby suits and cloth caps, stood in groups on street corners, some sharing a cigarette, which they passed from one to the other, sometimes coughing and spitting into the gutter. Others squatted on the pavement curbs, hands dangling between their knees. These men should have been employed in the mills and factories but the economic depression, and changes in the cotton trade, meant they had come home from the war, to find jobs few and far between.

Women in black, dusty looking coats and close-fitting dark hats, scurried like so many beetles anxiously searching the shops for affordable food and remnants of cloth in order to feed and clothe their families. Ellie felt at one with them, her own sadness echoed theirs. Every now and again people hailed each other across the street, or stopped to gossip; they might be tired and struggling but there was warmth in community.

A tram trundled to a stop just ahead of her and an elderly woman clambered down from the platform, using a stout walking stick. As she drew nearer, Ellie noticed the stick's beautifully carved handle, in the shape of a bear. Ellie stared at that stick, surely it was the stick carved from ash wood that Annette's husband had made. He had carved the bear, the emblem of Switzerland, to remind Annette of her homeland. Ellie caught up with the old woman and spoke her name.

"Annette, Annette Hamilton?"

The old woman turned and stared up into Ellie's face, her eyes clouded by cataracts.

"Oh my word! It's Ellie Elkson, isn't it? Well, bless my soul," the voice quavered but there was no mistaking that Swiss inflection. The delighted woman would have reached out to Ellie but with her stick in one hand and shopping bag in the other she was too encumbered.

"Annette? But I didn't think you lived here anymore?" Ellie only just stopped herself from saying, "I thought you were dead."

"I did move away. I went to live with my son in Yorkshire when my husband died. Then my son was killed in the war and I came back to live with Bertha and her children. Her husband came back from the war but he'd lost an arm and the sight in one eye. She's still working in the Hartsbeck hospital, but as a cleaner. They won't let her nurse now she's married. She needs to work, because of her husband's disability. They've three growing boys and need the money."

Annette began to breathe heavily and Ellie took her arm.

"I've been too long away from my clean mountain air," Annette sounded wistful, "the Hartsbeck chest has caught me at last," she laughed ruefully.

"You need to get inside, out of this cold air," said Ellie. "Where were you going?"

"I'm on my way home. I'd heard there was some bacon on offer down at Hindle's grocers. I managed to get some too, Bertha will be pleased. Her boys are always hungry."

"I'll walk you home. I'm on holiday, so I'm in no hurry."

"How lovely! See - we only live there, across the road from the tram stop. Come in and have a cup of tea with me, before any of the family come home."

Bertha's house was part of a row of terraced cottages. Inside it was small but comfortable and neat as a new pin. Annette had her own rocking chair in a corner of the living room near the fireplace. A dining table stood in the bay window which looked out over a small back garden showing winter vegetables and evergreens and well-ordered beds ready for spring and summer planting. Annette stirred up the fire and put the kettle on and soon the two women were deep in conversation, catching up on all that had happened and reminiscing about the past. With warmth and rest Annette's breathing settled down and she revelled in a rare opportunity to talk.

"We always hoped you would come back and nurse in Hartsbeck. Bertha was Sister- in -charge of the Maternity at Hartsbeck Victoria Hospital, before she married. She says they badly need a proper Maternity Ward with new equipment and delivery rooms and an operating theatre for emergencies. At the moment, they have to rely on the operating theatre of the main hospital being available; which is rarely the case. Actually, she thinks the whole hospital needs over-hauling and refurbishing but it takes money and there's not much of that about just now. She's glad to be a cleaner there, she sees it as a crucial hospital job and it allows her to chat with the patients and help keep an eye on them."

"Well, medical science is rushing forward at a tremendous rate; it's important not to be stuck in the past. I do very little hospital work now, only if I have to go for extra training, when some new-fangled method comes into fashion! I'm involved with home- births and helping mothers and fathers cope with rearing healthy children in their own homes. It's a bit like working with you in the early days, except that I'm a lot more experienced. Still, I often fall back on what you taught me Annette, it's got me out of many a tight spot. I owe you such a lot."

Annette was pleased and Ellie felt a warm stream of normality begin to soothe away some of the strangeness and tension of the years since she'd left home in 1899. She began to see the pattern her life had taken; some of it pleased her but other parts troubled her; these parts she could not share with Annette. Ellie refused to pollute Annette's innocent, unadulterated Christian Faith with any talk of Theosophy and the occult and she hoped Annette would never hear about the séance.

It was half past four by the time Ellie arrived home in Aspen Lane. She felt relaxed and rested, as if the whole affair of the séance had been a nightmare from which she'd now woken. Sarah had come back from school and was sitting at her piano. She was playing a lively polka, her fingers flying over the keys and her head moving back and forth in concentration, she ended with two loud, rhythmic chords and spun round to face Ellie.

"The children are learning to dance the polka and I have to play for them," she laughed, "it's easier playing without them, than with them!"

Memories of hopping round the school hall to 'Oh can you dance the polka?' hammered out on the old school-piano, prompted Ellie to lift her skirts and try a few steps round the room, singing the words of the old song. Sarah jumped up and joined her. When Jeannie came downstairs from her afternoon rest, her daughters were prancing round the room dancing the Polka together, and laughing uncontrollably. Eventually they collapsed onto the sofa.

"Girls, girls. How old do you think you are! We'll have Miss Webster in from next door!" her girls stared at her, then saw the spark of humour in their mother's eyes and laughed.

"It must be over twenty years, since Miss Webster died," gasped Ellie, remembering the sweet old lady who'd been their neighbour.

Whenever they had made too much noise as children their mother would threaten them with Miss Webster, "She'll turn herself into a monster and come storming round to find you."

"Even you would have a fit, Ellie, if she came knocking at the door right now," Sarah risked a sly dig at her sister.

"Poor Miss Webster, what a shock for her to be 'brought back'-by our shinanikins!" said Ellie and the three laughed till the tears ran. The sting of the séance had been removed. Only a faint after-taste remained as a warning in Rebecca and Tom's continued wari-ness of their Aunt Ellie. Otherwise, family relationships were chiefly restored. When Ellie returned to London, it was with a promise to visit again soon.

"I'll write as often as I can," shouted Sarah, as Ellie boarded the train and Ellie waved until her mother, father and sister disappeared from view.

It was not the end of Ellie's interest in Theosophy and its esoteric teachings but she never again dabbled in séances. Instead, together with Amelia she further developed her interest in alternative medi-cine, in particular hydrotherapy and even practised some of these water-cures on her-self. She promoted the healing properties of water to her patients and if appropriate, introduced some of the milder remedies, but she refused to inflict on them any of the more drastic treatments.

The following year, 1921, Ellie's father, Dave Elkson, died. He'd been failing slowly for some time. On the evening of the twenty first of June, he walked home from work and sank wearily into his chair without even removing his boots. Sarah made him a cup of tea and left him to rest but half an hour later she found it impos-sible to rouse him. Dr Waters was called. After examining his old friend, the doctor shook his head sadly and declared him to be dead.

"Would that we could all go so peacefully," he said soberly to Jeannie and the family members hovering in the room, "I shall miss him, he was a good friend. I'm sorry Jeannie and all of you, for your loss."

The family gathered again, for the funeral. Ellie came from London and Stephen, as the eldest son, escorted their mother to the church. George and Hannah were there with Tom and Rebecca, the children unusually large eyed and quiet. Hannah looked weary and heavy eyed, (she confided in Ellie that she was expecting another baby in December.) Edwin and Annie had with them their three year old son, Jack, named for the uncle he never knew. They all noticed how Jeannie's hands trembled constantly and how slowly and carefully she moved.

Cousin Hugh took the service. The other cousins came from Preston with Aunt Alice and Uncle Arthur. Ellie hadn't seen her uncle and aunt since before Grandma Jane died, well before the Great War. It seemed strange to see them without her.

Ellie thought of the days when there had been only herself and Stephen as children at home with her mother and father. She felt a great sorrow that the time of early intimacy with her parents hadn't lasted into her father's later years. She remembered the row when she told him she was going to London and how he'd waited for her to come home from walking on the Tops and hugged her so tightly. Now he was gone, hopefully to a better spiritual plane, but Ellie was uneasy. She knew her father's failings and regretted that she hadn't been around to help him more. Would he be able to make that great leap forward of the spirit, or would he be trapped in the weakness of his own nature. The whole gamut of her studies in Theosophy came pouring into her thoughts, threatening to crowd out Hugh's words, as he intoned the glorious liturgy of the funeral service. Nevertheless, certain of the powerful phrases registered in her mind.

"Heavenly Father—," it was a long time since Ellie had referred to God in that way and it gave her an almost physical ache.

—" raise us from the death of sin into the life of righteousness; that we may rest in Him",

—"May our brother David be found acceptable in thy sight"

—"Enter the place in God's kingdom prepared for you" –

—"Let light perpetual shine upon him–"

—"Work in him the good purpose of thy perfect will–"

l—May he know the consolation of Thy love, through Jesus Christ our Saviour,"

The words echoed and seemed to Ellie to come from the stone pillars and wooden beams of the church, the pillars swayed and came towards her; Hugh rocked from side to side his white surplice waving, ghost-like, around him. Ellie felt herself slipping sideways into some dark space. The acrid smell of ammonia brought her sharply to her senses and she was aware of Sarah waving a phial of smelling salts under her nose.

"Ellie," Sarah whispered urgently, "it's nearly over, hang on."

In fact it wasn't nearly over, they were only half way through but it gave Ellie time to recover and by the end she was able to walk out behind the coffin by hanging on to Sarah's arm.

"Whatever happened to you, Ellie? It's not like you to be like that, you've always been the strong one," Sarah asked anxiously as they walked towards the funeral cars.

"I don't know," said Ellie sickly and fainted clean away in a corner of the churchyard.

Edwin and George lifted her into one of the waiting cars. This time she was too unwell to continue to the burial or to the funeral tea. She was whisked home and put to bed by Annette Hamilton's daughter, Bertha, who'd been at the funeral. Bertha had gone out of respect for the family and on behalf of her mother, who'd died a few months previously.

Bertha quickly discovered that Ellie had been on a water-only fast for the past two days.

"Why on earth go on such a fast at the time of the funeral. Surely your nurses' training should have told you that you needed extra energy, not less, to face such an ordeal!"

"I've committed myself to a forty- eight hour fast of water only, once every month. I keep to careful timing and it usually falls on my off duty days. This time it fell yesterday and today. I would have allowed myself a bite at the funeral tea later. Just give me an aspirin and let me sleep; please Bertha."

Bertha was not sympathetic. She stood over Ellie insisting she drank hot, sweet tea and ate buttered toast and jam before she would give her an aspirin and allow her to sleep. Ellie said nothing about her mental turmoil and realised that with the help of Bertha's efficient ministrations it was receding. Bertha's matronly figure with her square, determined jaw and down to earth manner had a stabilising effect. At last Bertha sank down in the easy chair beside the bedroom window and took up a magazine to read. Ellie's eyes drooped and she slept.

A few days after her father's funeral Ellie returned to London and Felix Square. She had begun to feel restless under the Truby King regime. Certain aspects of Dr. King's methods disturbed her. She disagreed with his doctrine that to pick up babies, simply to cuddle them, was bad for their character, although she did agree that to give in to them up every time they demanded attention was not always good.

A method of 'controlled crying' was now popular, in which the baby's crying was monitored by the mother until she learnt when it was necessary attend to her infant or safe to leave her or him to cry for a while. Hannah would have said that all that was just common sense and experience and was nothing new and Ellie was inclined to agree, except that all mothers were not as sensible as Hannah.

As for the question of eugenics, although Dr. King had renounced its more extreme practices, she still detected some aspects of it in his teachings, which made her uneasy. Also, she was chiefly working with families who could afford private nursing care and she still felt called to be amongst the poorer element in society. At her request she was transferred to the Mother-Care centre in Trebovir Road and for a year was happier, working amongst mothers from the poorer districts but she was still restless. She decided to move away from the Truby King Conclave and back into the main- stream of nursing and midwifery.

First Ellie needed to find her own accommodation. She counted up her savings together with the share of inheritance from her father and found an affordable Georgian terraced house, in Redcliffe Street near Earls Court. She then applied for a nursing position in one of the local community clinics. These clinics were free and open to all but the less wealthy tended to use them more frequently.

Eliza Fizakerly fully approved of this change for her friend and made enquiries from two businessmen she knew who understood property and the buying of it. She persuaded them to help Ellie with her choice of house.

Ellie's brother, George, also gave his official stamp of approval; having come from Hartsbeck to inspect the property and make sure all was in order.

Back in Hartsbeck, Hannah had been experiencing a hard time carrying her third baby. In December Ellie was able to take a holiday in Hartsbeck and be with Hannah when she gave birth to a wiry, if rather small boy, Richard. He was particularly demanding and Hannah was glad of Ellie's experienced ministrations both to the baby and herself.

Ellie was not present eighteen months later when Hannah was delivered of a daughter, Alice. A deceptively delicate and sickly child, Alice quickly overcame any feebleness of body by her strong spirit and sheer love of life. By the time Ellie met her she was running around and long past baby-hood.

PART SIX

The Broad Shoulders Of Women.
Ellie And Sarah 1927-1929

CHAPTER 53

*Ellie in Redcliffe Street and
a letter from Stephen.*

By nineteen twenty-seven, Ellie had been happily established at 19, Redcliffe Street for five years. It had become almost home to her and life had settled into another regular and fulfilling routine. After working for two years in the Community Clinic, she'd been promoted to the position of Sister and proved competent in her extra responsibilities.

Since 1920 Ellie had begun to see changes in the city, which warmed her heart. New housing schemes, activated after the Great War, meant that many London slum-dwellers had now been re-housed in the greener suburbs with subsidised rents they could afford.. However, as she went about her work in the community it became obvious to Ellie that too many families had fallen through the net and remained in abject poverty.

Another innovation was the growing interest in birth control. Ellie attended several talks by Dr Marie Stopes, who in March 1921 had opened 'The Mothers' Clinic' in Holloway, north London. The clinic was run by midwives and visiting doctors and offered mothers birth control advice and taught them how to use a cervical cap. Ellie was tempted to offer her services but it was too specialised, she preferred the wider spectrum of her present work. As with her Truby King knowledge, she was still able to promote Dr Stopes' birth control ideas when applicable.

One Tuesday lunch time Ellie set out for her afternoon duties at the clinic. She wheeled her bicycle out of the back yard of 19,

Redcliffe Street. As she cycled on among rows of crowded terraced houses, she was reminded of the poorer areas of Hartsbeck although it was sounds of London accents which called to her.

"'Afternoon, Nurse!"

Her bicycle jolted over the cobbles as Ellie nodded to the group of men standing on the corner.

"Aye- up, Nursey! When are you off duty? 'ow about a nice ride by the river with me?"

A lanky young fellow, waving a half empty bottle, swayed into the road in front of her. It was impossible to swerve neatly past him and Ellie was forced to put her foot down and stop. The man lurched towards her, arms wide open to take her in his embrace. A flush of indignation swept through Ellie but in a moment two men from the group on the corner had moved forward. A fist from one of them landed on the point of her assailant's jaw, he staggered, unconscious, into a second man's arms and was pulled out of Ellie's way.

"'On you go Missy.'E won't remember a dickey- bird when 'e comes round. We'll look out for you again, when you're coming home. No need to fear the streets when we're around."

The man with the hard fist punched the air and drew a chorus of laughs from the others. For a moment they stood taller and Ellie glimpsed a younger, livelier spirit, behind their wearied eyes. These weren't the homeless tramps who had watched out for her in earlier years. These were men with homes and families but no jobs, no money coming in; wives and children waited at home for food, clothes and warmth, longing for a husband and dad who wasn't weighed down with depression and fear. Even the drunken lad, now propped against a wall, looked pathetically thin in a limp jacket that would have fitted two of him and trousers hoisted round his waist with a belt of string.

Ellie rode on round the corner to the clinic and wheeled her bike through the queue of mothers with babes in their arms and toddlers clinging to their skirts, waiting for the two-thirty session.

One of the mothers called out to Ellie; "Good morning Sister Elkson!" It was Mrs Fielding, a near neighbour of Ellie's who was struggling to bring up four children while her husband was in prison for robbery. The latest Fielding child, Ruby, was now six months old born two weeks after Mr Fielding had been sentenced. The eldest Fielding child, Kitty, who was twelve years old, had knocked on Ellie's door late at night to say that her mother was in labour three weeks before she was due. Ellie had delivered baby Ruby an hour later, helped by Kitty. They'd been watched from the doorway by two boys, Billy who was seven, and four year old Toby. Kitty had been born with a cleft palette which had only been partly rectified, her speech was full of clicks and whistles but she was able to make herself understood.

With a surge of satisfaction Ellie sped efficiently through the afternoon's work, dealing capably with every maternal problem posed to her and if some of the women whispered, "What does she know about it?" She simply told herself, "They can take it or leave it!"

Time went quickly by for Ellie. Her few leisure hours were spent pleasantly enough, sometimes with Eliza or Amelia, or attending women's empowerment meetings and public lectures and reading. On fine days she sometimes took walks. She rarely had time to think of Hartsbeck, it seemed so far away, but if on a fine day, she took a walk on Putney Heath or Wimbledon Common, memories of the Lancashire moors came flooding back.

On the morning of the first day of spring, nineteen twenty nine the clatter of the letter box broke into Ellie's thoughts as she washed her breakfast pots, almost making her drop her favourite, willow patterned cup. She delayed the moment of picking up her post, taking her time drying the pots and carefully rinsing the dish-cloth, before putting it to soak in bleach. When she'd taken off her apron and folded it away, she couldn't put off the moment any longer and walked deliberately into the hallway.

The letter she picked up had an English stamp, a Lancashire post-mark and her brother Stephen's scrawl on the envelope. She glared at it, blaming it for not being from Alex. It was always like this, on the first day of spring, the anniversary of his last meeting with her at Netley, before he left to join the Canadian Forces. It was fourteen years since they had said goodbye and twelve years since the note to say he was in Belgium. No record of him among the Canadian dead had ever been found. He had simply disappeared. Most of the time Ellie kept her memories of him locked away but on this anniversary, Alex always pushed his way to the forefront of her mind and a glimmer of foolish hope would raise its head. Maybe it was the effect of springtime. Many times she'd told herself that, if he had survived the war, he would probably be back in Canada, engrossed in his work, probably married with a family and not even thinking about her.

Ellie paused in front of a small, oval mirror on the wall. She scrutinised her face. The city air had taken the healthy bloom from her skin, leaving it pastry pale. Only when something angered or upset her, would a hot redness spread slowly over her neck and upwards across her nose and cheek-bones.

"Not even a pretty pink blush; just an embarrassing middle-age flush, making me look as if I've been on the gin."

Her hair was still dark and thick and appreciatively she patted its smoothly-rolled neatness. Forty-four years may be later middle-age but she considered herself strong and healthy. There had been another influenza epidemic raging through London since February and she'd avoided catching it; this in itself, spoke for her increased stamina.

Back in the kitchen Ellie poured water from the kettle into a glass and drank it meditatively. She preferred her water cool but boiled - it was safer that way. Even now in nineteen twenty nine, with treated drinking water in the taps, she couldn't forget the typhoid cases she'd seen when she began her nursing training, thirty years ago. Strangely, it was Alex who had first alerted her to the health-giving properties of water; Alex, who was against anything unorthodox in medicine or religion. There was such a thin line between acknowledging what was true and wholesome in both orthodox and unorthodox disciplines and what amounted to misuse and even abuse, within them.

"Don't forget to drink four pints of water every day. It is nature's doctor for all the body; clears out everything that is bad in you and helps all those tiny cells to work properly, do it for me, my little Ellie."

Alex's gentle French lilt behind his Canadian drawl had given a charming simplicity to his advice. Ellie smiled wryly; she was straight and tall, some would say awkward and unbending. Alex had been the only person to call her 'little', except her father, when she was a child. She had taken it as an endearment but now she wondered if Alex had been sneering at her. Still, he had been one of the few men who could look down on her. Well, he was safely out of her reach now. Ellie snatched up her brother's letter and ripped it open. It was dated two days previously. His boyish style soon made her smile:

174, Aspen Lane,
Hartsbeck,
Lancashire
19th March 1929

Dear Ellie,

Looking forward to you coming home for Easter. Can't believe you'll be here in just over a week. We've made an excellent plan to travel out to Estwick Village on the Saturday of Easter weekend and stay till Tuesday morning. Hope we won't get the end of the March winds as Easter day is 31ˢᵗ March. Most of the Hartsbeck NATS should be coming. Some will sleep at night in the wooden cabin and we hardy lads will take to the tents. Camp fires and sausages- you know you love them. You're a born hypocrite with all your talk of vegetarianism but always giving in to sausages. George and Hannah will be bringing the children. The oldies plan to book 'bed and breakfast' at the Inn in Estwick, for the Friday and Saturday nights. It will be the first time we've done anything like this since the end of that damnable war. Cousin Hugh will no doubt coerce some of our bunch into his church on Easter Day- (did you know he is to be made Vicar of Estwick just before Easter?) I think I'll find other things to do, such as taking a closer look at the rocks on Norber - plenty for the spirit to marvel at there. I've bought a new camera -it should pick out more detail than my old one. I can't wait to try it out. Lots of specimens for my geological collection in this area of the Craven Fault.

I hope city life hasn't made you too prim and proper for all this, Ellie. I'm expecting you to put on your walking legs and come with us. I'm worried about Sarah, she's looking very tired. Maybe it's that end- of-term feeling; teaching seven to nine year olds every day is a lot more soul destroying than my lecturing to nineteen and twenty year olds on a subject I'm crazy about. Even so, I get that longing to be free, after ten weeks of it. We should be glad we've got jobs. You should see the state of some of the fellows round here, the print works and the mills are all laying people off. I feel guilty just walking past the queues at the labour exchange and seeing old friends looking like layabouts.

Sarah must come with us, she needs the fresh air and a break but she won't come without you. You're good at doctoring people - look at it as your duty to your sister's health if you won't come for yourself. Don't mention any more of your theosophy, spiritualist or Buddhist notions to the others - you can talk about what you like to me!

Mother has gone down-hill over the last year or more. She's never completely got over Jack's death and then Dad's - but it's more than that. She's been having attacks of weakness and violent trembling but in between she seems to be alright. The problem is she never knows when an attack will happen. Sarah has booked her an appointment with Dr. Waters. Edwin's stammer looks like being permanent but he's learning to manage it so it's not as obvious as it was. Young Jack is growing into a fine young lad and has his father's interest in nature- bugs especially- at the moment. I don't see as much of Tom and Rebecca as I did, it will be good to be with them at Easter.

I've missed you Ellie. There's no-one at home now, who wants to listen to my constant ramblings about rock formations and water courses and changes in landscape. Oh, they enjoy the odd lecture down at the Naturalists but even the NATS can only take so much. You've a surprisingly scientific mind for a woman.

When you come for Easter please will you bring me a supply of that special dope for preserving the colour in mounted butter-flies. I've over 150 in my collection now but if I don't preserve them properly, their wings fade to a nondescript mud colour. They don't stock the right stuff up here but they have it in 'Gurphy's Supplies for the Natural Historian'- next to Earls Court underground station, just round the corner from you, you could buy a selection of preparation pins and setting strips as well. Bring the receipt and I'll pay you back. I've been reading 'The Old Red Sandstone' again. I wish I'd known Hugh Miller, his knowledge is incredible but the way he makes those rocks live is sheer poetry. By the way, did you know that your Dr Marie Stopes was a specialist in my field before she became a leading light in yours? I used to study her papers on the formation and constitution of coal when I was in mining engineering. She is still writing excellent papers on paleobotany i.e. the study of ancient plants; this was her first passion before marriage relations and birth control took over! It seems a strange shift from geology and ancient plants to human contraception, but we scientists often make strange connections.

Looking forward to seeing you soon. Tell me the time of your train and I'll meet you.

Your affectionate brother,

Stephen

Ps. George has surprised us all by taking up gliding! One of his clients persuaded him to try and he's hooked. Hannah is on pins whenever he goes to meet his gliding friends- usually on Pendle Hill or Beacon Fell. No accidents so far. Stephen.

Unwittingly, Stephen had stirred a latent desire in Ellie. She was aware that Marie Stopes had deeply personal reasons for writing about marriage relations and it reminded Ellie of her own unmarried, childless state. She read her brother's letter three times, frowning over the remarks about Sarah and her mother and began to feel she was about to become a more active part of the family again. George's new venture did surprise her. She had never thought of him as a dare-devil, at least it would stop him becoming stuffy. In her early days in London she had deliberately shut out thoughts of home, but now she desperately wanted to recapture them and be part of the family again. At least she knew to keep her theosophist leanings under wraps, when in Hartsbeck.

Her mood was happy as she made herself ready for work, thinking how good it would be to be with Sarah again, walking together in their favourite spots. Checking her watch again Ellie realised her sister would already be busy at school and she ought to be on her way to the clinic. She thought back to the small church primary school they'd all attended as children and wondered what had happened to the other girls she'd known; Ellie felt she'd lived through several life-times since those days.

CHAPTER 54

Sarah, a teacher's episode.

In the small town of Cubden, six miles outside Hartsbeck, Sarah sat alone at the piano in the school hall. Today was the last day of the Lenten term, nineteen twenty-nine. Tomorrow would be the start of the Easter holidays and she was almost thirty-nine years old. There had been a time when she would be filled with a contented joy at this time of year, the anticipation of Holy Week culminating in Good Friday, followed by the Easter festival. There would be days of walking in the countryside with her brothers and sister and a few friends. They would search out wild plants and insects, examine the rocks, hoping for fossils; glorying in sun or rain and the sound of moorland birds. Today she felt melancholy.

The war had added poignancy to such sacred festivals. The meaning of Gethsemane, Good Friday and Easter hit home to people of faith with a greater sense of reality. Sin; betrayal; despair; loss; suffering; forgiveness; love and new life; they'd been through them all, with good measure, during those war years and many wounds were still raw and sensitive. Celebrating these traumas again, in the life of Jesus, gave to many a sense of something strong and good, which had not and could not be defeated, regardless of the death and destruction and the awful losses among their families.

The seasons too had continued. In spring the sun still shone, the rain fell and winds blew; the mayflowers and the stitchwort appeared under the hedgerows, the swallows returned, the bees and wasps murmured their continual ways through the bracken. As for the rocks, they remained, year in year out, holding their ancient secrets. Even where hillsides had been ravaged by men, quarrying for good building stone, they had not lost their essential nature and the grass and moss soon dressed the wounds. Sarah thought of the trenches where Edwin and Jim had been and imagined them being re-clothed by nature.

Sarah leant across to the cupboard beside her, to search out the music for the children's final assembly. She caught her breath and gripped the edge of the piano keyboard as she felt a tightening in her breast, there wasn't really any pain, just a feeling of taut discomfort and the vague sensation of breathless panic. She breathed deeply, forcing herself to relax, the tightness ebbed away.

The noise of stoutly-booted feet, running in from outside, brought her abruptly back to the task in hand and she turned to see eleven year old Rachel Troop hurrying towards her, clothes torn and dishevelled, long hair flying loose from its blue ribbon and a livid red scratch across one muddy cheek. By the hand she dragged her younger brother Andrew, a delicate looking, pale-faced six year old with thick curly hair and large appealing brown eyes. The small boy's grey woollen socks sagged round his ankles revealing two bloodied knees and his shirt and jacket were splattered with mud. Rachel stalked up to the piano and faced Sarah.

"Please Miss Elkson; the big boys went for our Andrew again at playtime. They took 'is cap and threw it int' tree. I've given them a good hiding and I don't think they'll try it again, but mi brother's cap's stuck up t' tree and I'm reciting that poem to the school and parents in half an hour and Andrew's singing with the choir and we both look a right mess." Rachel placed her hand on her hip and stared despairingly at Andrew.

"Indeed you do," said Sarah. "Your mother will not be pleased when she sees you like that. She dressed you especially nicely, for the concert."

These two children did not come from a poor family but their parents were careful with what they had. Both mother and father had known poverty in their own childhood. Now that they were rising socially and financially, they (without being exactly snobbish) expected their children to stand a little above the others in the school, both in manners and educational progress. Sadly, their spoken grammar still left much to be desired.

"I could 'ave sorted it," muttered Andrew. "Rachel didn't ought to have butted in,"

Andrew's large, hazel eyes blinked short-sightedly, at his beloved teacher. Somehow Sarah kept her dignity but her lips twitched into a smile.

"Well, young man, you may be right but I would be thankful you've got a sister who looks out for you, the way Rachel does. Those big boys are three times the size of you. Rachel was very brave to stand up to them. However, I don't think it was a good idea to fight them, Rachel."

"No Miss, sorry Miss," Rachel hung her head. She had two older brothers and was used to holding her own with them. To her it had been natural to launch into the big boys.

"There isn't much time, you had better go and find Miss Harris, in the baby class. Ask her to clean you both up and to pin your dress Rachel. We'll sort out the matter of the cap, later."

"Yes miss!" Rachel was off like a shot, the reluctant Andrew in tow.

"And don't run!" Sarah was too late; the children careered into her cousin, the Reverend Hugh Nowell as he hurried into the hall.

"Watch out you two, you nearly had me over! Young Andrew isn't? Don't forget choir practice tonight, six o'clock sharp. Lots to do for Easter!"

"Yes Sir! I'll be there," Andrew brightened immediately, Choir was great and he felt at ease with the other choristers, not that any of them were saints but they weren't bullies and they nearly always kicked a football around after the practice.

"I'll make sure he is," bossed Rachel "I'm sorry we bumped into you."

"No harm done, this time!" the clergy man patted his slight paunch and turned his attention to Sarah.

"Good afternoon, Sarah, are we all set for the onslaught?"

Sarah looked up at her cousin with relief, "I don't know Hugh, I can't seem to find the right music and yet I know I set it out ready this morning, here, on the top shelf. The little ones are singing 'There is a Green Hill' and the older ones, 'When I survey the Wondrous Cross.' I was going to play a medley of Easter music from the Messiah and Steiner's crucifixion as they parade in and out.

"Let me have a look! Here we are, on the middle shelf with the Bible on top."

"Hugh, how did you know?"

"Ever seen a clergyman's study? You develop a sixth sense for these things."

Sarah laid out the music on top of the piano. Several mothers and some fathers came into the hall and two girls from the top class escorted them importantly to their seats as honoured guests. One or two had babies with them.

"I put a drop o' cough syrup with 'is last feed" whispered a large blousy woman loudly to her neighbour, "I 'opes it keeps 'im quiet, our Ernie'l never forgive me if he creates in middle of Rachel Troop's recitation. I reckon 'es sweet on 'er."

"It 'ad better work then, Gladys, or you'll be in for it," smiled her neighbour, surreptitiously popping a boiled sweet into her mouth.

Last of the guests were Mr and Mrs Troop, Rachel and Andrew's parents, smiling graciously as they were led to two empty chairs near the front.

"Everything alright, Miss Elkson?" the headmaster lent over Sarah and spoke quietly, "The children will be coming in shortly. Perhaps you would begin to play now and set the atmosphere. Miss Bury will bring in your class and Rachel will lead in the choir and performers."

"Thank you Mr Bolton. Sarah started to play her choice of Easter music. She linked the shepherds of Christmas to Jesus the good shepherd and Jesus the lamb of God slain for the salvation of all with 'Sheep may safely graze.' Her playing was gradually accompanied by the tap- tap of an army of small feet across the dusty wooden floor.

"Good choice," murmured Hugh as he took his seat at the side of the stage and watched as the children were marshalled to their places, older children at the back, younger ones at the front. Hugh half closed his eyes in thought. Next week he would be leaving for Estwick, his years as a Vicar here at Cubden would be over and this was his final assembly with these children. He could name each child and knew each family; the teachers had welcomed him as one of themselves. Soon another Vicar would take his place and Hugh would move on to shepherd yet another church. He wondered, had he done enough here? Had he been faithful enough to his calling to enable those he was leaving to remain faithful to theirs. It was in God's hands.

"Sit down on the floor please children, and cross your legs neatly." There was some pushing and shoving as the pupils wriggled into place on the floor but no real disorder; "That's right, now straight backs and no chattering," ordered Miss Bury, the assistant Head.

When all was quiet, a cleaned and tidied Rachel Troop led the choir of sixteen children onto the stage. They were followed by six more children who were to act out the story of Holy Week and Easter using short Bible readings and poems.

All went well until the little one's started to sing 'There is a Green Hill Far Away.' Baby Riley, roused from his sleep, cried out with all the power of his tiny lungs. The small singers faltered and would have stopped but for Sarah's pure, clear soprano, soaring strongly above the baby's crying and leading the childish voices back into their sweet rendition of the favourite hymn. Hugh smiled, watching Sarah from beneath his half-closed eyelids. One or two mothers dabbed their eyes and baby Riley was quieted with something produced from his mother's handbag.

The concert was over, the Easter play had been enacted once again, the choir had sung their praises (no Alleluias until Easter Day!) and prayers had been offered. Hugh had given a final blessing and now the children had gone home and Sarah and her cousin were alone in the school hall.

"I wish you would sing the solo at Estwick on Sunday, Sarah. Your voice is glorious; it plucks the heart strings. It's a sin not to let us hear it and it would be such a blessing for me, as I start in my new parish."

"I'm not sure Hugh, maybe as it's at Estwick and the family will be there -but I've been so afraid of the attacks of weakness I keep having. It would be awful if I suddenly lost the strength to sing in the middle of it, everyone would be so upset."

"Isn't it today you're going for your test results? Maybe Dr. Campbell will have some good news."

"Yes, I'm calling in at the surgery on my way home. The bus drops me right outside. Whether it will be good news, I don't know. I hope so, God knows we all need some good news but—we shall see. God's love stretches far beyond what happens to us here, we shouldn't be afraid. You've a tremendous new challenge to face yourself, Hugh. Everyone here will miss you."

"Bless you, Sarah," Hugh's eyes smiled his fondness for his cousin.

CHAPTER 55

Holiday in Estwick

Ellie didn't need to take much luggage home with her. Changes of underwear, a few pairs of stockings, a couple of blouses and a spare skirt were all she packed into the same leather holdall her brothers had given her when she first came to London. Everything else she would need was already at home and her travelling outfit would do for any formal outing. She checked the parcel from Gurphy's containing the items for Stephen's butterflies and an illustrated book entitled, 'Ferns and Flowering grasses of our Northern Moorlands,' for Sarah. Isobel Swarbrick, the author of the book, was an old student friend of Sarah's. Isobel had been to stay with them in Hartsbeck, for a week, during one summer holiday. Ellie had been home and joined them on their long country walks. She remembered the banter between Sarah and her friend.

"Oh not again Izzie, surely you drew that same species ten minutes ago! We'll never make it home before dark at this rate," Sarah would moan.

"I need to be sure of every detail and there is something unusual about this one, anyway it's growing in a different habitat." She preferred to draw her specimens growing within their natural environment rather than take them home in a box.

As it was late, Isobel had compromised by sketching as she walked. Glancing through the book Ellie thought it well worth the vexation.

To read on the train Ellie bought one of H.G. Wells' strange science fiction stories, 'The Island of Dr. Moreau', one of George's old favourites. Its macabre tale gripped her imagination and between reading and dozing she hardly noticed the miles flying past.

The train was late arriving at Hartsbeck and Ellie couldn't see Stephen on the station. Wearily, she allowed the porter to help her down from the carriage.

"Ellie! Ellie! I thought you were never coming."

Thin but vivacious, her light brown hair flying out from under a close fitting hat of brown felt, Sarah came hurrying down the platform her face alight with welcome,

"Sarah!"

The two sisters hugged each other and made their way to where mother was waiting in a taxi.

"Mother had to see the doctor, so we came on in a taxi to meet you. Oh, it's so good to have you home, Ellie."

They arrived at Aspen Lane to find Stephen organising the holiday luggage. Most of it was to be taken to the station by taxi early the following morning. Several bulging haversacks, two rolled up tents and four sleeping bags, filled the hallway.

Stephen briefed them all, ticking of instructions on his fingers:

"Mother you are to go in the taxi with Ellie, Sarah and Hannah and the two little ones. I'll walk to the station with George, Tom and Rebecca, Edwin, Annie and young Jack. The train for Hellifield leaves at quarter past nine. Samuel Whewel from the farm will meet us at Hellifield with his horse and cart and I've hired a horse and trap as well to take us on to Estwick. We should all be settled in by teatime tomorrow." It sounded like a military exercise.

In the flurry of preparing picnics for the next day's journey, eating an evening meal and having an early night, there was no time for conversation other than that related to the preparations. They were all up and ready on time the following morning, (with Stephen's military organising, dare they be anything else?) After a day of tumbling from taxi to train, to cart and trap it was a relief when they all arrived at Estwick. The menfolk and boys soon put up their tents in the farmer's field and Hannah with five year old Alice, six year old Richard and fourteen year old Rebecca had rooms in the farmhouse. Ellie, Sarah and their mother settled into comfortable rooms at the Inn.

The tranquillity of the landscape and the relaxed friendliness of the villagers soon calmed the harassed town dwellers. The weather was kind, the sun shone as if it was midsummer. Ellie and Sarah took a walk together, on the slopes of Ingleborough. The white limestone pavements stretched around them set among chalky-green grass and brilliant emerald mosses turning to brownie-orange where the sun had scorched them. Ingleborough's squared summit seemed just a short scramble away up a rock strewn slope but they both knew it was deceptively further and were content not to attempt the climb.

"Let's sit here awhile in the shade."

Ellie sank down in the shelter of a rocky outcrop and Sarah eased herself down beside her. The grass under them was bone dry and all they need worry about were the creepy crawlies finding their way inside their skirts. Ellie reached inside the outcrop and from its cool interior pulled out two moist shoots the white root ball still attached.

"I remember this," laughed Sarah taking one and sucking the bitter-sweet moisture from the plant, "I haven't a clue what it's called but Edwin used to find them for me when I was tiny,"

"I can't remember its name either, dad used to find them for mother and myself when we first came up here. I must have been about three or four years old. It certainly takes the edge off your thirst."

Sarah reached out and squeezed Ellie's hand, "such a lot has happened since we were children. Are you glad you went to London, Ellie?"

Ellie looked into Sarah's pale, strained face and felt a pang for the years they had missed together.

"It was something I had to do, Sarah. I missed all of you, but I believed that as women, we had to step out of the rut we were in and I'm glad I managed to step out of mine. At the time I just wanted to learn to nurse in the big city, like lots of other girls but it developed into something much larger than just my own career. Don't ask me to explain, I'm not one for words," Ellie stopped talking and gazed at the great sweep of the landscape before them.

Sarah too, stared at the landscape. "I think I know what you mean. Our English way of life has been changing dramatically and it's not just the war, it started before that. It makes me think of the 'sea-change' Shakespeare describes in 'The Tempest'. It's as if we've been shaken awake, as women. We're finding our own special place in this 'new order of things'. You and I weren't suffragettes but what we've done in our own careers has been just as much part of this 'sea-change' in society."

"Rather like evolution," Ellie laughed wryly. The sisters had drifted easily into one of the life-pondering moods of their girlhood bedtimes.

Ellie lay back and stared at the sky, "you sound just like my friend, Eliza. It does seem odd that all this beauty, all these rocks and hills and streams look the same as when we were children and it feels just as good to be here. But I feel different. I've become harder, colder, more brittle in some ways but more flexible and less shockable in others. I sometimes think I'm a bit like one of Stephen's ancient rocks."

"Or fossils!" Sarah quipped.

"Thank you, Sarah," Ellie lent across and tickled her sister's nose with a long piece of grass. Sarah giggled, then continued more seriously,

"But think, Ellie, you're bound to have changed. You had to learn to stand on your own two feet pretty quickly, in London, and you've had to face traumatic situations as a nurse. Then the war and losing Jack and Becky Nelson and then Dad. These things are bound to make us all harder but hopefully, stronger. Ellie, I'm glad you came on this holiday. I wish you were back home, in the family. I miss you." Suddenly Sarah started to sob.

Ellie took her sister's hand, feeling neither cold nor brittle.

Sarah turned her face away and asked, "you've seen lots of people die in your job. What's it like?"

Ellie tried to answer lightly, "Well, not lots, I wouldn't be very good at my job if there were lots but yes, I've seen people die. It's hard to watch children die. Strangely enough they seem to accept death like a friend; they don't fight it as adults do. Death is so personal, there are as many ways of dying as there are people. During the war, death was all around us but we carried on living our everyday lives. It changed us but we are still very much alive. Don't dwell on death, Sarah."

"But the moment of death, Ellie, I've not seen a person actually die. Is it very terrible?"

"No, Sarah. I can tell you that death itself is nothing to fear, the moment a person has 'passed on', as they say, there is just a great, enormous quiet and peace, where a few minutes before there may have been the sound of laboured breathing."

"So, is that struggling for breath, painful?"

"No, and I wouldn't call it ' struggling for breath.' It's just the body gradually letting go of its life support. Why do you want to know this Sarah? It's a morbid subject for such a lovely day?"

"I know, but I can't stop thinking about it. I think I may be dying Ellie, Dr. Campbell says I have breast cancer."

Ellie sat bolt upright, "Sarah! Are you sure?"

"Yes. I found a lump, here," she pointed to her breast, "Dr. Campbell sent me to a specialist in Preston, he took some tests and there's no doubt. They think it may have been left too long to cure."

Ellie swallowed hard. "Nonsense! A lot can be done these days, especially in London. We've got some of the most advanced cancer specialists. The Middlesex Hospital has been having a lot of success with breast cancer surgery."

Sarah looked hopeful, "Ellie, do you think they could help me?"

A hard stone had lodged in Ellie's chest; "we can find out. Come and stay with me in London, I'll make sure you see the best people."

In the shock of the moment, Ellie didn't stop to think things through, she daren't. All she could think of was that she must save

Sarah, at all costs. If the doctors couldn't help her sister then she would by using the water cures and other types of alternative medicine, she'd learnt about. Sarah must come back with her.

The sisters walked slowly down the hill to join the others, talking and making plans. Sarah's cheeks were pink with excitement and she'd lost her sad expression.

"Sarah, you look a new woman already! I knew this place would put fresh life into both of you. Supper's nearly ready!" Stephen grinned with satisfaction, as he cooked sausages and onions for them all over an open camp fire.

Easter day dawned with a breeze which blew the clouds away and welcomed the sun. As Stephen had predicted in his letter to Ellie, cousin Hugh had persuaded the church-goers amongst them, to come to the village church for morning service. Afterwards everyone, whether they'd been to church or not, were invited to the Vicarage for a grand Sunday lunch cooked by Hugh's wife, Margaret, helped and hindered by their two small children, Ruth and Gordon.

Hugh had asked Sarah, if she felt well enough, to sing the solo, 'I know that my Redeemer Liveth'. She sang and her pure soprano had never sounded more lovely, or her intonation of the words more meaningful. Ellie was lifted beyond herself, in a way she had longed for but never quite found in all her explorations into theosophy and its mysteries. Her love for Sarah swelled inside her but Sarah's singing was leading her towards an even greater love; she had almost reached it, when the solo ended. Sarah, trembling and exhausted, came back to sit beside her and Ellie, the nurse, became immediately concerned for her sister's obvious frailty.

"Oh, Sarah. You shouldn't have done it," she scolded taking her sister's hand.

"I wanted to do it, Ellie. It was my special gift to you all."

Ellie's eyes filled with tears, "It was a beautiful gift, thank you my dear; sit quietly now."

Later, when they'd returned to Hartsbeck and Sarah's illness was made clear to the family, Ellie had difficulty persuading them that Sarah should come back with her to London to find the best treatment for breast cancer. It was discussed when Sarah was out of the way, resting in her bedroom.

"There are good hospitals and specialists here in the North. Manchester has an excellent reputation and Leeds, even Preston has some excellent specialists," declared George.

"I understand that, but recent major breakthroughs have been made by doctors at the Middlesex Hospital in London. It's the first hospital to perform successful mastectomy operations. They have life-saving treatments there, Sarah ought to be given the opportunity and I shall be there with her and can help in all sorts of ways."

"Well, I'm not sure that Sarah is as ill as you all seem to think. She tires easily but she teaches full time and what with your father's death and helping me cope with my disabilities, she's bound to be tired. She keeps going, like we all do. I think a quiet holiday by the sea would put her right," Jeannie's words were defiant.

It was Dr Waters who tipped the balance in the end. He spoke directly to Jeannie in Stephen's presence.

"Jeannie, you must understand that we are not talking about measles or chickenpox here. Sarah has cancer and I'm afraid she may have kept it to herself for too long, before consulting me. Ellie is right, the work being done with breast cancer patients at the Middlesex Hospital is a real break-through and there is also a specialist cancer hospital in London. If Sarah goes to live with Ellie for a time, she will be eligible for treatment at these hospitals and I'm happy to write a letter, outlining her condition as I know it."

"Well if you are really sure, doctor. I wouldn't want to prevent her receiving the treatment she needs."

"I am sure, Jeannie. What's more she will have Ellie alongside her, to look after her in between any hospital treatment. Your eldest is a fine nurse, Jeannie. Stephen, I trust you agree with me?"

"About Ellie, yes definitely. About medical treatment in London, I'd have to give it some thought. Will it be expensive, can we afford it?"

"Good question. I'll look into it. I would say that if you all pool together, you should be able to afford treatment. Also, these hospitals are glad to have patients to try out their new methods and treatments. I'm sure they will take Sarah without asking an exorbitant fee,"

"As long as Sarah is treated with respect as a human being and not a mere guinea pig!" expostulated Stephen.

"That is why I'm glad that Ellie will be with her. There can be doctors who care less about the patient and more about exploring the disease and experimenting with their ideas. We need to persuade ourselves, that in the end their work will benefit future patients. Don't forget, our formidable Sister Elkson is used to handling doctors and their ways. She won't let Sarah suffer more, on their account."

"What do you think, mother? I think we must allow Sarah to go to London with Ellie. We've always trusted Dr. Waters in the past."

"I'll be sorry to see Sarah go and I shall insist on going up to London to visit. But yes, I agree, we must let her go." Jeanie's right hand began to shake suddenly and uncontrollably. The shaking seemed to spread up her arm and down the side of her body and her right foot could be seen tapping up and down against the carpet, her head jerked and tears ran down her face.

"It's as I suspected," declared the doctor as he held Jeanie's wrist to take her pulse. "A classic case of Parkinson's disease, still in the early stages. You'll feel alright again shortly Jeannie, a bit tired but nothing too drastic."

He turned to Stephen, "Parkinson's usually develops slowly. Your mother will need someone to be always nearby, in case of sudden attacks of weakness, or shaking like this. Otherwise, she could carry on leading a quieter but fairly normal life for several years. Over time she'll become much weaker and less able. With your permission, Jeannie, I'd like to refer you to a specialist in Manchester and I would strongly advise you to employ a housekeeper to help you and to be on hand during the day. Please, do not tell Sarah about this, she may refuse to go to London."

Stephen looked as if he had just woken into a bad dream. The prospect of being left alone with an ailing mother, threatened to curtail his freedom. The doctor assured him that practical help could be found and reminded him that Edwin and George and their wives lived nearby. They would cope and Sarah must take her chance in London.

CHAPTER 56

Sarah in London

Ellie travelled back to London alone to make the medical arrangements for her sister. She had letters with her from Dr Waters and from Mr Edward Gormley, the consultant in Preston, who'd confirmed the diagnosis of breast cancer. Both these letters Ellie took to Dr. Collins, asking him if he would take Sarah onto his panel when she came to London. He agreed. This was the first step towards Sarah being seen by a consultant at the Cancer Hospital in Chelsea, where new treatments for breast cancer, including groundbreaking surgery, were being practised with some success.

Sarah, escorted by Stephen, arrived in London a week later and the following day Ellie took her along to Dr Collins' surgery. Behind a screen Ellie helped remove Sarah's upper clothing so that the doctor could examine her. The tight swelling beneath the skin of Sarah's left breast, showed a lump similar in shape to a cauliflower floret. Ellie was aware of the doctor's quick intake of breath and the compression of his lips. First, he examined the right breast, which, on the surface, appeared normal. Moving to the left breast the doctor gently touched the knobbly lump and then, very carefully felt the area around it, which was stretched and taught. He asked Sarah to lift her arm, which she did with some difficulty. Ellie came forward and supported the arm while Dr. Collins explored the site of the glands around the arm- pit, pressing the slightly swollen tissue, Sarah winced and he stopped immediately.

"Thank you, Miss Elkson, I'm sorry if I hurt you but that is all I need to do for today," he searched her face as he spoke further;

"that must have been quite an ordeal for you, my dear; you were very patient. Tell me does your breast give you much pain?"

"It feels tight and hot if I use my arm too much and underneath my arm it throbs and aches sometimes but nothing too bad."

"I'm sure I can give you something to help ease that," the middle-aged doctor gave her an encouraging smile then left the cubicle, speaking to Ellie as he went.

"Sister, please help Miss Elkson to dress, then I would like to speak with you both."

When both sisters were sitting before his desk, Dr. Collins told them he would immediately refer Sarah to Sir Francis Oliver, a specialist at the Cancer Hospital. "You should hear from him within a few days, with the date of an appointment."

"Will he be able to cure me?" whispered Sarah

"Sir Francis and his team will certainly do their very best to help you, Miss Elkson. If anyone can bring about a cure, it will be the staff at the Cancer Hospital; recently they've had some excellent results from their new treatments."

Ellie noted that, while he had carefully built up her sister's trust in the hospital's capabilities, Dr Collins didn't make any promises, or offer any specific hope of a cure, in Sarah's case.

Sarah settled in thankfully with Ellie at 19, Redcliffe Street, while they awaited the letter from the Cancer Hospital. In the meantime Ellie planned an agenda, using her knowledge of water-cures, to try and cleanse Sarah's bodily systems of impurities and improve her chances of recovery. Amelia Antrim had renewed her friendship with Ellie and helped her with this.

"It's no good putting Sarah onto a water-only fast, Ellie. She isn't strong enough to take anything so drastic. Try to include raw vegetables, such as carrot and celery into her meals and salad stuffs such as beetroot, onion and lettuce and fresh fruit, mainly apples and pears. Nothing too acidic. Lightly steamed vegetables and white fish with herbs such as parsley and the occasional egg. A watery chicken broth with onions, barley and sage and consommé soups with herbs. Calves foot jelly and beef tea are good in moderation. If we aim to build up her strength with foods like this which are nourishing and purifying and have plenty of water content, she might manage twelve hours on water only. All of this will help to clear a good percentage of the toxins from her body and give her a better chance of fighting the cancer."

Ellie busily wrote down the list of foods Amelia was reading out to her from pamphlets written by her employer, the esteemed Dr Meyler. The good doctor was now retired from main stream medical practice and his idea was to complement the work of his more orthodox colleagues. He studied hard to alleviate suffering by natural remedies, diet being an important part of his alternative medical method. Many of his patients had been recommended to him because they had become the despair of their own doctors, this meant Meyler had nothing to lose if his methods didn't succeed. Others came to him because they preferred 'mother nature' to what they saw as 'the experimental dabblings' of medical science. Amelia understood Ellie's strong belief in water therapies and used her own intelligence to temper the more rigorous hydrotherapy practices to suit Sarah.

Sarah was happy to follow Ellie's eating plan. The food was light and easy to digest and suited her failing appetite. Ellie was on duty at the clinic or paying home visits at varying times each day and occasionally in the evenings, according to her rota. On Saturdays and Sundays she was at home. Her flexible hours also allowed her two free half days, during the week. At least she had no night duties in her present job and was also able to be with Sarah at every meal time.

Sarah spent her first few days restfully. Before going to work, Ellie would settle her sister comfortably, in a chair near the window of the front room, where she could see people going about their business in the street below.

"I feel like old Grandma Jane," she giggled, looking at her feet resting on a footstool and her legs covered with a woollen rug.

"I only need the lace cap and blue shawl round my shoulders."

"Nonsense," replied Ellie "you haven't a grey or white hair to be seen. Not like me!"

Forced to act like an invalid, Sarah busied herself writing letters and reading. She tried knitting, but the tight discomfort in her breast from holding up the needles soon made her stop. Amelia and other friends of Ellie would call in from time to time but dear Eliza became a regular visitor. She would call in whenever she knew Ellie had to be on duty at the clinic. Sarah soon came to love the astute, warm- hearted older woman.

Eliza soon discovered Sarah's love of music. One morning, the taxi driver, with much huffing and puffing, followed Eliza up the steps to Ellie's front door carrying a gramophone and a pile of records.

"I hope you approve of my choice of music. I'm afraid I've developed rather a varied taste. I've brought a selection to cover all moods. You can disapprove and call me vulgar, I shan't mind a bit, but then you must educate me properly, Sarah!"

Sarah laughed, "Eliza, this is wonderful! Remember I've grown up with brothers around me who had very lively musical tastes, if you could call them musical. Oh look, you've brought 'The Mikado' and 'The Pirates of Penzance'. I love Gilbert and Sullivan, I was once one of the 'three little girls from school' in the Mikado. It was only a local production, I must have been seventeen."

The two women had great fun, winding up the gramophone and playing the slightly wobbly recordings of Gilbert and Sullivan Operas, and singing quietly along with the well - known songs.

Over the next week Eliza came most days, sometimes in the morning, sometimes afternoon and the small house echoed with melody. Strauss; Verdi and Puccini; a few risqué music hall numbers and sacred music from such works as Mendelssohn's 'Elijah' and Handel's 'Messiah'. Sarah would have loved to continue listening to the music, when she was alone but found it too difficult to wind the gramophone herself. One of her favourite records was of a set of old English folk songs, sung by famous soloists. In her mind, her voice soared with the soprano, as she sang 'The Lark in the Pure Air.' It was one of the first solo pieces Sarah remembered singing, in a concert when she was eighteen. A record of folk -dance music, reminded her of playing the piano at school, for the elderly Miss Dukes, who had done her best to teach the children the traditional steps and moves of the dances. What muddles the children made, to the annoyance of the passionate Miss Dukes who believed wholeheartedly in the passing on of these ancient skills.

"I long to have one of those new wireless sets that are appearing in the shops," Eliza said. "They are enclosed in such beautifully designed wooden cabinets, to look just like a piece of furniture and not like the heap of metal and wires that my clergyman friend still has!"

Sarah too, thought that to have a wireless set would be wonderful but didn't say so as she knew Eliza would move heaven and earth to obtain one for her. She already felt overwhelmed by the older woman's generosity. Instead, Sarah's reply took a new direction.

"Two of my cousins are clergymen," she remarked. "Eliza, I know Ellie doesn't attend church but I would rather like to go, especially now, when I feel I need all the spiritual support I can find. I think a full Sunday service might be rather much. Do you know of a shorter mid-week one, nearby, which I could go to?"

Eliza beamed with delight. "Why yes. A few of us gather at St. Stephen's, at eleven o'clock each Wednesday morning for a simple Holy Communion service. It only lasts half an hour. I could come and collect you in a taxi and afterwards, if you wish, you could come and take a cup of tea with me, I live close by the church."

"That would be perfect, thank you Eliza. I want to come to the service but I'll wait and see how I stand up to it, before accepting your kind offer of tea. I'd enjoy coming to your house but I might just feel I need to come straight home from the church. I seem to find every-day things such an effort."

Eliza's keen eyes had not missed the dark shadows under Sarah's own and her gradually thinning features. She wished wholeheartedly, that the appointment at the Cancer Hospital would come quickly for her new friend. A full week had gone by with no sign of a letter. Eliza understood, all too well, the importance of catching breast cancer as early as possible for any chance of a cure. She also knew that Ellie was not using her influence to push the appointment, because she wanted her water therapies and special diets to have taken full effect, before Sarah was submitted to more invasive treatment,

"I remember, when I first began my nursing training, noticing how women who had had a poor diet, couldn't fight disease as well as those who'd eaten healthily," she argued.

"But Ellie, Sarah didn't have an unhealthy diet before and remember your training began in the 1890's. Medical science and cancer treatments have come on in leaps and bounds since then!"

"I began my training late in 1899 so I'd call it the 1900's and they haven't progressed as far as you may think, Eliza, much of it is still in the experimental stages. Remember, Hartsbeck was hit badly by depression, before and after the war, and I think Sarah skimped herself to provide better food for some of the poorer children at school. In any case, good or bad diet, the body still harbours dangerous toxins which the water therapies can help to eliminate."

Ellie was adamant and Eliza saw behind it Ellie's fear that she was going to lose Sarah. Secretly, Ellie guessed that Dr Waters had been right and Sarah had left it too late, when she'd first sought medical help. She dreaded Sarah finding this out from the hospital. Ellie had interpreted the look on Dr Collin's face, when he'd first seen Sarah's breast and she suspected, that he too, thought it was past hope of a conventional cure.

Nevertheless, Ellie didn't deliberately hold up the appointment, she just didn't use her influence to interfere and hurry it along. She encouraged Sarah to wait patiently for a letter and watched her sister like a hawk for signs of any real distress. She took it at face value when Sarah insisted that the medicine Dr Collins had prescribed, "wonderfully eases the discomfort."

Despite her increasing frailty, Sarah developed new interests. A few days after Sarah had arrived, Ellie had hired Kitty Fielding, now thirteen years old, to do some of the cleaning and cooking for the household. She came three half days a week, two mornings and one afternoon. It eased Ellie's anxiety to know that, for part of the time when she was away, there was officially, someone in the house with her sister.

Sarah took a great interest in Kitty from the start and encouraged the girl to talk with her. As a teacher, she realised how much schooling Kitty had missed and offered to help her catch up. In addition to her housework, Kitty started to come every afternoon at half past three, for half an hour's tuition. To begin with, Sarah helped her with the three 'r's' but soon discovered that the girl had already managed to build up her reading and writing skills on her own, by using her brothers' school books. Sarah quickly moved on to more interesting subjects such as history, geography and literature. Ellie and Eliza were detailed to bring books from the library and Stephen sent some books from Preston, on natural history and science. The half hour's tuition turned into an hour and Kitty became more of a companion to Sarah than a pupil and grew adept at understanding Sarah's needs. She made them cups of tea and when she saw that her teacher was tiring Kitty made her put her feet up and they would listen to music, or Kitty would read to her. The young girl's halting speech had much improved and had an unusually attractive lilt. Short and small-boned, Kitty was neat and clean in appearance with her mousey brown hair always tied back with a black shoe lace, ending with a small bow on top of her head. Her thin, sharp features were softened by a slightly lopsided mouth and an anxious to please expression. Sarah found Kitty comfortable to have around and always relaxed when she heard the girl's light step about the house.

It was a full two weeks later, on the nineteenth of June, that the letter arrived. It offered Sarah an appointment with the eminent Sir Francis Oliver on the afternoon of Wednesday, 3rd of July at two o'clock, at his clinic, in the Cancer Hospital. The letter stated that, until the appointment, Dr Collins would continue to attend Miss Elkson and he should contact the hospital immediately if further developments warranted it. Dr Collins visited Sarah later that same day and promised to drop in at least twice a week and more if he was needed.

The wait of another fortnight was frustrating but Sarah didn't have time to brood. Her days were already filling up with interesting projects. Kitty had realised how much Sarah missed the garden at Hartsbeck and how she longed to see her Lancashire moors with their wide expanse of greens, browns and purples of grass, bracken and heather. At Kitty's suggestion the two of them planted flower seeds in trays, on the windowsills of the London house. Eliza joined in the project and brought pots of red and white geraniums and purple and yellow pansies.

Sensing that Ellie might feel left out, Eliza placed a small rose bush, in a large pot, outside the front door, to cheer Ellie with its fragrant pink blooms, when she came home from a hard day at the clinic.

On Wednesday morning Eliza collected Sarah in a taxi and took her to the Communion service at St. Stephen's Church. It was a quiet, said service, with about fifteen others in the congregation.

"I feel so much stronger for coming here," she told Eliza. "Thank you for taking the trouble to bring me. Being amongst other Christians helps and receiving the bread and wine brings me so near to our Lord. I can face anything when I know He's with me. I'm sure you understand that, Eliza."

Eliza patted Sarah's hand, "Indeed I do understand Sarah. Sometimes I'm so aware of the hundreds of people who've been in this church, over the years, who must have experienced inner peace and healing from the services. Hundreds who've been baptised and married here and gone on through death, into new life. It gives me great comfort and courage to face my own life."

"I knew you would understand," was all Sarah could say and she sat quietly, mulling over the service, in the taxi home.

One beautifully sunny day, when Sarah felt well and Ellie was off duty, they took a taxi to St. James's Park where Eliza hired one of the open landaus, which waited at the park gates for visitors. Smiling they rode through the park, nodding to groups of people sauntering by who turned to stare at them. The women savoured the beauty of the flowers with their attendant butterflies and bees, the pools and fountains, the spreading shade of the mature trees and the green-ness of the grass after the grey city pavements.

"It's so good to hear the birds," sighed Sarah leaning back in quiet ecstasy on the cushions of the open carriage. For a few moments she closed her eyes, against the glare of the sun and enjoyed the sensa-tion of movement and the rhythmic clip- clop of the horses' hooves. She imagined herself on the road to Estwick.

Kitty was thrilled to be included in this outing and her head bobbed excitedly from side to side taking in all the sights. This was the first time she had been out of her own, small London borough. When they reached the end of the park and saw Buckingham Palace in the near distance, her eyes nearly popped out of her head and she had to be restrained from standing up in the carriage.

"Whatever would we do if King George and the Queen decided to ride out in the park?" said Eliza jokingly. Jean's eyes opened wider,

"Oh, do you think they might? Oh my! I would love to see the King and Queen. I wish my Mam could be with us!"

"We'll have to see if we can bring her next time," laughed Sarah.

Ellie smiled at the enjoyment of it all and locked away the pre-cious moments in her memory, knowing she would need to draw on them in the time ahead.

CHAPTER 57

Sarah consults Sir William Oliver

With so much activity the days leading up to the hospital appointment did not drag. Quite suddenly it was the nineteenth of June and Ellie and Sarah found themselves on their way to the Cancer Hospital to meet Sir William Oliver. Ellie was pleased that Sarah's complexion looked clear and her eyes had lost the dull look that had clouded them when she first arrived in London. Together with Amelia, she felt they had worked something of a miracle with their diet and water therapy and Kitty and Eliza had kept up Sarah's spirits with their various activities.

As the sisters climbed out of the taxi and walked towards the main doors of the hospital, Sarah longed to be back at Hartsbeck, walking through the doors of the friendly cottage hospital she had known in childhood. This hospital was large and cold. Austere nurses walked along narrow pathways to and from the buildings. They wore black capes over starched dresses, with veils, or frilled white caps perched unnaturally on top of severe hair arrangements and their faces were set purposefully looking neither to right or left with their flat, shiny black shoes hardly seeming to touch the ground as they sped along without appearing to rush. Ellie was used to this pattern of the nurses' walk; their minds set on where they were going, every moment counting and no distraction allowed. She also knew that inside these austere looking forms, were real, warm-hearted women and possibly some that she knew.

Sarah shivered. "It's all so strange," she whispered, "those nurses; they're like machines."

"It's all a front," chuckled Ellie. "They're just like you and me but they have to look cool, calm, collected and efficient at all costs, in case Matron happens to be around. Matron commands them like an army officer, especially when they're in uniform and in the grounds where the public see them. Just wait till you really need them, you'll see them in their true light then. I'm one of them - don't forget!"

"Yes, I know," Sarah peered mischievously into Ellie's face.

"Don't be cheeky," snapped Ellie but was pleased that Sarah's humour hadn't deserted her. Ellie wore a plain, dark tailored coat and hat, not unlike the uniform hat she wore for house visits. Her nurse's badge was pinned prominently on her lapel and her own flat, shiny, black shoes were reigned back, to keep in step with Sarah's slow ones.

Sarah had dressed in a loose, two piece costume of soft grey with a pale blue silk blouse. She'd chosen it so that she could slip off her jacket and blouse easily, for examination by the great doctor. She wore a narrow brimmed, navy blue straw hat with a white trim. Altogether she looked sweetly attractive, with her small, slender figure and kind, calm face. Ellie, glancing sideways at her, swallowed a lump in her throat.

They were shown the way to Sir William's clinic but by the time they had walked the length of three long corridors, Sarah was noticeably wilting. Ellie stopped a passing Sister, explaining Sarah's situation and asking if there was a wheel chair to be had.

The Sister stared at Ellie, "Ellie Elkson? Yes, it is you! It must be twenty years since–."

"Lettie,-Lettie Parrish. Am I glad to meet someone I know! This is my sister, Sarah, she's not at all well and has an appointment with Sir William Oliver in twenty minutes but she can't walk much further."

"These long corridors are lethal. I'll get the wheel chair from my ward, it's just in here. I'm ward Sister, it's a women's surgical, Parrish Ward. I'll not keep you, be back in a jiffy."

Lettie was back in two minutes with a wheel chair and a glass of iced water which she insisted Sarah sipped as soon as she was settled in the chair.

Giving Sarah a moment to recover, Ellie looked at her old colleague,

"It seems an age since Netley, Lettie, almost another life. I'm a Sister in a community mother and baby clinic. I left Felix Square years ago, I wasn't happy with all of Dr King's methods. You look well."

"I love my work here. So much progress is being made in cancer surgery. I'm glad to be part of it," she glanced at her watch, "you'd better be on your way, best not to keep Sir. William waiting,"

Lettie patted Sarah's hand as she retrieved the glass, "you'll find him very kind. Ellie, wheel your sister right back to the main entrance afterwards. I'll send someone for another chair for the Ward."

The colour had come back to Sarah's cheeks and she smiled her thanks. Ellie took charge of the chair and promising to look up her old friend later, sped away on her black shiny feet.

The dreaded inspection, by the awesome Sir William Oliver, revealed a growth larger and deeper than Ellie had imagined. Having been silent during much of the examination, Sir William guided the two sisters into a more comfortable interview room. Here he spoke with them, long and earnestly. Sarah listened to him and despite the fact that he addressed her personally, had the feeling that he wasn't speaking about herself but talking of somebody quite different.

"I'm very much afraid your cancer is quite advanced, Miss Elkson. It is my opinion, that surgery to remove the growth or to remove your breast at this stage, would not be beneficial. I fear the cancer must have gone unnoticed for over a year. I will be able to ease your condition with injections and other medication, which will help to reduce any swelling in the surrounding tissue and lessen pain. I would like you to stay here in the hospital for two nights, so that I will be able to initiate such therapy and do some other small tests."

Sir William turned to Ellie, "Sister Elkson, I would suggest that after these tests, your sister should return to your London house. That is, if you are able to make arrangements there, for her care. I want your sister to visit me here, at my clinic, every three weeks. I shall ask Dr Collins to visit her between times. Is this acceptable to you both or do you have questions you'd like to ask?"

"I'm in your hands, Sir William. For the moment I have no further questions," replied Sarah formally.

He stood up and pressed a bell on his desk and spoke directly to Sarah, "Good. Now, my dear young lady, I shall ask one of my efficient- looking young nurses to take you to Hepple Ward. Sister Hepple will make you very comfortable and I shall see you later this afternoon."

A softly- rounded body of a nurse entered the room. She took charge of Sarah with such warm friendliness that Sarah mentally withdrew her idea of nurses as machines. As she was whisked away in her wheel- chair Sarah waved her fingers at Ellie,

"See you in a day or two! Enjoy your break from me!"

No-one was deceived by her joking tone but Sarah still felt, that this wasn't really happening to her. Sir William turned to Ellie,

"Would you be willing to care for your sister at home?

"Yes, of course, Sir William."

"As a qualified nursing sister I take it you have had experience of nursing patients with breast cancer?"

"Yes, Sir William, but it's over twenty years ago since I nursed adult cancer patients specifically. I am sure the methods must have changed,"

"Only in certain areas. The basics are still the same. In a condition such as your sister's you will need to administer palliative care, including any drugs I prescribe. You must watch for any ulceration in the breast, or any discharge from the nipple and contact Dr Collins immediately. No doubt you know the appropriate cleaning and dressing procedures."

"Yes, of course, Doctor," Ellie was dismayed as she realised that nursing Sarah was going to be a full- time job. "Only, I am at the moment, employed as a child and family welfare, community nurse. It is my, or rather our, livelihood."

"Perhaps you could arrange for a reduction of hours, or work out a more flexible timetable. If it becomes necessary, I would be able to arrange for a nurse from the Cancer Hospital to come in certain times during the week. At the moment I am sure that your sister will be alright left alone for short periods, or with someone in the house who could always send for you, if needed," he hesitated before continuing.

"My dear, I should warn you that your sister may not have long to live. We can only ease her way through this disease. We will help, in every possible way, to enable her to enjoy some pleasure and peace, during this time. While she's in the hospital, I'll test your sister for anaemia and any other such deficiencies so that we can give her supplements to help her feel as well as possible during the next few months," he looked meaningfully at Ellie.

"If you wish I could write a letter to your superiors, explaining the situation and asking them to allow you time off when necessary and in the meantime, a temporary reduction in hours."

"Thank you, yes please, that would be most kind, Sir William," relief spilled through Ellie at this practical offer of support.

"Are you quite sure surgery would not help her?" she dared to ask.

"At this stage it could accelerate the disease. It would also cause her terrible pain and suffering, which would have to be controlled by mind and body numbing drugs. The palliative care which I have described, would give her a decent, if reduced, quality of life -until very near the end. However, if the growth in her breast becomes unbearable and suppurates badly, then we shall consider a surgical operation to remove what we can of the main growth but it will only ease, not cure her. You must be alert to the cancer spreading to other organs. A watchful, professional eye is needed but you must allow her to enjoy life when she feels like it. Short outings on good days; visits from friends who won't tire her too much; pleasant, quiet occupations; a light nutritious diet. She's fortunate to have you my dear. Encourage family members to come for short visits."

"Thank you, Sir William, we are fortunate to have you as our specialist."

Sir William bowed graciously and Ellie left to walk the long corridors back to the main entrance. As she passed Parrish Ward a familiar figure darted out and Lettie took her arm.

"I've been looking out for you; the ward is always quiet at this time. I'm going for my tea break. Will you come and join me?" Lettie looked round for Sarah, "Where's your sister?"

"Sir William is keeping her in for two nights, for tests and treatment. Then she's coming home to me. He says it will probably only be for a few months. Oh, Lettie, it's too cruel. First the war, now this. Is there any joy left in life? It's one nightmare after another!"

Lettie linked arms with her old colleague and steered her to a quiet room next to the staff dining hall. She plied Ellie with hot, sweet tea and allowed her to vent her grief and anger. Then she calmed her by talking practicalities of up-to-date cancer care. Ellie was soon taking a professional interest and gathering relevant information for nursing Sarah. Lettie breathed a sigh of relief, if Ellie was to break down now it would be terrible for Sarah and Ellie wouldn't be able to forgive herself. The two nurses lapsed into silence until Lettie gave Ellie a further shock.

"By the way, did you receive the letters from your friend, Alex Dobson? Sally the girl in charge of the post at Netley, said three had arrived, all together, after you'd left. Later that same day, there was a fire in the office block and a lot of correspondence was lost. I hoped your letters had been posted on to you, before the fire. Did you receive them?"

Ellie's heart quickened and her face went hot. "Three letters, after I left? No, I've never had them. In fact, I've heard nothing from or about Alex, since the war. I've kept hoping. All this time, I've not known whether he's dead or alive, or where he is."

"Oh Ellie, I'm so sorry. At least you now know that he did try to contact you. I think Sally said the letters were from Canada. I wish I'd taken them and posted them on to you, myself.

Ellie laughed with hysterical relief, "I don't feel so upset with him, now I know he did write. I expect he's angry with me, for not replying. After all this time, I think I'd better let things lie. I need to concentrate on Sarah. I'm so thankful I'm here for her; maybe I wouldn't have been, if Alex and I had come together again. Lettie, you've been an angel but you must go back to your ward. I'm feeling much better and it's good to know that you're here, if I need advice."

"Ellie, it's been so good to meet up again. I hope I'll be able to help you with Sarah. I'll pop along to Hepple Ward and see her, when I go off duty. Do take care of yourself, Ellie; you'll need all your strength. Don't just come for advice, come for a chat."

The two nurses clasped each other's hands with the old feeling of comradeship.

Ellie left the hospital and walked abstractedly through the streets of Chelsea in the late afternoon sunshine. It amazed her that people were going about their everyday business as usual.

"I suppose no-one could tell, from looking at me, what's going on in my personal life and I've no idea what may be going on in theirs," she mused. "We all simply 'carry on regardless'."

She haled a homebound bus and arrived back at Redcliffe Street by half past five to find Kitty Fielding on the doorstep.

"I've been so worried about you and Miss Sarah. I had to come round to make sure you were alright. Have they kept her in the hospital?"

"Just for two nights, Kitty, then she's coming home to us."

Kitty held out a basket covered with a clean white cloth, "Mam's been baking and she's sent this round specially. She thought as you might not feel like cooking when you came in and says you've got to keep your strength up. She knows how you're fond of cheese and onion and says if you can't eat it all, it'll keep a day or two in the cold cupboard, as long as it's covered." Kitty lifted a corner of the cloth and Ellie's mouth watered as the savoury smell of warm pastry, melting cheese with onions and a hint of nutmeg, wafted upwards.

"That smells so good, Kitty, would you like to come in and share it with me?"

"Thank you Sister Elkson, but I've to mind the young uns while Mam sees to old Mrs Lamb's supper and helps her to bed. She only lives across the street but I daren't leave my brothers and the baby on their own in the house."

"No, indeed. We don't want any more problems tonight. Please thank your mother for the pie. I'm going to have a slice now with a mug of tea and an apple and then I'll put my feet up. Oh, and Kitty, there's no need for you to come in to work until my sister comes home; she should be back the day after tomorrow. I think we'll be needing you a lot more during the next few months. I'll come and talk with you and your mother tomorrow. Will four o'clock be convenient?"

"Yes Sister, Mam and I will both be at home," Kitty's eyes took on their big wondering look but she said goodnight and tripped away down the street.

After supper Ellie put her feet up and closed her eyes for half an hour. Her thoughts played on the news of Alex's letters and on the interview with Sir William. She could do little about the letters but she could act on Sir William's advice. At seven o'clock Ellie decided she must contact the family at Hartsbeck. Usually she would write a letter but with the urgency of the situation she decided to telephone George. She knew he had a telephone at home because of his work and because he could now afford such things. Ellie hurried round to Mr. and Mrs Mason the couple who lived next door. They were so proud of their recently installed telephone, that they'd offered its use to their immediate neighbours.

"Of course, we don't want all and sundry using it but if you, Sister Elkson, are ever in urgent need of a telephone, please do feel free to ask us."

True to their word the Masons beamed expansively and ushered Ellie into their hallway where the telephone was installed. They simpered their sympathy concerning Sarah, hovering over Ellie as they explained the mechanics of "this wonderful machine."

When she was through to George, Ellie had to say quite firmly, "thank you so much, but I would like to speak to my brother privately; it is a very personal matter."

"Oh yes, of course, of course. We'll be in here if you need us," and the couple hastened into another room, leaving the door slightly ajar.

Ellie explained to George all that had happened with Sir William and his advice that the family should be informed as soon as possible,

"Sir William said Sarah may only have a short time to live. About three months; possibly less, maybe more. It's hard to tell. He said she should stay here at my house, where he can give her the treatment to help her through."

"Can they not operate?" George's tone was brusque,

"Not now, it would do no good, just make things worse. They may operate, to ease the pain, later. She left it too late, George. She must have kept it hidden for at least a year. Please will you tell mother and the others. You'll want to come and visit. You can stay with me, but not all at once; Sarah tires easily, better to spread it out."

"Will you cope, Ellie? It won't be easy," George spoke kindly and Ellie's eyes filled with tears, she blinked them away.

"I'll cope. There are people who'll help and I can arrange time off work. I'm ringing from a neighbour's house." Ellie gave George the number.

"Ellie, you must have your own telephone installed as soon as possible. We need to be able telephone straight to you and you to us and you'll be able to get medical assistance quickly. It will do Sarah good to have the use of it too, if she's to be housebound. I'll help with the expense, it's the least we can do. Go to the Post Office, they'll arrange it all."

"Good idea, thanks George, I'll sort that out tomorrow. How do I find out how much this call has cost?"

"Get back to the operator when we've finished and she'll tell you. In future ask to reverse the charges when you telephone us."

"I'll do that. Thank you George. Goodbye."

"Goodbye, Ellie. I'll go round and tell mother now. Keep us posted."

The telephone clicked. Ellie found out the cost of the call and went to pay the Mason's. She declined their offer of a drink and crawled home to bed. She slept through sheer weariness until she woke in the early hours and lay going over every small detail of the situation, until it was time to get up. At six o'clock she cycled off to her early duties, visiting families where babies of a few weeks were not feeding properly. Their mothers were becoming as worn down and fretful as their offspring. These early visits meant she was greeted by bad-tempered fathers, stamping about trying to get themselves off to work and resenting her presence. She'd learnt to diffuse the situation by taking charge of baby, so that mother could act as a wife, sorting her husband's breakfast and packed- lunch and seeing to any other children. In the meantime Ellie would wash and change the baby ready for feeding time. Sometimes the mother was so weary and badly nourished that she had only a little, poor quality, breast milk. In such cases Ellie had to explain a feeding routine using a breast milk supplement, of which Dr Truby King's formula was, to her mind, still the best. It took several visits for the jaded mothers to learn the strict hygiene of cleaning feeding bottles and preparing the formula. Ellie still imposed the strict rules she'd learnt from Dr King, of feeding by the clock and not on demand. This gave the mothers longer rests in between feeds and conserved their energy for other household duties. It worked as long as the mothers were stoical enough to ignore their infant's hunger cries and learnt to differentiate these cries, from those of real distress.

Her early visits completed, Ellie cycled to the clinic and talked over the circumstances of Sarah's illness with Sister Allinson, who was in over- all charge of staffing the clinic and senior to Ellie.

"I'm sure we can jiggle your hours around so that you can be at home with your sister when she will need you most, such as early morning for washing and dressing." Ellie agreed, thankful for her colleague's professional outlook.

"I think it will be best for you to work late morning and after-noon hours for the time being. We'll have a confab with the rest of the staff. You'll need plenty of stamina to keep on your job here, as well as caring for your sister. We don't want you to end up as a patient!"

"I can't afford to stop work altogether. I've the maintenance of the house to keep up, as well as other things," Ellie suddenly visualised all the complications pouring in on top of her.

"My dear, you're not on your own. Your brothers and your mother should contribute and surely your sister must have some savings."

"Yes, of course. I'm not thinking straight. I've been independent for so long, I forget I'm part of a family."

"Well, I suggest you discuss it with them. Now, we have a quiet afternoon here so I propose you have the rest of today off and prepare as much as you can for your sister. Tomorrow is Friday, so take the whole day off and don't come back on duty until Monday afternoon for the two o'clock clinic. We'll talk then."

Sister Allinson took Ellie's hand in her own strong one, "I'm sure you realise that the time will come when you will have to give yourself, full-time, to nursing your sister. We'll face that as we come to it. Sometimes our responsibilities take us in unexpected directions, God bless you my dear."

Ellie felt hugely encouraged by her colleague's use of 'we' and the weight of her responsibilities lightened.

CHAPTER 58

Caring for Sarah

Ellie left the clinic and went straight to the Post Office and arranged for a telephone to be installed at 19, Redcliffe Street.

"Mr Bradley, our telephone engineer and his assistant, will be with you at three o'clock tomorrow afternoon. Your telephone should be in working order by half past five, Miss Elkson. You'll wonder how you ever did without one."

"It's going to be very important to us. You do understand the urgency? We need to be able to contact medical help at a moment's notice." Ellie felt anxious.

"I understand perfectly. I've made it a priority."

Back at home, Ellie stripped Sarah's bed and remade it with fresh linen. She checked the food cupboard and made a list of items needed. She gathered up a pile of finished library books and after drinking a long glass of cooled, boiled water and nibbling an apple, locked the house and caught the bus to the Cancer Hospital. Sarah was in the middle of some procedure with the doctors but the staff nurse assured Ellie that Sarah would be ready to come home by eleven- thirty the following morning.

"Your sister will be extremely weak for a few days, after all the tests, and will need to be taken home by taxi. I'm quite sure you realise this without my telling you, Sister Elkson."

"Thank you, you are very kind," Ellie's insides did a strange wobble at the staff nurse's no-nonsense picture of Sarah's condition.

Ellie took a bus to the shopping centre near Earls Court and bought the food and toiletries on her list. She returned the books to the library and as well as a couple of light novels, which wouldn't tax Sarah's powers of concentration, she selected 'The White Passion' by Ada Teetgen, the tale of the struggle of an isolated community in Canada to set up a local hospital. The story was set during the three years prior to the Great War and was recommended for the romance and adventure entwined within its serious theme. Ellie was sure it would captivate Sarah and maybe even herself; it might even make her feel closer to Alex. Thinking of something for Sarah to read with Kitty, Ellie chose the children's classic, 'Little Women,' and a colour-fully illustrated travel book about the Far East.

By this time it was two o'clock and Ellie, laden with bags, called in at the tea shop where she often met Eliza. She was glad to see her friend's gaudily dressed, buxom figure, sitting at their usual table. The cockade of purple pansies on Eliza's broad brimmed straw hat trembled as she beamed a welcome at Ellie. For half an hour the two of them talked and planned, over a plate of salmon and cucumber sandwiches and slices of Dundee cake. Two pots of tea, hot and strong, revived Ellie. Her feeling of helplessness lessened as Eliza made it plain that she would be there to support Ellie and Sarah, through the next few months.

"Sarah and I get on very well together, despite my being a decrepit old woman. I haven't enough energy to wear her out and there will be times when she just wants another presence in the room with her. I can sit and do my crosswords, or read quietly, probably snooze a bit. When she's well enough we can have short outings like the one to St. James's Park."

Ellie squeezed her friends hand, "Dear Eliza, you'll wear yourself out with all this caring, it takes an emotional toll even when you just sit and watch. I know. But I'll be grateful for you to do these things. I'm seeing the Fieldings at four this afternoon. I want to ask if Kitty will come in every day and if her mother would do the laundry for us. There may come a time when Sarah will need her bedding changed frequently, day and night. I'm sure the Fieldings would be glad of the extra money."

The two women batted ideas backwards and forwards, deal-ing with the practicalities so as not to allow themselves to dwell on the details of Sarah's illness, or her dying. It helped them to keep positive.

"If she doesn't feel strong enough to come to church on Wednesdays, I'll ask the Vicar to bring her Holy Communion at home. It means such a lot to her, bless her. You wouldn't mind that, would you Ellie; despite your different religious leanings?"

"Oh, Eliza, of course I wouldn't mind. I'm glad Sarah has such a strong faith. I'm still searching for mine. Theosophy is only a path I've been exploring. I wouldn't deny a person the faith they've found. I shall still practise water therapy with Sarah. Amelia and I are convinced it will be good for her and make her feel better, even if it doesn't cure her." Deep down Ellie had a burning desire to cure Sarah and the water cures were a crucial part of that hope. Eliza knew this and it worried her but she smiled and said, "We shall all do the best we can for Sarah. But don't you dare drown her, Sister Elkson!" and they parted on a cheery note.

Ellie hurried home and collected Sarah's bedding and clothes for washing and was knocking on the Fielding's door by four o'clock. All went well; Mrs Fielding was more than glad to take on Sarah's laundry.

"And put your own in with it, at no extra cost. I'm pleased to help out. I'm that sorry for the lass and all your trouble. Our Kitty will be pleased to work more time for you." She turned to her daughter, "you've nothing else on at the moment, have you love?"

"Only helping out with work here at home and looking after our Ruby and the boys, when you're out. I'll fit everything in, if Mam says it's alright."

"Kitty, you go to work for Sister Elkson. I'll sort the rest. Beattie Mason will help us out with the young 'uns, she likes to have them. In any case Toby and Billy will be at school most days. There'll only be baby Ruby at home and you know how she loves Beattie, and old Mrs Mason dotes on her."

Beattie Mason was a single woman about Ellie's age. She'd been born badly disfigured by a large facial birth mark and a club-foot, so she'd never been out to work, instead she lived with and cared for her elderly mother. The club-foot had given her such a pronounced lob-sided limp that she had to wear a heavy leg brace. She managed well enough in her own home and was a familiar sight hobbling to the corner shop, at a surprisingly active pace. There was always a lot of laughter around Beattie. Her lively personality and raucous humour often embarrassed her more discreet mother.

Baby Ruby was the light of the Mason's life and Toby and Billy were welcome in small doses. Their house was only two doors away from the Fielding's and the two boys had often been enticed to Beattie's by the lure of home- made biscuits, which she baked to sell in the local market. A friend, who had a market stall, took Beattie's produce and sold it for her. The crisp, spicy ginger biscuits; melt in the mouth shortbreads; lemon dreams and oat crunchies, were much sought after and provided a regular small income. There were always a few 'misshapes', as Beattie called them, made up from left over mixture after the biscuits were cut. These misshapes were stored, ready for any local children - especially Toby and Billy. The hot, spicy smell of baking met you at the door of the Mason's house and children quickly changed their idea of her as, "that limping lady with the funny face," to "Beattie, the magic biscuit maker."

During the months that followed Sarah's return from hospital, the Fielding boys became regular callers at number 19, Redcliffe Street. In the early weeks Ellie would often come home to find Toby or Billy, playing cards or draughts with Sarah.

"I only let them come one at a time, that way there's no chance of them quarrelling or making a nuisance," explained Kitty, the first time, seeing Ellie's disapproving look.

"Miss Sarah asked to meet them. I think she misses having school children around."

Ellie relented but she noticed how much more relaxed the children were with Sarah than they'd ever been with her. One day Ellie entered the house to hear Sarah's, now soft, soprano quietly singing the old folk song, 'we'll build the Keel Row, the keel row the keel row.' The notes ended rather breathlessly and immediately Billy's boyish soprano, roughened by his life on the streets, burst into, 'Pack up your troubles in your own kit bag.'

They both started guiltily when Ellie came into the room, "we were having a song competition- seeing how many we knew," laughed Sarah, her eyes bright and cheeks flushed with excitement. Ellie merely smiled and went to make tea, Billy left for home, humming to himself.

Another day, Billy told Sarah about Beattie Mason and her biscuits.

"I'll bring you some next time. You'll like them, everybody does."

"That would be lovely, Billy. I think I'd like to meet Beattie, she sounds an interesting person."

Beattie came. It was an overcast afternoon and Sarah woke from a nap feeling sad and flat in spirits. The doorbell rang and Sarah sighed, she'd hoped none of the children would call, she didn't want the effort of putting on a happy face. Kitty put her head round the door:

"Are you feeling up to a visitor, Miss Sarah? She says she won't come up if you're not and she won't stay long in any case but she just popped round."

"Who has just popped round, Kitty?"

"Beattie Mason and she's brought some of her biscuits- a special selection,"

"O, you must bring her in, Kitty. Can she manage the front steps?"

"She's come to the back; it's all on the flat from there."

Beattie came hesitantly into the room, her marked face shaded by a large brimmed hat and her leg iron hidden under an old fashioned, ankle length skirt. She walked awkwardly with a one-sided lurch and her obvious embarrassment went straight to Sarah's heart and she stood up carefully, her own legs wobbly from weakness and sitting too long. Beattie lifted her face and smiled into Sarah's troubled eyes, she took Sarah's thin, dry hand.

"I've been wanting to meet you, Miss Elkson, I'm Beattie Mason, the biscuit lady that Billy's been telling you about but I think we'd better both sit down fairly quickly, or Kitty may find two helpless women on the floor,"

They both sank down into chairs laughing self-consciously. Sarah soon found her own low spirits forgotten as she talked with her visitor. Beattie found she could relax and be herself, without having to put on the loud jollity, which disguised a sense of shame at her disfigurements. They discovered things about each other. By the time Kitty came in with a tray of tea and a selection of Beattie's best biscuits, they'd shared some of their own deepest fears and sorrows. Far from making each other miserable they both felt a sense of contentment.

"My word, I've never spoken like this to a stranger in my whole life," remarked Beattie.

"I don't think we are strangers, Beattie. We've both had to face up to what's happened to our own bodies and so we've met on some kind of common ground. You couldn't have come on a better day for me. I was weary of trying to put a brave face on things but with you I was able to drop my guard."

"Me too," said Beattie, realising with surprise that she'd removed her hat as they talked, clearly exposing her birth-mark.

The conversation lightened over a discussion of baking and the secret of creating biscuits with just the right texture. Beattie went home with two new recipes to try and the promise to come again.

Sarah lay back in her chair and dozed peacefully until Ellie came home. When she told her about Beattie's visit Ellie experienced that strange, jealous niggle again. She thrust it away, hating herself for it and forcing a smile, set about preparing for Sarah's evening routine.

Sir William had sent Sarah home with a collection of medicines

"There are sedatives to calm me down and tonics to pep me up; pain relievers and infection-fighters and something to hit my lump and keep it dormant as long as possible. I'm a human medicine chest," joked Sarah to Eliza.

Ellie took charge of administering the drugs but also used treatments of her own. She gave Sarah warm or cooling water baths and tried the method of rubbing her sister's body briskly through a wrapping of wet sheets, to improve her patients circulation and vitality.

She was confident these remedies would improve Sarah's circulation and increase her vitality. She administered gentle, warm water enemas, to help Sarah eliminate her bowels and made sure that she drank at least two pints of plain, boiled water each day.

She was relieved that the lumpy growth in Sarah's breast didn't appear to grow larger during the first month under her care but a tender, swollen place, under Sarah's left arm worried her.

With cooperation from friends and working colleagues, Ellie was managing much better than she'd imagined. Her hours at the community clinic were scheduled to fit in with Sarah's routine; the telephone was in place and a rota had been worked out with Kitty, Eliza and Beatty so that someone was always on hand for her sister. The medicines kept any pain at bay and although she was often tired, Sarah was still able to tutor Kitty most days and enjoy Eliza's visits and go with her to the Wednesday Communion services. Visits from Toby and Billy and even baby Ruby, kept Sarah on her toes.

The telephone was a great boon and Sarah and Ellie spoke weekly, to the family at Hartsbeck.

Stephen had a battle persuading their mother to allow the installation of a phone at 74, Aspen Lane. He convinced her that it was important for his work as well as enabling them to speak to Sarah and Ellie, from their own fireside. Jeannie succumbed and soon became used to this, "unnatural instrument." The sisters usually telephoned home on Sunday evening. Sarah was so excited to hear the familiar voices that she spoke naturally from the start but Ellie was awkward and stilted. It irritated her to hear Sarah talking so easily and happily to the family. It was as if she, the eldest Elkson daughter, had become an outsider.

"I can't blame them. I've been living my own life away from them for so long," she told herself.

Unaware of Ellie's feelings, Sarah joyfully opened letters and small parcels which arrived for her from George and Hannah and their children. She showed Ellie drawings and notes from five year old Alice and seven year old Richard. Ellie felt even more disgruntled at the small messages and childish drawings, "for our dear Auntie Sarah, we miss you."

Ellie would love to have received messages like this.

Edwin sent a collection of his latest photographs of wild birds, each one beautifully set against backgrounds of moor or woodland and even one under the sycamore tree in the back garden.

"See how beautifully he's caught the light. He must have waited ages to get this just right," drooled Sarah.

It was the photograph of a lapwing on the moors hovering near to where his nest must be. Edwin had captured the early morning light as it touched the clouds and glistened on the dewy mist, rising from the grass.

"Can't you just imagine yourself there, Ellie," Sarah's yearning was so infectious that Ellie's heart melted and she bent over the photographs with her sister. At first glance, one image seemed to be simply of a patch of bracken, growing by the edge of a grassy path, shaded by hedges. On a closer look, Ellie saw a tiny butterfly, resting on one of the bracken fronds. The pictures were in black and white but with his new camera, Edwin had homed in on the tiny creature and they could just make out the markings on its wings.

"Sarah, look it's a Gatekeeper. I always think of it as our butterfly. There was one in our garden the day you were born."

"Yes, and when you first took me walking in the woods when I was small and then, when I stayed with you in Oxford, we saw them again. I loved them more than all the showy, coloured ones. They seemed like guardians, fluttering alongside and in front of us, just as if they were showing us the way."

"Clever Edwin, to take it for us," Ellie's sore heart was soothed.

"Look what he says about it," Sarah spread out their brother's letter.

"I hope you recognise the Gatekeeper butterfly, Annie says it will have a special message for you and Ellie and will help bring you special comfort in the days ahead. Trust my dear wife to have such fanciful thoughts but I hope it brings cheer to you both."

The sisters smiled warmly at each other and Ellie clutched at Edwin's mention of her by name.

"We won't forget the 'Gatekeeper' Ellie. We must keep it as a kind of symbol between us. When things get tough, whisper 'Gatekeeper' to me and I'll do the same for you."

CHAPTER 59

Visitors from Hartsbeck

Plans were made for Stephen to bring their mother up to London by train. They were to travel in three weeks' time and mother would stay for five nights. Stephen had some business to attend to at the Royal Geological Society in the city but he would call in to see Sarah and take mother home to Hartsbeck, at the end of her stay.

Jeannie Elkson had never been to London before and Eliza Fazakerley determined to arrange a simple outing, to give her a flavour of the city. Knowing that Jeannie herself was frail and Sarah would not be able to manage anything too demanding, Eliza decided on a short drive past some of the historical sites, such as Westminster Abbey and the Houses of Parliament and ending with a visit to the famous Heal's furniture store in Tottenham Court Road. 'Heal's' was one of Eliza's favourite places, browsing through floors of exquisitely designed ceramics, striking fabrics and exclusively crafted furniture, soothed Eliza's soul. The store's aim was that every item on show was designed for both beauty and practicality and she usually bought some small object that lifted the everyday to a higher plane. Eliza was sure that Mrs Elkson would enjoy a visit to this long established, exclusive London store, which was compact enough not to overwhelm the two invalids. There were lifts to each level and plenty of places to rest and admire the merchandise. If they wanted more, there was the Mansard Gallery on the fourth floor, which held exhibitions of modern art which could appeal or repel. The gallery had earned a reputation for introducing the latest styles in art; Picasso, Matisse, Modigliani and other modern French artists had all exhibited there, since the gallery opened twelve years ago. Eliza just hoped there would be nothing too outrageous on show for her friends. Above all, there was a wonderfully appointed tea- room, right next door to Heals, with delicious cakes and sandwiches which drew Eliza like a magnet. Even if Sarah was not well enough to come, Eliza felt sure such an outing would please Mrs Elkson.

Stephen and Jeannie Elkson arrived in the gentle warmth of an English August. Ellie was shocked to see the constant trembling of her mother's hands but Jeannie hadn't lost any of her steely, uprightness of character and refused to give in to any weakness. She spent precious hours alone with Sarah and came to terms with the probability of her daughter dying, there in London, in the not too distant future. Jeannie had already lost a son and a husband; bereavement no longer frightened her but she was deeply anxious for both her daughters. She noticed Ellie's tight-lipped silences and the tired lines around her eyes. She noticed how people did their best to entertain Sarah but as soon as Ellie came home they felt free to disappear and attend to their own affairs. Dear Ellie was losing out on the cheerful companionship of her friends and neighbours, although they were making it easier for her, by being with Sarah during her working hours. By six thirty every evening Sarah was wilting and Ellie would settle her sister down for the night.

"I'm back to being a little girl again, mother. Do you remember how strict you were about me being upstairs and in bed by half past six? Well I go with no arguments now but I don't go out like a light, as I did at six years old!"

"As long as you're resting your body and thinking good thoughts, my dear," Jeannie enfolded Sarah in a gentle embrace, careful not to press against her left side. Jeannie had been conscious of Sarah's involuntary wince, when she had hugged her a little too enthusiastically on her arrival.

Ellie helped Sarah to get ready for bed with a soothing bath followed by wrapping her in a warm towel with no rubbing or patting dry. To be true to the water therapy, Sarah should have slept in this towel but she'd begged to be allowed to put on her dry nightdress so Ellie let her lie in the towel for just quarter of an hour, before allowing her to put on her nightie.

"I still find it all very soothing, Ellie. You are good to me."

Ellie sighed as she gave Sarah her night time medication. The cancer was not lessening and she knew that before too long, Sarah would feel its presence more aggressively.

Once Sarah was settled Ellie would come and sit with her mother and Jeannie gave her eldest daughter all her attention and companionship. They talked of old times, before Sarah's birth, of the time in the grocery shop in Preston, before the move to Hartsbeck and laughed over shared memories.

"Dear Ellie, you were our first born. How your Dad and I marvelled at you when you lay in our arms. We wondered what kind of person you'd grow into, we never imagined what wonderful things you would do. But, it hasn't been easy for you, has it lass?"

Ellie wanted to weep at her mother's unexpected tenderness but she replied tersely,

"Life is never easy, for anyone," and broke the spell of intimacy by going to make a bedtime drink for them both.

"I must be away to bed mother, and so must you. I'm off to work at six o'clock and you'll have a full day as well." She saw her mother's crestfallen look and spoke more gently, "You need to rest, mother," she put a tentative hand on Jeannie's shoulder "I know how you struggle. You're very brave."

"We have to accept what's given to us, rough or smooth," Jeannie was back to her stern self. They looked at each other and laughed, "We're too much alike, you and I."

Jeannie was delighted with the proposed trip to Heal's.

"I've read so much about it in advertisements. My friends at home will be green with envy. We sometimes imagine the kind of things we would buy from Heal's, if we had the money!"

"Some things are very affordable, that's the beauty of Heal's. I'm sure we'll be able to find something for you to take home." Eliza reassured her.

Jeannie was sure that Eliza's idea of affordable was far above her own.

The day of the outing dawned fine and warm, with a friendly breeze and a few fluffy white clouds high up in the blue. Sarah was well enough join the group and preening herself that she'd persuaded Beattie Mason to come. Kitty Fielding was to join them as well.

"As part of her education in art and design," stipulated Sarah.

"I wish you could have time off, to come with us, Ellie," Jeannie said as she watched her elder daughter pin on her uniform hat and wheel out her bicycle ready for work.

"I'm alright, Mother. I've patients who need me and I'll be happy knowing you are enjoying yourselves. Make sure you don't over-do it and keep an eye on Sarah. I'll try and join you in the café later."

Ellie felt only a tiny bit resentful, as she bicycled away. Her mother made her realise again the importance of her nursing but there was another reason why she was glad not to go with them. The Mansard Gallery was one of the places she and Alex Dobson had visited together and she wasn't sure how she would react.

At half past nine Kitty served Sarah and Jeannie a good breakfast of porridge, followed by lightly- scrambled eggs and toast which they ate with relish, followed by several cups of tea. The promised meal of sandwiches and cake at the café wouldn't be until well after two o'clock. Beattie arrived and at eleven, Eliza came in a taxi-cab. They all tucked themselves comfortably inside, Kitty sitting on the fold up seat facing the others. The young girl leant forward eagerly, staring at the sights as they drove slowly over Westminster Bridge and past the Houses of Parliament and Westminster Abbey. Sarah recited Wordsworth's poem, 'On Westminster Bridge' and promised to teach it to an enthralled Kitty, sometime soon. After an hour's site-seeing drive the cab drew up in Tottenham Court Road at the 'Sign of the Four-poster', which was Heal's special emblem. The tall building with its pillars and high, arched windows and the 'By Royal Appointment' crest above the door gave Jeannie Elkson a shiver of anticipation. Kitty's eyes were wide with excitement. She helped

Sarah from the cab, linking her arm to give support, as they made their way into the softly lighted interior. Beattie was struggling to control her limp and kept her head down, to ensure that her hat brim hid her disfigured face.

Eliza had hurried ahead of them into the store and by the time they entered a smiling assistant was waiting to greet them. She invited the party to sit down while a short introduction to the store would be given. Chairs had been arranged strategically so that when seated, they had a good view of the main displays of furniture on the ground floor. A tall, thin gentleman in a smart suit came forward and introduced himself with a bow.

"Ladies, welcome to Heal and Sons. My name is Samuel Henson and I have worked here since I was a young errand boy. I won't tell you how many years ago that was,"

The ladies laughed demurely, hardly noticing the twisted features of their welcomer's face so warm and confident was his manner.

"We hope you will have a wonderful time here and enjoy the goods we have on display. This card will help you find your way around."

He handed them each a prettily coloured card, about double the size of a post card. When he came to Beattie he kept hold of the card as he placed it in her outstretched hand so she was compelled to lift her head and look into the strangest of faces. It was a kind, smiling face but twisted and scarred, so that his mouth and nose were pulled to one side and one eye lifted higher than the other. She gasped and grinned foolishly at him and he gave her a comical wink before continuing his spiel.

"It's the copy of a poster which was specially designed for us last year, by the agency of the artist Robert Percy Gossop."

The card showed all six floors of the shop, open to view like a dolls house with the front fully open and each room exposed to the observer. Beattie Mason forgot herself entirely, in looking at the exquisitely drawn, tiny pictures and working out what to find on each floor. She was relieved to see the picture of a lift looking like a large Chinese lantern in wrought iron, suspended between floors.

The eloquent gentleman was telling them a little of the history of Heal's and she lifted her head to hear him better.

"Ambrose Heal, who joined the family firm as a furniture designer in 1893, did much to promote the ethos of the firm. He emphasised the golden dictum of William Morris, 'Have nothing in your home that you do not know to be useful or believe to be beautiful.' He insisted that 'nothing need be ugly'." he gave the group a quizzical look, "Obviously he hadn't met me at the time."

Eliza laughed comfortably; she was well acquainted with Mr Samuel Henson and found his manners and personality far from ugly.

"Ambrose Heal also saw the importance of the imaginative display of merchandise. We have, as you know, an art gallery on the fourth floor, but I hope you will see the whole of our store as a display of art and realise the importance we place on beauty of form in everyday objects. Many of our customers also patronise the excellent tea room, which is right next door to the store. It doesn't belong to us but has almost become part of our facilities! All our assistants will help you in any way they can. The lift attendant will take you to the different floors and there are plenty of rest areas. Do enjoy your visit." Mr Henson gave a perfect bow and moved away to allow them to organise themselves.

So began a delightful two hours. Eliza was well known and much respected in the shop and the assistants fell over backwards to please her. From the variety of beds and general furnishings on the ground floor, they went to the basement to wander among the garden furniture and even more bedsteads. Beattie crowed with delight and longing when she discovered the array of kitchen equipment displayed in a corner of the basement. Sarah secretly bought her a set of unusually shaped biscuit cutters and a large baking tray, which was to be kept behind the counter until they were ready to leave. Jeannie found blankets and sheets of such excellent quality, that she didn't demur at the price and bought two pairs of sheets and pillowcases for Ellie, knowing how welcome they would be if Sarah became really ill. They marvelled over the display of electric light fittings and reminisced about the old gas lights.

They travelled in the lift to the first floor, where they found living room and bedroom furniture, unusually patterned fabrics, easy chairs (which they were allowed to rest in) and cushions of all shapes and sizes, colours and materials.

The second floor was fun, young Kitty enjoyed this one most of all, with its toys and gifts and nursery equipment. She longed for a toy to take home for her sister Ruby and the boys. Jeannie and Sarah sat among displays of pottery and glassware, enjoying the aesthetic quality of the shapes and patterns.

Then, on to the third floor, with its antique furniture, where Eliza fell in love with a grandfather clock and an Indian style rug.

Part of the fourth floor was laid out as a fully furnished flat, with a parlour; dining room; bedroom and dressing room; kitchen and nursery. Beside the flat was a garden bench and table flanked by two live bay trees in pots. In the bedroom area was a strikingly modern dressing table of such pure lines and unusual materials that it held their gaze. On examination the drawers were of a silvery metallic material, which reflected light. From between the drawers rose a rectangular, full length, unframed mirror. The effect was like liquid light. The name of the designer, written next to it, was Robert Block.

"How clean and pure the lines are," said Sarah "it's cold but beautiful, almost ethereal but strong as well." She suddenly turned away; the reflected light making her dizzy.

A middle-aged female assistant came in at that moment. She looked at Sarah and the rest of the gallant party and told them they must sit down and rest. She showed them to the garden bench and brought extra chairs then, hurried away and returned with a tray of coffee and biscuits, which she placed on the garden table.

"For medicinal purposes," she whispered tapping her nose, "we have facilities to make coffee for ourselves and we are told to offer refreshment to any visitors who need resuscitating. Without meaning any offence, I think you fit the bill," she gave Eliza a huge grin.

"Miss Broughton, you are an angel," said Eliza.

"If anyone comes, I shall say you are part of the display – live art. They'll like that. You may use the Ladies room if you wish which is just through the door on your right. Call me if you need anything."

Jeannie looked anxiously at Sarah who had turned a sickly green colour and sagged in her chair. Eliza whisked a miniature bottle of brandy from her capacious handbag and poured a good dose into Sarah's coffee, adding a spoonful of sugar. Kitty supported Sarah and persuaded her to sip it slowly. Sarah did so, taking it a small amount at a time and gradually her colour improved and she sat back in her chair with a great sigh,

"I'll just rest awhile before we go on," she said and closed her eyes. The others looked at each other in consternation. Jeannie Elkson spoke up;

"I think we should all have our coffee and biscuits and see how Sarah is afterwards."

They drank and ate silently, the joy suddenly gone from the day. Revived by the hot coffee, they sat and waited while Sarah seemed to sleep.

"If any of you want to look round the Mansard Gallery, I'll sit here with Sarah. I think she's just very tired. Hopefully, she'll wake up before the store closes, or we'll have to make use of some of those amazing beds!" Jeannie said this to cheer young Kitty who looked near to tears.

Beattie assessed the situation and offered to go with Kitty into the gallery to give Sarah's mother the chance to find out how her daughter really was.

"I'll stay here till we know how Sarah is and then go and find someone to help; I know most of the staff," said Eliza. "I think we should forget about the café. Beattie and Kitty, I'll let you know when we decide to leave, you must both go and see the gallery. Sarah particularly wanted you to see the exhibition, Kitty. She'll want to know all about it."

Reluctantly Kitty went with Beattie. Jeannie and Eliza were worried about Sarah's state, "I'm not sure whether she's unconscious, or just asleep," said Jeannie.

They tried to wake her, as gently as they could. After rubbing and slapping her daughter's hands and speaking sharply to her, Jeannie managed to make Sarah open her eyes. She was drowsy but much better and agreed that she should go straight home. Eliza disappeared to ask for help to take Sarah down in the lift. Miss Broughton went to find Beattie and Kitty. They came hurrying back just as Mr Samuel Henson and a young male assistant arrived, with a cunningly designed wheel-chair.

"I've asked the door-man to have a taxi ready for you," Mr Henson told Eliza.

"I feel like a living advertisement for your designer invalid carriages," Sarah spoke with a breathless attempt at humour, as they lifted her into the chair. There was a shaky laugh from Beattie and a general sigh of relief that Sarah was recovering.

The lift was overfull, so Kitty and Eliza, as the more able ones, walked down the spectacular spiral staircase enjoying another view of each floor as they went. When they came to the ground floor they found that Ellie and Stephen had arrived, expecting to join them for sandwiches and cake in the Café. Eliza explained that Sarah had been taken ill and the party were preparing to go straight home. Fashionably dressed people, who were drifting round the store, turned to look at them momentarily but were too well-bred to stare. The door-man hurried forward announcing that two taxi-cabs were waiting outside. Eliza had taken the initiative to order a separate one for her-self and Beatty. Stephen and Ellie took their places in the taxi with Jeannie, Sarah and Kitty.

Once home, Ellie helped her weary sister to bed. Kitty served everyone with bread and bowls of chicken broth, which she'd prepared the day before. Ellie helped Sarah to eat her broth and after dosing her with a sedative, left her to sleep.

CHAPTER 60

The Family rallies round

Jeannie stayed an extra two nights at Redcliffe Street, just to make sure that Sarah had recovered from her collapse in Heal's. After a night's rest, Sarah had appeared much the same as when her mother had first arrived. It was a relief to Jeannie, who was herself becoming very tired and also had hospital appointments to attend in Lancashire. Stephen had willingly stayed on, happy to see more of his sisters and to be near to his beloved Royal Geological Society Headquarters but he recognised it was time to escort his mother home.

When Jeannie reached Hartsbeck she reacted to the strain of the previous week and was too weak to leave her bed for several days and even then, could do very little. Her appointments with the specialist confirmed a progression of the Parkinson's disease but not a great acceleration. She was advised not to travel long distances and to limit her activities to those she found she could manage with ease,

"It will be trial and error, Mrs Elkson. No climbing ladders and no walking without your stick. You'll find your balance will be unpredictable and your legs shaky at times. You'll tire easily, as your body and your mind will be working extra hard, to cope with your condition."

The medication, prescribed to calm Jeannie's symptoms, also added to a general lethargy. The family realised their mother would not travel to see Sarah again. George and Edwin made two weekend visits to London, during the next few weeks. They stayed with their sisters in Redcliffe Street and did what they could to help them.

They travelled back to Hartsbeck by the Sunday afternoon train with feelings of helplessness and inadequacy. George had expressed his unhappiness to Ellie, about some of the water therapies she was using.

"Ellie, I don't think your water treatments are doing Sarah much good. They're tiring her out. I think we need to ask for a second opinion. Sir William what's his name, should be doing more than just giving her the once over every few weeks."

Edwin had unexpectedly supported Ellie, "I think you're wrong about Ellie's water treatments," he told them, "I saw them being used out in France during the war and they worked wonders. Lads unconscious from cold and shock, were brought round with hot and cold water rubs and others, who were very sick or in great pain, found the treatments intensely soothing. George, you must know that Sarah's illness is probably terminal."

"No, I don't know and from your use of the word 'probably,' neither do you. I think a second opinion is needed."

"Alright George, I'll arrange it as soon as possible," Ellie had promised wearily. She'd already toned down the water therapy and was using only soothing and non- stimulating applications, which Sarah insisted helped her considerably.

Stephen occasionally came to see them midweek, suddenly arriving with no warning, doubling up with a visit to the London scientific institutions, with which he was connected. He would spend an hour or two with Sarah and sleep the night on the sofa. Ellie was grateful for his visits; she'd always had a better rapport with him than with her other brothers and they were able to talk after Sarah was in bed. They discussed the idea of a second opinion, Ellie pouring out thoughts which had been flooding through her mind since George's visit.

"I'm afraid it will only cause Sarah more distress. I don't believe there can be a cure for her cancer. I'd be afraid of eager young doctors and researchers, trying all sorts of painful treatments on her, knowing they can't change the outcome but using her to learn new methods for future cases."

Stephen was more circumspect; "I think we should ask Sarah, what she wants. She may feel happy to be used as a guinea pig if she thinks it will help other cancer cases. You know what she's like. Surely the doctors would take care not to induce undue suffering, Sir William would still be involved wouldn't he?"

"It depends whether Sir William and the 'second opinion' are willing to accept each other and work as a team."

Ellie knew all too well how jealous specialists could be of their own methods.

The pain in Sarah's breast and surrounding areas was increasing. Some nights she woke in such agony that she tore her bed sheet in an effort to control herself, so she wouldn't wake Ellie. Mrs Fielding noticed the tears when she did the laundry; she mended the sheets but questioned Kitty about it. Kitty mentioned the mended sheets to Sarah, when she brought the clean bedding back.

"Oh, I get restless and tied up in the sheets, trying to get comfortable. Please, do apologise to your mother on my behalf for the extra work, Kitty. No need to say anything to Sister Ellie," was all Sarah would say.

During the day it was easier for Sarah to ask for extra pain-killers and as they worked quite quickly, nobody noticed how bad her discomfort was, especially if Ellie was away at the clinic.

In the middle of the night, a week after her talk with Stephen, Ellie was woken by the sound of a crash and a cry from her sister's room. Ellie found Sarah curled on the floor, weeping. The bedside table had been knocked over, the water glass broken and Sarah's Bible and prayer book sprinkled with shards of glass. Sarah's nightdress was wet from spilled water but she lay with her arms folded tightly around her chest and her knees drawn up;

"I'm sorry Ellie; I was trying to find a painkiller."

"Is it so bad, dear? You should have called me," Ellie found Sarah's dressing gown and knelt down to wrap it round her sister.

"I didn't want to disturb you," Sarah gasped.

Ellie quickly straightened Sarah's bed, and then helped her sister up.

"I need the lavatory Ellie, can you take me?"

"No. You must use the chamber pot; I'll put it on this chair and hold you."

Still tense with pain Sarah allowed Ellie to support her and was soon more comfortable and back in bed wearing a clean, dry nightdress. Ellie brought an increased dose of analgesic with fresh water and Sarah swallowed it gratefully. The light and Ellie's presence and the small activities had helped distract her from the worst of the pain. Ellie swept up the broken glass and put the table back in place.

"I'm going to make a warm, milky drink and sit with you till you feel better," Ellie padded away to the kitchen and when she came back with two beakers of warm milk and honey, she found tears running down Sarah's face. Smoothing her sister's forehead, Ellie spoke gently,

"The painkillers will take about half an hour to work fully, just relax and breathe deeply, it will help."

As she'd changed her sister's nightie, Ellie had noticed that the swelling in Sarah's breast had increased and it felt hot and hard, with a reddish- purple rash showing. She was tempted to put a warm water poultice against it but decided it was too tender and best left untouched. Soon Sarah became drowsy and slept. Ellie brought a blanket from her own room and slept fitfully in an arm chair beside the bed. By the time Sarah woke, restless and feverish at six o'clock Ellie was already washed and dressed. Sarah clawed at her breast through her night clothes.

"Look Ellie, it's wet and sticky."

Sarah pointed to the top of her nightdress to show a damp patch where something had seeped through. Opening the nightie Ellie found the skin around the lumps on Sarah's breast hot and livid and a watery discharge was oozing from her nipple. The smell was unmistakable to Ellie and her heart turned a somersault. She realised too, that Sarah had soiled the sheets during her sleep.

"We'll ask Dr Collins to come and take a look at you this morning. You probably need some different medication."

She spoke casually as she helped a rather dizzy and unsteady Sarah to use the chamber pot, wash and change into another clean nightdress.

"Now, sit in the arm chair, while I put fresh linen on the bed," Ellie stripped off the dirty sheets and remade the bed with clean ones laid ready. A pleasing scent of lemon mixed with lavender wafted through the room as she tucked the fresh, well- ironed sheets into place,

"What a god-send Mrs Fielding is," whispered Sarah with an attempt at a smile.

"You're right, we're lucky to have her. There, you can get straight back in now and I'll bring a cup of tea."

Sarah leant wearily against her sister, as she was helped back into bed. Then Ellie ran downstairs and while waiting for the kettle to boil, telephoned Dr Collins. He promised to come within the hour. Sarah was restless, refusing everything but drinks and complained of headache and back-ache.

Ellie telephoned Sister Allinson to explain that she would have to stay at home today. Kitty arrived, ready for work and quickly bundled the piles of soiled bedding and nightwear into a bag and hurried away with them to her mother. She was back within ten minutes.

"Mam's doing them first thing, so as to have them drying quickly. She's built up a good fire, even though it's only early September. Thank goodness your mother bought those lovely new sheets from Heals."

"It was very far-sighted of her," agreed Ellie and set Kitty to preparing her a simple breakfast while she waited for the doctor.

Dr Collins soon came. He sat quietly beside Sarah taking her pulse and temperature and speaking with her alone before asking Ellie in, to show him Sarah's breast.

The doctor drew in his breath, almost imperceptibly. He busied himself by scribbling a prescription, before speaking.

"Well young lady, Sir William led me to expect this, so it's nothing out of the ordinary for your condition. Your body is fighting away at this nasty disease and that's why you have a fever. I'm giving you medicine to help you cope with that. Also, I've prescribed a soothing lotion for your to sister apply to your breast and I'll leave you something to help you sleep."

Downstairs he took Ellie into the living room and closed the door.

"My dear, now is the time for you to ask to be released from your outside nursing duties and devote your skills to nursing your sister. Her condition is deteriorating, as you can tell. The malignancy is winning but good careful nursing will help ease her through."

Ellie fought back tears. She knew better than to ask how long her sister would live in this condition. Reluctantly she told Dr Collins of George's and Stephen's wishes.

"Doctor, my brothers insist that we have a second, specialist opinion. One of my brothers in particular, is demanding this in no uncertain terms. He's convinced that there may be some other modern treatment, not yet known to Sir William. He refuses to accept that Sarah' cancer is irreversibly terminal."

"From your tone, I take it you don't agree with your brother?"

"Not entirely. I'm afraid that obtaining a second opinion, with all that it involves, will cause my sister more suffering and distress."

"I'm inclined to agree with you, Sister." As always Dr Collins acknowledged Ellie's profession.

Ellie continued. "Nevertheless, I have promised my brothers that I would put their suggestion in motion."

Dr Collins walked to the window and tapped his fingers on the sill, deep in thought. At last he turned back to Ellie. "We need to go about this very carefully; another opinion may help Sarah to an easier death, who knows? We can try it, while keeping a close watch on her. As Sarah's GP, I have special privileges and could put a stop to anything you don't want. Suffering cannot be avoided whatever we do but we can avoid adding to it."

"How would you go about it, doctor?"

"For the moment Sarah can be kept comfortable here with you. Don't forget we can do nothing without Sarah's consent. She's in her right mind and can decide for herself. If she says 'No,' to a second opinion, then it's decided for us. If she agrees, I will explain the situation to Sir William and invite another, younger specialist, to come to the house and examine Sarah. You and I must be present."

After a day's rest on the new medication and a better night's sleep, Ellie and Dr Collins felt they could broach the subject with their patient.

Sarah agreed to a second opinion, "I don't mind if they do experiment on me, if it's going to help someone else later," she announced bravely. "At least some good will have come out of my horrid illness."

Ellie marvelled at her sister's intelligent grasp of the situation. Sarah sighed impatiently;

"I may not be a nurse, but I am a teacher, Ellie, I know what goes on in the world!" she snapped.

CHAPTER 61

A Second Opinion

On the tenth of September, Dr Collins received a formal letter from George Elkson to say that, together with his brother Stephen, he had researched the medical lists. As a result, they would be grateful if Dr Collins would invite Mr Mark Saunders, a reputable and forward-looking cancer specialist and surgeon, to give his opinion on their sister Sarah's case.

The situation was again put before Sarah and again she acquiesced. Two days later, the earnest, forward-looking Mr Saunders, a man in his late thirties, came to examine Sarah. As a result, he persuaded her to consider surgery, to remove the offending breast and to allow him to explore the adjoining glands and tissues under anaesthetic.

"It would have been preferable to have had such an operation, earlier in your illness, Miss Elkson. Nevertheless, it may ease your condition, even at this point and it will give my team an opportunity to observe the disease at this advanced stage. We could gain valuable knowledge for our research. You will receive the very best of treatment under my care, Miss Elkson, and our cancer nurses are second to none."

Ellie's blood boiled. She saw the eagerness in the surgeon's eyes. To her he was a predator with Sarah as choice prey. Immaculately dark suited, his head held high by his stiff white collar, the young specialist turned and flashed his perfect teeth in a wide smile at Ellie, his eyes, cold as steel, cut through her.

"Sister Elkson, please do reassure your sister that she has nothing to fear. We shall do our very best for her."

Ellie drew herself up to matron-like stature and returned his cold look with an even icier stare.

"Will you allow Sir William Oliver to be part of your team?" asked Dr Collins.

"Sir William is a remarkable man, of his generation. However, it would be unreasonable to expect him to work with ideas which are new to the field," was Mr Saunders' smooth reply.

"I see," said Dr Collins.

"I would like to arrange for you to come onto the surgical ward at the Cancer Hospital, next week, Miss Elkson; we shall need to run some tests before operating." He took out a slim diary. "Shall we say the twentieth of September?"

Having made up her mind, Sarah simply went along with all that the young surgeon said. She was too weary by now to think of a clear argument against him but was hurt by his dismissal of Sir William.

"Sir William has helped me considerably. I think he has still much to offer in his field. I'm sorry he won't be working with you," Sarah's voice had a severe tone.

"Which ward will it be, Mr Saunders?" asked Ellie

"The women's surgical, Parrish Ward. Sister Parrish is one of the old school but an excellent nurse never-the-less."

"I have nursed with Sister Parrish, we are old friends," Ellie felt a glimmer of comfort in this helpless on-rush of events.

"Well, there we are. Not all bad then, eh, Sister Elkson?"

The specialist's patronising tone made Ellie want to hit out at him but she was aware of Dr Collins' restraining hand on her arm.

"I shall expect you to contact me with the details of Miss Elkson's admittance to the cancer hospital. I will arrange for her transferral from here, Mr Saunders." Dr Collin's voice was equally patronising.

"Of course Doctor. My secretary will confirm the date in writing. Good day, ladies. We shall meet again soon." Mr Saunders saw himself out.

"Young whippersnapper!" expostulated Dr Collins. "I hope your brother will be satisfied with this 'second opinion'. Make sure your sister has the new prescription I wrote out as soon as possible and use a gentle poultice if it eases her. I can trust you to keep her as clean and comfortable as possible Sister Elkson. I'm going to speak to Sir William," and slamming on his top hat, he stormed from the house.

Sarah looked at Ellie, panic showing behind her eyes.

"Ellie, I'm frightened. What's going to happen? That man; I'm not sure I trusted him."

Ellie gave a short laugh, "Oh he'll be perfectly competent. He's one of the new, bright, young doctors, who can't always see their patient for the bright goal of success and the tantalising glitter of new science! He needs to learn from experience. Sir William was probably much like that at the same age."

She went to her sister and took her hand, "Sarah, you know how much l love you. I won't let him harm you. He can't do anything to you, unless you agree. Now, I'm sending Kitty to the chemist with the new prescription. In the meantime let's concentrate on making you more comfortable.

Dr. Collins hurried back to his surgery and telephoned Sir William. Fortunately the great man was in his office and available.

"I'm afraid there is little I can do, Dr Collins. Miss Elkson and her family are perfectly entitled to have a second opinion. If it is different from mine, they must then choose which they prefer to go along with; I can only offer the very best of nursing and palliative care. In my opinion, nothing can be done to cure Miss Elkson, or to bring her cancer into remission. She is dying and my experience tells me that she probably has one, or possibly, two months to live. I can help make those months more peaceful and comfortable, a time for Miss Elkson to enjoy her family and friends and make her peace with God. Innovative treatment may appear to offer more hope but in her case, could bring the end more quickly and in a more distressing manner. I'm certain that better treatments and cures are on their way for the future but I don't think operating or experimenting on Sarah Elkson will further research, or help her at this stage."

Phone calls flew backwards and forwards between Redcliffe Street and Hartsbeck. George travelled up to London for a day and met with both Sir William and the 'second opinion.'

"Well, Sarah, in my opinion, Mark Saunders should be given his chance. He offers us some hope and however slim that hope is, I think we should grasp it. Sarah, we don't want to lose you. If Mr Saunders thinks something can be done, please let him try. God knows I don't want you to suffer more but—I" –George's normally cool and calculating eyes, filled with tears. For a moment, Ellie saw the young boy of long ago, who had clutched her hand on the way to school. Sarah submitted to her brother's wishes.

When George had returned to Hartsbeck, Ellie was filled with trepidation, bad memories of the cancer patients she had nursed in the early 1900's raced through her mind.

Confirmation came in writing. The following week on the twentieth of September, Sarah was to be transferred to 'Parrish Ward,' under the care of the young specialist. In the days leading up to this, Ellie felt constantly nauseous, she ate little and slept less. Sarah noticed her sister's restlessness, how she fidgeted and walked from room to room, settling to nothing.

"I would like to take communion before going," Sarah had confided to Eliza.

"Of course you shall, my dear. I'll go and ask the Vicar straight away, he'll be only too glad to come to you."

"I would like you to be here, to take it with me, Eliza. I believe communion should be shared with others, when possible. I often think of Jesus feeding the five thousand, so many people fed by Him, that to me was an early Communion service."

"Why, yes. I hadn't thought of it that way but you're right; the gospel goes on straight away to say Jesus is the bread of life and whoever eats of Him will never be hungry and of course that means spiritual food."

"And think of all the millions of people He has fed and is still feeding, down the centuries. I've had plenty of time to sit and ponder these things in the last few weeks. Whenever He feeds me, I feel He gives me the spiritual strength to face anything. Oh, I don't think the bread and wine are magical or anything like that, but when I think of all that it means, I do feel stronger, Eliza and not so fearful."

"Well, our Lord himself was strengthened in the hours before his death," Eliza lent forward and kissed her young companion gently on the forehead.

"Thank you for not pretending death isn't coming, Eliza," Sarah's eyes became troubled, "but, I'm afraid for Ellie, she seems very disturbed."

"I think the situation has just hit her. She hoped she could heal you with her water therapies and her theosophist meditations. She'll calm down, as soon as she accepts it's out of her hands, then her common sense and nursing instincts will take over, I'm sure of it," Eliza spoke reassuringly but inwardly she too was concerned at Ellie's reaction.

That night Ellie tossed feverishly in her bed. Tomorrow would be the fifteenth of September, there were five days left before Sarah was to go into hospital. Ellie knew she had let her sister down, she hadn't been rigorous enough with the water therapy. If she'd really tried she could have rid Sarah's body of all the toxins causing the cancer and boosted up her immune system to fight off the disease. Accusing voices in Ellie's head told her the things she should have done, the douches and the rubbing sheets, the water fasts, hot and cold baths, wet wraps. More voices insistently told her it may not be too late; she should try harder in these next few days. It was all the time she had left, to help her sister.

Rising like a sleep walker, Ellie filled a bath tub with cold water and soaked a sheet in it. When Sarah woke to be attended to during the night, Ellie wrapped her in the wet, rung out sheet rubbing her sister's frail body vigorously until Sarah cried out for her to stop. Then Ellie wrapped a dry sheet over the wet one and tucked a blanket on top so that the wet sheet next to her sister's body would become warm and steamy as she slept and draw out the poisons from her body. She dare not stop the medication prescribed by Dr. Collins because she knew Sarah's pain would become intolerable but she forced Sarah to drink more water with them. The sleeping medicine and the gradually comforting feel of damp warmth enfolding her, soon sent Sarah into a deep sleep.

When her sister woke in the morning, Ellie removed the damp sheet and plunged Sarah into a cold bath which made the young woman gasp and cry out, Ellie wild-eyed and determined, splashed the chilly water over Sarah. While Sarah shivered in the cold bath Ellie soaked a towel in hot water. Helping Sarah out of the bath she covered her with the hot, wet towel and began the firm, rhythmic rubbing again. Sarah was white with exhaustion and shock but could do nothing against the demented strength of her sister. As Ellie rubbed, Sarah was glad to feel warmth welling through her. Her breast reacted to the heat with a searing pain and she clutched it, feeling an ooze of putrid liquid. All this time Ellie had worked silently but at the sight of the discharge she spoke jubilantly:

"That's just what we want my girl, I'll soon have you right with a few days of this treatment."

"Please, Ellie, I've had enough. Let me lie down in a dry nightie and have some rest."

Ellie looked at her trembling sister and seemed to come to her-self. Helping Sarah to the chair she patted her dry with another towel and dressed her in a clean nightie. Dry sheets were put on the bed and Sarah lay down thankfully but still gritting her teeth from pain. In silence, Ellie brought Sarah's pain-killing medicine and gave it to her with a glass of boiled, warm water.

"Please, may I have some milk or something to eat with it? It makes me feel sick otherwise," pleaded Sarah.

"You'll be alright, if you drink plenty of water," Ellie spoke firmly and refilled the glass helping Sarah to drink.

All that day Ellie gave Sarah more douches and rubs and allowed her to eat nothing and to drink only water. Ellie herself took noth-ing but water.

There had been no visitors and Ellie told Kitty that Sarah didn't want to eat. By evening Sarah was weak and felt sick and light- headed. Her fragile skin was becoming sore and flaky. Still Ellie didn't give in.

441

A mad determination to cure her sister had seized her and all night she worked on Sarah with the water therapies, allowing her little rest between.

The following day Eliza arrived, to say that the Vicar would call at three o'clock that afternoon, with Holy Communion, if that was convenient. Ellie stared at her friend as though she were a stranger.

"I'm afraid that's impossible. My patient is not allowed anything but plain water and visitors would be far too exhausting for her."

"May I see Sarah for a moment?" Eliza walked towards the bedroom. Ellie moved to block her way.

"I'm sorry, she's sleeping."

"I see," said Eliza carefully, "I'll just give a message to Kitty, in the kitchen and then I'll be on my way, Ellie."

"Sister Elkson, if you please," Ellie spoke stiffly and walked away into the bedroom, closing the door behind her.

Eliza was now fully alarmed. Had Ellie even known her ?

"Sister Elkson's been like this for two days and won't let Miss Sarah have anything but water, even though I've heard her beg for milk or something to eat, to stop the medicine making her sick. She keeps giving Miss Sarah cold baths and then takes hot water to rub her with afterwards but she won't let me in to see her. Sometimes Miss Sarah cries out for it to stop. There was a wet sheet yesterday morning and another today but it's only clean water that it's wet with. I'm fair worried, Mrs Fazakerley. Something's not right. If you hadn't called in today, I'd have come round for you."

"I'd have come yesterday but my breathing and my old joints wouldn't let me. Now, I'm going for Dr. Collins, Kitty, but don't tell Sister Elkson. She's obviously not well herself. Just carry on with your work as usual, but don't leave the house till I come back. If Sarah cries out, go into the bedroom, I'm sure Ellie doesn't mean to hurt her but I think our nurse is getting a little too enthusiastic for comfort."

Eliza puffed her way painfully along the street to Dr. Collin's surgery and was relieved to find him there, having just returned from a visit. When he heard her story the doctor groaned and put his head in his hands.

"When illness strikes, it's never just the patient who is affected but this situation is more complicated than most. I'll go round straight away but you, Mrs Fazakerley, are going to sit here and rest. My housekeeper will bring you a cup of tea. When you are rested she will call you a cab, no more hurrying around the streets for you today!"

Dr Collins arrived in time to find Ellie forcefully persuading Sarah to have yet another cold douche. Sarah was pleading with her;

"No Ellie, no more. You've tried your best but please, no more, you're hurting me,"

Dr Collins swept in and took Sarah from Ellie, gently laying her down on her bed and arranging pillows behind her. He examined the suppurating breast.

"Why have you not been dressing this, as I told you to, Sister Elkson?"

"Another doctor told me to use water-therapy and to allow the discharge to flow freely," Ellie spoke defensively.

"What other doctor?"

"I'm not sure but I think the voice was Dr. Alex Dobson's, I can't be sure but he was very insistent that I did as he told me."

"Did this doctor telephone you? Could it have been Mr Mark Saunders?"

"Oh no, this doctor spoke to me from another spiritual plain. He's gone over you see and so has far more knowledge than any doctor here, on this plain."

Dr. Collins observed Ellie carefully, "You mean the doctor who spoke to you has died? That he spoke to you from the dead?"

"He's dead to this world but he's alive on another plain. We must do as he says. He has the knowledge to heal my sister. I must keep working on her. Please, don't make me stop."

Dr. Collins thought quickly. He could see that Ellie had become deluded and needed careful handling.

"Sit down, Nurse!" he spoke abruptly with authority as a doctor might address an inexperienced student nurse. He deliberately dropped the title of Sister. Ellie sat, her mind taking her back to her early training.

"You have disobeyed orders and I am taking you off this case. I am bringing in another nurse to take your place. Do you understand, Nurse Elkson?"

"Yes, doctor, I'm very sorry sir," to Ellie's confused mind she was a student nurse again, who had made a bad mistake.

"Now, we are going to leave the patient to rest, until the new nurse comes,"

The doctor ushered Ellie from the bedroom into the living room. Ellie sank into a chair while he telephoned a nursing agency, which he used for such emergencies.

"I need a reliable, experienced nurse to be here within the next hour, earlier if possible. She will need to stay all day and I will also need a nurse to stay overnight with my patient." Dr. Collins relied on his knowledge of George Elkson to trust there would be no problem in paying for private nursing.

He remembered that Eliza had said Kitty Fielding would be in the kitchen and he called to the girl.

"Kitty, we need hot tea for Sister Elkson and myself and I want you to take one to Miss Sarah with a good spoonful of sugar. Sit with her while she drinks it and make sure she sips it slowly," he ordered.

Then he turned to Ellie and started the attempt to bring her back to reality. He added sugar to her tea and made her drink. Owing to her water-fast her blood sugars had dropped low enough to confuse her mind. The sugary tea helped. As she grasped the truth of the situation, Ellie began to cry, the tears streamed endlessly down her cheeks and she covered them with her hands hiding her face from Dr. Collins.

"My dear young woman, you have completely overtaxed yourself. I blame myself for not noticing the warning signs. Overtaxing your body and your emotions, can play silly tricks on the mind."

At that moment the doorbell rang and Eliza's voice could be heard asking Kitty if Dr. Collins was still there.

"In here Mrs Fazakerley," the doctor called out and Eliza walked in to a shaky welcome from Ellie. The two friends sat close together, Ellie hanging on tightly to Eliza's hands.

It seemed no time before the bell rang again, to announce the arrival of Nurse Audrey Canter, a jolly, competent looking, middle-aged woman. She disappeared into Sarah's bedroom with Dr Collins to be briefed on the whole case.

Ellie found herself opening her heart to Eliza and her friend decided that she would whisk Ellie away to her own house, at least for the rest of that day.

"A complete break away from this house and the sick room for a few hours is what you need. No need to change, come as you are, I've a cab waiting. Bring some night clothes and you can stay the night and come back early tomorrow; unless you want to stay with me longer. A good meal and a good night's sleep will soon put you right."

"A wonderful idea, just what the doctor orders," said Dr Collins coming back into the room. Nurse Canter is well known to me and is extremely capable. Kitty has promised to stay the night here as well as the night nurse, when she comes, so there is no need to worry. I'll prescribe you a mild sedative, Ellie, you should feel much better in the morning and Sarah has come to no real harm but she too will benefit from food and undisturbed sleep."

Ellie looked down sheepishly.

"Right, we mustn't keep the cab waiting any longer. Pack your night things and we'll be away," Eliza spoke briskly and Ellie hurried to get ready.

"Dr Collins, do I have to watch out for anything? Her mind did seem very disturbed earlier?"

"Just keep her resting and occupy her mind with something other than her sister, or that strange religion she seems obsessed with. A change of scene and some decent food should do the trick. I'll call round at your home in an hour, with a sedative for her and to check you over at the same time! Any worries and I'm on the end of the phone but I don't anticipate any more problems. Thank you for your kindness, Mrs Fazakerley."

The incident was over and dealt with so competently and Ellie returned to her normal self so quickly, after her rest and overnight stay with Eliza, that it could almost have been just a bad dream. The establishment of Nurse Carter as one of the household seemed a natural progression in Sarah's need of full-time care and she and Ellie soon settled into a routine together, although Ellie was never again left in the house alone with her sister. An equally competent Nurse Gregory took over from Nurse Carter at six o'clock each evening and stayed until Nurse Carter returned at half past seven each morning.

Cheery cards and letters arrived from Hartsbeck, for Sarah.

Ellie's own heart was warmed by a childish but carefully drawn picture of a nurse in a blue dress and white apron and a ridiculously high and frilly white cap, holding out something in a glass to a person lying on a couch wrapped in a blue shawl. The drawing was in an envelope addressed to Sister Ellie Elkson and inside a painstakingly wobbly message said, "Thank you Auntie Ellie for taking care of Auntie Sarah. I want to be a nurse like you, one day,. Love from Alice."

The Vicar arrived with Eliza to give Sarah Holy Communion. He invited Ellie to join them but she felt uncomfortable and made the excuse of having other work to do. Sarah's sad expression nearly made her change her mind but she turned away, unable to feel at one with them; her spirituality lay elsewhere. She still sought 'the wisdom of those who lived on higher plains beyond the grave,' as her books on Theosophy and spiritualism encouraged. The fact that she failed to make contact with these spiritual beings, gave her no comfort. She saw very little of Amelia these days. The would-be spiritualist medium felt it wrong to come to the house when Sarah was so obviously against any kind of occult activity. Sarah could see nothing positive in it at all.

"It's against all I believe in, Ellie and it disturbs me terribly to know that you and Amelia are so taken in by it. Jesus Christ is my

Lord and my Saviour and he tells us not to contact the dead. I believe He knows what is best for us."

After calling once at Redcliffe Street, Amelia quickly discovered Sarah's feelings and was sensitive enough to decide to keep away in future.

"Ellie, it would be cruel to cause Sarah any extra distress. You know where to find me, if you need me," and she had simply waved her hand and gone down the steps. With her hair tucked into a turban of orange and green velvet, topped by a gaudy red feather and her gaunt form wrapped in a loose black and yellow garment Amelia cut an eccentric and rather vulnerable figure as she walked away and Ellie wanted to run after her and bring her back but she let her go.

"Gives me the eeby jeebies," Kitty had said, "reminds me of one of those witch-doctors."

"Don't you dare speak of my friends or any other guest in this house like that again, Kitty, you are becoming far too familiar." Ellie had turned on the girl furiously, then gone quickly to her own bed-room and closed the door.

Sarah felt sorry for her sister when she heard about the incident.

"You spoke out of turn, Kitty, and Amelia is my sister's friend. You must learn to keep some thoughts to yourself. Don't upset your-self dear, we all learn by our mistakes; my sister won't be angry for long. Make her some of your special scones for tea and when she's had time to calm down, you must apologise."

Ellie soon forgave Kitty but the young girl had learnt a lesson, as the paid help she must not treat Miss Sarah and Sister Ellie as equals, no matter how close she felt to them. Ellie however was full of remorse and patted Kitty's arm repentantly, when she came in with the loaded tea-tray.

"Kitty, I'm sorry I spoke so sharply. You are a great comfort to us both, and especially to me. I've known you a long time. Do you remember the time when your Billy came running round to fetch me because Toby had swallowed a button and was choking? I was impressed with how you coped that day and you were a grand help

447

to me when your Ruby was born. If I'd married, I would have liked a daughter like you."

Kitty glowed with relief and pride and Ellie tucked into her tea-time scones.

CHAPTER 62

In Parrish Ward

When Ellie brought Sarah for admission to the cancer hospital the following week, she was comforted by the sight of Lettie Parrish with her sister's cap bobbing as she came swiftly down the ward to greet them. Lettie noticed that both sisters seemed calm and accepting of the situation and hoped fervently that this attitude would last.

"Welcome to Parrish Ward." She grinned at Ellie, "it still gives me a funny feeling when I call it that. I pinch myself to make sure I'm awake. However, Sarah (or perhaps I should call you Miss Elkson on the ward), I can assure you, we have an excellent team of nurses and we shall do our best for you."

"Thank you, Sister," said Sarah gravely, "but please, do call me Sarah, even on the Ward."

"You'll be alright with us, ducks! We're all in this together but there's plenty of fun when we get going!" a tiny elderly lady, with a lined, ravaged face and bright dark eyes, called to Sarah from the bed opposite,

"Now you behave yourself, Nellie Barnes, you'll burst your stitches with all your laughing." Sister Parrish smiled fondly at the old lady, "she's alright really; keeps us all from being miserable."

Another woman, who looked in her twenties, her pale face framed with thick, dark hair that spread across her pillow, smiled and waved from her bed and then carried on reading a magazine.

"Some of the patients are in the operating theatre or recovery rooms but they'll want plenty of sleep when they come back on the ward, so you'll have chance for some peace and quiet."

Ellie helped Sarah unpack her bag. There were two pretty new night gowns, one cream and one pale blue with soft lacy collars and cuffs, both presents from Eliza. Beattie Mason had knitted a bed-jacket in pastel rainbow shades of soft baby wool making a warm splash of colour in the clinical surroundings. Toiletries, handker-chiefs, hair-brush and comb, were put carefully in the bedside locker. Sarah's Bible and prayer book and a photograph of the family, on that last holiday in Estwick, were placed within reach on the locker top. Ellie gave her sister a copy of 'Berry and Co,' by Dornford Yates and 'Anne's House of Dreams' by L.M. Montgomery,

"In case you get bored," smiled Ellie, "'Berry and Co,' should make you laugh and I know you loved 'Anne of Green Gables,' this is a later one, about Anne's early days of marriage. It's girlish but an easy read and you know all the characters."

Sarah was touched, she knew neither of the books were her sis-ter's taste. Ellie must have chosen them specially for her. Secretly she didn't think she would feel like reading but gave Ellie a grateful kiss.

As it happened, Sarah was glad to have both books to dip into on that first day. The ward was quiet and between tests there were hours with little to do. After chatting with Nellie Barnes and the young, dark haired woman who was called Bernice, Sarah sat in her pale blue nightie with her bed jacket around her shoulders and tried to lose herself in the antics of 'Berry and Co' and revel nostal-gically, in the heart-twisting incidents of the life of the red-headed girl of 'Green Gables'.

When Sarah woke on the second day there were more patients on the ward, some recovering from surgery. Sarah felt ill and mis-erable, she'd slept poorly and was conscious of the foul smell from her breast and of intermittent pain. She had no appetite and drink-ing made her feel sick. For the first time she was forced to accept that she was a real cancer patient and dealing with this disease was to be the main purpose of her life in the hospital. Everything the nurses did for her was in connection with her illness. Even the ordi-nary bodily functions were watched over and monitored, "bowels opened"; "loose stools;" "hard stools;" "urine clear", "urine cloudy" and a trace of blood in any of these was of serious interest. Nellie Barnes had a field day with lavatorial jokes and helped them keep a sense of proportion, while losing all sense of propriety.

After three days of tests, Mr Mark Saunders declared that it would benefit Sarah, to have the offending breast removed as soon as possible. Sarah was relieved. She imagined herself free of the foul smelling, lumpy organ and the pain, which alternated between a constant throb and a vice-like grip.

"Of course we don't expect this operation will cure you, or even prolong your life but it should bring you much relief. Your heart is strong and you could live for some time. A mastectomy could make things easier for you."

Sister Parrish stood, frowning and tight lipped, beside the specialist as he spoke such brutal words. She did not agree with him and felt sure that Sarah's pain could be eased and controlled by other gentler methods; surgery would initially bring more pain and side effects. From her experience, Sister Parrish was aware that Sarah only had a short time left. She didn't speak of this in front of her patient but put her feelings strongly to Mr Saunders later, in her office.

"As a senior and experienced nurse, I am sure that this procedure will cause unnecessary suffering to my patient," she declared.

"Thank you for your opinion, Sister. I think we must now allow the patient to decide. Miss Elkson is in her right mind, whatever she decides I will accept."

Sarah asked that the breast be removed.

Nellie Barnes came over to Sarah's bedside for a chat later and Sarah told her about her decision. "Maybe, deep down I'm hoping for a cure, even though I know that can't be. But I can't bear the thought of being cosseted towards death, Nellie. I want something more positive to happen, even if it kills me!"

"That's the spirit lass, I'm not sure I'd be as brave as you and I'm quite partial to a bit of cosseting. Still, you're a lot younger and if you want to go out with a bang, then go for it! I'll keep praying for you." Nellie was a devout Roman Catholic.

"Oh Nellie, I'm not sure about the bang but with you around I'm going to die laughing, if nothing else," she gripped Nellie's hand tightly, tears threatening.

"Now ducky, you don't have to put a brave face on things all the time, have a good cry if you want to, nothing wrong in that."

Sarah had her cry, hanging on to Nellie's gnarled hand. The old woman sat with her, as she'd sat with her own children many a time, pouring all her motherly love and strength out towards Sarah.

Ellie felt shocked and helpless when she came to visit next day and heard the news about the decision to operate. Nothing she could say would change Sarah's mind and in the end she had to accept it. Sarah was to be prepared for surgery the following day.

Ellie went home and telephoned Hartsbeck. She spoke to her mother and left messages for George, Stephen and Edwin, who were all at work. Jeannie Elkson took the news robustly and the familiar, feisty spirit in her mother gave Ellie courage.

"Ellie, you know I'd be there with you, if I could be. I'm thinking of you both all the time. It's hard for you but don't feel you're on your own with this. One of the boys will come to you, as soon as they can."

Sarah had a welcome visit from the hospital chaplain. She'd shied away from picking up her bible or prayer book, even though in her heart she had been shouting out prayers to God. Her mind had been too addled to think of which passages to read but in the chaplain's presence, she listened gratefully, while he read from the psalms and the New Testament, familiar passages which soothed and strengthened her soul. Surprisingly, Sarah slept well that night and was woken at quarter past six by Parrish Ward coming to life with 'the march of tea and wash bowls' to quote Nellie Barnes. After all the pre-op procedures she was wheeled away to the theatre, smiling and waving a brave goodbye to her ward-mates.

"See you later, ducky," called out Nellie Barnes.

Mr Mark Saunders met her at the door of the theatre. "It's good to see you smiling, Miss Elkson, I don't often get such a treat from a patient about to have surgery," he remarked.

The operation went well. Sarah woke to hear Sister Parrish calling her name and patting her cheek.

"Wake up now, Sarah, it's all over and you're back on the ward."

The smell and taste of anaesthetic was still in Sarah's mouth and nostrils and as soon as she opened her eyes and moved her head she felt woozy and nauseated. She was lying on her side and a nurse was removing a long rubber tube from her mouth. Her hand moved to her breast but all she could feel was thick bandaging and a kind of numb ache, an earlier injection of morphine masking any deeper pain. Sister Parrish helped her to sit up and she immediately vomited into a bowl held out for her.

"That's right, get rid of all that nasty anaesthetic, you'll feel much better."

Afterwards a young nurse propped Sarah up with pillows and swabbed out her mouth with a pleasant lemony-tasting liquid and gave her a piece of ice to suck. The young nurse stayed beside the bed filling in charts and watching her patient. Sarah shivered and struggled to come round properly.

"I'm so cold," she whispered, her body shaking slightly.

"That's a normal reaction after an operation. You'll soon warm up," the nurse took her temperature and blood pressure, checked her pulse and respiration, then tucked an extra blanket around Sarah's trembling body.

"It's better to feel cold than too warm, it means your body is protecting itself – don't ask me the details but believe me that is so," the young nurse prattled comfortingly on, until Sarah closed her eyes and drifted into a drug-induced sleep.

Over the next five days Sarah struggled to recover. She developed a slight fever and remained in bed most of the time, except for the occasional, painful transfer to a bedside chair. Ellie visited each day and these were precious times with shared silences and quiet reminiscences. Eliza came once but stayed only a short time.

"She needs rest and quiet, I'll not come again, until she's much stronger."

Fruit and small gifts arrived from Beattie and Kitty and her family. On the sixth day, which was the twenty ninth of September,

Stephen came from Hartsbeck. He sat with Ellie, beside Sarah's bed. He thought how pretty she looked in her cream nightgown and rainbow bed-jacket. Her cheeks were faintly flushed and her greenish-blue eyes dreamily content.

"How's mother," asked Sarah, smiling at her brother.

"Annoyed that she's not able enough to come and see you. She finds walking a great trial now but still rules us with a rod of iron, from that old rocking chair in the kitchen."

Sarah laughed, then gave a sudden gasp and clutched her chest, she leant forward panting for breath. Ellie was up in a minute, her hand on Sarah's pulse;

"Nurse!" she called loudly and pressed the emergency button by the bed.

"What's happening to her?" Stephen watched in shock as Sarah's lips turned blue and her skin from pink flush to dirty grey. She rocked forward, her hands clenched, fighting for breath.

Sister Parrish rushed up the ward calling for a nurse to contact the duty doctor and Mr Saunders. Two other nurses joined her. Ellie and Stephen were shooed away. Curtains were drawn round the bed hiding Sister Parrish and her small team as they worked to save Sarah. Ellie and Stephen went to sit in the corridor. Mercifully, as they tiptoed out they saw that Nellie Barnes was fast asleep and snoring, her mouth wide open.

"Do you know what was happening to Sarah? Was it some kind of heart attack?" asked Stephen abrupt in his anxiety, Ellie was white and withdrawn, "It looked like a pulmonary embolism. Sit down, Stephen and stop hovering, it makes me nervous."

They watched the duty doctor rush past, followed shortly by Mr Mark Saunders, the tails of his dark suit lifting behind him as he strode past, a deep frown clouding his face.

Fifteen minutes later, Lettie Parrish came out and asked them both to come into her office. They noticed the curtains were still drawn round Sarah's bed and the striped trousers of the specialist could be seen moving about below them. Ellie guessed what was coming. She had the sensation of being disembodied; watching herself walking with Stephen into the Sister's office. She tried to imagine herself somewhere else, not wanting to hear what her old colleague was about to say. She caught sight of Stephen's face, which seemed to have shrunk and she reached for his hand as they sat facing Lettie. Her old colleagues face was pink with distress,

Lettie came forward and bent towards them,

"My dears, I'm so sorry. Sarah had an acute pulmonary embolism, which can happen a few days after such a big operation. The attack lasted only a few minutes and then she was gone."

Ellie covered her face and moaned, "No, not Sarah. Please, not my Sarah," she felt Stephen's arm go round her and Lettie's hand on her shoulder.

A young nurse arrived with a tray of tea which Sister Parrish quickly poured and laced with sugar, giving the brother and sister time to recover from their initial shock. She handed out the cups while explaining what had happened.

"There was nothing we could do. We tried our best to prevent this happening, moving her legs and helping her to sit up in the chair regularly though she didn't like to move around. Ellie, my dear, I would give anything for this not to have happened."

"Please," said Stephen, "don't blame yourself. It had to come soon, better for Sarah that it was so quick and not long and drawn out."

Ellie looked up, her face tense and white, "I'm glad you've been nursing her these last days, Lettie. You weren't a stranger to her, she knew you as my friend."

"Ellie, she was amazing, even though she was so weak and ill, she managed to be a great comfort to the other patients."

A knock on the door and Mr Mark Saunders entered. Ellie and Stephen stiffened. Anger at Sarah's death threatened to swamp them and the hostility in their eyes stopped the young man's gush of sympathy. He stood helplessly, hands hanging limply by his sides. He looked at the brother and sister and Ellie knew instinctively, that it was one of those moments in his career that he would carry with him always. This was one of those experiences, which would help to turn him from arrogance to humility, from a competent doctor to a great one. Her anger subsided and Mark Saunders found his voice:

"Your sister was very special; in the short time I knew her she taught me a lot. I don't mean medically but personally, in the way she faced her illness and death. You must feel angry with me for operating on her, I'm sorry. I hope it eased her pain a little and gave her hope. Sarah was very poorly and she knew it. Even if this hadn't happened, she would have only lived a few more weeks, but that can be no comfort to you, at the moment. Her chief thought, in submitting to the operation, was that it might help future cancer patients. Did you know that she sang to the other patients in the evenings? I heard her once when I came onto the ward, her voice was beautiful. She sang the old folk songs that everyone knew and then some of the hymns the others asked her to sing."

Ellie and Stephen swelled inside with pride for their sister.

"What a trump," said Stephen and they all smiled wistfully.

Another knock on the door and a student nurse announced that if the family wanted to go in to be with Sarah, she had been made ready for them.

The utter silence in the curtained cubicle was dramatic. Ellie and Stephen stood quietly side by side. Sarah lay flat, her eyes and mouth closed, her skin creamy pale and her light brown hair, combed so as to hide the streaks of grey, spread softly over the pillow. The nurses had changed her into the pale blue nightgown and had folded her hands together on top of the tidily tucked sheet. Her Bible and prayer book were arranged beside her on the bed. No sound of breathing or struggle for life, just quietness and peace. Ellie breathed in that great quiet, it was full of a presence she hadn't felt before.

Stephen touched her and whispered, "If I wasn't an atheist I would say God is here."

Ellie nodded and moved forward to kiss her sister's cooling forehead, "Goodbye, my Sarah." She moved away to let Stephen take her place.

He took one of Sarah's hands and pressed it, "Well done, little sis, you've made it through," then gently laid her hand back in place and turned away.

Both too awe-struck for tears, they stayed until a nurse popped her head through the curtains to make sure all was well and Ellie and Stephen came away, leaving Sarah's body to be prepared for the undertakers.

As they crossed the ward, the young woman who'd waved to Sarah on her arrival, called them over. Shakily she told them how Sarah had come to her in the middle of the night, "she'd only been on the ward a couple of days. This particular night I was upset, worrying about my little girl and my husband and how they'd cope if I died. I was trying not to cry but couldn't help it. Sarah heard me and struggled across from her bed. She sat and we talked, then she held my hand until I calmed down and fell asleep. I know that I'm getting better and will go home but I'll never forget Sarah. I didn't have the chance to tell her my good news."

Ellie clasped the woman's hand, "thank you, I'm glad she was a comfort to you. I expect you helped her too, by needing her."

"We're so proud of our sister. She would be glad to know you're going home to your family," Stephen's voice shook and he walked quickly out followed by Ellie.

CHAPTER 63

Golders Green

The fortnight that followed was filled with periods of frantic activity and periods of uneasy quiet. There had to be a post- mortem because of the suddenness of Sarah's death despite her on-going illness. Afterwards Stephen signed Sarah's death certificate as witness and Mr Mark Saunders wrote out the cause of death as 'Pulmonary embolism'.

It was arranged that Sarah was to be cremated at the Golders Green Crematorium. Eliza had once taken Ellie, to this prestigious place of the dead, to show her where her husband's ashes were scattered. Then it had been a gentle spring day, Ellie remembered how they walked through the gates and past the elegant red brick crematorium building, while Eliza read aloud from the guide book.

"Designed in the Italian, Lombardic style, by the architect Sir Ernest George and his partner Alfred Yeates,"

Once past the building they entered the gardens, "twelve acres of them, laid out by William Robinson," intoned Eliza, following the book with her finger, "we should find two ponds, and a bridge, as well as several large tombs."

Turning a corner they'd gasped with delight at a large meadow covered with purple, saffron and white crocus blooms.

"It really is a heavenly place," Ellie had remarked.

"I think that's exactly what the designer had in mind," said Eliza, "it's the first crematorium to be opened in London and caters for people of all religious faiths or none. It was opened the year my

Harry died. I remember they told me that I could choose whatever kind of ceremony I wanted and any kind of music."

"So, what did you choose?"

"As my husband was Scottish, I found a Presbyterian minister to take a simple service and a young man to play a highland lament on the bagpipes. Harry would have liked that,"

"Sounds very appropriate."

Ellie had taken her friend's arm and together they'd wandered through the grounds till they found the remembrance garden, where Harry Fazakerley's ashes had been placed over thirty years ago. Ellie had walked quietly away, while Eliza stood a moment, remembering.

Ellie hoped that her mother and brothers would allow Sarah's ashes to remain here in this Garden of Remembrance, where she could come and meditate and feel close to her sister.

George and Edwin telephoned about the funeral arrangements. In deference to their younger sister's Christian Faith, it was agreed to hold a service at St. Stephen's Church, where Sarah had taken Holy Communion. Cousin Hugh begged to be allowed to take part in the service and the Vicar readily agreed and the date was fixed for Friday the fourth of October. Only the three brothers came from Hartsbeck. Jeannie Elkson was too unsteady to travel so far and Hannah and Annie had stayed at home with their children and "to keep an eye on mother."

George appeared moody and withdrawn when he arrived, greeting Ellie with a terse,

"Sad day, Ellie. Didn't expect this so soon."

Edwin grasped his elder sister's hands and kissed her. "It's been a bad time for you sis, wish we could have been with you."

Cousin Hugh clapped her fondly on the shoulder, "My mother and father and all the cousins send their love. Hope you received their letters,"

"Yes, thank you. It was good of them to write," Ellie swallowed hard. She was more affected by George's terseness than by the kindness of Hugh and Edwin.

It was when Ellie proposed that Sarah's ashes should remain in Golders Green that the reason for George's mood became clear.

"I would have thought, after all that's happened, you would have allowed our sister's remains to go home to Hartsbeck. At least mother and the rest of the family would then be able to share properly in mourning for her. Don't you think you did enough, bringing Sarah away from us to London to try your fancy water cures and see your so-called specialists? Do you know what I think, Ellie? I think, if you hadn't been so full of your daft notions, Sarah might have had a chance. She should have stayed up North, with us."

George was beside himself with pent up anger, curling his hands into fists he hammered them on the back of a chair, his face contorted. Ellie stiffened. White-faced she looked him in the eye. She'd seen this reaction in bereaved relatives so many times and knew it was caused by raw grief and helplessness. Someone had to be blamed. Ellie took the blow squarely, wincing as it caught her own open wounds. Again she saw before her the little boy she'd coped with in his early tantrums and she reached out her arms to him. Unmanly tears threatened and George flapped her hands away and left the room.

"Ellie, don't take it to heart. I'm sure none of the others feel like that," Hugh spoke out in the silence.

"I wouldn't blame them if they did. I'm sure I'd have felt the same. George is taking Sarah's death hard, he's grieving and he's lashing out. Why shouldn't he, we all want to – leave him be, he'll calm down. I've gone over and over whether I should have persuaded Sarah to come here. At least George has brought it out in the open."

"Ellie, I think you should know mother told me specifically, that she couldn't bear it if Sarah's ashes were carried home to Hartsbeck. She doesn't want her last memory to be a box of dust. She asked if the ashes could be put in some tranquil place among trees and flowers, here, near you."

"She's sent me a letter to that effect, it arrived today. I'll show it to you all, when George recovers."

"Do you mind if I give Hannah a phone call," asked Hugh, "if anyone can help George to see sense, it will be Hannah. I'll just ask her to telephone him. He doesn't need to know I've contacted her."

"Good idea, Hugh. Go into that bedroom and close the door. We had an extension put in there for Sarah." Ellie pointed Hugh towards Sarah's bedroom.

George did calm down and was able to speak sensibly to Hannah when she rang. Jeannie also came to the phone and begged George to allow Sarah's ashes to remain in Golders Green.

"Don't bring her remains home, George. I can't think of my girl in a pile of ash. Her spirit will always be alive among us. Keep her ashes where her body died. Put them in that Garden of Remembrance which Eliza Fazakerley has told me about. It sounds beautiful, full of flowers, Sarah would love that. Don't make a fuss, George, and help Ellie through this. She's borne the brunt of it. I just wish I was with you all."

It was the longest speech Jeannie had ever made on the telephone and brought home to George how strongly his mother felt about this and how much she'd suffered. He thought of Jack's remains buried over in France, somehow this made his youngest brother seem more alive to them, somehow not quite dead. He felt that none of them would be surprised if he came walking in through the front door of 19, Redcliffe Street to join them.

"We'll arrange for Sarah's ashes to be placed in the Garden of Remembrance at Golders Green, if you are all in agreement," stated George, when they were gathered round the supper table later that evening.

George was used to taking charge of situations in his profession and though they smiled to themselves, none of the family resented it. They were proud of him.

George had become accepted as a leading figure in the Hartsbeck community. He was trusted with the administration of the legacies of wealthy inhabitants for the benefit of the town. He had been given free rein to choose the areas where monies, left to the town, were most needed. As a result he'd enabled new wings of the hospital to be opened and established educational and charitable trusts in the names of his prestigious clients. He was now a fully- fledged, highly respected family solicitor.

As George's spirits calmed, Ellie's grew more troubled. The sting of George's verbal attack began to weigh on her mind and she tortured herself with the thread of truth behind his words.

Sarah's funeral came and went. Ellie went through it as if in a dream. The church service was at eleven o'clock followed by the cremation. She dressed properly in black and made arrangements with Kitty and Mrs Fielding for refreshments to be laid out, ready for family and friends when they returned to the house. At the church the words of the funeral service swirled confusedly around her, registering only by their familiarity. She joined in the hymns chosen by Eliza and cousin Hugh but afterwards couldn't remember what they were. She did remember the final exhortation. It was spoken by Hugh and he seemed to be addressing her in particular; it stabbed at her jaded spirit, reminding her that she still had a job to do in the world.

"Go forth into the world in peace; be of good courage; hold fast that which is good; render to no man evil for evil; strengthen the faint hearted; support the weak; help the afflicted; honour all men; love and serve the Lord, rejoicing in the power of the Holy Spirit." The power in the words instilled into Ellie something of the strength that Sarah had spoken of finding, when she took Communion.

At the crematorium the organist played the music to 'I know that my Redeemer Liveth' and Ellie was back in the church in Estwick, at Easter time, when Sarah had sung this very aria.

She noticed Stephen bending forward in his seat, his head in his hands as if in prayer. She wondered how it was that, except for Sarah and Edwin and possibly Jack, they'd all turned away from the Church but here they were and the church and its ways were still there for them, speaking to them in their sorrow.

Cousin Hugh was not staying at Ellie's house with the rest of the family. One of his old university friends, Canon Ian Haworth, was the Precentor at Westminster Abbey and he and his wife had offered to put Hugh up for a few days. Ian had served his curacy in Hartsbeck about twenty years ago and he and his wife, Pauline, remembered Sarah and the Elkson family well. He came alone to the funeral, Pauline being engaged elsewhere. Ellie invited him back, for refreshments.

Stephen, George and Edwin, clustered together near the window, glad of the distraction of people passing in the street below. Eliza sat with Beattie Mason, near the glowing warmth of the fire. Cousin Hugh and the Vicar of St. Stephen's hovered between them, finding something to talk about with each. Kitty and her mother passed around glasses of sherry and plates of sandwiches. Homemade cakes and Beattie's biscuits were then followed by cups of hot tea and coffee.

Ellie and Canon Ian were left to themselves. Ian was thankful to tuck into the food offered; he had eaten nothing else that day. Ellie drank cup after cup of hot tea and nibbled on one of Beattie's biscuits. Aware of Ellie's inner turmoil, Ian led her into a conversation of happier times and she soon found herself smiling and talking with him of past years in Hartsbeck.

After an hour or so, the party broke up and Ian and Hugh prepared to leave together.

"You must come and visit us at Westminster Abbey, Ellie. We live in the precincts and Pauline, my wife, would love to meet you."

"My word, Ellie, you'll soon become too 'upperty' to worry about poor cousin Hugh in his little country parish," teased Hugh as he kissed Ellie goodbye, "but I'll keep in touch Ellie. Remember, I never stop praying for you."

Tears sprang to Ellie's eyes and for a moment she clung to him as he embraced her. She felt she was being launched alone into an open sea and in a very flimsy craft. The same sensation hit her the following day, when her brothers took their leave.

George was still a little cool but kissed his older sister and promised to contact her about Sarah's Will, which she'd made before coming to London. Sarah had made him the executor.

Edwin hugged her and told her to come home soon and visit them, in Hartsbeck.

Stephen patted her companionably on the back, then he took her by the shoulders and looked deep into her eyes,

"I'll be back in London in about six weeks. Don't forget, Ellie, you and I have been together the longest."

Although she knew he was just cementing their own special bond, from the time when they'd been the only two children in the Elkson household, Ellie felt Stephen was overdoing the sentiment to make her feel better. Embarrassed, she turned away. Once they had all gone she slipped away to her room, her emotions in turmoil.

CHAPTER 64

Sarah's Bequests

O nce the family had gone, Kitty helped Ellie to sort through the few things Sarah had accumulated while in London. They put them in piles of those to keep and those to give or throw away and disposed of them accordingly.

Eliza insisted that Ellie keep the gramophone and some of the records. "You may not want to play them at the moment but in time you will and music is always a great healer," she said to Ellie knowing that she herself couldn't bear to play the music she'd shared with Sarah, just yet.

For the next week Ellie and Kitty flung themselves into giving the house a thorough clean from top to bottom.

An "autumn clean", Kitty called it; "same as a spring clean." The activity stopped them from brooding and helped cleanse the house of bad memories, as well as dirt. Ellie was mentally and physically exhausted by the time they'd finished and slept soundly and dreamlessly.

Eliza insisted on taking Ellie for a few days holiday to a quiet seaside resort in Kent.

"You're trying to make a genteel, elderly lady, of me, Eliza," Ellie teased as they promenaded by the ocean in the fresh, autumn weather and took afternoon tea and dinner in glass enclosed restaurants, which made them feel they were out at sea. Once they went to the evening performance of a light comedy but otherwise they simply relaxed in Eliza's choice of a fashionable hotel and watched the world go by. "Dull and undemanding, just what we need," declared

Eliza. Ellie laughed, she was beginning to miss her work in the community.

Towards the end of October Ellie went to visit Sister Allinson at the Family Welfare Clinic.

The Sister was delighted to see her "My condolences to you on your sister's death, Sister Elkson. You did well to nurse her; it must have been hard for you," her keen eyes noted how refreshed and calm Ellie appeared.

"Thank you Sister, it wasn't easy but I've had a good rest and I'm eager to return to work at the clinic. If you will have me."

"We'll be more than glad to have you back with us. We've missed you on the team," Sister Allinson rifled through her large desk diary, "Would you be able to take up your old position again, straight away?"

"Why, yes Sister. I'm ready to start tomorrow, if you need me." Ellie's heart lifted.

"Let's take it gently. Why not start on Friday, November first. That will give you a day to settle in and to organise your timetable before the weekend. Then you can start straight in on Monday, the fourth. It will make it easier for pay and administration, if you begin on the first of the month. We'll be relieved to have you back, Sister Elkson."

By Armistice Day Ellie was back in the swing of the routine of the clinic. She wore the emblem of the red Flanders' poppy as an act of personal remembrance. Together with her colleagues and patients from the clinic she stood respectfully for the two minutes silence. She tried to keep the memories at bay of Jack and Becky and of the young men she'd nursed through horrendous injuries, so that they could be sent back to the front and maybe to their death. These memories and those of Sarah, were still too raw. Ellie drowned them out by immersing herself in her work, propagating her slightly modified form of Dr. Truby King's methods. She'd been surprised at how fashionable Dr. King's ideas were becoming and often found one of his booklets already in use, in some of the homes she visited.

"My mother brought me this, Sister. She told me her friends say it's all the rage now, to follow the Truby King way."

"Well, he's an excellent nutritionist, knows all about the right food to give babies whatever condition they're in and he believes healthy and well-rested mothers are essential to good nurturing of children. Nevertheless, just occasionally, it's alright to break his rules and cuddle your baby," she would tell them, surprising herself at her own, confidently flexible, approach.

"I would never have dared to have my own opinion, or think of bending the great doctor's rules when I was working with him," she confided to Eliza, "I must be getting old."

"Shows you've developed a mature mind of your own and you've regained your Northern common sense," Eliza had replied heartily, relieved that Ellie had recovered so quickly from Sarah's illness and death.

"Far too quickly, to my mind," declared Beattie Mason, as she thumped away with her rolling pin at her weekly biscuit making; "I've seen it too often. We'll have to watch our Sister Elkson, it'll catch up with her and then she'll go down with a thump."

"Like she's been hit with your rolling pin!" chuckled her now close friend, Samuel Henson, the assistant from Heals.

A friendship had grown from that first meeting in the furniture store and Sam would often be found sitting in Beattie's kitchen, chatting as she baked. It was a warm and happy respite for him to call in on Beattie after work, instead of hurrying straight back to his bachelor digs.

Sometimes he stayed for a meal, other times he would sweep Beattie up and take her out for a steak supper. They would sit in a quiet corner of the pub, where Beattie could relax, the shadows masking her disfigured face.

"I don't mind one bit if the whole world sees it, Beattie, it's the real you I love and your face has helped to make you the lovely person you are," he'd leant over and kissed her on the livid mark.

Beattie gasped, it had been his first real declaration of love and she wasn't sure how to react,

"Well, it had to be someone with a wonky eye, to see anything lovely in me!" she joked.

Sam had looked surprised, then he'd started to laugh till the tears ran, "We're a right pair, Beattie Mason!"

"Yes, Sam," Beattie had spoken tenderly, "I do believe we are."

That had sealed it and a few weeks later Beattie and Sam announced to each other (and a few close friends), that they had an on-going friendship "with marriage in mind".

"No reason to rush things," Sam would say but secretly they laid their plans. Beattie's mother Enid and Sam soon grew fond of each other and Enid was always included in the household which the couple planned to set up together.

Beattie still worried about Ellie, "She's throwing herself into her nursing too soon and not allowing herself to grieve properly," she told Sam.

Beattie was partly right. Beneath the surface Ellie grieved constantly for her sister but her work as a nurse never faltered; in fact she was becoming more and more competent and skilled in her job and earning even greater respect from staff and patients.

Then, three months after Sarah's death, Ellie had a visit from Amelia Antrim with a message from Mrs Dempster.

"She says it's very important that you meet with her, Ellie. She's sure Sarah is trying to contact you, through her. She says if you don't come, you will have no rest and neither will Sarah. She thinks Sarah will find another way to get through to you, in time, but it will be quicker and easier for you both, if you allow Mrs Dempster to help."

Ellie was angry and refused to go, she didn't trust Mrs Dempster. Amelia begged her to listen.

"Mrs Dempster can be very difficult; she can cause all sorts of trouble if you don't do as she asks. She's poisonous Ellie. Play along with her and then back out slowly."

"I certainly won't play along with her. If Sarah wants me, she doesn't have to come to me through that manipulative old fraud."

Ellie was adamant and Amelia had to let it go but the seed had been sown in Ellie's mind that Sarah might be trying to contact her.

Weekly letters began to come from Mrs Dempster, describing how a voice from the spirit world was desperately crying out for Ellie. The medium was sure it was Sarah. Ellie tore up the letters and threw them away, such was her contempt for the woman who sent them but they kept coming and the contents became more urgent. Ellie couldn't stop herself from reading them and their subtle poison seeped into her thoughts.

Her previous dabbling in spiritualism and theosophy now came back to her with thoughts of ectoplasm and spirits reaching out from other planes by using anything strange and ethereal they could find in this world.

Ellie was becoming addicted to the pull of her sister's last resting place, persuading herself that Sarah wanted her there. She began to take the underground to Golders Green once or twice a week, usually in the late afternoon or early morning. Walking through the grounds of the Crematorium she would make her way to the Garden of Remembrance where she would sit on a bench, for over an hour, staring at the plants and thinking of her sister. Sarah's name had been inscribed in the book of remembrance but Ellie didn't look it up. It would have made her sister's death too official. Autumn was ending and she could feel winter setting in as she wandered through the crematorium gardens, depending on when she was free. Only the dark, formal evergreens had kept their leaves; the beech and sycamore, the silver birch and oak, held out bone-bare branches. Ellie found herself searching for her sister's shape in the swathes of fog and mist swirling around corners of the paths and among the silent trees.

Wandering and sitting in the chilly damp air, brought on aches and pains in her limbs. At night, in bed, she would wind a warmed scarf round her head and face to soothe the neuralgia, which had begun to trouble her. Such discomforts didn't stop her walks; she welcomed them. The constant nagging guilt, about her part in adding to Sarah's suffering and hastening her death, had returned. Ellie embraced the rheumatic pains, as a kind of penance.

At last George contacted Ellie about Sarah's last will and testament. All her sisters' possessions had been meticulously divided between family members or friends. She'd left some money to charities but most of it had gone into the family trust, for future generations. Her precious piano she'd left to George and Hannah, on condition that all their children had piano lessons and it should be given to Rebecca, if she ever set up a home of her own.

During her stay in Redcliffe Street, Sarah had written to George and attached several codicils to her will. Her leather bound set of Dickens' works, she had asked to be given to Kitty Fielding, "who will know how to use and enjoy them!" Her recorder, which she had played since she was eight years old, she asked to be given to Billy- "he has a good ear for a tune." For Beattie Mason there was a small sum of money "to use as she sees fit", and for Mrs Fielding a pretty china tea service, which had been given to Sarah when she was twenty-one, "something pretty to serve tea to all your friends."

For Ellie there were two special gifts, a gold locket containing an icon of the black Madonna and child and in the opposite half, a tiny, solemn photograph of Sarah, when she was ten years old. The other gift was a small watercolour, about twelve by six inches, in a carved wood frame. It depicted the view from Norber hill above Estwick. Ellie never tired of looking at it. The artist was a friend of George's who had once been in love with Sarah and had given her this painting, as a seventeenth birthday present. The young artist had captured the light as it focused on the greens, golds and purples in the undulating landscape of rough moorlands and soft pastures set amongst the soft greys and whites of the limestone rocks. The sunlit clouds chased their shadows across the landscape to the distant sea. Ellie hung it on her bedroom wall. Often, at bedtime she would sit in front of this scene and meditate, and then touch it gently with her finger-tips before putting out the light. In between waking and sleeping she would dream of walking in the Yorkshire dales with her sister and brothers. She remembered Stephen saying to her, that if ever he was to find God, he thought it would be through learning the silent secrets of these ancient rocks. Always such happy dreams would darken, ending with Ellie stumbling through grey, clinging mists, towards a faintly glowing light ahead of her, searching for Sarah's spirit. Sarah's legacies to Ellie were proving to be far beyond her material gifts and were filled with a mixture of light and darkness.

PART SEVEN

ELLIE LABOURS ON. 1929-1933

CHAPTER 65

Goodbye to Eliza.

During the whole of the winter of 1929 Eliza complained of feeling her age.

"After all, I am coming up to my eightieth birthday," she would remark time and again.

She became more housebound, especially in frosty weather and winter fogs, which seemed to be worse than ever that year. She was thankful that the influenza epidemic, which had reached its peak the previous May, had passed her by.

Ellie hadn't visited her elderly friend since her return to work following Sarah's death and as Christmas approached Eliza became concerned. She sent a note to Ellie, begging her to call and see her;

'I'm still recovering from a nasty bout of bronchitis and can't leave the house, but I do want to see you before Christmas,' she wrote.

It had been a demanding few weeks at the clinic and Ellie was tired but filled with guilt and remorse, as soon as she was free she hurried round to her old friend.

During the visit, Eliza noticed Ellie's attention repeatedly drifting away in the middle of a conversation. She would stop mid-sentence and stare into the distance as if trying to focus on something. Then shaking her head she would say; "no, it's gone. Strange, very strange. Now, what was I saying?"

This happened several times and rang alarm bells for Eliza, "whatever is the matter with you Ellie? Is there something you can see that I can't? You're not dabbling with the spirits again are you?"

Ellie didn't want to upset Eliza by telling her about Mrs Dempster, but perhaps Eliza would understand the other things that were happening to her. The answer she gave was vague and evasive, "no, no of course not. Well maybe just a little bit. - It was just, I thought I saw- through the window- it must have been a trick of the light. Oh yes, I did go to a Theosophy meeting last week. It was very interesting; about oriental mystics. There's a lot going on in the spirit realms that we don't know about."

"And don't need to know about if you ask me. Some things are best left alone, or we'll drive ourselves mad," Eliza ejaculated in her outspoken way but Ellie didn't laugh, or raise an eyebrow, she just stared into space again. Suddenly she stood up, fastened her outdoor coat, said she was glad Eliza felt better and left the house.

Shaken, Eliza sat and pondered deeply over this. During the next few days she made some discreet enquiries, through her contacts in the nursing world, about Sister Ellie Elkson.

It appeared that at work Ellie appeared to be her normal self. Colleagues suggested that she was perhaps a little too ardent and conscientious, but in no way confused or lacking in concentration. Her ability to relate to patients and colleagues was a little more stilted than usual but quite acceptable. Eliza was puzzled.

When April came, with its spring weather, Eliza suggested that she would accompany Ellie to Golders Green. Ellie was alarmed and tried to discourage her, she much preferred her visits to be solitary.

Eliza, however, knew how to manipulate her friend. "My dear, I can feel age and infirmity creeping up on me and I don't know how many more times I will be able to visit my dear Harry's resting place. I would like to see it again in the spring time before my ashes join his. I know, it's only earthly remains but as you said yourself, in spring those gardens make you think of Heaven. It'll help me prepare for it. Come now, Ellie, you won't deny an old friend her little fancies?" Eliza hoped she wasn't laying it on too thickly. It worked.

"Of course we'll go together, Eliza. I've neglected you lately. We've been so busy at the clinic with all the epidemics and vaccination programmes, on top of the everyday work."

She could have added that they'd also had a short fall of staff, owing to three of the younger nurses recently leaving to be married. This had irritated Ellie in a new way. Since Sarah's death the Elkson children and young folk from Hartsbeck had stopped writing and sending pictures. Letters from her brothers and sisters- in-law had become fewer. She knew it was partly her own fault for not corresponding with them more often herself; "But there are more of them. You'd think one or two would think to write to me, now I'm on my own," she grumbled to herself.

As she watched the young mothers in the clinic with their babies, the longing for children of her own would sweep through Ellie reminding her that Sarah too had been deprived of marriage and children. She spoke about it to Geraldine, one of her colleagues at the clinic.

"Why should I start to have these longings now at my age? I'm forty-nine, not far off fifty years old. It's ridiculous, even to think of the possibility of conceiving children at my age! Especially with no husband in the offing!"

Geraldine, who was a similar age to Ellie and also single, laughed.

"That's the trouble Ellie, 'our age'. We realise we're more or less past it -we've lost our chance of going down that particular road. Although, Mrs Jenkins gave us all a surprise, when her test proved positive! Expecting again at forty six, when she's a grandmother of three!"

"Well at least she has a husband, which is more than could be said for us," Ellie tried to laugh it off but she didn't feel like laughing. She wanted to hit out at someone, preferably Alex Dobson for disappearing. He'd been her last hope of a husband. She snapped at Geraldine when she reminded Ellie that lots of women were in the same boat, because of the war.

"We shouldn't grumble; at least we've a worthwhile job," Geraldine ended.

"It doesn't make it any easier. That bloody war's got too much to answer for;" Ellie bit her tongue; it wasn't like her to swear.

"I trust that was a factual observation and not an expletive, Sister Elkson,"

Sister Allinson had walked in and was frowning at Ellie.

"A bit of both! I'm sorry Sister but that war—," Ellie was in no mood to be patronised.

"Apology accepted. In fact I fully agree. Nevertheless, we mustn't let it poison the rest of our lives. Now, let me have your reports for today."

Routine took over and Ellie pushed the intrusive longings to the back of her mind, firmly shutting the door on them once again but not before Sister Allinson had registered her colleague's emotional stress.

Eliza Fazakerley talked with her friend, Agnes Little, who was now retired but still actively interested in all around her, especially in connection with her old students from Juniper Ward. Relaxing over a night-cap in Eliza's living room the two friends mulled over the problem of Ellie.

"I think that if Ellie and I go together to Golders Green, she may give me some inkling as to what is unbalancing her mind. Believe me Agnes, something is. It can't be grief alone. You and I have been through bereavement and yet seem quite balanced in our minds."

"Yes, maybe now; but how did we seem in the first throws of bereavement? I remember expecting to find my brother, walking about among the crowds in London, for at least a year after his death."

"You're right. It's not quite eight months since Sarah's death but over ten years since the Great War ended. Instead of improving, Ellie's state of mind seems to be growing even stranger. She suddenly drifts away from whatever we are talking about and acts as if she's entered another dimension."

"But she snaps back when you challenge her?"

"Oh yes, so far; but I'm always afraid that one of these days, she won't."

"I think someone or something, connected with Sarah's death, has recently had some impact on her and this has disturbed her. Is she still in touch with those spiritualist friends?"

"I think she may well be. She deviously fed me some clap-trap about going to hear a speaker on Oriental Mysticism. I think it was to hide something else. She left me rather abruptly, before I could delve further," Eliza started coughing into her handkerchief.

"You're still very congested, Eliza. Has your doctor put you in touch with a specialist? I can recommend a very good one at Bart's."

"Oh, don't worry about my chest, bronchitis is such an old friend I'd be lost without his regular winter visits. My doctor understands my condition and soon puts me to rights. I can't be bothered with specialists and all that palaver, at my age."

Agnes grunted but looked at her friend appraisingly; she hadn't missed the specks of blood on Eliza's handkerchief. "Eliza, there's more than the occasional bout of bronchitis troubling that chest of yours."

"Oh stop fussing, Sister! I'm quite ready to go, Agnes. Dr. Collins, my GP, will keep me comfortable till the time comes. But, I do want to sort Ellie out, before anything happens to me."

The trip with Ellie to Golders Green never came about. Eliza succumbed at last to the tail end of the influenza epidemic. She collapsed in the street, a few days after her talk with Agnes Little. Kind neighbours took her home and put her to bed. Dr Collins arranged for day and night nurses to care for her. Influenza turned to pneumonia but it was six weeks before Eliza died, just as the spring weather arrived.

Ellie, Agnes and the Vicar of St. Stephen's were with Eliza at home when she died, but it was Ellie's hand she reached for near the end, whispering, "all will be well, all manner of things shall be well," before slipping into a pain-relieving sleep which, an hour later, moved gently into death.

"A grand old soldier," the Vicar said quietly, after saying a prayer commending her soul into God's keeping. "Quoting Julian of Norwich as her final words, dear soul. We need that message more than ever nowadays, to trust God that in the end all will be well."

"If a soul is commended into God's keeping, will that soul be safe and content, not wanting to return here?" Ellie asked him.

"Ellie, once in her new life (which is in God's nearer presence and in His safe-keeping,) Eliza, or any other soul, won't need to come back here for anything. We look forward to the time when we'll all go to where she is, when it's our turn to go through death's doorway and home to God."

"I see," Ellie looked at the priest. He seemed an ordinary middle-aged man, a little bald and portly, slightly pedantic in his speech but with a quiet confidence which made her feel calm and rested. She longed to stay near him and soak up some of his peaceful assurance into her own troubled soul, but the practical necessities of Eliza's death had to be attended to and Ellie found herself shaking the Vicar's hand and bidding him farewell.

She walked home, desolate and weary, wishing she'd agreed to go with Sister Juniper to have tea in a café but it would have reminded her too much of her times with Eliza. She was numb with grief.

To compound this, a further flare up of the influenza epidemic meant that all the nursing staff had to work at full stretch and Ellie was unable to attend Eliza's funeral. Now tired and run down, Ellie caught a very mild dose of 'flu. She quickly recovered and was back at work within a week with some of her old energy renewed.

"We must have developed a partial immunity," said Geraldine "it's about time we enjoyed some perks from this job."

CHAPTER 66

Epidemics and Vaccinations

Ellie and her medical colleagues were taken by surprise in the following summer of 1930. London was unexpectedly alerted to the possibility of a smallpox epidemic.

Sister Allinson had called all her staff together and addressed them as if she were a General mustering the troops.

"This has come as a shock to us. Over the last twenty years we have seen a vast decrease in smallpox cases and thought it was dying out altogether in the British Isles owing to the vaccination and health care programmes. There have always been some who have been against vaccination resulting in a few small outbreaks of recent years but these were quickly dealt with and did not spread. However, this outbreak is different and threatens to become a full-scale epidemic, unless we work hard. Parents have become lax about having their children vaccinated simply because smallpox seemed no longer a threat. I want you all to make sure your own vaccination certificates are up to date; you will be exposed to infection on a daily basis. Do I make myself clear, Nurses?"

Those who came regularly to the clinic and most of Ellie's home families had already been vaccinated but others had either been lax or suspicious of the procedure or preferred to 'let nature take its course.'

During that summer, more and more children were diagnosed with smallpox. Panic set in; the majority of the young parents and children hadn't seen smallpox before and when it began to spread among their neighbours and horror stories from grandparents began to circulate, they rushed to the clinic demanding vaccination or even revaccination.

"My Granddad remembers people being taken to special small-pox camps. They were put in tents, 'under canvas' my Granddad called it. I wouldn't mind that!" said one skinny boy of eight, with a shock of red hair and wide green eyes.

His mother cuffed him gently, "You wouldn't like it, if you were sick with the smallpox. Come on now, let nurse vaccinate you, no fussing. There's a queue a mile long behind us."

The next boy bravely rolled up his sleeve saying loudly, "My Dad remembers 'is mate being taken by boat to a hospital ship. He says it was a big gunner in t' Royal Navy before it was made into a place for smallpox. I wouldn't mind going on that ship, if I 'appened to catch smallpox. But I'd rather not catch it, my dad's mate died of it."

"I remember those ships," said Nurse Geraldine to Ellie, as they took a well-earned tea break.

They'd worked as smoothly as a conveyor belt for two hours, taking it in turns, one vaccinating while the other prepared the next dose, so no time was wasted between children.

"The ships were moored off Greenwich," Geraldine reminisced. "I nursed there for a few months. We lived in a smaller frigate, the 'Endymion', moored between the 'Atlas', a ninety gunner, which was for men patients only and a cross channel ferry boat the 'Castalia'. It needed getting used to, I can tell you. A bit grim on the 'Atlas' but well-equipped. We had speaking tubes to contact the other wards and a lift between decks. Three ordinary wards and six small isolation wards and a mortuary, plus bathrooms and cooking facilities. We had a lot of fatalities and they all died separated from their loved ones, it was heart-breaking. Thank goodness they went on to build permanent isolation hospitals on shore at Dartford."

"The 'Longreach,' the 'Orchard' and then the 'Joyce Green'! I remember all the fuss about the Longreach. There was some delay in changing it from temporary to permanent structures. They had access to the river 'cause they used the paddle steamers to bring the infected patients from London. The 'Joyce Green' is further inland. I'm sure they still use the river ambulance to take patients as far as Longreach and then transport them overland."

"Yes, but not for much longer. It's rumoured they plan to close all but the 'Joyce Green' down next year and stop using the river route as roads and motor transport are much faster nowadays. The 'Joyce Green' has come into its own again with this epidemic."

They went back on duty just as a four year old girl in the queue was violently sick. It was nearly her turn, so Ellie directed Geraldine to steer the rest of the queue away from the child and set up the vaccination equipment in a different part of the room. Geraldine continued vaccinating with one of the two junior nurses on duty while Ellie helped the other young nurse deal with the very sick child.

"What's your little girl's name?" Ellie asked the distraught mother.

"Trudy, Trudy Bold. She was a bit out of sorts this morning, wouldn't eat her breakfast and was that niggly; I thought I'd never get her here. She's our only one, nurse. She'll be alright, won't she?"

"We hope so, Mrs Bold," said Ellie and sent the distraught mother to the top of the queue, to have immediate vaccination. "Just in case, Mrs Bold. Now, we'll sort out your little girl. You have your vaccination and then you'll be able to be with her."

"My back hurts," sobbed Trudy as she finished vomiting and tried to curl up on the floor. An orderly came in with a bucket of sand and disinfectant and the two nurses lifted the child and took her to an isolation room where Ellie ascertained that Trudy had a high fever and the beginnings of a rash.

"Early signs of smallpox!" Ellie declared, "But we can't be certain, so many other childhood diseases start similarly."

They made the child comfortable and sent for the doctor on duty. Dr. Jordan, a sensible woman in her thirties, examined the child and then spoke decisively. "I think we must assume that this is smallpox and arrange for Trudy to go to the 'Joyce Green' immediately. She needs to have her vaccination first. It will help her fight the smallpox if she does have it and if she hasn't it will protect her from infection in the hospital. We've caught it early. Hopefully she'll pull through."

There were more, similar cases, over the days and weeks following, of children and adults showed the first symptoms of smallpox. Happily, the majority of them recovered within a few weeks with no side effects. The medical authorities announced that the strain of smallpox was 'variola minor', a milder form which had evolved due to the mass introduction of vaccination over the preceding twenty years. The stronger strain, 'Variola major,' which had been prevalent in the past, had a death rate of five to forty per cent. This present, weaker strain had a death rate of only nought point one to two per cent.

There were some fatalities. Ellie, going about the district visiting family homes witnessed several infant deaths over the following months. Each time she witnessed a child's death, Ellie searched for ways of coping with the anguish. She found herself again and again turning from theosophy to the church community at St. Stephens and the comforting presence of the priest who had been with her at Eliza's death. She never approached him but would creep in at the back during a service and listen to his voice intoning the words of faith. She didn't allow herself to delve deeper; she didn't want to break the spell his words wove around her. She had a fear that if she uncovered his feet of clay, she might find his words untrue and make-believe. She knew Eliza would have made her see sense and taken her to talk with the man, but Eliza wasn't there anymore.

Confused by her own thoughts, Ellie turned back to her theosophy acquaintances and similar groups and searched again for answers among their teachings. She moved backwards and forwards between church and theosophy until a strange mix of mystical notions were floating around in her mind, none of which she could grasp satisfactorily.

1930 became 1931 and then 1932. During those years Ellie and her colleagues dealt with continuing outbreaks of smallpox and measles. The measles epidemics were bad for the younger children and babies, there was no known cure and the disease had to take its course. It needed careful nursing to avoid the worst side effects of blindness and respiratory problems. The community nurses taught mothers how to shield their sick children's eyes from the light and to give steam inhalations. Most important was how to keep a hygienic sick room. Ignorance exacerbated the spread of disease and Ellie encouraged older brothers and sisters, in her families, to join local branches of the St. John's Ambulance Brigade where they would be taught home-nursing and how to keep fit and healthy bodies, as well as first aid.

"You would smile to see me pushing the Brigade so hard, Edwin," she wrote to her brother, "but, I can see what vital, practical knowledge it spreads."

"Jack and Becky Nelson will be cheering you on, Ellie! We have a lot of fun in the brigade as well as the serious stuff, friendship and team work—keep up the promotion!"

There was a particularly bad measles outbreak in the summer of 1932 and Ellie took on extra duties. She'd built close relationships with many of the families she dealt with and some of the children she almost regarded as her own.

One of these was the three month old baby of Mrs Brierley, a grandmother who, at forty years old, had given birth to her seventh child. In April 1932, she was delivered of a small but perfectly formed baby boy. She'd had a fairly easy birth but was left weary and lethargic, her once strong body battered and worn by years of child bearing and hard physical work.

"I never felt like this after the others," she'd moaned, when her son was a week old, "and this little 'un doesn't seem to thrive like them. He turns away from my breast and doesn't know what to do with a bottle. He doesn't seem to cotton-on how to suck. He's losing weight, not putting it on like he should. Can you 'elp the little tyke, Sister?"

This situation was just what Ellie had been trained for and she took charge with alacrity. The baby was baptised Job, but the family called him Jobo. With meticulous care Ellie worked out the suitable strength of Dr. Truby King's baby- milk formula for Jobo. She fed it to him, a few drops at a time, from a dropper fixed to his bottle. As soon as he was used to the taste, she put a rubber teat over her finger and dipped it into the formula, encouraging him to suck it off the teat. From there he progressed to sucking the baby milk through the teat from a bottle. Slowly Jobo gained weight. He was never eager to feed and didn't cry when he was hungry but Ellie fed him by the clock and delighted in seeing him come alive. She trained one of his older sisters to feed him in the same way and visited the Brierley's home three or four times a day, even when she was off-duty. She began to feel for little Jobo as if he was her own son. By the end of July, Jobo was definitely showing signs of becoming a healthy six month old but hadn't quite caught up on the ground he'd lost.

Then three months later, in early September, Jobo's ten year old sister, Carrie, rushed into the clinic.

"Please Sister Elkson, can you come? Little Jobo and mi Mam have been taken badly. I've only just got home from school and found them; Mam's making no sense and can't do nothing."

It was half past four and Ellie had been about to set off on her late afternoon visits. She went immediately with Carrie, to the Brierley's home.

As soon as she saw Jobo and his mother, she realised it was small-pox. Whether it was the milder strain or the strong one she couldn't tell.

"I thought the epidemic was over ages ago," cried young Carrie.

"Hopefully it is but there will still be the odd case popping up from time to time," Ellie told the girl and sent her away, with an encouraging smile, to bring the doctor.

Mrs Brierley was too sick to be of any help. Despite everything they tried, little Jobo died an hour after Ellie had arrived; jerking his way into the next world from Ellie's arms, not strong enough to fight against the early stages of the disease. Jobo's body had to be taken away quickly for cremation, as a precaution against the infection spreading throughout the family. Mrs Brierley had been taken to the Joyce Green Hospital, unaware of her baby's death. Other adult members of the family came, to take charge of the younger

Brierley's. These new adults were strangers to Ellie and to them she was just a nurse who had simply done her expected work with their sick ones. After checking that they had all been vaccinated, Ellie took her leave of the family and walked home.

If Ellie had been at the clinic she would have had to change from her uniform and leave it to be sterilized. As it was, she buttoned her coat and walked home along back streets, avoiding meeting people.

Once home in Redcliffe Street she switched on the newly installed water heater and set a match to the fire which Kitty had laid ready. After scrubbing her hands with carbolic soap and cold water she boiled the kettle and brewed tea. Kitty had laid out a tray, for her to come home to, with milk and sugar, cup and saucer and a covered plate hiding a generous slice of raison cake and a lump of cheese. Ellie had eaten nothing since breakfast and it was now past six o'clock. She drank the hot tea and nibbled at the cheese and cake, her appetite increasing with the savoury tang of cheese against the sweet juiciness of raisins.

As soon as there was enough hot water for a bath, she stripped off her clothes and bundled them into an old laundry bag, to take to the clinic next day. She poured a good cupful of disinfectant into the bath water, then stepped gingerly in and lay down. It was so good to feel the heat of the water lapping over her aching body. Leaning back she closed her eyes and lost herself in nothingness. The water began to cool and sighing she picked up the soap and loofa and scrubbed every bit of her body- no germ would escape her thoroughness. She let out the bath water and stood to sponge herself down with cold water, fresh from the tap. Shivering she took a large towel and rubbed herself vigorously, till her skin tingled. Gently massaging a niggling pain in her lower back Ellie wandered into the bedroom. Her flannel nightgown lay folded on the turned down corner of the sheet – (Kitty again; bless her). A covered glass of cool, boiled water was on her bedside table and Ellie took a long drink before climbing between the smooth sheets. Pulling the blanket and eiderdown over her weary body, she settled down to sleep.

Not once, since leaving the Brierley's home, had she allowed herself to think of baby Jobo and what had happened in that house. She'd withdrawn her mind from it and concentrated on the practicalities of walking home, eating, drinking and cleansing herself. The other home visits, on her list for that day, had been crowded out of her memory. Now, when sleep came, the guard slipped from her mind and all her disturbing feelings and introspections of the last few months rushed together in the mish-mash of nightmare.

First she thought she saw Alex Dobson, waving to her from a long way off. He had on a white doctor's coat and a stethoscope round his neck and was pointing urgently to something in front of him mouthing silent words. Slowly he faded away and what he'd been pointing to became clearer. In a dark landscape along a road white with fallen snow, a group of small creatures was moving towards her. Ellie could hear the wind moaning and see shining, icy particles floating around the tiny beings which were the colour and form of clear water but held in recognisable shapes by a transparent outer skin which stretched and flowed around them, as they drifted along in the ice- laden wind. Vaporous, silvery forms, reminiscent of angels, flew around and above them shepherding them along. As they came nearer, they reminded Ellie of unformed babies in their foetal mould. In her dream Ellie realised she was sitting in Sarah's chair, by the window in Redcliffe Street. Looking out she saw that the snow-white road led straight to her house. The leading one of the strange foetal beings floated right up to the window and pressed against it trying to get in. She stared into strange milky- blue baby eyes,

"Jobo?" she whispered.

Then, she understood. These must be spirit babies.

Ellie's deranged thoughts dredged up memories of all the babies she'd seen die, all the ones she had been helpless to save and she imagined the amorphous forms swimming towards her being the spirits of these babes. She heard their soft voices calling and whispering to her,

"Help us to come back, help us to be re- born, you can give us birth. Let us in. Let us inside you."

Behind their voices came another, "I can help you with this Ellie, let me help you," they were the deeper drawling tone tones of Dr Alex Dobson, "My little Ellie. Please, let me in too."

A great yearning pain grew in Ellie's womb. The longing to give birth, as well as the grief for these dead children and for Alex, gripped her. So real was the pain that Ellie woke, moaning and clutching at herself. She sat up feeling a warm stream coming from her and throwing off the bed clothes discovered she had a heavy flow of menstrual blood. This was nothing new, she had reached the early stages of her menopause and her monthly periods had become haywire in their timing. Sometimes the flow of blood was scanty and at other times, such as this, it was heavy and debilitating. She clambered out of bed and sorted herself out, feeling sick from her nightmare and from pain and the loss of fluids. It was quarter to six. Ellie washed and dressed, packing herself with protective pads, hoping that the flooding would quickly subside. She made tea and took two aspirin to ease the dragging pain. As the tea and medicine helped her to relax she sat in her chair by the cold embers of the fire and began to cry, silent, hopeless tears that dripped unheeded down her face. She felt entirely alone.

"I'm going mad and I've no-one I can turn to," she spoke aloud "who would ever understand what I saw in my dream. Were they spirits, trying to make contact from the other side, or were they just images formed from my own sick mind? Why couldn't it have been Sarah trying to come to me? She wasn't there at all. Of course I helped her to be born. She didn't die as a baby as those poor creatures had. Alex was there. Does that mean he's passed over? I still don't know if he's dead or alive."

Ellie's thoughts wandered randomly as each thought triggered another. She wondered about calling Amelia but thought her old acquaintance would try to persuade her to go to Mrs Dempster.

Kitty Fielding arrived for work and was startled by the whiteness of Ellie's face and the deep shadows under her eyes.

"Pardon my saying so, Sister Elkson, but you don't look fit for work today. I can telephone the clinic for you. Why don't I make you some breakfast and then you go back to bed for a bit."

At first Ellie looked at Kitty as if she didn't recognise her, then she answered the girl;

"I'm not on duty this morning. I had a bad night, Kitty, I just need to rest."

She refused breakfast but allowed Kitty to relight the fire and continued to sit in front of it, staring blankly into the flames until lunch time, moving only to use the bathroom or to drink the boiled water she asked Kitty to bring her. Twice she drifted into sleep but the nightmares started to return and she cried out in such a way that Kitty was frightened and shook her awake. At twelve o'clock Kitty decided she would go and bring Beattie Mason. If anyone could draw Ellie out of herself, it would surely be her.

"I'm just taking your sheets home for washing. I'll be back in half an hour," she called as she let herself out of the back door.

CHAPTER 67

Mrs Dempster re-appears.

Ellie listened to Kitty leaving the house and reassessed her situation. She felt rested and was relieved that her bleeding had lessened. She looked at the calendar on the wall, it was 22nd of September, the anniversary of Sarah's death. She must visit the crematorium.

Ellie decided to leave the house quickly, before Kitty came back. She shivered as she left the fireside. For September the weather was certainly cool but this coldness seemed to come from inside her. She buttoned on her thick winter coat and pulled on her black felt hat, tugging the brim firmly down, to shadow her face. Then she gathered a few essentials into her handbag and left the house.

It had been raining all morning, a thin miserable drizzle but when Ellie stepped outside the rain had stopped and the air smelled sweet. Ellie noticed this especially, when she arrived at Golders Green and walked through the gates of the crematorium. Both her body and her spirits seemed to lighten as she made her way to the garden of remembrance and a slow smile crept over her face as she walked at a leisurely pace under the dripping trees beside rose beds still in full bloom from the late summer flowering. Beneath the trees water-drops gleamed in the sunlight on the petals of bright blue gentians and deep yellow oxalis. A faint rainbow spread across the sky and Ellie knew she was in a hair's breadth of meeting Sarah. She felt her sister to be walking so close beside her that she stretched out her hand almost expecting to touch Sarah's. Ellie wanted these moments to go on and on, the peace was tangible, nothing must disturb it. Wiping the rain from a bench, she sat for a while, feeling the sun on her face. Before long a cloud passed overhead and the rain began again. Ellie got up and moved under the shelter of the trees.

In the distance, walking towards her, she saw two figures. They were obviously women, wrapped in long coats, their old-fashioned, large-brimmed hats swathed in scarves, against the rain.

For a moment, Ellie thought one of the figures was her old friend, Eliza. She quickened her step towards them in a happy dream-like state of expectation. Before she could meet them, the woman, who she thought was Eliza, stopped, spoke with her companion and then walked away down a side avenue, vanishing from view. The other woman walked on towards Ellie. As she neared her Ellie felt a sudden chill; Sarah's presence went and Ellie found herself face to face with Mrs Dempster. The woman stretched her arms towards Ellie and cried out:

"My dear, Miss Elkson, Ellie- surely I may call you by your first name. I feel, through dear Sarah, that I know you quite intimately."

"You never met my sister, Mrs Dempster."

"Oh but my dear, I've tried, so many times, to tell you that Sarah has come to me, since she passed over. She's come each year on her birthday and on your birthday and always on the anniversary of her death. The dear girl begged me to get in touch with you. She has something very important to communicate to you, through me. Indeed, she must be very near to us at this moment, I can sense her aura, Ellie. We must be still and wait."

The horrid woman took hold of Ellie's arm and held it in a firm grip. Her face was hooded and eager, like a vulture sure of its next meal. Ellie was sickened. Mrs Dempster could never experience Sarah's calming presence in the way that she had just done.

"Let go of my arm! My sister doesn't need to contact me through you. She will come to me directly, if she needs to, leave her alone and stop poisoning her memory."

"You know that's not true, dear. You are not a medium. Sarah has already made it clear to me and to my spirit guides, that she trusts me and will make contact at our next séance, if you promise to be there."

491

Ellie was finding it difficult to breathe properly, "I wouldn't be seen dead at your séances, Mrs Dempster. Let go of my arm this minute," she tried to shake herself free of the medium's grasp but Mrs Dempster just hung on to her more tightly.

"My dear, why do you think we have met like this today, out of the blue? Is it not rather strange? I believe your sister prompted me to come here today, so that I could speak to you alone. I don't usually walk in the grounds of Golders Green crematorium; it's a long way from where I live. I had a premonition that I would meet you here today and so I came, alone. I believe your sister wants you to know that she forgives you, for something you did to her."

"But you didn't come alone! I saw you walking with another woman and talking with her. You both stopped just where that avenue joins the main path," Ellie pointed to where she had seen them, "then she left you walked down the avenue."

The look in Mrs Dempster's eyes turned cunning, "You are mistaken my dear. I was quite alone until I met you. What did this woman look like?"

"An older lady in a long coat similar to yours and a wide-brimmed blue hat swathed in a purple scarf. I remember the colours because my friend, Eliza, often wore bright blues and purples and for a moment I thought it was her. Of course it couldn't have been. She died over two years ago."

Such information was a gift to the medium.

"Now I begin to understand. The spirits must have used your friend Eliza to prompt me to come here. She appeared to you just now, so that you would feel more comfortable in accepting my message from the spirit world."

Ellie was dumbfounded. This woman was using her friendship with Eliza for her own ends. She didn't, for one minute, believe Eliza's spirit had appeared - it had been a flesh and blood woman. Or had it? Quite suddenly Ellie became unsure of anything except the words spoken in Mrs Dempster's sickly-sweet tones.

"I believe your sister knows how guilty you still feel about the things you did to her and how you delayed her hospital treatment in order to practise your own methods on her. I think she wants to tell you that she forgives you and that she understands why you did it. She knows you didn't mean to hurt her in the way you did."

Ellie thought she would faint. All the horrible fears and guilt she had felt about Sarah's death came sweeping over her. She pushed Mrs Dempster away with all her might. The woman stumbled, her arms flailing as she lost her balance and fell to her knees, her long coat and skirt tangled around her feet. She crawled towards a bench as Ellie turned and left. As she hurried towards the crematorium entrance Ellie could hear the angry voice of the medium crying after her.

"You are a wicked woman, Ellie Elkson, believe me the spirits don't like it, they'll find a way to punish you, mark my words."

Mrs Dempster's parting words filled Ellie with a sense of foreboding, making her quicken her footsteps to escape from the unnerving situation. She stumbled out of the crematorium gates and hurried to the underground station. Not wanting to go home, she took a ticket to Tottenham Court Road and from there began to walk the London streets, with no particular destination in mind.

"If I keep walking I shall be alright. I've always been a good walker. Mother said I was a good walker. I could always keep going longer than the others, through the fields, up into the woods onto the moors with no need of a rest, just walking, walking, walking the streets of London," Ellie gave a small giggle, "who would have thought that little Ellie Elkson from Aspen Lane, Hartsbeck, would know the streets of London as well as her own Lancashire moors. Better not to think at all."

Ellie stared down at the grey paving stones begrimed with oily dust and bits of straw, mixed with treadings of horse muck. Rain mingled with the debris, mulching it into a slippery brown film that coated the soles of her boots and squelched grittily. Her hand-bag banged against her knees, its handle drooping loosely from her fingers. Rain water gathered in her hat-brim and dribbled down, under her coat collar.

She walked on, not caring where she went. The cold crept beneath her clothes, around her waist and up to her shoulders. Her arms and legs turned heavy and numb, the discomfort acting as a welcome barrier to her thoughts.

Looking up at last she saw, across the street, the huge door of Westminster Abbey. School history lessons, about taking sanctuary in the Abbey, played over in her memory and directed her footsteps. Her breathing was urgent as she quickened her steps but on entering the cool shadows of the great building, her breath came more easily and her tensed muscles relaxed. Dwarfed to insignificance by the surroundings, Ellie crept anonymously along the shadowed side aisles until she entered the Abbey cloisters and sat down on a stone bench against the wall. She remembered that Cousin Hugh's friend, Ian Howarth, who had been present at Sarah's funeral, was the Precentor at the Abbey and had rooms somewhere in the precincts. If anybody asked her what she was doing, she would mention his name and ask to see him. In the meantime she just sat, cold and still, not thinking, not moving, neither sad nor happy but dulled and utterly weary.

Through the arches on the opposite side of the cloister she watched the rain falling steadily onto an open, grassed quadrangle. An elderly verger, important in his black gown, walked past her into the main building. A few minutes later he returned and spoke to her.

"I hope I'm not disturbing you, Ma'am but evensong will be sung in the Abbey in ten minutes time. Would you care to attend the service? The music is very beautiful and uplifting – I always find it so," the old gentleman smiled respectfully. Hypnotised by his persuasive manner, Ellie followed him into the Abbey where he placed her in a seat at the back of the choir stalls. About a dozen other people were there already, visitors like herself. A group of young women in dark winter coats and felt cloche hats were making their way, self- consciously, to a row of empty seats. They were accompanied by three purposeful, middle aged ladies.

"'Girls' Friendly Society' from the North, having a week in London. It's their autumn conference," her guide had whispered as he bowed her to her place. The low murmur of the young women's voices reached Ellie across the choir stalls – comfortable, familiar Lancashire accents; sounds of home. Sarah had been a member of the 'Girls' Friendly Society' in Hartsbeck and Ellie searched their faces, half expecting to find her sister among them.

A distant rhythmic patter of feet announced the procession of the choir and clergy. The small congregation fell silent. Before entering the chancel, the procession stopped. A lone voice, high and clear, soared like an arrow, honed and balanced, straight upwards through the cold Cathedral air to hit the rafters and dispel in a million vibrations. Harmony upon harmony was added as other voices surrounded and carried that first solo melody, tossing it upwards again and again until the whole choir was one kaleidoscope of sound. Ellie closed her eyes and stepped inside the music, her heart beat fast and she gasped for breath. Tears ran silently down her cheeks, just as they had the night previously. The introit music ended and she fished for a hanky to mop her runny nose as the choir, followed by two robed clergymen, entered their stalls.

Ellie hardly noticed that it was Canon Ian Howarth leading the service of evensong. The earlier effect of the music had lifted her to such a high state of euphoria that she needed time to come slowly back to earth. The words of the liturgy spilled softly over her. Certain sentences stood out and registered more clearly to her consciousness.

"Dearly beloved————"

"To the Lord our God belong mercies and forgivenesses. If we say that we have no sin, we deceive ourselves and the truth is not in us: but if we confess our sins, He is faithful and just to forgive us our sins and to cleanse us from all unrighteousness."

"Our Father, who art in Heaven—."

The words of the Lord's Prayer surrounded Ellie like her mother's arms in childhood.

The Magnificat, Mary's song, rang out with its message of good news for the poor and needy.

"...He hath scattered the proud in their conceit. He hath put down the mighty from their seat and exalted the humble and meek. He hath filled the hungry with good things and the rich he hath sent empty away."

Ellie groaned inwardly, hit by a futile sense of failure at the inadequate fulfilment of her own vision of helping the needy. When the choir sang the words from the Nunc Dimittis, the song of the old man Simeon; "Lord, now let thy servant depart in peace," Ellie wished she could echo his request.

The final blessing was given and the service finished. Ellie felt drained of energy. The choir processed out with the clergy but she didn't stand as did the 'Girls' Friendly Society' and other members of the congregation. She didn't move when the others walked slowly away, gazing about them as they drifted into the main body of the Abbey. One or two glanced curiously at her but she didn't care.

"Let them stare," she thought, "I'm only another gargoyle; a bit of ridicule, made to drain society of its unwanted waste."

Desolation wrapped around her like a thick cloak and she sank into it, shutting everything else out. She curled sideways on the seat and bent her head low with a peculiar sense of safety, as if she had reached the bottom, after a long, downwards fall into darkness.

CHAPTER 68

Rescue in the Abbey

"Excuse me Miss, we'll be locking up the Abbey in a few minutes." Ellie's will-power was paralysed. She made no reply to the verger's statement and drew further into herself. She was a tortoise in its shell and hoped the old man would leave her alone. She heard his steps moving away down the aisle, then a mutter of voices and two sets of footsteps returning, one quicker and firmer than the verger's. A more authoritative voice spoke to her:

"Now, my dear. It really is time you went home. You'll find it very cold and dark in here, when we turn out the lights and lock up."

Ellie lifted her head, feeling the solid kindness of the man and recognised Ian Howarth, leaning over her.

"Why it's Ellie, Ellie Elkson. Ellie, my dear, whatever is the matter?"

Tears welled again in Ellie's eyes and poured down her face, part of her knew what was happening but another part of her refused to respond properly.

"Please, Ellie, tell me what's wrong," Ian sat down beside her and waited.

"I don't know. I'm very, very tired. I just want to stay here. Please leave me here, let me stay. I don't mind the dark or the cold."

"No, Ellie! You're coming with me. My rooms are nearby and my wife will have a warm fire going and tea ready. Come along now, Hugh would never forgive me if I left you here – I'd probably lose my job as well!"

Ian and the verger put a hand under each of her arms and pulled her to her feet. She leant heavily on them as they forced her to walk between them into the cloisters. They came to an arched wooden door with Ian's name engraved on it. Ian let go of her arm to open the door and blackness engulfed Ellie and she slid to the floor.

When she came to, Ellie found herself seated in a large, wing-backed chair, in front of a brightly- burning coal fire. She could feel the heat on her chilled legs and feet but the rest of her body was shivering. A woman was kneeling beside the chair, busily chaffing Ellie's icy cold fingers in her own small, warm ones.

"I'm Pauline, Ian Haworth's wife. You're in our home, Ellie."

Ian came into the room with two blankets, one he spread over Ellie's knees, the other around her shoulders. As Ellie warmed up, she felt an urgent need for the lavatory and tried to rise from the chair, Hugh put out a restraining hand,

"You're alright, Ellie; just stay still and get warm," he commanded.

His wife was more astute, "What is it Ellie, do you need something?"

"I need to use the lavatory," Ellie blushed, "but my legs won't hold me up."

"Hugh, you go and make a pot of tea in the kitchen. I'll fetch the bedpan we had for your mother. Don't come back in, till I call you."

Without turning a hair, Pauline sorted Ellie out and made her comfortable.

"You've had quite a heavy bleed Ellie, that might be why you fainted," she remarked as she matter-of-factly brought Ellie clean pads and removed the soiled ones."

"Are you a nurse?" whispered Ellie, recognising her competence.

"No," Pauline laughed "but I looked after Ian's mother. She was in a wheel chair during her last few years and I had to do most things for her. I'll go and tell Ian that he can come back in, now all is decent."

Ellie leant back and closed her eyes; the desolation wasn't far away but she felt she'd been temporarily drawn away from it, into a place of warmth and light.

Pauline went into the kitchen and closed the door. She faced Ian.

"She's obviously not fit to go back to her own home, Ian. We really must call a doctor. Geoffrey Hennessey is just round the corner. I'm sure he'll come."

"You're right. I'll go for him now," Ian went into the hallway for his coat. "Maybe she's had some kind of shock. A bad shock could have brought all her tragic memories of the past back with a vengeance. See if she'll take some of that hot tea I've made and put plenty of sugar in it."

"Good idea," replied Pauline as she turned up her face for her husband's kiss. They were a good team and over their twenty years of marriage had ministered together to people in all kinds of circumstances.

Ellie was drowsy but awake enough to sip the hot sweet tea. Pauline was relieved that the stark whiteness of her guest's face had softened to a creamier pallor. Rescuing the tea-cup from Ellie's slackening grip, she let her sleep and then, with a watchful eye, Pauline settled down in the chair opposite, to wait for Ian and the doctor.

Dr. Geoffrey Hennessy bounced into the room ahead of Ian. A sensible, jolly man, in his late forties, he regarded illness as an everyday occurrence that needed quick initial recognition followed by quick resolution, wherever possible. His experience was vast. He'd travelled the Far and Middle East, in pursuance of his profession and had developed an assured diagnostic eye. He valued the findings of both ancient and modern medicine.

Ian had filled the doctor in with what he knew of Ellie's background including the death of her sister. Ellie woke at the touch of Dr. Hennessy's hand on hers and the sound of his slightly high-pitched but commanding voice. She opened her eyes, sharp and inquiring and the doctor noticed how heavy the lids seemed and how dark the rings around them. He noted the sinewy, work-worn hands, the nails cut short and smooth and realised this was no over-imaginative, love-starved spinster but a strong, weary woman, who had worked hard all

499

her life and seen much suffering. Her pulse was weak and fluttery and his experienced eye noted signs of anaemia.

"When did you last eat, Miss Elkson?" he asked.

Ellie stared at him, not answering. She needed to focus properly on who he was and why he was questioning her.

"Who are you?" she managed to croak at last.

"I apologise. My name is Dr Geoffrey Hennessy. Your friend, the Reverend Ian Howarth, asked me to come. You were taken ill in the Abbey and he brought you back here, to his home."

"Oh," was all Ellie could muster.

"Miss Elkson is a professional Nursing Sister," Ian quickly interposed.

"In that case Sister Elkson. You will know that the questions I'm going to ask you are important. When did you last eat and can you remember what food you ate?"

Painstakingly he unravelled Ellie's eating habits, discovering not only her regular water fasts but that over the last few weeks she had been existing mainly on tea and toast and Kitty's slices of cake and cheese, with the occasional apple. Ellie too was shocked, when she realised how she'd neglected her diet. The doctor delved deeper in order to find out why eating had recently become such a low priority in her life. Ellie found herself speaking of her compulsive visits to Golders Green Crematorium in between her working hours; of her constant search for Sarah in between coping with the smallpox epidemic and the death of baby Jobo being the final straw.

At last Dr. Hennessy stood up and gave his verdict.

"Well, Sister Elkson. You are in full possession of your mental faculties, even though you were a little hazy to begin with. However, you are exhausted both in your mind and your body and neither are functioning well in this state. Initially, I advise absolute rest for at least six weeks and suggest you go into a reputable nursing home. While you are there, the medical staff will assess you to see if you need further treatment in a more specialist environment."

"You mean a mental hospital," stated Ellie sharply.

"Possibly, we shall wait and see. That may not be necessary. Rest in a Nursing Home first. I suggest that, this evening, you allow me to take you to a very good one I know. It's not very far from here. Before you ask, it is small and homely, run by well qualified staff and very affordable but don't worry about cost. They have a policy of always having some free places available."

Ellie lent forward in her chair, utterly defeated, "Do as you want with me," she muttered.

"My dear Sister Elkson, it's hard for any of us, in the medical profession, to accept the role of patient but while you are so unwell, you must trust yourself to us - your professional colleagues. I assure you, we'll do the very best we can for such a long serving member of our profession as you obviously are."

Ellie was taken by surprise at his words; they made her feel as if she mattered. She was Sister Elkson, long serving nurse, who didn't just need help but actually deserved it.

"Thank you doctor," she said and bowed her head in assent.

Dr. Hennessy made some telephone calls and all was soon arranged. Ellie submitted to being helped to the doctor's car and tucked warmly in the back seat with blankets. Pauline was to travel with them to the nursing home but before getting into the car, she took the doctor on one side and told him of the evidence of the heavy bleed Ellie must have had earlier that day. He nodded,

"I thought something like that may be happening to her. She's of that age. Thank you Pauline, you really should have been a nurse you know," and he patted her arm affectionately.

He turned back to Ian, "Ian, you say you are a family friend. Would you be so kind as to contact Miss Elkson's nearest relatives. They should know what's happening to her and it will help us to know what kind of care can be afforded."

CHAPTER 69

The Clergy in action.

As the car left the abbey precincts, Ian was already telephoning his friend Hugh Nowell, Ellie's cousin in Estwick. Thankfully, Hugh was at home. He was enjoying an early evening meal with his family after a fraught day, which had involved teaching at the village school; a farmer's funeral; an emergency call to the hospital and a controversial meeting with the churchwardens and the Archdeacon. He was looking forward to a relaxing hour or two of wood-turning and carpentry, with a group of boys from the village, once his own little ones were in bed. A resigned look came over his face when the telephone rang. His wife, Margaret, sprang to answer it, in protective mode. Ian, as a fellow clergyman recognised the exasperation in Margaret's voice. He knew she'd be ready to fend off the caller, if possible, to allow her husband a peaceful hour to eat with his family.

"Hello, Margaret, Ian Howarth from London here. Sorry to disturb you at tea time but it's urgent family business. Hugh's cousin, Ellie Elkson, has been taken ill and I need to speak to Hugh as soon as possible."

"Oh dear! I'll call Hugh right away, Ian. We were just having high tea, so he's here for once," She called her husband to the phone.

Ian quickly explained the situation to Hugh and obtained the details of how to get in touch with Ellie's brothers and her mother,

"You'd better explain it to them yourself, as you know the details first hand. Tell them I'll give them a ring later and see what I can do to help. Keep me posted if things get more serious, Ian, and thanks for all you and Pauline have already done. Poor Ellie, she always seemed the strongest of any of us."

"I think there's something else going on in the background. Whatever it is it's getting in the way of her normal resilience. Whether it's spiritual, or physical, or a mixture of both, I'm not sure. We don't realise how delicately we're balanced, till something tips the sails and over we go."

"Let's hope this doctor of yours can help. We must both keep Ellie in our prayers, Ian."

"That's a definite, Hugh. Now, I'd better ring George first, if I ring Stephen I might get his mother and I think it better if her sons tell her the news."

"Good thinking, Ian. I'll speak to you later—many thanks, again. Goodbye."

"God bless you, Hugh. My love to Margaret and the children."

George too was at home. He'd retreated to his study, with his pipe and a glass of whisky. He'd thankfully shut the door on the hub-bub of Rebecca preparing for her Girl Guide meeting and Hannah putting the two youngest to bed, helped by the latest young Irish girl she was training to go into service. Tom had shut himself in his bedroom with his homework.

George was sitting in the wing-backed chair by his study fire and cogitating over an awkward legal case which he'd been presented with that day. He sighed with annoyance, when the phone rang.

"Yes! George Elkson here."

"George. It's Ian Howarth; I was once a curate in Hartsbeck. You remember me? I'm your Cousin Hugh's friend and was with you at Sarah's funeral."

"Yes, of course I remember you. You're at Westminster Abbey. How are you? Is everything alright?"

"I'm well, thank you, but I'm afraid your older sister, Ellie, has been taken ill and the doctor has asked me to contact you."

"Ellie? Ill? Is it serious? I suppose it must be, if you're contacting us. It's not smallpox is it? Who is this doctor you mention? What happened to her? Where is she now?" George was firing questions as he would to a defendant but his insides had turned to water. He realised he was gripping the arms of his chair fiercely, daring some new tragedy to hit their family.

"She became unwell, after evensong in the Abbey, this afternoon. The verger and I helped her to my accommodation in the precincts but she collapsed on arrival. My wife and I brought her round and then sent for Dr. Hennessy, who lives nearby. He's an old friend of ours and a very reputable general physician. He believes that Ellie is suffering some kind of nervous collapse. He's admitted her into a nursing home for tonight and recommends at least six weeks complete rest there, or somewhere similar, depending on what she can afford. It's possible she may need further treatment, in a specialist hospital for mental illness but that's still to be decided."

"Good Heavens! It's strange she should be at evensong in the Abbey. Not like her at all."

"I think she'd wandered in out of the rain. It seems she'd had some kind of shock and had been walking the streets in a confused state, afterwards."

"One of us will come up to London straight away. If Ellie needs to be in a mental hospital, I'd rather it was nearer Hartsbeck, where we can keep an eye on her." George's mind flew back to his younger sister, Sarah, sick and dying so far away from home.

"It sounds impertinent, George, but do you know Ellie's financial state? The Nursing Home won't charge her for tonight and possibly not for another day or so, according to Dr. Hennessy. He did say the fees are not exorbitant but that it would depend on how much she could afford and how long before further treatment could be arranged."

"There's no problem there; Ellie has some savings and a little inherited money. Apart from that we, as a family, can afford to pay for further treatment. I'll look into the costs of good psychiatric hospitals and nursing homes in the north, straight away; I've contacts through my profession who will probably be available this evening. Now, Ian, please tell me the address and telephone number of the nursing home where my sister is and Dr. Hennessey's number as well. I must contact them myself."

George sounded cold and clinical but Ian detected the typical lawyer's fight for steely control. The clergyman in him longed to offer God's blessing but he was well aware of George's negative ideas about religious faith. He tried to give what comfort he could;

"I realise how very worrying this must be for you, George. We'll continue to do all we can for Ellie, at this end."

"Thank you, you're very kind. I'll be in touch with you again, as soon as I've made some arrangements." There was a click as George disconnected the call.

CHAPTER 70

The Reverend Ian's frustration

Inwardly, Ian, the scholarly Precentor, seethed with frustration at not being able to share with George the comfort of his faith. He was filled with anger at the naïve, unbending mind-set of clergy who mistakenly saw science as an enemy of Christianity and turned men like George away from the Church.

For Ian and most of his colleagues, science enhanced and complemented, rather than threatened or contradicted their faith.

"What's George Elkson said to rattle you so much?" queried Pauline, noting the angry flush on her husband's cheeks when he came back into their sitting room.

"Oh, it's not what he said, except that he's strung up tight enough to break. It's what I couldn't say, to him. He left the Church years ago, because of an argument with some narrow-minded cleric about evolution. He believes he's forfeited all rights to any of the Church's beliefs, including God."

"Surely, he's intelligent enough to know that accepting the theories of evolution doesn't mean he's to cut himself off from the Christian Faith and God. Where would you and I be, if that was the case? We both support evolution and science up to the hilt."

"I know, my love. To me, science and all its discoveries are an amazing part of God's truth. We live in an age where there are constant, new findings, about life and the universe. Rather than making God less, or pushing Him out of the picture, it shows Him to be even greater than we realised."

"Ah well, stop preaching and tell me about George. Why do you think he's near to breaking point?"

"He's obviously up-tight about the tragic deaths they've had in their family. I also think he feels guilty that he didn't go off to the war but stayed behind at Drake's solicitors. Hugh told me all about it when he came for Sarah's funeral. George did try to sign on with the Hartsbeck Pals but was told that his job in the law was essential to the home front and he was to go home and look after his family. Tom was eighteen months old and Rebecca just born, when the war was beginning. Old Mr Drake, the senior partner, put pressure on George to stay with the firm. Mr Drake's only son, Lewis, was killed at the Somme. George was devastated and had to face the fact that if he'd gone to the war, Lewis would have stayed in Hartsbeck and still be alive to practise law with his father. If George hadn't had to work his socks off to keep the solicitor's firm going, he could well have given way to guilt-driven melancholia. As it is, George drinks more whisky than he should. Luckily he seems able to hold it, according to Hugh."

"Poor Hannah. She's in the strange position of being one of the reasons George was persuaded to stay in Hartsbeck, she and the children."

"Yes, I think relations were a little strained for a while but Hannah has a wise head, she's very tenacious and knows when to stand back and allow things to take their course. As you know, I came to know them quite well when I was a curate. I had many a meal in their home. Sometimes I'd arrive back at my lonely curate's rooms to find that little Annie Elkson, Edwin's wife, had left a home- cooked apple pie or a fruit cake, carefully wrapped, on my doorstep."

"I'm glad these hospitable women were all married, or you might not have been free when I arrived on the scene. As it happened, they all made me very welcome, when we visited them after our wedding!"

Ian took Pauline in his arms and murmured sweetly into her hair. She squirmed and giggled. "Later, Ian, not now- you still have some phoning to do, but later, I promise," she kissed him strongly on his full, firm lips, and then pulled away, giving him a small push. With a dramatic sigh and a wink, Ian went back to his study.

After telephoning Dr. Hennessy with George's response, Ian sat in the peace of his study praying and thinking deeply. Again he mulled over the problem that had been tugging at the inner unity of the Church for years.

It boiled down to many people, including some church leaders, thinking of the Bible as a factual, scientific book. This put it into conflict with modern scientific discovery. The realisation that the earth was billions of years older than suggested by the biblical stories and that the earth was spherical rather than flat and orbits round the sun and not the other way round contradicted the biblical writings. Then Darwin and others, with their theories of evolution, seemed to deny God's creation of mankind as depicted in the Scriptures. All these developments and more had appeared, to some, as a threat to the authenticity of the Bible. Even the youngsters in Ian's confirmation classes were asking meaty questions.

"How come the Bible says the earth and all the plants and animals were made in seven days? Our teacher says it took billions of years."

"How can Adam and Eve be true? Our science teacher says that men and women evolved from apes and even the apes evolved from other creatures?"

"I'm puzzled about the virgin birth of Jesus, sir. My dad says it's silly to think that a woman could have a baby without a man. He says it's just a fairy story but my mum believes it. Is it true sir?"

The questions had been growing sharper and more penetrating with each new generation of Confirmees.

Ian taught them how to unravel the contents of the Bible for themselves and to discover meaning in all the different books.

"The scriptures are full of poetry, myth and allegory. Many of the narratives are set in ancient times and tell of the gradual development of a particular society and their growing relationship with the one God, leading right up to Our Lord Jesus Christ."

He taught them about Biblical criticism, about the historical and cultural conditions in which the different books of Bible were written;

"We can discern God at work in the Scriptures, so much more clearly, when we take on board that some things written in the Bible are not meant to be taken literally but express deep truths in story-form, using poetic and picturesque language."

In Ian's first year as a parish priest, he'd been invited to give a talk on 'The Authority of the Bible', at a meeting of different churches from the local deanery. Clergy and laity from fourteen Anglican parishes were present. As is the way with the Church of England, all the different types of churchmanship and ways of looking at the Bible, were represented. Four other Vicars present, shared Ian's more liberal understanding of the scriptures. However, for other clergy and most of the lay folk there, biblical criticism was a fairly new concept. Some of the audience were open-minded and interested, others were unsure, even suspicious and some openly hostile. Ian had invited his friend Hugh Nowell who was still a curate at the time.

Ian had described the stories about Creation in Genesis; the tales of Noah's Ark and Jonah and the whale and other well- loved biblical narratives, as myths. He said they were not to be taken literally but they expressed truths about God and our relationship with him, in an imaginative, picturesque way. He had hinted, ever so carefully, that many Christians would see the story of the Virgin birth of Christ in the same light, as a beautiful and memorable myth, helping us to understand and visualise the mystery of the incarnation as God coming among us in the person of Jesus.

At this point another local vicar, well-loved but with a strong, fundamentalist belief in the Bible, stood up and stormed out of the hall, slamming the door behind him.

After that, Ian had gone even further, suggesting that some of the miracle stories needed to be unravelled to discover the true miracle beneath the one described, which may not have happened in the way it was told. He had ended by saying that the holy scriptures of the Bible were like God's 'love letters to us'. We are 'the apple of His eye' as one of the psalms says, not in the literal but the figurative sense. As we look critically at the scriptures, we come to understand them better and God's love is revealed as stronger and more real in our own lives today.

Before Ian could sit down a tall, authoritative man of about sixty years old, had climbed onto the stage and deliberately turning his back on Ian, faced the audience. Ian recognised him as a doctor from the local hospital who had spent several years as a missionary in India.

"You don't have to listen to, or believe, a word that has just been said to you by this young, misguided clergyman. The devil himself could not have spoken more smoothly or with more deceit. We know that the Bible is the Holy Word of God. We know every syllable in it speaks truly. You can't choose to believe some parts and not others. We know that scientists have tried to seduce us with captivating tales of our having evolved from apes, or about the wonders of ancient rocks and fossils. All this is the Devil's work. Shun it and shun this young speaker. May God forgive him in his attempt to shake the beliefs of the faithful!" He deliberately turned towards Ian and held out a long thin hand, the other held a thick, black Bible, which he raised above his head. "Demon of deceit and lies; I command you to leave this young man, in Christ's name."

Ian remembered that he'd wanted to say to the doctor, "What if I was to walk into one of your medical meetings, where you were speaking on the modern medical breakthroughs in your specialist subject. If I was to tell everyone that what you were saying was bunkum and all modern medicine was balderdash and we should remember that illness is from evil spirits and that the practice of alchemy is the only true medical science! How would you react to that?"

Before Ian could say any of this, one of the organisers had led the man firmly from the stage and out of the hall. Several others from the same church stood and walked out with him, protesting loudly about unbelievers.

Ian had been shaken to the core. What had happened could have been a scene from the fifteenth century, not the twentieth! The rural dean, who had arranged the event, stood up and tried to smooth the waters with a vote of thanks to Ian for his scholarly and thought provoking address.

"The Reverend Ian Haworth has introduced us to some of the more modern and liberal ways of understanding the Bible. In no way should this disturb you. Nothing that the Reverend Ian Howarth has said tonight in any way alters or waters down the Christian Faith which most of you have been brought up in and come to love. As Mr Howarth stressed, God's truth is gradually revealed to us in many ways. The Holy Scriptures express that truth in the way that the ancient peoples came to understand it, in their time and culture. The Bible still speaks to us today in our generation, with all the new knowledge that we've gained. I can assure you that Ian Howarth is an honest Christian with a deep faith in our Lord Jesus Christ. He certainly does not speak with the forked tongue of the devil."

The Rural Dean had smiled round the slightly puzzled group of people gathered in the hall and a titter of relieved laughter slowly spread among them. Afterwards, alone with Ian he had spoken sharply.

"If you are going to pull anything like that out of the bag again in front of a faithful group of lay Christians of mixed church-man-ships, for heaven's sake warn me! I could have prepared them before-hand. Faith is a precious thing, but complicated. People build up sacred cows for themselves which can only be taken down with care and patience, so as not to disturb the foundations of their beliefs. You rattled a few fundamentalist cages tonight which isn't a bad thing but you could so easily shake the faith of some of the more vulnerable or conservative Christians. You're a young hot-head, Ian, learn to take things slowly when dealing with the flock- they need gentle leading sometimes."

"I do understand but I get so angry when I hear the atheists attack and ridicule Christianity by pointing the finger at uncritical biblical understanding. I've friends who've left the church because, if taken literally, the Bible seems to contradict so much that modern science is discovering. The laity deserves to hear what modern bibli-cal scholars are saying."

"I agree. However, my lad, it's probably best to begin in a small way. Why not start with more intimate seminars, where people can question and voice their fears and weigh up what's being said and discuss it. I think that, after tonight, we will do just that in the Deanery and advertise some smaller meetings for study. Are you game to take part? I know a senior clergyman who would be just the man to work alongside you, a man with a little more experience and diplomacy." The rural dean's eyes twinkled.

"Certainly, I'm game," Ian hadn't hesitated.

Hugh had been more circumspect, "I agree with what you are saying, Ian, but above all things I'm a parish priest and I need to deal with my flock according to where they are in there faith. Some of my parishioners would be completely shaken if I suggested the Virgin birth wasn't literally true. I must walk more gently with them, it would be cruel to confront their beliefs outright. New generations will come to understand what you say. In any case, the truth behind the stories is the same, whether you take them literally or mythically."

"Yes, but people are rejecting the message because they think we take these stories literally. Look at your brothers, Stephen and George. Both good scientists who've rejected the Church because they think it can't accept evolution. It's madness!"

Excited at the Rural Dean's proposal, Ian had decided to persuade some of his more sceptical friends from outside the church to join the discussion groups. After all, they loved nothing so much as a good debate with a whiff of controversy.

The unexpected bonus for Ian out of all this was that he had met Pauline. She had been in the audience on that fateful evening and joined the discussion groups. Remembering those times, Ian's desire for her rose. He looked at his watch, it was nearly eleven o'clock. Ian prayed quietly, commending Ellie and George and all the Elkson family to God before turning out the study light. Thanking God silently for the rich entwining of animal and spiritual instincts he crept upstairs to where his wife was already in bed, waiting for him.

CHAPTER 71

Ellie becomes a patient

Ellie spent a restless night in Dr. Hennessy's nursing home. It had been decided not to give her any drugs until her condition had been observed and assessed overnight.

"If she becomes too difficult you may give her a dose of aspirin," ordered Dr. Hennessy.

Ellie was thankful that she wasn't left alone. A nurse sat beside her bed all night, doing her best to soothe her when the fears and misery threatened to overwhelm her. Ellie would come to from a doze and with a groan, sit up in bed and covering her face with her hands, rock backwards and forwards, often silently but sometimes wracked with dry, choking sobs. One moment she would shiver with an icy coldness, only to throw off her bedclothes minutes later, feeling suffocatingly hot. Yet, when the nurse took her temperature, Ellie had no fever. At other times she would grip the nurse's hands and say, "I didn't know I was harming her. I only wanted to make her well—oh -what am I going to do – they'll never forgive me,"

Later she asked for the time. When the nurse told her it was half past two in the morning Ellie tried to get out of bed.

"It's past Jobo's feeding time, I must go to him. Where's his bottle?"

When the nurse restrained her, Ellie shouted, "If you won't let me feed him he's going to die. He must be fed a little every hour. Bring him to me, if you won't let me go to him. He's so frail. Please, don't let little Jobo die, please!" and the dreadful dry sobbing would start again.

The nurse rang the bell for another nurse to come and sent her to make cups of tea for Ellie and herself.

"I think we could give her some aspirin now. Dr. Hennessy said to try that if she was becoming over-excited."

The soothing effect of sweet tea and aspirin was aided by the motherly voice of the nurse, who spoke to Ellie as if she were a child who'd woken from a nightmare.

"Don't worry Ellie, everything's alright. Baby's been fed and is fast asleep. Now it's time for you to sleep," she held Ellie's hand and very softly sang the children's bedtime hymn, 'Now the day is over.' Ellie gave a great sigh and by half past three had fallen, exhausted, into a light sleep.

She opened her eyes two and a half hours later, at six o'clock. Her night nurse was leaving and the day staff starting their duties. Ellie's mind was in turmoil. One moment she felt reasonably calm, then, as she listened to the sounds of the nursing-home coming to life outside her room, panic seized her. She cried out, as her chest constricted and she sat up gasping for breath. At the sound of her cry the Sister in charge hurried to Ellie's room and soon had the panic attack under control. She read the report of the night nurse and, under cover of supervising the morning ablutions and breakfast distribution, she quietly assessed Ellie's state, By the time Dr. Hennessy arrived at ten o'clock, Sister was ready to give her assessment.

"In my opinion, Sister Elkson is in need of twenty four hour care, in a specialist psychiatric hospital. Although lucid at times, her mind becomes deranged quite suddenly and she imagines herself in another place and time. She has delusions of being in situations which obviously horrify and distress her to such an extent, both mentally and physically, that immediate medical attention has been necessary to control her reactions."

"You've made a very lucid and rapid assessment, Sister, thank you. However, don't you think a few more days of rest here might speed her recovery, rather than immediate transfer to a Mental Hospital?" Dr Hennessy was reluctant to take such drastic action so quickly.

"No, Doctor. I admit that Sister Elkson's condition is exacerbated by exhaustion. She won't be able to rest properly unless her mental state is treated under specialist conditions, which we can't provide here. In her best interests, she must have specialist psychiatric care."

"Very well, I've always found you a reliable diagnostician, Sister. I'll speak to Sister Elkson and decide which hospital would be best for her. Her brother may arrive sometime today. He would prefer her to be moved nearer to the family home, in Lancashire."

"That would be a good idea. I'm sure visits from family members could help a lot to stabilise her."

Ellie was delusional again when Dr. Hennessy entered her bedroom. Convinced that a whole group of new born babies were waiting for her to supervise their feeds, she was fighting against the nurse who was determined to keep her in bed.

"I must go to them. Dr. King will be very angry if I don't feed them on time. Their mothers can't breast feed, so I must give them Dr King's formula or they could die. How dare you keep me here, you stupid little nurse. Don't you know I'm a Sister?"

In her anguish Ellie slapped the young nurse across her face. The nurse flinched and sprang away from the bed. Dr. Hennessy strode in and took command.

"Thank you nurse, please go and report to Sister at once. Sister Elkson, be calm, there are no babies to feed here. You are a patient in my nursing-home. You have been very ill and need time to recover."

"But, where are my babies?" faltered Ellie, tears of bewilderment starting.

"They are in another mother and baby hospital at the other end of London, being well-looked after. Don't worry about them, you are off duty."

"I see," Ellie rubbed her forehead, "I must have been dreaming. This is your nursing home?"

"Yes, you have been resting here overnight but we may have to transfer you to a hospital for further treatment."

"I see," Ellie lay back wearily; too tired to ask what was the matter with her.

At midday, George arrived. Sister looked with surprise at the distinguished gentleman in a fitted grey suit and coat as he politely removing his homburg hat and greeted her.

"Good morning, Sister, my name is George Elkson; I believe my sister is a patient here?"

She hadn't expected someone so debonair and well-educated. Despite the Lancashire accent she noticed George spoke with a natural grammatical correctness and she quickly revised her ideas of people from the North of England. Dr. Hennessy too, was impressed by George's manner and competency. This north-country solicitor knew exactly what needed to be done. The previous evening George had listened carefully to all they had told him about Ellie and today he had come prepared. He had papers with him concerning two excellent psychiatric hospitals in the North West; one near Manchester, the other near Preston. It was decided that Ellie should be taken to the one near Manchester. The hospital agreed to accept her but suggested that before travelling she should remain for at least three more days rest, under sedation, in Dr. Hennessy's nursing home. Sister graciously accepted the situation and arranged round the clock supervision for her patient. Dr. Hennessy prescribed a sedative, which outwardly calmed Ellie but her dreams remained troubled.

Arrangements were made for Ellie to be driven to the Manchester hospital by private ambulance in three days' time, with a nurse in attendance. George stayed on in London for two days at the house in Redcliffe Street. Kitty was relieved to see him and to hear that Ellie was safe,

"We've been that worried. The clergyman from Westminster Abbey sent a message to say Sister Elkson had been taken ill. We'd been about to send for the police. She hadn't been well all morning. I left her and went to fetch Beattie Mason thinking she would know how to help her. When we came back, she'd gone. What will happen now, sir?" Kitty was nervous in front of George and her speech came out oddly.

"Sister Elkson is coming back to Lancashire to rest and be treated for her illness. I don't know whether she'll ever be back here, Kitty. I shall need all her clothes and belongings to be packed up ready to be sent to Hartsbeck and she'll need some fresh clothes and night-wear to wear for the next few days. Please can you see to that Kitty? I'll make sure you are paid properly for your work."

Kitty was almost in tears, "I'll do it gladly sir, without any extra pay. My mother and I and all her friends round here are very fond of Sister Elkson, we understood her ways. She showed me a trunk upstairs that she brought to London when she first came. I'll pack her things in that."

"Just the ticket, Kitty. Thank you. The house will have to be closed up, until we know whether my sister will be coming back."

Kitty busied herself doing George's bidding, as well as doing her best to make him comfortable during his stay but she kept out of his way as much as possible.

George went back to the nursing home and spoke gently with Ellie, "Come along now, lass. What's all this been about?" he lapsed comfortably into the familiar broad accent.

"I don't know George, I feel that peculiar. Where's Sarah? I thought she visited me earlier?"

George's eyes filled with tears and he squeezed Ellie's hand tightly. "She's gone home, Ellie. You're coming back to Lancashire, tomorrow. An ambulance is taking you to a hospital nearer home, where they can give you the best care and we can visit you. When you're better you can come home to Hartsbeck."

With all his heart George wished he was bringing Sarah home to Hartsbeck with Ellie.

"But, George, what about my babies?" Ellie looked distraught

"You'll have to leave all that behind. Those babies don't really belong to you. There are other nurses to look after them. You've more than done your bit, Ellie."

Dr. Hennessy sedated Ellie for the journey and by late evening Elli arrived at the large Royal Hospital for the mentally ill, fifteen miles outside Manchester. She was aware of very little on her arrival, only the cold air as she left the ambulance and the shadow of a great dark building. George had driven ahead and Stephen had driven down from Hartsbeck, so they were both there to meet her. They followed behind as the attendant nurse helped their sister up the stone steps and through an arched entrance into long corridors with a lingering smell of chemicals and drains. It reminded Ellie of Netley.

"Is that where they've brought me?" she wondered, "back to Netley? No, of course not; it can't' be. Maybe it's a prison?"

She believed, deep down, that George still blamed her for Sarah's early death. As a lawyer, maybe he'd brought up some charge against her that would put her in prison. Maybe the spirits were using him to work their evil plans against her.

"I know I deserve it, George, I'm a horrible person but don't put me away for ever," she muttered.

Stephen's hearing was acute and he stopped, struck by his sister's words and tone.

"Ellie, you're not here because you've done something wrong. You're ill and need treatment. As soon as you're well, we'll bring you home,"

"That's not what he thinks," Ellie nodded towards George, who was stung by the suspicion in her stare. They didn't answer her, knowing her mind was playing tricks but both bent down and kissed her on the cheek before leaving.

"Get well soon Ellie, love. We all want you home."

Tears came to Ellie's eyes. She touched her cheek where the kisses had been and that was how they left her.

Two well-built nurses escorted Ellie away to her Ward and George and Stephen were ushered into a room near the entrance, where the matron of the hospital spoke to them of Ellie's case and visiting times.

"We shall know better what treatment to give her in a few days' time. One of our senior psychiatrists will examine and talk with your sister, each day. All our members of staff are experienced in cases such as Sister Elkson's. You need have no fear of leaving her in our care. If you are worried at all, please telephone us. Family members are often particularly upset in cases of mental illness."

"What is the name of the specialist who will be caring for our sister?" asked George.

"Initially, it will be Dr. Samuel Kern but sometimes there is a personality clash between patient and psychiatrist; in which case, we would change her therapist."

"Thank you, we understand. We'll be keeping close contact with our sister through visits and telephone calls, but please keep us informed of any treatment you decide. I would like to know which drugs and if you wish to use any form of electrical treatment or hypnotic therapy, before you use them on her."

"Well, that's a little unusual. May we have your permission to use drugs at our discretion in an emergency, or if we feel it will benefit your sister in an immediate situation?"

"George, it would be unreasonable not to agree. After all we are putting Ellie in the care of the hospital and it is their special field. Matron, you must use what treatments you think will benefit our sister but do let us know if she is to have electrical treatment, we would prefer to discuss that with the doctor beforehand."

George pressed his lips together tightly, fuming inwardly but Stephen was the eldest and the scientist and so he bowed to his will.

CHAPTER 72

The Psychiatric Hospital 1931

The first two weeks in the 'Royal Northern Hospital for the Mentally Ill', passed in a blur of confusion for Ellie. Much of the time she spent sleeping. By the third week she felt more awake and was able to sit comfortable in the ward's day room, wearing her dressing gown and slippers. One morning, Gwen, a fellow patient, told her a gruesome tale of domestic abuse. At first Gwen's words wafted over Ellie but gradually, some of the bizarre horror of the tale reached her and Ellie realised her mind was re-focusing.

Gwen's husband had come home from the War, a changed man; he'd become morose and withdrawn, whereas before, he had been "jolly and carefree, full of fun."

"Then one day I was chopping onions in the kitchen and I heard him come in behind me. He was very quiet. He told me to turn round slowly and face him. He was pointing a gun at me, but I don't think it was me he saw, it was those deserters they'd made him shoot out in France. Poor blighters. Anyway, I shouts at him- 'don't be daft Stan; it's me Gwen, your wife. But he just kept staring at me and started squeezing the trigger. I puts me hands behind me and picks up the board with the chopped onions, knife and all and flings them right in his face. That put him right off his aim, the gun goes off but the shot goes wide, right through the kitchen window and sticks in the garden fence. I had the sense to drop to the floor and lie still. He just looked at me, turned away and walked upstairs."

"Good heavens," said Ellie heavily, her woolly mind trying to imagine the scene.

"Well, I got out of the back door pretty quick and went round to the people next door. They'd heard the shot. They sent for the police and the doctor. Then I seemed to go all funny, I couldn't seem to think straight. After the doctor had been, I ended up here. That's all." Gwen went off into a reverie staring into space, just as if she'd been shut down.

"Nothing as dramatic as that happened to me. I don't know why I should've ended up here. I've coped with death and illness and the sordid side of life for years, as a nurse. What was it that let me down all of a sudden?" Ellie felt chastened by Gwen's story.

A tall woman in a trailing dressing gown paused in her endless promenade of the room, "Probably your age, dearie," she murmured, and then drifted on, her long fingers carrying an imaginary cigarette to her lips again and again. Ellie pinched herself to make sure she was awake. It was like being part of a dream world interspersed with occasional wisps of 'almost-reality'.

Gwen, still staring at nothing, said, "It's that War, we've never got over it, leastways some of us haven't."

"I lost one brother and another came home with shellshock. And my sister-in-law died nursing sailors on board ship, I remember her funeral." Painfully, Ellie started to think back to those nightmare years of the War.

"There you are then, proves my point. I'll bet you that's the root of your trouble. Something else probably happened to you, more recently on top of that. Altogether it's just been too much for you to take. We've all got our breaking point," Gwen gave a wise nod.

Ellie felt disgusted with herself. Hundreds of people had lost family during the Great War but they hadn't collapsed as she had. Hundreds had lost family due to the influenza epidemics but they'd carried on bravely. She despised herself for her weakness and wanted to hide herself away where no-one could see her.

A young nurse tapped her on the shoulder, "Miss Elkson, I'm Nurse Mavis. Dr Kern would like to talk to you. I've come to take you down to his room.

"What, now?"

"Yes, straight away. We mustn't keep him waiting".

Ellie stood up quickly tucking stray ends of hair into place and searching for a handkerchief amongst the folds of her skirt. Her hands and face were sweating. Nurse Mavis laid her own calm hands over Ellie's.

"Come along, you look fit to meet the king himself."

Together they walked down the corridor and the wide, marbled staircase, to the doctor's offices on the floor below. Ellie stood hesitantly in the doorway, looking at the small man with his balding head and grey suit. He was certainly not the doctor she'd seen soon after she'd arrived at the hospital. This doctor was probably in his late thirties. He sat sideways behind a low desk, staring out of the window. Ellie looked beyond him and could see a corner of the garden and a huge sycamore tree, the tips of its branches nearly touching the glass and she longed to be outside.

Nurse Mavis cleared her throat loudly and announced, "Here is Miss Ellie Elkson, Doctor."

The little man jumped up and bounced round the desk to greet Ellie with a quick handshake. He peered at her through the thick lenses of horn-rimmed spectacles.

"Good morning, Sister Elkson. I am Dr. Samuel Kern, your psychiatrist. I've been away at a conference; otherwise I would have seen you earlier. I hope we shall enjoy many talks together."

Ellie began to perspire again. She sat down, trembling on the edge of the chair he offered her. He retreated behind the desk.

"Right, Miss Elkson. First of all I'll just need to ask you a few questions to make sure we have our records straight. What is your date of birth?"

"The eleventh of May 1881."

"Ah, a spring birthday. So, how old are you now?"

"Forty-nine."

"Good. Where were you born?"

"Surely Doctor, you already have all this information? You must know who I am?"

Dr Kern leant back in his chair and looked at his folded hands,

"I do know a little about you, Sister Elkson but I need to hear it from you. Suffice it to say that something has happened to upset the balance of your life. This in turn has upset the balance of your mind. Whatever it is that caused this has been too strong for your personality to cope with in the normal way. In order to help you gain a right balance again, we need you to help us to build a picture of yourself, from the beginning of your life, until now. In building this picture, we hope to find the cause of your recent breakdown. Then together, we can tackle the beast. Does that make sense to you, my dear?"

Ellie looked carefully at the little man; she wasn't a bit sure of him and hated being called 'my dear' by a stranger. She decided to co-operate.

"I was born in Longford, near Preston, but I moved to Hartsbeck with my parents and younger brother when I was four years old."

"Where exactly is Hartsbeck?"

"In the North West, about fifteen miles north of Preston."

"A bit grim up there, isn't it?"

"It's my home, doctor. Nobody calls their own home, grim. I take it you don't come from Lancashire?"

"No, I come from Sussex. Manchester is as far North as I've been and I'm finding it grim enough." He forced a smile, "I'm not being fair am I? I've only lived here a few months and I'm still suffering from homesickness. I need to explore the countryside. Now, tell me about your brothers and sisters, Ellie. What are their names?"

The smile, the small personal confession of homesickness and the use of her Christian name slightly unnerved Ellie.

"Stephen and George, Edwin, Sarah and Jack. But I don't want to talk about them."

"I see. Well then let's think of something entirely different. Do you like word games, Ellie?

"Sometimes."

"How would you explain the meaning of this proverb - 'People in glass houses shouldn't throw stones'"

Ellie stared at the doctor suspiciously, "What has that got to do with my illness?"

"I need to assess how well your mind is working at the moment, so that I know the best way to treat you, Ellie."

Ellie could think no further than imagining her brother Edwin in his greenhouse picking up a stone and throwing it with all his might at the glass walls.

"Because the walls of the house would shatter," she replied, knowing that there was a different, sub-lineal meaning to the proverb but unable to focus her confused mind enough to unravel it.

"No other meaning that you can think of?"

"Of course there's bloody well another meaning; you'll have to work it out yourself," Ellie threw her answer at him, then stood up and started walking towards the door. Her swearing had shocked even her. The doctor's voice, calm and authoritative stopped her.

"Miss Elkson, that was extremely rude of you, I am sure you know better than to behave like that."

Ellie, mortified, turned back and sat down, her head in her hands, sweat was pouring from her.

"I'm sorry Doctor; I didn't mean to be rude. I can't seem to arrange my thoughts properly. I really didn't mean to be rude," and to her utter shame Ellie started to sob, horrid, tearless, choking sobs.

"I understand, Ellie. I know you didn't mean to be rude but your responses have helped me to understand how I can help you."

"Oh?" whispered Ellie.

"Yes, I needed to test your reactions. I didn't deliberately want to humiliate you but it helped me to discover just how confused your mind has become. You're not alone in your confusion. You've no idea how many people have become mentally disturbed by the happenings of these past twenty years. Now my dear, that's enough for today, it's time you had your tea and a rest. Nurse Mavis will take you back to the ward and we'll talk again tomorrow."

He placed a hand beneath her elbow and with great courtesy assisted her to rise and escorted her to the door. Nurse Mavis was waiting and took her back to the ward, chattering cheerfully about shepherd's pie for supper followed by apple crumble so that Ellie began to feel like Alice in Wonderland, wondering what was real and what was fabricated?

CHAPTER 73

Broken dreams and delusions

That night as Ellie tried to sleep, the words of the doctor about people in glass houses throwing stones went round and round in her mind until she slept, with the noise of shattering glass reverberating in her ears. The sound triggered memories. Into her dream came the hard-faced women she'd seen fighting for women's rights by swinging bricks and mallets as they smashed the shop windows in Oxford Street. She heard again the smash of glass as a father had gone berserk on Juniper Ward, following the death of his twelve year old child. She thought she heard the smash of the glass window breaking in the chapel, on the night she heard Jack had been killed. Although she knew no such window had actually been broken. She saw Jack's shocked face, crying out soundlessly as he was shot down, carrying his wounded colleague back from the lines. She saw Becky Nelson collapsing on board a listing ship and was aware of the stormy sea crashing around her. Then she was walking barefoot on broken glass in Becky's funeral procession. Becky's funeral turned into her father's funeral and Bertha Harris was standing over her with a large glass ready to smash it on her head as she said, "You've let us all down Ellie Elkson; all of Lancashire!"

"Sister Elkson," a firm voice spoke from somewhere far off; as she struggled awake the voice took on a gentler tone "Ellie, wake up dear. You've been having a nightmare and it's time for your medicine."

Ellie opened her eyes to see a woman in Sister's uniform standing over her with a tall glass of water and a smaller glass of brownish liquid. Ellie felt her sheets and night dress, they were soaking wet and she remembered the ship and the waves and shivered.

"We need to change your bed and night clothes, you've perspired a whole river in your dreams, goodness knows what you were up to!"

The night sister was a stranger to Ellie but she was kind and efficient and soon had her patient settled for the remainder of the night.

There were many more meetings for Ellie with Dr Kern and she grew more used to him, even to trust him a little. He managed to draw from her things about her early childhood and her father's drinking. Later she confided in him about her unresolved relationship with Alex Dobson and her dabbling in theosophy and water therapy. They spoke of the war and her brother Jack and about Becky Nelson. Dr Kern insinuated that she may have a hidden sense of envy about Becky's heroic death,

"After all your sister-in-law's short, war-time nursing career was highly-lauded, whereas your nursing was taken for granted," the doctor spoke so reasonably that although Ellie was at first shocked, as she mulled over the doctor's suggestion further, she persuaded herself that there might be a grain of truth in it.

"I have a very unpleasant side to me," she mused, "what a self-centred person I am."

Dr Kern also suggested that, as the first born, she'd long harboured a repressed feeling of being usurped and replaced in her parents' affections by the arrival of her siblings. This completely muddled Ellie. In her vulnerable state she began to imagine that she really had experienced the feelings the doctor suggested. Then, she remembered the happy relationship she'd always had with her brother Stephen and her younger brothers and the utter joy when she'd held Sarah in her arms, after helping at her birth. No, the psychiatrist was wrong there, she was almost sure of it but he was so persuasive. Confusion engulfed her again and she began to suspect Dr Kern of deliberately putting warped ideas into her head.

Dr Kern preferred to practice this type of psychoanalysis on his patients. He would only recourse to electro-convulsive therapy if he felt a more rapid route out of a patient's depressive state was necessary, or if psychoanalysis was proving too disturbing.

"He's not averse to using ECG," Nurse Mavis told Ellie, in her gossipy way. "Several of his patients have been given it quite successfully. It's just that he'd rather try talking with patients and delving into their minds to find out why they think and react in the way they do. I think he's just nosy about people."

"Nurse Mavis! You do not discuss the doctors or the patients' treatments in that manner. It is unprofessional and very disturbing for the patients. I shall see you in my office before you go off duty."

"Yes Sister, I'm sorry. It's just that Miss Elkson is a nursing sister and I thought it might stimulate her mind—."

"Here, Miss Elkson is a patient. She needs to be treated with as much sensitivity as any other patient in a confused and depressed state. Don't add to her fears, Nurse. Now, go about your duties."

There were other distractions provided, to help patients unwind and allow their minds to heal. Relaxation classes to music; occupational therapy, during which Ellie dutifully made a mosaic teapot stand by gluing fragments of broken tile onto a small, square base. Ellie also opted to do some simple embroidery, which she enjoyed. She could lose herself in choosing the colours and stitches for the pansies and daisies she embroidered onto a linen tray cloth. It was while sewing that she felt most normal. Her mother had taught her to embroider as they sat by the kitchen fire on winter evenings, when she was still school age. Sarah had joined them, when she was old enough and they had struggled and triumphed over stitches and patterns together.

The worst reminder of her mental state and that of her fellow patients was the scrupulous collecting in of sharp objects, or anything that they might use to harm themselves, after each craft session.

Gradually Ellie and the other patients, in the short term ward, began to relate to each other. Snatches of conversation, a shared joke, or consultation over a pattern began to replace the oppressive silences as they worked. Sometimes one of the patients would begin to weep for no apparent reason or rock backwards and forwards, as if unable to comfort herself.

One morning, Ellie was badly upset by Suzanne, a young woman working next to her. Suzanne had been helping Ellie to select embroidery silks, when she suddenly gave a strangled cry and ran across the room and underneath one of the tables. There she curled up, hiding her head in her arms and refusing to come out. The staff left her there for half an hour until lunch-time when she was coaxed to the dining table.

Ellie realised then, that however well they seemed at any one moment, by the next any of them could be knocked completely off balance.

"They are all mentally ill and I'm one of them. Will any of us ever recover? Will I ever be able to leave this place?" she asked herself, a hundred times a day.

The worse of it was never being alone, even in the bathrooms and lavatories you were watched over, always watched over.

Then, one sunny morning, in early October, a nurse had escorted Ellie out into the garden and left her in a quiet place of trees and grass, with no windows overlooking it. What bliss. Ellie sat in the sunshine, on a wooden bench facing a bed of dahlias, which were still in bloom. The hospital building was out of sight behind her. She unclasped her hands and rubbed them slowly together as she looked around. The sunshine and the quiet growing things momentarily soothed her tired brain but she felt uneasy and in order to keep bad thoughts from entering her mind, she concentrated on the flowers. After a short time, even they began to unsettle her.

"Dahlia's are far too showy. All those clashing colours make me tired. Then there's the digging up and storing away from the frost in winter. Edwin would be pleased with these continuing to bloom; he's always trying to make his last into October. Edwin lives for his dahlias and his roses and his runner beans and his lettuce and Annie and little Jack."

Half dreaming, Ellie stared idly at a gardener bending over the flower beds. He began to look familiar. Earth-engrained fingers trembling over tender seedlings for autumn planting. It was her brother Edwin. Ellie laughed and stood up, stretching out her arms to him.

"Edwin! What the dickens are you doing here?"

The man turned his head. It wasn't Edwin; it was a much older man, a stranger to Ellie but only the hospital gardener. He was a kindly old man and walked towards her, fork in hand. Already shaken by her earlier mistake, Ellie's addled thoughts twisted the gardener's advance into an attack. In her deluded state she believed it was her brother, George, storming towards her brandishing a garden fork. Ellie fell to her knees clutching her head and screaming.

"NO- NO-NO-NO!!" no other words would come.

The gardener hurried on towards her, shouting for help. His cries were heard and there came the sound of running feet along the garden path. A young male nurse from the men's section gripped Ellie's arm and led her back inside to the women's ward. Sister Doreen, stern as a Nanny bristling with nursery discipline, rose from her desk to meet them, her keen eyes taking in the state of her patient.

"Now then Miss Elkson. There'll be no more going out in the garden, for you, if this is what happens. A soothing drink and bed till dinnertime. That should settle you down. Nurse Mavis, please see Miss Elkson to bed, I'll bring a sedative."

It was quiet on the ward. The other patients were either outside or doing craft work in a separate room. Ellie was glad no-one had asked why she'd screamed. The incident was already rolling backwards into the past, a waking nightmare, a displaced thought - no longer important. The young trainee nurse helped her to take off her heavy black skirt and white blouse and loosened her corsets. Rolling down her thick stockings Ellie rubbed the aching veins now swelling and mottling her once smooth and shapely legs. She felt like a seventy year old.

"These have done their share of walking," Nurse Mavis felt the rough calluses on Ellie's feet as she helped her onto the bed and tucked the top coverlet over her.

Changing completely into your nightie and slipping between the sheets was not encouraged during the day. A doctor may want to talk with you at any time; you had to be dressed and ready to be walked down to the consulting rooms. To keep a consultant waiting was a mortal sin, Ellie knew that.

Sister Doreen, her white cap bobbing importantly on her pile of frizzy ginger hair, arrived with the sedative. Ellie recognised the sickly sweet smell of paraldehyde and drank it quickly. Satisfied with her patient, Sister Doreen went back to the day ward leaving Ellie in the care of Nurse Mavis and the Staff Nurse, Edith. The two nurses busied themselves with tidying beds as they waited for the drug to take effect. Lying back on the pillows, Ellie closed her eyes as a gentle floatiness engulfed her. The warm smell of dinner cooking drifted across the ward. Could it be fish pie? It would be ready when she woke up. She could hear the clear accents of Nurse Mavis and the gruff tones of Staff Nurse Edna, coming and going.

"A terrible shame."

"Did you see her hands, all rough and chapped - and her feet?"

"Aye, at least we can treat those while she's idle. She's been a good nurse, by all accounts.

Over thirty years. Sick children mostly."

"She must have nursed all through that 'flu epidemic after the War. I lost a little brother with that. He was only two."

"She's burnt herself out, I shouldn't wonder. How's she doing now?"

Ellie sensed the small, dark-haired nurse lean over her.

"She's away. Her face looks younger than forty nine, when she's asleep."

"Well, she's never been married. Nothing ages a face like marriage. In my opinion," Staff Nurse Edna turned her back deliberately on Mavis.

"O Staff, don't say that. It's only two months off my wedding. Anyway, my mum says its being wed and having kids, that keeps you young."

"Who does she think she's kidding?" Nurse Mavis decided Edna had a bad case of sour grape syndrome.

Ellie was half-shocked at the familiar chatter between Staff Nurse and trainee nurse. Things were changing. Maybe the Mental Hospitals encouraged a more relaxed atmosphere. The voices drifted into the distance, as the two women left the room and Ellie slept.

She woke to find a familiar figure sitting beside her bed,

"Cousin Hugh! I didn't expect to see you but I suppose your dog collar is a passport to most places." Ellie turned away resentfully and closed her eyes.

Hugh reached out and took her hand, holding it firmly. Ellie felt the strength and roughness of his carpenter's fingers. Even now that he was an ordained priest, Hugh still found joy in working with wood and in teaching the village lads carpentry and wood turning. Ellie had almost forgotten that her cousin been a carpenter's apprentice and then, for a few years, a carpenter in his own right.

"You had a good sleep, Ellie. I've been here for some time."

"Watching me, I suppose." Ellie's tone was truculent. "What did you expect to see, the devil on my shoulder?"

Hugh laughed, "If I did, I was disappointed. You looked at peace with the whole world, in a '*sleep that knitteth up the ravelled sleeve of care*'," he quoted.

"Macbeth," retorted Ellie, "an apt play for someone like me. Condemned for killing my own sister."

"I'm not condemning you," said Hugh.

"But others do. George especially, but Stephen and Mother must hold it against me too and there are probably others in the family who do the same."

Ellie re-opened her eyes and sat up suddenly. In an attempt to calm her Hugh picked up a cardigan from the chair and placed it round his cousin's shoulders, she shrugged it on and buttoned it over her vest then pulled away from Hugh. She banged the bedclothes with her fists.

"All I wanted was to kill off that damnable cancer. I was so sure I could do it. We lost Jack in the war and Becky Nelson; Edwin's only half the man he was because of shell shock and then mother's suffering from Parkinson's disease. I thought we'd had enough troubles and that I could at least save Sarah. I didn't prevent her going to the specialist but looking back, I think the water cures I tried hurt her unnecessarily. I wish I'd just let her be but I was sure it would help. Perhaps if I'd tried harder, I could have saved her."

"Ellie, we all hoped and prayed that you could. We are all as much to blame. We should have noticed sooner how ill she was. She kept things to herself for too long."

Hugh was alarmed at the flush of agitation deepening on Ellie's face and the tenseness of her body. He wondered if it had been wise for him to come. He reached into his inside pocket.

"I've brought you something. The boys from church had been making it for Sarah. Most of them are in the choir and they nearly worshipped her after she sang the solo on Easter Day. They were upset when she became ill and decided to make something to cheer her up, they chose the designs themselves. I helped a little. When they heard she'd died they decided you should have it. They're good-hearted lads and the woodcarving classes have really brought them on; you should see the pride in their faces when they take home something useful and beautiful, that they've made."

"I think those boys worship you, Hugh. Your woodwork touches them better than a sermon, any day." Ellie surprised herself with the normality and warmth of her words. She was feeling better.

Hugh smiled wryly, "anyway, a deputation of boys came to me at the vicarage, last night. They said they'd all been discussing how bad you must be feeling and they thought if I was to bring this for you, it might help."

Opening his hand he showed Ellie a three inch square box, beautifully fashioned in oak, with the carving of a squirrel holding an acorn in relief, on the lid. On one side of the box a small bird was carved, on another a daisy and on another a sprig of holly with leaves and berries. On the fourth side was a simple cross. The lid fitted snugly without hinges but with a carved edging which made it easy to grip and lift off.

Ellie's fingers shook as she took it and caressed the carvings with her index finger.

"It's very beautiful."

"I thought you'd like it," Hugh grinned. "I know you're more into Buddhism than Christianity, but I knew you'd love it."

"Theosophy, not Buddhism, but that doesn't matter now." Ellie gave an involuntary shudder and avoided Hugh's eyes. She touched the box again and gently lifted it into her lap. "Dear Sarah, how she would enjoy this," tears brimmed over and trickled down her cheeks, "I don't deserve it," but she held the box close to her and breathed in the spicy smell of polished wood.

They were interrupted by Nurse Mavis, walking in with a covered tray.

"I'm sorry to disturb you both but you slept all through lunch, Miss Elkson. Sister thought you would be hungry. She lifted the cover to reveal buttered toast with a poached egg, two cups of steaming tea and slices of iced sponge cake. Ellie's mouth watered and for the first time since her arrival at the hospital, attacked the food with relish. In companiable silence, Hugh sipped his tea and ate cake and was glad he'd come. It would mean a lot, to his wood-work boys, that their gift had worked its own small miracle for Ellie.

PART EIGHT

BACK TO HARTSBECK 1932-1933

CHAPTER 74

Home again.

After the affair in the garden, followed by Hugh's visit, Ellie began to turn the corner towards recovery. One morning she woke up feeling so at ease that she wondered whatever had been the matter with her. She found she could grieve over Sarah's death naturally, without the destructive sense of guilt and fear.

When she began to help the nurses in their more mundane duties and listen to patients' conversations in a more professional way, the medical staff reviewed her case and decided it was time for her to be discharged. She was escorted by Nurse Mavis to her last interview, not with Dr Kern but with the chief senior doctor of the hospital, a Dr Hepburn,

Nurse Mavis had, by now, left to be married, so it was Staff Nurse Edna who took her down the long corridors and into the lift, followed by more corridors to the big chief's sanctuary. His office was in the old part of the hospital, where the long term patients with serious or incurable mental conditions lived, many of them would stay there for the rest of their lives.

Dr Hepburn had more of a presence than Dr Kern. He stood as she entered. An older man, his face was closed and still, as he fixed his gaze on Ellie.

"Good afternoon, Miss Elkson, I am Dr Hepburn," he pronounced his name with a sigh, as if it was a burden to him. He motioned Ellie to a comfortable chair and sat opposite her with no forbidding desk between them.

Ellie sat before him, upright and calm, waiting for his verdict. The doctor's still face relaxed and the corners of his mouth lifted, as if he found her manner reassuring.

"Dr Kern and I, in consultation with the nursing staff on your ward, have discussed your case, Miss Elkson. At fifty years old we believe that, within a calm and relaxing environment, you will continue to make a reasonable recovery. Indeed you are already well along that road." He turned away to cough, before continuing. "I recommend that you now go home to live in Hartsbeck. Your family agree with me. You are very close to your mother, I believe. I hear she has Parkinson's disease, so she will welcome you living with her. Your brother Stephen is still at home and you will have two other brothers and their families nearby. You will have company and plenty to do, when you feel ready. I am sure this is the right way ahead for you, Miss Elkson."

"And what of my nursing career?"

"At the moment, pursuing that is out of the question. Don't forget you have been mentally ill."

"So, as a nurse, I am to be wiped off the books. From now on I am Miss Ellie Elkson, one time mental patient. I have been sick in a psychiatric hospital for just three months. I have been a nurse for over thirty years."

"Thirty years of sterling service to your profession, Sister. Not many nurses can boast of such long service. You can be rightly proud of your career. Now, your mother needs your nursing skills."

"The spinster daughter," Ellie smiled wryly. She stood and stretched out her hand to the doctor. "Dr Hepburn, I want to thank you for the care I've received during my time here. I've been a cantankerous patient at times, as Dr Kern will vouch. Without his patient perseverance, Nurse Mavis's friendliness and the vigilance of Staff Nurse Edna and Sister Doreen, I wouldn't have recovered to the extent I have."

Ellie finished her little speech. It had been worth it just to see Dr Hepburn's mournful face splinter into a surprised smile, at this praise of his hospital and staff. So many of his patients would never recover. He had been in charge here almost thirty years and had encouraged his staff in their care of the residents and in their never-ending study, of new approaches in psychiatry. During his time here he'd discovered that seeking to understand and treat the myriads of mental illnesses, was like trying to plumb the depths of an ocean, which grew deeper at each sounding.

Dr Hepburn felt pathetically grateful for the words of this austere, middle-aged nurse. He stood and gave a small bow as he wished her well. He watched her leave his room with the keenest hope that Sister Elkson would find fulfilment in the next phase of her life.

Ellie was fully discharged the following day. George had been contacted and Ellie waited in the hospital entrance hall, her bags packed and ready for him to take her home to Hartsbeck. The secretary in the reception office kept glancing at her through the office window but Ellie felt abandoned, standing there alone, waiting. She was no longer part of the hospital community and was not yet sure of her accepted place within her own family. Then George drew up, in his smart Austin, saloon motor-car with Annie, Edwin's tiny wife, beside him.

Annie scrambled out with an unmistakably glad smile and linked Ellie's arm companiably, chatting away, as she guided her sister-in-law to the back seat of the car, where they could sit together.

"We've all been looking forward to this day Ellie. It will be so good to have you at home. It only took us an hour and a half to get here."

"We thought you might be glad of another woman with you. Hannah's tied up with the children and Annie wanted to come," George's tone was gentle but he looked embarrassed as he took his sister's bags and stowed them in the car boot. He went into the hospital's reception office to receive any instructions concerning Ellie and to report that they were ready to leave. It only took a few minutes and then they were on their way.

Ellie was thankful that Annie was there, she liked Edwin's wife with her gentle ways and common sense. She'd been dreading the long drive home with George, not knowing how he felt about her. Annie's presence was always calming and she had an infectious air of contentment. The car's interior smelt of leather and lingering petrol fumes. Dr Kern had insisted on prescribing a light sedative for the journey and after the initial excitement and chatter with Annie, Ellie fell into a doze and imagined what it would be like to live back in Hartsbeck. Annie had been telling her that most of the main roads now had tarmacadam laid over the old cobblestones, to make it smoother for motor vehicles.

"But the side streets are still cobbled and all the backs, I'd be sorry to see them all go. The greengrocer and the milkman still come round with their horses and carts, and of course the rag and bone man."

Ellie enjoyed the chatter, Annie was completely undemanding, telling her bits of things, which might interest her and allowing restful silences in between.

"The men boiled the tar in vats at the side of the roads they were tarmacking and it became known that to breathe in the fumes was very good for anybody with a cold or bad chest. Well, there's a lot of bad chests in Hartsbeck, what with the damp and the smoke, so you can imagine quite a few folk would gather round the vats breathing in the vapours. Mothers would take their little ones along, especially babies with a touch of croup. It could have been a spa town, so many wanted to come and 'take the cure.'"

They both laughed at the picture Annie conjured up and when Ellie eventually slept, the dreams of her home town were warm and friendly ones. She awoke with an apprehensive jolt when George announced, "here we are then, one seventy four, Aspen Lane. Home, Ellie." He opened the car door for her. Seeing the anguish in her face, he unexpectedly leant towards her and kissed her pale cheek, "I'm glad you're back. I never liked you being away in London. Welcome home, sis."

Ellie's eyes filled with tears, "Thank you, George. I just wish we were all home together again."

George sighed, "Many have lost all the family they had. We're lucky to have each other," he smiled at Ellie in a way she'd thought never to see from him again and timidly, she smiled back.

Jeannie Elkson had come to the front door, leaning heavily on a walking stick. Her brown hair, now speckled with grey, was piled up in the old way and her eyes shone brightly from behind neat, round spectacles. She still wore the ankle length skirts and waisted blouses fashionable before the war.

"Come along in Ellie," she said, without fuss, "and you too Annie, come and have a cup of tea with us. George, you can put Ellie's bags in her old bedroom upstairs."

"I'll call back this afternoon, mother, if you don't mind," said Annie. "I've to see to Edwin's meal and Jack will be in from school for his lunch. I'll come at four o'clock and bring Jack; he's been looking forward to seeing his Auntie Ellie. Anyway mother, Ellie's tired. She'll be glad to have you to herself, for now." Annie waved to them as she ran across the lane to her own house. George came downstairs, out of breath from taking up Ellie's luggage.

"I'll go and tell Hannah that Ellie's home. I'll have a bite to eat with her, and then I really will have to get back to the office, mother. You'll both be alright now? I expect Hannah will want to come and see you, Ellie. She soon tires nowadays, with our houseful, but I know she'd love to see you."

"Off you go, George. Thank-you for bringing Ellie home," Jeannie patted George's arm affectionately. "We'll be alright. Gertie Foster's made us both a bit of dinner, so we shan't starve! Off with you now, before you get the sack or Hannah thinks you've left her!"

Jeannie waved her stick at him and Ellie mouthed her thanks from behind her mother's back. George laughed and waved his hat before driving up the lane.

"My word, whoever would have thought it, motor cars in our family," Jeannie watched till the car was out of sight, then linked her free arm in Ellie's.

"Now then, let's go inside and have a chat and that cup of tea I'm dying for and I'm sure you are an' all."

Ellie chuckled at the way her mother had of lapsing from talking 'proper' to the local idiom.

Ellie's presence at Aspen Lane soon became taken for granted. She dropped into a routine of housework shared with Mrs Gertie Foster, her mother's daily housekeeper. Gertie lived two streets away with her husband Albert, who was out of work, another casualty of the economic depression. A wiry, fussy little man, he made himself available to do odd jobs for people and was often round at 174, Aspen Lane, working in the back garden or up a ladder fixing something or other. He was handy at plumbing too and any badly blocked drain, or leaking pipe, put Albert in his element. Gertie came every day. She was a sensible woman in her late fifties and had known the Elksons all her life. She reminisced with Ellie about past years.

"D'you recall the NAT's children's picnic, when it rained and young Ephraim Haworth and Geoffrey Chadwick, the vicar's lad, were chased by the bull. Leastways Ephraim was; young Geoffrey got stuck in the mud. Mother and I baked for two days making bread and cakes and pies for that picnic. Eeh, they were grand times. That was in eighteen ninety-eight, the year before you left us to go and live in London. We thought you no end of a swell."

Ellie began to relax in Gertie Foster's company but she couldn't bring herself to use the housekeeper's Christian name and Gertie, out of deference, still called Ellie, Miss Ellie. It was an undeniable element of division still lingering from the relationship of servant to mistress, although Gertie and Ellie probably came from similar ancestral roots. It suited Ellie, in her present state, to keep this slight social difference. It allowed her a friendship but at a distance.

"I do remember that picnic, Mrs Foster. We had a grand feast in the barn up at Oak farm, out of the rain."

Ellie smiled, her spirits warmed by the memory of that day and others like it.

Sometimes Ellie and her mother would spend an evening with George and Hannah, in their newly- built, detached house, on the outskirts of Hartsbeck. George was earning enough money now to live "in the posh area" as Stephen called it, and had fulfilled his dream of having a house built to his own design.

It was in a part of the town that had been fields and farmland when George bought his plot. The farmer had decided to sell his land for housing development and several socially-rising families bought plots near to each other. Situated on the crest of a hill leading south out of Hartsbeck, the plots were flanked by parkland on one side and countryside on the other. In consultation with an architect acquaintance, George had eagerly designed the style of the house as he and Hannah wanted it and oversaw each stage. There was a roomy entrance hall, and all the rooms were large enough for hospitality and comfortable living for his growing family. A smaller room on the ground floor was designated as George's study and retreat. Furnished with a roll-topped desk, leather covered chairs and shelves of books lining the walls, the study soon gained its own distinctive smell of old documents, pipe tobacco and whisky.

The large garden at the back was well established by the time Ellie had come back to Hartsbeck. Immediately outside the living and dining room windows was a rose garden leading to a lawn the size of two tennis courts and ending in a small orchard with apple trees, raspberry canes, gooseberry bushes and three varieties of currant bushes. At the front of the house was an open driveway and garage and to one side a small, shadowy garden, hedged in and filled with gloomy, dark-leaved shrubs and a pathway leading to a green painted front door. Hannah had a special, sunshiny plot, at the side of the house, near the kitchen door, where she grew Sweet Williams and herbs.

The joy of young Alice and Richard was the laundry chute. It was hidden inside a walk-in linen cupboard on the upstairs landing. To push the laundry (and other objects) through a trap door at the top of the chute, then race down to the scullery to see them re-appear, was a never-tiring game. They dared each other to slide down inside the chute but after Richard became stuck and had to be rescued by a fuming George, such antics were banned.

High up on the wall of the breakfast room, hung a row of bells; each one was connected to a different room in the house so that anyone in need, could ring for the maid, or whoever else happened to be in the kitchen at the time.

A tarmacked road had been laid, in front of the new houses and was named Humboldt Drive, after the famous naturalist of the sixteenth century. As it was built at the very highest point of the Drive, George and Hannah named their house 'Hillcrest.'

On the evenings Ellie and Jeannie came to 'Hillcrest', they would play cards or board games and Tom would leave his books for a while and entertain them with his flute or tin whistle. Then, George would wind up the gramophone and they would listen to Gilbert and Sullivan, or for comic relief, a record of Harry Lauder, the Scottish music-hall comedian. Sometimes Rebecca could be prevailed upon to play Sarah's piano. She could manage the 'Merry Peasant' quite well but little else. She said it wasn't her forte, which saddened Ellie.

All of Hannah's family loved to recite poetry of all kinds, from the bloodcurdling and dramatic to the romantic and philosophical. A light supper usually ended these evenings, before George drove Ellie and Jeannie back to Aspen Lane.

Ellie tried to feel at home in these family gatherings but something prevented her. She felt like an interloper. Perhaps, if Stephen had been there, it would have been easier but he was so involved with his scientific work that he was away, more than he was at home. Ellie realised that they were all very different people from the ones she'd said goodbye to when she left for London at the age of seventeen. She too had changed. In many ways, she'd become a stranger to her own family. Sarah had always tried to understand her; she'd kept in touch by letters and visits all down the years, long before her breast cancer.

Ellie now had three reasons to believe the family viewed her with suspicion. First was the awful affair of the séance, soon after the war, then Sarah's death in London and now, the shame of her mental illness. Not that any of them ever said that her breakdown was anything to be ashamed of, Ellie decided the idea of shame was probably in her own head but it made her extra sensitive to their reactions. She supposed, they could never be sure that she was quite sane. She became conscious of half-finished sentences, fading into mutters as she entered a room. She imagined guarded looks flashing between them, quickly replaced by forced smiles and oh, such cheerful greetings,

"Why, Ellie! You're looking better. I can tell by the brightness of your eyes."

"And the dampness of my nose, I suppose." Ellie realised they hadn't liked that; she was an invalid, who'd caused them a lot of trouble, they weren't ready for her to be joking and light hearted. "Still," she thought, "they could have laughed." That was the same time Ellie had disgraced herself by bursting out in front of them all,

"None of you really care about me. I'm not family, any more. Sarah was the only one who kept in touch with me, all those years I was away. It would be different if she was here."

Then George had lost his cool and snapped back at Ellie with the old accusations,

"Well what do you expect? It's chiefly your fault she's not here. You allowed yourself to be brainwashed by that new-fangled religious sect you joined. Dragging mother into it after Jack was killed and frightening my child with your séance. Then all that rubbish about water being a cure-all. The doctors might have saved Sarah, if you hadn't interfered."

I hadn't tried to explain or make excuses; it wouldn't have done any good. There'd been more bitter words and Mother had been stung into action by George's reference to her and the séance.

"We are a family!" she shouted, sitting upright in her chair and banging her stick loudly on the floor. We all subsided into silence and turned towards her, just as we had when we'd squabbled as children.

"George, you talk of new-fangled ideas when you and Stephen and your cronies are part of new-fangled groups yourselves. Your 'Rationalists' and Herbert Spencer are just as much frowned on in some circles, as Ellie's and my spiritualist leanings."

"It's the times," Stephen had conceded, "what with the War and the new sciences. We've all questioned the old truths and been excited by new ideas."

"So, we lost Jack to the War and Sarah to new ideas!" George's sarcasm had stung but Mother had kept her authority,

"Don't you ever forget that, years ago, Ellie saved you boys from many a lathering by your Dad when he was in drink and she'd many a clip round the ear for it. Aye, she's been a good sister to you. She was the first to stand up to your father for the right to her own career and she succeeded. It was Ellie who dealt with the War Office, when our Jack was killed. You idolised Becky Nelson when she died of influenza, nursing the sailors on board ship. Did you ever think of your sister Ellie away from home and nursing all through that 'flu epidemic and more?"

George had had the grace to look ashamed and Ellie had slipped away to her room, thinking her mother was going a bit too far.

As the months went by Ellie's moods began to lighten. Some days she felt almost her old self and then, without warning, her mood would swing downwards and she would become stuck in a murky place. It was like floundering in thick, black mud, the horrid fears and dark memories sticking to her wherever she turned. These were the days she would wander round the house as if in another world, cut off from everyone around her, her mind struggling with thoughts and situations no one else could see. She didn't answer when spoken to because the words she heard seemed to come from a different dimension.

She was recovering from one of these times, when Tom and Rebecca called at 174, Aspen Lane. They'd just arrived and were in the vestibule by the front door as she came down the hall-way on her way upstairs. It was the middle of December and it was gloomy in the passage, the only light coming from a small fanlight over the front door. The youngsters saw Aunt Ellie's dim shape, as she moved silently up the staircase. She didn't stop to greet them, even though that morning, she had been feeling more in touch with things. They didn't call out to her but she heard Tom whisper to his sister.

"There's Aunt Ellie. She frightens me, that white face and the smell of moth-balls."

"Seventeen years old and frightened of a sad middle-aged woman", thought Ellie miserably. She paused on the stairs to hear her niece's reply.

"She is sinister. It would help if she wore something more colourful than black. Some of her skirts are Grandma's old ones; that's why they smell of moth-balls. Aunt Ellie won't go shopping for any new clothes; she's still grieving for Auntie Sarah."

"It's her coldness," said Tom, "there's no sympathy about her."

If he had seen the effect his words had on her, Tom might have changed his mind about his Aunt but as the hot tears scoured her cheeks, Ellie stumbled up the rest of the stairs to her bedroom and closed the door on them all.

"Cold and unsympathetic! I've had to cultivate that," Ellie sat on her bed talking to herself in a low agitated voice. "As an eighteen year old probationary nurse in London -what year was it?- Eighteen ninety nine- I faced horrors on the wards those two young things will never see. Children thin as sticks, their faces all eyes, coughing, vomiting, wasting away. Mothers writhing in pain- not of childbirth but of the prurient fever, which comes after. I was tearful and sick to my stomach every day. Sister told me straight:

'Ellie, it's no use allowing yourself to feel for every case. You'll never help your patients that way. Emotion wears you out. It drains the spirit. Stand back; look at the situation; assess what needs to be done, then do it. My nurses must be 'cool, calm and collected.' Allow the relatives the luxury of feeling for their loved ones. You are there to do a job; feelings can get in the way."

The Sister's clichés would come thick and fast, like bullets from a gun but Ellie remembered that it was her next words that had quickened her and strengthened her determination to 'toughen up'.

"When we review your probationary year, we may consider you too sensitive to make a good nurse."

CHAPTER 75

Rebecca and Aunt Ellie

Rebecca couldn't stop thinking about Aunt Ellie. The conversation with Tom in the hallway had given her an idea. Alone and without fear of interruption, she considered the idea as she lay in bed at night before settling to sleep. Her father had asked her to accompany him to a charity tea-dance to take place a few weeks before Christmas.

A large manor house, situated in the depths of the Ribble Valley, had been left to the town. It was to be converted into a holiday home, where needy Hartsbeck children could enjoy a week of fresh air and wholesome food. A project which Rebecca knew would please Aunt Ellie. Once converted the house would cater for twenty children at a time and be open annually, for the whole summer. The tea-dance was to help raise funds for furnishings and to provide staff and equipment. George was to present a large cheque from the legacy of one of his wealthy clients, a Miss Murgatroyd, the last member of a wealthy manufacturing family. She'd left instructions for her family's accumulated wealth to be used for the welfare of the Hartsbeck community. George, as Miss Murgatroyd's executor, was responsible for choosing the benefactors. Rebecca was expected to represent her mother on this occasion.

Rebecca was aware that her mother preferred not to be seen at public functions, nowadays. With the births of her two youngest children, Alice and Richard, Hannah had put on an enormous amount of weight which she hadn't been able to lose. Her size embarrassed her and also increased her breathing difficulties, making her weary and lethargic. Public engagements, which had never been easy for her because of her deafness, had become a torment. She felt that her presence let George down. If she had but realised it, Hannah was so well-loved and respected in the town, her intellect and personality out-shining any physical drawback, that people felt privileged by her presence.

Hannah was content that she'd enabled George to progress so far in his career, helping him through his exams and then keeping a comfortable home for him, which was always open to his friends or clients.

George adored his children but he'd been forced to temper this with sternness as all four of them, having been allowed to think for themselves, could be strong- minded and wilful.

Hannah was more relaxed. She encouraged her family to read widely and recited poetry to them before they could even walk. Her ready sense of humour was shared by Rebecca and counteracted the seriousness of George and Tom, which sometimes hung over them from the responsibilities of the legal profession.

Between them, George and Hannah had bred children who were disciplined, free thinking and resourceful.

None had been baptised into the church as infants. George insisted they should be allowed to make up their own minds about their religious faith, when they were ready.

This worried Rebecca, her friends came from various Christian denominations and most were baptised, although her closest friend, Enid Fisher, who lived next door, was from a family of Christian Scientists. Memories of her Aunties, Sarah and Becky, teaching her prayers and bible stories would often flash through Rebecca's mind, triggered by some event or chance remark.

To make up for not being a baptised church member, Rebecca took her role as a leader in the 'Girl Guides' very seriously. She attended Church Parades and took her 'duty to God' part of the Guide Law as a special commitment, her bubbly nature filling her with sheer joy at the generous gift of life.

Rebecca needed to buy something suitable to wear for the tea dance and her daring idea, was to ask Aunt Ellie to go with her to choose it. She hoped to persuade her aunt into buying some new garment for herself as an alternative to the black, moth-balled ones so derided by Tom.

She planned her strategy carefully and searched for ways of befriending Aunt Ellie. The next time they were together Rebecca asked her aunt what she thought of the Children's Holiday Home project. Surprised and pleased by her niece's enthusiasm, Ellie's old passion for children deprived of fresh air and sunshine, good food and cleanliness re-surfaced. She began to speak with Rebecca of her ideas and experiences and delighted this maturing young woman, with tales of the dramatic recoveries of children with rickets in Doxlee Hospital.

Rebecca's eyes were quickly opened to a different Aunt Ellie, who told her of a world of people starving for food and fresh air, worn down by financial anxiety and whose children were often born with terrible diseases. All these Aunt Ellie had seen and as a nurse, she'd been part of the team which helped the sick children either recover or die a more peaceful death. Rebecca compared this to her own fairly comfortable life and felt troubled. Could she ask such a person as Aunt Ellie to go with her on a frivolous shopping trip. Before she could make up her mind, Rebecca had a traumatic experience of her own.

Enid, her Christian Scientist friend from next door, had a sister, Phyllis, two years younger than herself. Phyllis came home from school complaining of a pain in her right side and feeling ill. Mr and Mrs Fisher, as Christian Scientists, put the question to her as they usually did when their girls had a tummy upset, "What have you been thinking?" in their belief bad thoughts made you ill far more than bad food. They did not believe in calling a doctor even when Phyllis became worse and ran a high temperature and was violently sick, they tried even harder to surround their daughter with positive and loving thoughts and told Enid to do the same, they read aloud calming passages from their sacred books and the writings of Mary Baker Eddie.

When Phyllis began to scream in pain, Enid terrified, left the house and ran round to Rebecca's. It was half past twelve at night and the Elkson's were all in bed but Enid hammered on the door calling out for Mrs Elkson. Hannah and George were great friends of the Fishers and when Enid blurted out what was happening Hannah put on her dressing gown and hurried next door followed shortly after by George. All their persuading could not make the Fishers forsake their beliefs and send for the doctor. By two o'clock when Phyllis was obviously slipping into unconsciousness, which the Fishers insisted was a healing sleep, George could stand it no longer and went home to phone for Dr Jenkins.

When the doctor arrived, there was nothing he could do and Phyllis died at three o'clock that morning. Mr and Mrs Fisher, overwhelmed with grief focused their anger on George and Hannah for introducing an atmosphere of unbelief into their home at the critical moment.

"Get out of my house and never set foot in it again," shouted Sam Fisher to his bewildered neighbours and Dr. Jenkins, "and I forbid my wife and Enid to have anything more to do with any member of your family, George. Now leave us, please."

"I'm afraid you must allow me to write out a death certificate, Mr Fisher," said Dr. Jenkins firmly, "it is the law."

"If you must, you must. Get it done then and be off with you."

The usually kind and gentlemanly Mr Fisher was beside himself with confusion and grief. None of the adults took offence at his outburst and left quietly, Hannah laying a gentle hand on Mrs. Fisher's shoulders as she passed her.

Enid was forbidden to talk about Phyllis's death with anyone outside her own family.

Rebecca was heartbroken, she had been used to seeing Enid every day, either in her own house or Enid's and she was disturbed by young Phyllis's death. This was the first time Rebecca had come into contact with the death of someone she knew well and so near to her own age and gave her a cold feeling of dread.

Hannah noticed and tried to talk with her daughter about it. Sensibly, she realised that Rebecca needed something to occupy her hands and mind, until the initial shock had passed. She organised a baking session and the two of them worked hard, making dozens of mince-pies and sweets for Christmas. Matilda, the current maid, scurried round them trying her best to prepare a decent midday meal for when George came home. When the last batch of pies was out of the oven and cooling Hannah wiped her hands and sank into a chair.

"Now Rebecca, pack up two dozen mince pies and after dinner, take them down to Grandma and Aunt Ellie. You can stay and visit with them for a while, they'll be glad to see you."

That was how Rebecca found herself pouring out to Aunt Ellie about Phyllis and Ellie found herself in the position of comforter and counsellor to her niece. To her surprise Ellie found she had much to say from her experience of sick and dying children and their parents, which helped Rebecca. She kept away from disclosing any ideas which smacked directly of theosophy but she did slip in ideas of a life beyond death which would have been acceptable to the most conformist of Anglicans. Rebecca felt she was at last relating to Aunt Ellie, through their common experience of death.

"But Rebecca, you wouldn't believe how things have progressed since I first started nursing in 1899. We know so much more about the control and treatment of diseases and how the body responds to its environment. What's needed is for people to educate ordinary folk about good healthy ways of living."

"That's why I've decided to go to college and train to teach Domestic Science. This way I can help young girls learn how to bring up healthy families, with good diets and clean homes."

"That really warms my heart, Rebecca. Don't forget the fresh air and exercise!"

"I start college in Manchester at the beginning of September next year. I just hope Enid and I are allowed to see each other before then," Rebecca sighed.

Ellie, like Hannah, felt the need to draw Rebecca's thoughts to lighter things and brought up the subject of the tea-dance. After that it was easy for Rebecca to invite her Aunt to help her choose a new outfit.

Ellie was flattered and agreed. She was in a flurry of nerves during the days leading up to the shopping expedition but decided, if she was to prove her sanity, she must take part in normal activities again and her niece seemed a pleasant girl.

On the following Saturday the two shoppers set forth. At first Rebecca found Aunt Ellie to be a quiet, rather stiff companion. The town was not busy, people were struggling with the economic depression and many couldn't afford to shop for the pleasure of it. Necessities were bought when they could be afforded; when they couldn't there were the charitable groups to turn to, run by the more affluent. Ellie, more aware of this underlying poverty than Rebecca, felt embarrassed at the thought of buying fashionable clothes for herself when her mother had some perfectly serviceable, if out-dated, garments lying unused at home.

She did, however, enjoy choosing an outfit for Rebecca. The girl needed it and Ellie was able to guide her niece's choice. Rebecca hadn't a clue what a tea-dance required and had to be told that an evening gown would be out of place, as would a tailored suit.

In the end they chose a soft blue dress in light wool with a gently flared hem and prettily-shaped navy- blue collar and cuffs. The bodice was modestly gathered, to fit loosely and had two rows of seed pearls sewn into it. A belt in the same soft blue, emphasised Rebecca's girlish waist.

"Very elegant," said the shop assistant and Aunt Ellie nodded her approval.

Rebecca was happy, she felt comfortable in the dress and believed it suited her. She knew her father liked her in blue.

"It matches your eyes," he would say.

The dress was bought and shoes and gloves to match. Rebecca then turned her attention to her Aunt. She was concerned to see how jaded and tired Aunt Ellie looked and guided her into a tea shop. Ellie perked up after tea and a toasted teacake and was persuaded into buying two plain silk blouses for herself, one in a deep burgundy colour, the other in a jade green. Rebecca thought the richness of the colours brought life to her Aunt's pale face and gradually greying hair. She wanted her Aunt to buy a new hat but Ellie put her foot down and declared she'd had enough;

"I've enjoyed our outing far more than I expected, Rebecca. Thank you, my dear, but I'm ready to go home now."

The tea-dance was a great success and young Rebecca turned a few heads. Thankfully, her life was too full for her to have romantic thoughts of young men.

Christmas provided a happy respite for the whole family. Hannah insisted on going to church on Christmas day and her children went with her. George grunted and stayed at home, enjoying the peace of a quiet house.

The whole extended family congregated at George and Hannah's home for an enormous Christmas high-tea. Rebecca beamed when Grandma Jeannie and Uncle Stephen arrived with Aunt Ellie resplendent in her new burgundy silk blouse. Rebecca exchanged a secret smile with her aunt and pointedly smoothed her own blue dress while Ellie patted the collar of her blouse.

"Are you two communicating by secret code?" Tom whispered to his sister.

"Of course we are. Aunt Ellie and I have things in common that you wouldn't understand." Rebecca declared for all to hear.

Ellie heard the small exchange and her heart warmed. The family feast lost some of its dread for her. Tears of happy emotion trickled down her cheeks as she watched her three brothers and their wives and children, tucking into the cold meats and pickles, trifles, mince pies and Christmas cake. She listened to the old family jokes and reminiscences passed on from year to year. When they drank a toast to "absent friends" she raised her glass with the rest and felt nothing but the homely presence of precious memories. When young Richard was sick through overeating, it was Aunt Ellie who whisked him away and cleaned him up and gave him a special drink to make him feel better.

"If only I could be sure that the blackness won't come back again," was her last thought before she slept that night.

CHAPTER 76

Ellie and baby May

Old Dr Waters, who'd been the Elkson's family doctor since Ellie was a child, had retired ten years previously in 1923. Dr Jenkins had taken over the practice, he'd been the junior partner since 1898 and now in his late fifties, was a much loved and respected figure in the borough. He'd served with the medical corps during the war and the families of Hartsbeck felt he understood all they had suffered.

It was now May, 1933 and Dr Jenkins had just finished examining four week old May Anderson. She'd been born on the first of May, three weeks earlier than expected but had seemed healthy with a low but reasonable birth weight of five pounds two ounces. Her mother had wanted to breast feed but her milk would not come. Try as they might, Dr Jenkins and the community nurse, could not find a baby milk formula which suited the infant.

May was losing weight and becoming fretful, any food she did take she soon regurgitated. The specialists said there was nothing organically wrong but Dr. Jenkins was very much afraid that they were going to lose this much-wanted baby.

May's parents, Winifred and Gilbert Anderson, had been over-joyed when Winifred had found she was pregnant. Gilbert was a well-liked dental surgeon and the news thrilled their little community on the outskirts of Hartsbeck. The couple had been married for ten years and had begun to think they were infertile, with no chance of children. When May was born and lay safely in Winifred's arms she felt that they had been granted a very special gift. Now, Winifred was frantic with worry, as she struggled helplessly to feed her child who seemed to be fading before her eyes.

"There must be something else we could try, or someone who could help us," she felt sure that such a gift would not be snatched away so cruelly.

Dr. Jenkins thought for a moment, staring down at baby May with her screwed-up face and small, thin legs feebly kicking the air. An angry clenching of tiny fists and frustrated crying led him to say, "you've a young fighter here, Winifred; she'll not give up easily. I may just know someone who can help her but I must make some enquiries first. I'll come back to you as soon as I can, hopefully within the hour. In the meantime, give May sips of plain, boiled water with half a tea-spoonful of sugar to a pint, every quarter of an hour."

Dr. Jenkins had thought of the one person he knew to be a fully-experienced professional, in the field of infant nurture and caring for sick children: Ellie Elkson. He'd been overseeing Ellie's recovery ever since she'd been discharged from the Royal Northern Psychiatric Hospital eighteen months ago. She'd continued to suffer intermittent attacks of depression during her first three months at home. He'd observed Ellie carefully and had noted how she'd gradu-ally regained stability in her moods and begun to participate more naturally in the activities of every-day life. For the first six months she had attended his surgery weekly and by then he had felt she was stable enough for him to begin weaning her from the drugs pre-scribed by the hospital. To verify his opinion he'd arranged for Ellie to visit the psychiatric hospital for a check-up with Dr Kern and Dr Hepworth.

The report they sent back was encouraging and in agreement with DrJenkins' suggestions. He'd continued to decrease the dose of barbiturate, which Ellie took each evening and halving the already weak dose she took each morning. He had seen her twice a week during this crucial period and after six weeks she was taking a much weaker dosage and every other day, instead of every day. At one point Ellie reacted to the change and a backward step was taken but gradually her system adapted to the slow withdrawal.

Ellie experienced a sense of coming slowly awake, after a long hibernation. She noticed things about her, with freshened eyes. Stephen took her with him on some of his local rock and fossil hunting expeditions and she revelled in the freedom of the moors and hills. As her powers of concentration improved, she rediscovered her voracious appetite for reading.

She wasn't the energetic, idealistic young woman of previous years but then, as she kept telling herself, "what can I expect, at fifty years old?"

This age, for women, is often a time when old energies give way to new ones. As Ellie grew more active she'd directed her energies into caring for her invalid mother.

The nursing skills she showed in the care of her mother were exemplary. As her own mental and physical health improved, Ellie had asked Dr Jenkins for any up-to-date articles on Parkinson's disease and he'd lent her his stack of medical journals to pour through. She'd written to some of her old colleagues and even to her old mentor, Dr Truby King, for advice on diet and care of those with the disease. Dr Jenkins himself learnt a great deal from Ellie's research efforts.

Between them, Ellie and Gertie Foster had worked out an acceptable and palatable diet for Jeannie, incorporating the particular nutrients recommended by Dr Truby King for those with Parkinson's disease. Jeannie's general health improved. Family and friends remarked how well she was looking under Ellie's care and progression of the condition was much slower than expected.

Dr Jenkins had gone to visit Jeannie on the 28th February, which happened to be Shrove Tuesday. He'd found the kitchen full of her grandchildren, eagerly watching Grandma frying and tossing pancakes for them all, a thing which she would have found impossible a few months before.

There was no doubt in Dr Jenkins's mind that, despite a decrease in her energy levels, Ellie was still an excellent nurse and he understood her frustration at the sudden curtailing of her career. Time hung heavily on Ellie's hands and this was not ideal for someone liable to depression. He knew of Ellie's work with Dr Truby King, the celebrated nutritionist and specialist in infant care and that she had earned a good reputation, in London, for nursing similar cases to May Anderson.

Dare he suggest her services to the Anderson family? He was quite sure she was fit to take on the case but he was aware that she would need persuading. If it worked, it would benefit both Ellie and baby May. If it didn't work and Ellie proved mentally incapable, he could be in trouble. Dr Jenkins' instinct as a physician told him that she would be alright. He would be able to keep a close watch on her and there was no-one else in the locality that had her skill and knowledge.

The good doctor had persuaded himself. He'd been considering the matter for some days but today the case had shouted its urgency and he hurried round to 174, Aspen Lane.

Ellie was surprised and delighted by Dr Jenkins' request. Her confidence had been badly knocked but now she felt instinctively capable of the task.

It was Jeannie, her mother who was uncertain: "Ellie, should you be doing this? I'm not sure if you are strong enough yet. Remember, a child's life is at stake. Supposing something went wrong?"

"Mother, nothing is going to go wrong! Yes, a child's life is at stake and I might just be able to save it. It's what I'm trained to do. Dr Jenkins wouldn't ask me, if I wasn't strong enough."

"What about me? Who will see to me?" Jeannie tried another tack to save her daughter.

"Mother, you are able enough to do some things for yourself and Mrs. Foster comes every day. I'll make sure she knows exactly what you need. In any case, you've a tongue in your head and the telephone to hand. You can ask, if you need anything! Stephen should be here most nights. I will, most likely, have to sleep at the Andersons. I'll ask Annie if she and young Jack will come and sleep here when Stephen's away. Baby May won't be in a critical state for long. It must go one way or the other in a week or two."

Twenty minutes after Ellie had agreed to take on the case, Dr Jenkins was back at the Anderson's home. The couple listened carefully to the doctor's plan.

He told them that Ellie had become run down, through overwork, while nursing in London. After a stay in hospital she had come home to care for her invalid mother. The quieter life style in Hartsbeck had allowed Ellie to recover her health but she missed her job of nursing sick children. He explained Ellie's excellent qualifications and practical skills. Gilbert asked one or two searching questions about Ellie's illness and was assured that Ellie could, in no way, be a danger to May. It helped that the Anderson's had known Hannah and George Elkson and their children, for many years. They were so desperate about May, that the couple begged Dr Jenkins to arrange for Ellie to come as soon as possible.

"She will need to be here day and night to begin with," Dr Jenkins insisted, "are you able to provide a bed for Sister Elkson, where she can be in easy reach and hearing distance of the baby?"

"We'll arrange all that, Doctor," said Gilbert "they can be together in one large bedroom, if that's needed."

"Good. I don't want Sister Elkson to have anything extra to do other than nursing May. She will need some time to rest herself. If that is understood, I think we may have a good chance of saving May."

Within an hour Ellie was packing her bags to move to the Anderson's. She'd looked out all her notes from Dr. Truby King and had telephoned London asking for supplies of Dr King's latest breast milk formula and a fortifier containing extra protein, iron, calcium and vitamins which Dr. King recommended should be added to the feed for premature babies or new borns who were not feeding properly. All this was to be sent to Hartsbeck by train from London and should arrive later that evening. Dr Jenkins promised to meet the train and have the supplies brought immediately to Ellie, at the Anderson's.

In the meantime, Ellie searched her notes and her memory, to find an alternative to the sugar and water solution which baby May was being given. By twelve o'clock, midday, Ellie was on her way to the Andersons. It wasn't until she was in Dr Jenkins's car being driven to the small Hartsbeck suburb where the Anderson's lived, that baby

Jobo flashed into her mind and for the first time, she faltered. Could she really do this? Would memories of baby Jobo interfere with her competence?

As soon as she met Mr and Mrs Anderson and Winifred placed baby May in her arms, Ellie knew all would be well. May was nothing like Jobo, her eyes fixed onto Ellie's with a determined look which mirrored Ellie's own and she knew that this child was a survivor. Nevertheless, when Ellie weighed May on that first day, she knew it was going to be a hard slog; the child had gone down to three pounds four ounces.

For a whole week, baby, nurse and parents worked together and slowly, very slowly, May began to feed. To begin with she didn't take much more than a teaspoonful of a very diluted solution of Dr King's fortified breast-milk formula every fifteen minutes. Gilbert and Winifred insisted that they should take turns with Ellie during the night, so that she should have some sleep but on the first night, Ellie was loth to leave her position by little May. She needed to monitor the child carefully, watching for any bowel movements; regurgitation; restlessness and any change in temperature or colour, as well as feeding her. She had to watch for and weigh every wet nappy and make sure May took enough fluid, to make up the loss.

However, Ellie knew she must have rest. At seven in the evening on the second day, she asked Gilbert and Winifred to sit with her for the next hour and watch carefully all that she did with May. She let them use the small dropper to drip breast milk formula into May's tiny mouth and watch to see if she swallowed it. She taught them to recognise the different signs of restlessness and to monitor her stool and urine output. Then she allowed herself an hours rest while the couple took charge of their daughter. The second night was split in this way between them, Gilbert took one hour then Ellie took over for an hour, then Winifred and so on until morning.

Ellie did the majority of the daytime care, except for an hour's break for lunch and tea, when Winifred took charge. May showed signs of responding well to all this attention and was becoming used to the taste of the formula. She began to open her mouth expectantly whenever the dropper appeared. Ellie worked out a new night timetable, with two hour shifts shared between the three of them. This meant they all had the chance of four consecutive hours sleep. They found it easiest to move May's crib into the living room for the night with whoever was on duty, allowing the other two to sleep undisturbed upstairs.

"You must promise to wake me, if you are concerned about May in any way. If she starts to regurgitate or cry with colic or there is anything at all that you are uneasy about, wake me whether it's my time to take over or not. Also, if either of you feel unwell or overtired, tell me and I shall take over. I'm here to help you all, not just May. You are a family unit, so the health of each one of you is important to the others."

"I worry about Gilbert, he has to be at work every morning and I feel he isn't getting his sleep properly."

"Winnie, stop fretting. I'm strong as an ox and this situation won't go on for ever. May is improving every day, thanks to Sister Elkson. Anyway, I've rearranged my days so that appointments don't start until ten o'clock."

Ellie looked at Gilbert with admiration, his deep authoritative voice and strong frame declared his manliness but, unlike most men of that time, he was willing to throw himself into the heart of domestic life. He was conscientious and gentle in his care of May and didn't flinch at changing nappies or at regurgitated milk on his clothes. He would make tea and toast for his wife and for Ellie, during their night vigils. He didn't look over-tired but it helped that his dental surgery was on their home premises and that he could arrange appointments to suit him. His patients and most of the community of their district, were hoping with bated breath, for baby May "to start thriving," so there were no complaints.

By the end of the second week May weighed four pounds six ounces and was gaining every day, taking two ounces of formula from a normal bottle every hour. By the end of the third week, her weight had increased to six pounds and she was feeding normally for a baby of her size. During the fourth week, Ellie gradually weaned

May onto a formula more suited to her age. By the end of a month, May was growing into a happy and contented child, demanding her food when hungry and drinking it with furious energy. Ellie had to slow her down, so that she had time to digest the food she craved. Dr Jenkins called in each day and was delighted at the result of Ellie's ministrations,

"Well, Ellie- Sister Elkson, you are a credit to your profession. You have developed skills and knowledge far beyond anything I expected. You've taught me a lot during the last few weeks. May has developed beyond recognition and I've no fears for her future health, beyond accident or illness. Thank you, for all you've done."

Winifred spoke for herself and her husband. "We can never forget what you've done for us and for May. We'll make sure she knows all about you, when she's old enough, Sister Ellie. We're going to miss you dreadfully. Please, do come back and visit us. You'll need to make sure we're treating May properly!"

Ellie was moved by their thanks. For her, it was enough to see baby May sitting up and looking around with steady alert eyes, the tiny dimples and folds on her wrists proclaiming her healthy appetite. Tiredness almost overwhelmed Ellie as she packed her bags and said goodbye to George and Winifred. It was strange to accept her wages from them, they'd become like family to her and it dampened her spirits to feel she'd really just been a paid employee in their home.

Winifred must have guessed this because she seized the pretty, rabbit -shaped alarm clock they had all used to time baby May's feeds in those first days.

"Here, Ellie, take this as a reminder of us and all we went through together," she pressed it into Ellie's hands with tears in her eyes and Ellie clasped it to her, as Gilbert drove her back home to Aspen Lane.

CHAPTER 77

Solace in fresh air and books.

At first it was a relief to be home without the responsibility of baby May. Ellie enjoyed again the regular routine of sleep and meals at the right hours. It was now mid-June 1933 and the weather was warm. Though slower and stiffer in her joints, Ellie took walks on the tops as she used to do, revelling in the hedgerow flowers and the wild rose bushes with their delicate pink and white petals.

Stephen was engrossed in his science teaching at Preston College and had increased his research into geology and other forms of natural history. His teaching timetable was erratic, sometimes he taught during the day, sometimes in the evening. This meant he was often able to spend time during the week, as well as weekends, exploring locally or travelling as far as the Lake District, Wales and even Dorset, with his knapsack of tools and his camera. He was a popular speaker at many scientific or natural history societies and Edwin would accompany him as his lantern slide operator. Between them they'd built up a fascinating collection of photographic slides.

Stephen continued to enjoy gentle flirtations with a variety of young women but had no intention of settling down with any of them. Often, he wouldn't come home until well after eleven o'clock at night and was known for sleeping in most mornings.

"He's a night-bird," Ellie corrected Gertie Foster who had remarked about him being lazy.

"He works long after you and I are in bed. Even when he comes in late, he gets out his papers and scientific journals and reads and writes till the early hours. I've seen him, still at his desk at three o'clock in the morning, when I've had to get up in the night. He leaves his door ajar."

"Doesn't seem natural to me. He's clever, though. My nephew was in his chemistry class and says he's the best teacher he ever had and he wouldn't be where he is today, if it weren't for Mr Elkson."

Ellie smiled, Gertie's nephew worked as a pharmacist in Hartsbeck.

One day, Stephen took Ellie with him on the bus to Cock Bridge, about five or six miles away and from there they walked over Whalley Nab and down into Whalley village. It was a day of blue sky and white scudding clouds, the summer heat cooled by a mischievous breeze that came and went as they trod through fields and wood-lands, farmyards and along the banks of streams. They quenched their thirst at a farm with glasses of home-made sarsaparilla sold to them by the farmer's wife. Stephen pointed out butterflies and other insects just as he used to do.

"Look Stephen, a Gatekeeper! Sarah's favourite."

The tiny brown tipped butterfly fluttered along beside them, going from plant to plant hovering but never quite resting on any of them.

"She used to say it guided us. It certainly wants our company," smiled Stephen.

Ellie had a notion that the tiny winged creature was Sarah's spirit, dancing along beside them. After that day Ellie began to be troubled again by the idea that Sarah was trying to contact her. It was fortunate that she found she was now able to concentrate enough to lose her-self in reading, as a distraction from such thoughts.

"You're turning into a real bookworm, Miss Ellie," Gertie Foster grumbled when she eventually found Ellie sitting under the syca-more tree, deep in a book, "I've been looking all over for you, to help me fold the sheets ready for ironing."

Gertie had partly herself to blame. During Ellie's first few months at home, when her power of concentration had been poor, she'd found a secret attraction to the stories of passion and romance in cheap peri-odicals brought to her by Gertie.

She'd soon progressed from the magazine stories to gripping tales of adventure and romantic novels and then, as her mind grew more receptive, to deeper works of fiction.

Ellie's eager perusal of papers concerning Parkinson's disease was different. She needed the information for practical use and scanned the documents competently for useful material.

Ellie had now been back at home for more than a year. Rebecca had become wrapped up in preparing to go away to college in Manchester in September. Ellie understood completely but she'd begun to enjoy her niece's company and felt bereft.

However, with a new confidence born from her success with baby May, Ellie walked alone into Hartsbeck town-centre and joined the public library. Its size and stock of books initially overwhelmed her but she found a competent guide in a friendly, library assistant and was soon reading widely. Inevitably she was eventually drawn to books on religion and like an addict delved deeply into the occult texts of theosophy.

The idea that men and women prepared their own future in the next life, without any intervention of a salvific God, alternately pleased or troubled her. She couldn't quite cut herself off from believing in a personal God who would enable her to come to terms with her own uncomfortable nature. There were days when she longed for someone who could forgive and take away all that weighed heavily on her conscience. She told herself that such thoughts were irresponsible, "Ellie Elkson you must find your own spiritual strength and face up to your own life, past and present," She wondered about seeking her own spiritual guide from the next world. In the novel section she selected Oscar Wilde's 'Picture of Dorian Gray' and tried to read it again. She soon discarded it. The book was too heavy with memories of the day she'd first met Eliza in Boots' library and of her early explorations into theosophy. Ellie decided that she'd come back to this story from time to time and use it as a test of her mental stability. When she was able to read it through with no adverse effects, she would consider herself completely well.

Whenever she walked into Hartsbeck town-centre, Ellie would see the unemployed men, victims of the economic depression, lounging on street corners. She would watch thin, poorly-clad children, queuing with their mothers at the soup kitchens and in the fish-market where they hoped for a fish-head or any fish trimmings the stalls may have. Irrationally, Ellie felt herself to blame, because she was doing nothing to alleviate their plight. She began to remember the suffering of the children and adults she'd nursed, especially the ones who'd died. Memories came tumbling back and her mind distorted each memory until she felt convinced that, in some way, it had been her own, warped nature that had caused their suffering or their deaths.

She began to drift back into that state of withdrawal which feeds on its own misery and delights in its own sad company, shunning others. Such mental misery upset Ellie's physical health and she took to having days in bed, taking no food and drinking only boiled water. Gertie Foster became concerned and spoke of it to Dr Jenkins on one of his visits to Jeannie Elkson.

"I'm not happy about Miss Ellie, doctor. She's not right side up at all. She's eating next to nothing and gone back to drinking glass after glass of cold, boiled water- very fussy she is, about it having been boiled- too fussy to my mind. She's taken to having whole days in bed and when she is up, she sees to her mother and then hides herself away with her nose in a book, rather than be in company. She's like a tortoise, retreating into its shell. I think she's getting that melancholia again," and Gertie nodded sagely at Dr Jenkins.

Jeannie Elkson had noticed only that Ellie seemed slower and quieter and that sometimes her daughter rested in bed during the day.

"She gets a bit weary, there's nothing wrong with her having a lie down during the day, if she feels the need." Jeannie had become too occupied with dealing with her own increasing infirmity and didn't detect the depth of Ellie's depression.

Dr Jenkins talked with Ellie and came to the conclusion that she was developing a type of religious mania, fed by certain of the books she was reading.

"Ellie, it would do you good to take a good walk in the fresh air every day. A good brisk walk with a companion, try not to go alone. Don't just walk into the town. Go to the country areas, or the parks. We've some beautiful parks in Hartsbeck, the tram goes past your house and will take you to almost all the parks and you'll see other people out enjoying themselves, as well."

The doctor felt like a tourist agent, or a parent persuading a child into something it had no inclination to do. He decided to ask Gertie Foster and Ellie's sister-in-laws to make sure Ellie always had a companion on her walks.

"Ellie, you've done so well and we want to keep you well and enjoying life. You've become anaemic again. I'm going to prescribe a vitamin and iron tonic."

The doctor sighed and looked seriously at Ellie before telling her that he was putting her back on a higher dose of the medicine prescribed earlier by Dr Kern. This shook Ellie and she decided she would do all that Dr Jenkins suggested. She realised that she'd been allowing herself to sink back towards the debilitating darkness.

After a month of following the doctor's advice Ellie began to feel better. August was coming to an end and September loomed. The weather was kind with just the hint of autumn and Ellie took walks each day. Hannah sometimes went with her or Annie, but more often it was Gertie Foster who would set aside an hour in the afternoons for these outings.

Stephen was full of encouragement; "See it as part of your working day, Gertie; it seems you have two semi-invalids to care for nowadays. Anyway the fresh air will do you good as much as Ellie."

"Better not let Miss Ellie hear you call her a semi-invalid; she's coming out of that shell of hers quick enough and would soon give you a piece of her mind;" muttered Gertie as she hurried about her daily chores.

A week or two later Ellie was in Dr Jenkin's surgery. "Well, Sister Elkson; Ellie," He put down his pen and leaned back in the chair.

He'd been seeing her every week, ever since her slight relapse into depression during July and August.

"You've overcome that last little slip backwards very well indeed. It shows that you are capable of coping with attacks of depression, when they come. You'll always be prone to such attacks, from time to time. To some extent you will learn to recognise what triggers them but sometimes they may come for no reason that you can see. Their frequency should lessen, especially if you watch your diet, eat proper meals and please, keep away from water fasts. Such things are not for you, your metabolism can't stand up to it. Carry on with your daily walks in the fresh air and find a hobby you can enjoy at home, something you can do when you are kept there by your mother's condition. I don't mean reading your deep, theological books. If you must read, choose something light; my wife always enjoys a good Ethel M Dell."

"I wonder, Dr Jenkins, if I could be employed, on a part time basis, at Hartsbeck hospital. They may be glad of more staff now that the maternity unit has been extended and newly equipped, or maybe I could be of use at one of the maternity homes in the area. I worry that my nursing skills are going to waste."

"Hmm. I'll give that some thought. It may be that I could put you on a supply list, which means you would be approached, if a shortage of staff occurred, or if a nurse or midwife needed to be off work for some reason. You certainly did well with the Anderson's baby, but you did have a slight relapse afterwards. Will you leave it with me for a while, Sister?"

Ellie noticed how the doctor often referred to her as Sister and had an inkling that it was his way of boosting her confidence, reminding her that she'd earned such a mark of respect.

"Thank you, Doctor," she listened as he continued.

"Another aspect to consider is your mother. You must realise, that although you're keeping her stabilized by your excellent nursing, her condition will deteriorate; she can't be cured. She'll become more and more dependent on you, in the months or years ahead."

"Yes, of course. I did know that. I must do my duty by her."

"Right, well I think we can say you are much improved and you don't need to come and see me for a month, unless you want to do so. Keep up that lower dose of the medicine I prescribed."

They both stood and Dr Jenkins shook Ellie's hand, smiling encouragingly.

"You are a remarkable person, Ellie. I've known you since you were seventeen. I came into this practice as a junior partner with old Dr Waters the year before you went off to London to start your training. You've achieved a tremendous amount in your life and you're not wasting your talents even now."

"Thank you, Dr Jenkins, you've always encouraged me. I owe you a great deal," Ellie meant it and the doctor knew it, his eyes were moist as he watched her leave the surgery. He remembered her as the earnest young girl assisting Annette Harrison in the poverty stricken, back streets of Hartsbeck and as the determined nineteen year old, setting out to begin her nurse's training in London. His heart ached for her.

CHAPTER 78

Hannah's Surprise.

Ellie was not the only person in the Elkson family giving Dr Jenkins cause for concern. Hannah, at forty-one, was pregnant again and far from well. She'd come to his surgery thinking she had some serious illness and was shocked to discover that she was four months pregnant.

Dr. Jenkins finished the consultation with an order, "Hannah, you are to go home this minute and lie down for at least an hour and you must do this every afternoon."

When George came home from work Matilda told him that "Mrs Elkson isn't well, she's resting on her bed, upstairs."

He hurried up the stairs to find his wife already up and sitting on the side of the bed waiting for him.

"What's this Hannah? Matilda says you're not well?"

Smiling, Hannah patted a place next to her and he sat down and waited.

"I heard you come in and I wanted to speak to you alone. George, we are expecting another baby," she touched his hand anxiously.

George stared at her and then groaned. He was remembering the nights, over the past year, when he'd lain in bed agonising over Ellie and all that had happened in the family. His anxiety had run over into Tom and his Law exams and Rebecca going off to college and the health of young Alice, who seemed to catch every illness going. Hannah had wrapped him in her arms and drawn him to her. How thankfully he'd melted into the living warmth and tenderness of his wife's body, finding relief in an outpouring of love.

George took his pregnant wife's hands gently into his.

"Dearest, Hannah. I used you unthinkingly. I understood the dangers of you having another baby but it went right out of my head when we made love, I'm so sorry."

Hannah's eyes filled with tears, "George, I took you to me on those nights. I love you so very much and couldn't abide your pain. There were times when we just forgot to take precautions. You needed me and you allowed me to love you then, more than you had for such a long time. I'm not sorry about this child -though it's a real surprise, I thought I was past it. It seems I'm not." A touch of humour crept into her voice.

George felt accused, till he saw the soft light of acceptance in his wife's eyes.

He had a flash of understanding. Here was a woman, his wife, submitting her own life to that of the child growing within her. This unplanned life had come as a consequence of all that had happened to them, out of grief and love. It couldn't be denied. His harsh judgements, of men who loaded their weary wives with children they could ill afford, now shamed him. George kissed Hannah tenderly on the lips and stroked her shoulders.

"When is the baby due?" he asked,

"I'm just over four months gone, so it should be early in January. A New Year; a new life," she laughed, "Dr. Jenkins says if I'm very careful and rest as much as possible, I should be alright. He suggests I take a short holiday, as soon as possible. Perhaps I could go to Nancy Taylor's in Wray? It isn't far and the country air and the quiet always do me good. Nancy takes such care of me."

"Of course you must go. Nancy's been a Godsend to us. Do you remember the first day she came to us from Ireland?"

Hannah nodded, thinking back to the freezing, winter's evening when seventeen year old Nancy Doherty had arrived at their door. Wrapped in layers of shawls she was sitting up front on the driving seat of the cart, next to young Matthew Taylor the carter's boy, who'd collected her from the boat train. Her two small boxes of luggage were strung together precariously behind them. Matthew had jumped down and secured the horse, then lifted the young girl bodily to the ground. One tiny red nose and two bright eyes were all that could be seen from the shawls in the darkness but her indignant voice with its Irish brogue, announced that a person of reckoning had descended upon the Elkson household.

"Will you please to be leaving me to handle meself, Maester Taylor. I'm obliged for your help but just a touch of your hand on mine would ha' done, no need to take me in your arms as if—" her voice had trailed off into silence, as Hannah and George had come forward to greet her. Matthew, chuckling quietly, had left Nancy to introduce herself and busied himself with her luggage.

Nancy was one of the many Irish girls coming over to escape the famines and poverty in Ireland. Hannah had offered to take girls fresh from their homes and train them in the ways of a house-maid. She was good at this, having an air of authority and knowledge without being patronising. She made friends with the girls but was not over familiar. In return the girls worked hard and gave loyalty and respect. Nancy had been the first and after a year working with Hannah, had obtained a good position with the family of a wealthy mill owner. Matthew Taylor had kept his interest in her and after four years of courtship they were married. The couple had gone to live in the village of Wray, where they raised a family and ran the village shop. They also took holiday guests and Hannah had spent a restful week with them most summers, especially after the birth of Richard and then Alice. Nancy was well aware that Hannah needed these short breaks and would lavish her with care and good country food, during her stay.

"Yes, a holiday with Nancy will set you right!" George agreed and took Hannah in his arms, holding her close,

"Take care, my Hannah, you are very precious to me."

"And you to me," she whispered, resting against him.

CHAPTER 79

News of Dr. Alex Dobson.

Ellie left Dr. Jenkins' surgery frustrated but determined to make the best of her life as it was. She needed something to interest her and decided to ask Stephen if she could help him, in any way, with his geological work

Stephen was delighted that Ellie wanted to assist him. He asked her to read through some of the papers he was writing and to check and label a pile of rock specimens he hadn't had time to sort through.

"Oh and, if you've time, Ellie, would you like to write the labels for my butterfly collection; they are so small and fiddly it's time consuming. I know you've a good hand. You need to write the Latin name and the common name and the date and place I found each specimen."

As the days passed, Ellie realised she was fast becoming Stephen's full-time assistant. She didn't mind. It was interesting work and something to do while she was sitting with mother.

One evening, when Stephen was out, Ellie had gone to his study with a pile of completed specimen labels. She noticed a headline in a copy of the 'American Science Journal,' which lay on his desk. It announced that, Syndetocrinus, a new crinoid genus, had been discovered in the Silurian of Canada. Ellie was beginning to recognise certain geological terms and felt pleased that she knew that crinoids were pretty, delicate-looking fossils and Silurian was a geologic period. She picked up the journal, intrigued to read more and intending to show off her knowledge to Stephen at some point.

Glancing down the page, a cold shock ran through Ellie as her eye caught another head-line: "Plastic Surgeon, Mr Alexander Dobson." The name hit her like a blow, her legs trembled and she sat quickly in Stephen's chair and rested her head on his desk.

When she felt calmer, Ellie read the article. It was an obituary. Apparently Alex, (if it was Alex,) had been involved in some scientific research, involving the treatment of burns victims after the War. It seemed that Alex had suffered massive burns himself, particularly on his face, which had become so badly- deformed that it had been some years before he'd felt able to appear in public. His lungs had also been affected. Apparently, none of this had prevented him from working untiringly, in the burns unit of a hospital in Vancouver and then training as a plastic surgeon. The article praised his bravery. Alex's identity was further confirmed for Ellie by the potted biography of his training as a doctor of medicine in Canada and England before 1914. The article recorded that he'd worked in Oxford with orthopaedics and also with the famous Dr. Truby King, "whose work in the field of psychiatry and nutrition had helped Dr. Dobson in his own work in the field of traumatic burns injury".

Ellie read that Alex's work had pioneered several breakthroughs in this field and that his colleagues would continue to build on the progress he'd made. Ellie learnt that he'd lived with his sister, her husband and their children but he had never married. His sister thought that he'd been fond of a nurse in London, before the war, but when he'd come home with his horrific burn injuries, he'd refused to contact any of his old friends in England. He didn't want them to be repulsed by his changed appearance. Back in Canada he'd learnt to cope with the psychological trauma of his injuries as well as the physical and was able to empathise with others in similar predicaments. He'd become a well-known and well-loved figure in Vancouver and beyond, despite being a very private person. The article ended by announcing that Alex's research and the practical application of it, was of immense value to humanity and to medical science and that his sudden death in a skiing accident, at only fifty five years old, was a great loss.

Ellie didn't know how to react. Myriads of feelings played for the upper-hand, grief, pride, horror, relief, anger, pity and love. She was angry that he'd thought she would be repulsed by his appearance.

"Even if I had been at first; it wouldn't have lasted," she wanted to shout at him. "It would still have been you."

Then came relief that he hadn't just rejected her, without reason; pride that he hadn't lain down under his wounds but fought on for the sake of others and for his profession; pity, for his suffering; grief, that she hadn't been there with him and now, never could be. Most of all she was filled with a warm, all- pervading love, as if she were wrapped safely in a warm blanket and held tightly. She could have sworn that it was Alex holding her and his love warming her. Ellie stayed at Stephen's desk, until her mother called sharply from downstairs. Placing the science journal exactly as she'd found it, Ellie hurried down to help Jeannie to bed.

The warm, loved-feeling, lasted all that night and the following day but the morning after that it had gone. The memory of it was still there but the physical awareness of it was gone. Ellie told no-one about the obituary. She didn't want their pity. She wondered about writing to Lettie Parrish. At least Lettie had met Alex and knew how Ellie had waited and waited for news of him. The thought of Lettie as the Sister of her own ward, stabbed Ellie's conscience; she too ought to be nursing again in the front line. It also brought back such sharp memories of Sarah's death, that she couldn't bear it and she pushed all thoughts of contacting Sister Parrish, firmly away. Instead she confided her thoughts and memories of Alex to her diary and hid it away in her writing desk.

All these mixed emotions and the shock of Alex's death forced her to retreat back into her tortoise-like state. She curled protectively round her old wounds, shielding them from this fresh onslaught.

None of the family noticed. They were used to her being quiet. In any case, it was nearing the anniversary of Sarah's death when the atmosphere in the house-hold always became subdued. Stephen usually went up to London, to Golders Green where he would donate a new plant for the Garden of Remembrance on behalf of them all. He told them how he would stand in the garden simply to remember Sarah, and always found himself praying to the God he thought he'd renounced. Sarah's ashes and Alex's body, now dead, preyed on Ellie's mind. She searched again among the works of theosophists such as Madame Blavatsky, May Besant and Charles. W. Ledbeater, for spiritual meaning beyond the grave.

These readings did nothing to ease her mind. They spoke of evil influences as well as good ones, from beyond the grave. This teased her into guilt and fear. She worried whether she had used her talents in this life to their full extent. Some of the writings even made her wonder if she'd allowed evil beings, from beyond the grave, to influence her. How would she escape from their evil machinations in the next life? Would they turn her into a malevolent spirit? Such researching fed her depression and gave her nightmares.

In desperation Ellie turned to Cousin Hugh for help.

Hugh had visited Ellie and her mother several times over the months since Ellie's return to Hartsbeck. Ever since he'd glimpsed the fear and anguish lurking within Ellie during his visit to her in the psychiatric hospital, Hugh had thought deeply of how he could help her. He'd often tried to speak with her of the love of Christ and God's forgiveness but her mind and emotions were too confused for her to grasp what he was saying. In any case, in the first instance, it was her brothers' forgiveness she craved, not God's. He'd written out a list of bible passages, which he hoped Ellie would read instead of the theosophy texts. He'd chosen the passages carefully, searching out those which spoke of God dealing graciously with sinful and vulnerable people.

Wryly, he considered what his atheist friends would say- "that's typical of religion -just dishing out meaningless platitudes. You're giving her sweeties to suck, to make her feel better. You should be helping her to face up to things, not feeding her bed-time stories!" Hugh sighed, they could be partly right but Ellie's mind and soul were sick and needed to hear words which could soothe and heal, before she would be strong enough to face up to all that had happened. He realised that above all, she needed to forgive herself. Continuing the imagined dialogue with his atheist friends, he reminded them that, when they were physically sick they would eat light food, nourishing but easy to digest, soothing to the stomach, until they were well enough to eat a full blooded meal again.

Ellie had read the passages Hugh had given her and considered them but then she would also read some theosophical idea, which disagreed with these Bible verses. She was becoming more and more confused in her struggle to make sense of it all.

She wrote to Hugh and begged him to come to her. He came. She trembled pitifully when he tried to encourage her to voice her fears and his heart ached. In the end, he just held his cousin's hand, while she talked. He listened and realised Ellie seemed to want to be punished, rather than be given promises of forgiveness and would not entertain being told that she had nothing to feel guilty about. He spoke firmly to her;

"Ellie! You're meeting out far greater punishment to yourself than you deserve. Stop beating yourself into the ground. What you're doing to yourself is far worse than anything you did to Sarah."

It was no good; years of floundering in a mix of the occult mysteries of theosophy and the open mysteries of the Christian faith had turned Ellie's mind into a maze in which she twisted and turned frantically, unable to find the right way.

Unable to isolate one particular fear from the turmoil in Ellie's mind, Hugh read to her the parable of the lost sheep. To his great relief this seemed to calm her. She clung onto the idea of being found and brought safely home by the good shepherd. She dare not name the good shepherd, she'd resisted him too long but she clung on to the picture painted of him in the biblical parable and that was enough for the moment. When Hugh left, to go back to his parish and home duties, Ellie was in a more peaceful mood. She was even able to talk of Sarah with her mother who was brimming with memories of her youngest daughter now that it was September and nearing the fourth anniversary of Sarah's death.

"I can't believe its four years ago. It still seems so fresh in my mind, and I remember her so clearly," Jeannie mused.

They reminisced of times past when Sarah and Ellie were growing up.

"I'll never forget the day Sarah was born," Ellie said, longing to be back in that warm, sunlit place where she'd held baby Sarah in her arms.

"You were grand that day, Ellie. Sarah and I would've been lost without you. Who would have thought, that you would have gone on to be a fine nurse and Sarah a teacher? I'm that proud of you both; the boys too, but you and Sarah and I are women and between us we've shown the world that women are a force to be reckoned with," Jeannie smiled broadly and nodded her head in proud contentment. Ellie smiled sadly. She noticed that her mother spoke of Sarah as if she was still here, living with them.

The sense of Sarah being close-by haunted Ellie all that night. She dreamt again of walking through the woods and fields with her, just as she had done so often in reality. Only this time Sarah was in front, leading the way. The tiny gate-keeper butterfly, as always, fluttered beside Ellie through the dream. Suddenly Sarah stopped and Ellie stopped behind her. Sarah turned and smiled at her sister before walking on ahead, into the sunlit wood. She turned round again and beckoned to Ellie but Ellie couldn't move. The Gate-keeper had increased in size and was guarding the path between them. She dare not push past the creature whose wings were now like the wings of an angel. Sarah's face looked sad but she smiled and beckoned once more to Ellie, before disappearing into the trees. Ellie woke wondering if Sarah could be her Spirit Guide. She slept again, this time dreamlessly, until morning.

CHAPTER 80

Ellie goes walking.

It was Tuesday, the fifteenth of September and Jeannie Elkson was to spend the day with Hannah and her family at Humboldt Drive and to stay the night with them. George felt that Ellie needed a break and it would be good to have his mother with them. Rebecca was now away at the College of Domestic Economy in Manchester and they missed her lively presence. Hannah needed something to lift her from the lethargy brought on by her pregnancy and grandma's visit would cheer up Alice and Richard.

Stephen, back from his visit to Golders Green, had taken some students away for a few days on a field trip. He was expected back sometime on the following day, Wednesday.

Jeannie wanted Ellie to come to Hannah's as well; "I don't like Ellie being alone in the house all night. It's alright during the day when Gertie Foster's there,"

George was firm; "the whole reason for your visit to us, is to give Ellie a rest from you, mother. She's at your beck and call day and night. She needs a break and she deserves it. She wants a bit of time to herself. Even Edwin and Annie have promised her they'll leave her alone, unless she needs them and they're only across the street. You and Hannah are to have a quiet two days together being waited on by our excellent maid, Matilda, who's longing to spoil you both. Stop fretting mother!"

Ellie was glad to stay at home. She'd dreamt again of Sarah and woken in the night longing for her. She didn't want such thoughts crowded out by clammering children, or having to be sociable.

Rebecca was away fulfilling her dream to train as a domestic science teacher so she wouldn't be there to act as a buffer between Tom and herself. For the last five years Tom had been articled to his father at 'Drake and Elkson's solicitor's firm while also studying for his law degree. Earlier this year he'd completed his Law Society Final exams and in June he'd graduated and was now working full-time with George in the Hartsbeck office. This meant he would be at home in the evening which would have disconcerted Ellie. She still felt the sting of her nephew's comments about her coldness.

"Yes," Ellie told herself, "I'm more than glad to stay here, at Aspen Lane."

A car came to collect Jeannie at ten o'clock and Gertie and Ellie waved off the frail old lady with a sigh of relief. It was raining. Gertie looked at Ellie, she was uneasy about her charge and decided some old-fashioned house-work would keep her from becoming maudlin.

"We'll give the house a good bottoming. We've no meals to worry about, there's enough broth from yesterday for our lunch and there's plenty of eggs and ham and such like for your tea."

"It's meant to be a day off for me," objected Ellie.

"It'll be a different kind of work from the usual. You can take a rest whenever you want to, lass; I'm no slave driver but I thought you might welcome some activity."

Ellie elected to help Gertie. She could work and think at the same time.

They worked hard till half past twelve and then took an hour's break to fortify themselves with bowls of steaming lamb broth and hunks of Gertie's homemade bread. After lunch they sat by the kitchen fire for half an hour, Gertie reading the magazines she'd brought, while Ellie dozed and hoped for another glimpse of Sarah.

Eventually Gertie gave a great sigh and looked up at the clothes-rack hanging from the ceiling above them. There were only some shirts belonging to Stephen and a couple of blouses of Jeannie Elkson's hanging up to dry.

"We can leave those few bits on the rack till tomorrow. I think it's time we went for our walk in the fresh air, before I have to go home." Gertie was keeping strictly to Dr. Jenkins's orders.

"A walk will be good. It's fine now, just a bit damp after this morning's shower. We'd better wrap up," Ellie tried to sound cheerful but her thoughts were busy elsewhere.

They walked briskly to the local park and took a steep path upwards through a grove of trees. They paused at the highest point, where the imposing, ten year old war memorial now dominated the scene. Gertie would have steered her companion away but Ellie determinedly went to it and read down the long lists of names of the war dead until she came to Elkson, J. They both stood a moment with heads bowed, lost in their own thoughts. The walk home took them past the bowling-green and tennis courts, the museum and the deserted bandstand. No-one else was about. Ellie mentioned the different buildings to Gertie, as they caught their eye. She felt as if she was seeing things clearly for the first time in years and warmed to the places and objects as if they were old friends. She found herself nodding to them as she passed, as if to say "You've been my lifelong acquaintances. Thank you for being here."

They arrived home feeling chilled but soon warmed up over a pot of hot tea. Gertie cast a quick look round to make sure all was in order.

"There's still a few jobs but they'll do tomorrow. I'm off home now, Miss Ellie. That little stroll did us both good, blew all the cobwebs away. I'll be back in the morning at half past seven and we'll have a go at cleaning Mr. Stephen's room, before he gets home. I daren't touch it when he's around! It'll keep us both busy. Now get a good rest tonight, don't you be reading them books of yours till all hours!"

Gathering up her bag and gloves, Mrs Foster made for the back door. Her hand was stretched out towards the sneck when she turned back.

"Think on, if you need me just knock next door and they'll fetch me, I'm only round the corner but I must go and see to my Bert's meal. He'll think I've left him. Good-night then."

"Good-night, Mrs Foster." Ellie moved closer to the older woman but didn't touch her, "You've been so good to me Gertie, thank you."

Mrs Foster hesitated at the uncharacteristic show of affection and use of her Christian name. She patted Ellie's shoulder, "I'm that glad you're getting better, lass."

Then she opened the back door and hurried away, to see to her Bert.

Ellie went into the back garden and leant against the sycamore tree. She drew deep gasps of the spicy, autumn air. Her legs trembled. Despite Gertie's kindness, she felt battered by the housekeeper's obvious crusade to ward off depression and dirt. All day she'd longed to be alone. The sycamore was an old friend. Closing her eyes Ellie called back the memory of the family planting it as a young sapling on Edwin's tenth birthday, how many years ago? She couldn't remember. She did remember that Sarah, Edwin, George, Stephen and Jack, Mother and Dad and herself, had been happy that evening.

In her memory, the children's faces were unfurrowed by the ravages of the following years and the sun was shining. She stretched out her hand to touch the greenish bark of the mature tree but its chilling dampness was like cold sweat and she flinched. The bright fallen leaves, which had looked like tiny hands, had ground to earth mould under her boots. She looked up at the late afternoon sky and saw the colours of bruised flesh, blue and grey, purple and yellow, shot through with old pink.... Sarah's favourite blouse had been that same pink; she'd never liked her in it. Ellie groaned.

"Oh Sarah, I wish you were here with me, we could talk together and walk in the woods, just as we used to do."

She remembered the dream she'd had, when recovering from a cold in Mrs Larsen's house, during her first few years in London. That was when she had first read about theosophy. She regretted ever becoming entrapped by that strange movement; it had been like being sucked into thick treacle. She knew she could never shake off its influence.

Ellie's directed her thoughts back to her sister; "We shall walk together again Sarah, I promise you. Be ready for me, little sister."

Ellie's thin lips quivered into an almost smile as Sarah's voice seemed to answer her, "It's time Ellie. Come now."

Back indoors Ellie set about preparing things as if working to a well-known routine. She toiled up the steep narrow stairway, carrying with her a large jug of fresh, cold water. Once in her bedroom she closed the curtains on the weeping rooftops and set out two bowls and a glass, pouring water from the jug into each. Opening the bottom drawer of an old oak chest, Ellie took out her neatly-folded nurse's uniform and laid it on her bed and quietly placed her Bible on top. Just for a moment she hesitated, something stirred in her mind but it slipped away before she could grasp it. She undressed and carefully washed herself all over, the coldness of the water sharpening her senses.

"I have purified my outer body with fresh water," she murmured as if reciting a liturgy.

Then she dressed in the clean under-wear and a skirt and blouse, all of which she had washed and ironed herself.

"Nobody else can have contaminated them. If they are unclean, it is from me and no-one else."

Again her words seemed part of a liturgy.

Sitting in front of the dressing table she unpinned her hair, it was still dark-brown where it flowed over her shoulders but Ellie noticed that near her scalp it was turning to silvery.

"You're nine years older than I am. How come you've no grey hairs?" Sarah had asked when they'd been together in Redcliffe Street, pointing out the grey streaks in her own light-brown hair. Again Ellie felt some stirring in her mind, puzzled she dipped her brush into the second bowl of clean water and began to brush it through her hair. This time, quite unexpectedly, instead of her own liturgy of cleansing, the words of Jesus from the Gospels came to her. They were words she remembered from Easter services she'd attended as a child;

"If I wash thee not, thou hast no part with me."

A small sob escaped her, just one.

"Then you too must wash me, Lord. I must be pure outside and in; please, make me clean so I can come to Sarah and to you, in the blissful place," Ellie's hands trembled and reached upwards, like a child's. This time the stirring in her mind formed into a whisper of words,

"Wait! Not yet, Ellie. Wait."

She chose not to recognise the voice. It wasn't Sarah's. The idea of stopping now, in the middle of her chosen task, frightened Ellie and she shook the words away. The moment passed and she brushed, rolled and pinned her long hair on top of her small neat head. She moved across the landing into Stephen's room.

The evening was closing in and as she switched on the electric light, she averted her eyes from the collection of butterflies, mounted and pinned in their glass topped cabinet. She walked across the squeaky linoleum to Stephen's desk. Finding pen and paper she wrote a note.

Tuesday, 15th September 1933

Dearest Stephen,
*   I have gone walking with Sarah. Please tell mother.*
*   Your loving sister Ellie.*

She wanted to sit in his chair and rest her head on the desk for a while and take in the familiar smell of ink and old leather, the pencil shavings and the dregs of whisky and tobacco, but her sense of duty was too strong. She must not keep Sarah waiting.

Stephen's climbing rope was behind his bedroom door and taking it, Ellie went downstairs to the kitchen. The rope was too long. She wound it round and round the struts of the clothes rack leaving a length hanging to form a noose. Gently, she touched her brother's shirts and mother's blouses still hanging on the rack to dry and sniffed in the clean familiar scent of starch and rinsed-out soap. Warm memories threatened to overwhelm her but she shut them out and pulled the rack up to the ceiling, securing it firmly. She looked up at the small pulley wheels bolted into the plastered wood and pulled on the climbing rope, to check it would take her weight. It held her easily, but she took off her boots. The grandfather clock in the hallway struck eight; no one would be back in the house for hours.

"I'm coming to you, Sarah, I'm really coming!" Ellie spoke the words firmly as she clambered onto the table and placed the noose around her neck.

At ten minutes to midnight Stephen was walking up the hill from the railway station, towards home. As he came up Aspen Lane he stopped under a street lamp to light his pipe. Through the rough cloth of his knapsack he could feel the rock samples and fossils he'd collected in the Yorkshire dales during the last few days. Very much a night bird, he planned to spend the next two hours sorting and cataloguing his finds. Ellie would have gone to bed hours ago and he knew that mother was staying with George and Hannah. Glancing up at the terrace where they lived, Stephen was surprised to see a light in his bedroom. He hurried to open the front door; another light, from the kitchen, shone along the hallway.

"Hello!" he shouted, "I'm home! Ellie!" The house was very still, no-one answered his call. "It's not like Ellie to leave lights on," he muttered and wondered about intruders. They could be upstairs, or in the kitchen, or anywhere in the house. Reasoning that they would try to get away through the back door, Stephen clutched his knapsack as a weapon and crept softly into the kitchen.

What Stephen found, was described in the inquest report printed a week later in the local newspaper:

Hartsbeck Chronicle: Thursday, Sept. 17th 1933

"On Saturday morning the witness (Stephen Elkson) left home for a weekend in Yorkshire. He returned home at 11.50pm on Monday night and noticed a light in his bedroom and also in the back kitchen. On entering the kitchen he found his sister in a "sagging" position with her feet resting on the floor, and round her neck a piece of rope, one end of which was secured to the clothes-rack suspended from the ceiling. The rack was about five and a

half feet from the floor. She was fully clothed. He immediately cut her down and laid her on the kitchen settle before sending for Dr. Jenkins. Her body was quite cold and the doctor pronounced her to have been dead for some hours. The jury returned a verdict that the deceased hanged herself while not of sound mind."

Stephen had stood and looked down at his sister as she lay still and silent on the settle. It was the silence which had unnerved him. Quickly he'd telephoned his brother, George. George had been in his study having a friendly conversation with Tom, who'd just arrived home from a late concert in Preston. George had listened to Stephen's garbled message and Tom had raced for the whisky bottle as shock had registered on his father's face, turning his complexion grey. George had put down the phone, sunk onto a chair and grabbed the tot of whisky from Tom downing it in one. Revived almost immediately he'd jumped up, staggering slightly against the desk.

"Fetch my coat, Tom. I must drive down to Aspen Lane straight away. Your Aunt Ellie's been taken ill. Don't wake your mother."

Tom had insisted on driving him; "Dad, you look awful. You're in no fit state to drive."

George had agreed thankfully. Twenty year old Tom was a competent driver. George had been unable to bring himself to tell his son what Stephen had said on the phone, it was too horrible. He'd wanted Tom to wait in the car when they'd arrived at Aspen Lane but Stephen had the front door open for them and Tom just followed his father inside. The twenty year-old lad remembered thinking that Uncle Stephen's usually twinkly eyes had looked clouded and bewildered behind his spectacles. Uncle Edwin, his hair standing on end and pyjama legs showing beneath his trouser bottoms, had come hurrying across from his house, his St. John's Ambulance bag slung over one shoulder. Uncle Stephen had simply pointed towards the kitchen.

They'd ignored Tom and he'd followed on behind them all.

At this point Uncle Stephen had found his voice, "I thought you ought to see how it is, George, in case of legalities. I had to take her

585

down, she was very cold but her body was limp and soft. There didn't seem to be any signs of life, but I couldn't be sure. I've sent for Dr. Jenkins; he's out on a maternity case but will come within half an hour."

Their eyes had followed Stephen's first to Ellie's body on the settle then to the frayed rope dangling from the rack. The noose had lain separately on the floor, like a killed snake.

George had forgotten that his eldest son was a fully trained member of the St. John's Ambulance brigade and was surprised when Tom had immediately taken charge of the situation. He'd run over to his Aunt and supporting her sagging body against his own strong, youthful one turned her onto her side, into the recovery position. Edwin had quickly joined him and easily explained away the slightly unnerving sound as air had moved from inside Ellie's body.

Edwin had learnt to keep calm in the face of the horrors in the trenches and though he had started to shake, with a return of the old shell shock, he'd taken hold of one of Ellie's cold hands. "It's n- not s-s-stiff yet," he'd stammered as he'd massaged her fingers desperately, willing life to come back into his sister. It had been Tom who'd gently felt his aunt's bruised neck for any sign of a pulse and, gritting his teeth, undone Ellie's blouse. Edwin had passed him an instrument from his ambulance bag, it was similar to a miniature hearing trumpet. Tom had placed the instrument on Ellie's cold chest and bent his ear over it. He'd detected no sign of breathing and no heart- beat. Edwin had produced a pencil torch and Tom had shone it into each of his aunt's wide-open eyes, there had been no response to the light and Edwin carefully closed his sister's eyes. Tom knew he'd never forget his uncle's great, shuddering, involuntary sob.

George had felt mesmerised as he'd watched his son working on Ellie with Edwin.

It had been with such cool professionalism that Tom had finally pronounced his aunt to be dead that both Stephen and George had been taken by surprise when Tom had made a sudden move to the kitchen sink, where he was violently sick. The older men had snapped back into the realisation that here was a twenty-year- old lad. Whatever his expertise, this had been his first real experience of death and it had been an unusually traumatic one.

A spasm of anger towards his sister had coursed through George;

"How could she be so thoughtless, she must have known how it would be for us when we found her. Tom, you shouldn't have had to deal with this at your age."

Edwin had put his arm round Tom's shoulders and had comforted his nephew, "It often t-takes you like th- that the f-f-first time, lad. You g-get used to controlling it after a while, but it's always hard. You did well to d-do what you did, before giving in." He didn't remind anyone that some of the lads in the trenches had been younger than Tom.

George had been thinking hard. Dr Jenkins would be here soon and would certify Ellie's death. The police would have to be informed. They would have to assess the evidence in order to present it to the coroner at an inquest.

"Listen, all of you," George had barked, "I don't want Tom to have to go through giving evidence at the inquest with all the publicity. If Tom were to disappear from the scene now, before Dr. Jenkins arrives, he need have nothing more to do with it."

"I think you're right, George. There's no doubt Ellie was already dead when Stephen came home and it would be far better if you and I were the only ones involved in the inquest. Edwin, you take Tom to your house now. Then come back across. We'll say I sent for you once George had come and seen the situation."

"Better come quickly, Tom," Edwin had gathered up his ambulance bag. "Dr Jenkins could be here any minute."

By then Tom had seemed in a world of his own and had allowed Edwin to lead him out through the back door. Nephew and Uncle had stumbled over the cobbles of the dark back street and then turned the corner onto the main road and crossed quickly to Edwin's house. They'd found Annie up and dressed. She'd been in the middle of making hot tea for them all.

"As you're going back across, Edwin, you'd better take a flask of tea for George and Stephen and the doctor, when he comes. Tom had watched her busily filling the flask and felt surprisingly comforted by the homely action. That, together with an niggling, inner resentment at being sent away from the scene of death as if he were a child, had helped to replace some of the horror for him.

Aunt Annie had prattled on, "No need to take cups, you can use your mother's crockery. Make sure George and Stephen have sugar with their tea, for the shock. They won't like it, but they need it."

Edwin had gone back to his brothers and administered the medicinal tea with sugar as Annie had ordered. They'd hardly finished drinking it when Dr Jenkins had arrived, followed soon afterwards by the police. Stephen had covered his sister with the eiderdown from her own bed and Dr Jenkins had carefully drawn it up over her face as soon as he'd certified her as dead. By this time rigor mortis had begun to set in and the doctor had suggested the time of death as being about three or four hours previously. He'd then shaken the hands of the Elkson brothers.

"I'm deeply saddened by this," he'd told them, "we've all lost a person very dear to us and an excellent nurse. I shall call in to see your mother in the morning but now, you all need to have some rest. Ellie's body will be taken away within the hour. If there's nothing else I can do for any of you, I'll bid you all goodnight until tomorrow."

The brother's had breathed a sigh of relief when he'd gone. "It was right to keep Tom out of it but I can't help feeling we were doing something not quite legal," Stephen had voiced all their feelings.

Another secret which Stephen kept to himself was Ellie's last note. He'd first read it on retiring to bed after the doctor and the police had left and George had gone home. Edwin had stayed in the house with him and had already gone to bed. Ellie's body had been taken away for a post-mortem. By then it was four o'clock in the morning and sitting at his desk, his unopened knapsack of fossils on the floor beside him, Stephen had found, read and re-read his sister's message. He'd asked himself why he didn't want to share it with anyone else. He wasn't sure. Perhaps, because once there'd been only Ellie and himself, as children, before George and Edwin, Sarah and Jack were born and he wanted to keep this last message to himself, just as the two of them had shared their first childish confidences. Perhaps, because in his turmoil of anger and grief, he rebelled against obeying Ellie's last request to tell mother. Perhaps, because he thought the message would be sullied by their mother's reaction. He imagined she would dramatise it and give it some unwholesome spiritualist twist. Perhaps he didn't want to hear again George's sarcastic anger. Certainly he hadn't wanted the note presented as evidence, the 'suicide note', for the entire world to read.

Now, over a week later, he read it for the twentieth time. What was he to do with it? With a great sigh Stephen removed his spectacles, he could see further without them. Rubbing a hand across his eyes to clear them, he scanned the room. The butterflies in their cabinet were catching the morning sun on their wings. Their fading colours glowed and receded and glowed again, as the light dappled through the sycamore branches outside the window. Stephen took a lump of dull, red, sealing wax from his desk drawer and folding Ellie's last message into a small square, lit a match and sealed the note with hot wax. He struggled from his chair like an old man and stumbled across to the butterfly cabinet. His fingers trembled as he secured the tiny package with a pin next to the corpse of the tiny, brownish-orange butterfly labelled, 'The Gatekeeper'. He closed the lid of the cabinet, then sat down again at his desk and wept.

CHAPTER 81

George is surprised.

George was angry, angry and confused. During the weeks since Ellie's death he'd not only had to cope with his own grief but with his children's bewilderment and with the public reaction to the tragedy. Even Alice, at ten years old, had faced ghoulish questions in the school playground from children with an unhealthy curiosity in the macabre. She had discussed it with her brother Richard, who was her elder by only eighteen months. Together they'd asked Hannah and Tom to tell them exactly what had happened. Tom had been unable to cope and walked away into the garden while Hannah had talked with the younger ones, explaining that Ellie had been ill and so unhappy that she hadn't known what she was doing.

"Now Alice and Richard, when things like this happen it's not good to talk about them outside the family. People may ask you all sorts of things. All you need to say to them is 'I'm sorry but we don't want to talk about it.' That's what daddy and I will say and I want you to promise to do the same."

Apparently Alice and Richard had promised solemnly.

"God, what a mess!" George pushed away the papers on his desk and ran nervous fingers through his greying hair until his usually neat quiff stood on end. Impetuously, he picked up a pile of papers and thrust them into his briefcase, then strode from the room. Snatching his hat from the stand by the door he tossed a message to his secretary,

"I'm out for the rest of the day Miss Crabtree, please deal with any calls appropriately. Refer to Mr Tom if necessary."

"Certainly, Mr Elkson," Miss Crabtree had years of experience behind her, first with Mr Drake and then George Elkson. She felt herself quite capable of running the office on her own and George thought so too, within reason.

George drove his car out into the countryside of the Ribble Valley and parked it at Cock Bridge near the beginning of a favourite walk up the steeply wooded hillside of Whalley Nab. He changed the jacket of his town suit for an old tweed one and his shoes for hefty walking boots which he always kept ready in the car. As he struggled into the stiff boots he had a vivid childhood memory of Ellie pushing his feet into his clogs and his childish cry, "Ellie, stop it! You're hurting me."

Conscious of the echo of that cry piercing his heart, George pocketed pipe and tobacco and strode out over the Nab. This walk was so familiar to him that his feet took the right paths while his thoughts ranged freely. He cut a sturdy cudgel from a fallen tree branch, to help him over the rough ground and walked on hard and determined. Gradually his anger abated as the stony paths opened up into grassy moorland interspersed with wooded areas. He crossed a deeply-flowing stream, balancing from rock to rock, then oozed his way up the muddy bank. Sheep lifted their heads and stared at him as they munched the last of the autumn grass but he met no-one. Low grey clouds scudded across the sky, releasing the occasional patch of blue. The earth was damp and cold but rich with leaf mould.

"Ellie, you damned idiot," he muttered, his thoughts a conversation in his head.

"Why on earth kill yourself? Haven't we all been through enough? Surely you could have spared us this, especially mother. How could you do this to our mother?"

Horror, grief, shame, all three fought to be uppermost in his emotions. The one emotion George fought to keep at bay was love for his sister and yet he knew that this was the emotion triggering all the others. He deliberately tried not to think of Ellie before her death; of her time in London struggling without family around her, valiantly nursing through an epidemic on his wedding day, while he'd selfishly declared she'd let him down; her feverish struggles to cure Sarah which he'd deliberately turned against her. If he thought too much, guilt would overwhelm him.

Then there was Tom,

"I should never have allowed him to come with me and see his aunt like that but he seemed to cope so well on the night, better than any of us."

Tom had begun to show signs of delayed reaction. He was more reserved than his siblings, quiet and studious but inside he hid a sensitive and romantic nature, Hannah and young Alice had always been aware of this gentler side to him.

After his aunt's suicide Tom had cut himself off from family and friends as much as possible. He'd skipped meals, taking bread and cheese to his room saying that he needed to study. This was just an excuse because he'd passed all his exams earlier in the summer. His boyish face looked continually drawn with lack of sleep and ten year old Alice, who'd always been close to him, obviously felt abandoned and uneasy. Tom had become so ill-tempered that the two younger ones had begun to avoid him. All this George had been conscious of but thought it best to allow his son to come through the experience in his own way.

Hannah had hardly seemed to notice Tom's moodiness. Reluctantly, George admitted how difficult Hannah was finding this latest pregnancy. He brooded over his wife, as he pressed on towards the summit of the hill. Her last two pregnancies had been difficult and although it was ten years since the birth of Alice, their youngest child, Hannah's body had never regained its former vigour. She'd gained more and more weight and her energy had waned. Her once handsome face had lost its distinctiveness and become sallow and heavy. The bronchitis and asthma, which had threatened in earlier years, was now a constant problem. Dr. Jenkins had warned against further pregnancies.

All this had come at a time when George was receiving invitations into the social circles of his wealthier clients and needed his wife beside him. By sheer will and personality, Hannah would rise to each occasion and with her interest in people, charmed those she met. Nevertheless, George couldn't help comparing her to the suave, fashionable wives of his clients. Sometimes he would persuade Rebecca to accompany them, which eased Hannah's predicament and filled him with pride.

George smiled in appreciation at the memory of his exuberant elder daughter with her straight-forward, outgoing personality which was quite unfazed by social snobbery. Her love of sport and the out-doors had given her a healthy complexion and good figure which attracted George's clients. She often embarrassed the more conventional Tom, with her wicked way of popping any bubbles of pomposity she encountered. Hannah was pleased when Rebecca joined them at the functions but was conscious of the reason for it. Nevertheless, people loved and admired Hannah. George knew he'd every reason to be proud of his wife and his love and admiration of her swelled when he thought how she'd constantly reassured him whenever her pregnancy had consumed him with guilt. "You don't deserve her, George Elkson. You've been a selfish cad." He shouted the reprimand out loud, which relieved him a little. Then he shuddered as the picture of Ellie hanging herself from the kitchen clothes rack flashed back to him.

These thoughts and others roved through George's mind as he walked. He tried to shed them behind him, like bits of old skin and allow the living touch of the unfolding countryside to refill and calm his mind.

He reached the crest of Whalley Nab and found a sheltered spot underneath one of those sturdy, isolated trees that grow on the upper slopes of Lancashire hills, their twisted branches bent permanently, to the prevailing wind. George spread out his waterproof and leaning back against the tree's gnarled trunk, settled down to light his pipe. He mused that, although such hilltop trees were not so tall and splendid as their counterparts in the rich, well-watered soil of the valleys, they had a magnificence all of their own. Their trunks and branches were shorter and more scarred, battered by full exposure to the violence of wind and weather of all seasons. They gripped the rocky soil with roots that travelled deep and wide searching for food and anchorage and in spring and summer their leaves gave shade and shelter and beauty to the rugged landscape. Sheep gathered under them, finding relief from hot sun or cold, windswept rain and snow; the more delicate moorland flowers bloomed around them and green moss glowed with pleasure at the cool dampness where roots and trunk joined.

George closed his eyes, enjoying the support of the tree and feeling an empathy with its daily battles for life. What was this motivation, even of a tree, to live and improve the life of others, against all the odds. He remembered his brother Jack, his sister- in- law Becky and all those others who'd died or were injured in the Great War. They'd been battling for a better life for everyone, whatever the cost. But surely, the cost had been too great; men had made mistakes; there'd been too much devastation. Hopelessness swept through George and a great shuddering sigh came from somewhere, deep inside him. He wondered about his own young family and what they might have to face in the future and how they would cope. How would he cope, in this hostile world? Feeling as helpless as the part-formed babe in Hannah's womb George longed with all his heart for God. The breeze blew gently around him, ruffling his hair and rustling the leaves on the tree. The branches stretched over him like the arms of a huge cross and he was conscious of the weight of pain and loss far beyond his own. What was this dreadful pain and whose was it? It must be the agony of some great love. He looked up through the dark branches to the scudding white clouds. Could it be the world's pain? Or maybe the anguish of the world's creator? The pain of God? George trembled, surely not. But the thought would not go away. Was God really there, telling him something.

"Hush! Listen," the breeze whispered.

In the quietness of listening, George was sure he heard an unmistakable chuckle. Surprised, he grinned as he shared the joke, the irony. He, George Elkson, had rejected God for nature and science. Through nature and science, God had come to him.

"Thank you," whispered the troubled man; influential solicitor; evolutionist; father; husband and guilt-riven brother. George's spirit eased and the dark, haunted places inside him began to brighten. He didn't completely understand but was content to believe that this was God.

Later, George would talk of this experience with cousin Hugh. For now, George simply put out his pipe and came down the hillside, a chastened and humbler man but with an unmistakable sense of hope.

It was dark when he arrived home and his two youngest children ran to the gate to meet him. He caught Alice in his arms and swung her round; for a ten year old she was far too light and thin.

George put her down gently and looked enquiringly at Richard who was eagerly waiting for his father's attention:

"Daddy, I want to show you something."

George followed his eleven year old son to a bush in the corner of the front garden, dead leaves were piled underneath and carefully moving them, Richard showed his father a plump hedgehog curled up and ready for a good winter's sleep. They all admired the small creature, tucked safely beneath his prickles.

"Now, cover him up warmly and leave him in peace, we mustn't disturb him till he's ready to wake up, when winter's over."

"How do you know it's a 'him'? I thought it was Mrs Tiggywinkle," said Alice teasingly. Although now too old for Beatrix Potter stories the characters had all stayed with her.

"I don't know. She may well be Mrs Tiggywinkle or it may be Mr Tiggywinkle. Maybe there will be baby hedgehogs in the Spring."

Richard said, "Oh, Mummy's resting on her bed. I've to tell her as soon as you're home. Then we can eat."

The three of them raced each other into the house, laughing loudly.

CHAPTER 82

Honouring Ellie

The inquest and preparations for Ellie's funeral were all dealt with by the men-folk of the family. The women kept their troubled thoughts at bay, by busying themselves with daily household tasks. Gertie Foster and Matilda held their respective households tightly in check with a regular supply of meals, warm fires and clean clothing. All the women were ready with hot tea, whenever they noticed anyone in danger of flagging.

Very little was said between them, about Ellie. Her suicide was too new and raw and they were all busy battling with the conflicting feelings of horror and guilt, anger and sorrow, which would attack each of them unexpectedly. Stephen turned to his work for comfort and also discovered an unexpected solace in one of his colleagues, a woman of his own age, a science teacher but also a devout Roman Catholic. The couple had warmed to each other and although it was to be over ten years before they would marry, it was during this time, after Ellie's death, that they first discovered the hidden depths in each other's characters.

Cousin Gilbert and Cousin Hugh, as clergymen, were the only members of the family who'd had experience of such situations. Gilbert had moved away some years ago and lost touch with his Hartsbeck cousins, whereas Hugh was still very close to them. Though numbed, by his personal grief for Ellie, Hugh turned naturally to God and as always, gained strength from Him. Edwin and Annie also experienced the calm assurance of their faith and were able to be a strong support to the others. The children especially, gravitated to Uncle Edwin and Auntie Annie for comfort.

There was to be no big funeral. Only Ellie's generation of the family and her mother were to be present and Gertie Foster and Matilda.

Jeannie was specific about Ellie's London friends, "I don't want them contacted. Some of them are spiritualists and I don't want any of them trying to reach her beyond the grave!" she seemed to have forgotten the people who'd surrounded her with friendship, when she visited Sarah in London.

Cousin Hugh ignored his great aunt's orders and telephoned Ian and Pauline Haworth. He felt they had a right to know about Ellie and he had an idea that Ian or Pauline would contact the group of friends who had been at Sarah's funeral.

"Ellie's mother doesn't want her London friends to know - she's frightened of Ellie's spiritualist connections. I'm sure the Fielding family and Beattie and her husband ought to be told. They were so close to Ellie and to Sarah. Perhaps if they were just told that she'd died, without mentioning suicide, they would be less distressed."

It was Pauline Haworth who went to visit the Fielding family and Beatty and Sam Henson. Together they decided to have a small informal gathering in one of the side chapels at Westminster Abbey. And so it was that Billy, Kitty, Toby, Ruby and Mrs Fielding; Old Mrs Mason, Beattie and Sam Henson, and Pauline Haworth came together in Westminster Abbey and led by the Reverend Ian had a short memorial service for Ellie. Afterwards they went to the Haworth's home, where Ellie had been taken on the night of her collapse. Pauline served tea and sandwiches and they reminisced warmly of Ellie and of Sarah and the Elkson family. Beattie had brought a batch of Ellie's favourite biscuits,

"She was always partial to my ginger-bread biscuits. We had many a gossip over a plate of these; I thought I'd bring them for her sake. She had her moments, we all do, but I was fond of Sister Ellie. She always had time for me." Sam Henson squeezed his wife's hand and old Mrs Mason sobbed into her handkerchief.

Toby proudly lifted his head and announced, "Nurse–I mean, Sister Elkson, once saved my life," and they all smiled, his choking on a button was an often repeated family story.

Ian was glad he hadn't told them of the exact manner of Ellie's death.

Kitty who'd been crying, dried her eyes and contributed her own statement; "I met that lady they used to call Sister Juniper the other day. She's a grand old lady now, nearly ninety. I told her about Sister Elkson's death and she said; 'Sister Elkson is one of the unsung heroines of our age.' I felt real proud to have known her," and she nodded vehemently in agreement with her own statement before her tears started afresh.

Back in Hartsbeck, the funeral service was to be taken at the Crematorium Chapel, on Monday, 28th September, by the Reverend Owen Griffiths, Vicar of Hartsbeck. He knew the entire family well, having long been a keen member of the Hartsbeck Naturalists and Antiquarian Society as were all the Elksons.

George and Owen had often enjoyed a debate over a pint of beer, or a glass of whisky, after a meeting of the NATS. Together they'd attemp to unearth the meaning behind all the fluctuations in nature, philosophy and religion, as well as chuckling over the latest book by P.G. Woodhouse.

"I'll say one thing about you, George Elkson; you're a searcher for Truth with a capital 'T'. Anything that smacks of clap-trap or humbug or just plain uncertainty and you're at it like a cat with a mouse. One day you'll hit that Truth – I'd like to be with you on that day!"- was a remark Owen had made more than once.

After the short, said service in the Crematorium Chapel, they were to walk to the grave where Ellie was to be buried and the Vicar would say the prayers of committal, for Ellie. To the sorrow of Edwin and Annie, it had been decided that no hymns would be sung. Neither would there be a eulogy or flowers. Jeannie could not yet grieve properly for Ellie; except for a helpless anger, her feelings for her daughter seemed frozen.

However, following George's unexpected recognition of God on Whalley Nab, the plans were changed. George had been the chief opponent to singing a hymn but now quite suddenly he wanted one. His own feelings towards Ellie had thawed and much to Hannah's surprise he'd attended a Sunday service with her. The hymn, 'Lead kindly light' by John Henry Newman, had been sung and the words had struck home to him forcibly, relating both to himself and to Ellie. As they left the church Hannah had remarked,

"That hymn fits you so well, George, it even draws a parallel with your fondness for walking

'O'er moor and fen, o'er crag and torrent, till the night is gone;'"

"Hannah, do you think the family would sing it at Ellie's funeral?"

"We could ask them. As it's your suggestion I think they'd agree and I'm sure we'd all join in. Some better than others," Hannah smiled, thinking of her own tone deafness and tucked her hand into the crook of George's arm; he squeezed her against him affectionately.

Cousin Hugh played the organ and good and poor singers alike, joined in the hymn of 'Lead kindly light'. To George the second verse brought new meaning,

'I was not ever thus, nor prayed that Thou should'st lead me on;

I loved to choose and see my path; but now, lead thou me on.

I loved the garish day, and, spite of fears,

Pride ruled my will: remember not past years.'

The final sentiments of the hymn broke through the frozen barrier of Jeannie's feelings for a moment and brought tears to her eyes and her voice faltered at the words:

"And with the morn, those angel faces smile,

Which I have loved long since and lost awhile."

Before they left the chapel, Canon Owen Griffiths spoke to the small congregation,

"I know you wanted no eulogy today. However, I can't let Ellen Elkson, Ellie, go to her grave without some acknowledgement of the heroism expressed in her life. She left home to follow a dream, a vocation to help lift the needy of our nation from their undeserved poverty and suffering. She nursed some terrible cases, most of them sick children and without the comfort of her family nearby.

She nursed the wounded in the Great War. Afterwards, she continued her work as part of that great movement to cut the numbers of infant mortality and lessen the dangers of childbirth. She nursed her beloved sister, Sarah during her final weeks and mourned her for the rest of her life. After Sarah's death, she returned again to her work among families who needed her skills. She became ill herself and came home to recuperate. In her times of respite she used her skills to care for her mother and to save the life of baby May Anderson, here in Hartsbeck. The tragedies in many of the cases she nursed led Ellie to search for spiritual meaning in strange places. In the end, all Ellie's struggles became too much for her and she took the decision to end her life here. I know she believed in the next life. We that are left, are naturally confused and grief stricken, our love for Ellie has been badly wounded. One day I hope we shall be able to speak naturally of her again, among ourselves. For now, we commend Ellie to God, her loving Father and ours; remembering our own weakness and need of Him."

To everyone's surprise, it was George who led the mourners in a loud and affirming 'Amen.'

THE END

Janet M. Reeves was born and raised in Accrington, Lancashire, the place that inspired Ellie Elkson's fictional hometown of Hartsbeck. A lifelong writer of stories and poetry, she's a former librarian. She and her husband, a clergyman, have two sons and a daughter. In 2004, she earned a bachelor of arts in religious studies from Lancaster University, where she also studied creative writing.

Her first novel, *Silence Unlocked*, was inspired by stories of a woman from her hometown who was all but forgotten after she died under unnatural circumstances. The idea that a family would refuse to discuss a beloved relation because of shame and social stigma fascinated her. Reeves decided to reconstruct the mysterious woman's life while examining a fascinating period in English history.

39636063R00345

Made in the USA
Charleston, SC
13 March 2015